For Harry

Courage is knowing what not to fear.
Attributed to Plato

The Missing Sister

Lucinda Riley was born in Ireland and, after an early career as an actress in film, theatre and television, wrote her first book aged twenty-four. Her books have been translated into thirty-seven languages and sold thirty million copies worldwide. She is a *Sunday Times* and *New York Times* bestselling author.

Lucinda's The Seven Sisters series, which tells the story of adopted sisters and is inspired by the mythology of the famous star cluster, has become a global phenomenon. The series is a number one bestseller across the world and is currently in development with a major TV production company.

Lucinda and her family divide their time between the UK and a farmhouse in West Cork, Ireland, where she writes her books.

Also by Lucinda Riley

Hothouse Flower

The Girl on the Cliff

The Light Behind the Window

The Midnight Rose

The Italian Girl

The Angel Tree

The Olive Tree

The Love Letter

The Butterfly Room

The Seven Sisters Series

The Seven Sisters

The Storm Sister

The Shadow Sister

The Pearl Sister

The Moon Sister

The Sun Sister

The Missing Sister

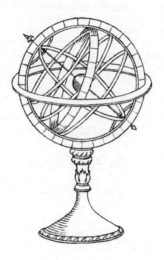

LUCINDA RILEY

MACMILLAN

First published 2021 by Macmillan
an imprint of Pan Macmillan
The Smithson, 6 Briset Street, London EC1M 5NR
EU representative: Macmillan Publishers Ireland Limited,
Mallard Lodge, Lansdowne Village, Dublin 4
Associated companies throughout the world
www.panmacmillan.com

ISBN 978-1-5098-4018-2

3 5 7 9 8 6 4

A CIP catalogue record for this book is available from the British Library.

Illustrations by Hemesh Alles

Typeset by Palimpsest Book Production Ltd, Falkirk, Stirlingshire
Printed and bound by CPI Group (UK) Ltd, Croydon, CR0 4YY

Visit **www.panmacmillan.com** to read more about all our books
and to buy them. You will also find features, author interviews and
news of any author events, and you can sign up for e-newsletters
so that you're always first to hear about our new releases.

Cast of characters

Mary-Kate
The Gibbston Valley, New Zealand
June 2008

1

I remember exactly where I was and what I was doing when I saw my father die. I was standing pretty much where I was now, leaning over the wooden veranda that surrounded our house and staring out at the grape pickers working their way along the neat rows of vines, heavily pregnant with this year's yield. I was just about to walk down the steps to join them when out of the corner of my eye I saw the man-mountain that was my father suddenly disappear from sight. At first I thought he had knelt down to collect a stray cluster of grapes – he detested waste of any kind, which he put down to the Presbyterian mindset of his Scottish parents – but then I saw the pickers from the rows nearby dash towards him. It was a good hundred-metre run from the veranda to reach him, and by the time I got there, someone had ripped open his shirt and was trying to resuscitate him, pumping his chest and giving mouth-to-mouth, while another had called 111. It took twenty minutes for the ambulance to arrive.

Even as he was lifted onto the stretcher, I could see from his already waxy complexion that I would never again hear his deep powerful voice that held so much gravitas, yet could turn to a throaty chuckle in a second. As tears streamed down my cheeks, I kissed him gently on his own ruddy, weather-beaten one, told him I loved him and said goodbye. Looking back, the whole dreadful experience had been surreal – the transition from being so full of life to, well . . . nothing but an empty, lifeless body, was impossible to take in.

After months of suffering pains in his chest, but pretending they were indigestion, Dad had finally been persuaded to go to the doctor. He'd been told that he had high cholesterol, and that he must stick to a strict diet. My mother and I had despaired as he'd continued to eat what he wanted *and* drink a bottle of his own red wine at dinner every night. So it should hardly have been a shock when the worst eventually happened. Perhaps we had believed him indestructible, his large personality and bonhomie aiding the illusion, but as my mother had rather darkly pointed out, we're all simply flesh and bone at the end of the day. At least he'd lived the way he wished to until the very end. He'd also been seventy-three, a fact I simply couldn't compute, given his physical strength and zest for life.

The upshot was that I felt cheated. After all, I was only twenty-two, and even though I'd always known I'd arrived late in my parents' lives, the significance of it only hit me when Dad died. In the few months since we'd lost him, I'd felt anger at the injustice: *why* hadn't I come into their lives sooner? My big brother Jack, who was thirty-two, had enjoyed a whole ten years more with Dad.

Mum could obviously sense my anger, even if I'd never said anything outright to her. And then I'd felt guilty, because it wasn't her fault in any way. I loved her so much – we'd always been very close, and I could see that she was grieving too. We'd done our best to comfort each other, and somehow, we'd got through it together.

Jack had been wonderful too, spending most of his time sorting through the dreadful bureaucratic aftermath of death. He'd also had to take sole charge of The Vinery, the business

Mum and Dad had started from scratch, but at least he'd already been well prepared by Dad to run it.

Since Jack was a toddler, Dad had taken him along as he went about the yearly cycle of caring for his precious vines that would, sometime between February and April, depending on the weather, bring forth the grapes that would then be harvested and ultimately result in the delicious – and recently, prize-winning – bottles of pinot noir that lay stacked in the warehouse, ready to be exported across New Zealand and Australia. He'd taken Jack through each step of the process, and by the time he was twelve, he could have probably directed the staff, such was the knowledge Dad had given him.

Jack had officially announced at sixteen that he wanted to join Dad and run The Vinery one day, which had pleased Dad enormously. He'd gone to uni to study business, and afterwards had begun working full-time in the vineyard.

'There's nothing better than passing on a healthy legacy,' Dad had toasted him a few years ago, after Jack had been on a six-month visit to a vineyard in the Adelaide Hills in Australia, and Dad had pronounced him ready.

'Maybe you'll come in with us too one day, Mary-Kate. Here's to there being McDougal winegrowers on this land for hundreds of years to come!'

While Jack had bought into Dad's dream, the opposite had happened to me. Maybe it was the fact that Jack was genuinely so enthralled by making beautiful wines; as well as having a nose that could spot a rogue grape a mile off, he was an excellent businessman. On the other hand, I had grown from a child to a young woman watching Dad and Jack patrolling the vines and working in what was affectionately known as the 'The Lab' (in fact, it was nothing more than a large shed with a tin roof atop it), but other things had caught my interest. Now I regarded The Vinery as a separate entity to me and my future. That hadn't stopped me working in our little shop during school and uni holidays, or helping out wherever I was needed, but wine just wasn't my passion. Even though Dad had looked disappointed when I'd said that I wanted to study music, he'd had the grace to understand.

'Good for you,' he'd said as he hugged me. 'Music is a big subject, Mary-Kate. Which bit of it do you actually see as your future career?'

I'd told him shyly that one day I would like to be a singer and write my own songs.

'That's a helluva dream to have, and I can only wish you luck and say that your mum and I are with you all the way, eh?'

'I think it's wonderful, Mary-Kate, I really do,' Mum had said. 'Expressing yourself through song is a magical thing.'

And study music I had, deciding on the University of Wellington, which offered a world-class degree, and I'd loved every minute of it. Having a state-of-the-art studio in which to record my songs, and being surrounded by other students who lived and breathed my passion, had been amazing. I'd formed a duo with Fletch, a great friend who played rhythm guitar and had a singing voice that harmonised well with mine. With me at the keyboard, we'd managed to get the odd gig in Wellington and had performed at our graduation concert last year, which was the first time my family had seen me sing and play live.

'I'm so proud of you, MK,' Dad had said, enveloping me in a hug. It had been one of the best moments of my life.

'Now here I am, a year on, chucked out the other end of my degree and still surrounded by vines,' I muttered. 'Honestly, MK, did you really think that Sony would come begging you to sign a record deal with them?'

Since leaving uni a year ago, I'd slowly become more and more depressed about my future career, and Dad's death had been a huge blow to my creativity. It felt like I'd lost two loves of my life at once, especially as one had been inextricably linked to the other. It had been Dad's love of female singer-songwriters that had first ignited my musical passion. I'd been brought up listening to Joni Mitchell, Joan Baez and Alanis Morissette.

My time in Wellington had also brought home to me just how protected and idyllic my childhood had been, living here in the glorious Garden of Eden that was the Gibbston Valley. The mountains that rose up around us provided a comforting physical barrier, while the fertile earth magically grew an abundance of succulent fruit.

I remembered a teenage Jack tricking me into eating the wild gooseberries that grew in prickly brambles behind our house, and his laughter as I'd spat out the sour fruit. I'd roamed free back then, my parents unconcerned; they'd known I was perfectly safe in the gorgeous countryside that surrounded us, playing in the cool, clear streams, and chasing rabbits across the coarse grass. While my parents had laboured in the vineyard, doing everything from planting the vines and protecting them from hungry wildlife, to picking and pressing the grapes, I'd lived in my own world.

The bright morning sun was suddenly eclipsed by a cloud, turning the valley a darker grey-green. It was a warning that winter was coming and, not for the first time, I wondered if I'd made the right decision to see it out here. A couple of months back, Mum had first mentioned her idea of taking off on what she called a 'Grand Tour' of the world to visit friends she hadn't seen for years. She had asked if I wanted to join her. At the time, I was still hoping that the demo tape I'd made with Fletch, which had gone out to record companies around the world just before Dad died, would produce some interest. Yet the replies that told us our music wasn't what the producer was 'looking for just now' were piling up on a shelf in my bedroom.

'Sweetheart, I don't need to tell you that the music business is one of the toughest to break into,' Mum had said.

'That's why I think I should stay here,' I'd replied. 'Fletch and I are working on some new stuff. I can't just abandon ship.'

'No, of course you can't. At least you have The Vinery to fall back on if it all goes wrong,' she'd added.

I knew that she was only being kind and I should be grateful for the fact I could earn money working in the shop and helping with the accounts. But as I looked out now on my Garden of Eden, I heaved a great big sigh, because the thought of staying here for the rest of my life was not a good one, however safe and beautiful it was. Everything had changed since I'd gone away to uni and even more so after Dad's death. It felt like the heart of this place had stopped beating with his passing. It didn't help that Jack – who, before Dad had died, had agreed to spend the summer in a Rhône Valley vineyard in France – had decided with Mum that he should still make the trip.

'The future of the business is in Jack's hands now and he needs to learn as much as he can,' Mum had told me. 'We have Doug on site to run the vineyard and besides, it's the quiet season and the perfect time for Jack to go.'

But since Mum had left on her Grand Tour yesterday, and with Jack away too, there was no doubt I was feeling very alone and in danger of sinking into further gloom. 'I miss you, Dad,' I murmured as I walked inside to get some brekkie, even though I wasn't hungry. The silent house did nothing to help my mood; all through my childhood, it had been buzzing with people – if it wasn't suppliers or pickers, it was visitors to the vineyard that Dad had got chatting to. As well as handing out samples of his wines, he'd often invite them to stay for a meal. Being hospitable and friendly was simply the Kiwi way and I was used to joining total strangers at our big pine table overlooking the valley. I had no idea how my mother was able to provide vats of tasty, plentiful food at a moment's notice, but she did, and with Dad providing the bonhomie, there had been a lot of fun and laughter.

I missed Jack too and the calm, positive energy he always exuded. He loved to tease me, but equally, I knew that he was always in my corner, my protector.

I took the orange juice carton from the fridge and poured the last of it into a glass, then did my best to hack through a loaf of day-old bread. I toasted it to make it edible, then began to write a quick shopping list to stock up on fridge supplies. The nearest supermarket was in Arrowtown, and I'd need to make the trip soon. Even though Mum had left plenty of casseroles in the freezer, it didn't feel right defrosting the big plastic tubs just for myself.

I shivered as I brought the list through to the sitting room and sat on the old sofa in front of the huge chimney breast, built out of the grey volcanic stone that abounded in the area. It had been the one thing that had convinced my parents thirty years ago that they should buy what was once a single-roomed hut in the middle of nowhere. It had no running water or facilities, and both Mum and Dad had liked to recall how that first summer, they and two-year-old Jack had used the stream that fell between the rocks behind the hut to bathe in, and a literal hole in the ground as a dunny. 'It was the happiest summer of my life,' Mum would say, 'and in the winter it got even better because of the fire.'

Mum was obsessed with real fires, and as soon as the first frost appeared in the valley, Dad, Jack and I would be sent out to collect the wood from the store, well seasoned in the months since it had been chopped. We'd stack it in the alcoves on either side of the chimney breast, then Mum would lay the wood in the grate and the ritual of what the family called 'the first light' would take place as she struck a match. From that moment on, the fire would burn merrily every day of the winter months, until the bluebells and snowdrops (the bulbs for which she'd had posted from Europe) bloomed under the trees between September and November, our spring.

Maybe I should light one now, I thought, thinking of the warm, welcoming glow that had greeted me on freezing days throughout my childhood when I'd come in from school. If Dad had been the metaphoric heart of the winery, Mum and her fire had been that of the home.

I stopped myself, feeling I really was too young to start looking back to childhood memories for comfort. I just needed some company, that was all. The problem was, most of my uni friends were either away abroad, enjoying their last moments of freedom before they settled down and found themselves jobs, or were working already.

Even though we had a landline, the internet signal in the valley was sporadic. Sending emails was a nightmare, and Dad had often resorted to driving the half hour to Queenstown and using his friend the travel agent's computer to send them. He'd always called our valley 'Brigadoon', after an old film about a village that only awakens for one day every hundred years, so that it would never be changed by the outside world. Well, maybe the valley was Brigadoon – it certainly remained more or less unchanged – but it was not the place for a budding singer-songwriter to make her mark. My dreams were full of Manhattan, London or Sydney, those towering buildings harbouring record producers who would take Fletch and me and make us stars . . .

The landline broke into my thoughts and I stood up to grab it before it rang off. 'You've reached The Vinery,' I parroted, as I had done since I was a child.

'Hi, MK, it's Fletch,' he said, using the nickname that everyone except my mum called me.

'Oh, hi there,' I said, my heart rate speeding up. 'Any news?'

'Nothing, other than I thought I might take you up on your offer to stay at yours. I have a couple of days off from the café and I need to get out of the city, eh?'

And I need to be in *it . . .*

'Hey, that's great! Come whenever you want. I'm here.'

'How about tomorrow? I'll be driving down, so that will take me most of the morning, as long as Sissy makes it, o'course.'

Sissy was the van in which Fletch and I had driven to our gigs. It was twenty years old and rusting everywhere it could rust, belching out smoke from the dodgy exhaust pipe that Fletch had temporarily fixed with string. I only hoped Sissy could manage the three-hour journey from Dunedin where Fletch lived with his family.

'So, I'll see you round lunchtime?' I said.

'Yeah, I can't wait. You know I love it down there. Perhaps we can spend a few hours on the piano, coming up with some new stuff?'

'Perhaps,' I answered, knowing I wasn't in a particularly creative space just now. 'Bye, Fletch, see you tomorrow.'

I finished the call and walked back to the sofa, feeling brighter now that Fletch was coming – he never failed to cheer me up with his sense of humour and positivity.

I heard a shout from outside and then a whistle, the sound Doug, our vineyard manager, used to alert us to the fact that he was on site. I stood up, went to the terrace and saw Doug and a group of burly Pacific Islanders walking through the bare vines.

'Hiya!' I shouted down.

'Hi, MK! Just taking the gang to show them where to begin the pulling out,' Doug replied.

'Fine. Good. Hi, guys,' I shouted down to his team and they waved up at me.

Their presence had broken the silence, and as the sun appeared from behind a cloud, the sight of other human beings, plus the thought that Fletch was coming tomorrow, lifted my spirits.

2

'You look pale, Maia. Are you feeling all right?' Ma said as she walked into the kitchen.

'I'm okay, I just didn't sleep very well last night thinking about Georg's bombshell.'

'Yes, it certainly was that. Coffee?' Ma asked her.

'Uh, no thanks. I'll have some chamomile tea if there is any.'

'There is, of course,' interjected Claudia. Her grey hair was pulled back tightly into a customary bun, and her usually dour face had a smile for Maia as she placed a basket of her freshly made rolls and pastries on the kitchen table. 'I take it before bed every night.'

'You must be feeling unwell, Maia. I have never known you to reject coffee first thing in the morning,' commented Ma as she collected her own.

'Habits are there to break,' Maia said wearily. 'I'm jet-lagged too, remember?'

'Of course you are, *chérie*. Why don't you eat some break-fast, then go back to bed and try to sleep?'

13

'No, Georg said he was coming later to discuss what we do about . . . the missing sister. How reliable do you think his sources are?'

'I have no idea,' Ma sighed.

'*Very*,' Claudia interrupted. 'He would not have arrived at midnight unless he was sure of his facts.'

'Morning, everyone,' said Ally as she joined the rest of the household in the kitchen. Bear was tucked up in a papoose strapped to her chest, his head lolling to one side as he dozed. One of his tiny fists was clutching a strand of Ally's red-gold curls.

'Would you like me to take him from you and put him in his cot?' asked Ma.

'No, because he's bound to wake up and howl the minute he realises he's alone. Oh Maia, you look pale,' said Ally.

'That is what I just said,' Ma murmured.

'Really, I'm okay,' Maia repeated. 'Is Christian around, by the way?' she asked Claudia.

'Yes, although he is just about to take the boat across the lake to Geneva to get some food supplies for me.'

'Then could you call him and say I'll hop on the boat with him? I have some things I need to do in the city and if we left soon, I'd be back in time to see Georg at noon.'

'Of course.' Claudia picked up the handset to dial Christian.

Ma put a cup of coffee in front of Ally. 'I have some chores to do, so I will leave you two to enjoy your breakfast.'

'Christian will have the boat ready in fifteen minutes,' said Claudia, putting down the handset. 'Now, I must go and help Marina.' She nodded at them both and left the kitchen.

'Are you sure you're okay?' Ally asked her sister when they were alone. 'You're as white as a sheet.'

'Please don't fuss, Ally. Maybe I caught a stomach bug on

the plane.' Maia took a sip of tea. 'Goodness, it's strange here, isn't it? I mean, the way everything carries on just as it did when Pa was alive? Except he isn't, so there's a gaping Pa-sized hole in everything.'

'I've been here a while already, so I'm sort of used to it, but yes, there is.'

'Talking of me looking unwell, Ally, you've lost a lot of weight.'

'Oh, that's just baby weight—'

'No, it isn't, not to me anyway. Remember, the last time I saw you was a year ago, when you left here to join Theo for the Fastnet Race. You weren't even pregnant then.'

'I actually was, but I didn't know it,' Ally pointed out.

'You mean, you didn't have any symptoms? No morning sickness or anything?'

'Not at the beginning. It kicked in at around eight weeks, if I remember rightly. And then I felt truly awful.'

'Well, you're definitely too thin. Maybe you're not looking after yourself well enough.'

'When I'm by myself, it never seems worth cooking a proper meal. And besides, even if I do sit down to eat, I'm normally jumping up from the table to go and sort this little one out.' Ally stroked Bear's cheek affectionately.

'It must be so hard bringing up a child by yourself.'

'It is. I mean, I do have my brother Thom, but as he's deputy conductor at the Bergen Philharmonic, I hardly see him, apart from Sundays. And sometimes not even then, if he's touring abroad with the orchestra. It's not the getting no sleep and the constant feeding and changing that bothers me; it's just the lack of someone to talk to, especially if Bear isn't well and I'm worried about him. So having Ma's been wonderful; she's a fount of knowledge on all things baby.'

'She's the ultimate grandmother,' Maia smiled. 'Pa would

have been so happy about Bear. He really is adorable. Now, I must go upstairs to get ready.'

As Maia stood up, Ally caught her older sister's hand. 'It is so good to see you. I've missed you so much.'

'And I you.' Maia kissed the top of Ally's head. 'I'll see you later.'

'Ally! Maia! Georg is here,' Ma shouted up the main staircase at noon.

A muffled 'Coming!' emanated from the top floor.

'Do you remember when Pa Salt bought you an old brass megaphone for Christmas?'

Georg smiled as he followed Ma into the kitchen and out onto the sun-filled terrace. He looked much more collected than he had the previous night, his steel-grey hair neatly brushed back and his pinstriped suit impeccable, accessorised tastefully with a small pocket square.

'I do,' Ma said, indicating for Georg to sit down under the parasol. 'Of course, it made no difference, because the girls all had their music on full blast, or were playing instruments, or arguing with each other. It was like the Tower of Babel on the attic floor. And I adored every moment of it. Now, I have Claudia's elderflower cordial, or a chilled bottle of your favourite Provençal rosé. Which is it to be?'

'As it is such a beautiful day, and I am yet to have my first glass of summer rosé, I will choose that. Thank you, Marina. May I do the honours for both of us?'

'Oh no, I shouldn't. I have work to do this afternoon and—'

'Come now, you're French! Surely a glass of rosé will not affect you adversely. In fact, I insist,' said Georg, as Maia and

Ally walked out onto the terrace to join them. 'Hello, girls.' Georg stood up. 'May I offer you both a glass of rosé?'

'I'll have a small glass, thank you, Georg,' said Ally, sitting down. 'Maybe it will help Bear sleep tonight,' she chuckled.

'None for me, thanks,' said Maia. 'You know, I'd almost forgotten how beautiful it is at Atlantis. In Brazil, everything is so . . . *big*: the noisy people, the vibrant colours of nature and the strong heat. Everything here feels comparatively soft and gentle.'

'It's certainly very peaceful,' said Ma. 'We are blessed to live in all the beauty that nature can provide.'

'How I've missed the winter snow,' murmured Maia.

'You should come to Norway for a winter; that will cure you,' smiled Ally. 'Or even worse, you'll get constant rain. Bergen gets far more of that than it does snow. Now, Georg, have you had any thoughts on what you told us last night?'

'Other than discussing where we go from here, no. One of us must visit the address I have, to verify if this woman is the missing sister.'

'If we do, how will we know whether she is or isn't?' asked Maia. 'Is there anything that we can identify her by?'

'I was handed a drawing of a . . . certain piece of jewellery, a ring that was apparently given to her. It is very unusual. If she has it, we will know without a doubt it is her. I have brought the drawing with me.' Georg reached into his slim leather briefcase to pull out a sheet of paper. He placed it on the table for them all to see.

Ally inspected it closely, with Maia looking over her shoulder.

'It is drawn from memory,' Georg explained. 'The gems in the setting are emeralds. The central stone is a diamond.'

'It's beautiful,' said Ally. 'Look, Maia, it's arranged in a star shape, with' – she paused to count – 'seven points.'

'Georg, do you know who originally made it?' Maia chimed in. 'It's a very unusual design.'

'I am afraid I do not,' Georg replied.

'Did Pa draw this?' Maia asked.

'He did, yes.'

'Seven points of a star for seven sisters . . .' Ally murmured.

'Georg, you said last night that her name was Mary,' said Maia.

'Yes.'

'Did Pa Salt find her, want to adopt her and then something happened and he lost her?'

'All I can say is that just before he . . . passed away, he was given some new information, which he asked me to follow up. Having discovered where she was born, it has taken me and others almost a year to trace where I believe she is now. Over the years I have taken many a false turn, and it has led to nothing. However, this time, your father was adamant his source was reliable.'

'Who was his source?' Maia asked.

'He did not say,' Georg replied.

'If it is the missing sister, it's a terrible shame that, after all these years of searching for her, she's found only a year after Pa's death,' Maia sighed.

'Wouldn't it be wonderful if it *was* her,' said Ally, 'and we could bring her back to Atlantis in time to board the *Titan* and go and lay the wreath?'

'It would,' Maia smiled. 'Although there is one big problem. According to your information, Georg, "Mary" hardly lives next door. And we leave for our cruise down to Greece in less than three weeks.'

'Yes, and sadly, I have a very busy schedule at present,' said Georg. 'Otherwise, I would go to find Mary myself.'

As if to underline the point, Georg's mobile rang. He excused himself and left the table.

'May I suggest something?' Ma spoke into the silence.

'Of course, Ma, go ahead,' said Maia.

'Given that Georg told us last night that Mary currently lives in New Zealand, I made some enquiries this morning to see how far it was to travel between Sydney and Auckland. Because—'

'CeCe is in Australia,' Maia finished for her. 'I thought about that last night too.'

'It is a three-hour flight from Sydney to Auckland,' Ma continued. 'If CeCe and her friend Chrissie left a day earlier than they are planning to, maybe they could take a detour to New Zealand to see if this Mary is who Georg thinks she is.'

'That's a great idea, Ma,' Ally said. 'I wonder if CeCe would do it. I know she hates flying.'

'If we explain, I'm sure she would,' said Ma. 'It would be so special to unite the missing sister with the family for your father's memorial.'

'The question is, does this Mary even know about Pa Salt and our family?' Ally asked. 'It's not often these days that all us sisters are gathered together,' she mused. 'It seems to me like the perfect moment – that is, if she *is* who Georg believes her to be. And if she's willing to meet us, of course. Now, I think the first thing to do is to contact CeCe, sooner rather than later, as it's already the evening in Australia.'

'What do we do about the rest of the sisters?' asked Maia. 'I mean, do we tell them?'

'Good point,' said Ally. 'We should email Star, Tiggy and Electra to let them know what's happening. Do you want to call CeCe, Maia, or shall I?'

'Why don't you do it, Ally? I think that, if it's okay with

everyone, I'll go and have a lie-down before lunch. I'm still feeling a bit queasy.'

'You poor darling,' said Ma, standing up. 'You definitely look a little green.'

'I'll come inside with you and make the call to CeCe,' said Ally. 'Let's just hope she isn't on one of her painting trips in the Outback with her grandfather. There's apparently no signal at all at his cabin.'

Claudia appeared on the terrace from the kitchen. 'I will start preparing lunch.' She turned to Georg who had walked back to the table. 'Would you like to stay?'

'No, thank you. I have some pressing matters to attend to and must leave immediately. What has been decided?' he asked Ma.

As Ally and Maia left the terrace, Ally saw that beads of sweat had appeared on Georg's forehead and he seemed distracted.

'We're contacting CeCe to see if she will go. Georg, you are convinced that this is her?' Ma asked.

'I have been convinced by others that would know, yes,' he replied. 'Now, I would have liked to chat further, but I must leave you.'

'I'm sure the girls can deal with this, Georg. They are grown women now, and very capable.' She put a reassuring hand on his arm. 'Try to relax. You seem very tense.'

'I will try, Marina, I will try,' he agreed with a sigh.

Ally found CeCe's Australian mobile number in her address book and picked up the receiver in the hallway to dial it.

'Come on, come on . . .' she whispered under her breath as

the line rang five or six times. She knew it was pointless leaving CeCe a message as she rarely listened to them.

'Damn,' she muttered as CeCe's voicemail kicked in. Putting the receiver down, she was about to go upstairs to feed Bear when the telephone rang.

'*Allô?*'

'Hello, is that Ma?'

'CeCe! It's me, Ally. Thanks so much for calling back.'

'No problem, I saw it was the Atlantis number. Is everything okay?'

'Yes, everything's good here. Maia flew in yesterday and it's so great to see her. When exactly is your flight to London, CeCe?'

'We leave the Alice the day after tomorrow to head for Sydney. I think I told you we're stopping over in London first for a few days, to sort out selling my apartment and to see Star. I'm dreading the flight, as usual.'

'I know, but listen, CeCe, Georg has brought some news. Don't worry, it isn't bad, but it's big news – or at least, it might be.'

'What is it?'

'He's had some information about . . . our missing sister. He thinks that she might be living in New Zealand.'

'You mean, the famous seventh sister? Wow!' CeCe breathed. 'That *is* news. How did Georg find her?'

'I'm not sure. You know how cagey he is. So—'

'You're going to ask me if I can just pop over to New Zealand to meet her, aren't you?' said CeCe.

'Full marks, Sherlock.' Ally smiled into the receiver. 'I know it would make your journey a little longer, but you're by far the closest to her. It would be so wonderful to have her with all of us when we lay Pa's wreath.'

'It would, yeah, but we don't know anything about this person. Does she know anything about us?'

'We're not sure. Georg says he only has a name and address. Oh! And a picture of a ring that proves it's her.'

'So what's the address? I mean, New Zealand's a big country.'

'I haven't got it on me, but I can get Georg to speak to you. Georg?' Ally beckoned him over as he emerged from the kitchen on his way to the front door. 'It's CeCe on the phone. She wants to know whereabouts in New Zealand Mary lives.'

'Mary? Is that her name?' said CeCe.

'Apparently. I'll pass you over to Georg.' Ally listened in as Georg read out the address.

'Thank you, CeCe,' said Georg. 'All costs will be covered by the trust. Giselle, my secretary, will book the flights. Now, I'm going to pass you back to your sister, as I must leave.' As Georg handed the receiver to Ally, he added, 'You have my office number, contact Giselle if you need anything. For now, adieu.'

'Okay. Hi, CeCe,' Ally said, giving Georg a small wave as he walked out of the front door. 'Do you know where in New Zealand that is?'

'Hold on. I'll ask Chrissie.'

There was a muffled discussion before CeCe came back to the phone.

'Chrissie says it's way down on the South Island. She thinks we should be able to fly to Queenstown from Sydney, which would make everything a lot easier than going to Auckland. We'll look into it.'

'Great. So, are you up for it?' Ally asked.

'You know me, I love a bit of travel and adventure, even when it involves planes. I've never been to New Zealand, so it'll be fun to get a glimpse of it.'

'Brilliant! Thanks, CeCe. If it's easier, email me the details and I'll call Georg's secretary about booking the flights. I'll fax a picture of the ring to you too.'

'Okay. Does Star know about this?'

'No, and nor do Electra or Tiggy. I'm going to email them all now.'

'Actually, Star's calling me in a bit to talk about meeting up in London, so I can fill her in. This is really exciting, isn't it?'

'It will be if it's actually *her*. Bye for now, CeCe. Keep in touch.'

'Bye, Ally, speak soon!'

3

CeCe
The Gibbston Valley

'Cee, you're holding the map upside down!' Chrissie said as she glanced over to the passenger seat.

'I am not . . . oh, maybe I am.' CeCe frowned. 'The words look the same to me either way, and as for the road squiggles . . . Jesus, when did we last see a signpost?'

'A while back. Wow, isn't this scenery spectacular?' Chrissie breathed as she pulled the hire car onto a verge and peered out at the majestic dark green mountains that unfolded under a ponderous cloudy sky. She reached to turn up the heating as raindrops began to splash onto the windscreen.

'Yup, I'm completely lost.' CeCe handed the map to Chrissie and looked in front and behind her at the empty road. 'It's ages since we left Queenstown. We should have stocked up on supplies when we were there, but I thought there would be other places along the way.'

'Right, according to the directions we printed off, we should come to a sign for The Vinery very soon. I guess we just have to keep going and hopefully find someone who can point us to it.' Chrissie tucked a lock of black curly hair back from her face and gave CeCe a weary smile. Their journey had involved stopovers in Melbourne and Christchurch, and they were both hungry and tired.

'There's hardly been a car for miles,' CeCe shrugged.

'Come on, Cee. Where's your spirit of adventure gone?'

'I dunno. Maybe I've gone soft in my old age and prefer home to sitting in a car completely lost, whilst it pisses down with rain. I'm actually cold!'

'It's coming into winter here. There'll be snow on those mountaintops before much longer. You're too used to the climate in the Alice, that's the problem,' said Chrissie as she put the car in gear and they set off once more. The windscreen wipers were working at full tilt, the downpour now rendering the mountains around them a washed-out blur.

'Yeah, I'm definitely a sunshine girl, and always have been. Can I borrow your hoody, Chrissie?'

'Sure. I did tell you, though, it was much colder here. Good job I packed a spare one for you, wasn't it?'

CeCe reached over into the back seat and opened one of the rucksacks. 'Thanks, Chrissie, I don't know what I'd do without you.'

'To be honest, nor do I.'

CeCe reached for Chrissie's hand and squeezed it. 'Sorry I'm so useless.'

'You're not useless, Cee, just not very . . . practical. Then again, I am, but I'm not as creative as you, so we make a good team, don't we?'

'We do.'

As Chrissie drove, CeCe felt comforted by her presence. The past few months had been the happiest of her life. Between spending time with Chrissie and going off on painting jaunts into the Outback with Francis, her grandfather, her life – and her heart – had never been so full. After the trauma of losing her close bond with Star, she'd thought she could never be happy again, but between them, Chrissie and Francis had filled the bit of her that had been missing; she had found a family where she fitted in, however unconventional it was.

'Look! There's a sign.' She pointed through the driving rain. 'Pull over and see what it says.'

'I can see it from here and it's saying left to The Vinery – woohoo! We made it!' Chrissie cheered. 'By the way,' she said as she steered the car down a narrow bumpy track, 'have you told your sisters yet that I'm coming with you to Atlantis?'

'The ones I've spoken to, yup, of course I have.'

'Do you think they'll be shocked . . . about us?'

'Pa brought us up to accept everyone, whatever their colour or orientation. Claudia, our housekeeper, might raise an eyebrow, but that's only because she's from the older generation and very traditional.'

'And what about you, Cee? Are *you* comfortable about us in front of your family?'

'You know I am. Why are you suddenly being so insecure?'

'Only because . . . even though you've told me all about your sisters and Atlantis, they didn't feel . . . *real*. But in just over a week, we'll actually *be* there. And I'm scared. Especially of meeting Star. I mean, you two were a team before I came along.'

'Before her boyfriend Mouse came along, you mean? Star was the one who wanted to get away from me, remember?'

'I know, but she still calls you every week, and I know you guys text all the time, and—'

'Chrissie! Star's my sister. And you, well, you're . . .'

'Yes?'

'You're my "other half". It's different, completely different, and I really hope there's room for both of you.'

26

'Of course there is, but it's a big deal, you know, "coming out".'

'Grrr, I hate that phrase.' CeCe shuddered. 'I'm just me, the same as I always have been. I hate being put in a box with a label. Look! There's another sign for The Vinery. Turn right just there.'

They set off down another narrow track. In the distance, CeCe could just make out row upon row of what looked like stripped, skeletal vines.

'Doesn't seem like this place is very successful. In the south of France at this time of year, the vines are covered in leaves and grapes.'

'Cee, you're forgetting the seasons are the other way round in this part of the world, like in Oz. I'd reckon the vines are harvested in the summer, so probably somewhere between February and April, which is why they look bare now. Okay, there's another signpost. "To Shop", "To Deliveries" and "To Reception". We'll head for reception, shall we?'

'Whatever you say, boss,' said CeCe, noticing the rain had now stopped and the sun was beginning to peep through the clouds. 'This weather's just like England,' she murmured. 'One minute rain, the next minute sun.'

'Maybe that's why so many English live here, although your grandfather was saying yesterday that the biggest group of migrants here is the Scots, closely followed by the Irish.'

'Setting off to the other side of the world to make their fortune. It's sort of what I did. Look, there's another sign to reception. Wow, what a lovely old stone house that is. It looks so cosy, set in its valley, with mountains shielding it on every side. It's a bit like our home in Geneva, without the lake,' CeCe commented as Chrissie drew the car to a halt.

The two-storey farmhouse was nestled in a hillside just above the vineyard, which extended down in terraces into the valley. Its walls were fashioned from sturdy grey rock, ruggedly cut and intricately laid together. The large windows reflected the burgeoning blue light of the sky, and a covered veranda hugged the house on all sides, with planters of cheerful red begonias hanging from the railings. CeCe could tell that the main house had been added to over the years, as the stone walls were different shades of grey, aged by the weather.

'The reception's over there,' Chrissie said, breaking into her thoughts as she pointed to a door on the left of the farmhouse. 'Maybe there'll be someone who can help us find Mary. Have you got that pic of the ring Ally faxed you?'

'I stuffed it in my rucksack before we left.' CeCe climbed out and grabbed it from the back seat. She unzipped the front pocket and pulled a couple of sheets of paper out of it.

'Honestly, Cee, they're all crumpled,' said Chrissie in dismay.

'That doesn't matter, does it? We can still see what the ring looks like.'

'Yeah, but it doesn't appear very professional. I mean, going to knock on the door of a complete stranger to tell her or someone in her family you believe she's your missing sister . . . She might think that you're nuts. I would,' Chrissie pointed out.

'Well, all we can do is ask. Wow, I suddenly feel nervous. You're right, they might think I'm crazy.'

'At least you've got that photo of your sisters and your father. You all look normal in that.'

'Yeah, but we don't look like sisters, do we?' CeCe said as Chrissie closed the car doors and locked them. 'Right, let's go before I chicken out.'

The reception – a small pine-clad showroom tacked onto the side of the main house – was deserted. CeCe rang the bell, as requested by the notice on the desk.

'Look at all these wines,' Chrissie said as she wandered round the showroom. 'Some of them have won awards. This is a pretty serious place. Maybe we should ask to try some.'

'It's only lunchtime and you go to sleep if you daytime drink. Besides, you're driving . . .'

'Hello, can I help you?' A tall young woman with blonde hair and bright blue eyes appeared from a door to the side of the showroom. CeCe thought how naturally pretty she was.

'Yes, I was wondering if we could speak to, um, Mary McDougal?' she said.

'That's me!' said the woman. 'I'm Mary McDougal. How can I help you?'

'Oh, er . . .'

'Well, I'm Chrissie and this is CeCe,' said Chrissie, taking over from a tongue-tied CeCe, 'and the situation is that CeCe's dad – who's dead, by the way – has a lawyer who has been hunting for someone who CeCe and her family have called the "missing sister" for years. Recently, the lawyer got some information that said the missing sister might be a woman called Mary McDougal, who lives at this address. Sorry, I know it all sounds a bit weird, but . . .'

'The thing is, Mary,' said CeCe, who by now had gathered her wits, 'Pa Salt – our father – adopted six of us girls as babies, and he used to speak about the "missing sister" – the one he couldn't find. We're all named after the Pleiades star cluster, and the youngest, Merope, has always been missing. She's technically the seventh sister, just like in all the Seven Sisters legends, right?'

As the woman stared blankly back at her, CeCe continued hastily.

'Actually, you probably don't know of them. It's just that we've been brought up with the myths, though most people, unless they're interested in stars and Greek legends, have never heard of the Seven Sisters.' CeCe realised she was rambling, so she shut her mouth before she could say more.

'Oh, I've heard of the Seven Sisters all right,' Mary smiled. 'My mother – who's also called Mary – read Classics at uni. She's always quoting Plato and the like.'

'Your mother's called Mary too?' CeCe stared at her.

'Yes, Mary McDougal, the same as me. My name's Mary-Kate officially, though everyone calls me MK. Er . . . do you have any other information about this missing sister?'

'Yes, just one thing. There's this picture of a ring,' said Chrissie. She placed the crumpled image in front of Mary-Kate on the slim counter that separated them. 'It's a ring with emeralds in a star shape with seven points and a diamond in the centre. Apparently, this Mary got it from, um, somebody, and it proves that it's her, if you know what I mean. Sadly, that's the only physical clue we have.'

Mary-Kate glanced at the picture, her brow furrowing slightly.

'It probably means nothing to you, and we'd better leave,' CeCe mumbled, her embarrassment growing by the second. She grabbed the piece of paper. 'So sorry for bothering you and—'

'Hold on! Can I take another look?'

CeCe stared at her in surprise. 'You recognise it?'

'I think I might do, yes.'

CeCe's stomach turned over. She looked at Chrissie, wishing she could reach for her hand and have her own comfortably squeezed, but she wasn't at *that* stage in public yet. She waited as the young woman studied the picture more closely.

'I couldn't say for sure, but it looks a lot like Mum's ring,' said Mary-Kate. 'Or actually – if it is the same one – it's mine now, as she gave it to me on my twenty-first.'

'Really?' CeCe gasped.

'Yeah, she's had it for as long as I can remember. It wasn't something she wore every day, but sometimes on special occasions, she'd take it out of her jewellery box and put it on. I always thought it was pretty. It's very small, you see, and she could only fit it on her little finger, which didn't look right, or her fourth finger, which already had an engagement and wedding ring on it. But as I'm not about to get engaged or married, it doesn't matter which finger I wear it on,' she added with a grin.

'So does that mean you've got it now?' CeCe said quickly. 'Could we take a look at it?'

'Actually, before she left on her trip, Mum asked me if she could take it with her, as I so rarely wear it anyway, though maybe she decided not to . . . Listen, why don't you come upstairs to the house?'

At that moment, a tall, well-muscled man wearing an Akubra hat put his head around the door.

'Hi, Doug,' said Mary-Kate. 'All okay?'

'Yeah, just popping in to get some more water bottles for the gang.' Doug indicated the group of burly men standing outside.

'Hi,' he said to CeCe and Chrissie as he crossed to a fridge and pulled out a tray of water bottles. 'Are youse tourists?'

'Yeah, sort of. It's beaut round here,' said Chrissie, recognising the man's Aussie accent.

'It is, yeah.'

'I'm just going to pop upstairs with our visitors,' said Mary-Kate. 'They think I may have some family connection to them.'

'Really?' Doug stared at CeCe and Chrissie and frowned. 'Well, me and the boys will be having our tucker just out there, if ya need anything.'

Doug indicated a round wooden table where his men were gathering and sitting down.

31

'Thanks, Doug,' said Mary-Kate.

He nodded, gave CeCe and Chrissie a piercing look, then left.

'Blimey, you wouldn't mess with them, would you?' breathed CeCe, staring at the group outside.

'No,' Mary-Kate said with a grin. 'Don't mind Doug, he's our manager – it's just that since Mum and my brother Jack left, he's gone all protective, y'know? The boys are great actually. I had a meal with them last night. Now, come through.'

'Seriously, we can wait outside if you want,' Chrissie said.

'It's fine, although I'll admit I'm finding this all a bit weird. Anyway, as you've just seen, I'm well protected.'

'Thanks,' said CeCe, as Mary-Kate pulled up part of the counter to let them in. She led them up some steep wooden steps and along a hallway into an airy beamed sitting room, which faced the valley and mountains beyond on one side, and was dominated by a huge stone fireplace on the other.

'Please, sit down and I'll go take a look for the ring.'

'Thank you for trusting us,' CeCe said as Mary-Kate crossed the room towards a door.

'No worries. I'll tell my mate Fletch to come in and keep you company,' she replied.

After Mary-Kate left and the two of them sat down on the old but comfortable sofa in front of the fireplace, Chrissie squeezed CeCe's hand. 'You okay?'

'Yup. What a sweet girl she is. I'm not sure I would have let two strangers into my house after that story.'

'No, but people round these parts are probably a lot more trusting than they are in cities. Besides, as she says, she has a team of minders just outside.'

'She reminds me of Star, with her blonde colouring and big blue eyes.'

'I know what you mean from the pictures you've shown me, but remember, none of you sisters are related by blood, so the chances are high that Mary-Kate isn't blood-related to any of you either,' Chrissie pointed out.

The door opened and a tall, lanky man in his early twenties entered. His long, light brown hair hung down from underneath a woollen beanie, and his ears sported several silver piercings.

'Hi there, I'm Fletch, good to meet you.'

The girls introduced themselves as Fletch sat down in an armchair across from them.

'So, MK's sent me in to make sure you guys won't hold her at gunpoint over her jewellery,' he grinned. 'What's the story?'

CeCe left it all to Chrissie to explain, because she did stuff like that so much better.

'I know it sounds strange,' Chrissie finished, 'but CeCe comes from a weird family. I mean, *they're* not weird, but the fact their father adopted them from all over the world *is*.'

'D'ya know why he adopted all of you? I mean, specifically?' asked Fletch.

'Not a clue,' said CeCe. 'I guess it was probably random, like, on his travels. We happened to be there, and he swept us up and took us home with him.'

'I see. I mean, I don't see, but . . .'

At that moment, Mary-Kate arrived back in the sitting room.

'I've looked through my jewellery box and Mum's, but the ring isn't there. She must have taken it with her after all.'

'How long is she away for?' asked CeCe.

'Well, what she said when she left was, "for as long as I want to be".' Mary-Kate shrugged. 'My dad died recently, and she decided she wanted to take a world tour and visit all the friends she hasn't seen for years, whilst she was still young enough to do it.'

'I'm sorry your dad died. As we said, so did mine recently,' said CeCe.

'Thanks,' said Mary-Kate. 'It's been really tough, y'know? It was only a few months ago.'

'Must have been a shock for your mum too,' said Chrissie.

'Oh, it was. Even though Dad was actually seventy-three, we never thought of him as old. Mum's quite a bit younger – she has the big Six-O coming up next year. But you'd never know how old she was either – she looks so youthful. See, there's a photo of her over there, taken last year with me, my brother Jack and my dad. Dad always liked to say that Mum looked like an actress called Grace Kelly.'

When Mary-Kate brought it over, both girls stared at the photo. If young Mary-Kate was pretty, Mary senior was still displaying the signs of a true beauty, despite being in her late fifties.

'Wow! I'd take her for not much older than forty,' whistled Chrissie.

'Me too,' said CeCe. 'She's . . . well, she's stunning.'

'She is, but more importantly, she's a great human being. Everyone loves my mum,' Mary-Kate said with a smile.

'I'll second that,' said Fletch. 'She's just one of those special people; very warm and welcoming, y'know?'

'Yeah, our adoptive mum, Ma, is like that – she just makes all of us feel good about ourselves,' said CeCe as she studied the other pictures arranged on the mantelpiece. One was a black and white shot of what looked like a younger Mary senior, dressed in a dark academic robe and cap, with a bright smile on her face. In the background were stone columns flanking the entrance of a grand building.

'So that's your mum too?' CeCe pointed to the photo.

'Yeah, that was her graduation from Trinity College in Dublin,' Mary-Kate nodded.

'She's Irish?'

'Yup, she is.'

'So, you really don't know how long she'll be abroad for?' Chrissie asked.

'No, as I said, the trip is open-ended; Mum said that not having a deadline on when she had to return was part of the treat. Although she did plan out her first few weeks.'

'Sorry to hassle you, but we'd love to meet up with her and ask her about that ring. Do you know where your mum is now?' said CeCe.

'Her schedule's stuck to the fridge; I'll go take a look, but I'm pretty sure she's still on Norfolk Island,' Mary-Kate said as she left the room.

'Norfolk?' frowned CeCe. 'Isn't that a county in England?'

'It is,' said Fletch, 'but it's also a tiny island that sits in the South Pacific between Australia and New Zealand. It's a beaut place, and when MK's mum's oldest friend Bridget came here to visit a couple of years back, they took a trip there together. Her friend liked it so much, she decided to up sticks from London and retire there.'

'Yup, Mum's still on the island, according to her fridge schedule,' Mary-Kate said as she reappeared.

'When does she leave? And how do we get there?' asked CeCe.

'In a couple of days' time, but the island's only a short plane ride from Auckland. I know that the planes don't fly every day, mind. We'd have to find out when they do,' warned Mary-Kate.

'Shit!' CeCe murmured under her breath. She glanced at Chrissie. 'We're meant to be flying out to London late tomorrow night. Have we got time?'

'We'll have to make time, won't we?' Chrissie shrugged. 'I mean, she's just down the road, compared to coming all this way back from Europe. And if the missing sister can be identified by this ring, then . . .'

'I'll check flights to Norfolk Island, and Queenstown to Auckland, 'cos it'd be faster to fly than drive,' said Fletch, standing up and moving to a long wooden dining table covered in papers, magazines and an old-fashioned fat-bottomed computer. 'It might take some time because the internet around here is dodgy, to put it mildly.' He tapped on the keyboard. 'Yup, no connection at the moment,' he sighed.

'I saw your brother in that photo. Is he in New Zealand at the moment?' CeCe asked Mary-Kate.

'He is normally, but he just went off to the south of France to learn more about French wine-making.'

'So he's gonna take over the vineyard from your dad?' Chrissie clarified.

'Yup. Hey, are you guys hungry? It's way past lunchtime.'

'Starving,' both Chrissie and CeCe answered at the same time.

After the four of them had put together some bread, local cheese and cold meats, they cleared space on the dining table and sat down to eat.

'So where do you guys actually live?' Fletch asked.

'In the Alice,' said CeCe. 'But my family home is called Atlantis, which is on the shores of Lake Geneva in Switzerland.'

'Atlantis, the mythical home of Atlas, father of the Seven Sisters,' smiled Mary-Kate. 'Your dad really was into his Greek legends.'

'He was, yeah. We have this big telescope that still stands in an observatory at the top of the house. By the time we could talk, we knew all the names of the stars in and around the Orion and Taurus constellations by heart,' said CeCe. 'I wasn't interested, to be honest, until I came to the Alice and realised that the Seven Sisters are goddesses in Aboriginal mythology. It made me wonder how there could be all these legends about them literally everywhere. Like, in Mayan culture, Greek, Japanese . . . these sisters are famous all over the world.'

'The Maori have stories about the sisters too,' Mary-Kate added. 'They're called the daughters of Matariki here. They each have special skills and gifts that they bring to the people.'

'So how did each culture know about the other back then?' Chrissie questioned. 'I mean, there was no internet or even a postal service or telephone, so how can all the legends be so similar without there being any communication between people?'

'You really need to meet my mum,' chuckled Mary-Kate. 'She doesn't half ramble on about subjects like that. She's a total brainbox – not like me, I'm afraid. I'm more into my music than philosophy.'

'You look like your mum, though,' said Chrissie.

'Yeah, a lot of people say that, but actually, I'm adopted.'

CeCe shot Chrissie a look. 'Wow,' she said. 'Like me and my sisters. Do you know exactly where you were adopted from? And who your birth parents are?'

'I don't. Mum and Dad told me as soon as I was old enough to understand, but I've always felt that my mum is my mum, and my dad is . . . *was* my dad. End of.'

'Sorry to pry,' CeCe said quickly. 'It's just . . . it's just that if you *are* adopted, then . . .'

'Then you really might be the missing sister,' Chrissie finished for her.

'Look, I understand your family have been searching for this person for a while,' Mary-Kate said gently, 'but I've never heard my mum mention anything about a "missing sister". All I know is that it was a closed adoption, and it happened here in NZ. I'm sure Mum will clear it all up if you get to see her.'

'Right.' Fletch stood up. 'I'm gonna try getting online again, so you guys have some idea of whether you can travel to Norfolk Island in the next twenty-four hours.' He moved along the table to sit in front of the computer.

'Does your mum have a mobile?' Chrissie asked.

'She does,' said Mary-Kate, 'but if you're about to ask me whether we can contact her on it, there's only the tiniest chance that she'll have a signal on Norfolk Island. Part of the beauty of living there is the fact they're fifty years behind everywhere else, especially in the modern technology department.'

'Okay, Houston, we have lift-off!' Fletch exclaimed. 'There's a seven a.m. flight from Queenstown to Auckland tomorrow morning, landing at eight. The flight for Norfolk Island leaves at ten a.m. and lands just shy of a couple of hours later. What time does your onward flight leave Sydney tomorrow night?'

'Around eleven p.m.,' said Chrissie. 'Are there any flights to Sydney leaving Norfolk Island late afternoon?'

'I'll take a look,' said Fletch, going back to his computer screen.

'Even if we can get a flight out at the right time, it would only give us a few hours on Norfolk Island,' said CeCe.

'It's a tiny island, though, eh?' Fletch commented.

'Mary-Kate, do you think you could just try your mum's mobile?' Chrissie asked. 'I mean, to go all that way and then find she isn't there would be a real pain.'

'I can try, for sure. And I can call Bridget, the friend she's staying with, too. Mum left her number on the fridge – I'll go and get it, then call both of them.'

'We're in luck!' said Fletch. 'There's a flight at five p.m.

from the island into Sydney. If you land in the morning at ten forty Norfolk time, that should give you plenty of time to meet up with Mary-Kate's mum. Who, by the way, is always known as "Merry" – she was apparently called that when she was little because she never stopped giggling.'

'That's cute,' smiled Chrissie.

'Not a nickname I was ever given as a baby,' muttered CeCe under her breath. 'Me and Electra were the angry, shouty sisters.'

'I've just tried my mum and Bridget, but I only got their voicemails on the mobile and the landline,' Mary-Kate said as she appeared from the kitchen. 'I left messages saying you were trying to get in contact with Mum about the ring and that you're planning to visit tomorrow, so if they manage to listen to their answer services, they'll know you're coming.'

'Well?' Fletch peered at them over the computer screen. 'There are three seats left on the flights to Auckland and Norfolk Island, and only two back to Sydney. Are you gonna go or not?'

CeCe looked at Chrissie, who shrugged. 'Whilst we're here, we should at least try to get to see Mary-Kate's mum, Cee.'

'Yup, you're right, even if it is an early wake-up tomorrow. If I give you my credit card details, Fletch, can you book us on the flights? Sorry to ask, but I doubt we'll find an internet café anywhere locally.'

'You won't, and course I will, no hassle, eh?'

'Oh, and just one last thing: can you recommend anywhere that we can stay the night?' Chrissie said, always the practical one.

'Sure, right here in the annexe,' said Mary-Kate. 'We use the dorms for the workers, but I'm pretty sure there's one room spare just now. It's not fancy or anything – just bunk beds – but it's the nearest place to rest your heads.'

'Thanks a million,' said Chrissie. 'We'll get out of your hair now. I'd like to take a wander outside. The countryside around here is incredible.'

'Okay, I'll just show you to your dorms and . . .' Mary-Kate glanced at Fletch before saying, 'Mum left the freezer full, and I can defrost a chook casserole for dinner tonight. You guys want in? I'd love to hear more about your family and what the connection might be to me.'

'Yeah, it would be great if you turned out to be the missing sister. And that's so kind of you to invite us,' CeCe smiled. 'Thanks for being so hospitable.'

'It's the New Zealand way, eh?' shrugged Fletch. 'Share and share alike.'

'Thanks,' said Chrissie. 'See you guys later.'

Outside, the air felt cool and fresh, and the sky was now a deep azure blue. 'It's so different from Australia here – it reminds me of Switzerland with all these mountains, but it's wilder and more untamed,' CeCe commented as they walked side by side past the sweeping acres of vines. They found a narrow path that led up an undulating hillside, and as they walked, the vegetation became coarser and less civilised. CeCe brushed her fingers over the leaves of the shrubs they passed to release the bright green scents of nature.

She could hear the calls of unfamiliar birds from the trees, and a faint rush of water, so she pulled Chrissie off the path towards it. They navigated their way through brambles – still wet from the earlier downpour and now glistening in the sunshine – until they stood beside a fast-running crystal-clear stream, splashing across smooth grey rock. As they watched dragonflies skimming over the surface, CeCe turned to smile at Chrissie.

'I wish we could stay here for longer,' she said. 'It's beautiful, and so peaceful.'

'I'd love to come back one day and explore properly,' Chrissie agreed. 'So . . . what do you think about Mary-Kate not wanting to know about her birth parents? I mean, you defo had your doubts when you went in search of your own birth family.'

'That was different.' CeCe swatted a bug from her face, panting as they followed the stream uphill. 'Pa had just died, Star had gone all weird and distant . . . I needed something – or someone else of my own, y'know? Mary-Kate still has a loving mum and brother, so she probably hasn't felt the urge to shake things up.'

Chrissie nodded, then reached out to CeCe's arm to tug her back. 'Can we stop for a second? My leg's aching.'

They sat down on a patch of mossy grass to catch their breath, and Chrissie swung her legs onto CeCe's lap. In comfortable silence, they gazed out over the valley, the farmhouse below and the neatly ordered lines of the vine terraces the only sign of human habitation.

'So, have we found her?' CeCe asked eventually.

'You know what?' Chrissie replied. 'I think we might have done.'

Dinner with Mary-Kate and Fletch that night was very relaxed, and it was after midnight and two bottles of excellent house pinot noir when CeCe and Chrissie said their goodbyes and made their way outside to the annexe. As Mary-Kate had said, the room was basic but had everything they needed, including a shower and thick woollen blankets to ward off the creeping cold of night.

'Wow, in the Alice I'm normally throwing the sheets off me 'cos I'm dripping with sweat, and here I am huddled under the covers,' chuckled CeCe. 'What do you think of Mary-Kate?'

'I think she's cool,' commented Chrissie. 'And if she did turn out to be your missing sister, it would be fun to have her around.'

'She said she was twenty-two, which would fit in perfectly with the rest of us. Electra, who's the youngest, is twenty-six. Or maybe we're just on a complete wild goose chase,' CeCe added sleepily. 'Sorry, but I'm about to drop off . . .'

Chrissie reached for her hand from the bunk opposite. 'Night night, honey, sleep tight. We've got an early morning call tomorrow, that's for sure.'

4

'Time to wake up, Cee. We're about to land and you need to fasten your seat belt.'

Chrissie's voice broke into CeCe's dreams and she opened her eyes to see Chrissie reaching for the seat belt to strap her in.

'Where are we?'

'About a thousand feet above Norfolk Island. Wow! It's tiny! Like one of those atolls you see in ads for the Maldives. Look down there; it's so green, and the water is such an amazing turquoise colour. I wonder if Merry or her friend Bridget got our messages?'

CeCe peered nervously out of her window. 'We'll find out when we land, I suppose. Mary-Kate said she left them both details of our flight time, so you never know, they might even be there to meet us. Oh my God, have you seen that? It looks like the runway's headed right out to sea! I don't think I can look.'

CeCe turned her head away as the plane's engines roared and it prepared to land.

'Phew! I'm glad that's over,' she said as the pilot put the brakes on hard and the plane skidded to a halt.

The two of them piled off the small aircraft with their rucksacks and headed for the tiny building that was Norfolk

Island's airport terminal. They passed by a small crowd of onlookers waiting behind a fence for passengers, then through customs control, where a beagle on a lead was sniffing around the new arrivals.

'It's a bit different to arriving on the Aussie mainland, isn't it?' CeCe commented. 'I reckon the Aussie border-force guys would prefer to have you stark naked before they let you through,' she giggled, as they emerged into a small arrivals area where the same handful of onlookers had moved inside to greet their visitors.

'Remember that I've never flown into Oz before, because this is the first time I've ever left the country.' Chrissie nudged her. 'Now, can you see a woman who looks like that photo we saw of Merry yesterday?'

Both of them scanned the group, most of whom had already collected their visitors and were walking away.

'Seems like they didn't get our messages,' Chrissie shrugged. 'Anyway, Mary-Kate said it was just a twenty-minute walk to Bridget's house from here. But which way?'

'If in doubt, go to the tourist information desk, which is right over there.' CeCe nodded to a young man sitting behind a desk piled with leaflets. The two of them walked over to it.

'Hi there, can I help you guys?'

'Yes, we're looking for a road called . . .' – Chrissie pulled a piece of paper out of her jean pocket – 'Headstone.'

'That's easy enough; it's at the end of the runway over there.' The man pointed into the distance. 'Just walk round the airport perimeter and turn left. That'll take you up to Headstone Road.'

'Thanks,' said CeCe.

'You guys looking for anywhere to stay? I can suggest a few ideas, eh?' the man encouraged them.

'No, we're going back to Sydney this arvo.'

'A flying visit f'sure, mate,' the man joked. 'Well, why don't you check in your rucksacks now so you don't have to carry them with you? Take your togs, though, in case you fancy a dip before you leave. There's a few ripper beaches around and about.'

'Thanks, we will.'

The man pointed them in the direction of the airline desk and to their surprise, they were able to check in to the flight for Sydney immediately.

'Wow, I love it here,' said CeCe as she dug into her rucksack for swimming costumes and towels. 'It's all so casual.'

'The beauty of small-island living,' said Chrissie as they set off. 'And it's so green – I love those trees,' she gestured to the tall firs that stood sentinel in rows ahead of them.

'They're called Norfolk pines,' said CeCe. 'Pa had some planted along the edge of our garden at Atlantis when I was younger.'

'I'm impressed, Cee, I didn't take you for a botanist.'

'You know I'm not, but a Norfolk pine was one of the first things that I ever drew when I was younger. It was terrible, of course, but Ma had it framed and I gave it to Pa for Christmas. I think it's still on the wall of his study to this day.'

'That's cool. So . . . what are we meant to say when we turn up on these guys' doorstep?' Chrissie asked.

'Same as we did with Mary-Kate, I suppose. After all this, I just hope they're in. I feel wrecked from an early wake-up, two flights and now two more to go later on!'

'I know, but it'll be worth it if we get to meet Merry and see that ring. Whatever happens, we should defo go for a dip in that amazing sea before we leave for the airport. That'll wake us up.'

A few minutes later, they saw a sign saying *Headstone Road.*

'What's the house number?'

'I can't see any numbers,' CeCe said as they passed the wooden bungalows, all sitting in immaculate gardens and surrounded by manicured hibiscus hedges studded with bright flowers.

'The house is called . . .' Chrissie studied the word on the note Mary-Kate had written. 'I've no idea how to pronounce this.'

'Well, don't ask me to try,' CeCe chuckled. 'They're all very house-proud round here, aren't they? It reminds me a bit of an English village, what with all the perfectly trimmed lawns.'

'Look! There it is.' Chrissie nudged her, pointing to a neatly painted sign saying *Síochán*.

They stood in front of the cattle grid that marked the entrance to the property. The bungalow was pristine like all the others, and had a couple of large gnomes standing guard at either side of the grid.

'Those two are dressed in the colours of the Irish flag, and I think that house name might be Gaelic, so I reckon the occupants are too,' said Chrissie as they carefully crossed the cattle grid.

'Right' – CeCe lowered her voice as they walked up to the door – 'who's going to do the talking?'

'You begin, and I'll help you out if you're struggling,' Chrissie suggested.

'Here goes,' said CeCe before ringing the doorbell, which sang a little tune that sounded like an Irish jig. There was no reply. On the fourth press of the bell, Chrissie turned to her.

'How about taking a wander round the back? They might be out in the garden – it's a beaut day.'

'Worth a try,' CeCe shrugged, so they walked round the side of the bungalow to the back of the house, edged by banana palms. The terrace, table and chairs, all protected by a sun awning, were deserted.

46

'Damn!' CeCe said, feeling her heart sink. 'There's no one in.'

'Look!' Chrissie pointed to the bottom of the long garden, where a figure with a spade was digging in the earth. 'Let's go and ask him, shall we?'

'Hellooo!' Chrissie called as they drew closer, and eventually a man – who was broad-shouldered and probably in his mid-sixties – looked up and waved at them from what was clearly a vegetable patch. 'Maybe he's expecting us.'

'Or maybe he's just friendly. Didn't you notice that everyone in the passing cars waved at us too?' said CeCe.

'Hello, girls,' said the man, leaning on his spade as they approached him. 'What can I do for the two of youse?' he asked in a pronounced Australian accent.

'Uh, yeah, hi. Do you, um, live here? I mean, is this your house?' CeCe asked.

'It is, yeah. And you are?'

'I'm CeCe and this is my friend Chrissie. We're looking for a woman – in fact, two women: one called Bridget Dempsey and the other called Mary – or Merry – McDougal. Do you know either of them?'

'I most certainly do,' the man nodded. 'Especially Bridge. She's my missus.'

'Great! That's fantastic. Are they in?'

'I'm afraid not, girls. They've both buggered off to Sydney, leaving me all on my lonesome.'

'You're joking!' CeCe muttered to Chrissie. 'We could've flown straight there. Merry's daughter, Mary-Kate, said she wasn't flying out until tomorrow.'

'She's right,' said the man. 'Merry was staying here, but she suddenly changed her mind and suggested that she and Bridge get the afternoon flight to Sydney, so they could spend what they called a "girls' night" together in the big city and do some shopping.'

'Shit,' CeCe said. 'That's a shame, because we've come a long way to see her and we're off to Sydney ourselves tonight. Do you happen to know how long Merry is in Sydney for?'

'I think she said she was flying out of Oz tonight. I'm due to pick up Bridge on the incoming flight this afternoon.'

'That must be the plane we're flying *out* on,' said Chrissie, rolling her eyes at CeCe in despair.

'Can I help you in any way?' the man said, sweeping off his Akubra hat and dabbing his sweating forehead with a handkerchief.

'Thanks, but it's Merry we came to speak to,' said CeCe.

'Well, why don't we step out of this glaring sun and go sit on the terrace? We can crack a couple of tinnies and you can explain why you need to see Merry. I'm Tony, by the way,' he said as they followed him back up the garden and under the cool shade of the awning. 'I'll just go grab those beers, and then we'll have a chat.'

'He seems like a good guy,' commented Chrissie as they sat down.

'Yeah, but he's not the person we want to speak to,' CeCe sighed.

'There y'go.' Tony returned and put the ice-cold beers down in front of them. They each took a grateful swig. 'So, what's the story?'

CeCe did her best to explain, with Chrissie filling in details when needed.

'Now that's a tall tale,' he chuckled, 'although I still don't fully get the connection between your folks and Merry.'

'Nor do I, to be honest, and I get the feeling we're probably barking up the wrong tree, but we thought we'd try anyway,' CeCe said, feeling deflated and exhausted.

'Mary-Kate did leave messages for her mum saying we

were coming. And one for Bridget. Didn't they get them?' said Chrissie.

'I dunno, 'cos I was out all day yesterday fixing up a bathroom for a mate of mine. To be honest, I don't know much about Merry, love. I met Bridge two years ago when she asked me to build this for her.' He indicated the bungalow. 'My parents brought me across from Brisbane when I was a kid, and I'm a builder by trade. My first wife died some years past, and when Bridge moved here, she was single too. Never thought I'd find another woman at my age, but we clicked right from the start. We got hitched six months ago,' he beamed.

'So you haven't known Merry long?'

'No, I only met her for the first time at our wedding.'

'Is your wife Irish by any chance?' continued Chrissie doggedly.

'Ya guessed then,' Tony nodded. 'She is, and proud of her heritage too.'

'We were told that Merry is originally Irish as well,' said CeCe.

'All I know is that they were at school and then uni in Dublin together. They lost contact for a long time – it happens, doesn't it, when people move away after uni? But now they're thick as thieves again. Can I get you guys a sarnie? My belly's rumbling f'sure.'

'If it's no trouble, that would be fantastic,' CeCe put in before Chrissie could politely decline. Her belly was rumbling too. 'We can come in and help you,' she added.

They followed Tony into a neat kitchen, which he proudly said he'd built himself.

'Never thought I'd get ta live in it, mind,' he said as he pulled cheese and ham out of the fridge. 'We're a bit low on supplies – everything has to be brought in by boat or plane, y'see. A new delivery isn't until tomorrow.'

'It must be amazing living here,' said Chrissie as she buttered the bread.

'For the main part, yeah,' Tony agreed. 'But like Robinson Crusoe, island living has its drawbacks. There's not much here for the young 'uns and a lot o' them leave the island to go to uni or find work. The internet is bloody terrible and unless you've got your own business like me, tourism's the only main industry. It's becoming an island of old folks, though there are changes coming to improve things, get some new blood. It's a beaut place to bring up kids. Everyone knows everyone here and there's a real sense of community. It's dead friendly and there's very little crime. Right, shall we take our tucker outside, eh?'

The girls followed Tony back out onto the terrace and launched into their sandwiches.

'Tony?'

'Yeah, CeCe?'

'I just wondered if, while she was here, you'd seen Merry wearing an emerald ring?'

Tony burst into a deep throaty chuckle.

'Can't say I look at stuff like that. Bridge says I'd never even notice if she came in dressed as Santa Claus, and she's probably right. Although . . . hang on a minute . . .' He put his fingers to his short beard and stroked it. 'Come ta think of it, I do remember a couple of nights ago, Bridge and Merry comparing rings. The one I bought for Bridge as an engagement ring had a green stone, of course . . . her being Irish an' all.'

'And . . . ?' CeCe leant forward.

'Merry was wearing an emerald ring too – they put their fingers together and shared one of those looks girls share, y'know?'

'So, she was actually wearing an emerald ring?'

'Yeah, she was. They were laughing, because Bridge said her emerald was bigger than Merry's.'

'Right.' CeCe and Chrissie exchanged a glance. 'That's encouraging,' CeCe nodded. 'Maybe we're on the right path after all. Do you happen to know where she's going after Sydney?'

'Yeah, she's headed to Canada – Toronto, I think she said, but I can check with Bridge.'

Chrissie looked at her watch. 'Thanks for your help and the sarnie, Tony. We're gonna get in a swim before we go to the airport.'

'Well, why don't we get the plates cleaned up – I don't want ta leave any mess around the place for Bridge to complain about – then you can jump in my pick-up and we'll do a quick tour of the island and finish off with a swim?'

'Wow! We'd love to,' smiled CeCe.

After a whistle-stop tour of the island, which could be reached end to end within twenty minutes, Tony drove them down a narrow road.

'Check out those.' Tony pointed at the row of ancient trees which towered above them.

'They look prehistoric. What are they?' asked CeCe.

'They're Moreton Bay fig trees; some of them are over a hundred years old,' Tony told her as the road led them past the airport runway and wound downwards, opening out at a small bridge and a cluster of stone buildings. They arrived in front of an almost deserted beach, where gentle waves lapped at the shore. In the distance a line of foaming white breakers indicated a reef. Tony led them to the hut that provided changing facilities and they emerged in their swimwear with their towels around their waists.

'Race ya!' called Tony, beginning to run across the warm

sand towards the waves. 'Last one in's a sissy!' he said as he splashed up to his waist then dived in. A few metres from the water's edge, CeCe helped Chrissie take off her prosthetic leg. Chrissie wrapped it up in a towel and placed it a safe distance from the waves.

'It always freaks me out that someone will come and steal it,' said Chrissie as CeCe helped her move towards the sea.

'Even I can't imagine anyone being mean enough to do that,' said CeCe. 'Right, off we go. Try not to leave me behind,' she called as Chrissie immediately dived in. Even though she only had one leg to propel her forwards, being an ex-champion swimmer, she always left CeCe playing catch-up within a few strokes.

'Isn't it fantastic?' Tony shouted from where he was treading water a few metres away.

'It sure is,' said Chrissie, who was floating on her back, her face in the sun. 'Wow, I hadn't realised how much I miss the sea, now that we live in the Alice,' she said as she turned to head out further.

'Chrissie, please don't go out too far!' she shouted. 'I don't want you getting into trouble, 'cos I'm not strong enough to save you.'

As usual, Chrissie took no notice of her, and eventually, CeCe swam back to shore and lay down on the sand to dry off.

'Your mate's quite a swimmer, isn't she?' said Tony, who had also come out of the water and sat down next to her. 'What happened to her leg?'

CeCe told him how Chrissie had lost her leg when she was fifteen, due to complications with meningitis, which had led to septicaemia.

'Before that,' CeCe sighed, 'she was the best swimmer in all of Western Australia. She was about to try out for the Olympic team.'

'Life's a bitch sometimes, isn't it? It's good ta see she's still at it, though, eh?'

'Yeah, but I'm shit-scared she's gonna disappear under those waves and never come up again.'

'I doubt it, look at her go,' smiled Tony. 'Well, we should be off if ya need ta catch that plane.'

CeCe stood up and waved her arms above her head to summon Chrissie back to shore. Once they were dressed, Tony drove them the few minutes to the airport.

'If we're lucky, Bridge might come through before you're called for your flight,' he said as he parked his truck in front of the terminal. They heard the thrum of a plane coming in to land.

'How do you fancy a trip here when we're back from Europe, Chrissie?' said CeCe as they followed Tony to the terminal building. 'I love this island.'

'Okay, but let's do Europe first, eh, Cee? I can't tell you how stoked I am to see it.'

'Oh, it's very boring compared to this. Chock-full of people and old monuments.'

'Hey, I'll see it for myself and then decide what I think,' Chrissie smiled. 'Look, the plane has landed.'

'We'll go to the veranda in the viewing area, eh?' said Tony. 'At least ya might get ta say hello.'

'Okay, great,' said CeCe. The doors of the tiny plane had just opened and the first passengers were disembarking.

'Look, there she is! Bridge, I'm over here!' he shouted at a loudly dressed, buxom woman with red hair, who was clutching a number of shopping bags as she descended the steps from the plane. Tony received a smile and a wave back. 'Come on, let's go say hi.'

CeCe's heart thumped in her chest as the woman approached the fence that separated the arriving passengers yet to clear customs from people waiting to greet them. Bridget came to a halt in front of them and perched her huge sunglasses on top of her head.

'How are ya, doll? Missed ya.' He kissed her over the fence. 'Listen, I've had two young ladies visit me whilst you were away. They came because they thought Merry was still on the island. Bridge, this is CeCe and Chrissie.'

Perhaps it's just me being oversensitive, CeCe thought, *but her whole expression has changed since Tony said who we are, and she doesn't look happy.*

'Hello there,' Bridget said as she forced a smile.

'They wanted ta know whether Merry was wearing an emerald ring when she was staying with us?' Tony continued. 'I said she was. Was I right for a change?'

'I can't be remembering details like that, love,' she said, lowering her sunglasses back down over her eyes.

'I thought I heard the two of youse chatting about having similar rings?'

'I think you'd been dreaming or had a skinful that night, Tony, 'cos I'm not remembering any talk of rings.'

'But—'

'Now, I'd better be getting myself through customs. They'll probably stop me, what with all the shopping I've done in Sydney. 'Twas nice to meet the two of you,' Bridget said. 'I'll see you on the other side,' she said pointedly to Tony.

As she disappeared inside the terminal, Tony turned to the girls.

'We'd better be getting ourselves inside too, because they'll be calling f'youse ta board any second.'

The flight call was already up on the display board and Sydney passengers were beginning to queue for security.

'Can we swap mobile numbers?' CeCe asked him as she produced her phone. They did so as they drew nearer to security.

'It really was lovely to meet you and to see a bit of Norfolk Island,' said CeCe. 'And thank you so much for your hospitality.'

'It was fun ta meet you two. And if you do decide to come back, just bowl round to our place for a visit, eh?' he said.

'Bye, Tony, and thank you again!'

'Oh! How cute is this?!' Chrissie said as they reached security and she pulled out a tray that still had a sticky label on it telling the passenger it was for cat litter.

'Yeah,' commented CeCe as they watched their mobiles and wet swimming clothes disappear into the tunnel. 'Bridget wasn't very happy to see us, was she?'

'No,' said Chrissie as they passed through the scanner and began to collect their belongings. 'She definitely wasn't.'

'I wonder why?' CeCe mused. 'What does she know that we don't?'

'At this moment in time,' Chrissie replied as they walked towards the boarding queue, 'everything.'

5

Atlantis

'It's for you,' Claudia said as she handed Maia the receiver. 'It's CeCe.'

'Ally!' Maia called onto the terrace, where her sister was sitting in the sunshine, finishing lunch. 'Hi, CeCe,' she said as Ally walked inside and they put their heads together to listen. 'Where are you?'

'We're in Sydney. We're about to check in for London, but I thought I'd call before we do and bring you up to date.'

'Have you found her?'

'Well, we met Mary-Kate McDougal. We think she could be the missing sister, 'cos she told us she was adopted, which would fit 'cos we all are. She's twenty-two, by the way, so that would fit too.'

'Fantastic!' said Ally.

'What about the emerald ring?' Maia asked. 'Did she recognise it?'

'She thinks she did. If it's the same one, then it was given to her by her mum on her twenty-first.'

'Wow!' said Ally. 'Maybe you *have* found her then! Did you see the ring?'

'Er, no, we didn't, 'cos her mum, who's also called Mary,

but goes by the nickname of "Merry", asked Mary-Kate if she could take it with her on this world tour she's on. Apparently it was hers originally. We actually managed to miss her twice – the first time by just a couple of days. And the second time . . . well, Chrissie and I have discussed it, and we wonder if it was because she knew we were coming that Merry left Norfolk Island a night early.'

'Norfolk Island? Where on earth is that?' Maia asked.

'It's in the South Pacific, just between New Zealand and Australia. It's really beautiful, but kinda stuck in the past – there's hardly any phone signal,' said CeCe. 'Mary-Kate said her mum was heading to the island to see her best friend Bridget. So we followed her there, but she'd already left.'

'Damn!' Ally muttered. 'So she's in Sydney now?'

'No. Looking at the departures board here, we think her plane's just left and is headed for Toronto in Canada. We're just checking that we're okay to get on our London flight?'

'I'm totally confused,' Ally sighed, 'but if she's left, then yes, of course. Are you sure she's headed for Toronto?'

'Yup. I just called Mary-Kate, her daughter, who confirmed it was the next destination on her schedule. She said she'd try to find out where her mum is staying. Sorry to disappoint you, Ally. We did our best.'

'Don't be silly, CeCe. You and Chrissie have done a fantastic job, so thank you.'

'I think we're on the right track, but we still need to see that ring,' said CeCe. 'Listen, we have to go check in right now, but there's more to tell you, like Merry is apparently Irish, and Mary-Kate has a brother and—'

'You go,' Ally said, 'and call us when you've landed. Thanks for finding all that out for us.'

Putting the phone down, Ally and Maia looked at each other and wandered back onto the terrace.

'So . . . could you make sense of all that?' said Maia.

'Let me get a pad and a pen so we can write down what she said.' Ally darted back into the kitchen and returned with what she needed. She began to write.

'Number one: we have a young woman called Mary-Kate McDougal who is twenty-two. Number two: we've identified that the emerald ring might be the one originally owned by her mum. She was given it on her twenty-first birthday.'

'Number three, and probably most importantly: we know Mary-Kate was adopted,' cut in Maia.

'Number four: her mum is also called Mary, commonly known as "Merry",' said Ally. 'Number five: Merry currently has the emerald ring which we need to see if we're to confirm that Mary-Kate is our missing sister.'

'And CeCe said there's a brother, remember . . .'

Ally wrote that down too, chewed her pen and then wrote *Toronto*.

'So, if we find out where she's staying, who should we send to Toronto?' asked Ally.

'You think it's worth pursuing?'

'Don't you?'

Maia's eyes travelled to the path which led to Pa Salt's garden.

'Merope's name was engraved on one band of the armillary sphere along with ours,' said Maia. 'Pa wouldn't have had it included unless she existed, surely?'

'Unless it was wishful thinking. But more importantly, Georg really believes this is her. He said that the information came from Pa just before he died. The proof was that her name is Mary McDougal, who lives at The Vinery in New Zealand, which we now know is true. *And* she owns an unusual emerald ring. Which Mary-Kate thought she recognised from the picture, but . . .'

'Maybe Georg has more information. Let's give him a call, shall we?' Maia suggested.

Ally went into the kitchen and dialled the number to Georg's office. After a few seconds, she was greeted by the light voice of his secretary.

'Hello, Giselle, it's Ally D'Aplièse here. Is Georg in?'

'*Désolée*, Mademoiselle D'Aplièse, Monsieur Hoffman has been called away.'

'Oh, I see. When will he be back?'

'I am afraid I do not know, but he wanted me to reassure your family that he would return in time for the boat trip later this month,' said Giselle.

'Can you pass on a message to him, please?' Ally asked. 'It's urgent.'

'I am so sorry, Mademoiselle D'Aplièse, but I am not able to contact him until he returns. I will make sure he calls you when he is back. *Au revoir*.'

Before Ally could respond, Giselle hung up the phone. Ally returned to the terrace, shaking her head in confusion.

'Maia, Georg's gone.'

'What do you mean "gone"?'

'His secretary says he's been called away and can't be contacted. Apparently he won't be back until the boat trip.'

'He's a busy man; Pa can't have been his only client.'

'Of course, but he probably has the information we need,' said Ally, 'and he left in such a rush when he was last here. All we have is a name and a picture of a ring. Well, I suppose we'll just have to continue without him.'

'So we should try and track down Mary-Kate's mum in Canada?'

'Surely we have to at least try? What do we have to lose?' said Ally.

'Nothing, I suppose,' Maia agreed. 'But who do we send to Toronto?'

'Well, our nearest sister is Electra, but I'd have to see how far Toronto is from New York,' Ally replied.

'I don't think it's far,' said Maia. 'We could ask Electra if she can go in the next few days, but I know she's been inundated by the media since the Concert for Africa the other night. She may not have the time. When I was in Geneva yesterday, her face was all over the newspapers.'

'She certainly knows how to grab the attention, doesn't she?'

'Honestly, Ally, she's sounded so much better since she came out of rehab. I don't think her speech at the concert was about getting attention. She's serious about helping others with addiction problems and it's wonderful that she can use her fame for good, don't you think? She's become an inspiring role model.'

'Yes, of course she is.' Ally yawned. 'Forgive me; I've become a ratty old bag in the past few weeks.'

'It's only because you're permanently exhausted,' Maia comforted her.

'Yup, I am. I thought that after all I've been through in my sailing career, having a baby alone would be easy, but you know what? It's the hardest thing I've ever done, especially the "alone" bit.'

'Everyone says it gets easier after the initial months, and at least for the next few weeks, Bear will have lots of aunties around to look after him.'

'I know, and Ma has been wonderful. It's just that sometimes, well . . .'

'What?'

'I look into the future and see myself alone,' Ally admitted. 'I can't imagine meeting anyone I can love as much as I loved

Theo. I know we were only together a short time – which is what everyone says when they try to comfort me – but it felt like forever to me. And . . .' Ally shook her head as tears fell down her pale cheeks.

'I'm so, so sorry, darling.' Maia put her arms around her younger sister. 'There's no point in trying to tell you that time heals, that you're still young and of course you've got a future ahead of you, because for now, you can't see it. But it is there, I promise.'

'Maybe, but then I feel so guilty. I should just be happy because I've got Bear. Of course I love him to the depths of my soul and yes, he's the best thing that's ever happened to me but . . . I miss Theo so, so much. Sorry, sorry . . . I never normally cry.'

'I know you don't, but it's good to let it out, Ally. You're so very strong, or at least, your pride doesn't allow you to be weak, but everyone has their breaking point.'

'I think I just need some sleep – proper sleep. Even when Ma is doing the night shift, I still wake up when I hear Bear cry.'

'Maybe we could arrange for you to take a short holiday – I'm sure Ma and I could cope with Bear here.'

Ally looked at her in horror. 'What kind of mother takes a "holiday" from her baby?'

'Those that can, I should think,' replied Maia pragmatically. 'If you look back to the old days, new mums didn't rely on their husbands; they had plenty of female relatives who would support them. You've had none of that support since you moved to Norway. Please don't beat yourself up, Ally, I know how hard it is to settle in a new country, and at least I speak the language in Brazil.'

'I've done my best to learn, but Norwegian is so difficult. There were a few nice mums at my antenatal classes who spoke some English, but since we've all had our babies, we've gone our separate ways. They have their own families around them, you know? I've begun to wonder whether it was a mistake moving there in the first place. It would be fine if I was playing in the orchestra, keeping busy, but for now I'm just stuck at home in the middle of nowhere with Bear.' Ally wiped her eyes harshly with her hands. 'Oh God, I'm sounding so self-indulgent.'

'You're not at all, and decisions can always be reversed, you know. Maybe these few weeks here at Atlantis, and then being back on your beloved ocean, will give you some time to reflect.'

'Yes, but where would I go? I mean, I love Ma and Claudia dearly, but I don't think I could ever move back to Atlantis permanently.'

'Nor could I, but there are other places in the world, Ally. You could say it's your oyster.'

'So you reckon I should just stick a pin in the map and go wherever it points to, do you? It doesn't work like that. Got a tissue?'

'Here,' said Maia, digging into a jean pocket and producing a tissue. 'Well, Auntie Maia suggests that you take a nap now, then let me and Ma sort Bear out tonight. I'm jet-lagged anyway, so I'll be up until all hours. Truly, Ally, I think that your brain has just been scrambled by exhaustion. It's important you get some rest before our sisters start arriving.'

'You're right,' Ally sighed, as she slipped a hairband from her wrist and twisted her curls into a knot on top of her head. 'Okay, if you're offering, I'll take you up on it. I'll stuff earplugs in tonight and try to ignore the squalling.'

'Why don't you sleep in one of the spare bedrooms below us on Pa's floor? That way you won't be woken if Bear starts crying. For now, I'll check flights from New York to Toronto and then give Electra a call to see if she wouldn't mind going.'

'Okay. Right, I'm going to take that nap. Bear's bottles are all in the fridge if you need them – the nappies are on his changing unit and—'

'I know the drill, Ally,' replied Maia gently. 'Now, go upstairs and get some sleep.'

Once the internet had informed her that Toronto was under two hours' flight from Manhattan, Maia picked up her mobile and dialled Electra's number. Not expecting her to answer as it was so early in New York, she was surprised to hear her sister's voice at the other end of the line.

'Maia! How are you?'

Even her phone response is different now . . . Maia thought. Before, Electra would never have asked how *she* was.

'I'm jet-lagged from the flight here, but it's great to be at Atlantis and see Ma, Claudia and Ally. And how are you, Miss Global Superstar?'

'OMG, Maia! I never, ever expected the kinda feedback I got from my speech. It feels like every newspaper and TV channel in the world wants to speak to me. Mariam – remember my assistant? – has had to hire a temp to help her. I'm . . . overwhelmed.'

'I bet you are, but at least it's for all the right reasons, isn't it?'

'Yeah, it is, and Stella – my grandmother – has been great. She's been dealing with a lot of the charity stuff. From what she said, we've already had enough donations to open *five* drop-in centres, and there's also been tons of charities offering me seats on their boards to act as a spokeswoman and stuff. Best of all, UNICEF have been in touch to ask if I'd consider becoming a global ambassador for them. That made Stella real proud, which was nice.'

'That all sounds fantastic, Electra! It's no more than you deserve. You're a true inspiration to those who are struggling like you have. Just make sure you don't end up relapsing under the pressure.'

'Oh, don't worry, I won't relapse. This is happy pressure, not sad, if you know what I mean. I feel . . . exhilarated. And Miles has also been great.'

'Miles . . . isn't he the guy you were in rehab with?'

'Yeah, and, well . . . we've become real close over the past few weeks. In fact, I was thinking that if he can spare the time, maybe I'd bring him along with me to Atlantis. He's a super-hot lawyer, so I can just send him into battle when I need to fight my corner against all you sisters.'

Electra chuckled, and it was a blissful, natural sound that Maia hadn't heard from her in years.

'If any of us can fight our corner in this crazy family of ours, then it's you, Electra, but of course he's welcome. I think everyone's bringing someone with them, except Ally. Her brother Thom can't come as he's on tour with the Bergen Philharmonic.'

'Well, at least she has Bear.'

'She does, yes, but she's feeling pretty low at the moment.'

'Yeah, I got that from the phone call we had recently. Never mind, we'll all be around to cheer her up and do some babysitting. So, is this just a call to see how I'm doing, or was there a reason for it?'

'Both, actually. Did you read the email Ally sent to you, Tiggy and Star?'

'I didn't. As I said, I've been inundated. Even Mariam hasn't been able to get up to date yet. What was it about?'

Maia explained as succinctly as she could the events since

Georg's surprise visit to them on the night of the Concert for Africa.

'. . . So we now know that Mary-Kate's mum, more commonly known as Merry, has apparently flown on to Toronto. She has the emerald ring with her, which Georg told us is the proof we need to identify the missing sister. We're still waiting to see if we can get an address for Merry over there, but if we can – and I'm sorry to ask you this when you're so busy – could you possibly spare a day to fly up to meet with her? It's only an hour and forty minutes to Toronto from NYC, so . . .'

'I'm sure I could, Maia. In fact, I'd actually appreciate a chance to get out of the city right now. I'll bring Mariam with me; she's great at getting information out of people.'

'Okay, well, that's fantastic, Electra! I just hope we get to find out where she's staying and then I'll be in touch.'

'Do you think this really might lead us to the missing sister?'

'I don't know, but Georg seemed certain about this information.'

'Wow, wouldn't it be incredible if we could get her to come lay the wreath with us? That would have made Pa so happy.'

'Yes, it would, and with your help, we just might. Now, I'm sure you have a busy day ahead of you, so I'll let you go. Congratulations again, little sister. What you did – and want to do – is incredible.'

'Gee, thanks, big sis. Let me know if you get that address and see you soon!'

After ending the call, Maia left the house and walked across to enter the Pavilion, closing the door behind her. Although she had chosen to sleep in her childhood room in the main house to be closer to Ally, her old home here – where she had lived alone for so long as an adult – had been kept clean and aired by Claudia. And it was where she, Floriano and Valentina would stay when they arrived. She went into the bedroom and opened her underwear drawer. Feeling around at the bottom of it, she drew out what she was looking for, then stared at it.

Yes, it was still there. Secreting it back in the drawer, Maia walked to the bed and sat down. She thought about what Ally had said earlier; about how she felt guilty because she was low at a time when she should be happy. This was partly true of her too just now, because something she'd wanted for a long time had finally happened. Yet at the same time, it had produced a metamorphosis inside her brain, which seemed determined to drag up painful events from her past . . .

As she forced herself to stand up, she decided that she was glad she had some space from Floriano, some time to work out her thoughts and feelings before she spoke to him.

'There's no rush,' she whispered as she looked around her at the rooms she had lived in for so long. Being back here, where she now acknowledged she'd hidden herself away from the world like a wounded animal, made tears prick her eyes. Atlantis had been such a safe, secure universe where day-to-day problems were few. And just now, she only wished she could recapture that feeling, and that Pa was still next door, because she was scared . . .

6

Mary-Kate
The Gibbston Valley

As the rain lashed against the windows and a wind howled through the valley, I finally gave up on the lyrics to a new song I'd been trying to compose on the keyboard. Yesterday, Fletch and I had worked together in the sitting room as a storm raged outside.

'We could do with a fire, mate,' Fletch had said. 'Winter's here.'

I'd swallowed hard, because Mum's lighting of the first fire of the year was something that only *she* did, but she wasn't here, and nor were Dad or Jack . . .

Then I'd reminded myself that I was twenty-two years old and an adult. So, getting Fletch to take a photograph – Dad had always marked the annual occasion this way, like other families did with birthdays or Christmas – I lit the fire.

After Fletch had taken off back to Dunedin this afternoon (Sissy having needed a jump-start), I'd been determined to improve on the lyrics I'd been tinkering with. Fletch had worked on a great tune, but he said my lyrics were 'depressing'. He was right. I didn't know whether it was the fact I felt so alone just now, or the general confusion after CeCe and Chrissie had left to find Mum on Norfolk Island, but nothing was coming creatively.

'What do you reckon about those girls then, eh?' Fletch had asked over a bottle of wine. 'They could be a link to your long-lost family, and they seem pretty cool – not to mention rich, if they've got this boat in the Med.'

'I don't know what to make of it. I wasn't lying when I told them I've never thought of finding my birth family. I'm a McDougal,' I'd added firmly.

But now, alone with my thoughts and rattling around in a house that was full of memories of Dad, the question of my birth family wouldn't leave me alone.

I played a dissonant chord in frustration, and looked up at the clock. It was midnight now, which meant that it was the morning in Toronto.

You have to speak to her . . .

Gulping down my nerves, I reached for the house phone to dial Mum's mobile number. *She probably won't answer anyway,* I comforted myself.

'Hi, sweetheart, is that you?' came Mum's voice after a couple of rings. I could hear how tired she sounded.

'Yes, hi, Mum. Where are you?'

'I've just checked into the Radisson here in Toronto. Is everything all right?'

'Yup, fine,' I said. 'Um, did you get my message the other day? About those two girls, CeCe and Chrissie, who wanted to meet you?'

'Yes, I did.' There was a pause on the line. Eventually she said, 'Unfortunately I'd already left for Sydney with Bridget when they arrived on the island. What were they like?'

'Honestly, Mum, they were really sweet. Fletch was here and we had them stay for dinner. They just genuinely want to find this "missing sister", as they kept calling her. I did explain on my message—'

'Did they say if they were working with others?' Mum cut in.

'Well, yes, if you mean the other sisters helping to find you – CeCe said she had five of them. They're all adopted too, like me. Umm, Mum . . .'

'Yes, sweetheart?'

I shut my eyes and took a deep breath. 'Mum, I know I've never needed to know about my . . . birth family, but their questions got me wondering if maybe I *should* know more about them.'

'Of course, darling, I understand. Please don't be embarrassed about saying it.'

'I love you and Dad and Jack more than anything and *you* are my family,' I said quickly. 'But I've been talking to Fletch about it, and I think it might be good to know a little more about this other part of me. Oh Mum, I don't want to upset you . . .' My voice broke, and I wished with all my heart that she were here with me, to take me into her comforting arms as she had always done.

'It's all right, Mary-Kate, really. Listen, why don't we sit down together when I'm home again, and then we can talk about it?'

'Thanks, yeah, that'd be great.'

'Those girls haven't contacted you again, have they?'

'Well . . . I spoke to CeCe briefly on the phone, but honestly, Mum, all they want is to see the emerald ring – the one you gave me on my twenty-first. They've got a drawing of it.'

'You said so in your message. Did they say where they got the drawing from?'

'Their lawyer, apparently. Mum, are you all right? You sound . . . a bit unlike yourself.'

'I'm absolutely fine, Mary-Kate, just worried about you. Is Fletch still there?'

'No, he left this arvo.'

'Okay, but Doug's around?'

'Yup. And the guys doing the pulling out are in the annexe. I'm perfectly safe.'

'Okay, well, don't go letting any more strangers into the house, will you?'

'You and Dad always did,' I countered.

'I know, but you're all alone there, sweetheart. It's different. Are you sure you don't want to fly out and join me in Toronto?'

'Where's all this come from, Mum? You and Dad always said the Valley was the safest place on earth! You're freaking me out!'

'Sorry, I'm sorry. I just don't like to think of my little girl all on her own. Keep in touch, won't you?'

''Course. Oh, also . . .' – I swallowed hard because I really needed to be sure – 'just before you go, can I check that I was adopted locally?'

'Yes, you were. It was an agency in Christchurch. Green and something.'

'Okay, thanks, Mum. Well, I'm gonna head for bed. Love you.'

'Love you too, darling, and take care, please.'

'I will. Bye.'

I put the phone back on the hook and sat down heavily on the sofa. Mum had sounded so strange and tense, not like herself at all. Even if she said she didn't mind about a link to my possible birth family turning up, she almost certainly did.

We'd speak when she got home, she'd said . . .

'But when is that going to be?' I said aloud to the empty room. Given all the countries she wanted to visit, it could be months before we could have a real conversation, and now that the spark had been ignited, I had a burning need for answers. I'd also give CeCe a call tomorrow to say Mum was at the Radisson – if that ring could be identified, it might identify *me*, and I needed to know, even if it wasn't what Mum wanted.

Coming to a decision, I got up and turned on the old computer on the table. My foot tapping impatiently as it loaded, I opened the web browser and went to Google.

Green and . . . adoption agency Christchurch New Zealand, I typed into the search bar.

Then I held my breath and hit *Enter*.

7

Atlantis

'I never thought I'd say this but, wow, sleeping is great,' Ally announced as she joined Maia in the kitchen for a late breakfast the next morning. 'You're as white as a sheet again. I'm presuming you didn't get much yourself?'

'No. I just can't seem to shake the jet lag,' Maia shrugged.

'You should have done by now; you've been back four days. Are you sure you're okay? How's the tummy?'

'Not great, but I'll be fine.'

'Maybe you should go to Dr Krause in Geneva and get checked over.'

'I will if I'm not feeling better in the next couple of days. Anyway, I'm glad *you* slept, Ally. You look like a different person.'

'I feel it. Where is His Majesty, by the way?'

'Ma took him out for a walk around the garden. You remember how obsessed she was with all of us kids being outside?'

'I do. And how much I hated walking that great big Silver Cross pram around and around the garden, trying to get Electra or Tiggy off to sleep!'

'Talking of Tiggy, I haven't heard back from her or Star

since you sent the email about the missing sister,' said Maia. 'Have you?'

'No, although CeCe said she'd mention it to Star, and you know what communications are like where Tiggy lives. She may not even have got the email yet. I just don't understand how people can live so cut off from the rest of the world.'

'You were when you were sailing, though, weren't you?'

'I suppose so, but there have been very few times when I've spent more than a couple of days away from any contact. There's normally a handy port where I can catch up on texts and emails.'

'You're a real people person, aren't you, Ally?'

'I've never really thought about it,' she mused, sitting down with her mug of coffee. 'I suppose I am.'

'Maybe that's why you find it so hard living in Norway: you don't know many people there and even if you do, it's hard to communicate with them.'

Ally stared at Maia, then nodded. 'You know what? You might be right. I'm used to living with a lot of people around me. All the sisters here at Atlantis, then sleeping with crews in tiny spaces. I don't do "alone", do I?'

'No. Whereas I love my own space.'

'You've had the opposite experience to me,' Ally pointed out. 'I've had to get used to being by myself, but after years alone here, you've had Floriano and Valentina living with you.'

'Yes, and it's been difficult to adjust to, especially as our apartment is so small and in the middle of a crowded city. That's why I enjoy going out to the *fazenda* – the farm I inherited. I can have some headspace there, some peace. Without it, I might go mad. We hope to get a bigger apartment at some point when cash flow allows.'

'Talking of cash flow,' said Ally, 'I'm going to have to speak to Georg when he gets back, because I'm almost broke. I haven't worked for months, so I'm reliant on the small income I get from the trust. I used all my savings and sold Theo's boat to renovate the Bergen house, but the cash didn't cover everything that needed doing so I had to ask Georg for a bit extra. I feel weird about asking him for more now, mainly because of pride – I've always supported myself in the past.'

'I know you have, Ally,' Maia said gently.

'I've got no choice, unless I sell the old barn Theo left me on the Greek island he always called "Somewhere". Besides, no one would buy it until I've renovated it – which I don't have the finances to do – and I should try to keep it for Bear.'

'Of course you should.'

'I'm not even sure how much money Pa left us. Are you?' Ally asked her.

'No. Those few days last year after Pa died are just a blur, and I can't remember exactly what Georg said about the finances,' Maia admitted. 'I think it would be a good idea if, when we're all back here after the cruise down to Delos, we ask him to explain how the trust works, so we can be clear about how much we have, and what we can use it for.'

'That would be good, yes, but I still feel awful having to ask for help in the first place. Pa taught us to stand on our own two feet,' sighed Ally.

'On the other hand, when a parent . . . dies, the children get left money in the will, which they are free to spend as they choose,' said Maia. 'We need to understand that *we* are in charge now – even if we find it difficult to remember that Georg works for *us*, not the other way round. It's our money and we shouldn't be scared of asking for it. Georg isn't our moral compass; that was Pa, remember? And he taught us not to abuse what we were lucky enough to be given. Being a single mother because your partner has died is one of the best reasons for needing financial support, Ally. If Pa was alive today, I know he would think so too.'

'You're right. Thank you, Maia.' Ally stretched out her hand to her sister. 'I've missed you a lot, you know. You've always been the calming voice of reason. I just wish you didn't live so far away.'

'I'm hoping that you and Bear will come and visit Brazil soon. It's an amazing country and . . .'

The telephone rang and Ally jumped up to catch the call.

'*Allô*, Ally D'Aplièse speaking. Who? Oh, hi, Mary-Kate,' she said as she beckoned Maia over to listen. 'It's very nice to speak to you. CeCe has told me all about meeting you in New Zealand. I have Maia – our eldest sister – here with me too.'

'Hi, Mary-Kate,' Maia said.

'Hi, Maia,' came Mary-Kate's gentle voice, 'it's good to talk to you too. CeCe left me this number and as I can't get hold of her, I hope it's okay that I've rung you.'

'Of course it is.' Ally took over again.

'I know CeCe and her friend Chrissie were trying to find out which hotel my mum is staying at in Toronto. I spoke to Mum last night and she said she's staying at the Radisson. I have all the details.' Both Maia and Ally could hear the tinge of excitement in Mary-Kate's voice. 'Shall I give them to you or wait until I get hold of CeCe?'

'To us, please,' said Ally, grabbing the pen and notepad that sat by the kitchen phone. 'Fire away.' Ally scribbled the address and the telephone number down. 'Thanks, Mary-Kate, that's fantastic.'

'So, what will you do? Will you guys fly over to see her?'

'We have a sister who lives in Manhattan. She's only a short plane ride away, so she's said that she might go.'

75

'Wow, your family sounds interesting. Odd, but interesting,' Mary-Kate chuckled. 'Whoops! I didn't mean to be rude or anything . . .'

'Oh, don't worry, we're used to it,' said Ally. 'I'm sure CeCe told you that if we confirm that ring of yours that your mum has got with her is the right one, then it would be fantastic for you to fly over to visit and come with us later this month on our boat trip for our father's memorial.'

'That's so nice of you, but I don't think I could afford it.'

'Oh, all costs of flights would be covered by our family trust,' Ally said hastily.

'Okay, thanks, I'll think about it. Anyway, let's see if your sister manages to hook up with my mum and ask her about that ring. Just . . . well, I think Mum's feeling a bit weird about CeCe and Chrissie turning up on the doorstep, y'know? I haven't said yet that another sister might be coming to see her in Toronto. I think that after Dad's death, she's feeling vulnerable.'

'I understand completely, Mary-Kate. We can always leave it if you'd prefer,' Maia replied diplomatically.

'I don't want to upset her or anything, but actually, I'd really like to know if I am your missing sister. Does that sound mean?'

'No, not at all. I'm sure it's a very difficult thing for the adoptive mum when a possible set of relatives turns up, especially out of the blue. That's our fault, Mary-Kate. We should have written to you first, but we were all so excited that we might have found you, we didn't think.'

'Well, I'm glad CeCe and Chrissie came, but . . .'

'I promise to tell Electra to tread carefully.'

'Electra . . . so she's the sixth sister?'

'She is,' Ally confirmed, surprise in her voice. 'You know your mythology.'

'Oh, I do. I was telling CeCe that Mum studied Classics at uni and had a bit of an obsession with all those Greek myths. Electra's such an unusual name, isn't it? There's only one Electra I know of, and that's the supermodel. I caught her speech on TV a few nights ago. That's not your sister, is it?'

'It is, actually.'

'Shit! I mean . . . seriously? She's, like, well, she's always been an idol of mine. She's so beautiful and elegant and that speech showed she's got a brain and compassion in spades. I think I might collapse on the spot if I met her!'

'Don't worry, we'll hold you up,' said Ally, sharing a smile with Maia. 'Right then, speak soon.'

'Yes. And if you do speak to Electra, tell her from me that I think she's amazing.'

'I will, and going back to what you were saying before, I do think we should give your mum some warning that Electra's coming tomorrow. If you like, I'll leave a message at the hotel reception later, saying that my sister might be visiting.'

'Okay, yes, that would be good. Thanks, Maia. Bye.'

'Bye, Mary-Kate, and thanks for calling.'

Maia hung up the phone, and stared at Ally for a few seconds.

'She sounds so sweet. And very young,' she said eventually as they walked back to the table.

'You know what? I think she sounded . . . normal.'

'Are you saying we're not?' Maia smiled.

'I think we're a bunch of women with different personalities. Just like most sisters are. And anyway, what is "normal?"'

'I am feeling guilty about her mum, though,' Maia sighed. 'It must be devastating to suddenly hear contact has been made about the possible birth family. Normally, it would have happened through official channels.'

'Yes, you're right. We should have thought,' Ally agreed. 'It was different for us; Pa was actively encouraging us to go and find our birth families.'

'It just shows how amazing Ma has been through all this as we've found our relatives,' said Maia. 'She's loved us all like a mother. I mean, I couldn't love her more, she *is* my mother.'

'And mine,' Ally agreed. 'And a fantastic granny to Bear.'

'So . . . do you think Mary-Kate is our missing sister?'

'Who knows? But if she is, how did Pa lose her?'

'I have absolutely no idea, and I hate these conversations,' Maia sighed. 'Remember we all used to chat about why he'd adopted us when we were younger? And what his obsession with the Seven Sisters was?'

'Of course I do.'

'Back then, we could just have walked downstairs to Pa's study and asked him outright, but none of us ever had the courage to do it. Now that he's gone, that isn't an option any longer. It makes me wish I had been brave enough, because now we'll never know.' Maia shook her head wearily.

'Probably not, although I reckon Georg knows far more than he'll ever say.'

'I agree, but I guess he's bound by whatever a lawyer's oath is not to reveal his clients' secrets.'

'Well, Pa certainly seems to have had a lot of those,' said Ally. 'Like, did you know there's a lift in this house?'

'What?' Maia gasped. 'Where?'

'There's a panel that hides it off the corridor from the kitchen,' said Ally, lowering her voice. 'Tiggy found out about it when she was staying here after being so ill in the spring. Apparently, Ma said that Pa had it installed not long before he died – he'd been struggling with the stairs, but kept it a secret because he didn't want any of us to worry.'

'I see,' said Maia slowly. 'That doesn't seem too suspicious, though, Ally.'

'No, but what *is* suspicious is that the lift goes down to a hidden wine cellar that no one has ever told us about!' said Ally.

'I'm sure there's an explanation for it—'

'When Electra was here a few months ago, Ma took both of us down there. And Electra confirmed what Tiggy found when she sneaked down into the cellar when Ma and Claudia were asleep – there's a door hidden behind one of the wine racks.'

'So what's behind it?'

'I don't know,' Ally sighed. 'I sneaked down there myself one night when I was up with Bear – the key to the lift is in the key box in the kitchen. I saw the door, but couldn't budge the wine rack in front of it.'

'Well, when we're all here together we'll go and take a look. Maybe Georg knows where and what it leads to. Anyway, getting back to the missing sister, now that we know where Mary-Kate's mum is staying in Toronto, let's call Electra again,' said Maia, looking at her watch. 'It's about six a.m. in New York – that might be too early.'

This time, Electra didn't answer her mobile, so Maia left a message for her to get back to them urgently. Ma arrived in from the garden with Bear, and Ally fed him as she sat in the kitchen waiting for Electra's call.

'You can go out or upstairs if you wish,' Ma commented as Claudia began preparing lunch. 'I won't leave the phone unattended.'

'If Electra doesn't call back soon, I might,' said Ally, as Maia excused herself to go to the bathroom. 'Can I leave Bear here with you? I thought I might take the Laser out on the lake after lunch.'

'Of course. You know it is my pleasure to look after him, Ally, and I'm sure an hour or two of sailing would do you the world of good. Maybe Maia could come with you,' said Ma, watching the kitchen door for Maia's return. 'Between you and me, she does not look well. Maybe some fresh air would do her good.'

'Maybe,' agreed Ally. 'I said she should go to the doctor if she doesn't improve over the next couple of days.'

'I hope she is better for when your sisters start to arrive. I want it to be a wonderful celebration.'

Ally caught the glimpse of anticipation in Ma's eyes.

'I hope so too, Ma. It must be very exciting for you, having all your girls back together again.'

'Oh, it is, but with all their families coming too, I must work out how to accommodate them. Do you think the couples will mind sharing the smaller beds you have in the rooms on the attic floor, or should I put them on your father's floor in the double rooms?'

Ally and Ma were discussing this when Maia walked back into the kitchen. 'Any news?' she asked.

'Not yet, but I'm sure Electra will contact us as soon as she gets the message. Ma was wondering whether you wanted to come out and take a spin round the lake on the Laser with me?'

'Not today, thank you. I'm not sure my stomach is quite settled enough yet,' Maia sighed.

'I have soup,' said Claudia from her station at the range. 'Will you eat inside or out?'

'Outside, I think, don't you, Maia?' said Ally.

'Err . . . I had a late breakfast so I'm not hungry. In fact, I think I'll go upstairs for a lie-down while you eat. I'll see you later.'

As Maia left the room, Ally and Ma shared a glance.

Having put Bear back in his pram, tucked into a shady spot under the big oak tree where Ma had always stationed the babies for a nap, Ally was just sitting down to drink her soup when the telephone rang. She dashed inside to pick it up, but Claudia had reached it first.

'Is it Electra?'

'No, it is Star. Here.' Claudia handed over the receiver and went back to her washing-up.

'Hello, Star! How are you?'

'Oh, I'm good, thank you, Ally.'

'How is Mouse? And Rory?'

'They're fine as well. Sorry I haven't replied to your email yet; we've been doing some stocktaking at the bookshop and it's been chaos. Anyway, I thought I'd call you rather than write. It seems ages since we last spoke.'

'That's because it has been,' Ally said with a smile, 'but don't worry. So you got my email?'

'Yes, and CeCe has filled me in too – we're meeting up in London in the next few days. Isn't it exciting? I mean, that Georg might have found the missing sister just in time to go and lay the wreath. Is there any more news?'

Ally explained that they were hoping Electra would go to Toronto tomorrow.

'Well, anything I can do from my end, let me know. Is it okay if I tell Orlando, Mouse's brother, about all this? He's actually a really good sleuth. It must be all those Conan Doyle stories he reads,' Star chuckled.

'I don't see why not. Have you decided when you're coming over to Atlantis yet?'

'As I said, I'll be meeting CeCe and Chrissie in London, but I won't be able to fly to Geneva with them – Mouse is very busy with the restoration of High Weald, so I don't want to leave Rory alone with him for too long. He'll only get fed

81

crisps and chocolate, knowing Mouse. Rory's school term finishes the day before we leave for the cruise, so I'll fly over with him then, and hopefully with Mouse too.'

'Just let us know, because it's not long now, is it?'

'No, and I'm so excited to see everybody. Goodness, Ally, it feels like so much has happened to all of us in the past year. And of course, I can't wait to meet Bear either. Keep in touch, won't you? I'm going to have to go actually – I promised to cook forty-eight muffins and a lemon drizzle cake for Rory's school fete tomorrow.'

'No problem, Star. Speak soon, bye.'

Ally wandered back outside to finish her soup, and tried not to feel envy that all her sisters' lives were so full and busy. And how all of them sounded happy.

I really do need that spin on the lake, she thought as she sat down.

Out on the water, the warm June breeze whipped Ally's curls around her face. She took in a lungful of pure air, then let it out slowly. It felt almost as if a physical weight had been lifted off her shoulders – or rather, out of her arms. She looked back at the silhouette of Atlantis, the pale pink turrets peeping out from behind the row of spruce trees that shielded it from prying eyes.

Veering sharply to avoid the path of other sailors, para-gliders and holidaymakers who were cluttering up the lake on this beautiful summer afternoon, Ally guided the Laser to an inlet and lay back, enjoying the sensation of the sun on her face. It reminded her of lying in Theo's arms only a year ago, feeling as happy as she'd ever felt.

'I miss you so much, my darling,' she whispered to the

heavens. 'Please show me how to move on, because I don't even know where my home is anymore.'

'Hello,' Maia greeted her sister as Ally walked back into the kitchen a couple of hours later. 'You've really caught the sun out there. Did you enjoy that?'

'It was wonderful, thanks. I'd forgotten how much I love it,' Ally smiled. 'Is Bear okay?'

'Ma's just about to give him a bath, and he's absolutely fine.'

'Great, then I'll head up and take a shower while I can. How are you feeling, Maia, any better?'

'I'm fine, Ally. Oh, just before you go up, Electra called while you were out. I've given her the name of the hotel in Toronto and Mariam has called the private jet company, so it's currently on hold for tomorrow.'

'Okay, perfect. See you in a bit,' Ally said as she left the kitchen.

After calling Merry's hotel to confirm with the receptionist that she was still there, Maia dialled Mariam's number.

'Hello, is that Mariam? It's Maia here.'

'Hi, Maia, all okay?'

'All is fine. I just wanted to tell you that Mary McDougal is definitely staying at the hotel for another couple of nights. She was out, but I've left a message saying Electra will be in touch to confirm a time to meet her tomorrow. I didn't say her name in case it caused too much of a fuss.'

'Thank you. That'll be me making the call then. Your sister's snowed under; everyone wants to speak to her right now,' said Mariam, her soft tone like a spoonful of melting honey. 'Miles and I think that it's very important she paces herself, as it's not so long since she came out of rehab.'

'Absolutely. I said the same to her, though I'm sure Electra has other ideas.'

'Actually, she's being very calm about the situation. She doesn't want to go back to that dark place either. We've decided to pick out a couple of trusted journalists and a major chat show she'll be interviewed on, which will give the charity lots of coverage, but won't be exploitative in any way.'

'I'm so grateful she has you, Mariam. Thank you so much for being there for her.'

'It really is no problem, Maia. Apart from the fact my job *is* to take care of her, I love her. She's such a strong person and I think she's going to do great things. Now, what is the full name of the lady we're meeting?'

'Mrs Mary McDougal, also known as "Merry".'

'Great,' said Mariam. 'I'll call the hotel now, try to talk to Merry and arrange a time and a place, shall I? I would think meeting at the hotel would be the easiest as it's close to Billy Bishop airport. Do you have her room number?'

'I'm afraid I don't. I'm not sure hotels give that kind of information these days. You'll just have to ask to be put through to her room.'

'Is it okay if I use my name instead of Electra's? As you said, the last thing we want is anyone finding out she's going to be there. She hasn't been out in public since the concert. We've decided she's going to have to be in disguise.'

'What it must be like to be world famous!' Maia chuckled.

'What do I say if this Mary asks me what the meeting is about?'

'Maybe just that you're calling on behalf of the sister of CeCe D'Aplièse, who visited Mary-Kate at the vineyard, and you'd like to arrange a meeting with her at the hotel,' Maia suggested.

'Right, I'll confirm the jet, then try to contact her and get back to you. Bye, Maia.'

'Bye, Mariam.'

Claudia arrived in the kitchen, followed by Ma and a delicious-smelling Bear, fresh and clean in a babygro.

'Ooh, pass him over for a cuddle with his auntie,' said Maia.

'Of course,' Ma said as she handed a wriggling Bear to her. 'Bath-times were always my favourite moment of the day when you were all small.'

'It was probably because bedtime wasn't that far off,' said Maia. 'Seriously, Ma, now I look back, I don't know how you coped.'

'Nor do I, but I did.' Ma shrugged as she poured herself a glass of water. 'And remember, as you grew up, you kept each other amused. Is Electra going to Toronto tomorrow?'

'Yes, but I just don't know what will happen,' said Maia. 'Apart from Georg being convinced that Mary McDougal is our missing sister, plus the emerald ring, we don't have a lot to go on. And when I spoke to Mary-Kate, she was worried her adoptive mum was upset by our sudden appearance in her daughter's life.'

'I can imagine,' Ma agreed. 'But it is up to Mary-Kate to decide if she wishes to know more, and it sounds as if she does.'

'Yes. Why do you think Georg is so certain it's her?'

'I know no more than you do, Maia. All I can say is that, throughout all the years I have known Georg, he has never said that he truly believed anyone else he has investigated could be the missing sister, so he must be convinced that this *is* her.'

'Did Pa ever mention a missing sister to you over the years, Ma?'

'Occasionally. There was always a sadness in his eyes when he spoke of the fact that he couldn't find her.'

'What about to you, Claudia?' asked Maia.

'Me?' Claudia looked up from the vegetables she was chopping for supper. 'Oh, I know nothing. I am not one for gossip,' she added, and Ma and Maia shared a smile. Claudia loved nothing more than a big pile of trashy magazines, which they both knew she hid under her recipe folder if anyone walked into the kitchen.

Maia's mobile rang again, and she handed Bear over to Ma as she answered it.

'Hi, Maia, Mariam here again. Mary McDougal wasn't in her room, but I left a message with the concierge to say we were coming tomorrow. I suggested one p.m., and that we meet in the lobby. I left my cell number too, so hopefully she'll call me back. If she doesn't, do we still go ahead?' Mariam asked.

'I . . . don't know, to be honest. It's a long way to go for nothing, and that might be the result.'

'I'm up for it,' said a voice in the background.

'One moment, Maia, I'll pass you over to Electra.'

'Hi there,' came Electra's voice. 'I think we should go, even if Mary doesn't get back to us. I mean, CeCe and Chrissie turned up unannounced, and look at the heap of information they managed to get. Besides, we know she's staying in the hotel, so if she's out, we'll just ask the concierge to tell us when she returns, and we'll sit in the lobby until she does. Remind me what she looks like?'

'From the photograph CeCe saw, she's a beautiful, petite blonde who looks around forty. Like the actress Grace Kelly apparently. Are you sure you're okay to go?'

'Hey, don't sweat; it's a day trip there and back. Normally

I'm on a plane twice a week to who knows where. I'll let you know how we get on. I think we owe it to Pa to at least try to identify the missing sister, don't we?'

'Yes, Electra, I think we do,' said Maia.

8

Electra
Toronto, Canada

The six-seater Cessna jet gained altitude as it flew due north away from New York. Electra gazed out of the window and thought how, in the 'old days', she'd be itching to access the well-stocked bar and grab a large vodka tonic. The urge – the habit – to do so was still strong inside her, but she accepted that it would probably never leave her and she'd simply have to fight every day not to give in to it.

'Hey, can you grab me a Coke?' she asked Mariam, who was sitting closer to the bar at the front than she was.

'Of course.' Mariam unstrapped herself and went to open the small refrigerator.

'Get me some pretzels too, will you? Geez, have I had an appetite for junk food since I came off the booze,' Electra sighed. 'Good job I seem to have a new career ahead of me, 'cos I'm getting far too fat to shimmy down the runway.'

'Really, Electra, you don't look as though you've put on an ounce. I think you must have a very good metabolism. Unlike me.' Mariam sat down, indicated her belly and shrugged.

'Maybe it's love that makes a person hungry,' Electra said as she opened the Coke. 'Are you and Tommy good?'

'I think we are, yes. He is so happy to work for you in an official capacity and he looks so handsome in his new suits.' A gentle blush appeared on Mariam's cheeks as she sipped her water.

'He's a great guy and also perfectly qualified for the job, what with his military background. As he's my bodyguard, I know I should have brought him with us today, but it's just a short hop, and in my disguise, nobody will even recognise me. It'll be just like that night we went out together for dinner in Paris. Without the booze and drugs on my part, of course,' Electra chuckled. 'Have you mentioned anything about Tommy to your family yet?'

'No, we're going to take it slowly. There's no rush, is there? I am just happy to have the chance to be with him when I can.'

'I for one can't wait to dance at your wedding, and I know you'll have such cute kids,' said Electra. 'Miles and I were talking baby names last night. He's got some seriously bad taste – every one of his suggestions for a boy were the names of his favourite basketball players!'

'He's a good man, Electra, and so protective of you. Hold on to him, won't you?'

'I sure will, as long as he holds on to me too. The fact he's a lawyer irritates me sometimes because he's so logical, but he does talk sense. And he's just so proud, y'know? He gets paid diddly-squat because so much of his work is pro bono. I mean, you should see his apartment in Harlem; it's above a bodega and about half the size of my closet! I suggested it might be great if we bought a place together where we could spread out, but he won't hear of it.'

'I can understand why he doesn't want to feel like a kept man,' Mariam replied.

'So why is it okay for women to be "kept"? Where's the difference?'

'It's just the way some men are,' Mariam shrugged. 'To be honest, it is good that Miles refuses to take advantage of your wealth. So many would.'

'Yeah, I know, but *I'd* like to take advantage of my wealth and buy a real nice house or apartment in Manhattan that would feel like mine. I know I have the ranch in Arizona now, but it'll be a while before it's ready for me to move into and it's too far away to be a permanent home. I need a base in the city. I've been thinking lately how important home is.'

'Maybe because you are due to return to it soon. Are you looking forward to going back to Atlantis and seeing all your sisters?'

'Good question.' Electra paused. 'The answer is, I'm not sure. They all find me difficult, and I know I *have* been, but that's just who I am. Even if I'm off the booze and drugs, I'm not going to suddenly grow wings overnight and become an angel.'

'If it helps, I think you have become a completely different person since you got sober.'

'You haven't seen me when I'm with my sisters.' Electra raised an eyebrow. 'Especially CeCe. She and I have always rubbed each other up the wrong way.'

'Remember, I come from a big family too and I promise you, there is always one sibling that others struggle to get along with. I mean, I love Shez, my younger sister, but she is so patronising just because she did a law degree and I went straight into work.'

'Yup, exactly,' nodded Electra. 'So how do you cope?'

'I try to understand that she and I have always competed. I want to be better than her, and I cannot help that feeling. But if I accept why I feel that way, I can cope.'

'Maybe CeCe's competition for me too, though not in the same way as you and Shez. I mean, she can holler louder than I can, but I think I throw the best tantrums,' Electra chuckled.

'You never know, both of you could have changed in the past year. From what you've said about CeCe, it sounds as though she's much happier now. I think so many of our struggles with our siblings come from feeling insecure that they're more favoured by a parent than we are. Then we start to have lives apart from our families, we build careers of our own and we're maybe with someone we care for who is *ours*, who we don't have to share with our siblings, which makes us feel stronger and more in control.'

'You know what, Mariam? You're wasted as a PA. You should become a counsellor. I think I've learnt more from you in the past few months than from any of the therapists I've paid shedloads to talk too.'

'Well, thank you for that compliment,' Mariam smiled. 'But remember, you pay me too. And talking of which, could we go through your interview schedule for the next few days?'

'I haven't been to Toronto in years,' commented Electra as they stepped off of the jet and were ushered into a limo that was waiting on the tarmac.

'I have never been,' said Mariam, 'but I have heard it is a beautiful city. I was reading about it last night, and apparently we have to get on a ferry that takes ninety seconds to cross Lake Ontario. They're thinking of building a tunnel underground so passengers can walk to the mainland.'

'You're a mine of information, Mariam,' said Electra. 'Looking back, I now feel bad that I've never bothered to find out anything about the places I've visited for photoshoots.

One city melts into another, one golden beach looks like everywhere else, y'know?'

'Not really, but I understand what you're saying. Look, there's the ferry.' Mariam pointed towards the slim strip of water separating them from the Canadian mainland.

'By the way, you did bring my disguise, didn't you?'

'I did,' Mariam nodded, digging inside her satchel, which had begun to remind Electra of Mary Poppins's carpet bag, as it never failed to produce whatever it was she needed.

'Do you want me to help you put it on?' Mariam asked as the limo moved forward onto the ferry and then parked up.

'Yes please. If we do manage to meet this woman in the hotel lobby, it's best that I'm not recognised or we'll be surrounded. Hopefully I can explain who I really am once we get Merry somewhere private.'

'Here's the top you wore in Paris, which you can put on over your T-shirt.'

'Thanks,' said Electra as she pulled the garment over her head and put her arms through the wide sleeves. She bent her head towards Mariam so she could wrap a colourful scarf around her head and pin it into place. After Mariam had added a little eyeliner around her eyes, she sat back. 'So, how do I look?'

'Just as you should. We are two Muslim women on a sight-seeing holiday in Canada, yes? Look, we're off the ferry already. The hotel is only a couple of minutes away,' added Mariam.

As they stepped out of the limousine in front of the Radisson, Electra's stomach gave a lurch. It felt like the butterflies she used to get when she had to return to boarding school. 'Which means you're nervous,' she muttered under her breath as they walked into the lobby. 'Right,' Electra said. 'What do we do now?'

'You go sit down and I'll ask the concierge if he can call Merry's room and let her know we're here. In case she's out, I suggest you find a spot to sit where we can see the entrance as well as the elevators just over there,' Mariam pointed. 'There's a free couch right in that corner which will give us a perfect view.'

'Okay,' Electra said, feeling very glad Mariam was with her. She always knew what to do and would calmly set about doing it. Having crossed the polished floor of the lobby and sat down where Mariam had suggested, Electra looked around and saw not one head turning towards her as it usually would.

Mariam returned and sat down beside her.

'No one has noticed me so far,' Electra whispered.

'Good, and I am sure Allah won't mind you borrowing the symbols of our faith occasionally, but if it's going to be more permanent, then you may have to convert,' Mariam replied. Electra wasn't sure if she was being serious or not. 'Anyway,' she continued, 'the concierge said he'd spoken to Mrs McDougal last night, and also put a note under her door, confirming we were coming and would meet her in the lobby at one o'clock.'

'I never open those notes that get left under the door, mind you,' said Electra. 'It's normally either your bill, or to say that housekeeping couldn't get access to turn down your bed. Did the concierge call her room when you were with him?'

'He did, yes, but she did not pick up.'

'Then maybe she's not coming.'

'Electra, we are ten minutes early, so let's be positive and give Mrs McDougal a chance, shall we?'

'Okay, okay, but if she doesn't show, it must mean she's avoiding us.'

'Her daughter, Mary-Kate, thinks – quite understandably –

that it might be because she is unhappy about potential relatives turning up suddenly. We must be sensitive, Electra.'

'I'll do my best, promise. Remind me what she looks like again?'

'Maia said we are looking for a small, slim, middle-aged woman with blonde hair . . . like Grace Kelly.'

'Oh yeah, I think Maia mentioned her. Who is she again?' Electra asked.

'*She* was one of the most beautiful women to ever walk the earth. My dad was in love with her for years. Here, let me see if I can bring up a picture of her.'

Mariam opened her satchel and pulled out her laptop. She typed in the password for the Wi-Fi that the concierge had given her and found what she was looking for.

'There – you have to admit she was stunning, and she even married a real-life prince! My dad was only a teenager when she got married, but he says he still remembers it because she looked so beautiful.'

'She sure is,' agreed Electra. 'And the polar opposite of me.' She gestured to her tall frame and ebony skin. 'That means that this Merry isn't genetically related to me in any way, but her colouring does remind me a little of Star . . . Now, why don't you watch the elevators over there, and I'll keep a close eye on the entrance?'

Both of them sat for twenty minutes staring at their allotted targets, until Electra shook herself. 'You know what? I'm starving.'

'Shall we order some food?' Mariam picked up the menu from the table and studied it. 'They don't have a halal menu here, so you can go veggie if you want, to keep in character.'

'Damn! I was going to have a cheeseburger, but I'll make do with a salad and French fries.'

'Okay.' Mariam checked her watch. 'It's now just after ten

past one, so she's either late or just not coming. We'll call the waitress over and order, then I'll go see the concierge again.'

Mariam did as she'd suggested, but Electra could already see from her face as she walked back to the couch that it wasn't good news. 'He's tried her room again, but no reply. I guess we're just going to have to sit here and wait.'

'If she *is* actively avoiding us, it could mean she feels threatened by us.'

'I am not surprised. She must find it strange that a bunch of adopted sisters are following her around the globe,' Mariam pointed out. 'Your family is not exactly standard, is it?'

'Well, if she actually came to meet me, then I could explain it all to her, couldn't I?'

'Explain that you need to see an emerald ring to prove that Mary-Kate is who Georg, your lawyer, thinks she is, i.e. the "missing sister"? Even that sounds odd, Electra, because none of you are your father's biological daughters. Did Georg tell you whether she has been left a legacy of some kind? Maybe that would help her think it was worthwhile meeting us. I mean, if there was money her daughter might inherit.'

'I don't know,' said Electra despairingly as the waitress brought them their lunch. 'Thanks, and can I have some extra ketchup and mayo for my fries?' she asked.

The waitress nodded and sped away.

Electra took a fry and chewed on it. 'I mean, as usual with Pa, everything is a mystery. What am I doing in Toronto, masquerading as a Muslim woman and eating fries in the lobby of some hotel? Waiting with you for someone I'd never heard of until a couple of days ago, who looks like she won't be showing up anyway?'

'You are right. Put like that, it does sound weird,' Mariam agreed, and both of them began to giggle.

'Seriously, Mariam, this is just ridiculous. If I were Mary-Kate's mom, I wouldn't show up either. Maybe you could ask the concierge if he'd try her room one last time? Then we're leaving.'

'After I've finished my sandwich, I will, yes,' said Mariam. 'And if she doesn't answer, perhaps you could write her a personal note? Then we could leave it with the concierge to hand over to her.'

'That's a good idea,' Electra agreed. 'Bring me some paper and an envelope back from the desk.'

It was almost two o'clock by the time Electra was satisfied with what she'd written.

'Right, this is the final draft,' she said, indicating all the screwed-up previous versions littering the coffee table.

'Go ahead, I'm listening,' said Mariam.

Dear Mary McDougal,

My name is Electra D'Aplièse, and I am one of six adopted sisters. Our father, Pa Salt (we're not sure of his actual name because that's all we ever called him), died a year ago. He'd adopted us from all over the globe, but had always told us that there was a seventh sister who was missing.

Our lawyer, Georg Hoffman, said that he'd found some information which proved a Mary McDougal was almost certainly the missing sister. We know from my sister CeCe's visit to your daughter Mary-Kate that she was adopted as a baby by you and your husband. The proof it's her is a star-shaped emerald ring, which Mary-Kate says you have with you.

I promise you, we are just normal women with no motive other than to fulfil our late father's wish to find the missing sister. Please feel free to contact me on my cell number, or the landline for our family home in Geneva.

I'm sorry we couldn't get to meet you today, but if your daughter is who our lawyer thinks she is, we'd all love to meet her – and you – at some point.

With best wishes,
Electra D'Aplièse

'That's perfect. It is good that you said you would like to meet both of them,' Mariam said as she snatched the letter before Electra could find further fault with it, then folded it and put it, together with a card containing the appropriate phone numbers, in an envelope. 'Should I address it to her?'

'Yeah, thanks.' Electra sighed. 'Wow, what a waste of a day. I'm going back with nothing to report. I'm a failed detective.'

'If you are, so am I,' said Mariam as she sealed the envelope. 'Okay. I'll give the concierge the letter, then should I call the limo to pull up outside?'

'Yes, although I need to use the restroom before we leave.'

'Sure,' Mariam agreed as Electra went in search of it.

Walking in, she saw one of the stalls was occupied, and chose the furthest stall from the door.

'No, they're still there,' came a woman's low voice from the other stall. 'The concierge told me on the phone my visitors were two Muslim women. But what would they want with me? I mean, you don't think that . . . it's *him*?'

Inside her cubicle, Electra had frozen.

Oh my God, oh my God, it's her . . . what the hell do I do?

'I came down to have a look at them. They're both young, but no, of course I didn't recognise them . . . I'm going to go back to my room now. I've decided to leave for London tonight, just in case – I'm too uncomfortable to stay.'

There was another pause as the woman listened to whoever

it was she was speaking to. 'Yes, of course I'll keep in touch, Bridget. I'll call Claridge's now and tell them I'm arriving early, then ask the concierge to change my flight . . . All right then, my love, thank you and I'll speak to you soon. Bye.'

Electra heard the woman open the stall door, the tapping of shoes across the tiled floor, then the main door to the restroom opening and closing.

Trying to think fast, Electra pulled off her top and head scarf, dropping them in a heap on the floor. Then she ran out of the restroom and along the corridor back to the lobby. She spotted a petite, well-dressed blonde, still holding a cell phone in her hand, standing with others as they waited in front of the elevator for it to arrive.

'Oh my God! Is it you? I'm sure it is! Oh my God! You *are* Electra, aren't you?' Long nails dug into Electra's shoulder from behind.

'Ouch! Can you get off me, please?' she said as she turned round to find an overexcited teenager behind her. 'Look, I'm not being rude, but I need to get into that elevator—'

'It *is* her, it's Electra!' shouted another woman waiting for the elevator, and instantly a crowd began to gather around her. She tried to walk forwards as the elevator doors began to open, but again she felt a firm grip on her shoulder holding her back and her path became blocked by people in front of her.

'*Please*, Electra, I just can't let you go until my friend takes a photo of us together. You were sooo great on TV the other night!'

'Let me through!' she shouted as she watched the blonde woman walk into the open elevator. She wriggled out of the teenager's grip and reached an arm forward to try and stop the doors from closing.

'Merry!' she shouted desperately.

But it was too late, and the doors were firmly shut. Electra looked up at the panel and saw the elevator was already on the third floor. She swore harshly under her breath and turned round to try and find Mariam, but the crowd had grown thick around her.

'Hey, Miss Electra, what are you doing here?' asked a young man as he began taking pictures on his camera.

'Yeah, we didn't know you were visiting Toronto,' called someone else. 'Can I have a photo too?'

'I . . .' Electra could feel beads of sweat gathering on her neck. 'Please, let me through, I have a car waiting for me outside. I . . .'

She was just on the verge of punching her way through the ever-deepening crowd when Mariam appeared in front of her and Electra gasped in relief.

'Hey, everyone, can you all move back a little, give Electra some space?' said Mariam in her calm, even tone.

'Yeah, ladies and gents, can we ask you to move away; you're blocking the elevator access, which could be dangerous.'

A man dressed in a black suit with an earpiece, which marked him out as security, appeared beside Mariam. 'This lady has a car waiting for her outside,' he said. 'Would you be so kind as to let her pass?'

Eventually, after Electra had posed for a number of pictures and signed autographs because she didn't want to be seen as mean or difficult, two hotel security guards escorted her and Mariam out onto the street and opened the limo door for them. It closed behind them with a bang. Inside, Electra groaned in frustration.

'Are you okay?' Mariam asked. 'Why did you take your headscarf and smock off?'

'Because *she* – Merry – was in the restroom! She was in a cubicle and I heard her on her cell phone, discussing how the concierge had said there were two Muslim women waiting for her. She seemed frightened – talked about whether it was "him", whoever "he" is. So obviously, when she finished her call, I threw off my disguise, hoping she wouldn't run if she saw *me* as me. But then I got recognised and I just missed getting in the elevator with her by a second. Damn it, damn it, damn it!' she swore as the limo moved off. 'Merry was right there, and I can't believe I missed her. Do you think there's any way the hotel would give us her room number? Maybe if we made up a life and death situation or—'

'I'm afraid I already tried that,' Mariam cut in. 'All the concierge was prepared to do was to call her again.' Mariam suddenly let out a chuckle. 'I'll never forget his face as he came over to see what the fuss was about, and recognised you standing next to me. He must have wondered what on earth was going on.'

'I'm wondering what on earth is going on too,' Electra said. 'It's now obvious that Merry is avoiding us. She also told her friend – who she called Bridget – that she was leaving a day early and flying to London tonight.'

'Ooh, Electra! So at least we know where she's going next. Did you get a good look at her when she was by the elevator?'

'I got a back view of blonde shoulder-length hair, and I remember thinking what a neat little tush she had. From the back she could have been anywhere between eighteen and sixty, but she definitely looked smart and attractive. Oh, and she'll be staying at Claridge's Hotel.'

'That is even better! It hasn't been a waste of time coming after all. You must call your sisters and let them know what's happened.'

'Sure,' Electra agreed. 'I suppose that at least we managed to learn a bit more.'

'Oh, I think you definitely did. Now, do you have a sister conveniently located anywhere near London?'

Electra turned to Mariam and smiled. 'As a matter of fact, I do.'

* * *

Once they were settled on the jet, waiting to take off, Electra placed a call to Atlantis.

'*Allô?*'

'Hi, Ally, it's Electra, reporting in from Toronto.'

'Hi, Electra! Did you get to meet Merry McDougal and see the ring?'

'Well, I did and I didn't.'

'What does that mean?'

Electra explained the afternoon's events. When she'd finished, there was a long silence.

'Right. So, apart from the fact your day sounds a bit like a scene from a farce, at least you were able to find out where she's going next. Claridge's, eh? She must be a wealthy woman,' said Ally.

'I just want to know why she's doing her best to avoid us. None of us mean her any harm, but she's definitely afraid. She talked about "him". I wonder now if she meant Pa?'

'But she knows that Pa is dead, and can't be any threat, even if she thought he was once, which I find hard to believe.'

There was a pause on the line.

'So,' Electra sighed, 'where do we go from here?'

'I'm not sure. I'll have to speak to Maia and see what she thinks.'

'What about Star? She lives very close to London, doesn't she?'

'Good point, she does.'

'Would she mind going to Claridge's and staking out the lobby for a blonde woman with a neat behind?' Electra chuckled. 'Problem is, I'm sure that blondes with good asses are two a penny there, but maybe it's worth a try, especially as Star lives so close.'

'There's no harm in giving Star a buzz to see if she's up for it. If Merry is leaving tonight, Toronto time, she'll probably arrive there tomorrow morning.'

'If she does go, I suggest she doesn't leave Merry McDougal any messages saying that yet another of the D'Aplièse sisters wants to meet up with her,' said Electra. 'It's obviously freaking her out.'

'I agree. We have to find other ways and means of gaining an audience with her,' said Ally. 'I'll talk to Star.'

'Okay, well, my jet's about to take off, so speak tomorrow, Ally.'

'Thanks so much for your help, Electra. Safe flight.'

Electra switched off her cell phone as the engines began to roar.

9

Star
High Weald, Kent, England

'Night night, darling, sleep tight,' Star said as she both spoke and signed the words to Rory.

He did the same, then held her to him tightly for a hug, his small arms wrapped round her neck. 'Love you, Star,' he said into her ear.

'I love you too, darling. See you in the morning.'

At the door, Star watched Rory roll over in his bed, then she switched off the overhead light, leaving the small night light on. She walked down the creaking stairs and into the kitchen, which was still a mess from supper earlier. Through the window above the sink, Star could see Mouse sitting at the ageing iron table they had set up on the grass to catch the evening sun.

Pouring herself a small glass of wine, she went to join him outside.

'Hello, darling,' he said, looking up from the plans for High Weald, his family's ancient Tudor mansion that had seen so much neglect in the past few decades. She remembered how bowled over she'd been when she'd first seen it last year, and how strange it was that she now knew every inch of decaying beam and damp, peeling paintwork inside it.

'How's everything coming along?' she asked him as she sat down.

'Slowly, as usual. I must have visited every reclamation yard in the south of England, looking for those two beams we need to replace the ones in the drawing room. But sixteenth-century beams that are the right thickness and colour aren't exactly just lying around.'

'Couldn't we do what your builder suggested, and make some that are a good approximation of the original? Giles said we could distress them and stain the wood the right colour so no one would even notice.'

'*I* would notice,' said Mouse. 'Anyway, there's an old pub in East Grinstead that's being refurbed into one of those gastro places, and they're knocking out the insides. The beams there are around the right time period, so maybe I'll find a match.'

'Let's hope so. I mean, it's fine here at Home Farm, but I wouldn't want to spend a winter here, especially as Rory is so prone to chest infections and there's no heating.'

'I know, darling.' Mouse finally looked up from his plans, his green eyes tired. 'But the point is that High Weald hasn't been properly updated in so long – and I'm talking structur-ally, not just a new flashy kitchen – so I want to ensure that not only is it as authentic as I can make it, but that it lasts for another two hundred years.'

'Of course.' Star stifled a sigh, because she'd heard this all so many times before. When it came to High Weald – and other houses Mouse worked on for clients – he was a perfectionist. Which was all very laudable, apart from the fact that the three of them were living in the freezing and impractical farmhouse down the lane from High Weald until the renovations were done. *And at this rate*, she thought, *I could be drawing my pension by the time we've moved.*

'If you're busy, would you mind if I popped over to see Orlando? I have a . . . situation I want to pick his brains about,' she said.

'Oh yes? And what's that?'

'It's complicated – to do with my family – but I'll tell you when we both have more time.' Star stood up and kissed Mouse on the top of his handsome head, noticing that stress had recently brought a few grey strands to his rich auburn hair. 'Remember to check on Rory in an hour. He's been having bad dreams recently and he can't call out properly yet.'

'I will, of course. I'll take my work inside,' Mouse nodded.

'Thanks, darling. I'll see you later.'

Star walked to her old Mini, started the engine and let out the sigh she'd been holding in. She did love Mouse dearly, but wow, was he hard work sometimes.

'It's almost as if the rest of the world doesn't exist outside his sixteenth-century beams and his porticoes and . . . grrrr,' she muttered as she drove off down the country lane towards the village of Tenterden. After a ten-minute drive, she parked the car outside the bookshop and let herself in with the old-fashioned brass key.

'Orlando? Are you upstairs?' she called, as she walked through to the back of the shop and opened the door that led to the flat above where he lived.

'I am,' came the reply. 'Do come up and join me.'

Star arrived at the top of the stairs and opened the door to the sitting room. Orlando was in his favourite leather chair, a white linen napkin tucked into his shirt, as he finished his dessert.

'Mmm . . . summer pudding. I truly adore it,' he said as he took his napkin and dabbed it round his mouth. 'Now then, to what do I owe this pleasure? We only said adieu an hour or two ago.'

'I'm not disturbing you, am I?'

'Goodness, no, although I was just about to go on a date with T. E. Lawrence and his purportedly real adventures in Arabia,' he replied, tapping the leather-bound book sitting on the table next to him. 'So, how can I help you?' Orlando wound his long, manicured fingers around each other and gazed up at her. His green eyes were so like Mouse's, and yet the two men couldn't have been more different. Star often forgot that Orlando was the younger brother, due to his penchant for dressing as if it was 1908 rather than 2008.

'I have a mystery for you: do you remember that I've sometimes mentioned Georg Hoffman, our family lawyer?'

'I do indeed. I never forget anything.'

'I know you don't, Orlando. Anyway, he arrived at Atlantis a few days ago and announced that he thought he'd found the missing sister – our seventh sister.'

'What?!' Even the usually unflappable Orlando looked shocked. 'Are you talking about Merope, the missing sister of the Pleiades? Of course, some legends say that honour goes to Electra, although your youngest sister is very much present.'

'She certainly is. You should have seen her speech at the Concert for Africa. It was amazing.'

'You know I don't approve of television – it is literal anaesthesia for the brain – but I did read about Electra's speech in the *Telegraph*. Obviously a reformed character, after her little trip into the funny farm.'

'Orlando! Please don't call it that. It's beyond rude and totally inappropriate.'

'Forgive me for my lack of political correctness. As you are well aware, my language comes from another era where "funny farm" would be an amusing phrase for an asylum. Once upon a time they called it Bedl—'

'Enough, Orlando!' Star reprimanded him. 'I know you do it on purpose to annoy me, but for the last time, Electra was simply getting help for her addictions. Anyway, do you want to hear where we've got to with the missing sister, or not?'

'Of course I do. If you would kindly remove my supper tray to the kitchen and furnish me with a nip of brandy, using the second glass to the left on the middle shelf in that cabinet, I will be all ears.'

As Star did as he asked, she wondered whether it was Orlando who needed treatment. *He definitely has OCD*, she thought as she allowed his instructions to guide her to the right glass on the right shelf.

'There we are,' she said as she put the stopper back in the crystal decanter and passed the brandy to him. Then she sat down in the leather chair on the other side of the fireplace. She thought how this room – modelled exactly on the sitting room of his old flat above the bookshop in Kensington, with its red-painted walls, antique furniture and rows of leather-bound books upon the shelves – would be the perfect setting for any Dickens novel. Orlando lived a good hundred years behind everybody else, which was mostly endearing, but sometimes irritating.

'So, dearest Star, do tell all,' Orlando said as he laced his fingers below his chin, ready to listen.

Star did so, and it took far longer than if she was telling anyone else, because Orlando constantly butted in with questions.

'What does that razor-sharp brain of yours deduce?' she finally asked.

'Rather sadly, not much more than you already have: that this Merry of yours, who has the emerald ring which is the clue to her adopted daughter's true heritage, does not want to be found. Or at least, she does not want to be found by *your* family. So the only question worth asking is, why?'

'Exactly,' said Star. 'I was hoping you might have some ideas.'

'I doubt it's anything personal towards any of your sisters. You say that none of you have ever met or heard of the McDougals before. So this story and the key to the mystery must go much further back in time. Yes,' Orlando nodded in affirmation, 'it's definitely something to do with the past.'

'I wonder if Pa was going to adopt Mary-Kate as a baby, then something went wrong, and he lost her?' Star mused.

'Perhaps. New Zealand is about as far away as you can get,' agreed Orlando. 'At least her mother might know who Mary-Kate's birth parents are.'

'Which is why you and I need to somehow arrange a meeting with her, so we can find out. *And* finally get a glimpse of that ring to match it to the drawing Ally has faxed me.'

'Are you saying you want to embroil me in a dangerous mission to London tomorrow?'

'Absolutely, and I know you wouldn't miss it for the world,' she countered.

'You know me too well, dear Star. Now, I want to go over everything again in detail . . .'

When Star had finished and there were no more questions, she watched Orlando sitting in his chair, eyes closed and obviously deep in concentration.

'Sorry not to be able to play Watson to your Holmes for much longer, but I need to get back home,' she prompted.

'Of course,' Orlando said, opening his eyes. 'So, you're serious about meeting with this woman tomorrow?'

'You know I am. Maia and Ally have asked me to.'

'Well then, I fear it will cost your family a fortune, but you need to reserve one suite, and a smaller single room, at Clar-idge's hotel.'

Star narrowed her eyes. 'Orlando, this isn't simply a ruse to spend a night in what I know is your favourite hotel?'

'My dear Star, it is you that will be making use of the luxury suite, whilst I am no doubt billeted in an attic room next to the maids. Although their afternoon tea is quite the ticket.'

'Hmmm . . . If you could tell me what this plan involves, then I could run it past Maia and Ally to see if they would allow us to spend what must be an astronomical amount for rooms there. Maia says Georg's secretary is booking anything we need. He's away apparently.'

'I am still finessing the plan, but please assure your sisters I believe it is almost foolproof. Tell them I will provide a refund of all costs if we fail in our endeavour. Now, I must get to work too; I have a lot of preparation to do overnight if I'm to pull this off.'

'What do you mean, *you* are going to pull this off? Am I not involved?'

'Oh, you are deeply involved, and must play your part to perfection. I am presuming that you have a smart dress or a suit in your wardrobe?'

'Um . . . I think I could probably pull something together, yes.'

'And any pearls?'

'I have a fake necklace and earrings that I bought once and have never worn.'

'Perfect. Oh, and of course, some heels, but not too high. Tomorrow, my dear Star, you will be Lady Sabrina Vaughan.'

'You mean, I have to act?'

'Hardly.' Orlando rolled his eyes. 'Think of it merely as preparation for your future wedding to my brother. You will be a real lady then anyway.'

'That's different . . . I'm not sure acting is my *métier*, Orlando. I've always had the most terrible stage fright.'

'You will just be playing yourself, only with more lucre, and it is I who will be doing most of the acting.'

'That's a relief. Do we need any help from CeCe and Chrissie?' asked Star. 'They're in London now, although CeCe is busy putting her flat on the market and sorting her stuff out to be shipped to Australia.'

'No.' Orlando waved the thought away. 'Under the circumstances, the last thing we require is another D'Aplièse sister. This is a delicate operation. Have the suite booked under your pseudonym, and mine under "Orlando Sackville".'

Star had to chuckle at the literary allusion. 'All right then.'

'Now, be gone and leave me to work,' he intoned. 'I shall meet you on the platform tomorrow, in time to catch the nine forty-six train to London. Goodnight.'

By the time Star arrived home, Mouse had gone to bed. She put in a quick call to Atlantis and explained the situation to Ally.

'Well, if Orlando thinks it will help, I'll send an email to Claridge's now to reserve the rooms,' Ally said. 'What exactly do you think he has up his sleeve?'

'I don't have a clue, but he's awfully clever and has helped me solve a couple of mysteries before.'

'I'm intrigued. Now, he said I should book your rooms under pseudonyms?'

'Yes. Orlando Sackville.' Star spelt it out for her. 'I'm sure he chose it in honour of Vita Sackville-West, who inspired the book *Orlando*, written by her friend Virginia Woolf.'

'Well, at least we're not the only family with obscure names,' Ally chuckled. 'And what pseudonym are you using?'

'I'm to be Lady Sabrina Vaughan. Anyway, I'd better try to get some sleep if I'm going to practise being a lady tomorrow.'

'Let's just hope that whatever your boss has planned, it works. I'll call Georg's secretary in the morning so she can arrange for the bill to be sent to her.'

'Okay. I'll keep in touch as often as Orlando allows. Night, Ally.'

'Night, Star.'

Orlando was already waiting on the platform at Ashford station when Star ran to join him, just as the train was approaching.

'Good morning. One might say you were cutting that fine,' he noted as the doors opened and they stepped inside.

'I had to take Rory to school, then hunt through my wardrobe to find something suitable to wear,' Star panted as she sat down. 'Will I do?'

'You look perfect,' said Orlando, admiring the elegant summer dress that showed off her slim figure. 'Although perhaps you could style your hair in a chignon? It might help make you look a little more stately.'

'Orlando,' Star whispered into his ear, 'we're not putting on an Oscar Wilde play, you know. These days, actresses and supermodels – common people to you – marry into the aristocracy all the time.'

'I am aware of that, but given that you told me our Mrs McDougal has lived in New Zealand for over thirty years, she, like me, may be a little behind the English times. But no matter, I think you look ravishing and will fit into our upcoming surroundings perfectly.'

'I wish Mouse could have joined me this evening. We could do with a couple of nights away together. Isn't it ironic that he is the real thing – a lord – yet not in a million years could he afford to stay at Claridge's?'

'Of course he could, Star. He has a houseful – or currently a storage facility full – of precious antiques, paintings and objets d'art that are worth a small fortune. But he, very sensibly in my book, would not think staying in a luxury hotel is worth spending his money on.'

'You're right, of course, and besides, the renovation of the house is costing everything he has. I do sometimes dream of moving into a modern semi where it's warm and everything actually works. And where my boyfriend comes home to me in time for supper and we chat about our days . . . or anything other than dado rails and RSJs – whatever they are.'

'High Weald is the other woman in Mouse's life,' Orlando declared.

'I know, and the worst thing is, I have to live with her forever.'

'Oh, come now, Star, it was obvious from the start that you fell in love with High Weald too.'

'Of course I did, and yes, it will be worth it when it's finished. Anyway, far more urgently, please tell me what exactly you have planned.'

'If all goes well, it should be a most pleasant way to pass the time,' Orlando said. 'We will arrive, unpack, then wander downstairs separately to take a light lunch in the Foyer restaurant that overlooks the entrance. Having researched all the flights that took off last night from Toronto, there are only four that our Mrs McDougal could be on. They all land between half past noon and three p.m. I have drawn a map of the ground floor at Claridge's. We will choose where we sit accordingly, so that we can espy the entrance and anyone who checks in to the hotel with luggage between those hours. Look.' Orlando dug a sheet of paper out of his ancient leather briefcase and pointed out the entrance, the Foyer and the reception desk drawn neatly onto it. 'When we check in, we must make sure to reserve tables in the restaurant with the best view.'

'But there may be any number of women arriving in the entrance area between those times.'

'We know that Mrs McDougal is in her late fifties – although she looks younger – and is slim with blonde hair. Plus, her suitcases will have airline luggage tags on them.' Orlando produced another piece of paper from his briefcase. 'This is a picture of the tag that would indicate Merry has travelled from Toronto Pearson. The airport code is YYZ.'

'Okay, but even if we do manage to spot her and her luggage, how will we introduce ourselves?'

'Aha!' said Orlando. 'You can leave that part to me. But of course, I must first introduce myself officially to *you*,' he said, dipping once more into his briefcase and handing Star a beautifully embossed business card.

VISCOUNT ORLANDO SACKVILLE
FOOD AND WINE JOURNALIST

Orlando had put his mobile number at the bottom of it. 'Viscount?' Star smiled. 'Food and wine journalist, eh?'

'I feel I jolly well could be, given the amount of fine fare and quality wines I have ingested over the course of my life. Besides, my brother is a lord, so me being a viscount is not too much of a stretch.'

'Okay, but how is you having a business card going to help? And how did you get these printed so quickly?'

'Ways and means, my dear girl. The printing shop down the street knows me well, and as to how it will help, I simply took into account everything that you have told me. I looked up The Vinery, and it tells me the proprietors are Jock and Mary McDougal. The business was started in the early eighties and is now one of the region's most successful vineyards, mainly selling wine within New Zealand, but also beginning to sell in Europe. In other words, given that New Zealand wine did not appear on any dining table further afield than Australia up until a few years ago, Jock and Mary McDougal have built up a business they must be very proud of.'

'Yes, but her husband – Jock – died a few months ago.'

'Exactly, and you have told me that their son Jack is taking over from where his father left off. If he is currently in France learning from the masters of the craft, it is easy to deduce he is aiming to grow the business further. Agreed?'

'Probably, yes.'

'Now, from what I understand of human nature, I do know that the maternal instinct normally overrides any other. Therefore, Mrs McDougal will wish to give her son any help that she can.'

'And?'

'What better than to bump into a food and wine writer whilst staying at Claridge's? Especially if he has an "in" with the well-known food and wine magazines and newspaper columns in Great Britain. *What such an article could do for our vineyard*, she thinks to herself. *And for my beloved son.* Are you getting the gist now, Star?'

'I think I am, yes. So, in a nutshell, you're going to introduce yourself to her as an aristocratic journalist – how you may get that introduction, I don't yet know – and then ask her if she'd be happy to be interviewed by you about her vineyard.'

'And her son, too, as he is the new official proprietor. It is patently obvious to me that we need to find some way of making contact with Master Jack to help establish further facts about his younger sister. For example, we have no idea if he too is adopted. Mummy dearest is bound to give me his contact details.' Orlando clapped his hands together in glee. 'Isn't it brilliant?'

'It's pretty good, yes, but where exactly do I come in?'

'Well, I need Mrs McDougal to feel reassured that I am not some charlatan trying to gather information about her surreptitiously. Therefore, after I have spotted her, then introduced myself at the reception desk, you will stand up from your table and walk past us. I will turn and stare in surprise. "Why! Sabrina!" I shall say. "What on earth are you doing here?" I will ask as we kiss each other politely on each cheek. Then you will reply that you're up from the country with your husband, doing a little light shopping. You will ask me to join you for drinks in your suite tonight at six p.m. I utter, "Delighted to," and you go on your way, having told me which suite you're in,' Orlando added. 'If all goes well with our little charade, Mrs McDougal will be convinced of my excellent credentials and social gravitas, which will warm her up for when I ask her for an interview.'

Star breathed in deeply. 'Goodness, I really do have to act! I hope that I can pull it off without saying something that will give us away.'

'Do not fear, Star. I've made your part short and sweet.'

'But when are we actually going to get to the crux of the matter? I mean, when do I come clean about who I am and why I'm masquerading as Lady Sabrina in an enormous suite?' she asked as the train pulled into Charing Cross station.

'As you said earlier, this is not an Oscar Wilde play, dear Star, merely a real-life improvisation. We will have to see whether we get past the first hurdle, which is spotting her entering the hotel and me being able to entrap her before she can escape to her room. There are many imponderables that I simply cannot take into account, but let us go one step at a time, shall we?'

'Okay,' she sighed as they left the train to head to the taxi rank and she felt her stomach turn over.

'Oh my goodness!' Star exclaimed as the general manager – who had shown them to her suite personally – left the sitting room. 'Isn't this amazing?'

'I have to admit that it is rather, yes. I've always adored Claridge's; it's an art deco triumph, and how wonderful that they have kept it so,' Orlando said as his fingers brushed across a tiger-striped desk, before sitting down in one of the velvet smoking chairs.

'They've left us a bottle of free champagne! Can we have some? It might help to calm my nerves.'

'My dear Star, you're acting like an excited child on Christmas morning. Of course we can open the champagne if you want, although I do wish people would not regard such things as "free". You – or in fact, your family – has just paid the equivalent of your month's salary at my bookshop to stay in a set of rooms for a single night. Your champagne is not free and if you decide to partake of the other accoutrements, such as those little bottles of whatever it is you ladies need to pour into the bath, or even the towels and bathrobes, then please do so. For none of it is "free". Yet people delight in saying they "stole" things when they return from such a jaunt. Utterly ridiculous,' sniffed Orlando, standing up and walking over to the ice bucket. 'What shall we drink to?' he asked her as he lifted out the champagne.

'Either living here forever, or not getting arrested for impersonating other people; you decide.'

'Let's drink to both!' Orlando said as he popped the cork. 'There you are,' he said, taking a flute of champagne across to her. 'I also brought you the paid-for chocolates they left next to the champagne.'

'I'm queen for a day,' Star said as she popped one of the gorgeously glazed delicacies into her mouth.

'From what you've told me of your family, you almost certainly have enough filthy lucre from your trust to live like this every day.'

'I'm not sure how much it actually is and even though it is ours, we run everything by Georg, our lawyer.'

'I have never met this Georg, but he is merely a member of staff that your family employs. It is your money, dear Star, and it's very important you and your sisters don't forget that.'

'You're right, of course, but Georg is quite scary. I'm sure he wouldn't approve of me asking him for a year's worth of money to live in a suite at Claridge's,' she chuckled. 'Besides, part of the fun is what a treat it is. It wouldn't be if I could live here every day, would it?'

'True, true,' agreed Orlando. 'Now then, while you were checking in, I was casing the joint. In other words, working out the best tables in the Foyer restaurant for you and I to sit, and I booked two. I will arrive first, then you ten minutes later. We can't be seen together by anybody before we bump into each other near the reception desk. So, you shall sit here' – Orlando indicated the position of her table on the floor plan – 'and I shall sit there, which gives us both a good view of the entrance, but means the enormous flower arrangement in the centre blocks us from each other's sight.'

'Okay, but how do we communicate? By carrier pigeon across the room?' she giggled.

'Star, I do hope that the alcohol isn't going to your head. We use the rather dull modern method of the mobile phone. If you or I spot a woman who may be Mrs McDougal, then we text each other. I will follow her progress, which will hopefully take her to the reception desk, give her a couple of minutes, then swoop in behind her. At this point, you will stand up, and make your way slowly across to us. You will stop at the flower arrangement and admire it, while checking that I have made verbal contact with her. Then, you will walk towards us and we will enact our little play. Just remember to ask me to your suite for drinks at six p.m.'

'Right, okay,' Star breathed, taking another gulp of champagne. 'We can do this, Orlando, can't we?'

'We surely can, my dear, we surely can. Now, given it is eleven thirty, I will take a wander downstairs and leave you to titivate. Good luck.'

'Good luck to you too,' Star called as Orlando walked towards the front door of their suite. 'And Orlando?'

'Yes?'

'Thank you.'

Merry
London
June 2008

10

I sat in the back of the taxi, and even though I felt exhausted from another sleepless night on a plane, I had to give a small smile of pleasure at the fact I was actually *sitting* in the back of a black cab. All those years ago, when I had last been in London during that terrible time, it had been my dream to put out a hand and hail one. But they, like anything else that hadn't been an absolute necessity, had been completely out of my budget. In fact, I could have equally contemplated getting on a rocket and flying to the moon, which had come true for Neil Armstrong just a few years before I'd arrived here in London.

I could hardly believe how the city had changed since I'd last visited. Great flyovers led out from Heathrow, the traffic backed up in a long, never-ending stream. Tall office blocks and apartment buildings rose out of the ground all around me, and I felt tears pricking at my eyes because it could have been Sydney or Toronto, or any big city across the world. I'd held on to my vision of London for so long; in my mind's eye, I saw the elegant architecture, the green swathes of open parks, and the National Gallery, which were about the only things that had been free to me back then.

Merry, I told myself firmly, *you know very well that at least*

Big Ben and the Houses of Parliament are still there, and the River Thames . . .

I closed my eyes to block out the view, praying it would improve as we drew closer to my treasured memories of the centre of this great city. I'd hoped I would be able to enjoy it properly this time, yet since Mary-Kate had left her messages for me and Bridget, and those women had sat waiting for me in the lobby at the Radisson, I'd been taken back to the last time I'd been here. And all the fear and dread I had felt then.

It has *to be him, surely . . . ?*

The line repeated in my head for the thousandth time. But why? Why after all these years? And how had he – *they* – found me?

Yet again, my heart began to slam against my chest. They must be serious as well, to use so many of them and be able to follow me all the way from New Zealand to Canada.

Admittedly, I'd come on my trip partly for pleasure, but also to search for both of them, know for sure where they were. And – certainly with one of them – to finally find out *why*. I hadn't uttered either of their names since I'd arrived in New Zealand thirty-seven years ago, knowing that to survive, I had to put my past behind me and begin again. But then, after my darling Jock had died out of the blue, it was as if the buffer he had always provided had collapsed and the memories had come rushing back. When I'd seen Bridget on Norfolk Island, fuelled by Irish whiskey, we'd reminisced about the old days and I'd admitted my 'Grand Tour' contained an ulterior motive.

'I just want to find out whether they're alive or dead,' I'd said as she'd refilled my glass. 'I can't live the rest of my life not knowing, *or* hiding, for that matter. I'd like to go home to Ireland and see my family. Hopefully, by the time I'm due to get there, I'll know. And feel it's safe, for them and me. Do you understand?'

'I do, of course, but in my view, both of them ruined your life in their different ways,' she said.

'That just isn't fair, Bridget. There *had* to be a reason why he never came. He loved me, you know he did, and—'

'Jaysus!' Bridget had studied me closely. 'You're sounding to me like you're still holding a candle for him! You're not, are you?'

'No, of course I'm not. You know how much I adored Jock. He saved me, Bridget, and I miss him terribly.'

'Maybe 'tis because he's gone that you've decided to rekindle the flame for your first love. But let me tell you, if you want to meet a man, get yourself on one of those cruises. My friend Priscilla went on one to Norway and said there were heaps of horny widowers looking for a wife,' she'd cackled.

'Looking for someone to nurse them through their dotage, more like.' I'd rolled my eyes. 'I don't think a cruise is for me, Bridget. And truly, it's got nothing to do with me looking for another man. It's about trying to find out what happened to my first love. *And* the man that I believe was responsible for destroying it.'

'Well, I'd say don't go digging up the past. Especially *your* past.'

Bridget always told it how it was and I respected her for that. We'd known each other since childhood, and despite her bossiness, which precluded anyone else's opinion being right except hers, I was very fond of her.

It was in her tiny flat that I'd stayed on the sofa during those awful three weeks in London. She'd been a good friend to me then when I'd needed her. Especially given that I'd lied and said I was going back to Ireland when I'd left her and

London behind. It was just safer she didn't know anything in case *he'd* come knocking on her door.

It was Bridget who had discovered my whereabouts two years ago, when a bottle of our 2005 pinot noir had won a gold medal at the prestigious Air New Zealand wine awards. The *Otago Daily Times* had taken a photograph of me, Jock and Jack, and printed a piece on The Vinery.

Bridget, retired and on holiday in New Zealand, had recognised me from the photograph and turned up one day, giving me a near heart attack when I'd opened the door and seen her. I'd had to tell her fast that neither Jock nor my children knew anything of my past, and, thinking she'd come to tell me of a family death, was hugely relieved when she told me it was simple serendipity that she'd seen the photograph.

I'd been thrilled when, a few weeks after moving to Norfolk Island, having fallen in love with it during our trip there, she'd met Tony – and after a short time, had decided to marry him. Given that Bridget had been a spinster all her life, I'd been very surprised.

'It's only because Tony just does whatever Bridget tells him to, Mum,' Jack had commented before he'd left for France – he was not a Bridget fan. 'I reckon she secretly beats him, then locks him in a kennel outside at night,' he'd added for good measure.

It was true that Tony was very mild-mannered and actively appeared to enjoy being ordered around. They certainly seemed very happy together anyway, though it had really put the wind up Bridget when we'd both heard the messages from Mary-Kate about the 'missing sister', and the two women who wanted to meet me.

'What did I tell you only last night about digging up the past?!' she'd exclaimed.

'But I've never even mentioned anything about all that to Mary-Kate. It must be coincidence, surely? After all, Mary-Kate is adopted, so one of these girls might just be part of her birth family.'

'They might be, yes, but I remember the "missing sister" is what he used to call you. After all these years, and Tony and me just getting hitched, I don't want anything to do with all that.'

So the two of us had decided to take the afternoon flight to Sydney, just in case. 'If these women do arrive on the island and knock on the door, Tony might spill some beans,' I'd fretted. 'Do you think we should tell him to be out?'

'No, Merry. Tony knows nothing, and if we told him not to say anything, then he'd just ask me a load of questions neither of us would have answers to. All he needs to know is we want a girls' night in Sydney. Best just to leave it and let them arrive unexpectedly.'

I could still feel the shiver of terror after hearing Mary-Kate's mention of the search for the missing sister.

I will hunt you down, wherever you try to hide . . .

Then there was the emerald ring. *He'd* hated it from the first moment he'd seen it. Because it was a twenty-first birthday gift to me from someone he loathed.

Looks like an engagement ring, so, he'd muttered. *Him, at his age, with all his money and his English accent . . . He's a pervert, that's what he is . . .*

Maybe when I arrived at Claridge's, I should just take the ring out of my bag and throw it in the River Thames. Yet I knew I couldn't, because aside from the fact it now belonged to Mary-Kate, it had been given to me by one of the most precious people in my life – by the man who had loved me unconditionally and never betrayed me . . . Ambrose.

Thankfully, the buildings around me were starting to

become lower, and some of the ones I remembered seeing from the top of a double-decker bus were appearing. The sight of them comforted me, and made the memory of the two women who had appeared in the lobby yesterday, and then the voice that had shouted my name as I stepped into the lift in Toronto, less frightening. Even though Mary-Kate, and the letter from a woman called Electra, had reassured me these sisters just wanted to see my ring, I couldn't work out how they had got to me so fast. Anyway, the good news was that the trail had ended in Canada. Not a soul other than Bridget, whom I could trust with my life, knew where I was today. For now, I was in London and there'd be no one tracking me down at Claridge's . . .

I felt a sudden and much-needed flip of excitement as the taxi pulled up outside the hotel. Porters rushed to take my luggage as I paid the driver. I'd been told about this famous and beautiful hotel by Ambrose all those years ago in Dublin, when I'd been thinking of taking an exploratory trip with Bridget to London during our summer break from uni.

'It's a magnificent city, Mary. Full of beautiful architecture and many historic buildings,' he'd said. 'If you do go, you must take tea at Claridge's, just to see the wonderful art deco interior. If my parents had to be in London for business or a social event, they would always stay there.'

So travel to London we had, but rather than Bridget and I taking tea at Claridge's, we had stayed at a grotty bed and breakfast off the Gloucester Road. Nevertheless, we had both fallen in love with the city itself, prompting Bridget to move there soon after university, and me fleeing to it when I'd needed to escape from Dublin . . .

And here I was now, being ushered through the lobby of Claridge's as a paying guest.

'Did you have a good journey, madam?' the receptionist

asked as I stood in front of the check-in desk, my eyes taking in the sheer elegance and luxury of my surroundings.

'I did indeed, thank you.'

'I see you flew in from Toronto. Canada's a country I've always wanted to visit. Do you have your passport, madam?'

I handed it over to her and watched her tap the details into her computer. 'So, your home address is The Vinery, Gibbston Valley, New Zealand?'

'It is, yes.'

'Another country I've always wanted to see,' she smiled, all charm.

'Do excuse me for butting in like this,' came a voice from behind me, 'but did I hear you say that you reside at The Vinery in the Gibbston Valley?'

I turned to see a very tall, angular man, whose three-piece suit looked as if it had been modelled on something Oscar Wilde would have worn in his heyday.

'Er, yes,' I replied, wondering if he was the manager of the hotel, because he looked terribly official. 'Is there a problem?'

'Good grief, no.' The man smiled, then reached into the top pocket of his jacket to pass me a card. 'Allow me to introduce myself.' He pointed to the name on the card. 'Viscount Orlando Sackville and, for my sins, I am a food and wine journalist. The reason I so rudely interrupted you was because only last week I was having lunch with a friend of mine. He's a wine importer, you see. And he mentioned to me that New Zealand wines were casting off their reputation for being the lesser sibling of Australian wines and producing some very good bottles. The Vinery was one of the vineyards he mentioned. I believe you won a gold medal for your 2005 pinot noir. May I ask if you are the proprietor?'

'Well, my husband – who sadly died recently – and I ran

the business together for many years. Now my son Jack is taking over.'

'May I offer you my condolences for your loss,' the man said, looking genuinely sad. 'Now, I must not take up any more of your time, but may I enquire whether you are staying here at the hotel?'

'I am, yes.'

'Then might I beg you to spare me an hour or so later on this evening? I would very much like to write a feature on The Vinery – it's the kind of thing that the food and wine pages of the broadsheets here just adore. And of course, I know the editor of the *Sunday Times* Wine Club well. I'm sure you will know that if one's wine is included in the selection, well, one is *made*, so to speak.'

'Can I think about it? I am rather jet-lagged, you see, and—'

'Sabrina! Darling girl, what on earth are you doing here?'

I turned around and saw a thin, willowy blonde, who rather reminded me of Mary-Kate, approaching before being kissed on both cheeks by my new friend.

'Oh, I'm up from the country with Julian. We're staying here for a couple of nights while he works and I do a little shopping,' she replied.

'That sounds divine, darling,' he said to the young woman, who seemed rather nervous, before he caught my eye and drew the woman in closer.

'May I introduce Lady Sabrina Vaughan? She's a very old friend of both my family and myself.'

'Hello, er . . . ?'

'Mary. Mrs Mary McDougal,' I said as I extended my hand to shake hers.

'Mrs McDougal here is the co-owner of a wonderful vineyard in New Zealand. I was just telling her how dear

Sebastian Fairclough was waxing lyrical about her wines only the other day. I am determined to entice her into giving me an interview about the vineyard.'

'I see,' Sabrina nodded. 'It's lovely to meet you, Mary.' There was a pause as my new friend eyed her.

'Oh!' she continued. 'Why don't you come to my suite for drinks at six tonight? It's room number, er . . . 106. You are very welcome too, Mrs McDougal,' she added.

'Wonderful! See you then, Sabrina,' answered Orlando.

'Excuse me, Mrs McDougal, may I take your credit card?' asked the receptionist as Sabrina walked off towards the lift.

'Why, yes, of course,' I said, digging into my purse and handing it over.

'Mrs McDougal, forgive me again for interrupting, but do come tonight for drinks with Sabrina and me if you can. Then we can discuss your vineyard and all things wine.'

'As I said, I might be a little jet-lagged, but I'll try.'

'Excellent. Adieu until then.' He began to walk away as the receptionist handed over my key, but then halted and turned back.

'Forgive me, but I didn't catch your room number.'

I looked down at the key. 'It's 112. Goodbye, Orlando.'

Upstairs in my beautiful room, with its high ceiling, exquisite furnishings and views onto the bustling London road beneath me, I unpacked a couple of summer dresses, a skirt and a blouse, then dialled room service to order tea for one. Even though there were tea-making facilities in the room, I wanted to drink it out of a bone-china cup, poured from an elegant teapot, just as Ambrose had described. It duly arrived, and I sat in a chair savouring the moment.

I studied the card that the very posh Englishman had thrust into my hand. If he was who he said he was (and the details on the card and the fact that another woman had greeted him in the lobby surely confirmed it), then it presented a wonderful opportunity to get The Vinery some British – and perhaps international – attention.

I decided I should call Jack. Out of habit, I looked at my watch to gauge the time difference, then realised that I was no longer in New Zealand, Australia or, in fact, Canada, and only an hour behind France.

I picked up the receiver on the bedside table and dialled Jack's mobile. It took a while to connect and then gave that strange dialling tone which meant you were calling a foreign country.

'Hello?'

'It's Mum here, Jack. The phone's very crackly – can you hear me?'

'Yes, loud and clear. How are you? Or more to the point, where are you?'

'I'm well, Jack, I'm well,' I said and, hoping he wasn't familiar with either American or British dialling codes, I told my son a lie. 'I'm in New York!'

'Wow! The Big Apple! How is it?'

'Oh . . . noisy, busy, amazing!' I bluffed, because I'd never visited New York in my life. 'Just as you would imagine. Now then, how are you, sweetheart?'

'Happy, Mum, very happy. It's hard work communicating as my French is pathetic, but I'm learning a lot from François, and the Rhône Valley is something else! Just mile after mile of vines, pastel-coloured houses and blue skies. We even have mountains behind us to remind me of home. Although it's nothing at all like home,' Jack chuckled. 'So, after New York, you're off to London?'

'I am, yes.'

'Well, François said he'd be happy to host you here after

the harvest, if you'd return the favour when he and his family visit New Zealand next year.'

'That goes without saying, Jack, of course I will. I'd love to see Provence, but I've Ireland on the schedule after London, remember?'

'The big return to the homeland . . . I'd enjoy taking a trip over there to see where my mysterious mum came from. Actually, I don't think you've ever said exactly where in Ireland, other than talking about uni in Dublin.'

'To be fair, Jack, you've never asked,' I countered.

'"To be fair", is it Mum? You sound Irish when just thinking about going back! Anyway, are you enjoying your Grand Tour?'

'I'm loving it, but I miss your dad terribly. We always said we'd do this when he retired, but of course, him being him, he never did.'

'I know, Mum, but I don't like you travelling by yourself.'

'Oh, Jack, don't worry about me, I'm perfectly capable of taking care of myself. Anyway, I wanted to tell you about someone I met at the hotel . . .' – I suddenly remembered that I was meant to be in New York – '. . . last night. He's a wine writer for some big international newspapers. We got chatting and he asked me whether I'd be up for doing an interview on The Vinery, its history, and so on. What do you think?'

'It sounds exactly like what we need. Wow, Mum, we let you out of our sight for more than two minutes, and you're chatting up wine journos in hotels!'

'Oh, very funny, Jack. This man was around half my age. He's called' – I consulted the card – 'Orlando Sackville. Have you heard of him, by any chance?'

'No, but then again, I'm not exactly an expert on wine journalists yet. Dad did all that kind of thing, y'know? Anyway, it can't do any harm to talk to him, can it? You can do the history of how you and Dad built the business up from nothing. If he needs to know the technical details of the grapes we use and stuff, then just give him my mobile number and I'd be happy to speak to him.'

'I will, of course,' I said. 'Right, I'd better leave you to get on. I've missed you, Jack, and I know your sister misses you as well.'

'I miss you guys too. Okay, Mum, keep in touch. Love you.'

'Love you too.' I ended the call, then picked up the journalist's card to dial the mobile number written on it.

'Orlando Sackville,' answered the dulcet tones of the man I'd met earlier.

'Hello, it's Mary McDougal here, the lady you met downstairs, from The Vinery in Otago. I'm not disturbing you, am I?'

'That's the last thing you're doing. What a delight! Does this call mean that you're prepared for me to interview you?'

'I discussed it with my son, Jack – the one who's in Provence – and he thinks it would be a good idea for me to speak to you. Although he's the person for any technical detail you'll need.'

'Wonderful! Six p.m. in Sabrina's suite then?'

'Yes. Although I won't stay for long, or I might fall asleep where I sit.'

'I understand completely. Sabrina is looking forward to seeing you too.'

Even though Orlando had not struck me as a man who would jump me, and was half my age anyway, I was still glad Sabrina would be there.

'I'll see you at six then. Goodbye, Orlando,' I said.

'*À bientôt*, Mrs McDougal.'

I hung up the phone, immediately taken back to my Dublin days when I'd first gone to Trinity College and encountered similar types to Orlando and Sabrina, with their cultivated English accents and their worry-free lives.

'I'm meeting an English viscount and a lady for drinks tonight,' I said aloud, and thought how much *he* would have hated that.

Lying back on the downy pillows, I went over the facts that I'd gathered so far on both men I'd been searching for. There were certainly no males of either name of the right age living in New Zealand – I had exhausted all possibilities before I'd left. And after going through pages of marriages and deaths at the records office in Toronto had drawn a blank, the only place that was left for me to search before I headed home to Ireland was right here in London.

Come on, Merry, stop thinking about all that. It was so long ago and this is meant to be a relaxing holiday! I reprimanded myself.

I pulled my bottle of duty-free Jameson's whiskey out of its box and poured myself a finger, deciding that, having travelled across so many time zones, my body was completely confused anyway. Normally I'd never have allowed myself to drink alcohol until the evening and it was barely two p.m. here, but I took a deep swig anyway. The sudden vivid memory floated back to me of the first night I'd ever seen him. I'd looked like a complete fright, turning up at some Dublin bar to hear Bridget's latest boyfriend play in a band.

That night, he'd told me I was the most beautiful girl he'd ever laid eyes on, but I'd just taken it as part of the chat. He'd not needed to say a word to charm me, because it had only taken one look at those warm hazel eyes to fall in love with him.

Dublin . . .

How could it be that I had been drawn back into the past so vividly since Jock had died? And was it just coincidence that, since my thoughts had travelled back in time, these women had begun pursuing me?

I'd also realised that by tentatively opening up the memories that had been sealed for so long, it had unleashed a torrent of further ones, some stemming way back into my childhood.

I remembered *him*, the young boy I'd known when we were both at school together and walking home across the fields – and how passionate he'd been even then. Fiercely set in his beliefs and determined to convince me too.

'You read this, Merry, and you'll understand,' he'd said as he'd pressed the notebook into my hands. It had been the day I'd left for boarding school in Dublin.

'I'll be after calling you the missing sister till you're back,' he'd said.

I remembered how his intensity had always been unsettling, especially as it was always so focused on *me*.

'I want you to read about my grandmother Nuala's life and see what the British did to us, and how my family fought for Ireland and freedom . . . 'Tis my gift to you, Merry . . .'

The first page of the black exercise book had been inscribed with the words *Nuala Murphy's diary, age 19*. I had kept it for forty-eight years, yet never read it. I remembered flipping through the pages when I had arrived at boarding school, but the cramped untidy writing – as well as the atrocious spelling – had put me off, besides which there had been so much else to occupy me in my new life in Dublin. And then, as he and I had got older, I had tried to distance myself as much as I could from him and his beliefs, yet still I'd taken the diary with me when I left Ireland. I had found it again in a box when I had gone about the painful process of packing up Jock's things. And instinctively brought it with me on this trip.

I stood up, opened my suitcase, and found the diary in the

inside pocket, wrapped in a canvas bag to protect it. Why hadn't I simply thrown it away, just as I had cast off almost everything else to do with my past?

Taking out my jewellery box, I went to put it in the room safe, but something urged me to open it. I picked up the ring, the seven tiny emeralds glittering in the light. Then I lay down on the bed, slid on my reading glasses and picked up the diary.

It's time, Merry . . .

I opened it, tracing my fingers over the faded black script that covered the pages.

28th July, 1920 . . .

Nuala

The Argideen Valley,
West Cork, Ireland

July 1920

Cumann na mBan

The Irishwomen's Council

11

Nuala Murphy was hanging out the washing on the line. Over the past few months it had extended to three times its size, what with all the laundry she was doing for the brave men of the local brigades of the Irish Republican Army, known as the IRA for short.

The washing line stood at the front of the farmhouse, which overlooked the valley and caught the morning sun. Nuala put her hands on her hips and surveyed the lanes beneath for any sign of the Black and Tans, the dreaded British constables named for their mix of khaki army trousers and the Royal Irish Constabulary dark green tunics that looked almost black. They trundled around the countryside in their lorries of destruction, their only mission to root out the men fighting the British as volunteers for the IRA. They had arrived in their thousands the year before to support the local police force, who had been struggling to contain the Irish uprising. Thankfully, Nuala could see that the lanes beneath the farmhouse were deserted.

Her friend Florence who, like Nuala, was a member of Cumann na mBan, the women's volunteer outfit, arrived once a week on her pony and trap with a new load of laundry concealed beneath squares of peat turf. Nuala allowed herself a small smile as the line of laundry flapped in the wind. There was something satisfying about displaying some of the most wanted men in West Cork's underthings for all to see.

Nuala cast one more glance around her and walked inside the farmhouse. The low-beamed kitchen-cum-living area was stifling today, what with the fire burning to cook lunch for the household. Her mother Eileen had already peeled all the vegetables and they were boiling away in a pot above the fire. Heading for the pantry, Nuala collected eggs that she had taken from the henhouse earlier, along with flour and the precious dried fruit soaked in cold tea, then set about making a mixture that would provide enough for three or four brack cakes. These days, they never knew when an IRA volunteer might arrive at the door, exhausted from being on the run and in need of food and shelter.

Once she had tipped the mixture into the bastable pot, ready to be hung over the fire when the vegetables were cooked, Nuala wiped the sweat from her brow and walked to the front door to take in some gulps of fresh air. She thought how, as a child, life here at Cross Farm had been hard work, but comparatively carefree. But that was before her Irish brethren had decided it was time to rise up against their British overlords, who had dominated and controlled Ireland for hundreds of years. After the initial killings of British constables in Tipperary in January of 1919, which had sparked the hostilities, ten thousand British soldiers had been sent to Ireland to subdue the uprising. Of all the British army troops in Ireland, the Essex Regiment was the most ruthless, raiding not only IRA safehouses, but also the homes of civilians. Then the Black and Tans had joined the soldiers to quell the insurrection.

Ireland had become an occupied country, where the freedoms Nuala had once taken for granted were being chipped away at every day. They had now been at war with the might of the British Empire for over a year, battling not just for their own freedom, but for that of Mother Ireland herself.

Nuala stifled a yawn – she couldn't remember the last time she'd had more than three hours' sleep, what with volunteers arriving at the farmhouse for food and a billet. Cross Farm was known to all of the local IRA as a safehouse, partly because of its position nestling in a valley, with the advantage of being able to post scouts at the top of the heavily forested hillside behind them, giving a bird's eye view of the lanes below. This gave the occupants of the farmhouse enough time to leave and scatter into the surrounding countryside.

'We will prevail,' Nuala whispered under her breath as she went inside to check on the vegetables. Her father Daniel and her older brother Fergus were committed volunteers, and both she and her big sister Hannah worked with Cumann na mBan. While it didn't require as much direct action as that of her brother, Nuala prided herself that their work acted as a strong foundation for the men – without the women delivering secret communications, smuggling ammunition and gelignite for bombs, or simply providing food and fresh clothing, the cause would have floundered in its first few weeks.

Her second cousin Christy had been living with the family too for almost ten years now. The Murphys had taken him in after both his parents had died, and Nuala had heard whispers that he had an older brother called Colin, who was soft in the head and up in Cork City at a hospital for people like him. This contrasted strongly with the sturdy presence that Christy brought to her life. At fifteen, he'd had an accident with a thresher on the farm, and although his leg had been saved, he now walked with a limp. Christy had carved himself a handsome oak stick, and though he was only a few years older than her, the stick seemed to lend him an air of wisdom. Despite his injury, Christy was as strong as an ox, and was an adjutant to the Ballinascarthy Brigade of the IRA, working alongside her father. Neither Christy nor her father were on active duty, but their brains helped plan the ambushes and made sure that supplies and intelligence were coordinated. He also worked at the pub down in Clogagh, and every evening, after labouring a full day at the farm, Christy got on his old nag and rode down to the village to pour glasses of porter. There, he listened out for useful information if a group of Tans or Essexes were in the pub, their tongues loosened from the drink.

'Hello, daughter,' her father said, as he rinsed his hands in the water barrel that stood outside the front door. 'Is lunch ready? I've a fierce hunger on me today,' he added as he dipped his head to pass through the doorway and sit down at the table. Her father was a bear of a man, and even though Fergus was a tall lad, Daniel was proud he could best his son in height. Out of all the passionate anti-British feelings that permeated the very walls of Cross Farm, her daddy's ran the deepest and most vociferous. His parents had been victims of the famine, then when he was a young lad he had witnessed the Land Wars – a rising against the British landowners who charged outrageous rents for the hovels their tenant farmers lived in. Daniel was a true Fenian through and through. Inspired by the Fianna, the warrior bands of Irish legend, Fenians were firm believers that Ireland should be independent – and that the only way to achieve this was through armed revolution.

Her daddy was also a fluent Gaelic speaker, and had brought up his children with a great pride in their Irishness, teaching them to speak the language almost before they could speak English. All the children knew it was dangerous to speak Gaelic in public, lest the British heard you, so they only spoke it behind the closed doors of Cross Farm.

After the Land Wars, her grandfather had managed to buy four acres of fertile farmland from their British landowners, the Fitzgeralds. When Daniel took over, he had succeeded in purchasing another acre to expand the farm. Being free of 'the oppressors', as he called the British, was, Nuala knew, the most important thing in her daddy's life.

His hero was Michael Collins – 'Mick', or 'the Big Fellow' as he was commonly known around these parts. Also a son of West Cork, born only a few miles away near Clonakilty, Mick had taken part in the Easter Rising alongside Daniel, then after two years in a British prison, had climbed the ranks to become chief of the IRA volunteers across Ireland. As Daddy said so often, it was Mick Collins who ran the show, especially while Éamon de Valera, the president of the fledgling Irish republican government, was in America raising funds for the Irish battle against their British masters. Michael Collins's name was spoken in hallowed tones, and Nuala's sister Hannah had a newspaper clipping of his photograph pinned up on the wall opposite the bed, so she could wake to the sight of him every morning. Nuala wondered if any man would ever match up to the Big Fellow for her. At twenty, her older sister remained steadfastly unmarried.

'Where's your mam, Nuala?' asked Daniel.

'Out digging up spuds, Daddy. I'll be calling her in.'

Nuala walked outside, put two fingers in her mouth and gave a shrill whistle. 'Where are Fergus and Christy?' she asked as she returned and began to dole out the potatoes, cabbage and boiled ham into bowls.

'Still sowing the fields with winter barley.' Daniel looked up at his daughter as she put his bowl down in front of him. They were all on half-rations of ham just now, saving what they could for hungry volunteers. 'Any news?'

'Not so far today, but . . .'

Nuala turned towards the open door as she saw Hannah flying up the track towards the farmhouse on her bicycle. Her sister worked in a dressmaker's shop in Timoleague and wouldn't normally return home for the midday meal. Nuala knew something was up. Her heart began to beat against her chest, the feeling so familiar to her now it was almost constant.

'What's happened?' she asked as Hannah came in through the door. Her mother Eileen, and Fergus and Christy, followed in her wake. The door was closed tightly, then bolted.

'I've just heard that Tom Hales and Pat Harte have been arrested by the Essexes,' Hannah said, panting hard with both exertion and emotion.

'Jaysus,' said Daniel, his hand covering his eyes. The rest of the family sank down onto the nearest chair or stool.

'How? Where?' asked Eileen.

'Who knew where they were?' demanded Christy.

Hannah put out her hands to quiet them all as Nuala stood there, the bowl she'd been placing on the table frozen in mid-air. Tom Hales was the commandant of the Third West Cork Brigade – he made all the main decisions, and his men trusted him with their lives. Pat Harte, always a steady soul, was his brigade quartermaster, in charge of its organisational and practical side.

'Was it a spy?' asked Fergus.

'We don't know who informed on them,' said Hannah. 'All I know is that they were captured at the Hurley farm. Ellie Sheehy was there too, but managed to talk her way out of it. She's the one who sent me the message.'

'Jesus, Mary and Joseph!' Daniel thumped the table with his fist. 'Not Tom and Pat. O'course, we all know why. 'Twas in retaliation for Sergeant Mulhern being shot and killed outside St Patrick's Church yesterday morning.'

'And may God have mercy on his merciless soul,' said Christy.

In the silence, Nuala managed to find her wits and serve out food to the shocked gathering.

'We can't expect that Mulhern could be murdered without reprisals – he was chief intelligence officer for West Cork, after all,' said Hannah. 'To be fair, 'twas a low attack, as the man was going into Mass. 'Twas brutal.'

'War is brutal, daughter, and that fecker had it coming to him. How many Irish lives are on his conscience as he stands before his maker?' demanded Daniel.

'What's done is done,' Nuala said, after crossing herself discreetly. 'Hannah, do you know where Tom and Pat have been taken?'

'Ellie said that they were tortured in the outhouse at the Hurley farm, then led out with their hands tied behind their backs. She said . . . she said that neither man could hardly stand up. They forced Pat to wave a Union Jack.' Hannah spat out the words. 'I've been told they're held at Bandon Barracks, but I'll be betting they'll be moved off fast to Cork City, before the volunteers launch a full ambush to rescue them.'

'I'd say you're right, daughter,' said Eileen. 'Are the other brigades alerted?'

'I don't know, Mammy, but I'm sure I'll be hearing later on.' Hannah shovelled some now cold potatoes and cabbage into her mouth. 'And Nuala, I've news for you.'

'What?'

'I've had Lady Fitzgerald's maid into the shop this morning. She was asking whether you'd go up to the Big House this afternoon to mind her son Philip? His nurse has left unexpectedly.'

The whole family stared at Hannah in disbelief. Eventually, Nuala managed to speak.

'Ah, Hannah, after what you've just told me, Argideen House is not the place I'd be choosing to spend my time. And besides, why me? I've only gone up there to help out at a dinner or a shoot sometimes, and I've never even met the son.'

'Lady Fitzgerald has heard that you were training to be a nurse before the hostilities started. Someone recommended you.'

'To be sure, I can't be going up there,' Nuala replied adamantly. 'I've sheets and clothes on the line, and who will make our tea?'

There was another silence, then her father looked up at her.

'I think you should go, daughter. The fact they'll have you inside their home means we're not suspected.'

'I . . . Daddy! No, please, I can't. Mammy, tell him!'

Eileen gave a shrug. Decisions like this were her husband's only.

'I'm with Daddy,' said Fergus. 'I think you should go. You'd never know what you'll be hearing when you're there.'

Nuala glared round at her family. ''Tis nothing less than sending me across enemy lines.'

'Now, Nuala, Sir Reginald might be a British Protestant who hosts the enemy, but I'd say he's a fair man whose family have lived in Ireland a long time,' Daniel replied. ''Tis easy in these situations to tar everyone with the same brush. You all know I'm an Irish republican through and through and I want the British out, but fair play to Sir Reginald, he's decent enough, given his kind. His father gave mine our land at a good price, and Sir Reginald handed me that extra acre for next to nothing.'

Nuala looked at her father and knew there was no argument to be brooked. Daddy's word was law. She gave a curt nod to indicate her compliance, and began to eat.

'What time am I meant to be there?' she asked.

'As soon as you can,' said Hannah.

'Go and clean yourself up and put on your best cotton dress,' Mammy ordered her after she'd finished her lunch.

Giving a heavy sigh of displeasure, Nuala did as she was told.

With her mother now in charge of the laundry and the cooking, Nuala wheeled her bicycle out of the barn to join Hannah on her journey towards Timoleague.

'What will the brigade do without Tom Hales in charge of them?' she asked her sister.

'I'd say they'll have Charlie Hurley replacing him as commandant,' Hannah said as they cycled downhill, following the lane at the bottom which ran beside the Argideen River, then heading along towards Inchybridge, where they would part.

'And my Finn?' Nuala whispered. 'Any news of him?'

'I heard he's with Charlie Hurley at a safehouse, so you're not to be worrying. Now then, I'm off back to the shop. Good luck to you at the Big House, sister.'

With a wave, Hannah cycled off, while Nuala headed reluctantly in the direction of Argideen House.

The narrow track ran alongside the railway line, which in turn ran alongside the river. The birds were singing and the sun was playing through the branches of the thick forest that surrounded her. She passed the special spot where she and Finn used to meet in secret and, stepping off her bicycle, she wheeled it into the woody interior and parked it against an old oak tree. Sitting down under its protective leaves, in the very place where Finn had first kissed her, Nuala took a few seconds to herself.

She'd first set eyes on Finnbar Casey at a Gaelic football match, when he'd been playing on the same team as Fergus. He'd been sixteen to her fourteen, and hadn't given her a second glance. But she had been hypnotised by this tall, dark-haired boy, who'd run with such grace, skilfully dodging his opponents as he kicked the ball into the goal. He had an easy laugh and kind blue eyes, and he'd stayed firmly in her memory, even after he'd gone off to complete his teacher training. They'd met again at a wedding a year ago, after he had taken up a position as teacher at the local school. Dancing together in the *ceilidh*, he had taken her hand in his, and she had known. At eighteen and twenty, the age gap hadn't mattered anymore. And that had been that. The wedding was set for August – only a few weeks' time.

'I'd always imagined we'd wed in a free Ireland . . .' Finn had said the last time they'd met.

'Sure, but I'm not waiting any longer to be your wife,' she'd told him. 'We'll fight for it together, so.'

Finn was also a committed member of the Third West Cork Brigade, alongside his best friend, Charlie Hurley. Only recently, the brigade had ambushed the Royal Irish Constabulary at Ahawadda and killed three policemen, then taken their rifles and ammunition. It was a valuable hoard as both were in short supply; while the British had an empire's worth of men and guns behind them, the volunteers were fighting with the few weapons that were either stolen or smuggled into the country from across the sea. Other men had already fallen around him, but Finn had managed to escape unharmed, which had earned him the nickname 'Finn o' the Nine Lives'. Nuala swallowed hard. He'd been lucky so far, but having been called on to tend to injured volunteers, Nuala knew all too well how luck could run out . . . Just like it had for Tom Hales and Pat Harte last night.

'And here I am, heading up to the Big House to serve the British,' she sighed as she climbed back onto the bicycle and moved off again. As she cycled along the high stone wall that marked the boundary of the house and parklands, then turned up the long, winding drive, she wondered what it would be like to live in a place that could probably sleep a hundred souls. The many windows of the house seemed to glint down at her, large columns flanking the front entrance, the building itself symmetrical and square in the way the British seemed to like everything.

Turning left as she approached the house, Nuala made her way around to the back to use the kitchen entrance. In the courtyard, five enormous, shiny horses poked their heads out of their stable doors.

If only we could get hold of a couple of those beauties, 'twould surely speed up the volunteers' journeys between their safehouses . . .

Stepping off her bike, she tidied her wind-strewn dark hair, straightened her dress, then walked to ring the bell at the kitchen door. She could hear the baying of the hunting dogs from their kennels.

'Hello there, Nuala, 'tis a grand day we're having for the weather, isn't it?' Lucy, one of the kitchen maids whom she knew from her school days, ushered her inside.

'I'd say any day it doesn't rain is a good day,' she replied.

'True,' Lucy agreed as she led her through the vast kitchen. 'Sit yerself down for five minutes.' She gestured to a stool by the huge hearth, a healthy fire burning within it and a pot of something that smelt delicious over it. 'Maureen, the parlour maid, is fetching Mrs Houghton, the housekeeper, to take you upstairs.'

'What's happened to the usual nurse?'

'Ah now, 'tis a good piece of gossip that's not to leave this kitchen.' Lucy pulled up a stool close to Nuala's and sat down. 'Laura only went and ran off with our stable lad!'

'And what would be wrong with that?'

'The thing that's wrong, Nuala, is that he's a local, and

149

she's British *and* a Protestant! Her ladyship had her brought over here especially to care for Philip. I'd be guessing they've caught a boat back to England by now. Her ladyship asked Mrs Houghton if she knew of anyone with nursing experience. Mrs Houghton asked us maids and I suggested you.'

''Tis thoughtful of you, Lucy, but I'm not properly qualified,' Nuala protested. 'I only did a year up at the North Infirmary in Cork, before I was needed to come back and help at the farm.'

'Her ladyship isn't to know that, is she? Besides, he's not sick, like, he just needs help washing and dressing himself and some company. Laura spent most of her time drinking tea and reading to him, so Maureen says. But then, she's a bit of a witch.' Lucy lowered her voice. 'Maureen's only the parlour maid, but she's all airs and graces on her. Nobody likes her. I . . .'

Lucy immediately shut up as a woman, who Nuala surmised was the unpopular Maureen, entered the kitchen. Dressed in her black maid's dress with its starched white apron, her pale face and long nose set off against her black hair, which was severely pinned back under her cap, Nuala guessed she was probably in her mid-twenties.

'Miss Murphy?' the woman asked her.

'Yes, I'm Nuala Murphy.'

'Please come with me.'

As Nuala walked across the kitchen to follow Maureen, she turned back to Lucy and rolled her eyes.

'So where did you train as a nurse?' Maureen asked as she led her across a vast hallway to the bottom of a flight of stairs so wide and big and grand that Nuala imagined they could lead to heaven.

'The North Infirmary in Cork.'

'And your family? Where are they from?'

'We live up at Cross Farm, between Clogagh and Timoleague. And you?' Nuala asked politely.

'I was born in Dublin, but my parents moved down here when they inherited a farm from my father's older brother. I've moved back to take care of my mother, who is ailing. Ah, Mrs Houghton, here is the girl who will fill the temporary nursing position.'

Nuala could hear the emphasis on the word 'temporary', as a tall woman in a long black dress without an apron, and a large bunch of keys hanging from her waist, appeared from one of the other rooms off the hall.

'Thank you, Maureen. Hello, Miss Murphy, I'll take you up to Philip's rooms,' the woman said in a pronounced British accent.

'May I ask what is wrong with the lad?' asked Nuala as she followed Mrs Houghton up the stairs.

'He was caught by an exploding mine while fighting in the Great War. He had his left leg shattered and they had to amputate to the knee. He's in a wheelchair and it's very unlikely he will ever leave it.'

Nuala hardly heard the housekeeper; she was staring at the huge paintings of people from the past that hung all the way up the stairs.

'And what are my duties?' she asked when she reached the top of the stairs and followed Mrs Houghton down a corridor wide enough to drive a Black and Tan truck along it.

'In the afternoons, Philip likes to be read to, then he will ring for tea and sandwiches around four o'clock. At seven, you will help him wash and put on his nightshirt and robe. He might listen to the radio, then at eight, you will help him into bed and he will take a hot drink and a biscuit, then his medicine. Once he is in bed, you are free to leave. Now' – Mrs Houghton turned to Nuala – 'I hope you are not squeamish?'

'I'm not, so,' Nuala replied, thinking 'squeamish' must be an English word for something she shouldn't be. 'Why?'

'Poor Philip's face was badly disfigured when he was caught in the blast. He lost one eye and can barely see out of the other.'

'Oh, that'll be no problem, I've seen the like in . . . hospital in Cork,' Nuala continued, horrified that she had been about to say 'in an ambush' when one of the IRA volunteers had been injured by an explosion.

'Good. Shall we go in?'

Mrs Houghton gave a light tap on the door and a voice called, 'Come.'

They walked into an airy sitting room, with windows facing out over the parkland beyond. The furnishings were so sumptuous that Nuala had an urge to simply run her hands over the soft silk damask that covered the sofa and chairs, and the shiny, elegant mahogany sideboards and tables that stood around the room. Sitting by the window with his back to them was a man in a wheelchair.

'Your new nurse is here, Philip.'

'Bring her over then,' a voice said in an English accent that had a slow thickness to it.

Nuala followed Mrs Houghton across the room, glad her mammy had insisted she put on her only good cotton dress.

The man turned his wheelchair round to face her, and Nuala did her best not to gulp in horror. His facial features had been cruelly rearranged: his empty eye socket, his nose and the left side of his mouth hung lower than his right. The skin in between was desperately scarred, and yet, the right side of his face remained untouched.

Nuala was able to see that, with his head of thick blond hair, he'd once been a handsome young man.

'Good afternoon, sir,' Nuala said as she dipped a small curtsey.

'Good afternoon, Miss . . . ?'

'Murphy, sir. Nuala Murphy.'

'I'm presuming you are Irish?'

'Indeed I am, sir. I live only a couple of miles away.'

'Your mother has already contacted staffing agencies in England,' cut in Mrs Houghton, 'but as Nuala has just said, she's local and a nurse.'

'As we both know, Mrs Houghton, I'm hardly in need of a nurse,' Philip shrugged. 'Come closer so I can see you properly.'

Philip beckoned Nuala towards him and only allowed her to halt when there were merely inches between them. He stared at her, and she could tell that even though he only had one eye that was apparently half-blind, there was a perceptiveness about him.

'She'll do fine, Mrs Houghton. Please' – he gave a dismissive wave with his hand – 'leave us to get to know each other.'

'Very good, Philip. Ring if you need anything.'

Mrs Houghton turned out of the room and Nuala was left alone with him. Despite her negative thoughts on coming over here, her big, warm heart immediately went out to this poor, disfigured man.

'Please,' he said, 'first of all, call me Philip, not "sir". As the staff already know, I can't bear it. Reminds me of a time I do not want to remember. Now, do sit down,' he said as he wheeled himself to the centre of the room.

Even though this was a simple request, given the fact that she had been drilled for her whole life to stand straight (and secretly proud) in front of any member of the British gentry, being asked to 'sit down' – especially on a damask sofa – was a confusing moment.

'Yes, sir, I mean, Philip,' Nuala replied, then did so. Now she had overcome the shock of seeing his face, her eyes travelled downwards to the half-empty trouser leg on his left side.

'So, Nuala, tell me about yourself.' Due to his twisted lip, she could see that it took effort for him to speak slowly and clearly.

'I . . . well, I'm one of three siblings, and I live at a farm with them and my cousin, my mammy and my daddy, Daniel Murphy.'

'Ah, yes, Mr Murphy. My father says he's a decent sort of Irishman. Sensible type,' Philip nodded. 'Not one to involve himself with the kind of activities that are going on around here and across Ireland at the moment, I'm sure.'

Jesus, Mary and Joseph! You can't let him see, I beg you, Face, don't be putting a blush up on my cheeks . . .

'No, Philip, not at all.'

He turned his head towards the windows.

'The one thing that kept me going throughout my time in the trenches was the thought of one day returning to the peace and tranquillity of my home here. And now . . .' He shook his head. 'At night I'm sometimes awoken by gunfire. I . . .'

Nuala watched his head droop, his shoulders shake slightly and realised the man was crying. She sat there, thinking she'd never seen a man cry, not even when she'd picked bits of stray bullet out of Sonny O'Neill's thigh after a Black and Tan raid on his farmhouse.

'I do apologise, Nuala. I tend to cry easily, I'm afraid. Especially when it comes to the subject of war. So many lives lost, so much suffering, and here we are in our quiet corner of the world, seemingly at war again.'

Nuala watched Philip dig into his trouser pocket for a handkerchief. He wiped his good eye, then his empty socket.

'May I get you anything, Philip?'

'A new eye and a leg would be just the ticket, but I doubt that'll be coming my way anytime soon. Until, of course, my spirit takes leave of the useless flesh it currently inhabits. I presume you believe in heaven, Nuala?'

'Yes, I do, Philip.'

'That's because you've never watched hundreds of men dying in agony, screaming for their mothers. Once you've heard that, it's pretty difficult to believe that there is a kind and benevolent father waiting for us upstairs. Don't you think?'

'Well, I . . .' Nuala bit her lip.

'Please, do go on. Nothing you say will offend me. You're the first young person I've seen in well over six months, not counting the nurse that you've taken over from – who was really quite the most stupid human being I've ever met. Mother and Father's friends are of a certain age, if you understand what I mean. You're a native of these parts, not to mention a Catholic to boot, so I'd like to hear your opinion.'

'I . . . suppose I'd say that whatever waits for all of us when we die must be so magnificent that we'd forget the pain we've suffered here on earth.'

'A true believer,' Philip replied, and Nuala wasn't sure if he was jesting or not. 'Although I can't stomach all that nonsense about being punished for sins on earth . . . What on earth has any seventeen-year-old soldier in the trenches done to deserve this, for example?' Philip indicated his face and lack of leg. 'I rather believe that the human race creates their own hell on earth.'

'War is a terrible thing, I'd agree. But sometimes 'tis necessary to fight for what is yours. Like you did against the Hun in France.'

'Of course you're right. I didn't fancy the Germans storming their way across our green and pleasant lands.'

Or you British occupying ours . . .

'I just hope it's worth all the sacrifice,' Philip continued. 'Now then, do you play chess, Nuala?'

'I don't, no.'

'Neither did the nurse before you. I did try to teach her, but she was too dim-witted to learn. Fancy having a go?'

'I'd be interested to learn a new game,' she replied, her mind scrambling to move on from the conversation they'd just had.

'Good. Then open the chess table that stands over there in front of the window.'

Philip instructed Nuala how it unfolded and she saw the top of the table was designed in a square, decorated in a dark and light chequered pattern.

'The chess pieces are in the cabinet underneath the tray holding the whiskey decanter. Pour me a drop whilst you're over there. I find the brain thinks better when it is calm, and let me tell you, a glass of Irish whiskey is worth twenty of my painkillers.'

For the first time, Nuala saw a smile appear on one side of his lips.

Nuala fetched him the drop of whiskey and a box that rattled, then wheeled him over to the table.

'Sit here opposite me; the light from the window helps me see better.' Philip dug in his trouser pocket and produced an eyeglass, which he put in place over his good eye.

'Now then,' he said as he took a gulp of whiskey, 'open the box and empty the chess pieces out. I will show you where to place yours.'

Nuala did so, and saw they were made of a black and cream material that was smooth and silky to the touch. Each one was beautifully carved, like a tiny sculpture.

'So . . . you can be white and I shall be black. Mirror your pieces to mine as I place them on the squares.'

Finally, the board was set up and after she had refilled Philip's glass, he taught her all the names of the different pieces, and the moves they could make across the board.

'Right, the only way to learn is to get stuck in and jolly well play,' he said. 'Are you game?'

Nuala said she was, whatever 'game' meant. Concentrating hard, she wasn't sure how much time passed as they moved their pieces across the board and she started to understand the rules.

There was a tap on the door. 'Damn!' Philip muttered. 'Come!'

Mrs Houghton stood in the doorway. 'I do apologise, but we were just wondering if you require tea? Normally the nurse would ring for it at four, and it is almost four and thirty.'

'That is because the last nurse was an idiot with stuffing for a brain. Whereas Nuala here has already grasped the rudimentary elements of chess. We will take tea and then continue the game afterwards.'

'Maureen will bring it up for you. It's smoked salmon and cucumber sandwiches.'

'Very good, Mrs Houghton.' The door closed and Philip glanced at Nuala. 'As we were so rudely interrupted, would you mind pushing me to the bathroom?'

Philip guided her through a door and into a bedroom with an enormous bed that had four posts, and what looked like a silk roof attached to them.

'To your right,' he ordered as he indicated another door. 'Push me in and I'll be fine from there.'

Nuala looked around in wonder at a big tub with a water pipe going into it, and a low round bowl that had a chain hanging above it from the ceiling.

'Are you sure you don't need some help?'

'I'll be grand, as you Irish say. Close the door behind you and I'll call when I'm ready.'

Standing in the beautiful bedroom, just for a moment Nuala imagined lying flat on the huge bed, looking up at its silk roof and staying here safe and sound forever. Away from the farmhouse that was under daily threat of raids, the lumpy straw pallet that formed her bed at night, and the hard work morning till dusk that was necessary just to put food in their mouths. She imagined having people to wait on her, and a bowl next door to her bedroom where she could discreetly relieve herself. And most of all, not living in fear every hour of every day . . .

But would I want to be him?

'Not in a million years,' she muttered.

'I'm ready,' came a call from the other room. Nuala shook herself and went to attend to him.

'All done,' he said as he smiled up at her. 'Would you kindly pull that chain above?'

She did so and water immediately rushed into the bowl below.

Trying not to stare at it, in case Philip were to take her for the peasant she was, she pushed him back into the sitting room, where Maureen had set up a three-tiered silver stand, brimming with sandwiches and cakes, as well as two beautiful china cups in front of the damask sofa.

'Afternoon tea is served,' said Maureen. As she gave a little bob, Nuala was sure the woman glanced in her direction and gave her a stare that was the opposite of warm.

'I hope you like fish,' Philip said as he reached for one of the sandwiches, made of a white-coloured bread with their crusts cut off.

'To be truthful, I've never tasted fish.'

'That doesn't surprise me in the least,' Philip commented.

'I've never understood why you Irish are so averse to the stuff. It is plentiful in the waters that surround us here, yet you stick to the flesh of animals.'

''Tis the way I've been brought up.'

'Well, after you have poured – tea first, milk last, by the way – I insist you try a sandwich. As you can see, there's enough for a party of ten.'

'I will so, thank you.'

Nuala poured the tea and the milk. Both teapot and milk jug were so heavy that she guessed they were made of solid silver.

'Please, pour some for yourself, Nuala. You must be parched.'

It was another word Nuala had never heard, but she was thirsty, so she did.

'Tchin-tchin,' Philip said, lifting his cup to hers, 'and well done on a couple of intelligent moves across the board. If your first try is anything to go by, we'll have you beating me in a few weeks' time.'

It was just past nine when Nuala finally left the house. Darkness was falling and she switched on her bicycle light to make sure she didn't ride into a ditch. Stopping at the same oak tree where she and Finn had always met, Nuala sat down and rested her back against the strength and wisdom of the old trunk.

She had entered a different world this afternoon, and her head was swimming with what she'd found there.

The game called chess had gone on for a fair old time after the tea (and the salmon, however pink and expensive, tasted a lot better than she'd imagined). Then Philip had insisted on another game, in which he'd stopped suggesting moves she should make. That had only lasted ten minutes, but then the next game had lasted almost an hour and he'd slapped his good thigh with his hand.

'Well done indeed,' he'd said as his milk and biscuits arrived with Maureen. 'Do you know, Maureen, Nuala might beat me at chess yet.'

Maureen had given a curt nod, then left. Not that Nuala was wanting praise, but there was something about the woman that made her hackles rise.

Wishing she could sit here for longer to take in the past few hours, Nuala saw that darkness had truly fallen and it was time she was home. Gathering her strength, she stood up and climbed back on her bicycle.

12

That night, Nuala and Hannah lay together in the bed they shared in the tiny attic room above the kitchen. Nuala had just snuffed out the candle and tucked the diary she'd been writing in safely under the mattress, having recorded the events of the day, as her teacher at school had once encouraged her to do. She'd had to leave school at the age of fourteen in order to help on the farm, but she was proud of the fact she was still practising her letters.

'So now, what was he like?' asked Hannah in the dark.

'He was . . . nice enough,' she said. 'He suffered terrible injuries in the Great War, so he sits in a wheelchair.'

'You're not feeling sympathy for him, are you? That family stole the land that was rightfully ours four hundred years ago, then they made us pay to get a tiny slice of it back!'

'He's only a bit older than you, Hannah, but has a face on him that could earn money in one of them circus fairs. He even cried when he was talking about the Great War—'

'Jaysus, girl!' Hannah sat bolt upright, removing the sheet and blanket with her. 'I'll not be hearing you feeling sorry for the enemy! I'll have you thrown out of Cumann na mBan before daylight.'

'No, no . . . Stop that now! Even Daddy says that for

Britishers, the Fitzgeralds are a decent enough family. Besides, there's none more wedded to the cause than me – I've my fiancé this very moment putting himself in danger to bring the British down. Now, as we've no visitors so far tonight, but a meeting of the brigade in our barn tomorrow, can we get some sleep whilst we can?'

'I can't help thinking about poor Tom Hales and Pat Harte,' Hannah sighed, lying down again. 'We've already sent word to our women spies; they'll find out where they are for sure. Now so, you're right: tomorrow will be a long day. The volunteers will be fierce hungry and Daddy says we have a lot of them coming.'

'At least we've clean clothes for them,' Nuala added, not daring to tell her sister that she'd been asked by Mrs Houghton to return to the Big House until a replacement nurse had been found.

I'll talk to Daddy in the morning, she thought as her eyelids drooped and she fell asleep.

'What do you think about it, Hannah?' Daniel asked, as the family sat round the table for breakfast the next morning. Even though it was only seven o'clock, the cows had been milked, and the pony and cart dispatched with Fergus to deliver the churns to the creamery.

'I'd say she shouldn't go again, Daddy. There's plenty to do here for a start, and that's without our work for Cumann na mBan. Who'll help Mammy with the extra cooking and washing we're doing these days? Never mind picking the vegetables and helping you with the harvest coming up. I've my job as a seamstress and . . . it's just not right to have one of our own working up at the Big House.'

'I'll cope, I have Fergus and Christy after all,' Eileen said, patting Christy's hand as he ate breakfast beside her. She looked at her husband. "Tis up to you, Daniel.'

Hannah made to open her mouth, but Daniel put up a hand to silence her. 'We've many volunteers who are spies working for us. And you women are some of the most successful, because the British don't suspect you.'

'Yet,' muttered Hannah.

'If Nuala's being offered a temporary position at the Big House, she'll be able to hear kitchen gossip from the other staff about who is visiting. Sir Reginald has plenty of military friends who might be inclined to be talking to him about any planned activities, especially after a few drops of whiskey.'

'I'm not likely to overhear chatter from the downstairs drawing room, Daddy,' Nuala interjected. "Tis an enormous house.'

'No, but sure, your young fellow might be chatting to his daddy from time to time about what's happening. 'Twould be useful to have an ear to hear it.'

'Philip's fond of a drop of whiskey himself,' Nuala smiled.

'Then feed him extra and find out what he knows,' Daniel said with a wink. 'Besides, how would it look if you turned them down? They'd be thinking 'twas an honour for you to work so closely with the family.'

'So you want me to carry on?'

'You have no choice, Nuala,' said Eileen. 'When the Big House calls . . .'

'We jump.' Hannah rolled her eyes. 'Come the grand day when we win, we'll be having that family out of there.'

'Is the son for us or against us, Nuala?' asked Christy.

'How can you even ask that question?' cried Hannah.

'Let your sister answer,' said Daniel.

'I'd say that Philip is against any war at all and just wants it to stop,' said Nuala.

'Philip, is it now?' Hannah's eyes glinted at her sister.

'Everyone calls him that, because being called "sir" reminds him of his time when he was a captain in the trenches,' Nuala shot back. 'I won't be doing this if I'm getting this pile of shite out of your mouth.'

'Nuala!' Eileen slammed the table. 'I'll not hear that kind of language under my roof. And you, miss,' she said, turning to Hannah, 'will keep your comments to yourself. Now then, I'd better be getting started. Do we know how many men we're expecting tonight?' she asked Daniel.

'Fifteen or twenty, and I've sent word to Timoleague to get some scouts to patrol up top whilst they're all here. There's a good few of them on the wanted list,' said Daniel.

'I've rounded up some local Cumann na mBan women to help with the cooking,' added Hannah.

'Make sure they hide their bicycles in the barn behind the hay bales,' Christy reminded her.

'Of course.' Hannah stood up. 'I'll be seeing ye.'

When Hannah had gone, Nuala helped her mother clear the bowls away, leaving them to soak in one of the water barrels outside.

'I'll be in the far field if you need me,' Daniel said as he strode out of the front door.

'Daddy?' Nuala caught up with him. 'Will Finn be here tonight?'

'I couldn't say; what with Tom and Pat taken, they're all on extra alert,' Daniel said and strode off with a wave of one of his large, brawny hands.

Hannah was as good as her word, and by the time she and
Nuala left, two women from Cumann na mBan were already
in the kitchen helping Mammy with the cooking for that
night.

Nuala's heart thumped as she cycled towards Argideen
House – not only at returning to it, but at the thought of the
men from the Third West Cork Brigade, which included her
beloved Finn, making their way in secret to convene at Cross
Farm's old barn.

'Wherever you are, darlin', I pray you're safe,' she whispered under her breath.

'Well, hello there, Nuala,' said Lucy as she walked into the
kitchen. 'I'm hearing you were a great hit with the young
master.'

'Was I?'

'Oh yes, Mrs Houghton told me he'd said that you had far
better nursing skills than the last girl.'

'I wasn't doing any nursing,' Nuala frowned. 'He'd a way
of doing most things for himself. All I did was give him a
quick wash before bed, then pop him under the covers and
feed him his pills.'

'Well, you got something right. Mrs Houghton's out at the
moment so 'twill be Maureen taking you to him.'

Maureen duly arrived and escorted Nuala upstairs without
saying a word. She stopped just outside Philip's door.

'I'd be grateful if you would ring down for the young
master's tea at four prompt. The sandwiches grow stale if
they're left for too long, and I've other things to be getting
on with.'

With that, she opened the door to let Nuala in.

Philip was sitting by the window in the same place she'd
first seen him yesterday. Remnants of his lunch were on a tray
on the table facing the damask sofa.

'I'll take these out for you now, if you're finished,' said Maureen.

'Thank you.'

Philip said no more until the door closed behind her.

'A real old sourpuss, isn't she? I've been told she lost her husband in the Great War, so I try to be forgiving,' Philip added. 'Sit down, Nuala.' He indicated the sofa. 'Have you had a pleasant morning?'

She suppressed a smile at the word 'pleasant', given she hadn't stopped for a second, without time to even eat any lunch herself after she had served it to her family.

'Nuala, you look quite pale. Can I ring for some tea? Sugar always perks one up, I find.'

'Oh, I'll be grand, Philip. My morning was pleasant enough, thank you.'

'No, I insist,' he said, grabbing the bell that hung by a string from his wheelchair. 'I can see hunger and fatigue at twenty paces and we simply cannot start another game of chess until you've put some sustenance inside you.'

'Really, Philip, I . . .' Nuala could feel a blush rising up her cheeks.

'It's no problem; these days the parlour maid is hardly rushed off her feet. None of Father's English friends – or Irish, for that matter – are particularly keen to travel down here, for fear of being taken hostage or shot at by the IRA along the way.'

To Nuala's continued embarrassment, Maureen appeared at the door. 'You rang, Philip?'

'Yes. Nuala and I are about to embark on a game of chess, and I don't wish to be disturbed. So I'd like you to bring up the tea and sandwiches before we begin. Nuala is hungry.'

'Yes, though that might take ten minutes, as I always make them fresh for you, Philip.' Maureen shot Nuala a look that could kill before she left the room.

'May I ask you, Nuala, do you and your family go hungry often?'

'Ah, no, Philip, not at all. We'd be lucky in that we have a field full of vegetables, and pigs for bacon. And the potato crop is looking well this year.'

'Unlike the dreadful potato famine last century. My father was only a boy at the time, but he remembers his father doing what he could to support his local tenants. The kitchen made batches of soup and extra bread, but of course, it could never be enough.'

'No.'

'Did many of your family leave for America?' he asked.

'I know my grandparents lost a number of their own to the famine, and brothers and sisters to America. I've cousins over there now who send parcels sometimes for Christmas. Have you been there yourself? It looks like a mighty fine place.'

'I have, as a matter of fact. We travelled on the poor doomed *Lusitania* over to New York, then went up to Boston to visit some of my mother's relatives. New York is indeed a sight to behold; Manhattan Island is filled with buildings that one has to crane one's neck backwards to see the top of.'

'Do you think anyone can make their fortune there?'

'Why do you ask?'

'Oh, me and my fiancé have talked of it sometimes.'

'I doubt there is an Irish family who hasn't,' said Philip. 'Certainly for some, it has been a success, but perhaps that has to be put in context against the bleak choices available to your ancestors: starve in Ireland or make a better life for themselves in America. I do remember my father pointing out a place called Brooklyn, which he said was a vast Irish settlement, due to the fact that many of the men there who had come over during the potato famine had found work building the Brooklyn Bridge. We drove through the area and the conditions were . . . uncomfortable, to say the least. The buildings were in disrepair and the streets crowded with filthy children playing outside. In answer to your question, yes, there are a lucky few who have flourished, but given the choice between living in poverty in a tenement building in Brooklyn, or being able to grow your own food and having fresh country air, I'd opt for Ireland.'

'Finn – my fiancé – is a teacher at Clogagh School and he was thinking that he'd like to give America a try. Me? I've told him fair and square that I'd not be setting foot on a ship after what happened to all those poor souls on the *Titanic*, and then the *Lusitania* after it.'

'I certainly understand your point of view, Nuala, but you must remember that the grand old *Lusitania* was torpedoed by the Germans. I promise you it was a mighty ship that otherwise would have continued to carry its human cargo safely across the Atlantic for many more years to come.'

'When Daddy heard of it sinking, he took his horse and rode down to the coast at Kinsale to help. I'll never forget him coming back and telling his tales of all the bodies floating in the water.' Nuala shuddered. 'Even though he's as fierce scared as me of the sea, he got in a boat and went out to help bring the bodies ashore.'

'I was deployed over in France at the time, but my father was there too and said the same. Well, if the sinking of that ship did anything, it certainly brought the Americans into the war. Ah, here is the tea. Let's have no more talk of darker times, eh? Leave the tray on the table in front of Nuala. She will pour,' Philip ordered Maureen.

The woman gave another nod and a bob, then, casting a further dark look at Nuala, left the room.

'She doesn't look happy,' Nuala sighed. 'She was only saying downstairs she likes to bring tea up at four o'clock sharp.'

'Goodness, don't worry about her. She's merely a parlour maid. Now then, get on with pouring the tea and eating as many sandwiches as you can, then we can begin our game.'

To her relief, Philip had pronounced himself fatigued and ready for bed at seven thirty, so having washed him, dressed him in his nightshirt, then put him in his bed and fed him his pills, she'd been away by eight thirty.

'It's the chess that's quite exhausted me,' he'd said with a smile as she'd left. 'I haven't had to exercise the muscle that sits in my head for far too long. I really had to work to win that last game, young lady. You've got the hang of it fast, and you'll be beating me soon enough, I shouldn't wonder.'

Now in the habit of stopping by her oak tree – almost as if she needed a few minutes to turn from Nuala the nurse at the Big House, to Nuala Murphy, daughter of a fiercely republican mother and father, and member of Cumann na mBan – she sank against the trunk and tucked her arms round her knees.

Of course, she could never tell anyone, not *anyone* ever, that she'd actually enjoyed the two afternoons she'd spent in Philip's company. He had said he wasn't hungry so soon after lunch, and besides, he could always call for more sandwiches if he needed them, so she was to eat as many as she wanted. Today they'd something inside Philip called potted meat, which she decided was one of the most delicious things she'd ever tasted. There'd been scones too, which the two of them had eaten together with cream and jam after the second game of chess had ended. Then they'd gone on to play two more. Philip was still beating her easily, whatever kind words he'd said, but she reckoned if she kept going, she might be able to hold her own in the game for longer. Having to concentrate so hard meant that all thoughts of anything else – which were mostly bad just now – had left her mind, and tonight she felt more relaxed than she'd been since before the bloody Easter Rising in 1916, four long years ago, which had been a watershed to her. It had marked the beginning of the concerted effort of the Irish to free themselves of their shackles, and Nuala had known then that her life would never be the same.

'But I like Philip, Oak Tree,' she confided to the thick, heavy branches above her. 'He's kind and gentle. And how he's suffered,' she sighed.

At least he hadn't cried today, she thought, as she got back on her bicycle, knowing she must get a spin on for home.

'It just shows that life's unfair on everyone, whether they're rich English or poor Irish,' she said to the wind as she prepared to tackle the steep hill up to Cross Farm.

'You're here at last, Nuala. We thought you might be sleeping over in one of their grand bedrooms,' Hannah commented as she walked into the kitchen.

'Jaysus, 'tis only just gone nine.' Nuala glanced around the kitchen and saw great tureens of vegetables on the table as Jenny and Lily, two women from the Clonakilty branch of Cumann na mBan, cut the ham and served it into numerous bowls.

'The men won't be coming in tonight to eat,' said Hannah, who was taking a cake off the hook over the fire. 'There was a patrol of the Essexes seen only an hour ago along the lane by the Shannons' farm.'

'Now then,' said her mother, 'we need to dole out these spuds and veg and get them to our visitors in the barn before they get cold. And yes, Himself has arrived already, Nuala, so I'd be suggesting you run a brush through that wild mane before you serve him his meal.' Eileen patted her daughter's hand. 'Take no notice of that sister of yours,' she said, lowering her voice further. 'She's stubborn as a mule, just like her daddy.'

Nuala made her way swiftly through the kitchen and ran upstairs to use the one pane of mirror in the house that hung in Mammy and Daddy's room. Brushing her long dark curly hair, that needed a good cut and some time she didn't have to sort it at the moment, she straightened her cotton dress that she'd had to wash out last night and wear again today. After checking for smudges on her face, she ran back downstairs, her heart banging in anticipation of seeing her love.

Dusk was beginning to fall as the women stepped out of the house to walk across the courtyard with food for the men inside the barn. It was almost fully enclosed, apart from one entrance along the side. Nuala knew there were scouts up above at the top of the hill, keeping watch for any trucks approaching below.

Eileen took the lead and gave the special knock on the barn door. Receiving the coded reply, she opened it and the five women walked in.

It was almost pitch black inside the barn, with only a small area lit by candlelight at one end. Nuala could make out the shapes of men sitting either cross-legged on the floor or on hay bales placed in a semicircle around one in the centre. As the women approached, the men, who had been talking in low voices, looked up. There were faces she knew and some she didn't. She cast her eyes around the men, all of whom looked thin and exhausted, until her eyes finally settled on one.

'Hello,' he mouthed and gave her a slight wave of his

fingertips. Nuala went with the other women around the semicircle, handing out the bowls and receiving whispered 'thank you's.

'You're looking well, Nuala,' Finn smiled up at her when she reached him. 'Will we meet afterwards in the usual place?'

She nodded, then left the barn with the other women.

'Wouldn't you love to be in there with them, to hear all the news and their plans?' Nuala commented to Hannah.

'We'll be getting them soon enough when we're sent with messages, or putting on our hooded cloaks to conceal ammunition or guns,' replied her sister.

Back in the kitchen, the women sat down to eat a hasty supper of their own. 'Any news of Tom and Pat?' Nuala asked.

'Yes,' said Jenny. 'I intercepted a telegram meant for Major Percival of the Essex Regiment. The lads have been moved to a hospital in Cork City.'

As Jenny worked in the post office in Bandon, she was a valuable spy for the cause and Nuala sometimes envied her for it.

'That means they're seriously hurt, God save them!' Eileen crossed herself.

'Be grateful for small mercies, girls,' Jenny piped up. 'At least our lads are not in jail and subject to further torture. They'll be looked after in hospital by our nurses.'

'I've already dropped a message to Florence – she'll catch the train to Cork City tomorrow and have one of the volunteers take a food parcel in, to see how they both are,' said Lily.

'Nuala, you go to the outhouse and bring in that pile of laundry, ready to take to the barn after the meeting,' said her mother.

Nuala stood up. 'Are they staying the night?'

'We've some straw pallets for them if they do. At least it's warm tonight; there's few enough blankets as it is.'

Nuala walked round to the outhouse and began piling the clean underclothes, trousers and shirts into two large baskets. As she carried one across the courtyard to the house, she stopped for a while, listening. Not a sound emanated from the barn. All was as it would normally be, except plans for guerrilla warfare were being made inside it.

'Ah, Philip, what would you be thinking of me if you knew?' she muttered.

It was past eleven when Daniel, Fergus and Christy entered the kitchen. The Cumann na mBan girls had done the cleaning and disappeared into the night, so only Hannah, Nuala and their mother were left in the kitchen.

'I'm for my bed, wife,' said Daniel. He turned to Nuala. 'There's someone waiting for you outside.' He indicated the back door. 'Don't you be long, I've eyes everywhere and you two aren't wed yet.'

Nuala's heart bounced at the thought of her fiancé waiting for her outside. Her a farmer's daughter with limited education and an unfinished nursing diploma, and him with a grand job as a teacher.

I wish I could tell him I can play chess, she thought as she walked towards the outhouse they were using to store the laundry, but she knew she couldn't.

In the dark, she could only see the glow of his cigarette.

'Is that you?' he whispered.

''Tis me,' she smiled.

Finn stamped out his cigarette and pulled her into his arms. He kissed her and, as always, her legs went shaky, and parts of her burnt with longing for what could only happen after they were married. Eventually, he led her out of the courtyard and onto the coarse grass, where they lay down and she snuggled into his arms.

'What if someone sees us here?' she whispered.

'Nuala, 'tis pitch black, but sure, I'd be more afraid of your daddy catching us like this than a whole patrol of Black and Tans,' he chuckled.

'We've no worries there, Finn, I could smell the whiskey on Daddy's breath from across the kitchen. He'll not surface until the cows are mooing for their milking in the morning.'

'Then I might just have my wicked way with you,' he murmured as he pulled her on top of him.

'Finnbar Casey! Don't you even be thinking such thoughts, so. I'm walking into that church as pure as the day I was born. Besides, what would all your schoolchildren think if they knew Mr Casey was taking a roll in the grass with his girl?'

'I'm sure they'd give me a round of applause, especially the boys.'

As Nuala's eyesight adjusted to the dimness and the moon appeared from behind a cloud, she could make out his features. She traced them with her fingertips.

'I love you, darlin', and I can't wait to be your wife.'

Some more gorgeous kissing happened, then Nuala rolled off of him and nestled her head on one of his arms, looking up at the stars.

''Tis a beautiful night. Calm, peaceful, so,' she said.

'It is, yes,' he murmured. 'And what's this I've been hearing about you nursing the Fitzgerald son up at the Big House?'

'Who told you?'

'Sure, I had a dispatch from one of the Cumann na mBan girls last night.'

Nuala sat up. 'You did not!'

'No, Nuala, I didn't, I'm just teasing you. Your daddy mentioned it earlier, said he'd told you 'twas a good idea.'

'And you, Finn? What do you think?'

'However much I'd prefer to stand waist-deep in a field of cow shite than have my girl carousing with the enemy, I think your daddy's right. What with me being a school teacher and you up the Fitzgeralds', 'twill mean we're not suspected. For now . . . The Black and Tan raids on local houses are after getting more frequent. I heard of three who had their farms searched last night, and their occupants scared half to death. The Buckleys' house was burnt to the ground. 'Twas in retaliation for the shooting of that louser, Mulhern.'

'Did Tom Hales order his shooting, d'you think?'

'I'd say he'd a hand in it, for sure. He's the commandant of the brigade – or was,' he sighed.

'What's going to happen now?'

'Charlie will take over until Tom's released. But there's no telling what kind of state the poor fellow will be in when he is. His family are all beside themselves, especially his brother Sean.'

'I won't ever let you fall into the hands of those British lousers,' she whispered fiercely to him.

'Sure, I'll be grand,' he chuckled. 'Though I'd like to see you take down the Essex Regiment, screaming like a banshee.'

'I would to save you, Finn, I swear. What else was discussed at the meeting?'

'Military business, darlin'. The less you know the better, so if you're ever interrogated, you have little to tell. One thing I will say is that Tom Barry was there tonight. You remember him, right?'

'I think so. Didn't he fight for the British in the Great War?'

'He did so, but he's one of the most committed volunteers I know. We discussed the idea of proper training,' Finn continued. 'What with Tom Barry being a military man, he'd be a good one to run it. The rest of us are amateurs at the game of war – and that's what we're fighting: a war. We've not a chance unless we organise ourselves properly.'

'I know, Finn. I keep thinking, how can a few Irish farmers, who've only held a pitchfork or a spade in their hands before now, take on the might of the British?' Nuala sighed.

''Tis those Black and Tans who are the most vicious, Nuala. They were recruited from the British soldiers that came back from the trenches in France. They're angry and used to bloodshed, which makes them savage. I'd say they've lost their consciences somewhere on those battlefields and they've scores to settle.'

'Don't frighten me, Finn, please.' Nuala shuddered. 'And you'll be part of this training thing?'

'I will indeed. It may make the difference between winning and losing. And we. Just. Can't. Lose. To the British. Again.' He gritted his teeth. 'We've finally got our own government in the Dáil in Dublin. We voted our own in, which gives us a remit to form a republic. 'Tis our right now for Irishmen to run our country. And don't you be listening to any of those up at the Big House if they tell you different.'

'Of course not. But I don't think Philip will. I've told him all about you.'

'Me?' Finn turned to look at her. 'Who's Philip?'

'The man I'm looking after; the son of Sir Reginald.'

'Don't you be saying too much, Nuala. You never know what could slip out of your mouth. Now then, let's talk of other things, like you and me being wed. Your daddy said we'll need to be using Timoleague church to fit all your friends and family in.'

The two of them argued gently over the size of the guest list, then spoke of the little cottage near the schoolhouse in Clogagh that came with Finn's job.

'We'll be brightening it up with a lick of paint, won't we?'

said Nuala. 'And Hannah can get material cheap from the dressmaker's, so I can make some pretty curtains.'

'Sure, you'll be having it look a picture.' Finn pulled her towards him and held her tightly in his arms. 'We'll be happy there, Nuala, I know we will.'

13

Nuala's new routine settled down after a couple of weeks: she'd be up at the crack of dawn to help as much as she could around the farm, and then cycle off to the Big House after lunch. There'd been further snipes from Hannah about what she'd termed Nuala's 'easy life up with the gentry'.

'As we women race around the country delivering dispatches, strapping ammunition round our waists and doing the fellows' laundry, you're up there playing games and eating cucumber sandwiches!'

Nuala rued the day she'd mentioned what she did for all the hours she spent with Philip. Even though she had tried to make it sound as boring as possible, her mother had listened with interest, and Hannah had latched on to the sandwiches and games of chess.

'Even though Daddy excuses you by saying you're a spy, I'm not seeing how you can be spying on anyone from an invalid's bedroom,' she'd sniffed.

Nuala had begun to pray that there would be some nugget of information she could take back to justify her time at the Big House, even though both her parents said there was no need, that the extra shillings helped pay the added cost of supplying the Third West Cork Brigade with food and fresh clothing. In truth, Hannah was right; even though Nuala had seen and reported a number of shiny black cars arriving, flanked by an Essex patrol, she couldn't identify the men inside them. All she could see was the tops of their hats or caps from her vantage point at the window above them.

'Look out for Major Percival,' Daddy had said, 'now, he's a prize we'd want to be having. He's the intelligence officer for the Essex Regiment and is responsible for a lot of the torture our lads have suffered. He's a habit of riding in his open-top car in the mornings, shooting his pistol about at farmers in the field just for the *craic*. We know 'tis him who was responsible for the capture of poor Tom and Pat.'

Through their network of female volunteers, details of the torture the men had endured had dripped out into West Cork. Charlie Hurley, now commandant of the brigade since Tom's capture, had arrived in the kitchen of Cross Farm to relay the details to the men of the family.

Banished from the room, Eileen, Hannah and Nuala had lurked at the top of the stairs, as Charlie had described the terrible beatings Tom Hales and Pat Harte had taken. The three women had wept when Charlie mentioned that Tom had had his fingernails pulled out one by one and his teeth broken, while Pat had been coshed so badly about the head with rifle butts that reports said he'd lost his brain inside it altogether. Pat was still in hospital, and Tom had been sentenced to two years in jail and shipped off to Pentonville Prison in London.

Finn had also been present that night at Cross Farm, ostensibly so they could discuss wedding plans, but their rendezvous afterwards had contained no such joy and Finn had held her close as she'd cried.

'I know what we're fighting for, Finn, and there's no one who believes in the cause more than me, but . . . sometimes I just wish I could go back to the way things were.'

'I know, darlin', but sure, doesn't it strengthen our resolve never to give in? We're in it now, and we can't give up. 'Tis a fight to the death, and that's that.'

'Please don't say that!' Nuala had begged him. 'We'll be wed at the end of next week and I'm not looking to be widowed just yet.'

'Oh, don't mind me, I'm fit enough to take on five of their side! They hide behind their weapons, but Charlie and me, we've been taking runs up and down the valley. Just feel the strength in this.' Finn had guided her hand to his thigh, which had felt like iron, but she'd quickly pulled her hand out of his grasp.

'There'll be none of that till our wedding night, remember?' She'd given him a weak smile as she'd wiped the tears from her eyes.

As Nuala cycled up the drive towards Argideen House, she prayed that one day she *would* see Major Percival, or identify *anyone* that visited Argideen House. But apart from Lucy, Maureen and Mrs Houghton, she'd not seen a single soul other than Philip since she'd arrived three weeks ago.

Parking her bicycle against the wall, she entered the quiet kitchen, feeling even more sorry for poor Philip. Nuala thought of when Christy had had his accident with the thresher, and had been laid up recovering for months.

In the heart of our home, being fussed over by everyone, not stuck upstairs with a stranger like me, she thought as she walked straight through the kitchen and up the staircase towards Philip's bedroom. It was a week ago since she'd been allowed to take herself upstairs, without waiting for Mrs Houghton or Maureen to escort her.

'That means you're trusted,' Mammy had said with a smile. 'Well done, Nuala.'

So many times she'd been tempted to dally on the grand staircase; to take in the big windows back and front that let light flood into the hall, the glass chandelier that had once held candles, which Philip said had recently been adapted for electric light. Still, to see them lit; she could hardly wait for the winter, when surely they'd have to have it turned on so you could climb safely up and down the stairs.

In truth, despite the guilt over her 'easy life', Nuala was glad of it. What with the wedding just around the corner, and all the preparations to be got on with, not to mention her household chores and her volunteer work, her hours up at the Big House were a welcome break.

'It's Nuala here, Philip, may I come in?' she called as she knocked on the door. A female voice answered that she could. Opening the door, she found a woman that she recognised to be Lady Fitzgerald standing in the room. She'd seen her occasionally at the dressmaker's in Timoleague, stepping out of a big car to choose some material or have a fitting. Even Hannah had said that she was 'not too grand with herself' considering, and spoke to the staff like they were human beings, not animals.

'Good morning, Nuala. Do come in and sit down.' She spoke in a low, warm tone, despite her crisp English accent.

'Good morning, Lady Fitzgerald.' Nuala bobbed a curtsey and did as she was bid. She looked up at the woman, who, with her blonde hair and blue eyes, was fierce pretty for an older lady. Compared to her own mammy, who must be of similar age, she looked twenty years younger. She had earrings with little pearls dangling off them, and her dress was made of a soft blue silk that matched her eyes. Nuala could only imagine what she wore for best if this was just for an ordinary August afternoon.

'Now, Philip here has been telling me how much he's enjoyed having you as his nurse over the past month.'

'I have indeed,' said Philip. 'I told Mother how you'd become quite the thing at playing chess. She's close to beating me now, Mother, she really is.'

Lady Fitzgerald gave Nuala a smile. 'It's obvious that you and Philip get along famously, but he also says you care for his medical needs too. As you know, we were looking for a fully trained nurse—'

'Mother, we've had this discussion over and over,' Philip butted in. 'I don't need a nurse anymore. My wounds are healed, and my overall health is stable. All I *need* is someone to push me to the lavvy, wash me, help me into bed and dole out my night-time medicine.'

'Yes, my dear, but you know the doctors have said you're at risk of seizures because of your head injuries and—'

'I haven't had one so far and it's been over two years since the whole bloody nightmare happened. What I need most is company that I enjoy.'

'I know, Philip.' Lady Fitzgerald turned back to Nuala. 'You can see how persuasive my son can be when he wants something. And he's persuaded me that he wishes to offer you a permanent position here as his nurse. How would you feel about that, Nuala?'

'I . . .'

'*Do* say yes, Nuala,' Philip pleaded. 'I mean, we can't have you leaving before you've won at chess, can we?' He gave her one of his lopsided smiles that always melted her heart.

'I'm honoured that you would offer me the position, given that I'm not fully qualified. May I ask my parents if they could spare me from the work on the farm? 'Twas the reason I came home from Cork in the first place and didn't complete my training.'

Nuala realised she was becoming more adept at lying every day.

'Of course you may.' Lady Fitzgerald gave her another of her sweet smiles that reminded Nuala so much of her son's. Even disfigured, the physical similarity between mother and son was pronounced.

'I presume you'll be wanting references?' asked Nuala.

'Mother already has those, don't you?'

'I do indeed. Your reference from the North Infirmary in Cork was glowing, although they did mention they're eager to have you back as soon as possible. *Is* that what you're planning, Nuala?'

'Oh no, your ladyship, things have changed since I left. I'm to be married this month to a teacher at Clogagh School, so I doubt I'll be leaving my husband to fend for himself.'

'Isn't that wonderful news, Philip?' Lady Fitzgerald's smile became even wider. 'About Nuala's marriage?'

It didn't look like it was much, as Philip tried his best to hide a frown. 'Then perhaps you should be asking your intended whether you're allowed to work here? He'll be in charge of you very soon.'

'I'll do that too, and have an answer for you tomorrow, I promise,' Nuala replied.

'Very good,' said Lady Fitzgerald. 'Now, doesn't your sister Hannah work in the dressmaker's in Timoleague?'

'She does, so, yes.'

'Have her take your measurements. You will need a uniform if you're staying with us permanently.'

'Mother, please, without risk of interfering in the women's clothing department, can I ask that Nuala have something simple made for her? Some blouses and plain skirts perhaps? I have had my fill of feeling as though I'm in a hospital, surrounded by nurses.'

'Very well, darling, but I must provide some aprons for when Nuala washes you. Now then, I should be getting on. We've General Strickland and his wife Barbara coming to take tea, which means I'm going to have to entertain her while he and your father talk business. Oh.' Lady Fitzgerald paused by the door and turned back. 'You'll receive eight shillings a week, with Sundays off and two weeks' annual holiday. Paid, of course,' she added. 'And another thing whilst I'm up here: do encourage Philip to get outside whilst the weather is so clement. Some fresh air would do you good, Philip. After all the trouble we went to in order to put the lift in, it seems a terrible shame that you never use it. I'll be up to kiss you goodnight at bedtime, darling. Goodbye, Nuala, it was a pleasure to meet you.'

When she'd left, Philip looked at her. 'I do hope you will take the job, Nuala. I've fought awfully hard for Mother to offer it to you.'

'I'd love to, I really would, Philip, but I have to ask if I'm allowed to first.'

'Of course, of course,' he nodded and looked up to her. 'Do you ever get tired of the control men have over your life? You might be surprised to hear that I've got a lot of time for the suffragette movement. Father abhors them, of course, and the Cumann na mBan here in Ireland is a little too radical even for me . . .'

Nuala fought the urge to correct his pronunciation of the Gaelic words, as he had called it '*bahn*' instead of '*mahn*', but the last thing she wanted was for him to know she was an active member of the 'radical' organisation.

'Having watched women working on the front line,' he was

saying, 'it occurs to me that the fairer sex are not only equal to men, but in many ways superior.'

'I'll be honest and say that I've not thought about it much; my family all work as hard as each other on the farm, doing our different jobs.'

'But does a man have to ask his father if he's allowed to take employment before he accepts it?' Philip pointed out.

'Well now, Christy, my cousin, who works in the pub in Clogagh, did ask my daddy if it was all right for him to do so.'

'Daddy's rule is law, eh?'

'Isn't it the same for you?' she asked him boldly.

'True. Nothing much happens around here without Father having agreed to it. Anyway, I do so hope your father will say yes to you working here, Nuala.'

'So do I, Philip,' she smiled at him. 'I'd like to more than you could ever know. Now then, what's this I hear about a lift? And why have you never mentioned it to me before?'

'Because our days have been given over to turning you into a worthy chess opponent,' Philip said defensively.

'We'd have had time for a walk occasionally, Philip. It might put some colour in your cheeks.'

'The cheek that sits somewhere below my nose, and is so scarred it looks like someone has scribbled all over it with a red ink pen? No, I prefer to stay up here, thank you.'

Nuala saw pain in his gaze, and realised the real reason.

'You're embarrassed, aren't you? You don't want anyone to see you.'

There was a pause as Philip turned his face away from her, which usually meant that he was about to cry.

'Of course I am,' he said quietly. 'Wouldn't you be? How would you feel if everyone gave you one glance and you saw the horror in their eyes? It was in yours when you first met me, Nuala.'

'Sure, I won't lie, it was. But then I got past that and saw the person you truly are.'

'That's because you're *you*. I'd have gardeners and maids screaming at the sight of me, let alone any of Mother and Father's visitors to the house. I . . . just . . . can't, all right?'

'I understand, Philip. Now then, will we be playing a game of chess or what?'

As she was cycling home, Nuala came up with what might be a plan. But first, she had to ask her family and fiancé whether they'd even allow her to stay on.

'Please, Holy Mother, let them.'

As she rode, she allowed herself to dream of a life where she no longer worked at the farm, with chickens, pigs and often cows to look after if Daddy was pushed. Just her own little cottage with Finn waking up beside her, and then spending afternoons with Philip . . .

''Twould be perfect,' she murmured as she cycled up the track to Cross Farm.

'Where are Hannah, Christy and Fergus?' she asked her mother, who was in her favourite chair by the hearth, knitting socks for the volunteers. Daddy sat opposite her, pipe in his mouth, reading a book in Gaelic.

'Christy's at the pub, Fergus is scouting at the top in case of a raid, and Hannah is after having an early night. She's to take the first train to Cork tomorrow to collect a dispatch from Dublin,' said Daniel. 'Any news?' He put his book down on his lap and looked up at her.

'Yes. I . . . well, I've been asked to stay on in a permanent position as nurse to Philip at the Big House.' She saw the look that passed between her parents. 'I wanted to ask you whether you thought 'twas a good idea. Oh, and' – Nuala added what she hoped was the icing on the cake – 'a big fancy car arrived today. A man called General Strickland was visiting Sir Reginald.'

'Jesus, Mary and Joseph!' Daniel exclaimed. 'He's the louser that runs the police force and all military operations up in Cork. He was there today?'

'Yes,' Nuala nodded.

'Do you know why?'

'I've not a clue, Daddy, but today I met Lady Fitzgerald. She spoke to me personally to offer me the position. And 'twas her who said about the general.'

'Our girl's infiltrating the heart of that family, Eileen,' Daniel beamed.

'And I've also an idea of how to see more.'

Nuala outlined her plan to persuade Philip downstairs and out into the garden.

There was a pause as her parents looked at each other again.

'Sure, Nuala, 'tis worth sticking with the work for now. But in a week's time, 'twill no longer be our decision what you do. You'll have to visit your fiancé tomorrow and ask him,' said Daniel.

'I'd say he mightn't be too pleased if his new wife is out until nine o'clock at night. Who will have his tea on the table when he comes home from the schoolroom?'

Nuala was fully prepared for this comment from her mother. 'Finn rarely gets home until after six o'clock. I'd leave his tea ready for him, so all he has to do is take the lid off the bowl and eat it.'

'I doubt he'll be wanting cold stew or vegetables a few

hours old,' said Daniel, 'but that's for him to decide, not us, daughter. A wife's place is by her husband's side, and I'm sure he'll not be wanting you cycling home in the dark and the rain when the nights draw in for winter.'

Nuala was reminded of the conversation she'd had with Philip earlier about the suffragettes.

'I'll be earning good money, which would help us,' she persisted. 'Finn's wages don't go far and we have no land to farm on to supplement it, so. Anyway, if he's after agreeing, would you think it's a good idea?'

'I've said what I think, but 'tis not for me to decide,' said Daniel. 'Now, I'm for my bed. Leave a lamp burning in the window. We've new calves in the barn, which'll be collected by dawn. Goodnight, daughter.'

'Goodnight,' she called as her parents made their way up the stairs to the bed that sometimes creaked in an odd way a while after they closed their bedroom door. She knew what the sound was, a sound that she herself would help make when she and Finn were wed . . . She blushed at the very thought of it.

Blowing out the candles, she left the oil lamp on the window ledge and went upstairs.

Only one more week of sleeping with my sister, she thought as she undressed, then crept in next to Hannah. They took turns to lie on the lumpy bit of the covered straw pallet because it was the worst place to sleep, but with Hannah up early to go to Cork City tomorrow, 'twas only fair that tonight she had the good side. Nuala shut her eyes and tried not to think about the 'new calves' in the barn. This was code for rifles that had been passed through many hands to reach them here in West Cork, and were currently lying in a dump in the woods behind the farmhouse. If they were found by the British before they were collected, the men in the family would be taken to Bandon Barracks to suffer the same fate as Tom and Pat. Comforting herself with the thought that Fergus was on watch up top, she did her best to go to sleep. After all, there had been 'calves' left here many times before . . .

'What's all this I hear about you carrying on working up at the Big House?' demanded Hannah the next day when she was back from Cork City. Nuala was mucking out the pigsty and replacing the straw, a job they both hated. 'What, I wonder, will Finn be thinking about that?'

'I'll be asking him, won't I? Then I'll tell you,' Nuala shot back.

''Tis all right for some: finding yourself a good husband with a proper job *and* working up at the Big House. All of this down at your cosy new cottage in Clogagh. We'll be calling you Lady Nuala soon enough, so we will. What about your volunteer work?'

'I'll take messages in the morning, and when I'm back at night, I swear. And I have Sundays off too. There.' Nuala threw in the last batch of fresh straw and moved over to the water barrel to wash the stench of pig from her hands. She'd skip eating lunch and bathe in the stream on her way to the Big House, because she'd not want to arrive smelling of pig.

'I'm sorry, Nuala,' Hannah sighed, 'I'm after turning into a grumpy old maid. I'm exhausted, I am. I had to cycle back the long way round from the station, as I saw a truck full of Tans.'

'Where were they headed?' Nuala asked as they walked towards the kitchen.

'They stopped at the Clogagh crossroads and didn't seem to know which way to turn. They were lost, since the volunteers took down the signposts,' she said with a giggle.

'I'll cook the lunch before I go, so, no bother.'

'Thanks.' Hannah gave her a wan smile as they entered the kitchen and she went upstairs.

'Did the calves leave the barn safely last night, Daddy?' she asked as Daniel arrived from the front entrance of the cottage.

'I'd say they did, yes. Now, where's my lunch?'

Having had no time to visit Finn, Nuala explained to Philip that he'd get her answer on Monday, for tomorrow was a Sunday, and her day off.

'But even if he says yes, Philip, I'd be having to take next Friday off for my wedding.'

'And I'd have thought the day after that too,' Philip said brusquely. 'Well, let me know for definite on Monday, and pity me having Maureen as my nurse all day tomorrow.'

Once she'd got that over with, they'd played their first game of chess, which took them straight up to tea time. As Nuala drank her tea, she decided to tackle him.

'I've been thinking . . .'

'About . . . ?'

'Well, what if I was to tell Mrs Houghton that you were wanting to come down to the garden but didn't want the staff around to disturb you? We could ring the bell to let her know we were coming, then I could take you out by the front entrance and into a place where the gardeners wouldn't be working. I'm sure there must be somewhere in that great big park outside where you can sit in peace? The weather's set fair for the next few days.'

'I don't know, Nuala,' Philip sighed. 'Like you, I'll think about it tomorrow and give you my answer on Monday.'

''Tis up to you, o'course, but for the love of God, you can't stay up here for the rest of your life,' she said, trying to keep her voice calm. 'All the flowers are in full bloom, and the air smells of cow parsley and . . . I just think 'twould do you a lot of good. We could put your trilby on your head to hide your face and—'

'Have you been in cahoots with Mother, Nuala?' he interrupted. 'I'm afraid you're beginning to sound just like her.'

'No, I haven't, but maybe we're thinking the same thoughts because we want the best for you.'

'What's best for me is if I never wake up again! I don't know which is worse,' he continued. 'The nightmares full of bangs and whistles and then the thud as the shells hit the ground and explode, or this waking hell.'

'Oh Philip, please don't be saying such things! You've suffered terribly, and it's understandable you're feeling like you do, but you're still here on God's green earth and I'd say that's because you're meant to be.'

'What use can I be to anyone like this?'

'For a start, you've taught me to play chess,' Nuala rallied. 'And maybe, once you've braved going downstairs, you could be enjoying more company, like that man who visited your parents yesterday.'

'General Strickland? Good Lord, I hardly think so, Nuala. The last thing I want is to listen to Father go on about the Boer War and hear Strickland complaining about the uprising down here. Father said that they're thinking about recruiting a new division of Auxiliaries to help us "crush the Irish".' He looked at her quickly. 'My apologies, Nuala, I meant no offence.'

'None taken.' Nuala was far too pleased with herself to care what he said, as she now had information to take home with her.

'I pray for you and your family's sake that you continue to stay out of it all,' he added. 'I'm only thinking of your safety, because Father said these new men will be highly trained and will stop at nothing to defeat this rebellion.'

'I will, so, Philip, I swear,' Nuala said, her best innocent expression on her face.

When she arrived home, Nuala was touched to see that Finn, who always came round to Cross Farm for his tea on a Saturday night, had waited for her so they could eat together.

'Hello, darlin',' he said, standing up to give her a hug as she walked into the kitchen.

'Where is everyone?' she asked.

'Oh, here and there; I'd say they're allowing us some time to ourselves.'

'Could you hang on for another few minutes before we eat?' Nuala asked. 'I've got important information to tell you all. I'll go and whistle for them.'

'What's this about important information?' said her mammy from the top of the stairs, where she'd obviously been listening in. 'Your daddy and Fergus are next door at the O'Hanlons', planning the harvest.'

'I'll go and fetch them,' said Finn, donning his cap and leaving the kitchen.

Hannah followed their mother down the stairs and fifteen minutes later the family was gathered together.

'So, Nuala,' said Daniel, 'what is it you have to tell us?'

Nuala recounted what Philip had told her about General Strickland's visit yesterday. She tried not to sound big with herself, being in possession of such knowledge before even headquarters in Dublin had sent a dispatch through about it.

'Now then, this is what I call news.' Daniel thumped the table. 'Did he say when exactly these Auxiliaries were coming?'

'No, but he said they'd be highly trained.'

'I'm assuming 'twould be soon,' said Fergus.

''Tis all we need,' Hannah sighed.

'Well done, Nuala. 'Tis obvious that you've won his trust if he's telling you things like that,' Eileen smiled at her.

'Hannah, will you write a message and get it sent off around the place?' said Daniel. 'It needs to go up to Dublin too, though I'm sure Mick Collins will already have heard the news.'

'He will, sure,' Hannah said, a glow in her cheeks at the mention of her hero. 'I'll be writing now.'

'Nuala, I'd say that decides it,' said Daniel. 'If Strickland and Sir Reginald are after discussing the British plans and Philip's being told them by his daddy, you'd be helping us by staying on there.'

'What's this?' Finn shot her a glance.

'Forgive me, Finn, I'd no time to see you yesterday,' said Nuala. 'I was going to tell you tonight that I've been offered a permanent position as nurse to Philip up at the Big House.'

'Have you now?' Finn's intelligent blue eyes appraised her.

'The money's good – eight shillings a week – and I'd reckon 'twould come in handy.'

'Though 'twould mean that you'd be missing your tea being ready on the table when you come in from a hard day's work,' her mother said pointedly.

There was a pause as Finn digested the news. Nuala felt utterly terrible and wished she'd just have said the words to him as soon as she'd got home, rather than him sitting here now with all the family staring at him.

'Sure,' he said, turning to her mother, ''tis school holidays at the moment and I've been a bachelor a while, so I know my way around a spud. Besides, if Nuala is there to help the cause, who am I to complain? 'Twill be harder for her than

me. You're having to learn to become a great actress, darlin'.'
He gave her a smile.

'We're all learning that, Finn,' Hannah put in.

'I'd say Daddy and Finn are right,' said Fergus. 'You should
take the job.'

The rest of the family nodded their agreement.

'That's that then, so. You have yourself a new job, daughter. Right. 'Tis time to leave these two alone to discuss
wedding plans.'

As the family dispersed, Nuala rekindled the fire to warm
up the pot, then served stew into two bowls, taking little for
herself as she was still full from the gorgeous Victoria sponge
cake Philip had insisted she try earlier. Even though it was
named after a British queen and was therefore a traitorous
thing to be eating, she'd savoured every mouthful. 'Can you
forgive me for not telling you the moment I came through the
door tonight?' she asked him.

'I'd have preferred it if we'd been able to discuss it alone
but—'

'Finn, you must say if you'd rather I didn't take the position. It doesn't matter about Mammy and Daddy – 'tis you I'll
be answering to this time next week.'

'And why would I be stopping you? As you say, Nuala,
'twill bring in some shillings to the household, and besides, it
means your nursing training hasn't been wasted. You're doing
what you were born to do.'

'Not really, Finn; 'tis hardly like I'm saving lives on a battle-
field.'

'From the sound of these Auxiliaries, there might be plenty
of that coming your way in the future. And isn't it you that's
always said to me it's not just about tending wounds, but tending souls? Seems like you're doing that for Philip. Oh, and one
more thing' – Finn took her hand across the table – 'let's have

none of this old-fashioned shite about answering to your husband. The only person you need to be answering to is yourself and your conscience. Within reason, of course,' he smiled.

She gazed at him and thought how well he and Philip would get on if they were to meet. Her heart was fit to burst with love for him.

'Thank you, though you must know I'd never do anything without discussing it with you first,' she said.

'Marriage is about being a team. We're both equals in it, and we must respect each other. I learnt that from the women up at teacher training in Waterford. I'd say half the students were women and just as bright as the men. If not brighter,' he grinned. 'Now then, with that agreed, tell me how the plans are going for our wedding?'

14

Nuala woke up on the morning of her marriage to Finn feeling as if she hadn't slept a wink. Every time she imagined taking her daddy's arm and walking down the aisle in front of two hundred souls, she thought she might be sick all over the beautiful white gown Hannah and the other dressmakers had sewn for her at the shop in their spare time.

Sitting up, she saw the sun was not yet showing its face above the other side of the valley, which meant it was before five.

Lying back down, she knew this was the last time she'd ever share a bed with Hannah. Which immediately sent her tummy into another loop of anxiety . . . She couldn't even ask her big sister what 'it' was like because she was the first to marry, and she could hardly be asking Mammy. She looked over at Hannah – she was so vivacious and quick-witted, though her temper came equally quickly, as Daddy always said. She'd had many fellows after her, but none had ever interested her.

Do you resent me for walking up the aisle before you . . . ?

Well, today, however many times Hannah would snipe at her, she'd ignore it. As Nuala had grown older, she'd also become aware that the eldest daughter had the hardest time on the farm. It was Hannah that Mammy looked to for the extra jobs, and Hannah did most things without complaint.

'I'll miss you . . .' she whispered to her sleeping sister. Hannah had inherited Mammy's pale skin, freckles and hair the colour of a shiny copper pan, whereas Nuala had her father's dark colouring. She'd always considered herself the plainer of the two, with any attention at weddings and *ceilidhs* going to Hannah. Fergus seemed disinterested in women in general, saving his affections for the cows in the field. So here she was, on the morning of her wedding, the youngest, but the first of her siblings to be wed . . .

Jumping out of bed, she decided she'd feed the hens and make breakfast just one last time.

As she crept downstairs so as not to wake anyone, she almost jumped out of her skin to see Mammy in her nightgown, stirring the pot over the fire.

'Why are you up so early?'

''Tis a stupid question to be asking on my daughter's wedding morn,' Eileen scolded her.

'I'm out to feed the hens and—'

'You'll be doing no such thing! Today is *your* day, daughter, and we'll be treating you like a princess right from the start of it. Now then, sit down in my chair and I'll be making you a mug of tea and then a bowl of porridge, so. After that, you're to be in the tub before everyone starts arriving.'

'But I—'

'None of that, miss; 'tis the last day that my word is law. For once, you'll be doing as you're told.' Then Eileen opened her hands and cupped her daughter's face inside them. 'I'm proud of you, Nuala. Finn's such a good fellow. Just remember to make the most of this time with him before the small ones start coming along, won't you?'

'I will, Mammy, I promise.'

Fourteen hours later, Nuala lay in her new bed in her new home, alongside her new husband. The sheet tucked firmly over the strange sensation of her own nakedness, she watched as her husband (equally naked) slept peacefully beside her. Even though she was utterly hanging – the most exhausted she'd ever felt in the whole of her exhausting life – she wanted to play the day back to herself so she could store it safely away in her memory without forgetting a moment.

She'd been taken to the church in a garland-streamed pony and cart, and all the way into Timoleague everyone had come out of their houses and shops and clapped her on her way. Then the walk down the aisle on her daddy's arm and the look in Finn's eyes as he turned round and saw her and whispered, 'You're beautiful,' in her ear, as Daddy had let go of her hand and had given it over to Finn's safekeeping. The fine spread laid on by friends and family, which even Finn's mammy, after a glass of sherry or two, was impressed by. The band that had struck up as the *ceilidh* had begun, with everyone in high spirits and dancing away as if they'd not a care in the world. She and Finn in the centre as he'd spun her round and round . . . Then the throwing of her bouquet, made up of wild fuchsia, violets and forget-me-nots. Hannah had been the one to catch it and everyone had cheered, especially as Nuala had seen that a young man had caught her eye.

Then the way Finn had carried her over the threshold of the little cottage that would be her new home. He hadn't put her down until he'd climbed the stairs and laid her gently on the bed. He'd struggled with all the tiny white buttons that had fastened her into the dress, but all the time he'd kept kissing her until she'd lain beneath him, and their lovemaking had begun.

She'd been amazed to find, after hearing gossip that men

liked 'it' better than women, that *she'd* liked it too. Yes, it had
hurt at first, but then it suddenly hadn't anymore as she'd
been swept along with all the new and wonderful sensations
her body and her mind had experienced.

It has been perfect, just perfect, she thought drowsily,
before she finally fell asleep.

'So, how is the new Mrs Casey faring?'

Philip looked up at her as she walked in, clad in her new
blouse of white poplin and the long grey skirt of such fine
fabric that it didn't itch her legs. She'd been provided with a
pair of new black boots too, and a stack of crisp, starched
white aprons.

'I'm well, thank you,' Nuala said. 'And yourself?'

'Oh, I'm the same as you left me. Whereas you . . . My
goodness, it's a positive metamorphosis! My dear Nuala, what
with the new togs and your hair pinned up like that, it seems
that you've turned from a girl to a woman overnight. Now,
do sit down.'

Nuala did so, feeling horribly embarrassed. Even though
the tone of Philip's voice had been light, she knew what he
was insinuating.

'Mrs Houghton said 'twould be more appropriate for my
position if my hair was put up,' she answered defensively.

'It suits you, although I must say I rather liked it tumbling
over your shoulders. At least Mother didn't insist on a nurse's
cap, so I'll be grateful for small mercies. How was the wedding?'

'It was perfect, thank you, Philip. The whole day went off
as well as it could have done.'

'And your new in-laws? Do they approve of the match?'

'Finn has no father – he died when he was very young. His mammy – mother,' she corrected herself, 'is a fine woman. She remarried a few years ago before Finn left to do his teaching diploma, and lives a good while away, near Howe's Strand in Kilbrittain.'

'Goodness, that all sounds very civilised,' said Philip. 'At least you don't have your mother-in-law living with you like so many Irish families do. I've often wondered how kindly my own dear mama would take to any woman I chose to marry. Not that it's a thought worth having any longer. Who would want me?'

'Many, I should think, when they got to know you.'

'You're being kind, Nuala, but let's neither of us delude ourselves. I'm a freak show, not fit to go out in public. I'll spend the rest of my days exactly where I am now. Anyway, I'm glad to see you happy, and I apologise if I appear maudlin. In truth, I can't help but feel envy for . . .' – Philip checked himself – 'for the fact that such a normal rite of passage has been denied me. Now then, I'd imagine you're quite exhausted today. So I thought I'd add in a little relief from the chess-board and teach you to play backgammon. The box is in the same cabinet as the chess pieces.'

'Whatever you wish,' replied Nuala, as she went to the sideboard to retrieve another beautifully turned wooden box full of small round black and white counters. She thought of Finn at home in their tiny cottage and, for the first time, resented being here with Philip.

Nuala would always remember those precious first few weeks after she and Finn were wed as the happiest of her life. She spent most of them in a dreamlike state of bliss; she'd wake in Finn's arms and stay there for a good while longer after they'd woken. Down they'd go for breakfast before Finn would cycle off to help her father and his neighbours with their harvests, as the new school term hadn't begun yet. Then she'd deal with the IRA men's laundry that her friend Florence delivered to the little outhouse. Having hung it out to dry in the small courtyard at the back of the cottage, she'd bake bread and make a cake for their tea before cycling off to the Big House to spend the afternoons with Philip. Returning in the evening, if Finn was home and not on volunteer duties, she'd find he'd already set out their evening meal. They'd sit together eating in the candlelight, before he'd take her hand and lead her upstairs to bed.

He'd shown her a way of lessening the chances of babies arriving too, assuring her it was only a small tweak to the usual procedure and not at all foolproof, and therefore not against any laws that God sent down to his Catholic servants on earth. Guiltily, she celebrated when her monthlies appeared, even though her mother began to cast her glances when she and Finn joined them at Mass at Timoleague church on Sundays. As was the family tradition, they all went afterwards to pray at the tiny graves of her mother's four lost babies; those souls that in another life would have grown to be her siblings. Nuala shuddered at the thought of birthing a babe only to have it die in her arms, and decided that for now, she and Finn were doing the right thing.

And all along, the fight against the British rumbled on. One night in September, Finn, now back to work at his school, which was just across the street, took her hand over the little table they used to eat on.

'I've been asked to attend a training camp, so I'll be gone from Friday till late next Sunday night,' he said.

'I . . . where? How? What about the school?'

'The "where" is the O'Briens' place up at Clonbuig; the "why" is as I told you: although we've fought hard, we need to get our men into better shape if we're going to prevail against the British and now your Auxies—'

'They're not *my* Auxies, Finn.'

'You know I didn't mean it like that. 'Twas heaven-sent that we were prepared for these monsters. They've only just arrived – one hundred and fifty of them, with more to come, I'm sure – and they're already terrorising ordinary Irish folk. Even though they're stationed up at Macroom, seems to be they're intent on coming down here. They're sending in their lorries to villages, then ordering everyone out of doors and firing shots. They're lining everyone – including our sick and elderly – up against the walls, poking them with their re-volvers and beating the men with ammunition belts.' Finn put his head in his hands. 'These men are animals, Nuala. They're fully trained servicemen, used to battle, and they're here to destroy the Irish by any means they can. With the Black and Tans, the Essexes and now these new lousers, if we're even to begin to compete, *we* have to have some training. Tom Barry's going to be running the camp.'

'You'll be away for the whole week then?'

'Yes. HQ in Dublin want an elite Flying Column, with only the finest volunteers picked for it. That means that we won't be working in a specific brigade or company, we'll be more flexible and can be deployed as and when we're needed.'

'But, Finn, you're a schoolteacher! Not a soldier.'

'That's the point. I *need* this training if I'm to be of use. You know I'm fit as a flea, strong and able to give and take orders – I can make a difference to the cause. I'll leave by night and on Monday morning, you're to walk to the school and tell Principal O'Driscoll I've some vomiting sickness and I'm not able to work. Then you're to come home and close every one of those curtains you've made. If anyone knocks to ask after me, you're to say I'm in bed and still sick.'

'What if these Auxie fellows, or the Tans, come and raid our village? If they're taking everyone outside their houses and lining them up, people will notice you're not here.'

'Then you'll simply say I'm too sick to be moved and pray your pretty smile will win the day, so they don't come inside after me.'

'What if they hear about the camp?'

''Tis only those going and the women of the Kilbrittain Cumann na mBan that know.'

'Then I'll come there next Sunday and help out, so.'

'No, Nuala, you'll go to Mass with your family as always and tell everyone that I'll be recovered enough to start school again the next morning. Try to remember that we're not suspected of any wrongdoing and we'll be wanting to keep it that way, not only for us, but for our families and the other men and women who are risking their lives for Ireland.'

'Oh Finn.' Nuala bit her lip. 'What'll I do without you in an empty house?'

'Sure, you'll manage, but while I'm here, will we go upstairs and have an early night?' he smiled.

'You look a little pale today, Nuala,' Philip observed as she sat down on the sofa.

'Ah, 'tis nothing, Philip. Finn has caught some vomiting sickness and I was up half the night minding him,' she answered as calmly as she could.

'The perfect wife, eh? Is he all right to be on his own?'

'It started last night and he was finally sleeping when I left. I doubt he'll be needing his tea tonight, though.'

'I had it once in the trenches – a can of tinned meat that had gone off. I was awfully sick for a few days – mind you, it earned me some good nights' kip inside the medical tent.' He shook his head as if dispelling the memories. 'It's a beautiful day, isn't it?'

'It is, yes, and I was thinking 'tis just the day to go out for a walk. Will you, Philip? Please?'

'I . . .'

'If you don't do it the once, you'll never do it. And you're a brave fighting man, and 'tis just a ride downstairs in the lift and out into the fresh air. Please, Philip . . . for me.'

He looked at her, his good eye showing her a range of emotions. Finally, he nodded.

'You win. I will do it for you, Nuala. You can take me into Mother's private garden at the side of the house. We shouldn't be disturbed there.'

'Thank you, Philip,' Nuala replied, hardly able to hold back her tears. What with Finn away, her barefaced lie to Principal O'Driscoll at the school that morning, and the dread of her treachery being discovered here, her nerves were in shreds. 'I'll ring the bell and tell Mrs Houghton we're coming down.'

She helped Philip into a tweed jacket he pointed out in the wardrobe, then insisted on a scarf in case there was a breeze.

'For goodness' sake, Nuala. I'm hardly likely to get a chill on a day like this.'

'Well, so, 'tis better to be prepared. Now then, I'll put your hat on.'

'Will you wheel me across to the mirror before we leave?'

Nuala did so. 'What with the scarf and the hat tipped across to the left, you'd hardly be noticing, would you?' she said.

'I wouldn't go that far, but, well, place the blanket over my legs – or leg, should I say – and let's get this over and done with.'

There was a knock on the door and Nuala opened it to find Mrs Houghton standing there.

'The lift door is open and I've alerted the rest of the staff to keep clear of the front hall and Lady Fitzgerald's private garden,' she said.

'Shall we go?' said Nuala.

'If I have to,' grunted Philip, his voice muffled by the thick woollen scarf in which he had buried half of his face.

Nuala pushed the wheelchair along the landing.

'Right,' said Mrs Houghton, 'there's only room for you and the chair, so I'll meet you downstairs. Press the button marked "G" and I'll close the cage.'

'I've never been in a lift before,' Nuala said. ''Twill be like flying!'

'That's the part when you come back up, Nuala,' Philip replied dryly.

The criss-crossed metal door was secured behind them and with a gentle jolt and a loud whirring noise, Nuala watched as Mrs Houghton's face disappeared from view. Five seconds later, the lift bumped to a halt. Turning round, Nuala saw the entrance hall beyond the metal grille.

''Tis magic, Philip! We've landed. What do I do now?'

'Open the cage, I would imagine.'

Nuala found the lever and pushed it back as Mrs Houghton approached from the other side.

'There we are, Philip, just a few more seconds and we'll be outside in the fresh air,' said Nuala.

She saw him slump deeper into his chair as they crossed the entrance hall. The wide front door was already open and Mrs Houghton indicated the ramp laid in front of it.

'It's not steep, but hold on tight to the chair,' she ordered.

'I will,' Nuala chuckled. 'We wouldn't want you flying off across the garden, Philip, would we? Now, which way do we go?'

'I'll accompany you, shall I?' Mrs Houghton asked.

'No need, I'm sure Nuala will not let me come to any harm,' said Philip. 'Go on then, get a move on!'

She did so, following the flagstone path around to the side of the house and arriving in a formal garden. There was a path leading through the beautifully tended beds, full to the brim with roses and other jewel-coloured flowers she'd never seen before. They arrived at a central paved area, in the middle of which was some kind of round ornament.

'Ah, Philip! This garden is just about the most beautiful thing I've ever seen!' Nuala said as she pulled him to a stop and turned around to take it all in.

'It's my mother's pride and joy,' said Philip. 'Despite the fact that we have gardeners, she's spent hours in here on her hands and knees, digging in all sorts of different specimens that Father would bring her back from his travels. She and I would sit on the bench over there and she'd tell me the names of all the things she was planting.'

'Well, you'd never have to be worried about being spotted here; what with the trees and bushes all around it, you can't be seen from the outside. 'Tis like a secret garden.'

'That's what Mother's always said. I reckon she comes here a lot to hide from Father,' he smiled.

'What is that?' Nuala pointed to the round metal ornament that stood on a plinth in the middle of the square.

'It's a sundial. Before we all had clocks and watches, it was used to tell people what time of day it was. As the sun moves around from its rising in the east to setting in the west, the shadows tell you if it is midday, or that dusk is approaching. Mother always says that when the sun is over the yardarm, it's time for a gin and tonic, or a whiskey,' he chuckled as he tipped his head upwards towards the sun. 'Good Lord, that feels nice. Push me closer to the bench and then you can sit down by me.'

They sat in the garden for a good while. Philip didn't say much, content to simply enjoy being outside. Nuala thought how to her 'being outside' always indicated work. It was a rare occasion when the family would simply sit in the fresh air and be still.

There was a sudden rustle and the sound of footsteps along the stone path. 'Who the blazes is that?! I thought Mrs Houghton had warned them . . .'

'Philip, darling, it's only me.'

Lady Fitzgerald appeared from behind the bushes. Nuala immediately stood up and gave a bob.

'Do sit down again, Nuala dear. I just wanted to come and see how you were, Philip.'

'I'm doing well, Mother, thank you.'

Lady Fitzgerald walked round to the front of her son's chair, knelt down and took his hands in hers. 'Darling boy, I'm so very glad you decided to come outside. How do you think my garden is looking?'

'Quite beautiful, Mother. It's certainly come on in the past few years.'

'I kept busy with my planting when you were away at the front. It took my mind off things. Nuala, would you mind if I took Philip around it? I want to show him the new herbaceous border. Now, darling, can you see those sprays of mauve flowers? They're *Hydrangea aspera*, then just over there I've planted some *Rosa moyesii* to get a splash of crimson. And those are my *Callistemon linearis*, which look rather like bright pink brushes. I planted those years ago, if you remember. I wasn't sure they'd like the soil, but as you can see, they haven't just taken, they've taken over!'

Nuala sat, enjoying the sight of mother and son outside together. She was also amazed that she was yet to meet Sir Reginald; she'd only caught glimpses of a rotund figure with an enormous grey moustache when he was seeing off a guest beneath the upstairs window. She felt a distinct coldness whenever Philip talked of him. They obviously weren't close.

Philip and Lady Fitzgerald came back towards the bench and Philip yawned. 'Perhaps it's time to take him inside, Nuala dear,' said Lady Fitzgerald. 'All that fresh air must have exhausted you, Philip. Oh, and also, your father has gone to London to meet with the builders. We're having the Eaton Square house renovated: proper bathrooms installed and a telephone line. I rather thought I'd come upstairs and take supper with you later. Which means you can leave early, Nuala. I'll see Philip into bed.'

'Thank you, your ladyship.'

'Will you push Philip back in?' she asked. 'Sadly, I have letters to write.' Once upstairs, Nuala took Philip to the bath-room and then they had tea.

Afterwards, she could see how drowsy he was.

'What about we forget playing a game today, and you sit quietly and have a rest?'

'I admit the trip has knocked me out a little. And to think a couple of years or so ago, I was marching thirty miles at a stretch through French ditches and fields. Why don't you read to me instead, Nuala?'

This was the moment she'd been dreading since she'd arrived at Argideen House.

'I will try, but I'm not sure I'll be up to your standard.'

'But you can read?' he asked.

'Oh yes, so, and I know my letters, but reading out loud, I . . .'

Nuala stopped herself. She'd been about to explain that the

only books they had at home were in Gaelic. But as that would probably be seen by Philip as some kind of heresy, she managed to close her mouth in time.

'No matter, we'll start gently. There's a book of poems by Wordsworth up there,' he pointed.

Nuala turned to the bookshelf placed on the back wall of the sitting room. 'Third shelf up and just to the left. Look for "Word".'

Nuala found a slim leather-bound copy and brought it over to him.

'Now then, Wordsworth is a very famous English poet,' he said. 'His most well-known is "I Wandered Lonely as a Cloud" and it's about daffodils. Do you know what a daffodil is?'

'No, so, I don't.'

'They are rather beautiful flowers and we have them here in our garden in springtime. They look like yellow trumpets with orange centres. Now, try reading the poem to me.'

Nuala took the book and looked down at the page Philip had pointed out. She felt as if she was back at school, having been chosen to stand at the front of the classroom and read a piece aloud.

'Right, I'll be giving it a go but . . .' She took a deep breath. '*I wandered lonely as a cloud, That floats on high o – o –*'

'The word is "o'er", as in "over". Go on, you're doing awfully well.'

Six lines later, Nuala was fit to throw the stupid book onto the fire, because it was making *her* look stupid.

'I told you, Philip, reading out loud is not my favourite. Especially not with these strange words that your man Wordsworth uses. I'd do better if 'twas the Bible, or descriptions of parts of the body, or sicknesses from my nursing training.'

'It's good to be given a challenge. You challenged me today, and I took it, remember?'

'Ah, you're right; so you're paying me back for dragging you outside?'

'I am, but I'm so glad you did. It'll be the same with you and your reading. All it takes is the bravery to give something a try. Why don't you take that book home with you tonight and look over the poem? Tomorrow I'll help you with any words that you can't pronounce. And honestly, Nuala, thank you for insisting I go outside. Why don't you take a read of some of the other poems whilst I have a short nap?'

Philip's eyes were still closed an hour later, when there was a soft tap at the door and his mother walked in.

Nuala put a finger to her lips.

'The dear boy is obviously wiped out,' said Lady Fitzgerald. 'He's had more excitement in the past few hours than in the year since he came home. I cannot thank you enough for persuading him outside. He told me it was all down to you. I'm so very grateful. Here.' She pressed a coin into Nuala's hand. 'I know you were married recently, so think of it as a small wedding gift from me, and please don't tell the other servants.'

'Thank you, Lady Fitzgerald, but there really is no need.'

'Now then, why don't you get home to your husband, and I'll see Philip to bed?'

'I will, so, thank you.'

'Look at you, persuading the young master outside,' Lucy the kitchen maid smiled as Nuala, now changed into her home clothes, walked through the kitchen towards the back door. 'Everyone's been talking about it, haven't they, Maureen?'

'They have, Lucy. I'd half wonder what Nuala has been doing upstairs to persuade him.'

As Maureen turned away and walked through the door that led to the front of the house, Nuala stared at Lucy openmouthed.

'Did she really just say what I'm thinking she said?' she breathed.

'She did, so, Nuala, but you're not to be taking any notice of the old witch. We all know she lost her husband in the Great War and her babe was stillborn, but that's no reason for being cruel.'

'Last week, she was telling me that my weight was affecting my work.' Cook turned round and shook her head. 'I told her straight, had she ever seen a thin cook?' Cook (whose real name was Mrs O'Sullivan) began to chuckle. 'And would you be trusting them if they had? Just ignore her, Nuala, she's jealous that you're in with the young master and Lady Fitzgerald.'

Having said goodnight, Nuala got on her bicycle, still seething. Under the oak tree, she let out her frustration.

'That witch knows I'm newly married! How could she even be thinking I'd be upstairs using my charms on Philip? Jaysus! I'm his nurse, 'twould almost be . . .'

The thought was so horrifying she didn't have the word for it. Her rage fuelling her flight along the valley in half the normal time, she was just leaning her bicycle against the side of her cottage when old Mrs Grady, her neighbour, appeared out of nowhere.

'Is your man sick, Nuala? I heard some talk in the village.'

'He is indeed, Mrs Grady.'

'I've not heard a peep from him since you left. I did tap on the door and look through the front window, but the curtains were closed.'

'He was probably sleeping after a bad night. I'll be up inside now to check on him.'

'If he's that sick, he shouldn't be left alone when you're at work,' Mrs Grady clucked. 'I'm happy to be popping in during the afternoons to see if there's anything he'd be needing while you're out.'

'That's very kind of you, Mrs Grady, and sure, I'll take you up on the offer if he's not improving.'

'You do that,' Mrs Grady said as Nuala unlocked the door. 'Would you like me to come inside with you? Just in case . . .'

'I'll be calling you if there's a problem. Goodnight, Mrs Grady, and thank you.'

Nuala shut the door behind her, wishing she could lock it, but knowing that would alert her friendly but nosy neighbour that something was up. Peeping through the front window and seeing Mrs Grady was still hanging around, she sighed and went upstairs to the bedroom she and Finn shared. She opened the curtains and the window to call down to her.

'He's alive and well, Mrs Grady, so you're not to be worrying now. Goodnight.'

Nuala closed the window, redrew the curtains and sat down on the bed, knowing it was going to be a long week.

True to his promise, Finn arrived home in the early hours of the following Monday. He was so quiet, she hadn't even heard the back door open.

'Finn! Oh Finn! You're home safe.'

'I am indeed,' he said as he divested himself of his clothes and slipped into bed beside her. 'Forgive me, I'm stinking from sweat and grime . . . It's been a long, hard week.'

'But you survived.'

'I did. Come here, my Nuala.' He stretched out his arm and she laid her head on his chest.

'Who was there?' she asked. 'What did you do? Were there any raids—?'

'Nuala, I'm hanging. I need some . . .'

Nuala saw his eyes had closed, but she lay awake, loving the feel of his warmth and listening to the steady beat of his heart beneath her ear. She could not be more grateful that he was home; every day she'd had the locals knocking on her door asking after Finn and when he'd be back at work. Shouldn't she call a doctor if he wasn't improving? Was it contagious, did she think? In the end, she'd cycled down to Timoleague to visit Hannah at work and explained that the locals were getting suspicious.

'I need to know the name for a bad illness that includes vomiting. I've a few ideas, but I need to pick the right one.'

'Go along to the chemist here – Susan behind the counter is a woman you can trust,' Hannah said in a low voice. 'Tell her that Finn has a vomiting bug and ask her for some powders. I'm sure she'll be able to give you a fancy name for an ailment.'

Nuala had duly done so, and Susan herself had cycled up with the powders and entered the cottage to see to the 'patient'. Her arrival and the fact that now Nuala could tell everyone Finn had 'gastroenteritis' had done nothing for her reputation as a cook, but had satisfied the neighbours. Hannah had also 'taken sick' from the dressmaker's shop, in order to assist the women cooking for the men up at the training camp in Kilbrittain, which had added strength to the myth.

The mad thing was that she knew Mrs Grady and the rest of the village would be cheering Finn on if they knew the truth. But that knowledge would only put everyone in danger.

My life is a constant lie . . . Nuala thought, before she finally drifted into a restless sleep.

At seven a.m., she had to shake Finn awake. She'd already made him tea and porridge and took it up to him to eat in bed.

'Will you be all right to go to teach today?' she asked.

'I have to be, don't I?'

'Yes. Everyone's been asking after your health so you need to show your face. How did the week go?'

'I'd say 'twas the proper thing; we were put into sections and taught to act as if an attack from the enemy could arrive at any time. We learnt how to detonate a Mills bomb, then we practised with the new Lee-Enfield rifles, aiming and trigger-pressing, and we even slept with our rifles on us. If an alarm was given and any man in the section was not out of their bed fast enough, we'd have to do it all over again. We took turns to be in command of a section, and then in the evenings, after our tea, we'd be together in the barn to listen to lectures or do written exercises.'

'It sounds serious, Finn. Are you sure that the enemy didn't know what you were doing up there? The farm is close by the Black and Tan post in Kilbrittain.'

'The Bandon and Kilbrittain battalions fielded the scouts, and did a grand job of protecting us. We all knew the whistle that would tell us if they were coming, but thanks be, they never did. We spent a lot of time out on the land, learning how to best use natural cover and how to navigate it quietly, keeping our formation when we were ambushing a road patrol.'

'At least now you'll all be ready if there is an attack,' she said.

'We will, so, but Nuala, here's the difference: *we're* going *on* the attack. We can't just be sitting around playing defensive – we've got to organise more of our own attacks if we're ever to triumph. There have been plans discussed which will be put into action soon. I'll be needing to take more time away from the school to fight for the cause in the coming months.'

'But how, Finn? You've a fine job as a teacher; you're not thinking of leaving it, are you?'

'Not leaving, no, but if necessary, I'll need to tell Principal O'Driscoll of my involvement in the Flying Column. Perhaps my "illness" has been worse than was thought, so I might have to take some more time to rest, if you see what I mean.'

'Well, what with your pale, thin face and your red eyes, you'll be looking the part this morning,' Nuala sighed. 'Are you sure the principal can be trusted?'

'I am. He wants Ireland back just as much as I do, and has often said he'd be out there fighting with the volunteers himself if he was a younger man. I have to trust him, Nuala,' Finn said as he finished the last spoonful of porridge.

Nuala sat there, staring at him. Eventually she said, 'You know I'm as committed to the cause as you are, Finn, but if that means losing you in the process, then I'd even get on a boat and cross the sea to America to start a safer life there. And you know how much I fear the sea.'

Finn put out a hand to caress her face. 'I do know, darlin'. But this is a fight we have to win, whatever the cost. Oh, and before I forget, Tom Barry was asking whether you'd seen Major Percival up at the Big House recently?'

'There's been a few fine cars, but I haven't heard Philip talk of anyone else since General Strickland.'

'Percival's the bastard we want more than any other. And we'll have him, Nuala, we will. Tom Barry's put out the word in Bandon for his movements to be watched day and night. Once we know his routine then—'

'You'll attempt to shoot him?' Nuala looked at her husband in horror. 'Holy Mother of God . . . You'd murder him?'

''Tis not murder in a war, Nuala. Now, I must be getting off to school.'

'You'll be here when I get back tonight?' Nuala asked as she watched him dress in a smart shirt, trousers and tie.

''Twas agreed we all needed a rest this week, but . . . I can't be promising anything any longer. And remember to put it round the village I'm still suffering from the effects of my illness, and that you're worried for my health. Bye, darlin', I'll be seeing ye.'

'Will we go for a walk and a sit in the gardens today, Philip?' she asked later that afternoon at Argideen House. She had just read the Wordsworth poem he'd given her and he'd pronounced her 'word perfect'.

'No, Father has that ghastly Major Percival coming round. Mother and I can't stand him – he's an arrogant arse, if you ask me. The very worst of the British here in Ireland.'

'Have you met him?'

'No, but Mother says he'd have every Irishman – and woman – dead if he could. He's never lived here, you see, doesn't understand how you're all needed around the place, to help run our farms and houses. And that up until a few years back, we've all rubbed along together quite well. Like you and I do, eh, Nuala?'

'Yes, Philip, o'course.'

Even though Nuala knew Philip meant well, the fact he took British superiority as his God-given right irritated her.

'So, will we go out to the garden or not?' she asked him brusquely.

'Major Percival was up visiting the Big House today.'

Finn stared at her across the table, where they were eating tea. 'Did you see him? Hear him?' he asked.

'No, Philip refused to take a walk in case the major saw him. He's too embarrassed about how he looks.'

'You make sure you try and find out what the two of them were talking about. Major Percival is the number one target and is under surveillance as we speak.'

'I'll try, Finn, but Philip's never even met the fellow. He only hears bits from his mammy. His daddy hardly speaks to him.'

'Perhaps he's ashamed of his son, if you say he's so disfigured.'

'Perhaps. How were things at school today? Did you speak to Principal O'Driscoll?'

'I did, yes. We went for a glass at the pub after school. Christy was serving and looked out for anyone overhearing the conversation.'

'And?'

'O'Driscoll's said he'll help me cover my tracks. There's a doctor down in Timoleague he knows, a supporter of us volunteers. He's going to send him to me tomorrow so that the village can see I've had a real doctor come to visit, so it must be serious.' Finn gave a weak smile, took her hand and squeezed it. 'We'll get through this, Nuala, I know we will. There'll be happier days to come for our small ones.'

'Ah, sure, but with the both of us up to our tricks and

living here where everyone wants to know our business, 'tis dangerous, Finn, there's no denying it.'

'Well, we're both here and together tonight. One day at a time, eh, darlin'? 'Tis the only way to deal with it.'

With no visitors the next afternoon, Philip was happy for her to take him back into the garden. She decided it was time to press him on another point that might help in his rehabilitation.

'Philip?'

'Mmm?' he replied as he sat next to her in his chair, eyes closed as he enjoyed the glorious scent of the flowers.

'I've been thinking . . .'

Philip opened his eyes and glanced at her. 'Always a bad sign. What do you have in store for me this time? A quick spot of swimming in the Argideen River? Or perhaps taking a hack on one of the stallions in the stables?'

'Oh no, nothing as advanced as that yet. It's just, well, I'm looking at your false leg standing idle in the bedroom and wondering why you never wear it. If you did, you'd be up and walking beside me, not sitting in that chair you hate so much.'

'Nuala, I shall answer this very shortly and simply: when the doctor strapped it on to what is left of my kneecap and insisted I stand and take my not very considerable weight on it, the agony was almost as bad as coming round after the mine had exploded. Actually, it was probably worse, because I was fully conscious. So, the answer is no.'

'You say you've only tried it on once?'

'Yes. And never again.'

'But . . . the wound where they amputated your leg has healed over now. Maybe it was still raw when the doctor asked you to stand on it before. So, yes, 'twould have been holy hell putting weight on it. I'd reckon 'twould be different now. Just imagine if you could walk again! Be independent! Wouldn't that be a mighty wonderful thing?'

'It would also be a wonderful thing if man could fly to the moon, but it's an impossibility. Now, will you please leave me alone, so that I can enjoy my time in the garden?'

Knowing Philip and his stubbornness all too well now, Nuala did not bring up the subject again. She did have something else she needed to talk to him about, and once they were back upstairs, she finally plucked up the courage to ask.

'Did your daddy enjoy his chat with Major Percival yesterday?' she said as Maureen brought afternoon tea into the room and began setting it out.

'I don't know if anyone can actually enjoy meeting the man. Mother did tell me, however, that my father said Percival was sure his movements were being watched by the IRA. He's noticed curtain twitching in the houses opposite Bandon Barracks whenever he walks a few doors down to have his evening meal. He believes the IRA are planning to assassinate him, but told my father he was prepared to send his forces to ransack every home in Bandon to find the culprits. Thank you, Maureen, you may leave us now,' Philip added to the woman. 'Nuala will pour.'

Nuala did her best not to let her hands shake as she did so.

'There you go.' Nuala handed the cup to Philip, then took a deep sip of her own tea. She'd been starving, having had no lunch again, but now she felt she might be sick if she put anything in her mouth.

'You look a bit queer, Nuala. Are you all right?'

'I'm grand, Philip, and eager to get on with that game of chess.'

Coming out of Argideen House that night, Nuala cycled to the oak tree and stood by it in a quandary as to who to take the message to, so it would reach those volunteers who were watching Major Percival the fastest. In the end, she plumped for Christy, working in the pub just across from her cottage, and cycled like a mad thing towards Clogagh.

Running into her house, she penned a quick note, then went across to the pub. Saying hello to a few of the locals hunched over their glasses at tables, she sidled up to the bar, where Christy was pouring three drops of whiskey.

'Hello, Nuala,' said Christy. 'What would you be doing in here at this time of night? Not looking for a drop of whiskey for yourself, are you?' he teased her. He'd brushed back his thick, dark brown hair today, so that Nuala could see his sincere warm brown eyes.

'There's a calf stuck in the womb up at the farm, and we'd be needing your help immediately.' Nuala used the sentence the family had constructed as code for an emergency.

'Right then, I'll speak to John; I'm sure he'll let me off early, as things aren't too busy.'

He eyed her hand as it slid across the bar to him. He put his over hers and squeezed it, then she pulled her hand away as he slid his back.

'I hope the calf survives,' she said, as she moved away back through the tables.

Heart pumping with adrenaline, she took some deep breaths as she walked back to the cottage.

'What's going on? Why did you run over to the pub?' Finn asked her as he stirred the soup in the pot over the fire.

'Philip told me that Major Percival suspects there are

people spying on him. He said he was prepared to destroy every house in Bandon to find the culprits. He knows our lot are after him,' Nuala panted, partly out of relief that she was home and able to let it out for the first time after three hours of trying to act normally in front of Philip. He said she'd played chess like a four-year-old, and to be fair, he was right.

'I'd already heard something about the house searches in Bandon, but not that they know there's any kind of a plot. We must get word to the men,' said Finn.

'I already passed Christy a note in the pub. He'll be off to Charlie Hurley's on his horse, who'll send word to Bandon.'

'Well done, Nuala,' Finn smiled. ''Tis worth all those hours of chess to think it might have saved some souls from a brutal beating and prison.'

'If we're in time.'

'Yes,' Finn agreed. 'If we're in time.'

15

Nuala heard nothing that night, or the following morning. Finn had left for school with a comforting, 'Bad news travels the fastest, Nuala,' but it hadn't eased her anxiety.

All she wanted to know for certain was whether Tom Barry – who Finn had confided in her was the one in charge of the Bandon spy party – had received the message to abort and flee in time.

'Jaysus,' she panted as she cycled up to the Big House. 'I'm a simple farmer's daughter, I'm not built for all this intrigue.'

She held her breath as she nodded to Lucy in the kitchen then headed upstairs to Philip's room. Only when he turned his wheelchair around to greet her with his half-smile did she let it out in relief.

'Hello, Nuala,' he said. 'You look as though you've been climbing Ben Nevis. Sit down and catch your breath.'

She sat down gratefully, wondering who or what Ben Nevis was.

'Today, I rather think I'd like *you* to teach me something,' said Philip. 'Refresh our minds before we play chess again,' he said.

Buoyed by relief that she'd not been found out, she smiled. 'What did you have in mind, so?'

'Have you any Irish games we could play? Although I'm

not up to hurling or Gaelic football. Perhaps a board game of sorts?'

She paused to think. 'I'll be honest with you, Philip, there's not much time for games like chess. The men sometimes play cards or drinking games but . . .'

Philip let out a chuckle. 'So did we, in the trenches. It was alcohol that kept us going more than anything else. But sadly, I don't think a drinking game will be quite as diverting with Darjeeling tea.'

Nuala tried hard to think, keen to give Philip something new that he wouldn't encounter in his small, English world, which didn't extend far beyond the borders of this parkland.

'Sometimes in the winter, Daddy used to tell us Irish fairy tales to pass the time. My sister Hannah always liked the scary tales of *púcaí*: spirit creatures who often appear as horses, then terrify any living soul who tries to ride them.'

'Let's stay away from any ghost stories, Nuala,' Philip shuddered. 'But I know you Irish believe in fairies and have a lot of tales to tell about them.'

''Tis part of our lore, of the earth and nature around us, so. I think you'd be liking Finvarra, king of the fairies. My Finn is named for him, and me for Nuala, the fairy queen.'

Nuala could not fail to note the slightest curl of his lip that she now recognised whenever she mentioned her husband.

'Well, why not regale me with the life of King Finn and Queen Nuala,' he said, giving her a thin smile.

So Nuala told him the story of how their namesakes had ruled a kingdom of fairies, or 'The Folk' as they were referred to in hushed tones. They were powerful creatures that lived close to the human world, lurking beneath fairy mounds and stone circles, waiting for a hapless wanderer to lose their way, only to be kidnapped by the all-powerful and charismatic Finvarra.

'Just as your Finn kidnapped you?' Philip put in, a hint of sarcasm in his voice.

'Ah, I was happy to be kidnapped. And just now, as 'tis close to the feast of Samhain, farmers are trying to appease Finvarra to ensure a good harvest,' she said.

'Like our druids used to in England. All humans have folk-lore of different kinds.'

'Do they?' Nuala asked in surprise.

'Oh yes, and this queen you've told me of – she shares traits with characters like Shakespeare's Titania and Morgan le Fay. They are all beautiful and enchanting, but clever too and often manipulative. Perhaps you are like your own fairy queen, Nuala.'

'Oh, I wouldn't be saying that now,' she countered, blush-ing. 'Who's this Morgan le Fay?'

'She was Merlin's apprentice in the old court of our British King Arthur. He taught her all he knew, his secret magics and ancient wisdoms. Then she betrayed him.'

'She sounds like a fierce bad woman. Our Queen Nuala would never betray Finvarra.'

'Oh, Morgan had her reasons. In fact, if you go to that shelf over there, you'll find a large green tome by a writer called Sir Thomas Malory: *Le Morte d'Arthur*.'

Nuala found it, then sat back down and opened the heavy book, internally sighing as she saw the pages covered in small text.

'I think we can skip over the Uther Pendragon stories,' he instructed her, 'and get right to chapter twenty-five – that's written XXV – when Merlin helps Arthur gain the sword Excalibur from the Lady of the Lake. Read it to me, Nuala.'

'I'll do my best, Philip.'

Having received word when she arrived home that Tom Barry and his men had escaped the clutches of the Essex Regiment in the nick of time, due to her intelligence from the Big House, Nuala walked around for the next week with a cautious optimism and pride. As autumn began and the leaves in the woods turned to red and bronze and gold, she spent her early mornings with Finn before he left for school, which provided a small window of calm in their young marriage. Then she would often cycle to other female volunteers' farmhouses to deliver dispatches – once with a pistol strapped to the outside of her thigh under her skirt – or do the volunteers' laundry. She spent the afternoons with Philip, now glad of the fire that burnt brightly in the large grate in his room as the nights drew in. They alternated between reading *Le Morte d'Arthur* (she was beginning to get the hang of the strange English it was written in), games of chess and walks around a garden rich with autumn colour.

Finn was increasingly away at night as the Flying Column gained confidence and mounted more attacks. When he arrived in their bed in the small hours of the morning, she only wished she could whisk him away to the land of the fairy folk, where the two of them ruled their kingdom together and there was only music, laughter and dancing . . .

Having had an idea about Philip, Nuala went to see Christy in the pub one night after work.

'Is all well, Nuala?' he asked, setting a drop of whiskey down in front of her with a wink.

'It is, thank you,' she said, taking a sip to warm her after her ride home. 'Christy, do you mind if I ask you something?'

'Ask and I'll answer,' he shrugged.

'Philip – the Fitzgeralds' son – you know he lost his leg in France?'

'Sure, you told me,' he nodded. 'Lucky he escaped with his

life, but I'd be thinking with all his family money, he's had the doctors at every hour and the best care.'

'He has, but . . . oh Christy, he's so stubborn! He won't take the help he's been offered. He's got a fine leg of wood made especially for him, but it gathers dust in a corner, because he won't even be looking at it. He says 'tis too painful.'

'How long has it been since it happened?' he asked as he walked around the counter and sat down on a stool beside her, easing the weight off his own bad leg.

'Over two years now. I've only just convinced him to go outside in his wheelchair. It's like he's given up, and all he wants is games of chess and his books. But there'd be so much more to life if he could only walk!'

'Sure, but you've got to be remembering that 'tis a mental wound as well as a physical one. When I had my accident, d'you remember how I was? Feeling sorry for myself, like I was no use to anyone any longer.'

'But you know that's not true. What would Mammy and Daddy be doing without you on the farm, and even more so with Fergus often . . . away. You work harder than any able-bodied man I know, Christy.'

'That may be' – Christy lowered his voice – 'but when I see Fergus and Finn going off, I feel like a useless eejit. There's not a day goes by that I don't remember the pain of my foot and shin being crushed by that thresher. I dream of it often, so, and I'm sure your Philip relives his war nightly too. I can only imagine how difficult it must have been for him to be coping with no leg, when at least I've still got use of mine. And the time it took to find the courage to stand up and use my stick.' He tapped it on the ground with a fond smile.

'So what got you to go on? To have hope?'

''Twas your family, and you, Nuala, with your care of me.'

She couldn't bear the intensity of his gaze, so she averted

her eyes and looked down at the large calloused hand that rested on his oak stick.

'If it hadn't been for your cheerful smile every day,' he continued, 'I wouldn't have been wanting to even get out of bed, the pain was so fierce. But you were there, even though you were no more than thirteen. You were born to be a nurse, Nuala. And if this Philip knows what's good for him, he'll listen to you.'

'Maybe, but I'm failing so far, Christy.'

'Well now, my stick has helped take the weight off my bad leg and I've got a spare. Perhaps your man might like to try it?'

'At least I could offer it to him,' she said. 'Thank you, Christy.'

'You never let me take no for an answer,' he called after her. 'Don't let him.'

The following afternoon, Christy drove Nuala on his pony and cart to Argideen House, because she had his spare stick with her. Arriving at the kitchen door, she bolted up the stairs and knocked.

'Come in, Nuala,' said Philip.

When she entered, she noted the big book on King Arthur was placed on the side table by the damask sofa, waiting for her.

'Hello, Philip. Now then, today we'll be doing something new,' she said briskly.

'Really? Just what have you got up your sleeve?' he said, warily eyeing the walking stick in her hand. 'If it's what I think it is, then I must put my foot down – so to speak – and say no.'

Nuala sat down on the sofa, the stick in her hand. 'Do you remember me telling you about my cousin Christy?'

'Yes. The fellow who works in the pub?'

'Well, this is his.' She tapped the stick on the floor. 'When he was fifteen, he was working the thresher during barley season. A thresher is—'

'I know what a thresher is, Nuala.'

'Then you'll also be knowing how dangerous they can be. Christy's always been a strong lad, and smart too, but he slipped and his right foot and part of his leg were caught in it. I don't have to be telling you what a terrible injury it was.'

'I can imagine. Did they amputate?'

'No, they saved it, but it took near to a year for Christy to recover, and he's not been able to walk without a stick since. He'll never run, or swing a girl round the place in a *ceilidh* again, but he's walking and can ride his horse.'

'Well, good for him, but I don't see what it's got to do with me,' Philip said irritably. 'Christy's got two legs, and I'm assuming both eyes, and his whole face.'

'And you've got a fine wooden leg made especially for you just a few yards away in your bedroom,' she countered.

'Nuala, I said no and I meant it!'

She ignored him and went into the bedroom to fetch the leg. It was leaning up as usual against the wall in the corner, and Mrs Houghton had already shown her the stack of cotton socks in the dresser drawer. They would fit snugly over his stump and protect the scarred, delicate skin of the wound.

Taking the surprisingly heavy leg into the sitting room, she saw the look of abject fear on his face.

'No, Nuala, please!'

'Sure, we'll go slow about it,' she soothed him. 'But you have to try. How about we just fix it on, and you can stay sitting with it while we have a game of chess? Just to get the feel of it, so.'

'I know you mean well, but it's no use. I'm perfectly all right here in my chair.'

'Are you, Philip?' She gave him a direct gaze. 'Every day I watch you and see how your pride is hurt by having to ask people for help. I'd feel the same way if 'twas me, and it's what got Christy out of bed and walking in the end. Besides, most soldiers I've seen in your position have little more than a wooden peg, when you have a fine custom-made leg! You've got to at least try it, so don't be letting your stubbornness get in the way of things.'

Flushed from speaking to him so forthrightly, she half expected him to fire her on the spot.

After a long silence in which neither of them moved, Philip let out a long sigh and gave a nod of acceptance.

'All right, but I'm not putting weight on it.'

'Thank you. So now, let's get going,' she said as she knelt down in front of him. 'I'll just be rolling up this trouser leg, so it won't be getting in the way,' she explained as she exposed the stump. Though he was used to being washed by her nightly, she could feel how tense he was. 'Now so, we've got a cotton sock to go on over,' she said as she slid it on. 'And I'll just be opening the clasps and bindings on it.'

The leg was made of a dark blond wood, which had been sanded, oiled and varnished. It had a foot carved at the end and leather laces so she could adjust the fit around Philip's thigh. She tried to work confidently, not betraying the fact that she'd never done this before.

Once the leg was fastened and she had checked with Philip that it wasn't too uncomfortable, she tested the hinge so it could move smoothly with his knee, and placed the foot next to his other on the wheelchair rest. Then she wheeled him over to the window and set up the chess table without another word.

They played in silence, the satisfying click on the wooden board as pieces were moved the only sound, other than the crackling fire. Once he had declared checkmate, rather than ringing for tea, she went down into the kitchen and brought the tray up herself so he wouldn't have Maureen gawking at the leg.

As she poured him his tea, then added his preferred amount of milk, he cleared his throat.

'So, did you see many . . . amputees when you were up in hospital in Cork?' he asked.

'Yes. 'Twas the end of the Great War and we had young fellows recovering from injuries not unlike yours. I was only in training at the time, so I was emptying bedpans and the like rather than doing the proper nursing, but I saw a lot of suffering. And bravery,' she added for good measure.

He chewed on his sandwich thoughtfully before replying. 'I'm sure you did. And I know I'm luckier than most living here, but I don't think I'll ever know true peace again.'

'I think you could, Philip, if you were more independent. Yes, it takes a good deal of work and courage, but you can do it, I know you can.'

'You're so unfailingly optimistic, Nuala.'

'I don't see the point in being anything else, do you? And I've faith, Philip, and a great deal of it in you.'

'Then I'd hate to let you down, but—'

'Then don't, Philip.'

After a long pause, he sighed. 'Go on then. Let's give this a try.'

Her heart giving a bounce of joy, she wheeled him over to the long bookshelf, where there was a variety of firm surfaces to hold on to at the right height. Placing his feet on the floor and handing him Christy's stick, she gently put her arms around his waist, as she did when she was helping him into bed at night.

'Now then, I've got you, Philip,' she said. 'We'll get you upright, and for now, balance your weight on your good leg. Once you feel comfortable, we'll try putting weight on the bad one.'

As she helped him to standing, she could feel him shaking with exertion and nerves, and saw his knuckles were white on the hand that clutched Christy's stick.

'Breathe, Philip, just in and out, so.'

With a gasp, he let out a breath and drew one in so quickly, she feared he would hyperventilate.

'Right. Hold on to the shelf there with your other hand . . .' Nuala indicated the right height. 'Now, 'tis time for you to try some weight on the leg. I promise it won't hurt as much as before,' she encouraged him.

She felt his body shift as he tentatively placed some weight on the wooden leg, and then heard another sharp intake of breath.

'How is it? Do you want to sit back down?' she asked.

'No,' he panted, beads of sweat on his forehead. 'No, no, I'm not giving up now I've come this far. It isn't as bad as it was. Let me get my balance and then I'll try standing alone.'

'Grand,' she said. 'You're being so brave. Now, when you're ready . . .'

Philip shifted about until he was comfortable. 'Ready,' he muttered.

'Balance on the stick and let go of the shelf . . . I'm here to catch you if you fall.'

He released his grip slowly, as she stood in front of him, arms stretched towards him.

'Look at you, Philip!' she said, feeling so proud of him she was fit to burst. 'You're standing by yourself! 'Tis a breeze, isn't it?'

There was a sudden knock on the door, and it opened before Nuala could shout for them to wait.

'Philip?' Lady Fitzgerald entered the room. 'Oh – oh my . . .'

Philip had frozen at his mother's arrival, and Nuala reached out to support him, so he wouldn't lose his balance.

'It's just an experiment, Mother, to see if the leg still fits,' he said, trying to sound nonchalant as Nuala helped him sit back down in his wheelchair.

Lady Fitzgerald looked at Nuala, who gave her a meaningful glance.

'Of course,' said Lady Fitzgerald, taking the hint. 'I've just come to ask if you'd like me to join you for supper up here tonight, as our guests have cancelled.'

'That would be lovely, Mother.'

'Good. I'll come up at seven,' said Lady Fitzgerald. 'Nuala,' she nodded, and gave her a look of such joy and gratitude, it brought tears to her eyes.

Once the door had closed behind Lady Fitzgerald, Philip looked up at Nuala and gave a chuckle.

'Did you see Mother's face when she came in?! Oh, the discomfort was worth it for that alone. Thank you, Nuala. I should have tried it long ago, but I . . . I was afraid.'

''Tis understandable,' she said as she wheeled him back to the window where the sun was now setting, casting a golden glow into the room. 'I won't lie to you, there's more work to do before you can walk on your own,' she said as she knelt to unstrap the leg.

'But you'll help me, won't you, Nuala?'

'O'course I will, Philip.'

Just before seven, Nuala was just about to leave for home,

when Lady Fitzgerald stopped her at the bottom of the staircase.

'Nuala, a moment, please,' she said.

'Of course, your ladyship.' Nuala noticed that Lady Fitzgerald's eyes looked red, as though she'd been crying.

'Nuala, what you've managed to do for Philip is nothing less than a miracle,' she said softly. 'I can only thank you from the bottom of my heart.'

"Twas your son that did it,' she answered. 'Goodnight, Lady Fitzgerald.'

Nuala walked home that night not even feeling the cold wind that whipped at her cheeks. All she could think of was the look on Philip's face when he had stood by himself, unsupported for the first time since his injury. And felt determined to help him find the peace *and* sense of pride that he so longed for.

16

As autumn held West Cork firmly in its grip, the war for Irish independence went into high gear. While the British continued to ride into villages and burn down farms in reprisal for the many successful ambushes, so the IRA volunteers thwarted them as best they could, blowing up bridges, moving signposts and cutting telegraph cables wherever they could find them. Finn was away at night regularly, and Nuala busier than ever, delivering or collecting dispatches or arms.

Lady Fitzgerald had arranged for the groom who worked in the stables at Argideen House to construct a frame with two wooden bars, so that Philip could hold on to them while he practised walking on his wooden leg. The frame had been set up in Philip's sitting room, and he allowed Nuala to subject him to a rigorous exercise regime to strengthen his leg muscles.

'I'd say 'tis time for you to come off those bars and try walking a few steps on your stick,' she said one misty October afternoon.

'If I had known what a slave driver you were, I'd never have convinced Mother to employ you,' Philip had said as, his arms trembling and sweat beading his face, he held himself up on the bars and hobbled up and down the carpet.

'We'll try tomorrow, shall we?' Nuala said as she sat him down and unstrapped his leg.

An hour after she arrived home, Finn, who'd been out on Flying Column activities for the past few nights, appeared through the back door, looking exhausted.

'Hello, darlin', that smells good,' he said as he embraced her, then sniffed the pot hanging over the fire.

'And you look as if you need the stew inside you, Finn Casey. You're after losing more weight.'

''Tis all the marching around the place that's done it. I've never been fitter, I swear. I'm all brawn now, Nuala.' He winked at her.

'Any news?' she asked him.

'Yes, and 'tis good for a change,' he said as Nuala passed him the bowl of stew and he ate it hungrily. 'The Column opened fire on the Essexes at Newcestown – we've killed two officers and wounded three. Finally, we've had a victory!'

Nuala crossed herself and sent up a prayer for the dead men. Finn saw her do so.

'Darlin', the last thing we want is to cause death to other souls, but . . .' he shrugged, ''tis the only way. It's either the British or us. Some of our volunteers have been rounded up and their homeplaces have been raided and burnt to the ground. Nuala, they're arresting women too – I know of three Cumann na mBan girls that have been sentenced to jail in Cork City. I'm worried about you here alone when I'm away at night, and it's going to become more frequent. You'd be safer away up with your family at Cross Farm.'

'I've Christy across the road who'd protect me and—'

'No one can protect a woman alone from the British,

especially at night. There was a report only this week that came down from Kerry, about a woman who'd been terrorised and molested by two Tans. So, from now on, you're to go up to the farm if I'm away overnight, and not return until you have word I'm back.'

'But, Finn, what will the neighbours think if both of us are gone?'

'I've talked to Christy, and Principal O'Driscoll. Both of them are sure there are no spies in the village, only support for us volunteers and the women who are working for the cause.'

'Maybe, but we can't be endangering my position with the Fitzgeralds. If it becomes known—'

'It won't, so. We can trust O'Driscoll and our friends in the village. And, darlin', if it comes down to it, I'd have you leave your position if it means you can be safe.'

'But I don't want to leave,' she protested. 'You said yourself what I'm doing is valuable – it saved Tom Barry and his men in Bandon!'

'It did, though you're not the only spy we've got, Nuala, but you are my only wife!' He took her hands in his and softened his voice. 'We might be past trying to pretend to be a normal couple, but it's still my duty to protect you. Now then, let's eat up this stew before it gets cold.'

As October turned to November, Finn was away so often that Nuala was spending at least half her nights up at Cross Farm. Nuala noticed that Philip rarely asked after her husband, perhaps because he was kept so busy strengthening his legs. They had finished reading *Le Morte D'Arthur*. The story of the British king had turned darker towards the end of it, although Nuala had approved of the knights' final mission to obtain the Holy Grail.

'And what is your Holy Grail, Nuala?' he had asked her as she'd finally closed the book.

Freedom for Ireland, she had thought, but instead had said, 'For you to be free of your wheelchair, so I haven't got to push you around any longer.'

Philip had chuckled and rung the bell for tea.

As Nuala lay in bed next to Hannah because Finn was away again, she thought how she'd never dreamt she'd be back here as a married woman. But at least she was kept busy: as the fighting had stepped up, volunteer casualties had grown, so she, with Hannah's help, had decided to organise a first-aid training day at Cross Farm for the women of Cumann na mBan. Aoife, one of her friends from her time nursing up in Cork, was travelling down to help her teach the basics of dressing and cleaning a wound, how to deal with an unconscious patient, and even how to extract a bullet. The women had been asked to collect as much antiseptic, bandages and basic medicines from the local pharmacies and hospitals as they could. They duly arrived and the haul was laid out at one end of the barn, with Aoife sorting it into a field kit for each woman to take away.

'I'm enjoying this,' said Nuala to Hannah as, after the first-aid training, they portioned out the stew that would be served in the barn.

'Yes, 'tis good for morale for us to gather together, *and* have the men scouting for the women for a change. Though I'd not trust them to cook for us,' Hannah chuckled.

After they'd eaten, the women, sixteen of them in all, listened to their local captains talk on various subjects, which covered everything from how their knitting needles should be clacking away in any spare time they had as the lads were in need of socks, scarves and jumpers, to being shown a Webley revolver and a rifle. Mary Walsh of the Kilbrittain brigade gave a demonstration on how to load and fire them, explaining the different ammunitions, as well as safe cleaning procedures. There was also a call for the women to renew their efforts to fundraise.

'I'm hardly going to be holding a tea party in the middle of our village asking the locals to support our efforts, am I?' countered Florence acerbically. 'I'd be under arrest before we'd have time to clear away the cups!'

'No, Florence, you're right, but ask all the women you trust to ask the women *they* trust in their villages to give anything they can to support our brave fellows.'

'We need support too, so!' piped up another woman. 'What with all the laundry coming my way, I'm going through bars of soap like a babe hungry for her milk!'

'And food . . .'

'And wool!'

'We'll just have to do what we can, girls,' said Hannah. 'Our lads are depending on us and we won't let them down, will we?'

A rousing cheer came up in the barn before it was quickly hushed, and everyone lay down on straw pallets and huddled under blankets, as it was bitingly cold. Nuala's feet were half frozen as the rain lashed down on the roof. Thinking of how Finn and his comrades had to endure this night after night, sometimes after hours of marching or lying in a sodden ditch waiting for the enemy to approach, she felt awed by their bravery.

Once the last woman had left after breakfast the following morning, Hannah, Nuala and their mother washed out the pots.

'I'd say that was a grand thing you organised, Nuala,' said Eileen.

'It was,' Hannah agreed. 'Everyone went away with a new fire in their bellies.'

'I'm away out to feed the pigs,' Eileen announced. 'You girls sit down now and warm up after your night outside.'

'Thank you, Mammy.'

The two sisters sat listening to the crackling of the fire for a while, before Hannah spoke.

'Now so, whilst no one else is around, I wanted to tell you something. But you have to swear to keep it a secret.'

'I will of course, Hannah. What is it?'

'Do you remember Ryan, Finn's friend from Kinsale, who came to your wedding?'

'I remember him dancing with you, yes. Why?'

'I've been seeing a bit of him since then, due to him working at the post office along the road from the dressmaker's shop. He took his civil service exams and was meant to travel to England, but then when the Easter Rising happened, he decided he shouldn't go.'

'You dark horse, you. You've said nothing,' Nuala smiled.

'Because there's been nothing to tell. We've been on walks in our lunch hours, and met up sometimes after work, when I've not been away taking messages, but then . . .'

'Yes?' Nuala could sense her sister's excitement.

'Last Wednesday on our half-day, he took me for a long walk along the strand and . . .'

'Ah, stop with the suspense, woman! What?'

'He proposed!'

'Holy Mary, Mother of God! Now that *is* news! And . . . ?'

'I said yes. Oh Nuala.' Hannah reached across and squeezed her sister's hands. 'I'm so happy I'm fit to burst!'

'And I'm so happy *for* you, sister! 'Tis wonderful news, and exactly what the family needs just now.'

'Maybe, but you know what Daddy's like about these things. Ryan's homeplace is in Kinsale, so he won't know the family.'

'Ah sure, Finn's a friend of his, Hannah.'

'Maybe, but when Ryan comes up here to ask Daddy for my hand, Daddy'll spend at least an hour interviewing him like he did Finn.'

'Sure, 'tis his right as our father, and Ryan will just have to be prepared. When's he coming up?'

'Next Sunday. Can I show you the ring?'

'O'course!'

Hannah's eyes searched round the empty kitchen, as though someone might be lurking under the table. Then she reached down the front of her blouse and pulled out a ring she'd hung on a piece of thread.

''Tis in the shape of the claddagh, and only silver-plated, because his wages don't go far after he's paid for his board, but I love it.'

Nuala admired the little ring, with its silver heart cupped between two hands. She looked at Hannah's sparkling eyes as her sister gave the ring a kiss.

''Tis beautiful. Is he a good man?'

'Ryan's so good that he puts me to shame! I doubt a bad thought ever crossed that man's mind. He told me that when he was younger, he'd a notion to join the priesthood. The only problem is . . .'

'Yes?'

'He doesn't know anything of my involvement in Cumann na mBan. He wouldn't be liking it if he did. He doesn't approve of war, you see.'

'Hannah, you told me earlier that he didn't go to England to further his career there after the Rising. Surely he'd support you?'

'I'd say there was a difference between hating the British and being actively involved in fighting. He's a pacifist, which means he's against violence for any reason.'

Nuala looked at her sister aghast. 'But Hannah, you're one of the most passionate members of our cause! Are you saying you'd give up your activities for him?'

'Of course not, but after we're wed I'll be needing to be more careful. Perhaps if I explained that everything we do is for Mick Collins, Ryan might understand. I think he loves Michael Collins more than I do,' Hannah giggled. 'Ryan says he's a true politician; he believes Mick uses his intelligence and not his muscle to sort things out.'

'We both know that's not true, Hannah. Michael Collins was a fine soldier before he was a politician. He helped lead the Rising with Éamon de Valera, and spent two years in a British jail because of it.'

'True, but now he's in the newspapers, all dressed in his suit and tie, looking smart and important.'

'Does Ryan know that his hero is also head of IRA intelligence?' Nuala asked. 'That there's not a thing the IRA does in any part of the country without him knowing about it? Or often ordering it himself?'

'Maybe he does, maybe he doesn't. The point is, he'd not be pleased if he found out his fiancée was so deep into supporting the violence that she'd be drowning in it any second.' Hannah let out a long sigh and then looked at her sister. 'What do I do, Nuala? I'd die if I lost him . . .'

'I don't know. We come from a family of fierce Fenians who are all prepared to lay down their lives for Ireland's freedom.'

'I know. What if Daddy says something that gives us all away?' Hannah worried aloud. 'Ryan might turn tail and run down the valley to his lodgings in Timoleague!'

'As you say, Ryan's not local. Sure, Daddy won't give anything away until he knows to trust him.'

'You're right,' Hannah agreed. 'And it's not because Ryan doesn't believe in the cause . . .'

'Just that he doesn't believe in war.' Nuala was immediately reminded of Philip. 'At least he's not an Englishman,' she chuckled.

'Or a Black and Tan.'

'Or an Auxie.'

'Or even a Protestant!' Hannah laughed and her face relaxed a little.

'To my thinking, if you love your man the way I love Finn, there's nothing you wouldn't do to be with him.'

'I do – love him, I mean. I'd still do what I could – knit and raise money – but . . . would you understand, Nuala?'

'I would try my hardest to, Hannah.' Nuala gave a sad shrug. 'Love changes everything.'

Sure enough, a week later, the family was alerted to the fact that Hannah had invited 'a friend' to Sunday lunch after Mass.

No one was fooled, especially not Eileen, who plagued Nuala, Christy and Fergus with questions.

'Will you stop asking me! I swear I know nothing,' Nuala pleaded as her father drove his family back in the pony and trap after Mass. Hannah was following on with her 'friend'.

When they eventually arrived, Nuala felt sympathy for the pale, slim, curly-headed man who stepped through the door behind Hannah.

'This is Ryan O'Reilly, whom you all might remember from Finn and Nuala's wedding,' said Hannah, a bright red blush travelling up her neck to her face.

Finn – who to Nuala's delight had arrived home a couple of days ago – stepped forward.

'How are you, Ryan?' he said, shaking his friend's hand. Nuala thought the poor fellow looked as terrified as if he was about to be shot by the Black and Tans.

Introductions to each member of the family were made, and they all sat down to eat. Her father was at the head of the table, silent for once as his gimlet stare fell upon Ryan, appraising him.

After lunch, fortified with plenty of porter from the barrel outside, Ryan cleared his throat and approached Daniel.

'May I have a word with you in private, sir?'

'There's little privacy to be had in here, as you can see, so I'd suggest we step outside,' said Daniel. 'The weather's set fair for a while.'

'Yes, sir.'

The whole family watched as Daniel led him outside. 'Like a lamb to the slaughter,' said Fergus.

'At least he's found a wife, unlike you, brother,' Nuala shot back, only half joking.

''Twould hardly be fair to ask a woman to be my wife when I'm not knowing if I'll see out the year,' Fergus replied. 'Besides, I'm thinking I'm happier alone. Some fellows are,' he shrugged.

'Your brother is becoming a confirmed bachelor,' sighed Eileen.

'Well, at least I don't have to put myself through all that.' Fergus indicated Ryan and Daniel talking on the bench outside.

'Ah sure, Ryan will be fine,' smiled Finn. 'He's a decent sort of a fellow, the quiet type, like none of you!'

Nuala was standing by the window, watching the two men. 'Ryan's standing up and—'

'Come away from that window, girl!' said Eileen. 'Give them some privacy now.'

All eyes turned to Hannah.

'Stop staring at me!' she shouted, and with that, ran up the stairs to her bedroom. While they were waiting, Finn, Christy and Fergus went into a huddle by the kitchen table. Nuala couldn't decide whether they were discussing the suitability of Ryan O'Reilly for Hannah, or volunteer business. Both – in their different ways – were equally important.

'Jesus, Mary and Joseph, will you be seeing the time? I'll be putting on the tea,' Eileen called far too loudly to those still gathered in the kitchen. As the water boiled, the back door opened and the two men walked in.

'I'd like to tell you that Ryan O'Reilly has asked for our Hannah's hand in marriage. And after some debate, permission has been granted,' Daniel announced.

With that, a rousing cheer broke out, and as the men shook Ryan's hand and welcomed him to the family, Daniel went to the pantry to extract the bottle of whiskey.

Nuala and Eileen looked expectantly up the stairs for the bride-to-be, who came down the steps and straight into her mother's arms.

'I'm so happy for you!' Eileen wept. 'I was worrying you'd become an old maid.'

'Jaysus, I'm only twenty, Mammy,' Hannah smiled. It was Nuala's turn to hug her big sister.

'Congratulations, sister. And don't be putting me in a gown that's pink if I'm to be your maid of honour.'

'Who says you are?' Hannah teased her then hugged her again. 'Thank you, Nuala. I don't know what I'd do without you.'

17

In late November, a day after what was already being called
'Bloody Sunday' in the newspapers, Nuala arrived at Argideen
House trying to contain a fury she knew she mustn't show.
Philip was now walking without the safety net of the bars, and
was using Christy's stick to wander in circles around the sitting
room, with Nuala at his side should he falter. It wasn't until
they sat down to have afternoon tea and scones that he asked
her outright if she was upset about the events at Croke Park.

Nuala took a long sip of tea to buy herself time. ''Tis tragic
what happened,' she said, trying to keep any emotion out of
her voice. 'Just a crowd sitting watching a game of Gaelic
football, and they're fired upon by the British with no warning. We've fourteen Irish dead, including children.'

'Only the dead have seen the end of war,' Philip said
gravely, which Nuala knew meant he was quoting someone
she'd never heard of.

'That's no use to their families, is it?' she said, heat creeping
into her voice. 'Is it a part of war to murder children?'

'No, of course not, and I'm as sorry as you are, Nuala,' he
sighed. 'Like you, I simply want the British and Irish to come
to a peaceful resolution. Although that might be a long way
off, considering how Major Percival sounded when he was
here yesterday.'

'Major Percival was here?' she said.

'Yes. Mother tried to convince me to come down and take tea with him, but I'd gladly stay in a wheelchair if it meant not having to set eyes on that man.'

'Do you know why he came yesterday?' she asked.

'From the sound of his self-congratulatory booming voice, I'd say he wanted to boast to Father about something or other. And given yesterday's horrific events, I think we can both imagine what it was.'

At that moment, Nuala decided this Major Percival deserved the most painful death that God could create for him. And knew she hated him just as much as any other of the brave volunteers who had suffered at his cruel, merciless hands.

Hannah and Ryan's wedding had been set for mid-December.

''Tisn't a perfect time to be wed, but with things as they are, the sooner the better,' Hannah had sighed.

No one understood Hannah's need for urgency better than Nuala. She'd comforted her with suggesting all the things that would make a winter wedding special. Philip had said a decorated fir tree usually stood in the entrance hall of Argideen House, and was a tradition of England's Queen Victoria, established by her German husband Albert. Nuala loved the idea, but knew it wouldn't be the right thing to have.

'We can decorate the church with sprays of holly and light candles and—'

'Have muddy puddles splashing the bottom of my white dress,' Hannah had grumbled. But it was happy grumbling, and there was a glow to her sister's cheeks that Nuala was pleased to see.

She had told Finn that Major Percival had been at the Big House again, but was frustrated with herself for not knowing more.

''Tis all right, darlin', just keep your ears pricked up,' Finn had said. He had gone out to a brigade council meeting in Kilbrittain that evening, and she knew he wouldn't be back until late. Even so, when he hadn't returned by three in the morning, Nuala's heart began to beat harder. Finally, at four thirty, she heard the back door open.

Flying down the stairs, she found Finn soaked to the skin and panting hard. Another figure stood behind him.

'Hello there, Nuala, will it be all right if I come in?' Charlie Hurley wiped his rain-matted hair from his gaunt, pale face.

'Of course, Charlie, come and sit a while.'

'I think we both need a drop of the hard stuff, Nuala,' said Finn, closing the back door as quietly as he could. Both men were still in their volunteer outfits – while the Flying Column had no regular uniform, they all wore peaky caps and long trench coats to stave off the rain and hide any weapons they were carrying beneath.

'What happened?' Nuala whispered, so as not to alert Mrs Grady, the old lady in the cottage next door.

'I'll get the whiskey first,' said Finn as he went to the cupboard, where he took out two glasses and poured a good measure into both.

As they took off their sodden clothes, Nuala ran upstairs to find shirts, trousers and socks for them to change into.

'We all started to leave after the meeting, going in parties of three,' began Finn. 'We were after getting to Coppeen and there was a truck of Auxies. They saw us before we saw them and they searched us all. Thanks be to God, none of us were carrying any papers on us.'

'We acted drunk,' put in Charlie. 'Said we'd been to the pub for a glass, but they shouldn't be telling our wives.'

'And they let you go?' asked Nuala.

'They did, so. Sean Hales and his crowd were following on, along with Con Crowley and John O'Mahoney, who had documents on them outlining what we'd discussed at the meeting. We doubled back to warn them, but we didn't get there in time,' Finn sighed. 'We hid in a ditch as the Auxies searched them. They found the evidence they needed and Con and John were herded onto the back of the truck.'

'There was nothing we could have done about it, Finn,' said Charlie, draining his whiskey and pouring himself another. 'Jaysus, those poor lads.'

'How incriminating were the documents?' she asked.

'Thank the lord Con uses code, but there's enough there to show that they're IRA volunteers, so.'

'And Sean?'

'Ah, now Sean, he has the blarney to talk his way out of Mountjoy Jail. He told Crake – that was the name of the commanding officer – that he was in the area buying cattle. He gave a false name and the eejit believed him! Said he had an honest face and wished more Irishmen were like him.'

Both Charlie and Finn laughed loudly as the whiskey calmed them. 'Shh,' warned Nuala. 'What about Con and John?'

'I'd not want to see the state of them now, if Tom Hales and Pat Harte are anything to go by.' Finn shuddered.

'These Auxies, they didn't get a good look at your faces, did they?' she said.

'What, apart from shining a torch right under our chins?' Charlie sighed. 'They saw us all right, but all we Irish look the same to them, so.'

'What do you think will happen now about what we discussed?' Finn asked Charlie.

'I'd say that Sean will be even more likely to.'

'To what?' Nuala asked.

Charlie looked at Finn.

'You can tell Nuala anything,' Finn reassured him. 'She's as good as our men any day of the week.'

'Then she'll know about it soon enough,' said Charlie. 'It's to involve all the volunteers around these parts . . . We're to blow up Timoleague RIC post and then set fire to Timoleague Castle and the Travers' house next door.'

Nuala stared at them, open-mouthed.

'You wouldn't dare! 'Tis right on our doorstep!' she gasped. 'They'll be searching every house around if you do.'

'I know, Nuala, but we've information down from Dublin HQ,' said Charlie. 'The British want to take over the castle and house and post more men in there because of the trouble we've been causing them. We can't have that happen. We'd be overrun with the lousers, so.'

'Timoleague RIC post has been evacuated already, hasn't it?'

'Yes,' said Charlie, 'but the British are looking to refill it. The company here in Clogagh will be raised, as well as others, and we're to collect gelignite from across town and hide it somewhere close. We were thinking of Cross Farm, Nuala, if your mam and dad would agree. 'Tis close enough to Timoleague.'

'But the Travers family and their servants up at the house haven't been evacuated! Will you set fire to them where they lie in their beds?' Nuala asked, aghast. She'd seen old Robert Travers from Timoleague House one day from the window of Argideen House, when he and his wife had come to visit the Fitzgeralds.

'The British would burn us in our beds and not be thinking twice about it, Nuala, but no, we'll have them taken to safety before, don't you worry,' Finn comforted her.

She drew in a breath and then exhaled slowly.

'Now then, Nuala, go back upstairs and get some rest,' said Finn, 'and I'll be getting a pallet from the outhouse for you, Charlie.'

'Sure, I'm grand where I am in this chair . . . You two go up . . . I'll be . . .'

'He's asleep already, poor fellow,' whispered Finn. 'He's got enough work for five men. Being commandant, he takes every injury or death in the company personally.'

Upstairs, Nuala put her arms around her husband, who had fallen asleep the moment his head had landed on the pillow.

'I love you, darlin',' she said as she caressed his hair, wondering darkly how many more days and nights she had left to feel his heart beating steadily against hers.

When Nuala went into Timoleague for the next monthly fair day, when all the farmers brought cattle to sell and stallholders set up along the street, hawking everything from homemade jam to saddles, the usual jollity of the event was completely lost. The Essex Regiment were a menacing presence, marching down the streets or clearing men out of the pubs so they could sit down in their places. Hannah joined her when the dressmaker's shop closed for lunch and they wandered along the street, glancing at the stalls.

'Have you heard what's about to happen?' Nuala asked her sister under her breath.

'I have indeed. The "manure" was delivered to Cross Farm two days ago.'

'Holy Mother of God, this will rouse mayhem around here.'

'Don't you be telling me, Nuala. 'Tis my wedding day in three weeks. I'm scared that half the guests will be locked up in Bandon Barracks, or worse, if they're caught.'

Nuala reached for her sister's hand. 'We have to believe they won't be,' she comforted her as they manoeuvred past a young bullock being walked down the street by his proud new owner.

'Now then, why don't we buy crubeens from Mrs MacNally's stall, eat them and then go to see your dress at the shop?' Nuala forced a bright smile onto her face. 'And mine, o'course, even though just the thought of it gives me the horrors!'

'I like lilac,' Hannah said defensively. ''Tis quite the thing in Paris, my magazine said.'

Nuala rolled her eyes and went off to buy their crubeens, then they sat themselves on their favourite bench overlooking Courtmacsherry Bay. The day was bright and mild, and they could see the ruins of the old stone abbey below them. The sound of the waves breaking on the shore calmed Nuala's fraught nerves.

'Does Himself know what's to happen?' she asked her sister.

'No, and I'll not be telling him,' Hannah said firmly. 'I'll be as surprised as Ryan is the day after.'

'I know it's none of my business, Hannah, but d'you think it's right to be lying about what you believe in and the brave things that you've been doing for your country – *his* country – before you're even wed?'

'This war can't go on forever, and if 'tis just a few months of pretence, I will, so. Aren't we all having to pretend?' she said pointedly.

'Not to our husbands, surely?'

'Nuala, will you leave it be for now? Everyone knows I'm to be wed to Ryan soon, so they're not asking me to take dispatches anyway. So I'm not lying to him, am I?'

Nuala wanted to say more, but knew it wasn't her place. 'Well now, will we go away up to the shop and try on that lilac rag you'll have me in?'

'Are you ready to be walking outside now?' Nuala said to Philip a few days later, as they paced around his sitting room for what felt like the thousandth time. A month of daily exercise had strengthened Philip's upper body as well as his legs, so his posture was now straighter even when sitting in the chair. Nuala had been surprised at how tall he was, standing at over six feet.

'Outside?' Philip gave a snort. 'It's December and you want to drag me into that damp, frigid air?'

'Yes,' she said. ''Twill be good for you. We'll wrap you up tight, and you'll warm up quick enough when you're walking,' she encouraged him.

'All right then,' he softened. 'After all, I did once live in a trench at below freezing point, so a walk in my mother's garden should be a breeze in comparison.'

'Right, so, I'll warn Mrs Houghton that we'll be going outside.'

'Oh, don't bother with that, Nuala, just get me ready, will you?'

She helped him dress in a woollen coat, his scarf and hat, then together they walked out onto the landing and into the lift. On arrival into the entrance hall, Maureen, who was carrying a tray across it, stopped short and looked at Philip in amazement. Nuala felt an inner sense of satisfaction.

Outside, the air was sharp and cold, and though their breath was visible in front of them, the sun had come out to shine on the barren winterscape of the parklands. With Philip using his stick, and Nuala having her arm tucked into the crook of his on the other side, they trod carefully on the path towards the garden, lest Philip slip on a patch of damp moss.

'Ahh,' Philip sniffed the air. 'The glorious Irish smell of peat fires burning. I rather think you *are* a fairy queen, Nuala,' he said as they arrived in Lady Fitzgerald's private garden, walking past stone planters full of winter pansies, which provided delightful splashes of purple and yellow against the slumbering perennials. 'I feel as if you have cast a spell on me. I could never have pictured myself walking again. Going where I please, having independence . . .'

''Tis not magic, Philip,' she replied. ''Tis your own strength and hard work.'

'And your encouragement,' he said, pausing to turn to her. 'Nuala, I can never thank you enough for what you have done for me. You have brought me back to life.' Then he took her hand and kissed it. 'Promise me you'll never leave me, Nuala. I swear I'd die without you. You've given me a reason to live again. Promise me, Nuala, please.'

She looked up at him and saw tears coursing down his face.

'I promise,' she answered. What else could she say?

With Philip declaring himself exhausted at seven that night, she changed out of her work clothes and was just about to leave for home when Mrs Houghton called her back.

'Her ladyship wants to see you, Nuala,' she said and led her across the hall into a pretty parlour, which contained a writing desk looking over the garden she and Philip had walked through earlier. Lady Fitzgerald was engaged in reading a letter, but turned round and stood up as Nuala walked in.

'Thank you, Mrs Houghton. You may leave us. Please, sit down, Nuala.' Lady Fitzgerald indicated a chair.

'Is everything all right, your ladyship? Philip was feeling up to walking around, but if you'd rather he stayed inside in the warm—'

'Goodness no, quite the opposite, Nuala. I simply wished to thank you,' said Lady Fitzgerald. 'This wonderful change in Philip is all down to you. Not just physically, but he's been so . . . hopeful again. I can hear the two of you laughing together, and the sound makes me so happy. I—' She broke off and took a deep breath. 'As a gesture of my thanks, I would like to increase your wages to ten shillings a week. I know how hard you have worked, and I hope you will be—'

A knock on the door interrupted Lady Fitzgerald, and Mrs Houghton entered. 'Excuse me, Lady Fitzgerald, but Mr Lewis has arrived about the painting in the Lily bedroom that you want reframing.'

'Thank you, Mrs Houghton, I will come out to see him.' Lady Fitzgerald turned to Nuala. 'I should only be a moment, my dear, then we will finish our discussion.'

As the two women left the room and shut the door to keep the heat in, Nuala allowed herself a little laugh of delight.

'Ten shillings,' she breathed, thinking what she and Finn could do with the much-needed extra money. She stood up and wandered around the beautiful room, admiring the landscape paintings gracing the wood-panelled walls and the leather-topped desk.

Without stopping to think, Nuala glanced down at the letter Lady Fitzgerald had just been reading.

My dear Laura and Reginald,

Once more I write to offer my grateful thank you for dinner the other evening; a delightful harbour in what is becoming an ever more stormy sea. At least some good news on that front: two of our spies acting as deserters have gained the enemy's trust and have arranged to meet the ringleader TB on 3rd December, at which point we will arrest him.

Nuala speed-read the rest and saw the signature at the bottom:

Arthur Percival

Nuala heard footsteps approach the door and hurried to sit back down in her chair.

'My apologies,' said Lady Fitzgerald as she entered the room, then opened a drawer to her desk and took out an envelope. 'Your wages for this week with two extra shillings inside.' She pressed the envelope into Nuala's hands. 'Thank you again, my dear. Now then, get home to that husband of yours.'

Nuala cycled to Clogagh as if the devil himself were chasing her. She arrived at the cottage and was relieved to find Finn in his shirtsleeves, marking schoolwork at the kitchen table.

'Finn,' she panted. 'I've urgent news for Tom Barry!'

In between sips of water from the glass he had placed in front of her, she explained the missive from Major Percival.

Finn paced in front of the fire as he took in what she was telling him.

'Nuala, the attack on Timoleague is tomorrow, and the whole Column is in high gear, with people in secret locations . . . I don't know how to find Tom in time to tell him . . .'

'We've got to!' Nuala cried. 'Those deserters he's meeting are spies for the British! The Essex will be lying in wait for Tom and we know what they'll do to him! They know he's the brains behind the Flying Column, so 'twill be even worse than what they did to Tom Hales and Pat!'

Finn crouched down by his wife and took her in his arms.

'I'll be sortin' it, darlin', don't you be worrying. What you've found out is vital, and we've a chance of stopping the meeting. Now, please eat something before you faint from exhaustion.'

18

Finn had gone out soon after, and when he returned, he had assured Nuala he'd left word for Tom Barry with as many volunteers as he could find. The following morning – the day of the planned burnings in Timoleague – he dressed calmly in his schoolmaster's clothes.

'Now so, after work tonight, you're to cycle straight up to Cross Farm and wait there until you hear the all-clear from me or another I'll send word with.'

'Are the explosives – I mean, the manure – still in the dump?' Nuala was so agitated, she was forgetting to talk in code.

'It's been moved closer to the place it will be needed in,' said Finn. 'I'm off away to help spread it.' He kissed her hard on the lips, then hugged her tightly to him. 'Goodbye, Nuala. I love you and I'll be seeing ye.'

With that, he was gone.

Up at the farmhouse that evening, the family (minus Fergus, who was out helping to 'spread the manure', and Christy, who'd helped move the 'manure' earlier but was now working as usual at the pub), went through their night-time routine.

Though the subject was not discussed when they all sat down for their tea, the air of tension was palpable. Even her father, who was usually able to hold a conversation with a fly, was quiet. Every one of them knew how many local fellows were involved in tonight's activities. 'Will we sing some of the old songs, husband?' asked Eileen as the women finished clearing up. 'Will you get out your fiddle?'

'Not tonight; even with scouts up above on the hill, I'd be afraid of a knock on the door.'

'To be sure, Daddy, once that manure is spread, they'll all be busy down below,' said Nuala.

'I'm sure you're right, daughter, but 'tis not the night to be taking any chances. Hannah will read to us from the Bible. How about Moses parting the Red Sea, then the passage where the people are led into the Promised Land?'

Daniel offered the family a grim smile, and they nodded at the appropriateness of the suggestions.

As she sat cross-legged by the fire, with Mammy and Daddy on either side of her, she listened to Hannah's reading. And it calmed her.

Oh, dear Lord, and Holy Mother Mary, keep my Finn and Fergus safe tonight, and let all us Irish have our own Promised Land delivered back to us . . .

The family were just in the process of turning out the oil lamps when Seamus O'Hanlon, their neighbour and one of the scouts, burst through the back door. The whole family froze where they were.

'Our lads have gone and done it! Come up to the top of the hill and see for yourself!'

The family followed him out through the back door and up the steep wooded hill to the top. And there, across the valley and down the hill again towards Timoleague, they saw great yellow flames jumping into the night sky.

The family crossed themselves, then sat down in a huddle on the soaking grass.

Nuala imagined she could smell the smoke hanging in the cold night air.

'I'm just hoping the fire doesn't spread,' muttered Hannah to Nuala.

'Ryan's not in his lodgings, is he?' Nuala whispered back. 'Did you not warn him?'

'How could I? Then he'd be knowing that *I* knew.'

'Sure, he'll be fine, Hannah, he lives a way away from the targets. I'm just praying my Finn and our Fergus come home safely tonight.'

'That'll show the British we mean business and no mistake!' Daniel punched his fist in the air.

'Shh, Daniel!' hushed his wife. 'You never know who's lurking close by.'

'Tonight it's just us, woman, and I'll be as joyful as I wish on my own land.'

As they walked back down towards the farmhouse, Eileen caught up with her girls. 'I've told your father there's to be no more using us as an ammunition dump for a while. There'll be reprisals for this, make no mistake.'

'And we'll all be ready for them, Mammy,' Nuala said firmly, while Hannah said nothing and just walked off down the hill alone.

To her relief, both Finn and Fergus returned safely in the early hours, but the next morning, the main street in Clogagh was silent, everyone hiding away indoors, both from fear of reprisals and the stench of burnt timber that still hung in the air.

'Hello, Lucy,' she said as she let herself into the kitchen of Argideen House.

Lucy looked up from the floor that she was scrubbing. 'Hello, Nuala. Don't go and change – Lady Fitzgerald is wanting to see you first.'

'Really? What about?'

'I've no idea. Mrs Houghton will come and take you through to her parlour.' Nuala sat down abruptly on the nearest stool.

Lucy wasn't in the mood for talking and silence reigned as she waited for Mrs Houghton to come and fetch her.

'Follow me, Nuala.'

Crossing the hall, Mrs Houghton knocked on the door of Lady Fitzgerald's parlour room.

'Come,' said a voice from within.

Lady Fitzgerald was standing looking out of the window onto her garden, her back straight in a dark green gown.

As she turned, Nuala could see that her lovely features were held as stiffly as her body.

'Sit down, Nuala,' Lady Fitzgerald gestured, and she did so.

'Now then,' she began, 'I wish to tell you about a call my husband received from Major Percival this morning, concerning the grave events of last night.'

'Oh,' Nuala said, summoning every ounce of acting skill she possessed to hold her features steady. 'You mean the fires? Sure, 'twas terrible to see.'

'It was, yes, and my friends, the Travers, who lived in Timoleague House, are sheltering here with us. They have only the clothes they stand up in, but are at least grateful that the Irish who attacked their home allowed them to leave. Anyway . . .'

Lady Fitzgerald brushed a hand across her forehead distractedly.

'These are dark times we live in, Nuala. It has been discovered that some . . . sensitive information was passed to the IRA, regarding details that were sent to this house by Major Percival himself. The man mentioned in the letter – or at least, by his initials – did not arrive to meet the spies, but sent others in his place. They were dealt with, of course, but the man Major Percival and his team had spent months hatching a plot to entrap still remains at large to plan and commit further atrocities like last night's.'

Nuala felt Lady Fitzgerald's gaze resting upon her.

'That letter was open here on this very desk two days ago. When you were sitting in that chair, and I left you alone to see Mr Lewis for a few minutes.'

Nuala could hardly breathe. 'I—'

'And this incident had me questioning other events,' Lady Fitzgerald continued. 'A few months ago, the major foiled an attempt on his life in Bandon, but the assassin had apparently been warned and had disappeared. Not a soul other than the major, his men and my husband knew that the Essex were to break into those houses to catch the perpetrator. Except for myself, of course, and my son, whom I told in confidence. Nuala, I am asking you now to tell the truth. Did Philip discuss it with you?'

'I . . . 'tis so long ago now, but I think Philip had said that Major Percival was coming over to see Sir Reginald the day before, and that he wouldn't want to walk in the gardens whilst there was a visitor. That was all.'

'Are you sure about that, Nuala?'

'I'm certain,' she nodded.

'Sadly' – Lady Fitzgerald gave a long sigh of resignation – 'it appears that you are lying. I mentioned in passing to Philip earlier whether he'd discussed Major Percival's plan with you and he said that he had. His story was also corroborated by

Maureen, who was most distressed to report that she was in the room serving tea when the conversation took place.'

'Yes, now I think about it, 'tis true, your ladyship. Philip did mention something about Major Percival. I didn't want to say that to you, in case I got him into trouble. We often talk about the . . . hostilities. We are, well, we are friends.'

'And he trusts you. I understand,' said Lady Fitzgerald. 'Which makes this situation even harder.'

'I swear that I'll tell him in future that I don't want to discuss anything with him. 'Tis only because he seemed to have no one else to talk to, other than you, of course,' Nuala added hastily. 'And I'd never be looking into your personal things, or reading letters—'

'Forgive me Nuala, I find that difficult to believe. You see, after I spoke to Maureen and she confirmed my son's story, the poor thing broke down. She said she felt torn by loyalty to you as another member of staff, but that she felt she must tell me that your family are noted Fenians, with your brother a known IRA volunteer. She also told me that your sister Hannah is a leading light of this Irish women's voluntary organisation. She suspects that you may be too, or at the very least, support your family's . . . activities from the sidelines. What do you have to say to that, Nuala?'

'Nothing, other than 'tis true my family are made of proud Irish stock, but beyond that I know no more. Besides, I'm no longer living under their roof. My husband is Finn Casey, a schoolmaster at Clogagh.'

'I know he is, Nuala, and I also know that he has been mysteriously absent from work a great deal in the last few months.'

'He's been sick, Lady Fitzgerald, with a bad stomach. What could be wrong with that?'

'On the surface, nothing, but Maureen has a friend who

lives close to you. Apparently, she went to call on your husband in the afternoons to see if he needed anything whilst you were working here. She told Maureen the curtains were all drawn and there was no response from inside. As if the house were empty.'

'He was very sick, Lady Fitzgerald, and not up to receiving neighbours.'

'So sick that you left him all those afternoons to come here for eight hours?'

The question hung in the air for a good few seconds before Lady Fitzgerald spoke again.

'This is Ireland, Nuala, and even though I may have been born English, it has been my home for over twenty-six years. I know very well how communities look out for each other. And how a newly married wife would not leave a seriously ill husband alone without someone to care for him. There would have been someone with him, Nuala, or at least checking on him regularly.'

'I . . .'

'I am not here to judge you, your family or your husband on your activities outside this house. In fact, I'd prefer it if I didn't know, because I like you very much, Nuala. And the most tragic thing of all is that so does my son.'

Nuala watched tears come into Lady Fitzgerald's eyes.

'However, given this new information, and the devastating fires in Timoleague last night, I can no longer trust you. Or your family.'

'But I hardly know Maureen! How come she thinks she knows so much about them? The truth is that she's never liked me.'

'Now, now, Nuala, please don't be churlish. It doesn't suit you. The simple truth is, I cannot take the risk of my dear innocent Philip imparting further information to the woman whom he believes is his friend. Therefore I am forced to terminate your employment here. You will leave the house immediately.' Lady Fitzgerald walked to the desk, opened it and pulled out a small brown envelope. 'That is your pay until the end of the week.'

Nuala stood up, open-mouthed in horror. 'May I not even say goodbye to Philip?'

'It's best that you don't. I have told him your husband is seriously unwell and you have decided you must be at home caring for him, as any good wife should.'

Nuala was crying openly now. 'Please . . . tell him that I'll miss him and thanks a million for teaching me to play chess – I never did get to beat him, because he was so brilliant and—'

'Of course I will, and rest assured that I will say nothing to anyone about our discussions this morning. Your secrets – if they are secrets – are safe with me, but know they are not so safe in other hands. Life is full of difficult choices, Nuala, and we are living in difficult times. I accept that your loyalty must always be towards your husband and your family.'

Nuala's nose was running so fast she was reduced to the indignity of wiping it on her hand.

'Forgive me, Lady Fitzgerald. You've been so kind to me . . .'

Nuala felt a hand on her shoulder. 'And you've been so good to Philip, and for that I thank you.'

When Nuala arrived home, she closed the curtains at the back and the front of the house. Then she sat down in the chair next to the fire and wept her heart out.

'Oh Philip, I'm so very sorry to have let you down. There

was no bad in you, and now I'll no longer be there to mind you.'

When she was empty of tears and desperate to talk to someone about what had happened, she splashed her face with water and tidied her hair in order to walk across the road to see Christy. No one could *ever* know how truly heart-broken about Philip she was – not even Finn – or they'd be calling her a traitor by the morning.

'Will you pop over and have a glass when you've finished here?' she asked him.

'O'course, there's few enough in today.'

Back in the cottage, Nuala forced down some bread and butter, then took out the whiskey bottle from the cupboard and found two mugs. Christy arrived twenty minutes later and she poured them both a drop.

'You on the hard stuff, Nuala?' Christy smiled.

'After the day I've had, you'll be understanding why I am.'

Then she told her cousin what had happened up at the Big House. He poured himself more whiskey.

'Jaysus,' he breathed. 'D'you think she's likely to tell Major Percival what she suspects? She'd have no reason not to, Nuala.'

'No, I don't. Maybe I'm being naive, but she was kind, Christy, even when she was saying I must leave her employment. 'Twas as if she understood and somehow sympathised.'

'She's a woman who's had a husband and a son fight through two wars. Now they're all involved in another. From what you say, seems she's the rare British person with a heart. The dangerous one is this Maureen. What a witch to be telling on you like that.'

'She hated me from the day I arrived. She didn't like the fact Philip and I were friends and she had to serve me tea every day.' That thought at least brought a smile to Nuala's lips.

'Sounds like she was jealous of you.'

'Lucy, my friend up there, told me she lost her husband and child. I reckon she's bitter, so she is.'

'War can make it that way. Listen, I need to be getting back. I'll ride over to Cross Farm later and tell the family what's happened. We'll be preparing ourselves for the worst. Finn will be back from school soon.'

'And then he's straight off out with the Column. I reckon they've something else planned.'

'You're to keep calm, Nuala. I'm across the road if you need me.' Christy stood up and kissed her on the top of her head. 'I'll be seeing ye,' he said as he walked out of the door.

The entire family were on tenterhooks in the following few days in case the reason for Nuala's abrupt departure from Argideen House reached the ears of the authorities. To their shared relief, neither Nuala and Finn's cottage nor Cross Farm were raided. When she was in town picking up a message from Hannah in Timoleague to take over to the captain of Cumann na mBan in Darrara, Nuala saw Lady Fitzgerald in the distance. She wished she could thank her for keeping her word, but instead, Nuala turned and walked in the opposite direction.

Luckily school finished for the Christmas holidays, so there was no need to give excuses when Finn announced he was off to a further Flying Column training camp.

'I'm not sure when I'll be back, darlin'. We've training and then an ambush to plan – the Auxies are moving further away from Macroom Castle and into our territory and we've to show them who's boss around here. Go up to Cross Farm with your family for a few days; I could be away for some time.'

The worry of Finn's absence was eased a little by spending her time helping to prepare for her sister's wedding and for Christmas itself. She often cycled down to Timoleague to meet Hannah at lunchtime.

'Have you been in to Ryan's lodgings yet?' Nuala asked her as they ate their lunch on the bench overlooking the bay.

'I have indeed. The house is owned by Mrs O'Flanaghan, and Ryan has the attic to himself.'

'Does it have a double bed?' she nudged her sister.

'Only a single, but 'twill do for now. We're looking for another place, as I'd like my own kitchen and facilities. With my wages and Ryan's, we can afford it, so, but there's nothing to be had in town just now.'

To while away the afternoon hours she would otherwise have spent with Philip, Nuala had embarked on making a patchwork quilt as a wedding present, using various bits of material she'd collected over the years. Never a seamstress like her sister, she was struggling, but wasn't it the thought that counted? she told herself, as she unstitched a patch for the umpteenth time. At least it took her mind off worrying if Philip was keeping up his walking practice and Finn was safe. Retribution for the burning of the barracks and castle was still taking place, and gruesome images of the kinds of torture other volunteers had suffered at the hands of the British haunted her.

If any bit of suffering was down to me being found out . . . She shuddered, then, telling herself that worrying helped nobody, she gritted her teeth and concentrated on sewing her quilt.

19

More bad news came a few days later when martial law was declared on County Cork. This meant that any man could be stopped and searched, and if he was found to have ammunition or weapons on him, he was immediately arrested and subject to a court martial. If found guilty, he could be shot. A curfew was also introduced across the county, with no resident allowed out between the hours of eight p.m. and six a.m.

'But what would happen if a family member was dying in the next village, or even in the next street?' said Nuala, showing Finn the *Cork Examiner* newspaper, in which the new laws had been printed.

'The patrols would arrest you on sight,' shrugged Finn.

'It says you can also be arrested for harbouring a suspected volunteer, for "loitering", or for simply having your hands in your pockets . . .' Nuala shook her head in disgust.

'The good news is that all the residents of the towns and villages are hating the British even more for the new ruling. Charlie told me he'd had forty new volunteers approach him, wanting to sign up. We'll win this war, Nuala, I swear to you, we will.'

Finn continued to disappear regularly after dark, despite the curfew, as the Tans and the Essexes marched down the streets of local villages to intimidate the residents. Insisting to Finn she was going to stay at the cottage, Nuala spent most evenings alone working on Hannah's quilt. At least she knew she could always call on Christy, who was having to stay the nights up above the pub because of the curfew. She cycled up to seek solace with her family whenever the curfew allowed.

'Jaysus! Have you seen this?' Daniel slapped a newspaper down on the table and pointed with his calloused finger to the headline. 'How could he do it to us all when we're fighting to free his flock from the tyranny of the British?'

The family gathered round to read in the newspaper that the Bishop of Cork had issued a decree, saying that any Catholic taking part in an ambush would be guilty of murder, and immediately excommunicated.

'Jesus, Mary and Joseph!' Eileen muttered, as she crossed herself and sat down heavily on the stool. 'Almost every volunteer is Catholic! They're needing to feel that God is on their side as they fight, not that he'll be throwing them out of heaven and placing them in hell if they do!'

'This is what he has to say,' spat Daniel, 'after the Black and Tans have set fire to half of Cork City!'

'Do you think he'd a British rifle pointing to his back when he did this?' said Fergus.

'You might be right, but I couldn't be more sure that 'twill be him refused from entering the Pearly Gates and not our brave men and women.'

'But will they fight on?' asked Nuala.

'Will it stop you from doing what you do?' Daniel looked at her. 'Would it stop either of you?'

Brother and sister looked at each other. ''Twill not stop me,' said Fergus.

'Or me,' muttered Nuala, reaching for the comfort of her mother's hand.

Needing the security of her family after such news, Nuala opted to stay the night. Hannah arrived from the dressmaker's shop, and after tea, the two of them went upstairs to talk.

'How's the husband-to-be?' Nuala said as they lay on their bed.

'He was off to Mass when I left him earlier,' Hannah sighed. 'He said he wanted time to think about the bishop's proclamation. I've told you before that Ryan's faith puts us all to shame.'

'Does he think the decree is right?'

'He said that at least 'twould deter some volunteers from carrying on with their violent activities, and that had to be a good thing. He wants peace, Nuala, that's all.'

'Does Ryan know that most of those attending his wedding are volunteers?'

'I haven't told him, and neither has anyone else. He's entitled to his views, fair enough.' Hannah shot her sister a look. 'He still wants freedom for the Irish, but has a different way of thinking how to get that.'

'So now, let's just sit here and wait until the military kill us all, shall we? I'd like to be showing him some dispatches signed by his hero Michael Collins. 'Twas his idea originally to form the Flying Column and—'

'D'you think I don't know that?! But what can I do? I'm marrying the man in a few days' time! And that's all there is to it.'

The morning before Hannah's wedding, there was a knock on the cottage door. Nuala opened it to see her friend Lucy, down from the Big House.

'Hello, Lucy, 'tis lovely to see you. Will you come in?'

'I'm on my way to work, but I thought I should drop by and tell you before you heard it from anyone else.'

'What is it?' Nuala asked as Lucy followed her in. Always slight, today Lucy looked like a frightened, fragile bird.

'Ah, Nuala, I'm thinking you need to sit down. I've some upsetting news for you.'

'What is it? What's wrong?'

'I don't know how to say this, but, yesterday . . . there was a loud bang from the young master's bedroom. Her ladyship ran upstairs as fast as she could, but the shot was to his head, and . . . he was already gone.'

'What?' Nuala shook her head in confusion. 'Who was already gone?'

'Philip. He took his service revolver from his drawer and shot himself in the head. I'm so sorry, Nuala. I know how fond of him you were.'

'No,' was all Nuala could manage to whisper. 'Why? He was getting better, walking by himself and going outside and . . .'

'There was no more of that after you left, Nuala. Maureen was put in charge of minding him whilst Lady Fitzgerald tried to find a new nurse. She said he sat in his chair staring out of the window and not speaking to her at all. Lady Fitzgerald was worried enough to call the doctor, who prescribed some tablets for him, but . . .'

'How is . . . she?'

'She's locked herself in her bedroom and won't let anyone in. You would be knowing more than most how much she loved that boy.'

'Yes, she did, and oh . . .'

Words failed her, and she put her head in her hands and wept.

'Listen, I've got to go, but can I call a neighbour to sit with you?'

'No! I can't be seen to be grieving for the enemy now, can I, Lucy?'

'You're right, so,' Lucy agreed. 'Take care of yourself, Nuala, and I'm so sorry.'

After Lucy had left, Nuala climbed onto her bicycle and headed for the one place she hoped could give her comfort. As the cold December rain drenched her to her bones, she looked up at the barren branches of the oak tree.

'Philip, if you can hear up there, it's me, Nuala,' she whispered. 'I'm so, so sorry I had to leave you, but this whole mess meant your mammy couldn't have me stay. 'Tis my fault, this; I betrayed your trust and I'll never forgive myself for it, never.'

Soaking wet, Nuala stood up and cycled into Timoleague as the rain poured so hard on her she thought that she might drown, and didn't care if she did. At the church door, she climbed off her bicycle and walked inside. Crossing herself and curtseying in front of the altar, she knelt to ask God and the Holy Mother for forgiveness. Then she stood up and went to the votive candle stand. Taking a penny out of her pocket and putting it into the pot, she lit a candle for the Honourable Philip Fitzgerald, Protestant son of the local landowner, and her friend.

'Rest in peace, Philip, and I'll never forget you,' she muttered as the candle burnt amongst others lit for Catholic souls.

Then she turned and walked out of the church.

20

I reached for a tissue and blew my nose hard. Then I turned the page of the battered notebook:

I cant be writin any mor.

After that, the remaining pages were blank.

I closed the notebook and lay back, thinking of this young woman who had carried the weight of the world on her shoulders, fighting a seemingly unwinnable war. She was younger than my own daughter, but had faced horrors that neither Mary-Kate nor myself, nor anyone who had never lived through war, could begin to understand. Yet I could now see that the seeds of violence that had been sown in Nuala's life almost ninety years ago had touched my own with disastrous consequences . . .

My head felt full of the voices of the past: that particular melodic West Cork cadence that Nuala had conveyed through her writing, the familiar place names that I had cut from my mind for so long.

He had given me this diary all those years ago to make me understand. And yes, if these had been his grandmother's words, it certainly explained his hatred of the British. One thing I remembered clearly about my days in Ireland was that everyone had long memories. And that old grievances were rarely forgiven and forgotten, but passed on from one generation to the next.

I yawned suddenly, and realised I felt exhausted. The past had been a foreign country for so long but, both metaphorically and physically, I was drawing ever closer to it . . .

21

Star
Claridge's Hotel

'Where is she? Do you think she isn't coming?'

Star paced round the sitting room of her suite and looked nervously at her watch. 'It's already ten past seven. We mustn't lose her now, Orlando.'

'Don't panic, Lady Sabrina, I'm sure nothing's gone awry with my plan,' he replied, taking a slurp of champagne.

'I wish I could be as relaxed as you,' Star muttered, then picked up the receiver and dialled 0. 'Hello, is this the front desk? Could you possibly put me through to Mrs Mary McDougal in Room 112? Thank you so much, that's very kind of you.' Star waited while the receptionist connected her, raising a disapproving eyebrow at Orlando, who was pouring them both a top-up of champagne. The line rang for an unbearably long time before it was answered.

'Hello?' a dazed voice answered.

'Mrs McDougal? It's Sabrina Vaughan here. Orlando and I were just wondering whether you were still coming?'

'I – I am. Oh dear, I'm afraid I sat down on the bed and

279

must have dropped off. How rude of me. I'll be there in ten minutes.'

'No problem at all, Mrs McDougal. We'll see you soon.'

As she hung up, Orlando raised his glass to her. 'And the fish is reeled into the net.'

'Honestly, Orlando, it's not as if we're hunting her, we just want to speak to her! I'll go and tidy myself up.'

Fifteen minutes later, there was a knock on the door. Nervously smoothing down the skirt of her dress, Star went to answer it.

Merry McDougal was standing in the corridor, wearing a tasteful jade-green dress, teamed with a pair of black court shoes. Her blonde hair hung in a wavy shoulder-length bob around a fine-featured face, her sapphire-blue eyes standing out against her pale skin. Star thought how elegant she looked, despite having just woken from an impromptu nap. She was clutching a small bag, and Star gulped as she saw an emerald-green glimmer on one finger.

'Hello, Mrs McDougal. Come in,' Star said, trying to sound as natural as possible.

She led Merry into the large sitting room and saw Orlando had disappeared into the bedroom. 'Please, sit down while I fetch Orlando. He was just on the phone to a . . . wine supplier. Back in a tick,' she said, then ducked into the bedroom. He was standing by the door and had obviously been listening behind it.

'It's her!' Star stage-whispered to Orlando. 'Oh my God, I feel so nervous. And guess what?'

'What?'

'I only got a quick glance, but it looks like she's wearing the ring.'

'As they say these days, high five!' Without actually offering Star the hand-clap, Orlando swept through the door.

'Mrs McDougal, thank you so much for coming. Please, don't bother to get up,' he said as the woman prepared to stand.

'I am so sorry about my lateness. As I said to Sabrina, I'm afraid the jet lag got to me and I fell asleep.'

Star noticed she had a slight, unplaceable accent underlying her pleasant, low tone.

'Please do not apologise, Mrs McDougal. It gave myself and my old chum, Sabrina here, a chance to catch up, although it might have to be you who has to catch up on the alcohol front.' Orlando nodded at his champagne glass. 'One too many of these has gone down a treat. It's from a new *cave*, more affordable than your Krug and Dom Pérignon, and really rather pleasant. I myself am not a particular fan of champagnes, especially when the sparkling element over-powers the taste, which it does in some brands, but this is very palatable. Now, will you join us in the remnants of the bottle, or would you prefer to drink something else?'

'I may sound rather dull, but I think I'd better stick to water while we have the interview. My brain's blurry as it is. Oh, and please call me Merry,' she added as Star walked across the room to an alcove and held up two water bottles.

'Still or sparkling?' asked Star.

'I'll have the sparkling, and then I'll at least feel a little more festive.'

Once the water had been poured, Orlando sat in the velvet smoking chair opposite Merry. He indicated the dictaphone lying on the table between them. 'Would you mind awfully if I record this? My shorthand is non-existent and I'd like to catch every word that falls from your lips.'

'Of course not,' Merry said, taking a sip of water. 'What exactly is it you'd like to know?'

'Let's start with how it all began. I think I can detect from your accent that you are not a native Kiwi. In fact, forgive me if I'm wrong,' he said, as Star sat down on the sofa, 'but I think I can hear just the slightest hint of an Irish burr in there somewhere.'

Star watched as a slight blush came to the woman's cheeks.

'You've a good ear, although I left Dublin straight after university. I've lived in New Zealand for some decades now.'

'Ah, one of the many millions of Irish emigrants?'

'Sadly, yes. We were all looking for a better life elsewhere in those days.'

'As a matter of fact, I had a couple of chums that went to Trinity College. Were you there, or at University College Dublin?'

'Trinity. I studied Classics.'

Orlando's face lit up. 'Then we may have far more to discuss than wine. Greek philosophy and mythology are great passions of mine, and I sometimes wish I'd pursued them after university.'

'They were certainly passions of mine too. I lived and breathed Greek myths when I was a child,' she said.

'It was my father who fuelled my passion,' Orlando commented. 'What about you?'

'I had a godfather who was a Fellow in Classics at Trinity when I first met him, then went on to become head of the department. Of course, he's long retired now, and may not even be alive any longer.'

'You lost contact with him?' Orlando prompted.

'Yes, I . . . well,' Merry shrugged. 'You know how it is. Anyway, shall I tell you about how my husband and I started The Vinery?'

'Please, I'm all ears, dear lady.'

'Well, Jock and I met when I arrived in New Zealand and we both worked at a hotel called The Hermitage. It's at the base of Mount Cook on the South Island. I was a waitress there when I met him. He'd started as a waiter, but had already worked his way up to maître d' and sommelier. Even back then, he had a passion for wine. I'm sorry, I've probably gone a bit too far back for your article . . .'

'Please, the floor is yours, Merry. Spout forth for as long as you wish, I find it fascinating.'

Star listened intently as the woman talked about how the two of them had married, then how, on a trip out to the Gibbston Valley in Central Otago, they'd come across an old stone ruin of a house, which Merry said had probably been built during the gold rush. They'd fallen in love with it and it had taken years to rebuild.

'We used to travel down there at weekends and holidays. Jack was only a toddler at the time but we all loved it, and the beauty of our valley, so much that Jock and I eventually decided to put all our savings into establishing a small vineyard there.'

As Merry found her stride, telling Orlando how she and Jock had worked like the devil, bathing in streams until they had been able to build a bathroom, Star let her eyes drop surreptitiously from Merry's face to her hands, which were small, pale and delicate. One hand came to rest on her lap, and Star saw that the ring was definitely made of emeralds and arranged in a star-shaped design around a diamond. She took a mental photograph of the ring, then stood up.

'Excuse me, but I must use the bathroom,' she said as she went out of the sitting room and into the bedroom, closing the door behind her. She ran to her holdall, pulled it onto the bed and ferreted inside the net holder for the envelope containing the drawing of the ring. In the bathroom, with the door firmly locked, Star drew it out and stared at it.

It was identical.

Flushing the toilet, then secreting the envelope in the bedside drawer, she walked back into the sitting room.

'As for the details on the actual mix of grapes we use now,'
Merry was saying, 'you need to speak to my son, Jack, who
is currently in the Rhône Valley, studying their viticulture and
looking for any techniques he can apply to our own vineyard.
Otago is famous for its pinot noir, as you know. Let me write
down his number.'

As Merry bent to find her mobile in the bag she'd
brought with her and Orlando offered her a pen and paper
from the hotel pad, Star stared at the ring again, just to
make sure.

'That's his French mobile. It's best to call after four p.m.
our time.'

'Thank you very much, Mrs McDougal. I think your story
will make the most inspiring article. Just in case I think of any
more questions, could you possibly furnish me with your own
mobile phone number?'

'Of course,' Merry said, adding it to the note.

'Now, are you sure you won't have a drink with us?'

'Ah, go on then, I'll have a small whiskey,' Merry agreed.

'So' – Star took over as Orlando headed for the mini-bar –
'how long will you be in London for?'

'I'm not sure yet, maybe a couple of days, maybe two
weeks or two months . . . Since Jock died and Jack took over
The Vinery, I'm as free as a bird. It's a shame my daughter
didn't join me. She's never seen Europe before,' Merry added
as she took the whiskey.

'As they say in Ireland, *sláinte!*' toasted Orlando.

'*Sláinte!*' Merry repeated as they clinked glasses.

'So, how old is your daughter?' Star asked, even though she
knew.

'Mary-Kate's twenty-two – there's ten years between Jack

and his sister. We had Jack, then struggled to conceive again, so we adopted.'

'Is Mary-Kate interested in joining the family firm?' asked Orlando.

'No, not at all. She studied music at university and wants to make that her career.'

'Well, one would hope that, with your son at the helm and this article, the legacy you and Jock nurtured can really begin to come to the attention of the wider wine world.'

'I do hope so. It was Jock's life passion.' Merry gave a small, sad smile.

'I find it interesting that you, like me, never pursued what you said earlier was your own passion beyond university,' mused Orlando. 'May I enquire why?'

'Well, I had started a Masters, thinking that perhaps I'd go on to a PhD, but . . . life had other plans.'

'As it does for so many of us,' Orlando agreed with a sigh.

'That's a very pretty ring,' said Star, knowing she must speak up before it was too late. 'The star shape is unusual.'

'Thank you. I received it from my godfather on my twenty-first birthday.'

'Are those seven points on it?' asked Star. 'It rather reminds me of the Seven Sisters – of the Pleiades cluster—'

'Yes, I've always been fascinated with their myths,' Orlando butted in. 'Particularly the story of the missing sister. I'd be delighted to chew the philosophical cud with you, if you have the time? Maybe dinner tomorrow night, after I've conducted my interviews, of course,' Orlando added quickly. 'Sabrina, you could join us, couldn't you?'

'Perhaps, although I'll have to check, um, what Julian is doing.' Star could feel her guard slipping, but while Merry was in captivity, she was absolutely desperate to ask more questions.

'Yes, that sounds lovely,' said Merry, who stood up abruptly and put her whiskey glass down on the table. 'Now, if you'll excuse me, I think I must go before I really do fall asleep here in my chair. Thank you for the whiskey and the interview.'

Star and Orlando stood up and watched her as she headed for the door.

'How does eight thirty tomorrow evening in Gordon Ramsay's downstairs sound?' Orlando called after her.

'Fine. Goodnight, Sabrina, Orlando.'

The door banged shut behind her before Star and Orlando could say another word.

They both stood there for a few seconds, staring at each other, then Orlando sat back down and took a swig of his champagne.

'Shit!' Star uttered a rare swear word in her frustration. 'The moment you mentioned the missing sister, she was spooked.'

'A miscalculation perhaps,' Orlando sighed. 'Although you had pointed out her unusual ring.'

'I had to say something, Orlando. When I left the room, I went to check that ring against the drawing Ally faxed me. There's no doubt, it *is* the ring. It's identical. She has it! I should call Atlantis and speak to Maia and Ally—'

'Hold on just one moment, Star. Let us think about this carefully. It was obvious to me that Mrs Merry McDougal has something to hide. And as her fear began the moment I mentioned the missing sister, we can surmise that it has something to do with that. One has to examine the facts: why did she leave Trinity so suddenly, before finishing her Masters?'

'I—'

'I understand it could be for a simple reason, but let me finish. This obviously highly intelligent woman moved about as far away from Ireland as she could possibly get, then buried herself in some beautiful but off-the-map valley and never again pursued a career in academia. In my opinion, she's spent the past several decades hiding. The question is, from what? Or more accurately, who?'

'Isn't that rather a big leap, Orlando? I mean, just because she didn't want a future in academia doesn't mean anything. Maybe she fell in love.'

'Perhaps, but if you put her life's trajectory alongside the fact that she has very obviously been avoiding your sisters' pursuit of her, when all her daughter told her was that she may have found a connection to your family, with the clue of the star-shaped emerald ring, then this all adds up to a woman who is fearful of what the revelation might mean for her. And for her daughter,' he added.

'Maybe you've been reading too many crime novels, but yes, I agree, there's definitely something she's afraid of. What's so frustrating is that the woman sleeping just a few doors down from us now has the answers to the puzzle, but we daren't push her further or we'll scare her off. CeCe said that Mary-Kate has never looked into her biological family. Though as we now think she really *could* be the missing sister, maybe we could call her now and ask her on our cruise. But . . .'

'Because of Mummy Mary's obvious reticence, you feel it would be inappropriate to do so.'

'Yes. We've just lied our way into meeting her and it's . . . morally wrong to use that information to go behind her back and contact her daughter. Oh dear, Orlando, we've got ourselves into a real mess here,' Star sighed.

Silence reigned as they both thought about it.

'Perhaps there's another way of gleaning information on Mary-Kate's adoption,' Orlando said eventually. 'For some reason only known to herself, Merry does not wish her daughter to explore her true heritage. However, we must not forget that Merry has a son called Jack. May I suggest something?'

'Go on.'

'I would call Atlantis and see if Maia can go to France to meet him. Geneva isn't far from Provence and I have the address of the *cave* he is staying at on the tape. She told us that Jack is thirty-two, and he was ten when Mary-Kate arrived in the family. He will definitely have a memory of that moment, and perhaps know more of his mother's heritage too.'

'He might, but Mary-Kate knows nothing of her adoptive parents, so why should Jack? Orlando, we can't just let Merry walk out of here without us seeing her again. I just want to come clean, tell her who we truly are. I feel terrible about all this deception. This isn't a game, Orlando, it really isn't.'

'No. Well, I promise that even if I have to sit cross-legged in front of Mrs McDougal's door all night, we will not let that happen,' Orlando said firmly. 'Now, I'm retiring to my room to think and we will speak by telephone later when I have cleared my brain. In the meantime, you call Atlantis and tell your sisters that one of them needs to get down to Provence. I will telephone you later with the exact address.'

He walked purposefully across the room, then paused at the door and turned to look at Star.

'Perchance one other question we should be asking is this: where did Merry get that ring from in the first place? Adieu for now.'

With that, Orlando left the suite.

Star heaved herself up and wearily walked into the bedroom so she could be comfortable while speaking to Maia and Ally. She tried to clarify in her mind the facts she needed to tell them.

Finding the Atlantis number on her mobile, she waited for it to connect and opened the bedside drawer to pull out the envelope with the drawing of the star-shaped ring.

'Hello, Ma, it's Star here. How are you?'

'I am well, *chérie*, and enjoying the beautiful summer weather here. And of course, your sisters' company. And you? Is all well?'

'Yes, it is, thank you. I . . .' Star stopped herself as she wasn't sure how much her sisters were telling Ma of the search for the missing sister. 'Can I possibly speak to one or both of them?'

'Of course; they are out on the terrace and I know they are eager to speak to you. I am very much looking forward to seeing you soon.'

As Star waited for Ma to fetch her sisters, she reminded herself to call Mouse straight afterwards and make sure he had fed Rory something and managed to get him to bed.

'Star! Ally here, and Maia is listening too.'

'Hi, Star,' Maia said. 'Have you any news for us?'

'I do. Orlando's master plan worked, and I've just spent an hour with Merry McDougal.'

There was silence at the other end. Then both her sisters talked at once.

'Oh wow!'

'What did she say?'

'Is Mary-Kate the missing sister . . . ?'

'Hold on, both of you, and I'll tell you as much as I can, though I'm still trying to process everything. Firstly, and probably most importantly, when she walked in, I noticed immediately that she was wearing the ring. While Orlando interviewed her about her vineyard, I went into the bedroom and checked it against the drawing you faxed me. Seriously, it's identical.'

'That's wonderful news! Did you ask her where she got it from?' Maia queried.

'She said it was a twenty-first birthday present from her godfather, who was apparently a professor of Classics at Trinity College in Dublin, where she herself did the same degree.'

'So, did you then say that the ring meant her daughter was the missing sister?' Ally cut in.

'No, because the minute I mentioned the design and how unusual it was, and Orlando said he had a particular interest in the missing sister of the Pleiades, she got up and left. She was totally spooked. Orlando and I have invited her to dinner tomorrow night – I just really want to tell her who we are – but we both think she might run again. It's obvious that, for whatever reason, she *was* avoiding CeCe and Chrissie when they went to that island, as well as Electra when she flew to Canada. And now she may well try to avoid us. Honestly, I feel truly awful for getting her here under false pretences.'

There was a pause as Star heard both her sisters whispering in the background.

'I understand, Star. The only reason we can think of is that she doesn't want her daughter to know who her birth parents were,' said Maia. 'That's got to be it, hasn't it?'

'I suppose so – but she looked genuinely frightened when she left,' Star sighed. 'Even Orlando seems stumped. He says he has a plan to make sure that she doesn't leave the hotel without him knowing about it – don't ask me how. But just in case we do lose her again, Orlando thinks that one of you two should go to Provence and speak to Mary-Kate's brother, Jack. Maybe he'll know more about his mum and her past.'

'Maybe, but how would he know any more about Mary-Kate's adoption than his sister did?' asked Ally.

'He's ten years older than Mary-Kate so he might remember

something. And also be less emotionally involved than his mum.'

'Do we know where he is in Provence?' Maia asked.

'I'll text you the address for the *cave* – Orlando has it on tape – but could one of you go? Like, tomorrow?'

'It's a good five to six hours' drive from Geneva,' said Maia.

'Send us that address and we'll get back to you in a bit when we've had a chat and sorted out the arrangements, okay?' Ally added.

'Okay,' said Star.

'And please thank Orlando for his help – so far you're actually the only ones that have managed to meet Merry face to face,' said Maia.

'Even if my Lady Sabrina acting was rubbish' – Star gave a low chuckle – 'Orlando was brilliant. You know, this sounds weird, but her face actually reminded me of someone I've seen before, I just can't think who.'

'If you do, let us know. Speak later, Star. And really, well done. Bye.'

Star ended the call, then lay back on the bed and closed her eyes for a few seconds. Then she took a deep breath, opened them and called Mouse's mobile. It rang for ages, but finally, he answered.

'Hello, darling, how are you?' his deep voice came into her ear.

'I'm fine, thanks. Just checking in to say goodnight and to make sure Rory's had dinner and you've put him to bed,' she smiled.

'Of course I did! I am capable of looking after my own child when you're not here, Star.'

'I know you are, but you're also very busy.'

'I am. So, how did the "thing" you and Orlando needed to do in London go?'

'Oh, it was . . . okay. It's complicated, Mouse. I'll explain when I'm home.'

'It all sounds very mysterious, darling.'

'As I said last night, it's just something to do with my family and organising things for Pa's memorial service. I'll be home either tomorrow or the following morning. You couldn't by any chance come to London tomorrow night, could you? The suite is just beautiful and I'm sure I could get Jenny the babysitter to stay overnight with Rory.'

'Sorry, but I'm snowed under here.'

'I . . . okay.'

'All right, darling. Well, keep in touch.'

'I will, and give Rory a hug from me. Goodnight.'

'Goodnight.'

Ending the call, Star let out a big sigh. Why did she still find it so difficult to say what she felt? Perhaps it was simply that after all the years with CeCe, it was inbuilt, or maybe it was just the kind of person she was. But keeping everything bottled up wasn't healthy and had nearly wrecked her relationship with her precious sister. She knew that Mouse loved her, but he was of that particular breed of Englishmen who were not good at expressing their feelings either. She understood that, but between her inability to say what she needed from him – that they should find even the occasional night when houses and work were forgotten and they could just be together – and Mouse's struggle with showing emotion, their communication wasn't what it should be. 'You have to try,' she muttered to herself as the room telephone rang on the bedside table beside her.

'Room 161 for you, madam. Shall I put the call through?'

'Yes, thank you.'

'Dear Star, did you manage to contact your sisters?' came Orlando's dulcet tones.

'I did and they're going to call me back when they've decided on a plan.'

'But you did insist that they went to Provence at the earliest opportunity?'

'Yes, Orlando. I'm sure Maia will go.'

'Good, good. Well, I have made sure that we will know if our Mrs McDougal exits the hotel at any point from now on. I will call you if and when I get word from my . . . contact that she is on the move.'

Star couldn't help but laugh. 'Honestly, Orlando, you've really enjoyed this, haven't you?'

'For my sins, I rather admit I have, although we are still far from solving this puzzle. Now, make sure you don't block your room telephone, and that your mobile is charged and turned on for the rest of the night.'

'I will, I promise. Oh, I need Jack's address in Provence.'

'It's the Minuet Cave in Châteauneuf-du-Pape. Now, I shall sit in my comparatively poky little room and continue to think. For now, I shall say goodnight.'

'Goodnight, Orlando, sleep well and thank you.'

After texting Ally the address, Star did her ablutions and, despite her guilty conscience, she had to chuckle at Orlando and his eccentricity. What with Mouse being so very serious and absorbed in his work, his brother so often brought a smile to her face. As she climbed into bed and turned off the light, she thanked the heavens that he was in her life.

22

Atlantis

'I found it,' said Ally, stepping through the French doors of the kitchen and onto the terrace where Maia was sitting. The sun was setting behind the mountains and turning the sky a vibrant shade of orange. 'The *cave* is in the village of Châteauneuf-du-Pape in the Rhône Valley, and the nearest airport is Marseille. Or you could just drive straight there, because by the time you've got to Geneva airport and faffed about, then hired a car from Marseille at the other end, it's probably faster.'

'Okay,' said Maia quietly.

'You're happy to go, aren't you?'

Maia let out a weary sigh. 'I'm not feeling all that well just now, Ally.'

'I told you, you should have gone to the doctor days ago. The sooner you can find out what it is, then—'

'Ally, I know what it is, that is not the problem!'

'You do?'

'Yes, I do. I didn't want to tell you before I saw Floriano next week, but . . .'

'What is it? Please, tell me, because my imagination is running riot.'

'Really, it's nothing to worry about. I am well, and—'

'Oh my God!' Ally looked at her, then threw back her head and laughed. 'It's okay, Maia, I know what it is. You're—'

'Pregnant. Yes, I am. When I went to Geneva with Christian, I bought a test and the result was positive. In fact, I bought three tests – which are hidden in my underwear drawer in the Pavilion – and they are all positive!'

'That's wonderful news!' Ally stood up and threw her arms around Maia. 'You are pleased, aren't you?'

'Of course, but it's stirred up some things from my past.'

'Oh.' Ally looked at her sister. 'I understand.'

'And apart from that, I'm feeling sick *all* the time! And when I'm not being sick, I am thinking that I will be, do you understand?'

'Of course I do, darling. I've been there.'

'And Floriano and I . . . well, we aren't married yet, and then there is Valentina to consider. How will she feel about a new brother or sister?'

'I don't think whether you're married or not makes any difference these days, Maia. You've lived with Floriano for almost a year and I've never seen you so happy. I honestly think he will be thrilled, and Valentina too. I'm certain it will bond you all even closer. If you feel it's important to get married, then I'm sure Floriano won't mind that either.'

'No.' Maia smiled for the first time. 'He won't mind at all. He proposed very soon after I moved in with him. It was me that wanted to wait. But you understand why this is sending me back to the past, don't you? I mean' – Maia bent her head and put a hand to her forehead – 'if I'm to have this child and raise it, then why couldn't I have kept my son all those years ago? Oh Ally, my head is in such a mess . . . Having all the same pregnancy sensations now just takes me back to that time at uni in Paris when I was so alone and scared. And then giving birth to a baby who would never know me as a mother and I would never know him as my son! I . . . how could I have given him away? How could I?'

Ally took her sister in her arms as she sobbed with all the grief of the past fifteen years.

'And to top it all, the father of my child is Zed Eszu! He's an evil man, Ally. We know that he's pursued Tiggy and Electra too. Why was he doing it? It cannot simply be random that he's been obsessed with us sisters. He doesn't leave our family alone!'

'No, I've thought about that too,' agreed Ally.

'I am the only one who has borne his child, and at least he will never know.'

'You don't want him to?'

'Never! I know nothing about his business dealings, but I do know him as a human being. He gets what he wants and then moves on. He's without any kind of scruples. Or guilt,' Maia added as Ally produced a tissue from her jean pocket and handed it to her sister.

'Well, the lack of guilt or empathy is an indication of being a psychopath. Maybe that's what he is.'

'I don't know,' said Maia, blowing her nose. 'But his fascination for me in Paris, and then two of our sisters more recently, is definitely not a coincidence.'

'What makes it even stranger is that his father's boat was next to Pa's when I radioed the *Titan* to try to rendezvous with it last June. The *Olympus* was on the radar. Anyway, Maia, enough of all that. I just wish that you could be happier about your wonderful news.'

'Were you when you were pregnant?'

'Yes and no. I was conflicted, just like you are. Maybe most women are to some degree initially, even if their circumstances are less complex than yours or mine.'

'But you went ahead and kept your baby, even though you had lost your beloved Theo. My circumstances all those years ago weren't all that different.'

'Maia, please, I wasn't nineteen and just starting out on my life and career like you were. I was a thirty-year-old woman who knew that she loved the baby's father desperately, and that the baby was a gift, a chance to have a part of Theo always with me. They were completely different circumstances.'

'Thank you for trying to make me feel better about giving my baby away, but nothing can, Ally, nothing.'

'Maybe not, but equally, you can't let guilt over the past affect your present and future, Maia. This baby is the start of a whole new life for you, Floriano and Valentina. It would be very sad if you weren't able to embrace it, for them, as well as yourself.'

Maia was silent for a while, then she looked at Ally, her beautiful dark eyes still wet with tears, and nodded. 'You're right. I must embrace it for them. Thank you, Ally.'

'You know,' Ally mused, 'even though we lost Pa last year, it feels like at least we've found each other again. All those years when you never really talked to me. I missed my big sister, I really did.'

'Please forgive me for that. I was so ashamed . . . I hated myself for so long. But you're right. I must move on.'

'Yes, you must. Just one last question: would you ever think about finding your son?'

'Even though every millimetre of me yearns to know him, to hold him in my arms and tell him I love him, and there hasn't been a day that has gone past since I gave him away that I haven't thought about him, or wondered where he is and how he's doing . . . I can't. It would be for *me*, not him. I don't even know if his parents have told him that he's adopted. Walking back into his life now could completely disrupt it. He's at such a vulnerable age – fifteen; no longer a baby or even a child. He's almost an adult. And then there are his parents: they've – or at least I hope they have – loved him like he was their own since he was a day old. How would they feel if the birth mother suddenly walked in?'

'I can't imagine, but I understand what you're saying.'

'Perhaps I'll see him one day in the future. If he wants to get in contact with me. I'm sure he could if he tried,' Maia sighed.

'Talking of that, I'm still convinced that's the problem for Merry: she obviously doesn't want to risk another family stealing her beloved daughter away.'

'I agree, but surely it's Mary-Kate's choice whether she wants to meet her birth family – or whatever we are to her? Like it would be my son's?' Maia pointed out.

'As CeCe told us, it's never occurred to Mary-Kate to search for her birth parents before. She was perfectly content not knowing about the past.'

'Then is it our place to interfere? She should talk to her mother about it first.'

'From the calls we've had with her, she now seems eager to know. Oh dear,' Ally sighed. 'I mean, from what Star has told us, that emerald ring suggests she is who we're looking for, but given she's in New Zealand and her mum's in London with no definite date to return home, it doesn't look like she'll be joining us on the cruise.'

'I'll say it for the thousandth time: I so wish Pa were here to tell us what to do,' said Maia.

'Well, he's not, and actually, before we go back to Mary-Kate and tell her that the ring is identical, I think Orlando is right: you should go down to Provence to meet Jack.'

'Ally' – Maia looked at her – 'I'm sorry, but I feel too

unwell to make such a journey. I'm sick all the time, and I just can't face the drive.'

'Okay, I understand. Well, that's that then. It's a shame, because I saw on the website that it has a very nice *gîte* set in the vineyard that visitors can rent. It's vacant at the moment. I know how much you love France, especially since you discovered your heritage there. It's part of who you are, Maia.'

'I am sorry, Ally; even though you're right, and I'd love to go to Provence, I just can't.'

'Then I'll call Tiggy and see if she can fly over. It's not that far from Scotland, is it?'

'No, but . . . Ally, why don't you go?'

'Me?! Can you imagine what Bear would be like on a five-hour car journey? I couldn't.'

'I think you could if you left Bear here at Atlantis with Ma and me for a couple of days. It would do you good, Ally. You've not been apart from him for more than a few hours since the moment he was born, and you've told me you've started supplementing his milk because he's such a hungry baby. You could express tonight and tomorrow morning before you leave.'

'Oh Maia, I couldn't. What if he got sick? Had a fever? How could I leave him here? I . . .'

'At the risk of sounding patronising, Ma brought up six babies and is quite capable of dealing with a fever and even worse. She absolutely adores Bear, and he seems to love her too. He quite likes me as well,' Maia added with a smile.

'Are you trying to say he doesn't need his mother?'

'No, Ally, of course not. What I am saying is that even *you* must admit that you've been exhausted and have found it a strain coping by yourself. I think a drive through beautiful countryside heading for a *gîte* in the Rhône Valley, and some time – and nights – alone, would do you the world of good.

It's completely normal for mothers to leave their babies in the care of a grandparent, *and* an auntie. Would you at least think about it?'

'Okay, but—'

'No buts, Ally. Just think about it. Now, I'm going to get an early night. Ma's insisted on making me a milky drink before bed like she used to when we were little,' Maia smiled. 'Have a good night's sleep, and thank you. Our conversation has really helped me. Please don't tell anyone about my news – not even Ma . . . I want to speak to Floriano first.'

'You know you can trust me.'

'Always. Goodnight, darling.' Maia kissed Ally's red curls and walked into the kitchen.

Ally sat back, watching insects buzzing around the lamps that lit up the garden. She thought about what Maia had suggested and at first rejected it out of hand because it seemed like such a foreign concept. It was almost a year now since Bear had become part of her. She'd lived every day with him either in her tummy or out of it. On the other hand, the thought of driving down to Provence alone *was* appealing. She could take the old open-topped Mercedes sports car that Pa kept in the garage just next to the pontoon in Geneva. He'd once collected her from the airport in it after a race and the two of them had driven down to Nice to meet the *Titan*. They'd played *The Magic Flute* at full blast as the wind had rushed through her hair.

'I felt so free then . . .' she murmured.

Looking at her watch, she saw it was past ten o'clock. She walked back into the kitchen to find Ma already preparing Bear's bottles.

'Ma, it's late. I could have done that.'

'It is no problem, Ally. I will do the night-time feeds again tonight. If I tell you I enjoy those moments when the rest of the world is still and a contented baby lies sleeping in my arms, would you think me mad?'

'I wouldn't at all.' Ally took a bottle from the steriliser and put it on the table, so she could take it upstairs to express some milk for tomorrow morning.

'Maia just mentioned to me that a trip to Provence is necessary,' said Ma. 'As Maia is not quite herself, she suggested that perhaps you should go. You know I am happy to look after little Bear whilst you are away. In fact, it would be my pleasure to do so.'

'Maia seems very keen on me going, but I'm not sure I want to.'

'It is up to you, of course, but if there is someone you must meet to find out more about this missing sister, then you should consider it. I know your father wanted to find her so very badly. Ah well,' Ma sighed, 'you must do what is right for you first, Ally. And if she cannot be found in time for the cruise, the most important thing is that she *is* found.'

'But what if she doesn't *want* or need to be a part of this family? From what CeCe and Chrissie said, Mary-Kate has her own very loving adoptive family, although she too has recently lost her father. And her mum is obviously not happy about our arrival in her daughter's life either. I know it's what Pa wanted, but sometimes things just can't happen, for whatever reason.'

'I know, Ally, I know. Do not upset yourself, please, it's the last thing your father would have wanted. Now, will you come upstairs to bed with me, or are you staying down here?'

'I'll come with you.'

They switched off the lights in the kitchen, and walked up the stairs.

'Goodnight, Ma,' she said as she turned for one of the guest rooms on the first floor. 'Ma?'

'Yes, *chérie?*'

'Is there . . . I mean, do you know anything about Pa and his life that can maybe help us?'

'I know very little, Ally, I promise. Your father was a private man and he never shared any of his secrets with me.'

'But there were secrets, weren't there?'

'Yes, *chérie*, I think there were. Goodnight.'

Walking along the corridor, Ally paused in front of Pa's bedroom. She put out a tentative hand to open the door, then decided against it. She needed to sleep tonight, not have the ghosts of the past haunt her.

Inside the very comfortable guest room, she undressed quickly and slipped into bed.

'Who were you, Pa? Who were you?' she murmured before she fell asleep.

23

'I'm going to go to Provence,' Ally said to Ma early the following morning as she entered Ma's suite. As if on cue, Bear began screaming. She headed to the cot, scooped the squalling baby out of it, then sat down in the chair and began to feed him. A beautiful silence descended. Ma sat down on the sofa opposite her, managing to look elegant in her peacock-blue silk robe, even this early in the morning.

'I think that is a very good idea, Ally.'

'It's only six now,' Ally said, looking out of the window at the sun already peeping over the mountains. 'If I leave in an hour or so, I can be in Provence by this afternoon.'

'Ally, would you not like Christian to drive you there? Then you can relax and enjoy the scenery.'

'No. It's been ages since I took a road trip, and if I'm doing this without Bear, I think it would do me good to have some space and blast out tunes on the way down.'

'I will take the best care of the little one until your return,' said Ma.

'I know you will, Ma. I was thinking last night that at some point, I'll have to get back to work – but where and what that will be, I'm not sure. So I'll just have to get used to leaving him in the care of others.'

'One step at a time, Ally. You have had a most traumatic year. There is plenty of time to decide on your future.'

'Well, I'm going to have to ask Georg if I can take some money out of the trust Pa set up for all of us. I know I only need to ask,' Ally said as she moved Bear from one breast to the other, 'but all us girls find him intimidating.'

'I can assure you that Georg is one of the kindest men I have ever met. I do know that once you are all gathered on the *Titan*, he wishes to talk to you about how the trust should be managed from here on in. As he puts it, he is only the temporary gatekeeper until the six of you are ready to manage it yourselves. Now, if you are comfortable, I will go and get dressed. Shall I call Christian and tell him to bring the boat round in an hour?'

'Yes please. And also say that I'm going to drive the old open-top Mercedes.'

'Of course, Ally. I will see you downstairs with Bear.'

'So the expressed milk is in the fridge and just keep an eye on his temperature – it was raised a little a couple of days ago and—'

'Ally, please trust me to take care of your precious little one and we will see you when you're back,' said Ma. She kissed Ally's cheek and stepped back onto the grass from the jetty where the speedboat was moored.

'Bye bye, Ally.' Maia hugged her. 'Keep in touch.'

'I will. *Au revoir!*'

She waved to them as Christian pulled the speedboat away from the jetty. Normally, she would have taken the wheel herself, but today, she decided to sit back and enjoy another glorious morning on the lake. The water shimmered under the sun as they began to speed towards Geneva. Christian knew he didn't have to worry about his passenger's sea legs, so he went full steam ahead. Ally could see how he felt in his element at the wheel of the boat, his skin tanned a deep brown and his broad shoulders relaxed.

Even though she felt choked at her first ever goodbye to Bear, being on the water comforted her and reminded her of who she had been before Bear had arrived.

This time last year, she'd been training with the crew, and at the full peak of her fitness.

And then she'd fallen in love . . .

'I will always remember those few weeks as the best of my life,' she murmured to the sky, as Christian began to slow the boat and steer it towards the pontoon. Ally jumped off to secure the ropes as Christian carried her holdall and joined her on dry land.

Parked next to the dock was the little sports car, its racing-green paintwork gleaming in the sun and its roof down. Ally watched as Christian took the keys from a young man in an immaculate white T-shirt and shorts. They chatted for a moment, then the young man waved and wandered off towards a bicycle.

'I asked Julien from the local garage to check the oil and fill up the tank,' said Christian. 'It's getting old now, but Julien says everything looks good, so you should have no problem with it.'

'It must be vintage by now,' Ally chuckled as she took the keys from Christian.

'You are sure you don't want me to drive you, Ally?'

'Quite sure,' she replied as she got in the car and turned on the engine. 'Thanks, Christian. I'll call you when I need you to come and collect me.'

'Take care, Ally, and drive safely,' he shouted above the noise of the engine as the car reversed.

'I will, bye!'

Ally made good time through Geneva and across the border into France. She'd brought a collection of CDs and spent the journey alternating between classical and pop, singing her heart out to some of her favourite anthems. She stopped at an *aire* for coffee, a baguette and to express milk – even though she was supplementing now, she didn't want to finish breastfeeding just yet.

Reaching Grenoble, she pulled off the *autoroute*, suddenly feeling exhausted. After a twenty-minute catnap, she began the final stretch down into Provence. She watched as the countryside visibly softened around her.

'It really is so beautiful here,' she murmured as she drove past a particularly lovely pale yellow farmhouse. Up a gentle slope covered in vineyards stood a grand château. The gates were open and part of her longed to drive up to the advertised *cave* to take a taste of one of her favourite wines: Provençal rosé. A road sign told her she was only three kilometres away from Châteauneuf-du-Pape. So close now, she decided to pull over and gather her thoughts. Reaching into her bag for her mobile, she saw there were a number of text messages, all from Star.

'Call me!' was the gist of most of them.

Ally rang Star's number and she answered immediately. 'Hi, Star, what's up?'

'Oh, don't worry, nothing awful has happened. As far as we know, Merry McDougal has not checked out of the hotel. She *has* left her room, however, and Orlando has followed her to see where she's going. Her bags are still here, according to the concierge.'

'Okay. I'm almost at the *cave* where this Jack's apparently staying and I've enjoyed the journey so much, I switched my brain off about what I'm going to say once I get there. I don't know whether I should pretend to be a tourist and casually engage Jack in conversation about his family, or just come clean immediately. What do you think?'

'Oh gosh, Ally, I suppose it depends whether Merry has already told him about CeCe and Electra's visits.'

'If I somehow manage to meet him and then get him to talk to me without having to kidnap him and tie him to a chair at gunpoint, I'll do my best. Honestly, Star, you're right: now that I'm actually here, this all feels very uncomfortable. If Merry doesn't want her daughter to know about her origins, then I don't think it's right that we force it. Despite whatever reasons Pa had for wanting to find her.'

'I agree. If I were you, I'd play it by ear. Just be yourself and let things progress naturally. Good luck, Ally, and please keep in touch.'

'And you. Bye, Star.'

With a sigh, Ally started up the engine and moved out onto the road. She thought about the fact that all of her sisters had had someone with them when they'd been on the trail of the missing sister. CeCe had Chrissie; Electra, Mariam; and Star with Orlando by her side.

'And here I am, going it alone again,' she muttered as she saw a sign to the Minuet Cave. The building she was heading towards looked very much like the others scattered around the countryside: an old stone farmhouse with terracotta roofs and large blue-shuttered windows. Pausing at the turning onto a lane, which ran along a chalky path through the vines, she took a deep breath and saw an image of Theo in her mind.

'Be by my side, won't you, darling?'

With that, she pulled onto the track and drove towards the farmhouse.

'Right, here goes,' she whispered as she stepped out of the car and followed the signs to the shop. Housed in a dark, cellar-like room at one end of the farmhouse, it was empty of people. Bottles of red Châteauneuf-du-Pape were stacked closely together, with every inch of space used. She was just about to go in search of someone when a teenage boy of around sixteen walked inside and smiled at her.

'*Je peux vous aider?*'

'Yes, I saw your sign advertising the *gîte* you have for rent and was wondering whether it was available?'

'For when, *mademoiselle*?' The teenager walked around the tiny counter jammed into a corner of the room and took out a book from a shelf beneath.

'For tonight actually.'

He thumbed through the book then nodded. 'Yes, it's available.'

'How much is it?'

The boy told her, and after saying she wanted to stay two nights minimum, she took her credit card from her purse.

'No, no, *mademoiselle*. You pay when you leave. One moment, and I will call *Maman* to come and take you down to the *gîte*.' Then he went to a small fridge and pulled out a bottle of rosé. 'Would you like a glass?'

'Do you know, I actually would,' Ally smiled. 'It's been a long drive.'

Once she had been furnished with the glass of pale pink wine, the boy walked towards the door. '*Excusez-moi, Maman* will be here soon.'

While she waited, Ally went outside into the courtyard and sat down on an ancient wrought-iron bench. The courtyard was full of wooden wine pallets, but also children's scooters, bikes and a rusty climbing frame. The sun was lower now in the azure-blue sky and Ally tilted her head back to enjoy its warmth on her face. The rosé tasted wonderful and she closed her eyes, breathing in deeply and trying to relax.

'*Bonjour, mademoiselle*, I am Ginette Valmer, and I will take you down to the *gîte*,' came a bright voice. Ally opened her eyes to see a dark-haired woman of around forty, wearing jeans, a T-shirt and a stained apron. She was carrying a small basket of food.

'I am pleased to meet you too. I am Ally D'Aplièse,' Ally said in formal French as she shook the woman's hand. She collected her holdall from the car and they walked along the chalky path towards the *gîte*, which was to the left of the farmhouse, nestled in an idyllic spot amongst the vines. She made polite conversation in response to Madame Valmer's questions.

'Yes, I live in Geneva, and I'm down here visiting for a few days.'

'To taste the wines?'

'Yes, and to also . . . look for a house round here.' The words fell out of Ally's mouth before she could stop them.

'Well, there are *immobiliers* in both Gigondas and Vac- queyras and also another in Beaumes-de-Venise. I can give you their telephone numbers or you can visit if you wish,' Madame Valmer replied as they reached the front door of the *gîte*. 'Now, here we are. It is very small, but okay for one person or a couple,' she said as they walked inside. Ally saw a basic but clean space with a small kitchenette along one side, a heavy French mahogany bed, and a sofa and two chairs placed in front of a tiny corner fireplace.

'The shower and toilet are through there,' Madame Valmer added, pointing to a wooden door at the back. She placed the basket on the small counter. 'Here is a fresh baguette, some butter, cheese and milk and there is already some rosé in the fridge.'

'Thank you, but really, I can go shopping.'

'Everything will be closed by now around here. You know

how it is in France,' Madame Valmer smiled, her dark eyes dancing. 'Nothing is ever open when you need it.'

'Then maybe you could tell me of a restaurant or a café close by where I could get something to eat? It's been a long journey from Geneva.'

'Ah, there are a few, but . . .'

There was a pause as Madame Valmer eyed her. 'Come for dinner with us.'

'Are you sure? I can easily find something in Gigondas,' said Ally.

'Another mouth will make no difference. I have three children and four hungry men who work in the *cave*, so' – Madame Valmer waved her hands at Ally expressively – 'one more is no problem. And it will be a change to have another female at the table!'

'I'd like that very much, if you don't mind.'

'It is simple food; we will eat at seven thirty. See you then.'

'*Merci, Madame Valmer, à ce soir.*'

'Call me Ginette!' she said as she left the *gîte*.

Ally went to the fridge and opened the ice-cold bottle of rosé. Walking outside, she saw an old worn table and two iron chairs placed just to the side of the *gîte*. She sat down to enjoy the sun on her face and to call Atlantis. The home number was engaged, so she rang Maia instead.

'Hi, just calling to say I've arrived safely. How is Bear?'

'In the bath with Ma clucking over him. He's fine, and I think Ma is really enjoying being in charge. So, have you met Jack yet?'

'No, just a son of the family and a woman who I presume is one of the owners of the *cave*. For some reason, when she asked me why I was here, I said I was house-hunting!' Ally chuckled. 'Anyway, the good news is, I've been invited to dinner with them all tonight. Hopefully this Jack will be at the table, and I can start a conversation with him.'

'Wonderful! Whatever happens, staying in a *gîte* in Provence and eating a home-cooked French supper sounds delightful to me.'

'Well, it's so beautiful here, I might be serious about buying a house. The thought of another freezing and rainy Bergen winter isn't appealing just now.'

'There's no harm in looking, is there?'

'I was only joking, Maia. I have Thom and my father there. Actually, I must give Felix a call too and make sure he isn't lying in a pool of whisky somewhere. Tell Ma to give Bear a big goodnight kiss from his *maman*, won't you?'

'Of course I will. And Ally?'

'Yes?'

'Forget Jack for now and just enjoy your time there. *À bientôt.*'

Eager to stretch her legs after the long drive, Ally took herself on a walk through the vines. Not quite ready to be harvested, the grapes hadn't yet developed the dark blue hue that would produce the world-famous Châteauneuf-du-Pape red wine. Around her was the sound of cicadas and insect life that vibrated in the hot, still air. In the distance, a farm dog lay panting in the shade of a parasol-shaped pine tree, as the softening afternoon light slanted to glint golden on the vine leaves.

Ally sat down in the shade next to a wild lavender bush. She brushed her hands over the heavy purple flower heads to fill her nostrils with their calming scent. And finally felt glad that Maia and Ma had persuaded her to come.

Eventually, she returned to the *gîte* for a quick shower in the tiny cubicle (the water was only lukewarm, but the weather was hot enough for it to be refreshing) then changed into a clean pair of jeans and a shirt, adding a touch of mascara and a dash of lipstick, and allowing her hair to flow freely around her shoulders.

'Wow, it's a long time since I've been out to dinner,' she said to herself as she walked up through the vines towards the farmhouse. Glad of the glass and a half of rosé she'd had to bolster her confidence, she knocked on the front door.

'Everyone is at the back!' Ginette's head appeared from a window. 'Walk round, Ally.'

She did so, and saw a loggia hung with vines jutting out from the back of the house, which faced what she knew were the Dentelles Mountains. In the fast descending dusk, small lanterns were placed around the loggia, ready to be lit when night fell. At the table sat four men, as well as the teenage boy she'd met earlier, another boy aged around twelve, and a smaller boy of seven or eight. As Ally approached, there was raucous laughter, then all the men turned to look at her. One of them – small, but brawny – stood up.

'Excuse me, *mademoiselle*, we were not laughing at you, just at our friend's strange Kiwi expressions! Please, come and sit down. I am François, the co-owner of the *cave*. This is Vincent and Pierre-Jean who work here with me, and these are my sons: Tomás, Olivier, and Gerard. And this' – François pointed to the man she was about to sit next to – 'is Jack McDougal, all the way from New Zealand.'

Ally stood behind her chair and watched as the man she'd come here to speak to turned round and stood up. Jack McDougal towered over her. He was very fair, with piercing blue eyes and wavy blond hair cut short.

'*Enchanté, mademoiselle*,' he said in a very strange accent.

'And I apologise now for my bad French. Please' – he put out a hand – 'sit down.'

'Do you speak English, *mademoiselle*?' François, the host, asked her.

'Yes, I do.'

'Ah, Jack, then tonight you will finally have someone who understands what you are talking about!'

Everyone around the table laughed again.

'And he is not lying when he says his French is bad,' François added.

'But then, our English is worse! Would you like some wine, *mademoiselle*?' Vincent, who was opposite her at the table, tapped a bottle of red. 'It is an early sample of our 2006 vintage, which we are all hoping may be one of our best yet.'

'Thank you,' Ally said as her glass was filled to the brim. 'I'm afraid I don't know much about wine, but *santé*!'

'*Santé*.' Everyone raised their glasses, and she noticed that even the young boy Gérard had a small amount in his glass.

Ally tasted the wine, which was smooth and rich and slipped down her throat like velvet. 'You are right, this wine is beautiful,' she said to François.

'We will hope and pray that in the future, when it is finally ready, we will be winning medals for it,' he said.

Ally noticed Jack was looking in mild bewilderment around the table.

'François was just saying that he hopes this wine will win him some awards,' she translated into English.

'Ah, thanks. I've been here for a few weeks, and even though I'm doing my best to build up my vocabulary, they speak too fast for me to understand more than the odd sentence.'

'French is a hard language to learn. I was lucky because my father made sure my sisters and I were bilingual from the cradle. It's the only way.'

'I agree. My mum can speak decent French and read Latin and Greek, but it wasn't a gift that was passed on to me, I'm afraid,' said Jack. 'Sorry, I didn't catch your name?'

'I'm Ally, Ally D'Aplièse.' Ally held her breath to see if he recognised her surname.

'Jack McDougal. As you've just been told, I'm from New Zealand. And where are you from?'

'Geneva, in Switzerland,' Ally said, relief flooding through her that he obviously didn't know who she was. Ginette brought out a tray of food and Jack immediately stood up to help her, loading platters of salad and bread onto the table.

'Geneva, eh? I've never been there, or anywhere else in Europe for that matter, other than France. Is it a good place to live?' he asked as people around the table began to help themselves to the food.

'Yes, it's beautiful. We live on the lake with a lovely view of the mountains. But actually, at the moment, I'm living in Norway. Geneva is my family home,' she said as Jack offered her a platter of tuna salad. 'Thanks,' she said, taking the wooden spoon and doling a good portion onto her plate because she was starving.

'A quick warning: don't eat too much of this – it's only the starter. We have steak coming up after, and then, of course, cheese,' he grinned. 'Wow, do the French eat well.'

Ally could hear that his accent sounded vaguely Australian, but softer.

'Thanks for the warning. I'm actually really hungry. It was a long drive down here today.'

'How far?'

'Oh, it's almost four hundred kilometres from Geneva, but there's a pretty good *autoroute*.'

'So, why are you down here?'

'I'm . . . house-hunting.'

'I don't blame you. If I didn't have a vineyard to run in New Zealand and the language wasn't so hard, I'd be here like a shot.'

'How come you're such a long way from home?' Ally asked as she took a forkful of the salad – a mix of crisp green beans, tomatoes, egg and tuna, with a sharp creamy dressing.

'I'm here to learn the whys and wherefores of French wine-making to see if I can apply some of their old traditions and new ideas to our own wines. And maybe try some new combos of grapes too. I mean,' he said, taking a swig of his wine, 'if I could make something that comes even close to this, I'd die happy.'

'So you're passionate about wine?'

'Totally. I grew up on the vineyard that my father founded. He was one of the first to set up in New Zealand, and he and Mum went through blood, sweat and a load of sacrifices to get the vineyard to where it is today. It's the family legacy, so to speak. My father died a few months ago, so now it's all down to me. I miss the old boy. He might have been a pain at times, but not having him there with me has been tough.'

As he reached for the bottle to pour himself another glass, Ally could hardly believe how the conversation was flowing between them. Jack seemed so open, so natural . . . no airs and graces whatsoever.

She helped clear the plates with Ginette, and then brought out dishes of tiny roasted potatoes and broad beans, while Ginette delivered a *filet de boeuf* to her husband to be portioned out between the diners.

'*Mon Dieu!*' Ally said as she tasted the tender steak – pink in the middle, just how she liked it. 'This is delicious.'

'Everything here is, and this steak is a real treat, as the meat in New Zealand is more lamb than beef,' Jack smiled. 'Mind you, we are getting more head of cattle around the place these days. So, Ally, you said earlier that you have sisters?'

'Yes, I do,' Ally said, suddenly realising she must tread carefully. 'Five in all.'

'Wow! I've got one sister, and she's quite enough, thanks.'

'Are you two close?' she asked, steering the conversation back to him.

'These days, yeah, we are. She's adopted, actually. I was ten when she arrived so we never really grew up together, but we've got closer as we've got older. She was very cut up about Dad dying. She's only twenty-two, y'see. She feels a bit cheated, I suppose, because she didn't have him around for long. And of course, my mum misses him like crazy.'

'I'll bet she does. I managed to lose both my father and my fiancé last year, so it sounds like we've both had a bit of a time.'

'Did you? I'm so sorry, Ally. The most I can say about the past year is that it's hopefully produced a pretty good pinot noir. It'll be my first batch,' said Jack. 'Is that why you're here?'

'What do you mean?'

'Well, my mum's off somewhere at the moment on a world tour. Maybe women need to get away when something bad happens . . . not that I mean you have, or anything. Sorry, I know nothing about your circumstances at all.'

Ally saw Jack's face reddening in embarrassment. 'Don't apologise. You might be right. I think everyone reacts in their different ways to grief – all my sisters definitely did. On the other hand . . .' Ally turned to Jack and smiled in the dimming light. 'You're a long way from home, too.'

'Touché!' he said, clinking his glass against hers. 'Although my trip was actually planned before my dad died, so I have an excuse. Whatever gets you through, that's what I say.'

There was another pause as both of them helped collect the used dishes and then bring the cheese to the table. Someone had lit the lanterns, which cast a soft glow under the loggia.

'So, Miss . . . Christ, I've forgotten your surname.'

'D'Aplièse.'

'So, Miss D'Aplièse,' Jack continued as the dessert wine was being passed around, 'I seem to have, as usual, blurted out everything about myself. What about you? I mean, what's your passion?'

'I trained as a flautist, but then I got sidetracked and ended up sailing in some pretty big races. This time last year I was down in Greece in the Aegean Sea. Then I did the Fastnet and—'

'*What?!* I can't believe you were racing the Fastnet! That's like, well, the ultimate sailing challenge, and means that you're at the top of your game. Where I live in the Gibbston Valley, the lakes are where it's at, so I took some lessons and loved it. Then during my gap year, I joined a crew and took sailing trips around the NZ coast. It was nothing like proper racing, of course – just for pleasure – but there's just something about being out on the ocean, isn't there?'

'There is, yes. I'm impressed, Jack. There aren't many people who even know what the Fastnet Race is! Sadly, that's when I lost my fiancé. He was captaining our boat. We ran into stormy weather, and . . . well, he died trying to save the life of one of our crew.'

'Christ, I'm so sorry, Ally. Actually, I think I may have read about the accident in a newspaper. They always say, don't they, that what the sea gives, it takes away. And you sure lost a lot.'

'Yes, I did, but at least . . .' Ally was about to tell Jack about Bear, but something stopped her. 'I'm recovering now.'

'So, how long are you staying here?'

'I don't know yet,' she hedged.

'Well, if you're around for a while, maybe we could head to Marseille and rent a boat for a day. I'll be second mate and you can show me how it's really done.'

'That sounds appealing, although I doubt I'll have time. I love the Med – it's a breeze compared to the Celtic Sea and the Atlantic.'

'So who's at home in Geneva? Your mum, your sisters?' he asked.

'Ma's still at home, but my sisters have flown the nest.' Again, Ally purposely turned the conversation back to Jack. 'Excuse me if I'm sounding nosy, but why do you think your parents adopted your sister ten years after you? I mean . . . had they always planned to adopt, or was it some other reason?'

'I'm not sure, to be honest. Y'know what parents are like with their kids – they don't go into detail. I was only ten and didn't ask. The way I remember it is, one day I came home from school and there was Mary-Kate in my mum's arms, with my dad looking on. He was completely besotted with her actually. In those early years it used to tick me off, t'be honest.'

'Being an only child for a long time and then suddenly being presented with a new baby sister must have been tough.'

'Yeah, too right,' Jack grinned. 'Suddenly I wasn't the centre of attention anymore. But once I turned eighteen, I went off to uni and got over myself. In retrospect, it was a good thing. I was probably a spoilt brat when I was growing up, and gave my sis a bit of a hard time, y'know? Teasing her and stuff. Mary-Kate's great these days and we get on really well, and Dad's death has defo brought us closer.'

Coffee arrived, which Ally drank, along with a large glass of water from the stoneware jug on the table.

'Try a little Beaumes-de-Venise? It's local nectar in a glass, literally,' Jack asked as he lifted up his own.

'No thanks. I've already drunk far more than I normally do.'

'I've drunk far more than I normally do every night since I arrived!' He laughed. 'Wine here is simply part of the daily menu. They even make my dad look sober, and he drank a bottle of wine a day. Just out of interest, how have you ended up in Norway?'

'As a matter of fact, I was adopted too. I traced my birth family to Norway, which is why I moved there. My birth mum is dead, but I live with my twin brother Thom. My biological dad, Felix – who would think all this alcohol was paradise – lives just up the hill from us in Bergen.'

'D'you think it's a good idea? I mean, to pursue your birth family? My sis told me over the phone recently that she'd had a couple of girls turn up on her doorstep, saying there might be some connection to their family. I don't know the details, but I just wonder what you think?'

Ally swallowed and wished she *had* taken a glass of the dessert wine. Having thought she'd have to prise information out of this man, it all seemed to be coming up more or less naturally in the conversation.

'To be honest, I don't think I ever considered it until Pa died,' said Ally. 'He was . . . well, he was just enough, if you know what I mean. For me, anyway. In answer to your question, finding my birth family was fantastic, but then again, I'd lost the two loves of my life within a few months of each other, so to find I had a brother and a biological father – no matter how much of a soak he is – was wonderful.'

'Well, maybe now Dad's gone and Mary-Kate seems to have been contacted by these girls, she'll look into her birth family too. I hope she's as lucky as you.'

'So she doesn't know who her birth parents were?'

'No,' Jack shrugged. 'As I can't remember Mum and Dad going far to get her or anything, it must have been a local adoption.' He took a swig of his dessert wine. 'Wow, this is some conversation we're having, Ally. I hope I haven't said anything to upset you.'

'Not at all. Sometimes it's easier to talk with strangers about these things than it is to talk to the people you love, isn't it?'

'True, though I hope you won't be a stranger over the next couple of days. It's been good to talk to someone in English for a change,' he grinned. 'So, are you off house-hunting tomorrow?'

'I've written down the names of some *immobiliers* that are very good,' Ginette piped up in French as she poured them both more coffee. 'I'll go to the kitchen and get them.'

'Actually, I'm tired from my drive today, so I think I'll be heading for my bed now anyway.' Ally stood up, feeling her breasts heavy with milk, ready for Bear's night-time feed. 'Goodnight, Jack, it's been a pleasure to meet you.'

'And you, Ally. Hopefully I'll see you around in the next couple o'days,' he said as Ally followed Ginette into the kitchen.

'*À bientôt,*' she replied with a smile.

'There you are.' Ginette handed her an old envelope on which she'd jotted down the names and numbers of three *immobiliers*.

'Thank you so much for a wonderful evening. The food was amazing.'

'*Merci*, Ally, I am happy you enjoyed yourself,' she said as she led Ally to the front door. 'You and Jack seemed to be getting on very well,' she added, opening the door.

'Oh, that's just because we both speak English,' Ally said,

feeling her face getting hot. 'He seems like a very nice guy, though.'

'He is, and it was good for him to have someone who spoke his language. I worry he feels left out from our conversations over dinner, but what can you do? *Bonne nuit*, Ally.'

'*Bonne nuit*, Ginette, and thank you again.'

24

Ally woke up the following morning, rolled over to check the time on the old clock radio, and was stunned to see it was past ten o'clock.

She rolled onto her back, spread out her arms and legs and enjoyed the sensation of feeling rested – albeit with a slight headache from too much wine. Reaching for her mobile, she checked there had been no overnight messages from Atlantis, then saw a text from Star saying, **Call me!**

Not inclined quite yet to break the feeling of peace, she got out of bed to make coffee, then sat cross-legged on the soft mattress, sipping it and looking out of the window across the vineyard. She couldn't remember when she'd last enjoyed an evening more than last night. The gorgeous setting, combined with the convivial and welcoming company, had been a joy. There'd been lots of laughter around the table, and of course, her conversation with Jack had been a minefield, but still, a pleasure too.

They'd spoken so openly, like she used to with Theo, yet the two men could not have been more different: Theo, an intellectual at heart, despite his 'day job' as a sailor, and Jack, intelligent and obviously thoughtful, but a less complex soul than her fiancé. Even in the looks department, Theo had not been tall, even though he was strong, and his tanned skin and dark hair contrasted completely with Jack's height and fair features. 'Ally, honestly!' she chided herself, feeling almost as if she was betraying Theo by enjoying another man's company. But it was the first time she had done so since his death, and it was okay to make a new friend, whether they be male or female, surely?

Is that all it is, though . . . ?

'So why didn't you tell him about Bear, or come clean about why you're really here?' she murmured as she stood to top up her coffee.

The truth was, she didn't know – or maybe didn't *want* to know – the reason just now.

Her mobile rang on the bed next to her, and having checked it wasn't Atlantis but Star again, Ally didn't feel up to speaking to her until she'd got her thoughts in order. Her feelings of guilt intensified as she thought about Jack's honesty, when she was here under completely false pretences.

Sighing, she picked up the mobile and placed a call to Atlantis. 'Hi, Ma, how's Bear?'

'He is perfect, Ally. I've just taken him for a walk, and now he is sleeping peacefully in his pram in the shade of the oak tree just beyond the terrace—'

'Where you used to put all of us,' Ally finished for her with a smile.

'And how are you, *chérie*? How is my beautiful Provence?'

'Beautiful indeed. The *cave* owners I'm staying with are lovely too and I slept really well last night. So thanks to both you and Maia for persuading me to come. How is she, by the way?'

'Oh, the same,' Ma said, 'but . . . well, it is the way these things are, *n'est-ce pas?*'

Ma knows Maia is pregnant, Ally thought instantly.

'She is in her Pavilion, sorting through a few things she

wishes to take back to Brazil,' Ma continued, 'and making it ready for when Floriano and Valentina arrive. She has her mobile if you wish to speak to her, but I should tell you that Star is eager to get in touch with you. Perhaps you can call her?'

'Of course.'

'When do you think you will be back, Ally?'

'As soon as possible, but I've still got some information to gather.'

'Take as long as you wish, *chérie*, I am loving my time being *grandmère* to your dear little boy.'

'Thanks, Ma. Give him the biggest hug from me, won't you?'

'Of course. Goodbye, Ally.'

Having dressed in a pair of shorts and a T-shirt, Ally munched on some now rather stale baguette with butter, and decided she must go and find the nearest supermarket to buy supplies. Pulling on a cap and sunglasses to try to stop the incessant march of the freckles across her already pink-tinged face, she went and sat outside to enjoy the mellow morning breeze while she spoke to Star.

'Hi, Ally, how are you?'

'I'm fine, thank you. You sound a bit breathless, is everything all right?'

'Yes, I just wanted to know if you managed to locate Mrs McDougal's son at the *cave*?'

'I did. In fact, I sat next to him at dinner all night.'

'Ooh! That's fantastic, Ally. Did you find out anything about Mary-Kate's birth parents?'

'Nothing, I'm afraid. Although we did have a very open conversation about adoption. He said he just remembers his parents arriving home with Mary-Kate one afternoon, so he thought it was a local adoption. His mother doesn't seem to

have warned him to avoid anything to do with us D'Aplièse
sisters, but he did say that Mary-Kate had mentioned CeCe
and Chrissie's visit to him when they last spoke on the phone.
And that he thought she might want to find out more about
her birth family. He was so friendly, I feel awful about not
coming clean to him about why I'm here. What's happened at
that end? Has Merry run away again?'

'We don't think so, no. Orlando followed her yesterday to
Clerkenwell – she was apparently headed for the records of
births, marriages and deaths. He trailed her back to the hotel,
then she disappeared into her room, and I got a call to my
suite at around six p.m. to say she wasn't feeling well and
could we leave having dinner together. She said she was going
to call back this morning to let us know how she felt and
whether she could have lunch with us. The problem is, that a)
I have to return to Kent to pick up Rory from school, and b)
Orlando needs to get back to the bookshop. Obviously he'll
stay on if Merry agrees to lunch, but . . . oh, I don't know, it
just all feels wrong. Even Orlando is depressed, which he very
rarely is. I just feel bad that she's scared of us and we're still
pursuing her. I mean, it's not the end of the world if Mary-
Kate can't be there for the laying of the wreath, is it, Ally?
Having seen that ring with my own eyes, I do think it's the
same one as in the picture, but maybe we should just wait
until poor Merry has enjoyed her world tour and is back
home with her daughter. Then they can decide together
whether Mary-Kate wants to meet us all.'

'I know what you mean,' Ally sighed. 'Well, I'll call you
later if I bump into Jack again, but I'm not going to engineer
it, Star.'

'No. I totally understand. I've got to go now. Bye, Ally,
speak soon.'

Ally came off the phone, like Orlando, feeling vaguely

depressed by the whole situation. There was part of her that just wanted to forget all about her initial motivation, and simply enjoy the feeling of calm she'd woken up with. She was about to get up and take a walk up to the farmhouse to see if Ginette could point her in the direction of the local supermarket when Jack suddenly appeared from around the corner.

'Morning. I'm not disturbing you, am I?' He pointed to the mobile still cradled in Ally's hands.

'Not at all. Would you like to sit down?'

'Sorry, I can't. I'm actually here to ask whether you need any food supplies. François is out at meetings about the upcoming harvest, so when I'm at a loose end, Ginette sends me to the village to do some shopping for her. She says it's good for my French,' he grinned.

'As a matter of fact, I was just about to go and ask her where the nearest supermarket was. And the local *immobilier*, of course,' she added quickly. 'I should get registered there at least.'

'Why don't I give you a lift into Gigondas? We can kill two birds with one stone and you can help me out in the supermarket, so I don't get my *ananas* mixed up with my *anis*!'

'Okay, but are you sure you don't want me to follow you in my car? Otherwise you'll have to wait for me to go to the *immobilier* office.'

'I don't mind. While François is out, it's either me sitting around, poring over a French dictionary to find out what a particular viticulture phrase means, or having a beer in the sun in beautiful Gigondas.'

'You could always do both at the same time,' Ally pointed out, and they chuckled.

'Right, I'll leave you to get whatever you need and meet you by the car in ten, okay?'

'Okay, thanks, Jack.'

'No problem.'

Arriving in the picturesque village of Gigondas, which Jack explained was one of the finest *appellations* in the region, Ally saw it was crammed with tourists, keen to sample the wines on offer from local *caves*. The cafés were humming with conversation, the diners seated at tables spilling out onto the pavements. They struggled to find a parking space for Ginette's battered Citroën.

'What a gorgeous little place this is,' Ally commented as they walked down the hill in the bright sunshine.

'It is, yeah. Right, let's dive into the supermarket and get the stuff from Ginette's list, shall we?' said Jack, entering a narrow shop which was like a Tardis on the inside, stretching right back and packed to the gills with foodstuffs.

'Okay, but I'm not going to help you,' Ally told him firmly. 'Making mistakes is the only way to learn languages.'

They each collected a basket and went their separate ways, before meeting at the till.

'Could you at least check that the stuff I've got corresponds with what's on the list?' he asked her as they waited in the queue to pay.

Ally did a quick search of the basket and checked the products off the list. 'Almost perfect, but she wants *demi-écrémé*, not *entier* milk.'

'Great, thanks,' he said and whizzed off to exchange the carton.

After dumping the bags in the car, Jack walked her along the street until they stood in front of the *immobilier* office. Ally tried the door, but it was firmly shut.

'Damn! It's literally one minute past midday and they've locked their door. Typical bloody French,' Jack chuckled.

'Lunch always comes first. Sorry – we're speaking in English, so I keep forgetting that you're actually French.'

'No, Jack, I'm Swiss, remember?'

'O'course, sorry,' he said as they walked back up through the village towards the car. 'Actually, I think the French have got their priorities absolutely right: enjoying the good things in life is what it's all about. You're only here once, after all,' said Jack.

'If you were my sister Tiggy, she'd disagree with you on that.'

'Really? Listen,' Jack said, pointing to an outdoor café swarming with lunchtime diners, 'why don't we hang around here until the *immobilier* reopens at two? Unless you have something else to do?'

'I don't, but doesn't Ginette need her shopping?'

'Not until later, and she's probably glad to see the back of me for a while. Shall we?'

'Why not?'

At the café, Jack indicated a free table for two and they sat down. 'Beer? Wine?' he asked. 'As I'm here, I'm going to grab some lunch too. You?'

'A glass of rosé for me, and yes, this menu looks delicious.'

'Well, if we can ever get any service, we'll order,' Jack rolled his eyes. 'I once waited twenty minutes for someone to even notice I was breathing over here. It wouldn't happen in New Zealand, that's for sure.'

'I've heard it's a beautiful country, from everyone who's been there.'

'It is, yeah, it just about has everything, y'know? Skiing in the winter, hot weather and beaches in the summer, and the interior – where I live – is sweet as. All it's lacking outside the towns and cities is people. Our nearest neighbour is a fifteen-minute drive away. So if you like solitude, it's great.'

'So, do you? Like solitude?'

'Not after I came back from uni, I didn't, but I suppose I got used to it. Then you come to a place like this, a little village that's just buzzing, and you wonder what the hell you're doing. Still, I'm not complaining. I love what I do, and I live in a stunning part of the world.'

'New Zealand's actually on my bucket list to visit one day,' she said as she raised her menu at a passing waiter, who blatantly ignored her.

'It goes without saying that we'd be happy to host you at The Vinery anytime. Another problem with the Gibbston Valley is that all the young have gone to the towns and cities, and it's mostly oldies living around me. I look forward to the company of backpackers touring the area, who sometimes hitch up in The Vinery to bag a bunk for the night.'

Ally flapped her menu at the waiter as he returned and finally, their order for beer, rosé, a jug of water and two steak hachés was taken.

'So, I presume your parents are Kiwis?' she said.

'No Kiwi is an "original", if you know what I mean, other than the Maori,' said Jack. 'Most of the population have emigrated from somewhere else. I was born there, but my dad's parents were originally from Scotland, hence the McDougal. And my mum hails from Dublin in Ireland. But yeah, I guess they'd both call themselves Kiwis, having lived there so long.'

'Do your parents ever go back to visit Scotland and Ireland?'

'I think Dad went back a couple of times with his parents, but Mum's never been back to Ireland as far as I know. I mean, there's a pic of her receiving a degree from uni there but I reckon that when people begin a new life, they want to focus on the present, not the past.'

'I'd agree,' she said as the waiter dumped two jugs, a bottle of beer and some glasses on the table. Ally peered into both of the jugs looking for the water.

'*Mon Dieu!* One jug is full of rosé. I only asked for a glass!'

'That's not the way they do things round here,' Jack smiled as he poured her both water and rosé. 'Cheers!'

'Cheers,' said Ally, raising her glass. 'Going back to your mum, as I told you last night, when I went in search of my own heritage, parts of it were painful and parts of it were fantastic.'

'Well, Mum did mention that she's going to visit Ireland at some point on her tour.'

'Right. Is she on this holiday by herself?'

'Yeah. MK – that's what I call my little sis – and I weren't too happy about it, but Mum's pretty independent and seriously clever, y'know? T'be honest, I've never understood why she buried herself in the Gibbston Valley with my dad and didn't use her degree.'

'Maybe because she loved your father,' Ally suggested. 'Love can change everything.'

'True, but I'm yet to experience that feeling, to be honest. You obviously have.'

'Yes, and even if I never feel it again, at least I know I had it once. So your sister's holding the fort in New Zealand while you and your mum are away?'

'Not really – we have a very good manager who sorts out the vineyard. My sister's a budding singer-songwriter, and she's working on stuff with a guy she met at uni.'

'Wow. This is a terrible question, but . . . is she any good?'

'As you're never likely to meet her, I can be honest,' Jack chuckled. 'And the answer is, I haven't a clue. She's obsessed with Joni Mitchell and her type – all angsty lyrics – whereas I was born a decade before her and like a good tune, y'know?'

'I do know,' Ally agreed. 'Something "feel good" that you

can bop along to and shout out the lyrics. I was playing that kind of music on the drive down here.'

'This might be a rude thing to ask a lady, but would you be near my age? I'm thirty-two.'

'I'm thirty-one.'

'So, we're from the same generation and like a good anthem,' he grinned. The two steak hachés arrived and Jack asked for another beer.

'You are driving,' Ally reminded him.

'Yeah, but there's a lot of me to soak up the booze. They're only small bottles, Ally, and I'd never take the risk of being over.'

'I understand, and the good news is, because you are driving, I can have as much of this as I want,' she smiled as she poured herself a second glass of rosé.

'So, tell me about your sister Tiggy. She sounds interesting,' Jack said as he dug into his steak.

'Oh, my sisters are all interesting, and we couldn't be more different from each other.'

'In what way?

As she ate, Ally regaled Jack with a potted biography of each of them, being careful to use CeCe's proper name, Celaeno, in case his sister had mentioned her. When she got to Electra, Jack gave the usual response.

'I can't believe you're related to her! Her pic has been everywhere here in the past week. Wow, it makes my family seem so dull,' sighed Jack. 'Your dad sounds like he was a real philanthropist to adopt you girls.'

'He was, and an incredible man too. Like your mum, he was very clever.'

'What did he do?'

'Believe it or not, none of us are actually sure. We knew he ran a business of some kind, but what exactly, I've no idea. He was away a lot, travelling.'

'D'you think he was a spy?'

'Maybe, but I'm not sure spies make as much money as Pa did,' Ally chuckled. 'We were brought up in real luxury, although interestingly, he never gave any of us more than a basic allowance. We've all had to fend for ourselves financially.'

'Well, if it's any comfort, you certainly don't come across as a spoilt brat.'

'It is. Thanks.'

'Apart from that swanky car you arrived in,' Jack teased her. 'That's a cracker, f'sure. Is it yours?'

'It belonged to Pa, but any of us could use it if we wanted to. Of course, when Pa died, none of us wanted to deal with the nuts and bolts of our finances. Luckily, we've had people to run the trust he left for us, but we're going to organise a meeting with our lawyer in the next few weeks to have it explained to us. It's time we all grew up and took responsibility.'

'That all sounds far too complicated to me. At least when you don't have much, you don't have a lot to sort out,' Jack shrugged. 'When my dad died, the house passed to Mum, and the wine business to the three of us. End of. Coffee?'

'I think I'd better,' Ally agreed. 'The *immobilier* should be open soon, so after coffee, I'll go and register.'

'Okay, and hey, Ally, don't think I've got a problem with you coming from money or anything. It's completely to your father's credit and yours that I'd never have guessed it.'

'Apart from the car,' they both said at the same time, then laughed.

'This is my treat,' Ally said when the waitress arrived, and she slapped some euros on the table.

'Actually, little rich girl, it's definitely mine,' Jack said, slapping his euros down equally hard.

Having agreed to go dutch, they walked to the *immobilier*, where Ally registered and, given the fact she was feeling uncomfortable about Jack thinking she was a spoilt princess, made a point of looking for properties under two hundred thousand euros.

'That one's nice,' said Jack, peering over her shoulder at the listings.

'It's an old wreck and the last thing I want is to have to employ a team of builders to renovate something. What about this one?'

As they debated about the imaginary properties she might buy, Ally felt like a complete charlatan.

'Come on, let's go back to the *cave*. I'm feeling too depressed now I've seen what's available for the money I've got to spend. And no, I can't go any higher,' she said pointedly as they walked outside and along the narrow street towards their car. 'So, are you actually managing to learn anything at all whilst you're here, considering the language barrier?'

'Yeah, I've learnt a sackload of stuff,' he said as they climbed into the car and he started up the engine. 'A lot of it is watching the practical process, so you don't need words to explain what they're doing. The problem is, the soil here is more alkaline than it is back at home, but I'm definitely gonna try growing a few different vines and test out the mix of grapes they use here for the Châteauneuf-du-Pape.'

'How much longer are you staying?'

'Technically, until after the harvest. In reality, I could stay in Europe longer if I wanted, because it's the quiet period for me at the vineyard back home. So I just might go visit some other countries whilst I've got the chance. Y'never know, I might pitch up in Norway.'

'Feel free to do so,' Ally said as they arrived back at the

cave, and she got out of the car to help Jack take the shopping inside.

'Good afternoon,' Ginette said as she stood in the court-yard. 'I wondered where you two had got to. Can you take that shopping into the kitchen? I have to collect the children from school.'

'O'course,' Jack agreed.

'Oh, and Ally? You are very welcome to eat with us again tonight.'

'Thanks, Ginette,' Ally said as she followed Jack into the kitchen. The room – in fact, the whole farmhouse – was in need of renovation, she thought, as she unpacked the bags and stowed perishables into the fridge.

'Does François make any money from his wine?' she asked Jack.

'Not a lot, because any spare profit he makes is just poured back into expanding the vineyard or updating the machinery. The oak barrels down in the cellar are over a hundred years old. Last winter, they got a shedload of rain, so he's had to spend a lot of money making it watertight. That's climate change for you,' Jack shrugged. 'All right, I need a cuppa.'

'A cuppa?'

'A cuppa tea,' Jack explained as he took the kettle and filled it from the tap. 'They don't go big on tea here in Provence. I had to go and buy this myself,' he added as he switched it on. 'And the teabags. Want one?'

'Oh, I'm fine, actually. I'm going to walk back to my *gîte*. I have a few phone calls to make.'

'Okay. You coming over tonight?'

'I . . . does Ginette invite all her guests to eat with the family?'

'Only the ones she likes. So she obviously likes you.'

'I don't want to impose.'

'Let me promise you that if Ginette didn't want you, she wouldn't have asked. It's her that rules the roost around here, not François. Like all women, I suppose,' Jack smiled. 'See you later?'

'Okay, yes. Bye, Jack.'

Ally walked back through the vines with her own bag of shopping, which would now be redundant as she was having supper at the farmhouse. Pouring herself a large glass of water to try and ward off the headache she always got if she drank at lunchtime, she went to sit outside and dug in her handbag to check her mobile, which had been on silent ever since she'd left for Gigondas with Jack this morning. As she'd expected, there were a number of missed calls. None of them were from Atlantis, thank God, just from Star. Ally dialled her number.

'Hi, Star, it's me. I haven't listened to any messages you've left, so tell me, what's happened?'

'I'm afraid we've lost her, Ally. Even though Orlando sat in the hotel lobby all day, he nipped to the loo and came back to find she'd gone. I'm back in Kent, just about to go and collect Rory, and Orlando is following on by train. We've no idea where she's gone, Ally. The trail is cold.'

'Oh dear.' Ally bit her lip. 'I'm sorry, Star. I know you tried really hard to get her to talk.'

'We did. Orlando's furious with himself for missing her. The doorman on duty was told to watch out for her, but apparently, a big party of guests had just arrived. She somehow managed to slip out. Are you still at the *cave*?'

'Yes. I've spent most of the day with Jack – he took me to the local village so I could visit the *immobilier*, but it was shut, so we had lunch. Honestly, Star, he doesn't know anything much about his family's past. He told me that his mum was from Dublin in Ireland and had a degree from Trinity – which we already knew – but I'm afraid that's all. I'm seeing him tonight as I'm having dinner up at the farmhouse again, but I feel really uncomfortable about probing him any further.'

'Orlando is convinced it's to do with any mention of the missing sister. Maybe you should ask Jack if that means anything to him.'

'No, Star, I couldn't. Sorry, but he's such a nice guy and I'm a terrible liar. It's now blatantly obvious his mum is avoiding us, and I'm thinking that maybe we should give the whole thing up for now.'

There was a pause on the line.

'I understand, Ally, and I agree. Anyway, it sounds like you've struck up a friendship with Jack at least. What's he like?'

'Lovely.' The word was out of Ally's mouth before she could stop it.

'Really?' Star chuckled. 'I haven't heard you say that about a man since, well . . . Anyway, just forget everything else and enjoy dinner tonight. I've got to be off now to fetch Rory. Bye, Ally.'

'Bye, Star.'

As she approached the farmhouse that evening, Ally felt totally conflicted. So much of her just wanted to enjoy the dinner and Jack's company, to go with the flow of the evening. Another part of her felt a need to tell Jack the real reason why she was here. She'd always tried to live her life as honestly as she could, albeit without hurting anyone by blurting out what she really thought, like Electra and CeCe often did. So if she were Jack, and down the line discovered that the friendly woman he had spent time with over the past twenty-four hours had only been trying to pump him for information, she wouldn't want anything to do with that person again.

Does it matter if that happens? she pondered. *And if so, why . . . ?*

'Because he's a nice, decent guy, who treated you like a normal human being, not a victim,' she told herself as she marched up to the front door. 'Just drink wine, lots of it,' she muttered as she went to say hello to Ginette in the kitchen.

'I've brought you something small just to say thank you for being an incredible host,' said Ally. 'Sorry if it's a bit boring, but it's quite hard to think of anything to bring when you're hosted by a *cave* in one of the most beautiful places in the world. Even your flower beds are full of gorgeous specimens.' Ally pointed to a freshly picked bunch displayed in a vase on the kitchen table.

'Oh! Ladurée macarons! What a treat, thank you. Please, put them in the drawer over there so I can eat them all myself! You are leaving tomorrow?'

'Yes, sadly I must, but I'd love to come back again another time and stay for longer.'

'Did you see any houses that interested you?'

'No, it seems that properties here are far more expensive than I had thought.'

'Or maybe you were too distracted to look . . .' Ginette's eyes danced as she held up a courgette. 'I hear Monsieur Jack and you enjoyed lunch together earlier.' She smiled mischievously as she took a sharp knife to the courgette and began to chop it.

'Jack and I enjoyed talking because I speak English.'

'*Mon Dieu!*' Ginette ran a hand through her wavy dark hair. 'Why is everyone so afraid of saying that they are attracted to each other these days? It was obvious from the moment you sat down at the table last night that the two of you had chemistry. Everyone who saw you commented on it. This is France, Ally, we invented the word "love". So what if you do want to spend a night, a week, a month or maybe a lifetime together? Those moments when you first meet someone who is as attracted to you as you are to them are so rare. And at the moment, everything is simple. No baggage has been unloaded, no soul explored . . .' Ginette gave a very Gallic shrug. 'What's not to enjoy? Now, if you are headed outside, can you take that tray of plates with you?'

'Of course,' Ally said, picking up the stacked tray, glad to have something to do. Maybe Ginette was right: she should just enjoy her last evening in the company of someone she liked. And – possibly – found attractive too.

Having received a warm welcome from everyone at the table, Ally was directed to the same seat as last night, next to Jack.

'Good evening,' he said, filling up her glass from a stoneware jug, rather than a bottle, as she sat down. 'We're on the usual Côtes du Rhône tonight, by the way. Basic table wine, but it's still a ripper.'

'Oh, I'm not fussy, I'll drink anything that's put in front of me.'

'Will you, eh? So it's vodka shots later, is it?'

'I didn't mean it like that, but if you're at sea for a while and you come into port with a load of thirsty men, you certainly learn how to handle your alcohol. *Santé.*' Ally raised her glass and smiled at him.

'*Santé.* I bet you kept them all in order, didn't you?' Jack teased her.

'As a matter of fact, I didn't at all. After the usual sexist comments, we'd push off out to sea and by the time we came back, they were calling me "Al" and barely noticed my gender.

I'd always pretend I was a rubbish cook so they wouldn't assign me to the galley on account of me being a woman.'

'And *are* you a rubbish cook?'

'Possibly,' Ally chuckled.

'What puzzles me is that in most of the houses I visited as a child, there were always mums in the kitchens, yet most of the really famous chefs are male. Why do you think that is?'

'I'm not sure I want to get into an argument about gender politics just now, Jack.' Ally knocked back another gulp of wine.

'You mean, you might end up slugging me over the head with that wine jug?'

'Hopefully it wouldn't be that dramatic, but after years in male-dominated environments, I certainly have a few things to say. Yup,' she agreed with herself and Jack poured her another glass of wine.

'Well, it's worth adding that my mum brought me up to have complete respect for the opposite sex, i.e. you lot,' he grinned. 'She taught me how to cook pasta, a roast and make a tuna salad – she said those three dishes would see me through any occasion.'

'Is she a good cook?'

'She's certainly no *cordon bleu*, but a legend at managing to produce a big pot of something tasty for large numbers from what's left lying around. Because of where we live, we can't just run round the corner to the local shop, y'know? She's fanatical about leftovers being eaten up – probably something to do with her childhood. These things usually are, from what little I know about psychology.'

'I . . .' Even though Ally was genuinely interested *beyond* gaining information on his mum, she still felt guilty for prob- ing. 'Do you think she had a tough childhood?'

'As I said, she doesn't talk about it, and I don't think any kid is interested in listening to the 'rents going on about their past. Now my dad is gone, and I can't ask him any more questions, I just keep wishing I had.'

'Same here,' Ally agreed as bowls of crudités and olive oil were placed on the table from anonymous hands above them. 'I can't tell you how many questions I've got now for Pa.'

'From the sound of things, you had a pretty idyllic childhood.' Jack offered her a bowl of crudités.

'Yes. We had just about everything we could ask for. A loving mother figure in our nanny, Ma, Pa's full attention whenever we needed it . . . and each other. I look back now and almost feel it was *too* idyllic. I think that's why Pa sent us all to boarding school when we were thirteen. He wanted us to know what the real world was like.'

'You're saying boarding school is the real world?' Jack queried. 'I mean, to get you there in the first place, your dad would have had to pay. Places like that were only available to the elite and still are, aren't they?'

'Yes, you're right, but mine didn't include any home comforts. It's a bit like being in a learning prison that you have to pay for, and you certainly get to know what humanity is like if you're living with it twenty-four hours a day. You have to learn to fight your own battles, without any kind of support from your parents.'

'So the rich go to boarding school to know what it feels like to be deprived?'

'I think that's a bit of a sweeping statement, but in essence, yes. Would I have wanted to go to a state-run school and be able to go home to my family every night? No matter what was on the table for supper or what kind of house we lived in? When I started boarding, I would have done. Then as I settled down to it and became more independent, I started to realise how privileged I was. The school offered me all sorts of extramural opportunities I'd never have had at a state school.'

'Actually, my mum boarded too and said it was the making of her for the reasons you just mentioned, even though she hated it at first. I wonder what you'll do with your own kids when they come along?'

Jack was looking her right in the eye and Ally could feel a blush rising in her cheeks. Turning her head away and concentrating on her crudités, she shrugged.

'I'm not sure,' she replied lamely.

After a fantastic main course of wild boar, which no one round the table questioned the provenance of, given that shooting was illegal at this time of year, Ally went to the nearest bathroom and expressed some of the milk in her breasts to relieve the pressure and risk of leaking.

After washing her face in cold water, she stared at herself in the mirror.

'Remember what Ginette said,' she whispered, 'and just enjoy. Tomorrow, you're gone.'

'I must head for bed,' Ally said after coffee and a glass of delicious, if unnecessary, Armagnac. 'I have an early start in the morning.'

'Okay, I'll walk you home, shall I?' offered Jack.

Having said her goodbyes, left promises to all that she would return and told Ginette she'd see her early tomorrow morning to settle the bill, she and Jack walked down the now moonlit path to her *gîte*.

'If I was going to buy something here, I think the *gîte* would be almost perfect,' she commented.

'Apart from at harvest time, when it would be pretty noisy.

Plus, you'd have loads of sweaty grape-pickers peering in through your windows first thing in the morning. And spiders creeping in to join you from the vines.'

'Sell it to me, why don't you?' she smiled. 'I was just thinking how picturesque it looked in the moonlight. I wouldn't mind the spiders, after once finding a rat on my mattress on board ship. It must have scuttled in whilst we were in port and had decided to join us for the onward leg.'

'Wow! I guess even I'd have a problem with that. What did you do?'

'Admittedly, I screamed and one of the boys came to my rescue,' Ally laughed.

'Don't worry, I'd have done the same, but you're a hardy lass underneath that delicate exterior, aren't you?'

'I'm not sure about that, but there's not much that scares me these days, apart from losing someone else I care about.'

'Yeah, death puts it all into perspective, doesn't it? The thing that scares me is that I might find myself still working on my vineyard in thirty years' time, old and alone. As I've mentioned, there's not a lot of chances to meet with my own age group – there are any number of ageing single farmers and vintners living around me.'

'Does anyone ever really want to be alone?' sighed Ally.

'Well, better that than settling for someone simply for the sake of not being alone, eh?'

'Absolutely,' Ally agreed.

'Were you and your fiancé together for a long time? Sorry, I don't mean to pry or anything.'

'No, it's fine. Actually, we weren't. It was a whirlwind romance. I just knew that he was The One, and he felt the same, so we got engaged pretty quickly.'

'I get the feeling that's how it was for my mum and dad, although of course, you can never tell what goes on behind closed doors. But when I compare their marriage to a lot of my mates' parents, they always seemed very happy. Never argued, y'know? Or at least, not within earshot of us. I worry about my mum now that dad's gone. She's almost sixty, so it's unlikely she'll meet anyone else.'

'What about all those bachelor farmers you just mentioned?'

'I doubt it. Mum and Dad were together for over thirty-five years. Talking of which, I got a strange call from Mum just before dinner tonight.'

'Really?' Ally's heart began to thump as they reached the entrance to the *gîte*. 'What about?'

'Oh, she wanted to tell me she'd flown over to Dublin earlier today, which is odd as I thought she was staying in New York for a bit to see old friends and then heading to London. I was, like, you must be excited to be back in the home country after all this time, and she was, like, yeah, well, I had to come back here, but you never know who you might meet from your past. It could have just been a joke, but to be honest, Ally, I thought she sounded, well,' Jack shrugged, 'frightened.'

'I . . . maybe everyone's nervous when they go back to the place they came from after so long?'

'Maybe, yeah, but then she said how much she loved me and how proud of me she was and all that kind of stuff. She sounded close to tears. I was wondering whether I should take a flight across to Ireland to make sure she's okay. It's only a couple of hours from Marseille to Dublin, and she just sounded . . . odd. What d'you think?'

Jack looked straight at her and Ally wanted to fall through the ground or disappear in a puff of smoke.

'Well, I – I . . . think that if you're worried about her, then maybe you should go. If it's not that far,' she stuttered.

'I'm still getting my head around the fact that nothing in Europe is that far,' he smiled. 'I'm used to it all being on the other side of the world.'

'Do you know where she's staying? I mean, with friends or . . . ?'

'Yeah, apparently the hotel she's at is called the Merrion, so she joked it was named after her – her nickname's "Merry". Anyway, I'll give her a bell tomorrow morning, see how she sounds and then decide.'

'Good idea. Right, time for my bed,' Ally said, once again feeling a blush running through her cheeks and just wanting to get inside.

'Listen, if I don't get to see you tomorrow, I just wanted to say it's been a pleasure to spend time with you. Could we keep in touch?'

'Of course we can, yes.'

'Great. I'll give you my NZ and my French mobile numbers.'

'And I'll give you my Swiss and Norwegian ones.'

They tapped their numbers into each other's phones.

'Well then, goodnight,' she said, reaching for the *gîte* key from her jean pocket and sticking it into the lock. As she turned it, she felt a pair of hands on her shoulders and jumped.

'Hey, sorry, Ally, I . . .' Jack was standing back with his hands up as though she was about to shoot him. 'I didn't mean to . . . I wasn't gonna . . . shit!'

'Seriously, don't worry. It's just, I'm not . . .'

'Ready?'

'Yes, not just now anyway, but I've really enjoyed spending time with you, Jack, and . . .' She looked up at him. 'Would a hug do?'

'O'course it would,' he smiled. 'Come here.' He pulled her

in towards him and everything about him smelt exactly as she had expected: fresh and natural and clean. She could feel the strength of him, and his height made her feel unusually like a fragile flower.

For all sorts of reasons, she pulled out of his grasp far sooner than she would have wanted to. He bent down and gave her a tender kiss on the cheek.

'*Bonne nuit*, Ally,' he said. 'I hope we meet again soon.'

With a rueful smile, he turned and ambled back up the gravel path to the farmhouse.

Inside, Ally felt short of breath and 'panty', as she'd once described the sensation to Ma when she'd had a panic attack just before she was about to sit her very first flute examination. Sitting down on the bed, she bent forward, trying to slow her breathing. Wondering exactly which part of the last ten minutes had caused this reaction, she reached for the bottle of water by the bed and took a swig from it. Finally, her breathing calmed, as did her pulse. Looking at her mobile, she saw there were no missed calls or new voice messages, which meant Bear was fine. There were texts from Star asking how the evening had gone and another from Maia saying basically the same thing.

Call me! they had both ended.

'Nope.' Ally shook her head. 'Not tonight.' She just wanted to keep the memory of the evening and that delicious hug exactly as it was for a few more hours, until she had to tell her sisters and it became another part of their joint subterfuge. Besides, she decided as she undressed, if Jack did fly to see his mum in Dublin tomorrow, she was bound to tell him about the strange women who were after her to try and claim his sister as one of their own . . .

'And he won't want to keep in touch after that, will he?' she muttered to herself as she got into bed, set the alarm and turned off the light. She lay there staring into the darkness, remembering not only the hug but all the laughter they'd shared. It had been a long time since she'd really laughed, and even if Jack had referred to his lack of academic cleverness, it was obvious to her that he was highly intelligent.

'You don't necessarily need a stack of certificates to be wise,' Pa had once said to her when she had told him how insecure she'd felt about having a degree in music, rather than science or literature.

Jack's wise, she thought, before she drifted off to sleep.

25

Having slept badly, Ally was awake by six thirty and ready to go an hour later. She knew that Ginette would be up, preparing to drop the children at school, so she popped into the kitchen to pay her bill and say goodbye.

'It has been a pleasure to host you, Ally, and please come back and visit us soon,' Ginette said as the children ran in and out of the door, collecting lunchboxes, sports kit and books.

'I'd love to,' Ally responded as all of them walked outside and Ginette planted the region's customary three kisses on Ally's cheeks.

Glad not to have bumped into Jack on her way out, Ally set off for Geneva. Once on the *autoroute*, she pulled into an *aire* to use the facilities and to phone Atlantis.

'Hi, Ma, I'm on my way home. Is Bear okay?'

'You would know already if he wasn't. He's very much looking forward to seeing his *maman*,' Ma added.

'I'm sure that's not true, but thanks for saying it anyway, Ma,' Ally smiled. 'I'll see you later.'

'Maia would like to speak to you.'

'Tell her we'll talk when I get home,' Ally said firmly. 'I have to go now, Ma. Bye.'

Back in the car, Ally switched CDs to some of her favourite

classical pieces and relived every second of the past two days. Which for now, were *hers*, and hers alone . . .

By the time she arrived back at Atlantis, Bear was nodding on Ma's shoulder, ready for his afternoon nap. Taking him up to her bedroom, Ally put him to her breast.

'*Maman*'s home, darling, and she's missed you so much.'

Bear suckled for a few seconds, then his tiny lips let go and he lay back in her arms, fast asleep.

Logically, she was glad he seemed to have suffered no ill effects from her absence, but as she laid him down in his cot, the fact he had so easily ceased to need her still hurt.

She wished she could clamber into bed for a nap herself, but it wasn't fair on Maia, or any of her sisters who had participated in the search for the elusive Merry. She'd already waited since last night to tell them she knew exactly where Merry was. However she felt about her part in the ongoing plot, she had to at least pass on the information.

'Hello, Ally,' said Maia as her sister walked into the kitchen. 'Sorry I wasn't here to greet you when you arrived, Floriano had just called and I needed to speak to him about his flight over here. So, how was Provence?'

'Beautiful, as I said on the phone. Listen, Maia, I'm really tired after the drive, so forgive me if I cut to the chase. Jack told me that he got a call from his mum saying she was in Dublin, Ireland. She's staying at the Merrion Hotel there. The only other detail I got out of him was that she sounded, as he put it, "odd" and "frightened". Given she left London so suddenly, we've definitely scared her and I feel terrible about it.'

'Oh dear, that isn't good,' Maia agreed, 'but I understand. I'm sure it's because she doesn't want the child she's cared for since birth to be claimed by another family. Perhaps she's scared that Mary-Kate might love them more.' Maia looked at Ally and bit her lip. 'Maybe we should just leave this whole thing?'

'That's what I said to Star last night. I mean, Jack is a decent, straightforward guy and I felt awful pretending I was somebody I wasn't – a passing tourist looking to buy a house in the area – especially when he said he was really worried about his mum's state of mind. I think we either have to come clean to Merry, or drop it completely. It's not a game, and I almost get the feeling that Orlando was treating it like one.'

'He was only trying to help, but maybe he enjoys the thrill of the chase too much. I mostly agree with you, Ally, but then again, I can't help thinking of Pa and how long Georg said he'd searched for the missing sister. I remember when I was a teenager, I asked him why our seventh sister had never arrived. And the look on his face was heartbreaking when he told me it was because he'd never found her.' Maia sighed. 'I don't know what we should do, I really don't.'

'Well, whatever it is, I think before we go any further we need to see Merry in person and put her mind at rest that we're not out to get her.'

Maia saw the tension on her sister's face. 'Oh Ally, I was hoping the trip to Provence would provide you with some time out to relax. You seem more tense now than when you left.'

'You know how I am about honesty. I'm just not comfortable with subterfuge and lies. I would have made the most terrible spy.'

'What about sending Tiggy? After all, she's the only other sister who hasn't participated in our search, and absolutely nobody could be frightened of her – she's the gentlest of us all. If anyone can explain to Merry that we mean no harm, then it's her.'

'Yes, that's a great idea, Maia. And Scotland's not very far from Ireland, is it?'

'No, it's not.'

'All right,' Ally said with a sigh, 'let's at least ask her and see what she says.'

Maia took out her mobile and placed the call to Tiggy. To her surprise, after a couple of rings, she heard Tiggy's voice.

'Hello, Maia. I've just read Ally's email about the missing sister and had picked up my mobile to call . . . Is everything all right?'

'Yes, everyone is well here,' Maia replied. 'Ally's with me. How are you?'

'Oh, I'm good, I can't wait to see you both soon. Have you traced the missing sister and her ring yet?' Tiggy asked.

'It's a long story but . . .' Maia explained as briefly as she could what had happened in the past few days.

'We think it might be because she doesn't want Mary-Kate, her daughter, to know about her birth parents,' Maia finished.

'What do you think, Tiggy?' asked Ally.

There was silence on the line for a bit before Tiggy replied. 'It feels to me as if she is . . . frightened.'

'That's interesting, because it's exactly what her son Jack told me after he'd spoken to her yesterday. Would you, and anyone you know . . . well, *upstairs*, have any idea why?' Ally blushed as she referenced Tiggy's spiritual powers, but having witnessed them for herself in Granada, she was definitely a convert.

'I would need to think about it, and it's far easier if I can talk to the person than sense things from far away. But yes, my instinct is that she's afraid.'

'Well' – it was Maia's turn to speak – 'Ally and I were

wondering whether it would be possible for you to do just that – speak to her in person.'

'You have her telephone number?'

'Yes, Orlando got it, but we really need someone to go to see her in person and explain we don't mean any harm,' said Ally. 'We know exactly where she is, which isn't very far from where you are.'

'Everything's far from where I am,' Tiggy chuckled. 'Is she in Scotland?'

'No, Dublin. It can't be more than an hour or two's flight.'

'I probably could – I'm sure Cal can cope without me for a couple of days. It's just, well, the ethical thing that worries me. There's obviously a reason why she's running away and I don't want to scare her further by just appearing out of the blue. Can I think about it?'

'Of course,' Maia agreed, 'and if you don't feel it's right, then we'll leave it.'

'Give me half an hour. Oh, and by the way, Maia, ginger tea might help with your symptoms. Bye.'

The line went dead and both Ally and Maia sat there, staring at each other in surprise.

'I thought you said you hadn't told anybody else about the . . . you know?' Ally whispered, her hand indicating her sister's stomach.

'Ally, I haven't! Truly.'

'Well, I certainly haven't.'

'Then how does she know?' Maia asked.

'She just does,' Ally shrugged. 'In Granada, just before Bear was born, she told me things about Theo and this necklace he'd given me that she couldn't possibly have known about. She . . . she said she saw him standing there. I . . .' Tears pricked Ally's eyes. 'It was a very special moment. Our little sister has a unique gift.'

'Coming from you, Ally, who is always sceptical of any-thing you can't work out logically, that's saying a lot. Let's see what she's decided to do when she calls back.'

The sound of a text pinging through on Ally's mobile made her look down.

Hi, Ally, Jack from Provence/NZ here. Just checking you got back to Geneva safely. It was so great to meet you. Keep in touch and maybe we can get together in Europe before I fly home. Jack.

At the end of the text was one kiss. The sight of it made Ally's stomach flip suddenly.

'Who's that from?' Maia enquired.

'Jack, Merry's son.'

'Really? From your expression, you two obviously got on well.'

'I had to get on with him, didn't I? I had to pump him for information on his mum. I'm going upstairs to see if Bear's awake yet.'

Maia watched her sister walk out of the kitchen, then smiled. 'The lady doth protest too much, methinks,' she quoted from Shakespeare's *Hamlet*.

Later that evening, just as Ally was getting into bed, there was a knock on her bedroom door and Maia appeared.

'Tiggy's said she'll go. She's looking to get on an afternoon flight to Dublin tomorrow. It's less than two hours from Aberdeen.'

'Right. Great. Well, let's hope Merry won't have disappeared again by then, and Tiggy can get a chance to explain.'

'As Tiggy put it, "I doubt she'll have gone far." Anyway, I just thought I'd tell you.'

'I'm so glad she's going. If she does meet Merry, at least she can set the record straight.'

'Yes. Sleep well, Ally.'

'And you.'

Once the door had shut behind Maia, Ally lay back, suddenly feeling conflicted over Tiggy's decision. Morally, it was the right thing to do, but of course it would mean Jack would eventually get to hear from his mother about *her* part in the deception . . .

'For God's sake, Ally, you only knew him for less than forty-eight hours,' she told herself firmly.

But still, she spent ages agonising over whether or what she should text back, and went to sleep thinking about that kiss at the end of his . . .

26

Merry
Dublin, Ireland

I woke up with the alarm, which I'd set for nine o'clock, and lay there feeling rested after the first proper night's sleep I'd had since I'd left New Zealand. Perhaps it was partly to do with the fact that I was on 'home territory' – it felt comforting to be back in Ireland, which was ironic, given why I'd left Dublin all those years ago. Yet knowing that part of me belonged here, that I'd come from the very soil of this proud, unique and beautiful island, had made me emotional since the moment the aeroplane had touched down.

Jock had asked me time and again whether I wanted to visit my family in the 'old country', but I'd always refused. However much I missed them, I knew that they might let something slip to Jock about my hasty departure and, more importantly, because I had to protect them too. The truth was that I hadn't spoken to a single member of my family for thirty-seven years.

Lies, lies, lies . . .

'Enough is enough,' I said out loud to yet another beautifully appointed and furnished hotel room. Just in case there

354

was anyone lurking outside my door listening, I added, 'I'm not afraid anymore!'

I reached over to dial room service and asked for a pot of tea and some biscuits. Biscuits for breakfast felt indulgent, especially the homemade ones that hotels like the Merrion provided, but why shouldn't I indulge myself? I picked up one of the shiny leaflets that had been left by the phone to tempt me. I'd never been to a spa – every time I saw one in my mind, I imagined an ancient Roman bath full of ladies enjoying its restorative properties. I'd recently discovered the modern-day equivalent, which always seemed to be in the hotel basement, where long corridors opened onto treatment rooms filled with tinkling background music emanating from a discreetly hidden CD player. I flicked through the leaflets, wondering whether I would take the plunge and treat myself to one of the many massages on offer, but the menu was as varied and confusing as a Chinese takeaway.

A knock at my door caused my heart to immediately beat faster, but I took a deep breath and answered it. As a waiter greeted me, I thought that perhaps it was the lilting accent, along with the intrinsic Irish friendliness, that put me at ease. He came into the room to set up my breakfast on a small table, and asked me where I'd come from.

'London.'

'Would that be your home?'

'No, I live in New Zealand.'

'Do you now? Well, 'tis a long way you've travelled. I hope you enjoy your stay, Mrs McDougal.'

He left and I picked up the tea he'd poured and drew one of my spare teabags out of my holdall to add it to the pot. I'd decided hotel tea was watery no matter where you were in the world, but then again, I'd grown up with a brew so strong, it could strip the skin from your hands, as Jock had liked to say about the way I made it.

Back on the bed with my teacup, I thought how much I'd wanted to come out of hiding the moment I'd arrived on Irish soil. At passport control, I'd longed to announce in my broad childhood accent that I'd been born here and once held an Irish passport, but that everything about me and where I'd come from had been stripped away on purpose to protect myself and those that I loved.

Well, here I was, with a different name and nationality, returned to the land which had birthed me – and given me all the troubles that had sent me flying away from it . . .

So today, I was going in search of the one person in the world whom I trusted more than any other, but whom I'd been forced to leave behind too. I needed his help, and in light of the pursuers who had hunted me since I'd left New Zealand, I had nowhere else to turn.

I looked down at the ring my dear Ambrose had given me on my twenty-first birthday. Who would have known that something so small and beautiful and given out of love could have caused all this, simply because it identified who I'd once been?

At least, I *believed* it had been given out of love . . .

No, Merry, don't start doubting him, *because if you do, then you're really lost*, I reprimanded myself. *Now then, my girl, time for a shower and then we're going for a walk around the corner.*

At noon, I was standing in Merrion Square outside the tall, elegant town house that used to contain Ambrose's ground and basement maisonette. I checked surreptitiously through the window and saw the curtains, the lamp and the bookshelves looked exactly the same as they had when I'd last seen it.

The worst-case scenario would be that he was dead, and either a relative or a new buyer or renter had taken over his home without bothering to change anything.

'Just walk up those steps and knock on the door, Merry,' I told myself. 'He's eighty-five, so he's hardly going to shoot you where you stand, is he?'

I climbed the steps and pressed his bell, which struck the same two notes I remembered from all those decades ago. There was no answer for a while, but then a voice – a dearly beloved voice which I knew so well – spoke to me through a speaker grille above the bell.

'Ambrose Lister. Who is calling?'

'I . . . it's me, Mary O'Reilly. The girl from years ago. Ambrose, it's me!' I entreated, and by this time, my lips were virtually kissing the grille. 'Can I come in?'

'Mary? Mary O'Reilly?'

'Yes, 'tis me, even if I've lost my accent a bit, Ambrose. 'Tis me.'

Silence reigned as I gulped back tears caused by the few seconds I'd spent being who I'd been back then, and by the thought of seeing him again. Then the door opened and he was there.

'Jesus, Mary and Joseph!' I gasped. 'I'm sorry, I'm crying.'

'Goodness, in eighty-five years I haven't been so surprised. Please come in, so that we don't disgrace ourselves on this very public doorstep.'

Ambrose ushered me inside and I saw that even though he now walked with a stick, and had less hair (which hadn't been much back then) he was still completely who I remembered him as. Dressed in an old tweed jacket and a checked shirt with a dark green bow tie, his kind brown eyes seemed owlish behind thick round glasses. He was the only one to ever call me Mary rather than 'Merry', and my heart swelled at hearing my name spoken in his clipped accent again.

Once the front door was closed, he led me along the hallway and into the sitting room. The desk in the window and two leather chairs situated opposite each other in front of a marble fireplace hadn't changed. Nor had the now threadbare sofa that sat against the wall, facing the overflowing bookshelves on either side of the fireplace. He closed the door, then turned around to look at me.

'Well now, well now . . .' was all he could manage.

I didn't do much better as I tried to gulp back my tears.

'I believe, even though it is only eleven o'clock, that some strong medicine is called for.'

Ambrose walked to one of the bookshelves and pulled out a bottle of whiskey, plus two glasses from the cupboard beneath it. As he placed the three items on his desk, I saw that his hands shook unsteadily.

'Shall I pour?' I asked.

'If you would, my dear. I find myself quite at a loss.'

'Sit down, and I'll sort us out.'

As Ambrose lowered himself into his favourite chair, I poured two generous measures, and handed one to him. Then I sat down in the chair opposite him.

'*Sláinte!*'

'*Sláinte!*'

We each took a large gulp that burnt my stomach a second later, but wasn't unpleasant. After we both drained our glasses in silence, Ambrose placed his down on the round side table next to his chair. I was glad to see that his hand was steadier now.

'I could use many quotes of renown to mark this moment, but I do not want to resort to either cliché or hyperbole,' he said. 'I will simply ask you where on earth you have been for the last thirty-seven years? And you, I'm sure' – he put up a finger which I knew meant that he hadn't finished – 'will tell me that it's a long story. They are the best, but perhaps you could be brief initially and, as they say these days, cut to the chase.'

'I've been living in New Zealand,' I said. 'I married a man called Jock and we have two children. One called Jack, who is thirty-two, and the other named Mary-Kate, who is twenty-two.'

'And now to the most important question: have you been happy?'

'When I left, I was desperately unhappy,' I admitted, 'but eventually, yes. When I met Jock, I realised I needed to forget about the past and live with what I had found. Once I had done that, I was able to enjoy and appreciate life again.'

Ambrose paused, resting his elbows on the arms of the leather chair, his fingers under his chin. 'The next question is, whether you have the time and the wherewithal to tell me the minutiae of the intervening years. Or are you leaving again sometime soon?'

'At this moment, I have nothing planned that will take me anywhere else. Ironically, for reasons I want to talk to you about, I embarked on a Grand Tour that was meant to take me months. So far, I have been to four countries in about a week. I had planned for Ireland to be my last stop.'

Ambrose smiled at this. 'The schemes of mice and men, or should I add "and women". What matters is that you are here now, and even if my eyesight is fading fast, you look no different. You are still the beautiful young woman I loved, and last saw in this very room when she was only twenty-two years old.'

'Then your eyesight *is* fading, dearest Ambrose. I am nearly fifty-nine years of age now, and getting old.'

'So, it is possible you can spare me some time over the next few hours – or days – to tell me why, in the first instance, you had to leave Ireland and cease all contact with me?'

'I intend to, yes. But that . . . well, that really depends on your response when I tell you about my current problem. Which has a lot to do with why I left Ireland in the first place.'

'Goodness! Are you in the midst of writing a Greek tragedy? Or are you describing the story of your life?' Ambrose raised an expressive eyebrow.

'Perhaps I am being overdramatic, but that's the reason I'm sitting here with you now. You're the only person left that I can truly ask for advice.'

'What about your husband? Jock?'

'My darling Jock died a few months ago. Which was when I decided to—'

'Revisit your past?'

'Yes.'

'And are you feeling that your past has perhaps caught up with you?' he asked, acutely perceptive as always.

'I am, yes. Completely . . .' I stood up. 'Would you mind if I helped myself to another whiskey?'

'Not at all, Mary. Pour me another drop too. I always think better when there's a rationed percentage of alcohol inside me, but please never tell any of my other ex-students that,' he said with a wink. 'There's also a tray of rather good sandwiches in the kitchen, which will soak it up. My daily, who does – or doesn't, as the case may be – everything for me, made them just before she left.'

'I'll go and get them.'

I walked down the dim corridor to the kitchen, and saw that not a single cabinet had been changed since I was last here, although there was a new cooker and even a microwave placed in one corner. The plate of sandwiches was made with soda bread and covered in cling film.

'Here we are,' I said as I returned and placed the plate on the side table next to him.

'Help yourself. One will be cheese and salad, the other ham and salad. It always is.'

'They look delicious; certainly better than anything Mrs Cavanagh ever provided,' I smiled, taking one.

'Ah, Mrs Cavanagh,' he sighed. 'Well, I may have missed out on a large portion of your life, dear Mary, but equally, you have missed out on a rather large portion of mine. And talking of portions, let us eat and continue the conversation once we have done so.'

Another silence descended as we ate the sandwiches. Ambrose had always taught me it was rude to talk with one's mouth full. And I had taught my own children the same.

'So, apart from your eyes, are you keeping well?' I asked when we had finished.

'I think the words "apart from" are the common denominator for anyone of my age. Apart from the rheumatism, and the rather high cholesterol – which I hasten to add I've lived with since my fifties – I'm as fit as a flea.'

'Do you get down to West Cork much these days?'

Ambrose's smile faded from his lips. 'Sadly I don't. In fact, I haven't been there since the early seventies, just a year or so after you left.'

'But what about Father O'Brien? You and he were such good friends.'

'Ah, now, Mary, that is a story for another day.'

I watched Ambrose's gaze move to the window and realised that whatever had ended their friendship had been a painful experience for him.

'I see you're still wearing the ring I gave you,' he said, turning back to me and pointing to it.

'Yes, although technically, it belongs to my daughter – I

gave it to her on *her* twenty-first birthday, but then I asked her if I might borrow it for this trip. I was worried that you might not recognise me after all these years, so I brought it with me as insurance.'

'Not recognise you? Mary, you are perhaps the most beloved person of my life! How could you possibly have thought that? Unless . . . ah.' Ambrose put up a finger to his head. 'You thought I may have lost my marbles, gone senile in my old age, eh?'

'To be truthful, it did occur to me that I may need something to jog your memory. Forgive me, Ambrose.'

'I will think about whether you deserve my forgiveness whilst you make us both a cup of coffee. I presume you remember the way I like it?'

'Strong, with just a hint of milk and one spoonful of brown sugar?' I asked him as I stood up.

'Precisely, my dear, precisely.'

I arrived back with the coffee five minutes later, having made myself a tea.

'So, where do you wish to start?' he asked me.

'I know it should be at the very beginning, but we may have to work backwards a little. If I give you the outline, would you let me fill in the blanks later?'

'Whatever you wish. I'm no longer needed at Trinity by my peers or students – I retired just over fifteen years ago – so the floor is yours for as long as you desire.'

'Actually, I didn't just bring the ring with me today to jog your memory, Ambrose, I brought it because it seems to have become a centre point of my problem. Back then and now.'

'Really? I'm most sorry to hear that.'

'The thing is . . . the reason I left Ireland was because I had to, well, escape from someone. I went to London first, but then I had no choice but to move on. I decided to go further afield, first to Canada, and then to New Zealand.'

Ambrose remained silent as I collected myself to say more.

'I changed my surname when I got married – I'm now McDougal – and became a New Zealand citizen a few years later. I had a new identity, which I truly believed had freed me from the threat of him finding me. As I said earlier, I was able to enjoy my life there, running a vineyard and bringing up my family with Jock. But then . . .'

'Yes?'

'I'd only just embarked on my Grand Tour and my first port of call was Norfolk Island – a tiny isle between New Zealand and Australia. I was visiting my old friend Bridget who'd recently moved there. Do you remember Bridget?'

'How can I forget her, given we have established I am definitely not senile? Your flame-haired enemy as a child and best friend at university.'

'That's the one, yes. Anyway, there I was on Norfolk Island, drinking with Bridget and her new husband, when I received a message from my daughter Mary-Kate. Apparently, she'd had two women enquiring about her, saying she could be the "missing sister" in their family of six other girls – all adopted by a very odd-sounding man, who died a year ago. The proof of the connection was supposedly an emerald ring shaped like a star, with seven points around a small diamond.' I lifted my hand and indicated my ring. 'Mary-Kate told me she'd seen a drawing of the ring that the women had brought with them. She said she was pretty sure it was this one.'

'Really? Pray, continue.'

'Anyway, these women were so desperate to track me and the ring down that Mary-Kate said they were flying over to Norfolk Island to see me.'

'Do you know why they were so desperate?'

'Some cock and bull story about their dead father; how it had been his dearest wish to find the "missing sister". Even though it was too late for him, these sisters are having some kind of a memorial service a year on from his death, by going to the spot where they think he was buried at sea. I mean, these girls even have the same names as the Seven Sisters of the Pleiades! Have you ever heard such a ridiculous story?'

'Well, I certainly recognise the theme of the missing sister from any number of mythological tales around the globe, as you must have done, Mary. You wrote your Bachelor's dissertation on Orion's chase of Merope, after all.'

'I know, Ambrose, but the Seven Sisters were . . . *are* imaginary, not a real-life human family.'

'If you'd said that to the ancient Greeks, Mary, they'd have you left on the top of Mount Olympus as a sacrifice to their gods.'

'Ambrose, please, this isn't a laughing matter.'

'Forgive me, Mary. Do continue. I am sure there must be a method behind the madness of these events.'

'Well, when I heard that they were going to fly over to Norfolk Island, I spoke with Bridget about it, given she knew all about my past, and she agreed that I should leave earlier so I didn't have to meet them. I flew to Canada, which was to be the next stop on my tour, but on my first day in Toronto, I got calls and messages from the concierge saying that two women were coming to see me. When they arrived in reception, I asked the concierge what they looked like and he told me that they were in Muslim dress.'

'So they are not the same two women who followed you to Norfolk Island, then?'

'No. From what I briefly saw of them, they were dark-skinned, and even though I told the concierge to tell them I was out, they simply sat there and waited in the lobby. In the end, I couldn't bear it any longer, so I came down to take a look at them for myself. One of them must have recognised me, because she called my name after she'd spotted me, as I was running for the lift. Thank God it closed before she could get to me. She also left me a letter that told the same story as the girls who had visited Mary-Kate. I was so frightened that I decided to fly straight to London.'

'Curiouser and curiouser,' said Ambrose as I took a breath and a sip of my tea.

'By chance, I bumped into what seemed like a very nice man in reception on my arrival at the hotel. He asked me whether I'd be interested in giving him an interview about the vineyard that myself and my husband built up and ran, as he was a wine journalist. He invited me to the suite of his friend, who introduced herself as Lady Sabrina. They really couldn't have seemed more above board. But then' – I took a sip of my tea – 'as this man Orlando was interviewing me, I noticed the woman was staring at my ring. Once the interview was over, she asked me about it. She said the seven points looked very unusual and then the man mentioned the Seven Sisters of the Pleiades, and the missing sister . . .' I shook my head despairingly. 'At that point, I stood up and left. And then the next day, I noticed that Orlando was tailing me when I went to Clerkenwell to look up the records of marriages and deaths. They'd invited me to dinner that evening, but I cancelled, and lay in my room that night, completely sleepless, watching the hours pass by. The next morning, thinking I'd slip out early, I saw the man was already reading a newspaper in the lobby by the front entrance. In the end, I had my baggage taken downstairs and stored by a porter. I had to wait for this Orlando to leave for the lavatory before I could slip out. And here I am! I . . .'

I put a hand to my brow, embarrassed that I felt like sobbing at his knee, as I'd sometimes done as a child when things had seemed too much. 'I'm so exhausted, Ambrose, really I am. They're after me again, I know they are.'

'Who are "they"?'

'Some very ugly, violent people – or rather a person who knew ugly, violent people and who threatened me a long time ago. He also threatened my family and anyone I loved, including you. Which is why I . . .'

'Ran away,' finished Ambrose.

'Yes. Do you have a tissue by any chance?'

'Here, Mary, dry your eyes.' He handed me his handkerchief, and it smelt so very much of my childhood with him that it brought more tears to my eyes.

'I'm just so worried for Mary-Kate. She's alone at the vineyard in New Zealand and knows nothing about my past. Nor does Jack, my son. He'd send them after my children, I know he would, and . . .'

'Hush now,' Ambrose said gently. 'Obviously I know little of the past scenario you are talking about, but—'

'The missing sister was what he always called me! Back then, when . . . oh,' I said, feeling totally out of words to describe the complexity of what had happened.

'So now, I presume you are talking about someone I knew of when you were living here with me?'

'Yes. I am, but please don't say his name. I can't bear to hear it. He's found me, Ambrose, I know he has.'

I watched as Ambrose steepled his fingers under his chin and stared at me for what felt like a very long time. A gamut of emotions that I couldn't easily read crossed his features. Eventually, he gave a long sigh.

'I understand, Mary dear, and I just might be able to allay your fears somewhat. But I'm afraid you will need to excuse me. My one nod to my age is to take a short nap in the afternoons. And rather than doze – or even worse – snore loudly within your hearing, would you mind if I retired to my bedroom for an hour or two? Your sudden appearance seems to have rather taken it out of me.'

'Oh Ambrose, of course not. I'll leave and come back later. I'm so sorry, really I am. After all these years, I hadn't expected our first meeting to be like this.'

'Please do not apologise, Mary dear. Just accept that I am not as young as I used to be.' Ambrose offered me a weak smile as he stood up and we walked along the narrow corridor towards the back of his maisonette. 'Please feel free to stay here. As you well know, there's a plethora of books at your disposal. If you wish to go out, the key is where it always was: in the Copenhagen Blue china pot on the table in the corridor.'

'Do you need any help?' I asked as he began to descend the steps to the basement, which housed two bedrooms and a bathroom.

'I seem to have managed quite well in the years since you left, and I hope to manage a few more in the same vein. I will see you at half past four, Mary, but . . . please be assured, I believe you are quite safe.'

As he disappeared from view, I decided that perhaps I too would go back to the hotel for a nap.

Taking the key, I left the maisonette and walked the few hundred yards round the corner, breathing in the familiarity of the atmosphere and the voices I could hear around me. This city had provided the backdrop to some of the happiest moments of my life, before it had gone so badly wrong.

Stepping inside the hotel, I went to the desk to retrieve my key.

'There you are, Mrs McDougal,' said the receptionist as he

handed it to me. 'Oh, and there's someone waiting for you in the lobby.'

My heart started to thud so fast that I thought I might faint where I stood. I hung on to the desk for support and bowed my head, trying to get my breath back.

'Are you all right, Mrs McDougal?'

'Yes, yes, I'm fine. I . . . did you get a name from this person?'

'I did, yes. He only arrived fifteen minutes or so ago. Now, let me see . . .'

A hand descended onto my shoulder from behind and I let out a small scream.

'Mum! It's me!'

'Oh, I . . .' I clutched the desk tighter as the world spun.

'Why don't you take your mammy to sit down in the lounge and we'll bring some water through for her?' the receptionist suggested.

'No, I'm all right, really.' I turned towards the great, tall man I had brought into this world, and rested my head against his chest as he hugged me.

'I'm so sorry I startled you, Mum. Why don't we go to the lounge like the man said, and maybe order some tea?'

'Okay,' I agreed, and Jack manoeuvred his arm around my waist to support me as we walked.

Once we were sitting on a sofa in the quiet lounge and tea had been ordered, I felt Jack's gaze upon me.

'Seriously, I'm fine now. So, tell me, what on earth are you doing here?' I asked him.

'It's simple, Mum: I was worried about you.'

'Why?'

'You just sounded . . . odd on the phone the other day. I tried calling you again early this morning, but you didn't pick up.'

'I'm perfectly fine, Jack. I'm sorry you felt you had to chase halfway across the world to see me.'

'It wasn't across the world, remember, Mum? It only took me a couple of hours to get here from Provence. The flight wasn't much longer than going from Christchurch to Auckland. Anyway, I'm here now, and after your reaction to my arrival at reception, I'm glad I am. What's going on, Mum?' he asked as the tea arrived.

'Let's drink the tea, shall we? You pour,' I said, not trusting my own hands to hold the pot steadily. 'Add an extra spoonful of sugar to mine.'

Eventually, a hot sweet, tea and Jack's comforting presence slowed my heart rate and cleared my head.

'I'm feeling much better now,' I said, to ease my son's concerned stare. 'I'm sorry about jumping the way I did.'

'That's okay,' Jack shrugged. 'You obviously thought I was someone you didn't want to see.'

My son glanced at me through eyes that were a bright blue, very like mine. 'Yes, I thought that maybe you were,' I sighed. I'd always found it extremely difficult to lie to Jack face-to-face; his intrinsic openness and honesty – along with an acute perceptiveness, especially when it came to me – made it almost impossible.

'So, who was it you were expecting?'

'Oh Jack, it's such a long story. In a nutshell, I think . . . well, I think that someone who used to live here in Dublin – a dangerous man – may be on my trail again.'

Jack sipped his tea calmly as he took this in. 'Okay. And how do you know this?'

'I just *do*.'

'Right. So, what has happened in the last week to make you think this?'

I glanced around nervously. 'I'd prefer not to talk about it in public. You never know who is listening.'

'Blimey, Mum, you sound completely paranoid! And a little crazy, to be honest, which worries me because you've always been the calmest and sanest person I know. For now, I'm going to give you the benefit of the doubt and not drag you off to the nearest shrink to find out if you've suddenly developed delusional tendencies, but you'd better explain who this man is.'

'I'm perfectly sane.' I lowered my voice just in case the waitress standing in the corner of the otherwise deserted lounge could hear us. 'It all started when those girls came to visit your sister at The Vinery, with some story about how she was the long-lost missing sister that their dead father had been looking for.'

'Ah,' Jack nodded. 'Okay. MK told me the proof was something to do with that emerald ring you're wearing at the moment. They just wanted to take a look at it.'

'Yes. Well, since they arrived, I've had strangers turning up at every hotel I've visited, asking to see me. Then when I was in London, do you remember I called you about the man who wanted to interview me about The Vinery for his newspaper?'

'I do, yes. Hold on, you told me you were in New York!' Jack narrowed his eyes.

'I'm sorry, Jack, I knew you'd worry and ask questions if you thought I'd derailed so much from my original trip itinerary. Anyway, this man definitely wasn't who he said he was. The woman he was with saw the ring and asked about it. He even followed me the next day when I left the hotel. That's when I decided to leave for Ireland and why I sounded odd on the phone when we spoke yesterday.'

'Okay,' Jack nodded. 'And do you know why these people are following you? I mean, what do they want? Is it just the ring? It's only small,' Jack said as he stared at it. 'It doesn't

look that valuable . . . oh Mum, you didn't steal it, did you?'
He gave me a wry smile.

'Of course I didn't steal it! I promise I'll tell you the whole
story at some point – it's time, I suppose.' I sighed, then
checked my watch. 'I'm going to have to leave in a bit. I've
only popped back to the hotel for an hour while my friend
has a nap, you see.'

'Your friend?'

'He's my godfather, Ambrose, actually. I paid him a call
earlier. I haven't seen him for thirty-seven years.'

'Your godfather?' Jack frowned. 'Why have you never mentioned him to any of us before?'

'Let's just say I wanted to leave the past behind me. For
everyone's sake. It was him that gave me this ring on my
twenty-first birthday.'

'So he's involved in all this, is he? . . . Whatever *this* is?'

'No, he wasn't.' I gave my son a sad smile. 'Have you heard
from Mary-Kate, by the way?'

'No, not for the past few days.'

'This may sound ridiculous, but I'm worried about her
there at The Vinery all by herself. You haven't had any visitors
recently in Provence, have you? People asking about me?'

'No, although I did meet a very nice woman who came to
stay at the *gîte* François and Ginette own and . . .' Jack
frowned suddenly. 'Wow,' he muttered.

'What?' I asked him as my heart rate began to rise again.

'Nothing, I'm sure it was nothing. I mean, we just got on
really well. I was so happy to have someone who spoke English to talk to over dinner. She said she had adopted sisters
and, actually, I suppose she did ask quite a lot of questions
about you and MK's adoption.'

'Oh no, Jack.' I put my fingers to my brow. 'They found
you as well.'

'Mum, who are "they"?' he urged me. 'This woman – Ally – was great, and it was pure coincidence that we were put next to each other at the dinner table. Actually, it was me who offered to drive her into the village the next day, because I really liked her. She didn't mention anything about a missing sister, or the Seven Sisters, or a ring . . .'

'Okay. Well, it might be coincidence, but until we know for sure, I'm going to ask Mary-Kate to leave The Vinery and fly over here.'

'Mum, what the hell?! Are you telling me that our lives are in danger?'

'They might be, yes, and until I'm certain they're not, we need to be together.'

I looked at my beloved son's expression, which contained a mixture of shock and doubt. I knew I had to tell him something before he carted me off to the local psychiatric hospital.

'The thing is, Jack, a long time ago, someone who was in a group of very dangerous people threatened to hunt me down and kill me.' I swallowed. 'It may sound ridiculous and overdramatic, but that was the way things were here back then. He'd always called me the missing sister and hated this ring, and by extension my godfather, because he'd given it to me. This goes back a very long way, Jack, and until I can find out if he's alive or dead, I'm not going to be able to relax, okay? That's why I'm here in Ireland. I have to put this to bed for good.'

'Okay.' Jack nodded. 'So you think that he and his . . . people are after you again?'

'Until it's been proved that they're not, I do believe it's possible, yes. You didn't know him, Jack, what he believed in, the cause he thought he was fighting for. He was' – I gulped – 'consumed by it. And had been for the whole of his life.'

'All right, at least you're making a bit more sense now. Is

this why you've never really talked about your past here in Ireland then? And why you ended up in New Zealand – as far away as you could possibly get?'

'It is. Now, I need to go and see Ambrose. He'll be wondering where I've got to.'

'Can I come with you, Mum? After what you've just told me, I think I should, just in case.'

'I . . . okay. Maybe it's about time you learnt about your heritage.' I signalled for the waitress.

The bill paid, the two of us left the hotel.

'Did you bring a bag with you?' I asked my son as we walked round the corner towards Merrion Square.

'Yes, it's stored with the porter for now and they have a room for me, but I just wanted to make sure you were actually here before I checked in. This man who you think is after you, was he part of some kind of extremist group?'

'Not when I first knew him, but he was definitely involved towards the end. Jack, I swear, I'm not exaggerating. I know the organisation he was with had a network. He said he was quite high up, so one order from him and things . . . well, they happened. Now,' I said as I paused outside Ambrose's building, 'remember, my godfather is very old, but don't let that fool you into thinking he's lost one ounce of his enormous brain. Ambrose was, and still is, the cleverest man I know.'

'Well,' Jack said as he looked up at the tall, elegant red-bricked building with its old-fashioned square-paned windows, 'he must be very rich to own one of these on such a beautiful garden square.'

'He only owns the ground and basement apartment, but you're right. Even that would sell for a lot these days. He bought it a long time ago. And Jack . . . ?'

'Don't worry, Mum,' Jack shrugged affably, 'I'll remember my manners.'

'I know you will, love. Right, let's go inside, shall we?'

I unlocked the door and stood in the entrance hall, with its original black and white patterned tiles.

'Ambrose? It's Mary here,' I announced as I opened the interior door that led into the sitting room.

'Good evening,' he said, already standing up from his favourite chair to greet me. I watched his eyes sweep over Jack, who was in his usual casual attire of shorts, T-shirt and not-so-white trainers.

'And who might this be?' said Ambrose.

'Jack McDougal, Merry's son.' He held out his hand. 'How d'you do?' he said and I could have kissed him for using such a formal expression, which I knew would endear him to Ambrose.

'I do very well, thank you, young man. Well, as there are three of us, I suggest you two sit down on the sofa. Mary, you didn't tell me your son was with you.'

'He wasn't when I saw you earlier, but he turned up in search of me.'

'I see. Now,' he said, 'would anyone like a drink? I'm afraid I have little to offer but the two staples of my life: whiskey and water.' Ambrose looked at the clock on the mantelpiece over the fireplace. 'It's almost five o'clock, therefore I'll take a whiskey. Your mother knows where the bottle and glasses are kept,' he added as Jack rose.

'I'll take some water for now, Jack, thank you,' I added. 'The kitchen is at the end of the corridor, and tap is fine.'

Jack nodded and left the room as I went to retrieve the whiskey bottle and a glass.

'A fine young man, who looks very like his mama,' Ambrose said. 'And not a bad bone in his body, I'd wager.'

'There really isn't, Ambrose, though he's not so young anymore. I worry that he'll get set in his ways as a bachelor and never settle down.'

'Would any woman ever be good enough for him? Or more accurately, for his mother?' Ambrose gave me a raise of an eyebrow as I handed him his whiskey.

'Probably not. He's so completely without guile,' I sighed. 'He's had his heart broken a few times because of it.'

'I must ask you before he returns: are you happy for us to talk openly in front of him?'

'I have to be, Ambrose. I told him what I think has been happening recently and it's all because of the past. It's time there were no more secrets. I've lived with them for too long.'

Jack returned with two glasses of water, handed one to me and sat down.

'*Sláinte!*' Ambrose raised his glass. 'That's "cheers" in Gaelic,' he added for Jack's benefit.

'*Sláinte!*' Jack and I toasted back.

'Are you Irish yourself, sir?' Jack asked.

'Please, call me Ambrose. And indeed, I am Irish. In fact, if I was a stick of traditional seaside rock, it would read "Made in Ireland" down the centre of it.'

'You don't have an Irish accent, though. And nor does Mum.'

'You should have heard your mother when she was a little girl, Jack. She had as broad a West Cork accent as it was possible to get. I, of course, drummed it out of her when she came to Dublin.'

'Where is West Cork?'

'Another county in Ireland, down in the south-west.'

'So you didn't grow up in Dublin, Mum?' said Jack.

'Oh no.' I shook my head. 'I grew up in the countryside . . . We didn't even have electricity until I was six!'

'But you're not that old, Mum. You were born in the late forties, weren't you?'

'West Cork was quite behind the times then,' Ambrose put in.

'So, did you know Mum's family well?'

'In a way,' said Ambrose, casting me a glance. 'You have never told your son about your childhood?'

'No. Nor my husband or Mary-Kate,' I admitted.

'May I ask why not?' said Ambrose.

'Because . . . as I've said, I wanted to leave the past behind and start afresh.'

'I'd love to know more, Mum, I really would,' Jack encouraged me.

'Well, perhaps now might be the time to tell young Jack a bit about his heritage?' Ambrose suggested gently. 'I'm here to expand on any details you don't quite remember, Mary – I'm sure my mind will just about stretch back to my long-lost youth.'

I turned to my son, who was looking at me imploringly. Reading Nuala's diary had certainly reminded me of the familiar spaces of my childhood. Closing my eyes, a wave of emotions and memories came over me, ones I had tried so hard to forget for well over half my life.

But you can't forget, Merry, it's who you are . . .

So, I let the wave engulf me without fighting it off, and realised for the first time that here, with my son and my beloved godfather, I could safely swim in the waters of the past without drowning in them.

I took a deep breath and began . . .

Merry
The Argideen Valley
October 1955

An Cláirseach
The Celtic Harp

27

Merry started as an arm swung onto her chest. Katie, her big sister, who was only two years older than her, was dreaming again. Merry removed the arm and placed it back where it belonged on Katie's side of the bed. Her sister rolled over and curled herself into a little ball, her red curls splayed on her pillow. Merry too turned over so their bottoms were touching on the narrow mattress, and looked out of the tiny window-pane to check how high the sun was and whether Daddy would be out in the milking shed yet. The sky was as it usually was: full of big pieces of grey cloud that looked fit to burst with raindrops. She reckoned she still had an hour to stay warm under the blankets before she'd need to be up and dressed to feed the chickens.

Opposite her, Nora, who shared a mattress with their oldest sister Ellen, was snoring gently. As her brain woke up, Merry felt excitement in her tummy and she remembered why it was.

Today was the day the electricity thing was to be switched on and they were to move across the yard to the New House. She'd watched Daddy and her older brother John, and some-times their neighbours if they could be spared from their own farms, build it ever since she could remember. If Daddy wasn't in the shed with the cows, or out in the barley fields, he was across the yard, making the New House go upwards.

Merry looked up at the ceiling, which was very low and made a triangle shape (she'd learnt about triangles at her new school) with a beam through it at the top to hold it up. Merry didn't like that beam because it was dark and big spiders liked to make their homes right above her. One time, she'd woken up and seen the biggest in the world hovering just above her on its silver thread. She'd screamed and Mammy had rushed in and caught it, telling her not to be a 'silly little eejit', and that spiders were good because they caught flies, but Merry didn't think they were good at all, whatever Mammy said.

In the new bedroom, there was a flat ceiling that was painted white, which meant it would be much easier to see any webs and take them away before the spiders could build their homes any bigger. Merry knew she'd sleep much better in the New House.

There were also four whole bedrooms upstairs, which meant Ellen and Nora would have a room to themselves, so just she and Katie would share theirs. The boys – John and little Bill – would have another room, and Mammy and Daddy the biggest room. There was a new baby in Mammy's tummy and Merry had prayed to Jesus that it would be a boy too, so she and Katie could keep their new room just to themselves for always. Even though she knew she had to love her brothers and sisters, it didn't say in the Bible she had to *like* them.

And Merry and Katie didn't like Nora. She was very bossy and gave them both jobs to do that Ellen, their older sister, had given to *her*.

Mammy and Daddy were hoping for a boy too – another big strong lad to help on the farm. Merry and Katie's hands were still too small to do the milking and Ellen was only interested in kissing her boyfriend, which Merry and Katie had seen her do behind the milking shed and thought was disgusting. There were lots of other chores on the farm and Daddy often said that John was the only useful one around, which Merry thought was very unfair because she looked after baby Bill the most. And besides, it wasn't her fault she'd been born a girl, was it?

Aside from Katie, Merry's favourite person to speak to was the man called Ambrose, who was sometimes up at Father O'Brien's house where Mammy cleaned on a Monday. Ambrose had begun teaching her letters even before she had started school last month. She wasn't sure why it had always been her who was chosen to go up to the priest's house to clean with Mammy, but she didn't mind a bit. It was better than not minding actually, because she *loved* it! Some of her best memories were sitting in front of a warm fire eating a little round cake hot from the oven, filled with strawberry jam and something that was creamy white, which tasted sweet and delicious. Now she was bigger, she knew the 'cakes' were called scones. While she was eating, Ambrose would talk to her, which made it quite difficult to answer as her mouth was so full of cake, and he didn't approve of talking while you were chewing. Other times, he'd read to her from a storybook about a princess who was put to sleep for one hundred years and only woken by a kiss from a prince.

Ambrose was very kind to her, but she didn't know why. When she'd asked Father O'Brien what he was to her, and why she was allowed to call him by his first name, rather than 'Mr Lister' like Mammy did, she watched him as he thought about it for quite a long time.

'Perhaps one could say that he is your godfather, Mary.'

She didn't like to ask what a 'godfather' actually was – Ambrose didn't look like God in Heaven *or* her father. He had round eyes like an owl behind thick glasses, and fluffs of blond hair on his head – a good deal less hair than Father

O'Brien or Daddy. He was a lot smaller than them too, but his face was always jollier and less serious.

Then, as if Father O'Brien could read her mind, he'd smiled at her. 'Think of him as your special protector down here on earth.'

'Oh. Do all my brothers and sisters have one too?'

'They all have godparents, yes, but because Ambrose is able to spoil you more than theirs, it's best you keep anything he gives you secret, or they may get jealous.'

'Mammy knows, though, doesn't she?'

'Yes, and your father, so you're not to worry you're doing anything wrong.'

'I understand,' she'd nodded gravely.

Last Christmas, Ambrose had given her a book, but it didn't have anything written in it, only lines on which she was to try practising her letters and forming them into words. Ambrose said it didn't matter if they were spelt wrong, because he would correct them and that's the way she would get better.

Reaching under the mattress, she pulled out the book. The light was very bad but she was used to it.

The cover was smooth and silky to the touch and she liked the feel of it, but when she had asked Ambrose what the cover was made of, he had told her it was leather, which came from a cow's skin. This didn't make sense at all, because all the cows she knew had hairy skin, covered in mud.

Opening it, she slid out the pencil, which had its own little band to attach it to the side of the book, and turned to the last page she'd written.

Mi familee
Ellen: aje 16. Bossi. Kisses her boyfrend.
John: aje 14. Helps Daddy. Likes cows. Smells like
   cows. My favorit brotha.

Nora: aje 12. Doesn't like anithin.
Katie: aje neerli 8. Mi best frend. VERRI pretty. dosnt
    help much wit babi Bill.
Me: aje nearly 6. Likes books. Not verri pretty. Caled
    Merry becos I giggel a LOT.
Bill: aje 2. Smells.
New babi: not here yet.

Deciding she should add something about Mammy and
Daddy, Merry thought what she might write about them.

Merry loved both her parents very much, but Mammy was
always so busy cooking and washing and having more babies,
it was difficult to ever talk about the things that went through
her mind. Whenever Mammy saw her she would just give her
another job to do, like putting fresh straw in for the pigs or
picking cabbages out of the ground for their tea.

As for Daddy, he was always out on the farm and wasn't
really one for talking anyway.

Daddy: works VERRI hard. Smells of cow.

Merry thought that didn't sound very nice, so she added:

VERRI hansom.

Before she had started school a month ago, Merry's favourite day of the week had always been Mondays, when she and
Mammy walked up to the priest's house together. They chatted about all sorts of things (Merry knew her brothers and
sisters thought her a chatterbox, but there were just so many
things to be interested in). Mammy would sometimes kiss her
on top of her head and call her 'my special girl'.

Mammy, she wrote carefully, *VERRI beautiful. kind. I love her VERRI much.* When up cleaning the priest's house, Mammy was always rushing around and muttering about Mrs Cavanagh. At home, Mammy called her 'that old crow', but Merry had been told never to repeat that outside the family, even if Mrs Cavanagh did look like one. Whenever she saw her at Mass on Sundays, perched on the pew at the front and looking around at the congregation, all beaky and disapproving, she'd see a great black bird instead. Father O'Brien had told Merry there was no need to be afraid of her; Mrs Cavanagh cleaned the priest's house every day except Monday and complained to anyone who would listen about how Mammy wasn't doing her job well enough, which made Merry even more cross.

Mrs Cavanagh often talked about having worked up at the Big House, and Merry's friend Bobby said it was because Mrs Cavanagh had worked for so long for a British family (and he said the word 'British' the same way Katie said the word 'slug') that she'd been taken over by 'colonist views' and took out her anger on the 'hardworking Irish'. When Merry had asked Bobby what a 'colonist' was, he'd gone all red, which made her think it was a word he'd heard at home but didn't really understand.

Bobby was in her class at school in Clogagh, and because his homeplace was in the same direction as Merry's farm, she and Katie walked home with him part of the way after school. As Merry and Bobby were at the same reading level, their teacher Miss Lucey, whom Merry adored because she was so pretty and seemed to know everything there was to know in the world, often placed them together. To begin with, Merry had been glad to know someone who liked reading too. Even though everyone else in the class kept away from him because of his temper and gossip about his family, Bobby could be kind when he set his mind to it. He'd given her a pink crayon once and said she could keep it, even though everyone knew his family was very poor. His jumper was full of holes and his long dark hair looked like it had never seen a brush. He lived with his mammy and his little sister (neither of whom she'd ever seen) in a tiny cottage that Nora had said didn't have a tap or electricity.

Katie said that he was stone mad and should be taken away by the Gardaí, but despite his bad and often strange behaviour, Merry only felt pity for him. She sometimes thought that the only one who loved him was his dog Hunter, a black and white collie who had probably never hunted anything. Hunter was always waiting for Bobby in the lane near Inchybridge, his tail wagging and his tongue hanging out in a smile. Sometimes, when she and Katie parted ways from Bobby, Merry would look back to watch Hunter padding faithfully beside Bobby. Hunter could always calm him down when he was in a rage, even when Merry couldn't.

She shut her writing book carefully, replaced the pencil in its holder and put it back under the mattress. Then she sat up again and stared out of the window at the New House. It was hard to believe that today it would become their home. They would even have an inside tap, drawn from the stream on the hillside behind it. She had been allowed to try it, and it *was* like magic; the water came out when you turned it on, and disappeared when you turned it the other way. There was a range oven for Mammy to cook on so she'd no longer have to use the pot over the fire, and a big kitchen table that Daddy had made out of wood, which could seat all eight and a half of them with room to spare. And then . . . the best thing of all: a little hut which she could walk to from the kitchen. Inside it was a contraption with a seat that she'd only ever seen up at Father O'Brien's house, and a chain above to flush it.

Anyway, it meant that none of them needed to go into the fields beyond to do their 'business', as Mammy called it. How it worked, Merry didn't know, but like everything else at the New House, it was magical.

Merry shivered as a blast of wind whistled through a crack in the windowpane, so she huddled under the blanket once more. And for one of the few times in her life, other than birthdays, Christmas and when she went up with Mammy to the priest's house, Merry could hardly wait until it was time to feed the chickens, because that meant the most exciting day of all had begun.

'Merry, will you be picking up that blanket? It's trailing behind you in the mud!' called Mammy, as she and Katie followed their mother across the yard for the hundredth time to put their things into the New House.

Both girls watched as Mammy dumped the pots she'd carried onto the long table, and used an old cloth to open the small door on the new range. She and Katie had been told very sharply not to touch it because it would be too hot. A delicious smell wafted out as it opened.

'Is that brack cake, Mammy?' Merry asked.

'It is, Merry. We'll be wanting something nice for our first tea inside.'

'Does it have the little black fruit in it?' asked Katie.

'It has currants in it, yes,' Mammy answered as she drew it out and put it on a table to the side of the range to cool. 'And don't either of you be touching it yet, or I'll have you cleaning out the pigsty. Merry, get back across and see to Bill, will you?'

'Where's Nora?' asked Merry. 'She's after disappearing again.'

'I'm not knowing, but see to Bill while me, Ellen and Katie make the beds upstairs.'

'Yes, Mammy,' Merry said, rolling her eyes and passing Katie a glance. As she walked back across, Merry felt so angry with Nora, it made her heart beat faster. Nora was always disappearing when there was work to be done. And now it meant another smelly napkin to change, when it was really Nora's turn. Bill was sitting in the small wooden pen placed in a corner of the old kitchen, the only room downstairs and where the whole family were when they were not in bed or outside. For the first time she could ever remember, Merry saw the fire that had been lit earlier in the big nook that took up almost the whole of one wall had been allowed to go out.

'Bye bye, fire,' Merry said out loud. 'We'll not be needing you anymore for our cooking.' Turning her attention to Bill, who smelt worse than the fields when Daddy and John spread the manure, she took a blanket from the sideboard and laid it out on the cold stone floor. Then she picked up Bill from his pen and placed him on it. Next, she found a clean napkin from the pile in the sideboard drawer and a pail of water which they used to clean Bill's mess.

'Do you know, Bill, that you'll be two soon, and 'tis time for you to get out of napkins altogether?'

Bill, who Merry thought was the spit of Daddy already, with his dark hair and blue eyes, giggled at her as Merry held her breath and unpinned the napkin, then slid it and the mess inside it from under him. Rolling the dirty napkin up to be scraped out and washed later, she took a cloth and dipped it in the pail of water to clean his bottom. Then she expertly fastened a clean napkin around him. Immediately after she'd done that, Bill rolled onto his side and then heaved himself up onto all fours. Even though he could walk a bit now, he still preferred to crawl, and did so very fast. He knew how to place himself under the table with the chairs about him, so hands could not easily reach him. He thought it was a grand game altogether, and would sit there chuckling as Merry had to move chairs to reach him.

'Aha!' Merry said as she dived under the table and grabbed him. 'No chairs today, Mr Bill! They've all gone over to the New House already.' Pulling him out, Bill protested heavily as she picked him up and placed him safely back in his pen. His howling grew louder, so she plucked up the empty bottle and refilled it with milk from the pail that stood outside the front door to keep it cool.

'There now, drink your milk and be good while we work away in the New House,' Merry told him. 'And there's your doggy to play with,' she said, picking up a wooden toy she herself remembered loving when she'd been little.

As Merry took the soiled napkin out to scrape away the contents in the bowl which would be disposed of later in the field, she wondered why Mammy wanted to have babies. Even though she loved her little brother, she still remembered the fierce look of fear on Mammy's face when she'd been standing in the kitchen and a large swish of water had appeared between her legs. At the time, Merry had thought that Mammy had disgraced herself, but it turned out it was the sign that Bill was on his way out of her tummy. The baby delivery lady had arrived soon after, and the family had sat in the kitchen, listening to the screaming from Mammy upstairs.

'Is she dying, Daddy?' Merry had dared to ask. 'Going up to heaven to be with Jesus?'

'No, Merry, she's giving birth to a babe, just like she gave birth to your brother and sisters.'

Merry thought now that, with the new babe coming soon, there'd be even more napkins for her to clean.

'And that's another thing that will be better, Bill,' she called to him as she dunked the napkin in the special fluid that took most of the brown stains away. 'We have a tap over at the New House, so maybe 'twill be easier to wash these.'

Leaving the door ajar so Bill could be heard if he screamed, Merry ran back across to the New House to help Mammy.

28

'I'll be on my way now, Father,' said Mrs Cavanagh as she stood in the doorway to James's study. 'Your friend's room has fresh sheets and I've dusted round. The fire is laid and your tea is in the range.'

'Thank you, Mrs Cavanagh. Enjoy your day of rest and I'll see you as usual on Tuesday.'

'Just make sure that Mrs O'Reilly spends more time clean-ing than she does yabbing. I'm getting tired of double work to do when I come back. Goodnight, Father.' With that, Mrs Cavanagh shut the door more firmly than she needed to just to underline her point. A point she made every single Sunday evening when she left for her day off. Over the last seven years, James had often wanted to tell her the truth: that young Maggie O'Reilly was a pleasure to have in the house, with her lovely smile and the way she sang in a high, sweet voice as she went about her chores. She was also a far better cook than Mrs Cavanagh could ever be, and in the few hours she spent at the house, she would leave it sparkling. However, having prayed on the subject, he'd realised that all he thought was exactly what Mrs Cavanagh knew herself if she were to look into her heart: she was threatened by the younger woman and that was why she behaved towards her as she did.

Behind his desk, Father James O'Brien stretched and

breathed a sigh of relief. His Sunday duties were over and this evening – the start of his unofficial day off (although his door was always open to members of his flock in trouble) – was made even better by the fact that his dearest friend Ambrose was on his way down from Dublin for his monthly visit.

James stood up to switch on the electric light that hung in the centre of the room.

The evenings were drawing in already, even though it was only the start of October.

Ambrose's visit prompted James to think how much had changed since he'd arrived here in the parish of Timoleague almost seven years ago. Ambrose had said then that it would take time for him to be accepted, and he'd been right. Now, he not only felt that he had been, but more importantly, that he was respected by the community he served. And rather than his youth being a negative, he had managed to turn it into a positive by lending a hand during the harvest and coun- selling rather than judging the wives if they came to him pregnant yet again, wondering how they could cope with another babe.

Having originally thought he'd move on to a more presti- gious post in a parish with a larger flock, when one such vacancy in Cork City had been offered to him, he'd decided against it after days of reflection and prayer. He was happy here, welcomed with a smile at the homes he visited and plied with enough cakes and scones to make up for Mrs Cavan- agh's lack of talent in that department.

The arrival of electricity in his home four years ago had been enormously helpful, because it had meant he could at least listen to the radio and keep in touch with what he thought of these days as 'the outside world'. When he'd taken a trip back to Dublin to visit Ambrose, the city he'd grown up in and loved with all his heart had felt claustrophobic and noisy. He'd realised the peace and beauty he'd found here in West Cork suited his temperament. Where better to contemplate one of his parishioner's dilemmas than to drive out to the magnificent Inchydoney Beach near Clonakilty, and walk along the sand as the waves roared and the wind whipped around the skirt of his cassock. Or on a long walk along the cliffs of Dunworley, where you'd not meet another soul until you stood on a headland that looked out on all sides onto the Atlantic Ocean beneath. Unless something changed, James had decided that he suited the countryside and would probably be happy staying here for the rest of the life God might choose to give him.

Ambrose, of course, who was a Senior Fellow in Classics at Trinity College, was always trying to persuade him to return to the bright lights of Dublin, where Ambrose could walk around the corner to see him, rather than driving for four or five hours down to visit him in Timoleague. But the roads had improved between Dublin and West Cork in the past few years – they'd had to, what with the advent of the working man being able to afford a car rather than just the gentry, and besides, James thought that his friend enjoyed his road trip in his bright red Beetle. James had nicknamed it the Ladybird, as it often arrived covered in large dark splotches of mud from the many puddles it had to drive through en route. And he would be here soon . . .

While he waited, James walked over to the gramophone and pulled out a record from its sleeve. Placing the vinyl circle on the turntable, he moved the needle to his favourite variation from *Rhapsody on a Theme of Paganini*. Ambrose had told him that Rachmaninoff had turned the main theme upside down to create the extraordinary classical piece. He sat in the leather chair as the pianist played the first very simple chords . . .

'My dear boy, I've woken you, after what I know is always a long hard day for you in the "office".'

James opened his eyes, doing his best to focus, and saw Ambrose standing above him. Which was rather novel, as it was normally him looking down on Ambrose.

'Forgive me, Ambrose. I . . . yes, I must have drifted off.'

'And to Rachmaninoff, I see.' Ambrose walked over to the gramophone and released the needle from its endless circle at the end of the recording. 'Goodness, the vinyl is covered in scratches; I'll bring you a new one next time I'm down.'

'There's no need; I rather like the scratches, because it gives the piece an air of antiquity that suits it.' James smiled as he clapped his arms around Ambrose's shoulders. 'As always, 'tis a pleasure to see you. Hungry?'

'If I'm honest, no.' Ambrose removed his cap and driving gloves and placed them on James's desk. 'Not for Mrs Cavanagh's fare, at least. I stopped and enjoyed a picnic from the hamper my own daily had provided just before I entered Cork City.'

'Wonderful, then I will treat myself to a hunk of bread, ham and the homemade chutney one of my parishioners provided me with. We'll tip Mrs Cavanagh's broth into the slop for the chickens,' James said with a wink.

An hour later, with a fire burning in the grate, and a new recording of Rimsky-Korsakov's *Scheherazade* that Ambrose had brought along with him playing on the gramophone, the two men were sitting opposite each other in their fireside chairs.

'I've been looking forward to our night and day of quiet contemplation and philosophical discussion,' Ambrose said with a wry smile. 'But I always worry that you'll try to save my soul for God while I'm here.'

'You know very well that I stopped trying to do that years ago. You are a lost cause.'

'Maybe I am. However, let it be a comfort to you that I surround myself with myth and legend within my own philosophical journey. Greek mythology was simply an earlier version of the Bible: tales of morality to tame the human being.'

'And perhaps to teach him,' James mused. 'My question would be, have we learnt anything since ancient times?'

'If you're asking whether we're more civilised, given that in the past forty or so years, we've faced two of the harshest world wars in history, I'd question it. Perhaps it seems politer to use aeroplanes or tanks to spit out death to thousands. Indeed, I'd prefer being blown up by a shell to being hanged, drawn and quartered, but—'

'I believe that the answer is no,' said James. 'Look at the way the Irish suffered under British rule. Their lands taken from them, many forced to change their religion during the Reformation. Being down here amongst a far simpler population than you'd find in Dublin has opened my eyes to just how hard their lives have been.'

'I sense a glimpse of republicanism appearing in your soul, Father O'Brien, but as a large part of Ireland *is* now a republic, I'd say civilisation has moved on. I think you should read that.' Ambrose pointed to the book he'd brought for his friend. 'Kierkegaard was a religious soul and a philosopher. As he says, life is not a problem to be solved, but a reality to be experienced.'

'Then perhaps we should no longer discuss the heavenly

and human condition and both follow his lead,' James commented as he glanced down at the title of the book. '*Fear and Trembling* . . . the title does not inspire confidence.'

'Read it. I promise you'll think it rather good, James, even if the man was a staunch Protestant.'

'Then I'd also add that my bishop would find you a bad influence on me,' James chuckled.

'Then I will have truly achieved my goal. Now, tell me how little Mary O'Reilly is getting on. Have they moved into their new house yet?'

'They have indeed. Yesterday, as it happens. I went over to bless it after Mass earlier today.'

'And?'

'Considering that John O'Reilly has built it mainly with his own hands block by block, it is certainly solid enough to keep the wind out, and three times the size of their old farmhouse. The electricity is on, and the range and the kitchen tap are working. The whole family looked exhausted, but very happy.'

'Thank heavens for that. Their old farmhouse was hardly better than a hovel,' Ambrose remarked.

'Well, Fergus Murphy, the last owner, had no funds to keep up with modern agricultural methods. Poor John inherited a museum, not a farm, after his uncle died.'

'They're finally moving into the twentieth century then.'

'At least now he is able to feed his children every day, and perhaps even make a little profit from his efforts.'

'And how is Mary?'

'As bright and sweet as she always is. She told me this morning she's enjoying school.'

'I'm only glad she's going; that bright head of hers needs stimulation. How's her reading coming along?'

'I knew you'd ask that, so while I was there, I asked her to read a few simple sentences from the "Parable of the Sower and the Seeds", which she'd been learning at school. She hardly hesitated with the words, though I worry she hasn't enough reading material at home. She's already surpassed her older brother and sisters and, to my knowledge, the O'Reillys only possess one book, which is, of course, the Bible. I told both Merry and her older sister Katie that they were to read and learn the words of the "Prodigal Son" and I'd test them the next time I visited. That way, it doesn't look as if Merry is being singled out.'

'Good man, and I know for a fact the O'Reillys have the means for her elder sisters to continue their education in future if they so desire, not just Mary. I'm sure it suits your purposes too, to know that Mary is receiving extra tuition in Bible study,' smiled Ambrose. 'It's a shame I don't see her as often as I have done due to her schooling, but I hope to see her in the Christmas holidays and it's far more important she receives at least some level of education.'

'Well, her teacher, Miss Lucey, is young and eager to bring the children on. I'd say that Merry's in a safe pair of hands. When I was last down there, she mentioned how surprised she was to see the new little O'Reilly girl already reading.'

'I only wish I could give her more reading material at home,' said Ambrose.

'We both know you can't, my friend. A gift to a child returning from the priest's house could be seen as suspicious.'

'Of course, James, of course. You know I would never do anything to compromise your position. As you have said, your parishioners have now begun to trust you.'

'I have come to understand their ways and they mine, although I did have an unfortunate incident recently with one young female member of my flock.'

'You don't even have to tell me what happened – she

caught you after Mass, seeming distressed; you took her for a walk around the cemetery. And there, she declared her undying love for you.'

James looked at Ambrose in utter astonishment. 'How did you know?'

'Because you are a handsome man in your prime, who comforts the sick and administers last rites to the dying. You act as the community's moral compass; you are approachable, yet untouchable. All that makes a tantalising recipe for young girls with no one else to idolise.'

'I am a priest!' exhorted James in frustration. 'As I said to Colleen, any special attention she told me I'd shown towards her had simply been because her mother had died recently, leaving her with five young siblings to care for at the age of just fourteen. I was being kind, nothing more.'

'I'm only surprised such a situation hasn't come up before, James. I'm sure it will happen many times more in the future, so you'd better be prepared.'

'I don't believe I handled the situation with Colleen well at all. I haven't seen her at Mass since it happened and when I went round to visit at her home, she refused to let me in.'

'Leave her be for now; she'll get over herself in time when she meets a more suitable target for her affections.'

'You're sounding like you're an expert, so,' James grinned.

'Hardly, and I'm warning you that you are starting to put the word "so" at the end of your sentences. You are becoming a true West Cork native.'

'What if I am?' James chuckled. 'It's my adopted home, where I will live for the rest of my life.'

'You also seem to have lost all ambition to move on to a more prestigious parish.'

'For now, I feel I am doing good here.'

'Well, from my point of view, even if I have to travel through the bogs of the Midlands to see you, at least I know you're close to my special little girl, and for that, I am grateful.'

That night, Ambrose settled himself as best he could on the narrow iron bed with its hard horse-hair mattress, and gave a deep sigh. Not for the first time, he wondered what he was doing, driving down every month to the godforsaken south-west coast to visit his old friend, when he could have enjoyed a far more relaxed day in his comfortable apartment in Merrion Square, perhaps sharing a light supper with Mairead O'Connell, an English Fellow at Trinity.

While the rest of the world was rocking around the clock to Bill Haley and his Comets, West Cork was still caught in a time warp, with a pig's head for a Saturday night's dinner treat. The notion of a radio in every home, or even the television screens that had started to pop up in Dublin since a transmitter had been erected in Belfast, was still far off. Let alone that, he was making the journey to visit a man whom he knew would only ever regard him as his closest friend.

Long ago, when they were at boarding school together, he had dreamt that James would see what Ambrose believed he truly was, accept it and change the course of his life plan to accommodate it. Which, of course, in Ambrose's dream scenario, would include him. But after twenty-five years, Ambrose had to accept that this was, and only ever could be, a dream because God himself was the love of James's life.

He knew he had a choice: he could give up and move on, enjoy his pleasant and fulfilling life teaching his students at

Trinity, or he could continue to hanker after something that could never be. Friendship was all James was prepared – or *able* – to offer him. But was that more painful than not having James in his life at all?

He knew the answer, of course: James loved him in his own way, and that would have to be enough, because the thought of a life without him in it was one Ambrose simply couldn't contemplate.

29

Merry woke up in her new bedroom as her stomach turned over and her heart began to beat faster. Today it was her birthday, the seventh of November, and Mammy had sewn her a special pink dress to wear to her very own party. Her class at school were coming, along with their parents.

Mammy had had them all scrubbing every surface, and even dusting the inside of the presses since yesterday morning.

'No one will say the O'Reillys are dirty,' Mammy repeated for the endless time. Merry's eldest brother John had said 'twas just a chance for Mammy and Daddy to show off their new place, but even if he was right, she was excited about the day. All her friends from school were invited, apart from Bobby Noiro, who for some reason she didn't know was never allowed up at the farm.

Merry also knew that Bridget O'Mahoney, who looked like Mammy and her sister Katie, with her pale skin and her flame hair, would be wearing a far more expensive dress than her, which would be made by the seamstress who worked for the tailor in Timoleague, like all her clothes were. Bridget came from the richest family around these parts; they lived in a house that was even bigger than the one Father O'Brien lived in. Her daddy drove her to school every day in a big shiny car, whereas the rest of her class had to walk across the fields (which were more of a bog in the winter, when it was raining). Miss Lucey always made them take off their boots and set them by the fire in the schoolroom to dry out while she did her teaching. It was fierce kind of her to think about that, but most times they got soaked again only a few yards into their journey home.

Merry wriggled her toes. She was amazed they were still on her feet and hadn't turned into fins like the fish, given the amount of time they spent in water. Sometimes the puddles she walked through came up to the bit of her body between her ankle and her knee (she must ask Miss Lucey what that bit was called). Still, today it wasn't raining and Merry decided to enjoy every moment of it.

As it was a Sunday, the family went to Mass, and outside afterwards Father O'Brien wished her a very happy sixth birthday.

Sunday was her second favourite day, after Mondays up at the priest's house. Merry looked forward to it all week, because it was the only day that all the siblings had time to play games together after lunch was cleared away. They'd go out into the fields, rain or shine, and run wild. They'd play at hurling, trying to get the small hard ball between the make-shift goalposts that Daddy or John had erected. Or sometimes tag, or hide-and-seek, when she would always be found first because she couldn't stop giggling. Today, as it was her birthday party, she had been allowed to choose all the games.

As the family climbed onto their pony and trap to head home, Merry decided that no matter how perfect Bridget O'Mahoney's dress was, and how many layers of net skirts it had, Merry wouldn't mind a bit, because it was *her* birthday, and today was a GOOD day.

'Mammy, you look so pretty in that dress,' Merry said admiringly as her mother came into the kitchen just before the party was about to start. 'Doesn't she, Daddy?'

'You're a picture, to be sure, love,' Daddy said, putting a hand protectively on Mammy's huge tummy, as Merry surveyed the feast laid out on the long wooden table.

There were sandwiches with different fillings, Mammy's special baked ham, scones and, in the centre of it all, a birthday cake iced in pink that said *Happy Birthday Merry* on the top of it.

Lined up on another table was an array of mugs ready to be dipped into the barrel that Daddy had brought back on the cart a few days ago. Daddy didn't go to the pub much, but she'd heard him say that nothing could make a party go with a swing like a glass of stout for the men.

'Ready?' her mammy asked her daddy. He gave her one of those secret looks and a smile.

'Ready.'

'Our first guests are here,' piped up Nora, as the Sheehy family appeared in the courtyard.

'Let the party begin,' Merry heard Mammy mutter under her breath, as she touched her great big tummy full of baby.

Only a few hours later, Merry lay in her bed with Katie. Both had their heads underneath the pillows to try and block out the sound of Mammy screaming. The water had come again from between her legs just after the last guests had left, and the baby delivery lady had been sent for. Mrs Moran had arrived and shooed the family away as she'd helped Mammy upstairs to her bedroom.

'Will Mammy die?' Katie asked her sisters, and Merry

could feel her slight body trembling against her. All four girls were in Merry and Katie's room, along with little Bill, because it was furthest away from the screaming.

'No, Katie,' said Ellen, ''tis just the way. 'Twas the same when Mammy had Bill.'

'Then I'll never have babies,' Katie said, mirroring Merry's own thoughts on the subject.

'Don't worry, 'twill stop soon and we'll have a beautiful baby brother or sister to play with. Mammy and Daddy will smile and be as proud as punch,' said Nora.

'What if something goes wrong?'

'It won't,' Ellen said firmly.

'Well, Orla's mammy died having her little sister,' Katie said staunchly.

''Twill be all right, try and sleep, Katie,' Ellen soothed her.

'How can I, when all I can hear is Mammy screaming?'

'Then we'll sing, shall we? How about "Be Thou My Vision"?'

So the four girls sang their favourite hymns and a couple of the 'old songs' that Daddy liked to play on his fiddle on a Sunday evening. The agonised screaming went on long into the night. Ellen and Nora went back to their room with Bill, and Merry and Katie dozed fitfully through the dark hours until dawn, when a weak cry was heard from their parents' room.

'The baby's here, Katie,' Merry muttered, as a silence as deafening as the screams fell like a blanket over the house.

'When can we see the new babe?'

All of the children clustered around Daddy the next morning. 'Is it a girl or a boy?' asked John. 'I want a boy!'

'It's a boy,' murmured a grey-faced Daddy.

'All boys are eejits,' sighed Nora.

'All girls are eejits,' John shot back.

'Can we see Mammy?' Merry asked.

'Not for now, Merry. The midwife's seeing to her. The birth took a lot out of her,' Daddy replied.

'She will be all right, though, won't she?' Merry asked, reading the concern on her father's face.

'Sure, the midwife says she'll be fine, and we're not to worry.'

But Merry did, even when Mrs Moran eventually came down with the new baby wrapped up in a sheet. They all peered down at him.

'He's tiny!'

'His eyes aren't open!'

'He looks like Daddy!'

'Now then, would Daddy like to hold his new son?' asked Mrs Moran. John O'Reilly held out his arms and she put the baby into them.

'Would you like a cup of tea, Mrs Moran?' Ellen, the eldest girl and therefore in charge of all things domestic if Mammy wasn't here, asked the woman politely.

'No thanks, my love, I've another lady in labour in Clogagh, who I must go to check on. Now then, why don't you walk outside with me, girls?'

As Ellen showed Mrs Moran to the door, Nora, Katie and Merry followed behind.

'Your mammy lost a lot of blood whilst birthing the babe, but thanks be to God, it's stopped for now,' said Mrs Moran in a low voice. 'You'll be needing to check on her regularly to make sure it doesn't start again, and she must have complete bedrest until she's stronger.'

Ellen nodded and as Mrs Moran waved goodbye, Merry

tugged on Ellen's skirt. 'Where does she want us to check?' Merry asked her.

'In between her legs, of course!' said Ellen impatiently. 'You're not to be worrying, any of you, I'll be doing all that. Mammy has to rest for the next few days, so Nora, Katie and you will be doing more chores, understand? As well as looking after Bill and the chickens, you'll be doing breakfasts and making broth from chicken bones for Mammy, to help her get stronger, because I won't be having time for any of that.'

'But it's school today and I don't know how to make broth,' Merry whispered.

'Then you'll just have to stay home and learn, won't you, girl?' Ellen said before she turned away to go inside and head back upstairs to Mammy. 'Oh, and one of you has to go up to the priest's house to tell Father O'Brien Mammy won't be in to clean today.'

Father O'Brien was just about to leave for Mass when he heard a tapping on the front door. He opened it and saw Katie O'Reilly, a diminutive version of her mother Maggie, standing there panting, and dripping wet from the rain.

'Hello, Father O'Brien, I've a message for you. Our new brother was born in the night and Mammy is very tired from the birth and she has to stay in bed to rest and she can't come up today to clean your house and we're not to go to school so we can help and Nora's feeding the chickens but Merry doesn't know how to make broth and Daddy wanted to know when you could church Mammy and baptise the babe and—'

'Slow down, Katie,' James said, putting a gentle hand on Katie's shoulder, 'and draw breath. You look soaked to the skin. Come in for a bit and warm yourself by my fire.'

'Oh Father, I should be getting back to help my sisters.'

'I'm sure five minutes won't harm.'

James gave her a slight push and propelled her through the door to his study, where Ambrose was sitting reading the *Cork Examiner*.

'This is my friend Ambrose Lister. Ambrose, this is Katie, Maggie O'Reilly's daughter. Now then, Katie, take off your boots and we'll put them by the fire to dry out a little. You sit down there.' James pointed to the chair opposite Ambrose, who was staring at the tiny girl with the flame-red curls.

'So, your mammy has had her new babe?' said James.

'Yes, and he's going to be called Patrick.'

'A fine name that is too. And you say Merry doesn't know how to make broth?'

'No, Father. Ellen told her to make it, but Ellen's been too busy taking care of Mammy to help her, and all we know is it's got chicken bones in it, and that Mammy should have it to make her strong again, but . . .'

James's heart broke as the little girl wrung her hands.

'Well now, I've Mass at the church, but after that, why don't I come down and see what I can do to help?' he suggested.

'Do you know how to make broth, Father?' Katie asked, her wide green eyes looking hopeful.

'I'm sure that I can get some guidance to help you, and also see to having your mother churched and getting your new brother baptised. Have you had breakfast?'

'No, Father, because Merry tried to make goodie, but 'twas disgusting.' Katie made a face. 'I don't think she's a very good cook.'

'You wait there and I'll be back in a trice.'

'I'm sorry to be bothering you, Father,' Katie said as her small feet reached instinctively for the warmth of the fire.

'And you, sir,' she said to Ambrose as James disappeared to the kitchen.

'Oh, don't worry about me. I'm happy to be bothered.'

Katie looked at him, her little face serious. 'You have a funny accent, if you don't mind me saying so.'

'I don't mind, Katie. And I'd agree with you.'

'You're not from round these parts, are you, sir?'

'I'm not, no. I live in Dublin.'

'Dublin! That's a very big city, isn't it, sir? And a very, very long way away?'

'It is indeed, Katie.'

'Is that your car outside? I like the colour.' Katie pointed out of the window at the red Beetle in the drive. ''Tis a funny shape for a car, though.'

'It's called a Beetle, because it looks a little like one, doesn't it? Would you like a ride in it?'

'Oh sir, I've never been in a car before. I might be very scared of the noise.'

James walked back in with a picnic basket and placed it at Katie's feet. 'There's half a loaf of bread in there and some cheese and ham as well, which should do all of you for the morning.'

'Oh, thank you, Father. 'Twill stop Merry fretting that we've nothing to serve Daddy and John when they're in from the fields.' She stood up, then collected her boots, and proceeded to put them on. Then she reached for the picnic basket. 'I'm sure Mammy will be back next week to clean,' she reassured both of them.

'Well now, I'll be straight down to you after Mass, Katie.'

'Are you sure you don't want a ride to your house in my red car?' Ambrose asked as the little girl walked towards the door clutching the basket, which was almost as big as she was.

'No thank you, sir, I'll be grand walking home.'

Once James had seen Katie out, he came back to the study.

'What a charming little thing she is,' Ambrose said. 'It sounds like chaos at the O'Reilly farm. Surely Mary and her sisters aren't meant to run the house whilst their mother recovers from the birth? Can't the older sister take care of the household while the younger ones attend school? And what on earth is "goodie"?!'

'A cheap version of porridge using stale bread, and no is the answer. 'Tis a large farm to run, and Merry and Katie are old enough now to help.'

'The poor mites,' sighed Ambrose. 'We must do what we can to help.'

'I can certainly take up the soup that neither of us ate last night, rather than putting it in the slop. I'll be able to see the lie of the land when I get down there.'

There was another knock on the front door, then the sound of the handle turning and the familiar *tap-tap* of a pair of sturdy brogues coming along the hall.

There was a sharp rap on the study door, and Mrs Cavanagh put her head around it.

'Excuse me for interrupting, but I've heard tell that Mrs O'Reilly won't be in to do her work today. So I thought 'twas my duty to come and offer myself in her place.'

She sounds as if she's giving herself up for sacrifice, thought Ambrose as he felt her usual piercing look of disapproval fall upon him.

'That's most kind of you, Mrs Cavanagh, but I'm sure that Mr Lister and I can mind ourselves for the day, if you've other things to be doing,' said James.

'Ah, I can put them off for you, Father. Have you had breakfast yet?'

'No, but—'

'Then I'll be sorting it out for you. It's a good job I don't have small ones that are likely to mean I'll be unable to work for you if you need me, Father.'

With that, Mrs Cavanagh turned and left the study.

Rather than looking at her new blanket, knitted out of colourful squares by Mammy for her birthday, or counting the pennies she'd been given by everyone who had come to her party, Merry was having the worst day of her life.

The truly terrible part was seeing Mammy as pale as the sheets on her bed. She was too weak to even take a sip of water, let alone hold Patrick. The new babe was smaller than Katie's wooden doll and as pale as Mammy. Ellen said he didn't even seem to know how to suckle. But at least, when Merry said a prayer to the Blessed Virgin on her knees at the bedside, Mammy smiled and patted Merry's arm. Ellen entered the bedroom and pushed her out of the way to check on their mother.

'Go down to the kitchen,' Ellen barked at her.

Merry watched through a crack in the wooden door as Ellen pulled back the sheet and looked between Mammy's legs. There was no big red patch like Mrs Moran had warned about, so she gave a sigh of relief.

'Merry, I told you to leave,' Ellen hissed. 'Go and make the broth, girl.'

Merry scarpered down the stairs and into the kitchen. Daddy, who rarely drank from the whiskey bottle he kept in the press in the New Room, was now fast asleep in his chair, the bottle by his side.

Katie was also in the kitchen, with Bill asleep in her lap.

'I need to make a broth for Mammy,' Merry said despairingly.

'Ellen said I must. What if she dies in the night, Katie, because I didn't know how?'

'Father O'Brien said he'll come down to show us. I'll carry Bill up and put him in our bed, and take up a fresh jug of water for Mammy. I'll take a spoon of sugar from the pantry to put in it as well. I heard Mrs Moran say sugar water was good for keeping up strength.'

Merry stood by the range, staring down at the pile of chicken bones that she was somehow supposed to turn into the watery soup Mammy sometimes made if any of them were sick. She thought hard and remembered that carrots and spuds had been involved, so she went to find some.

She peeled and chopped a few of them, put them in the pot with the bones, added some water and put it on the hotplate of the range. She watched it come to the boil, hoping that some magic would happen, but it didn't. Instead, the water began to spit everywhere, so she had to lift it off. The pot was heavy and some water splashed onto her fingers, sending a jolt of pain through them.

'Ouch!' she cried, as she put the pan down and went to the tap to put her fingers under cold water, tears spilling out of her eyes. At the same time, there was a knock on the door and Father O'Brien appeared with another basket.

'Merry, what has happened?'

'Oh, 'tis nothing, Father,' she said, drying her eyes on the nearest cloth. 'I was trying to make broth.'

'I've brought some soup for you.' Father O'Brien put the basket down and offered her two flasks. 'With a few of the carrots and potatoes added from that pot, it should be enough for your mammy for a couple of days. Where are your sisters?'

'Ellen's upstairs with Mammy, Nora's after helping John outside 'cos Daddy's sleeping, and Katie took Bill up to put him down for a sleep and hasn't come back yet.' Merry stared at Father O'Brien, remembering Mammy always offered him a cup of tea and some cake. But before she could, he'd picked up his basket.

'Right, if you'd be good enough to show me up to your mammy's room, I'll get on with the religious side of things.' He smiled at her, as he pulled out another flask, took the top off and sniffed it. 'I'm just checking this is the one with the holy water in it. 'Twouldn't do to be baptising your brother with soup now, would it?'

Merry giggled, and as she led him upstairs, thought how much she loved Father O'Brien because he always knew what to do.

After his arrival, the day got a lot better. Once Mammy had been churched (whatever that was), Daddy was woken up by Ellen and they all went upstairs to watch Patrick being baptised. Ellen took over the cooking after a gentle word from Father O'Brien about the dangers of small ones and boiling water, and Nora was dispatched upstairs with the soup and to sit with Mammy.

Eventually, night came and Merry and Katie were shooed up to bed by Ellen. 'Bill will sleep with you tonight – we don't want Mammy disturbed,' she'd added.

'You have him for now,' Katie said as she tucked Bill under the new blanket with Merry. Then she took the hairbrush they shared from the top of the chest of drawers. 'Count to one hundred for me,' Katie demanded, because Merry knew she got lost after the thirties.

She did so, and marvelled at the way her sister's hair shone like spun copper. 'Sure, you'll be getting yourself a handsome man to marry one day,' Merry said admiringly.

'I swear I'll be having myself a husband even richer than Bridget O'Mahoney's daddy, with a house ten times bigger than this one. Even if I don't love him and he has a nose longer than Mrs Cavanagh's,' Katie said firmly. 'Can I see how many birthday pennies you got yesterday?'

'If you promise not to tell anyone where they're hidden. On pain of death, Katie. Swear on all the saints first.'

Katie crossed herself. 'I swear on all the saints.'

Merry climbed out of her bed and opened the drawer she used for her pants and socks. Thinking that even her sisters on the search for pennies wouldn't touch her smalls, she pulled out a black sock, then took it over to the bed and poured out the contents.

'Jesus, Mary and Joseph! I'd reckon you could buy your own cow with that amount!' Katie took one of the shiny round coins in her small palm and stroked it. 'How many do you have?'

'Thirteen altogether.'

''Tis an unlucky number, Merry. Maybe you should give one to me for safekeeping.'

'Of course you can have one, Katie, but don't tell the others or they'll want one too.'

'Will we go to Timoleague to buy some sweeties this week?' Katie suggested.

'Maybe, but I'm saving the rest.'

'What for?'

'I don't know,' Merry said, 'but something.'

'John told me a secret once.'

'What secret?'

'Oh, about how we can get more sweeties if . . .'

'What?'

'I'm not sure I should tell.'

'Katie O'Reilly! I just told you where I hide my pennies. You tell me now, or I'll—'

''Tis your turn to swear on all the saints you won't say I said.'

Merry did so. 'Come on now, Katie, tell me.'

'John told me that when he was my age, some of the boys in his class at school who had pennies took them down to the railway line when the train was due to go by. When they heard the hoot of the train, they ran onto the tracks and laid their pennies on the rails. When the train passed, its wheels ran over them. And Mrs Delaney at the sweetie shop always gave them a few extra sweeties if the boys had flattened pennies. I'd say 'twas because it makes them larger,' Katie nodded knowledgeably.

'John's never done that, has he?'

At that point, Katie's pale skin flushed a deep crimson, even as she shook her head.

'You're not to go telling Mammy and Daddy.'

'But 'tis dangerous, Katie, he could have been killed!' Merry said as she collected her pennies and put them back in the drawer.

She'd just climbed back into bed when Nora came into their room.

'Merry, go sit with Mammy while I go downstairs to the laundry with this sheet.' She yawned loudly. 'I'm exhausted, and here you two are, tucked up cosy in your beds.' Nora swung round and marched back through the door.

'All she's done is sit with Mammy for most of the afternoon,' Katie complained. ''Twas me that was washing out the new babe's napkins.'

'Well, I'd better go and sit with Mammy like she said.'

Merry walked along the narrow landing, then unhooked the latch to Mammy and Daddy's room. With relief, she saw that both her mother and the new babe were asleep, even if they were as still and pale as the grave.

Getting down on her knees, she sent up another prayer, before gingerly lifting the sheet to check for blood like Ellen had done. It was clean.

'Thank you, Holy Mother, for protecting my own,' she whispered as she replaced the sheet and then sat down in the chair to wait for Nora to return.

The week after baby Patrick had arrived felt like the longest of Merry's whole life. At least she and Katie had been sent back to school, because Nora had announced it was time for her to leave the convent school in Clonakilty. With Mammy sick, Ellen, John and Daddy needed help around the place. Besides, Nora said, what did she need with letters and numbers?

When Merry was home, it felt like the new babe cried all the time, and Ellen and Nora were only ever complaining about all the work they had to do, while Daddy grumbled that he'd hardly had any sleep due to the baby screaming. Daddy had taken to sleeping in the New Room, because he said it was quieter downstairs. The New Room was just off the kitchen and the children were never allowed in it, because it was 'for best'. It had a big fire and two armchairs for Mammy and Daddy, where he now slept while still sitting upright.

Nora handed Bill over to Merry and Katie the moment they walked through the door. He was by now moving quite fast on his chubby little legs, and the two of them spent their lives chasing after him, indoors and out.

Merry went up to see Mammy every day when she got home. She'd be awake and ask her about what she had learnt, while she nursed little Pat, who seemed to have got the hang of feeding now. She told Mammy about the new reading book she was on, and how Miss Lucey was teaching them something called geography, which was all about other countries in the world. Then she went downstairs to start her home-work at the kitchen table.

One misty evening, Katie was sitting on the floor, throwing a ball to Bill.

'I swear, I'll never have babies. Ever,' Katie said yet again as Bill went after the ball, then fell over, bumping his head on a table leg and starting to yowl.

'But that's what God wants us to do, Katie. Father O'Brien said so. If no one had babies, then there would be no people on earth, would there? Anyway, Mammy says she's feeling much better and 'tis the last day Ellen is in charge,' Merry added, trying to cheer Katie up.

'Bridget O'Mahoney has a maid at home,' Katie said, as she gathered Bill in her small arms to comfort him. 'I'll have one too when I'm older.'

There was an unexpected knock on the front door. Merry looked at Katie in surprise, as no one ever used the front door.

'You'd better open it,' Katie shrugged.

Merry stood up and did so. Outside in the darkness stood a thin man wearing a tall hat.

'Hello there, I'm Dr Townsend,' he smiled down at her. 'And who might you be?'

'I'm Merry O'Reilly,' she replied politely, knowing his funny accent meant he was British.

'That you are, dear. Father O'Brien suggested I should call. Might I see your mother, please?'

He followed Merry into the kitchen, sweeping off his fine hat, then allowed Katie to lead him upstairs to Mammy's bedroom. He shut the door behind him.

Both Merry and Katie decided to send up a prayer to the Holy Mother that there was no bad news, because Bobby Noiro had told her that was the only time a doctor came to visit. It was a doctor who'd come to the door when his daddy had died in a fire in their barn, but that was all Bobby would say about it.

Ellen came in to start preparing the evening meal, and Nora appeared from wherever she'd been hiding to get out of doing chores.

'Who was that man?' she asked.

'A doctor. I let him in,' Merry said importantly.

A look passed between Ellen and Nora which filled Merry's heart with fear. A silence hung over the kitchen as the four girls waited for the doctor to come down the stairs.

Eventually he did, and Nora was sent to fetch Daddy in from the cowshed. 'May I have a word in private, Mr O'Reilly?'

Daddy led him into the New Room and the door was once again firmly shut. Fifteen minutes later, the two men re-appeared in the kitchen.

'Is everything all right, Doctor?' asked Katie, always first with the chat.

'Yes indeed, young miss,' the doctor said with a reassuring smile. 'Your mother will be very well and so will your little brother.'

Merry saw the expression on Daddy's face and thought that he looked as if Mammy were dead and had been sent to purgatory for all eternity.

'So now, Doctor, what's the cost?' Daddy asked him.

'As 'twas only advice, I won't be charging you. I'll let myself out,' he said. 'Good evening, everyone.'

With a touch of his hat, he was gone.

''Tis wonderful news Mammy's well, isn't it, Daddy?' said Merry.

'Yes,' he replied, but even though his mouth said the words, the expression on his face didn't change.

As the family sat down for their tea, chattering like a flock of birds, Daddy sat silently, his face like stone.

Later, after they'd finished the soup and bread, then said their prayers together, Katie and Merry went upstairs to their room.

'Daddy didn't look very happy about Mammy being well, did he?' said Merry.

'No, he didn't. Do you . . . do you think the doctor was just lying to us and Mammy's going to die?' Katie asked her.

'I don't know.' Merry shivered at the thought.

'Holy Mother, 'tis cold in this room,' Katie pronounced. 'Winter is coming in. Can I share your bed tonight?'

'O'course,' Merry agreed, wondering why Mammy and Daddy had chosen to give them separate beds in the first place, Katie was so rarely in her own.

They snuggled up together and finally the feeling began to flood back into Merry's frozen feet.

'Aren't adults a mystery, Katie?' she said aloud in the dark.

'They are indeed. And guess what, Merry?'

'I can't, Katie, what?'

'One day, we're going to be adults too!'

30

It was Christmastime and Merry had already been an angel in the little play Miss Lucey had put on in the school hall for any parents that wanted to come and watch. Katie had hated every moment of being a shepherd, but Merry had loved her own costume, even if it was only made out of an old sheet and a bit of tinsel that sat like a crown on her head. She had to concentrate hard as she'd had words to remember as well:

'And Mary will bring forth a son, and you shall call His name Jesus, for He will save His people from their sins.'

Being called Mary, she'd have preferred to be the Holy Virgin herself, but there were three other Marys in the school (which meant being called by her nickname was much better than being 'Mary M.' or 'Mary O.' or 'Mary D.'). None of the Marys had been given the part. That honour had gone to Bridget O'Mahoney. Of course, her mammy had had her costume made by their seamstress, and as Merry stared at Bridget, in a lovely blue dress that matched her eyes, she thought that if it were hers, she'd never take it off.

Mammy had come to watch, and even though baby Pat had screamed during the 'Silent Night' carol, Merry had decided she was the prettiest mother in the room. She was well now, with colour back in her cheeks and, as her brother John had said, 'a bit more meat on her bones'.

Bobby Noiro hadn't been given a role in the play, as punishment for hitting Seamus Daly on the head. Ever since, Seamus had been after saying that all of Bobby's family were traitors and murderers. Bobby would have most likely hit Seamus several times more if Mr Byrne, the caretaker, hadn't pulled them apart.

On the walk home, Bobby's favourite new thing was to disappear behind trees, then jump out shouting, 'Bang!' He told her he was shooting the 'Black and Tans'. Merry didn't know why he'd want to shoot at them, because those were colours, weren't they? Katie always got cross with him, flicking her red hair and walking faster ahead, so it was Merry and Bobby walking together and him recounting the stories of 'the old days' that his granny had told him, which were all to do with some war.

The next day, what with school being over for the Christmas holidays, she knew it would be the last time she walked home with Bobby, so she gave him the little card she'd drawn for him, spelling out the word 'Christmas' very carefully. She'd only made it because the day before, when the class had been exchanging cards, Bobby had been the only one who hadn't been given any. Even though he hadn't said, Merry could tell it had upset him something fierce.

When he saw the card she'd made him, he gave her a big smile and handed her a crumpled bit of stained ribbon.

''Tis blue, like your eyes,' he said, staring at his boots.

'Thanks a million, Bobby. I'll wear it for when Santy comes,' she said. Then he'd turned and run off with Hunter at his heels towards his cottage, while Katie made kissing noises at Merry all the way back home.

For some reason Merry couldn't quite work out, the atmosphere in the house felt different to normal Christmases. Even though the paper garlands had been made, and holly brought into the house and carols sung, something didn't feel the same.

Merry decided it was because Mammy and Daddy looked so miserable. Before Pat had been born and the visit from the doctor had happened, she'd often seen Daddy give Mammy a kiss on top of her head or squeeze her hand under the table at tea, as if they shared some secret that made them both smile. But these days, they hardly spoke and Merry had watched Daddy's whiskey bottle go down and down until there was almost none left.

Maybe I'm imagining it, she thought when she woke up on Christmas Eve and felt that lovely tingle of excitement in her belly. 'Today will be a GOOD day,' she announced to herself. This morning, she was up to the priest's house with Mammy to help her clean, because it was the Christmas holidays. She hoped Ambrose would be there as she hadn't seen him for what felt like a very long time. She loved sitting in Father O'Brien's study with the fire burning brightly in the grate. Last time, they'd had chats about how her schooling was getting on, then he'd taken a book of fairy stories by Mr Hans Christian Andersen and read her 'The Little Match Girl'. The story was all about a child on New Year's Eve, who burnt matches because they gave her light and warmth. She froze to death out on the street, but then her soul was sent into heaven and she was happy to be with her beloved grandmother.

'That sounds very sad,' Katie had pouted after Merry had told her the story. 'And it has no fairies in it at all!'

Merry heard Pat crying in their parents' room. The babe seemed to be always hungry, and sometimes Merry looked at her mammy with Pat to her breast, and thought she was like the cows being drained of their milk morning and night.

Anxious for the day to begin, she dressed in her warmest jumper, which was really too small for her now, a skirt and a pair of woollen socks, then made her way downstairs. Since Mammy had been so weak after the babe had been born, and had to feed Pat early in the morning, she was now an expert goodie maker, getting stale bread to mix with the milk and a dash of sugar. But this morning, in honour of it being Christmas Eve, Mammy had said that it was a proper porridge day. Merry switched on the overhead light, took the oats from the pantry and filled a jug with milk from the churn. As she stirred the porridge on the range, Merry looked outside and saw the fields in front of the farmhouse were sparkling with frost.

'To be sure, it looks like a Christmas picture,' she said to herself. She had actually started to enjoy the quiet moments in the kitchen before everyone tumbled down the stairs and Daddy and John came in from the milking shed, ready for their breakfast. While the porridge simmered, Merry took the loaf of soda bread Mammy had made yesterday and put that and the butter on the table. Placing the bowls to warm on the range, she thought of the presents she'd bought with her birthday pennies for her family. Beautiful new ribbons for Ellen and Nora, a special comb for Katie's hair, and a toy rabbit and a toy mouse for Pat and Bill. She'd bought some embroidery thread to make Mammy and Daddy handkerchiefs out of squares of cotton, though the 'D's were a little bit wonky. Now she'd only tuppence left, which she'd keep for a rainy day, as Mammy always called savings. As it rained most days, she supposed those savings were important.

'Morning, Merry,' said Mammy as she walked into the kitchen with baby Pat tucked into the sling strapped across her chest.

'Sit down, Mammy. Everything is done already.'

Mammy smiled up at her as she sat in the chair. 'Pat wouldn't settle last night, so I'm a little weary this morning. Thank you, Merry, you're a good girl, to be sure.'

''Tis Christmas Eve, Mammy, the best day of the year.'

'And I must go to clean the Father's house,' Mammy sighed.

'I'm there to help you, I promise.'

'Oh Merry, I didn't mean it like that. You do your fair share here and more. And Mr Lister is such a kind man. If it hadn't been for him, then . . .'

Merry, who was stirring the porridge to make sure it wasn't getting too thick, turned to look at her mother.

'What do you mean, Mammy?'

'Ah, nothing, Merry, only that he helps you with your letters. He teaches at a famous university and you can't be getting any more clever than that. I just hope this one settles whilst we're up there, so I can get on with my work and then be back home in time to get everything ready for tomorrow.'

'I can mind Pat for you there, Mammy, you know I can.'

'I know, pet,' Maggie smiled at her. 'I'll be having some of that porridge now, with maybe an extra dash of sugar on it for energy.'

'What are you having some of, Mammy?' asked Ellen as she walked in carrying a squirming Bill.

'Never you mind,' she said. 'We were talking about Santy, weren't we?'

'Yes, we were, Mammy.' Merry smiled to herself as she sprinkled a little sugar on the bowls and brought them to the table.

An hour later, the two of them were on their way up to the top of the hill that the priest's house sat on, looking down on the village of Timoleague. When they arrived, Mammy knocked politely and waited for an answer. Ambrose opened the door.

'Good day to you both,' he smiled. 'The father's out on his rounds already, visiting the sick and giving them a Christmas blessing. You know what to do, Mrs O'Reilly. Oh, and the father said to tell you that all the ingredients you need are in the pantry.'

'Very good, Mr Lister. I'm sorry I've had to bring baby Pat along, but he just wouldn't settle and all the other girls are busy at home . . .'

'That's no problem at all, Mrs O'Reilly. Now then, I've just boiled the kettle and filled the pot. May I offer you a nice hot cup of tea after your walk? It really is biting out there.'

Ten minutes later, after a cup of tea into which Merry had poured as much sugar as she wanted from the bowl Ambrose had left out for them, she carried Pat into the study with her, while Mammy got on with her work.

'I'm sure he'll settle in a minute, Ambrose, but he's a fierce screamer.'

'That was what my mother said of me when I was a baby,' Ambrose smiled as Merry gently rocked the baby in her arms, begging him silently to go to sleep. 'Maybe the warmth of the fire will soothe him.'

'I wish something would,' Merry sighed.

'So, Mary, how has school been since I last saw you?'

Ambrose always insisted on calling her Mary, as he'd told her he wasn't fond of nicknames.

'Oh, very good, Ambrose. I'm onto reading book ten, which Miss Lucey said is normally for older children. And my numbers are coming on well, I think, even though they're harder than reading letters. At least you don't have to add them up, do you?'

'No, you don't, Mary.'

'Look now, Pat has finally closed his eyes. I'll just lay him down on the mat over there, if you don't mind.'

'Not at all. Should we talk in whispers so as not to wake him?'

'Oh no, you should hear the noise my brothers and sisters make around the place when he's asleep. He'll be grand altogether, so.'

Ambrose watched the little girl as she laid the baby down carefully, then covered him with a worn blanket.

'And how's your family, Mary?'

'We all caught a cold a few weeks back, but we're better now, thank you,' Merry said as she sat down. 'Mammy is much better too, but this small one wants a lot of milk.'

'And your father?'

'Well, he has more glasses of his whiskey now than he used to and sometimes he looks sad . . .' Merry shook her head. 'I don't know why, Ambrose, because we're just after moving to our new house, the harvest was a healthy one and . . .' Merry shrugged. 'Sometimes, I just can't understand adults.'

'No, Mary,' Ambrose replied as he suppressed a smile, 'sometimes I can't either, and I am one! Now then, shall I read you a story?'

'Can it be "The Little Match Girl"?'

'Well now, as it's Christmas Eve, how about I read a new Christmas story to you?'

'Yes please.' Merry watched as he reached for what looked like a very old book on the table beside him.

'This story is by an English author called Charles Dickens. It's quite a grown-up story, Mary, and long too, so we may only get through part of it today. It also has things called ghosts in it. Do you know what ghosts are?'

'Oh yes, Ambrose! Mammy's after telling us fairy stories about the old times in Ireland and there are ghosts in those. Me and Katie think they're real, but Ellen and Nora say we're eejits because of it.'

'I wouldn't call you an eejit, Mary, but my opinion is the same as your sisters: ghosts don't exist. However, sometimes it's fun to be scared, isn't it?'

'I think so, but not at midnight, when everyone in the house is sleeping except for me.'

'I think that you are clever enough to understand the difference between real life and stories. Perhaps the best thing for me to do is to start reading and you must tell me to stop if you get frightened, all right?'

Merry nodded, her eyes wide.

'So, this story is called . . .' Ambrose held out the page to Mary and pointed at the title.

'A Christmas Carol!'

'Well done, Mary. It's the story of a man called Ebenezer Scrooge. Perhaps if you think of the meanest person you know, who always looks unhappy, you can imagine what he's like.'

'Like Mrs Cavanagh, you mean?' Merry asked, then clapped a hand over her mouth as she realised what she'd said.

Ambrose gave a chuckle. 'If you wish, though Father O'Brien would call that a bit un-Christian of us. Not that it matters to me, of course.'

'What do you mean? Are you not a Catholic?' Merry asked as she suddenly realised that, even though Ambrose was great friends with Father O'Brien, she never saw him at Mass on Sundays when he was down here from Dublin.

'Ah now,' he said, taking off his spectacles and cleaning them on his handkerchief. Without them, he looked like a little mole. 'That is a big question, Mary.'

'Is it? But everyone is Catholic,' she said.

'Actually, there are many different religions around the world,' he said, putting his spectacles back on his nose. 'And Catholicism is just one of them. There are Hindus in India, for example, who believe in many gods—'

'But there's only one god!' she protested.

'There is in the Catholic belief, yes, but there are people on this earth who worship different gods.'

'Does that mean that they will all go to hell?' she asked. 'Because they don't believe in the real God?'

'Is that what you think should happen to them, Mary?' he asked her.

Merry rubbed her nose in frustration because Ambrose had a habit of asking her questions back whenever she asked *him* something.

'I think . . .' She chewed her lip. 'I think if they're good on earth, they shouldn't go to hell, because hell is only for bad people. But if you don't believe in God at all, that makes you very bad.'

'So if I don't believe in God, it must make me bad?' he said.

She stared at him open-mouthed. 'No, I . . .'

'It's all right, Mary,' Ambrose said gently, 'I'm sorry to have upset you. I'm only trying to explain to you how people believe in different things. Like you and Katie believing in ghosts, while your other sisters don't. It doesn't make any of us wrong, it just means that you have different beliefs. And that's perfectly all right.'

'Yes,' she nodded, because she did sort of see what he meant, but God wasn't a ghost.

'Now, shall we get to the story?' he said. 'So, we will begin . . .'

Merry was so gripped by the story, it took Ambrose to point to baby Pat to rouse her from her listening. 'Perhaps we should stop there, Mary dear, as your little brother seems to be hungry.'

Merry came back into the real world with a jolt; they'd just got to the part where the Ghost of Christmas Past had arrived, seeming so jolly after the very scary Jacob Marley ghost. She turned her gaze towards the wailing Pat and only just stopped herself sticking out her tongue at him.

'I'll go and find Mammy.' Sweeping up the offending baby, she marched him into the kitchen, where her mother was rolling out pastry.

'Sorry, Mammy, but . . .'

Her mother sighed and brushed a floury hand across her brow, leaving a slight sprinkling of white dust across it.

'He also smells,' Merry added as she placed Pat in her mother's arms, then swiftly turned towards the kitchen door, eager to get back to the story.

'Now then, girl, would you not be changing him for me before you go? Unless you have better things to do.'

Merry rolled her eyes then turned back to her mother, resigned. 'O'course, Mammy,' she said.

It was almost time to leave for home when Ambrose beckoned Merry back into the study. She was still holding a grizzling Pat in her arms. Every time she'd put him down, he'd start up the racket all over again, so they hadn't carried on with the story.

'Today I'm nearly hating you, Patrick O'Reilly,' she whispered to him as she walked down the corridor towards the study.

'Why don't I take Pat for a while?' suggested Ambrose, and promptly took the babe from her. Pat stopped fussing immediately and just looked up into Ambrose's owl eyes. 'What a good boy he is,' said Ambrose. 'And that touch of dark hair, just like your daddy.'

'I was hoping he'd be blond like me, so I wouldn't be the only one in the family,' she said. 'Katie says 'tis because I'm the youngest sister. God ran out of colour and that's why my hair is so light.'

'Katie certainly has an imagination,' Ambrose chuckled. 'Now then, Mary, I'll be here with Father O'Brien over the next few days, so perhaps it will be possible for us to continue *A Christmas Carol* before I leave. But for now . . .'

He pointed to a flat package on Father O'Brien's desk that was wrapped in bright red paper with Santys all over it. It was proper Christmas paper, not the plain brown stuff that her family used for presents.

'Ooh! Ambrose, I . . .'

'Perhaps you should open it now, so your brothers and sisters don't get jealous, eh?'

'Do you think it's all right to do that before Santy comes?'

'Yes indeed, because this is from *me* for Christmas. Now then, sit down and open it.'

Merry did so, quivering with excitement about what could be inside, although from the shape and feel of it, she'd a pretty good guess. She undid the ribbon and the wrapping carefully, because if Ambrose would let her, she wanted to keep it and use it for some of her own presents. Peeling it back, she stared at the words on the front cover of what she'd already known was a book.

''Tis beautiful. Thank you, Ambrose.'

'Can you read the name of the book, Mary?'

'Um . . . could I have a go?'

'Please do.'

'*The My-thes and Leg-ends of the Gre . . . Greek Gods!*'
Merry looked up at him to see whether she'd got it right.

'That was a very good try indeed. It's actually *The Myths
and Legends of the Greek Gods*. Myths and legends are similar words for the old Irish tales you've heard from your
parents. These stories are about gods who lived in Greece long
ago, on top of a mountain called Olympus.'

Merry was still transfixed by the front cover. The letters were
all made of gold and she traced her fingers over them. The figure
on the front was a man with a bare chest, but at least he had
material covering his middle parts, so he looked like Jesus did
on the cross. Except he had a pair of wings on his back, which
Jesus didn't have, because wings belonged to birds and angels.

'We have to go home now, so maybe I could leave it here
with my other books and then 'twould be a treat to look at
each page slowly and read it when I come back to visit.' She
stroked the front cover lovingly. 'Thank you, Ambrose, 'tis the
most beautiful thing I've ever seen.'

'It's a pleasure, Mary, and a very merry Christmas to you.'

Walking home with Mammy, Merry tried to understand what
Ambrose had been telling her about God. In fact, her mind
felt overcrowded with new thoughts to think.

'You're very quiet, Merry, 'tis unlike you,' Mammy said, smiling down at her. 'Are you thinking of your Christmas presents?'

'I'm thinking that Ambrose told me he doesn't believe in
God. Does that mean he'll go to hell?' she blurted out.

'I . . . did he really say that?'

Merry could tell Mammy was shocked. 'I think so, but 'twas a bit confusing.'

'I'm sure he didn't mean it.'

'I'm sure too. Ambrose is a good person, Mammy, and always so patient with me.' 'Patient' was a word Mammy liked, because she was always telling her and Katie to be it.

'He is, Merry, and he's been so kind to you, helping you with your letters and giving you books. I've known Mr Lister since you were a little baby, and he *is* a very good man. Remember, he's from Dublin, and up in Dublin people think funny things, maybe different things from us, but I'm sure he has God in his heart.'

'Yes, so am I,' Merry nodded, feeling relieved that she could continue being Ambrose's friend without making God angry. Besides, she really wanted to hear the rest of *A Christmas Carol* . . .

'Dear little Mary had tears in her eyes when she looked at the book. She caressed the letters as if they were made of solid gold. It brought tears to my own eyes, James, it truly did.'

James sat opposite Ambrose, nursing a mug of tea, as Ambrose drank a large whiskey. It had been a long, busy day, as Christmas Eve always was, and James still had Midnight Mass to go. His stomach felt heavy from the amount of Christmas treats he'd been plied with by the kind parishioners, which he'd felt he must eat gratefully and comment on their wonderful flavour.

'Is all quite well in the O'Reilly household?' Ambrose was asking. 'I had the distinct feeling from Merry that her parents were less than happy. And her poor mother looks far too thin and completely exhausted.'

'I sent the doctor up to see her as you requested. He reported that Maggie O'Reilly's fatigue is simply the result of too many babies. I don't know the exact medical details, but the doctor has told both husband and wife that young Patrick must be their last child. Apparently, it's doubtful that Maggie could survive another pregnancy.'

'What does that mean in practice?'

'I'm sure you can understand what that means, Ambrose. 'Tis our Catholic ways; nothing must prevent God's children coming into the world, other than nature.'

'So in short, all conjugal rights have now become wrongs?' said Ambrose.

'Yes. Maggie and John can no longer indulge in the natural pleasures of the flesh, because any resulting child would surely kill her. Neither can they take safeguards to stop that happening, or they go against God and everything their faith stands for.'

'No wonder even a six-year-old has noticed her father is taking a nip of whiskey more often than he used to,' Ambrose remarked. 'Six years ago, Maggie O'Reilly was a beautiful young woman, and her husband a strong, handsome man. Now she looks as though she carries the weight of the world on her shoulders.'

'They both do,' sighed James. 'Sadly, they are just one of many young couples in the parish in the same predicament.'

'Do you think I should offer some extra support? If the family were able to employ domestic help, then—'

'No, Ambrose. No one except the richest farmers and tradespeople, and myself as a priest of course, can employ domestic staff. It would be seen as a move far above the O'Reillys' station, and would alienate them from their community.'

'Then there's nothing we can do?'

'I must leave now to prepare for Midnight Mass. We'll talk more when I'm back, but no, I don't think there is.'

Ambrose watched as James left the room to go and celebrate one of the most holy nights of the year in the Christian faith. He'd said before that the majority of his flock were even less well off than the O'Reillys. Hope of a heavenly existence beyond the hardship of their lives on earth was an easy myth to peddle to the poor.

The question was, was he himself playing 'God' with Mary, due to his fondness for her?

As a child, he'd been presented with his own first book of Greek fables, like the one he'd just given Mary. He'd read it with fascination, and it could be said that the book had brought him to where he was now: a Senior Fellow in Classics at Trinity College, Dublin.

Then, he'd imagined the gods on the top of Mount Olympus as puppet-masters: each one in charge of a few million human beings who lived like ants below them on the earth.

'The gods' games,' Ambrose muttered as he poured himself another glass of whiskey. Yet now he was a human god, capable of using money he'd never even earned himself to change the life of one young child. He was becoming sure that Mary had a bright academic future, but was he like all parents – albeit a quasi-one – and trying to model Mary in his own image?

His Greek philosophers had plenty to say on that score. But for once, Ambrose preferred to think for himself.

As the clock struck midnight, Ambrose crossed himself out of habit. James was right: they must trust the O'Reillys to be the reliable and steady cradle that Mary needed until she was older – and if fate took a hand he could step in sooner.

31

June 1960
(Five years later)

'I wish I'd lived in the days of the War of Independence against the British,' Bobby said as he and Merry walked across the fields from Clogagh to home. Her little brother Bill, who had started school last autumn, was following on behind, holding on to the hand of Bobby's little sister Helen, a quiet, shy girl who had Bobby's colouring, but none of his anger.

'Then you might have been shot, Bobby Noiro,' Merry replied as she watched him stop suddenly. His latest game was shooting stones from his slingshot, pretending he was something called a 'volunteer'.

'One day, I'll show you the gun my granddad used to kill the British colonists,' he said as he caught up with her.

'What's a colonist?' she asked him, just to test whether he really knew.

'Britishers who stole countries for themselves. My granny told me,' he said importantly.

Merry sighed and shook her head. As Bobby had grown, so had his aggression *and* his hatred for the British. And as she knew Ambrose came from a British family originally, even if they had arrived here hundreds of years ago, which really made him Irish anyway, she didn't like it when Bobby gave her the chat about the British being evil.

'Bang!' he shouted suddenly. 'Got yer!'

Merry looked on horrified as he started taking shots at the cows in the O'Hanlons' field.

'Stop that, Bobby!'

''Tis just target practice, Merry,' he protested as she pulled him away from the cows, who were lowing in distress. Helen had started to cry and looked genuinely frightened. 'They're for the slaughter soon anyway.'

'You can't be hurting creatures for sport,' she reprimanded him, taking Helen in her arms and grabbing Bill's hand. 'There's no reason for it.'

''Tis what the British did to us,' he muttered darkly, but he moved away from the cows and walked next to her the rest of the way.

Merry knew it was best not to talk to him once he went down this path. In the years that they'd been at school together, she'd learnt he was a boy whose moods could change like lightning. Even though the rest of their class barely acknowledged him anymore, due to his violent attacks if the boys were playing football in the playground and someone called his tactics 'foul', Merry still saw a different side to him when they were alone. In the classroom, he was the only one who was up to her reading standard and took an interest in the world beyond their small farming community. Bobby *wanted* to learn like she did, and that bond, and seeing the gentler side that the others didn't, gave Merry hope that Bobby would grow out of his bad behaviour. Besides, she felt sorry for him, what with him having no friends and having to be the man in his family because he'd no daddy.

She would never forget the day he'd cried like a baby on

Merry's shoulder. His dog, Hunter, had been shot by mistake by a neighbouring farmer out after rabbits. He'd crowed in delight when the farmer's pigsty was mysteriously set alight a few days later.

'"An eye for an eye" is what the Bible says, Merry,' Bobby had concluded, even though she'd endlessly tried to explain that Hunter's shooting had been an accident.

Yet however strange and sometimes downright cruel Bobby was, Merry knew she was his only friend, and she couldn't help her heart going out to him.

What made it worse was that Katie, now thirteen, had left school last Christmas, declaring herself 'bored of learning'.

'Besides, what with Ellen away and married, and Nora working up at the Big House during the shooting season and when the family are there in the summer, I'm the eldest girl and Mammy needs my help at home,' Katie had said.

Bobby had been scared of Katie, who always said exactly what she thought, so now it was just Merry and the little ones who walked home with him.

Since leaving six months ago, Katie never read anymore and was only interested in putting her hair up in different styles, or listening to loud music by someone called Elvis on the radio Daddy had bought a year ago. She and Nora often practised new dances together in the kitchen, and Merry felt left out, even though Katie insisted she was still her best friend.

'And I don't like you spending so much time with Bobby Noiro,' she'd said to Merry. 'Your man is mad as a box of frogs.'

'No, he isn't, he just has a vivid imagination, 'tis all,' Merry had defended him, but inside, part of her agreed with her sister. She'd found that the best way to calm him when he got into one of his moods was to tell him a story. She'd been telling him Greek myths and legends from the book Ambrose had once given her for Christmas. While Bobby enjoyed the violent tales of gods wreaking vengeance on other gods most, Merry's favourite was that of the Seven Sisters, as she was one of seven siblings herself.

'You know that the IRA stored arms in my family's barn during the revolution,' Bobby continued as they walked. 'My granny told me they were always gone by morn. She hates the British and so do I,' he added, just in case she hadn't understood from the thousands of times he'd told her before.

'Bobby, we shouldn't hate anyone. The Bible says that—' Merry began.

'I don't care what the Bible says. The British Protestants have ruled over our country for too long. They stole our lands, treated us like peasants and starved us! Granny says in the North they still do.' He turned to Merry, his black hair grown so long it blew in the wind, and his heavy dark eyebrows fierce over his blue eyes. 'You would think that any good god wouldn't have made us suffer like that, wouldn't you?'

'No, but to be sure, He had his reasons. And look! Ireland's a republic now, Bobby. We're free!' she said.

'But the English are still here, in the country that should be ours, *all* ours, even the North.'

'The world isn't perfect, is it? Besides, take a look at where we live,' she said, turning round and stretching out her arms. ''Tis beautiful!'

Merry stood looking down over the fields, as Bill picked up a ladybird and handed it to Helen, who immediately screamed and dropped it.

'Look at the lady's eardrops growing everywhere' – Merry pointed – 'and the coppertips in the woods. And then there's the green fields and the trees and the blue sea just beyond the valley.'

''Tis the trouble with girls,' Bobby grumbled. 'Your heads are in the clouds, dreaming the day away. That's why we men have to fight the wars and leave you behind at home with the babes.'

'Not fair, Bobby Noiro,' Merry retorted as they set off again towards Inchybridge. 'I'd beat you in reading any day. I bet you wouldn't even be knowing who Charles Dickens is.'

'No, but I'm sure he's a Britisher with that name, so.'

'And what if he is? Shakespeare, the greatest writer in the world, was an Englishman too. Now then, we're here,' she said with relief as they reached the narrow bridge that crossed the slim strip of the Argideen River. 'I'll be seeing you tomorrow, Bobby. Eight o'clock, or I'll be gone without you. Bye, Helen,' she said to the little girl, who nodded and trotted off behind her big brother. Merry felt sorry for her too – she was desperately thin and hardly ever said a word.

'I'll be seeing ye,' Bobby said as he turned and marched off along the lane to his homeplace further along the valley. Merry walked on with Bill, loving the rare feeling of sun on her face. There was a smell of what Merry could only describe as a freshness in the air, and the fields were dotted with daisies and dandelions. She sat down where she was and laid flat on her back, and Bill, who adored his older sister, followed suit. She was sad that there were only a few days to go before the end of term. Next year would be her last with Miss Lucey, because she would be eleven. After that, she didn't know where she would be sent to school; maybe St Mary's Convent in Clonakilty, where her sisters had all gone for a while.

'The nuns hit you with a ruler if your skirt's not down to your ankles or your shoes don't shine,' Katie had declared when she'd been there. 'And there are no boys,' she'd added with a sigh.

Merry had decided no boys sounded like a good thing, but the nuns definitely looked scary, and 'twas a long walk to meet the school bus every day.

As Merry stood up, she decided that, unlike Nora and Katie, she didn't want to grow up at all.

'Phew, 'tis hot in here!' Merry commented as she threw her satchel on the kitchen table.

'Don't be complaining it's too hot when you spend all winter complaining about the cold,' Katie reprimanded her.

'Want some bread and jam?' Merry asked her sister as she cut herself a slice and covered it in the rich strawberry preserve Father O'Brien had given Mammy last week. Merry thought it was the best thing she'd ever tasted. 'Where is Mammy today? Has she taken Pat out visiting?'

'I'd say she's resting. She's exhausted all the time, so 'tis a good thing I'm here to keep house.'

'I'm here, girls.' Their mammy gave a weak smile as she walked through the kitchen door.

'Where's Pat?'

'In the fields with Daddy and John,' said Katie.

Merry studied Mammy and thought she looked as wan as she had after Pat was born. She'd seemed better in the last few years, but as her mother turned towards the range to boil the kettle, Merry's own tummy turned over as she saw the slight outline of a bump.

'Katie, will you go call the boys in for their tea?' Mammy ordered her. Katie gave a toss of her flame-coloured curls and went outside.

'Mammy,' Merry said, lowering her voice as she walked towards her, 'are you, well, are you having another babe?'

Maggie turned to her daughter, then stroked the top of her blonde head.

'There's nothing you don't notice, is there, Merry? Yes, I am, but 'tis a secret from the rest of your brothers and sisters.'

'But, I thought the doctor had said no more babies, because then you'd get sick again?' Merry felt the panic rising inside her – she still remembered the time after Pat's birth as the worst few months of her life.

'I know, but sometimes, these things just . . . happen. God has put new life there and' – Merry watched her beloved mammy swallow hard as her eyes glinted with tears – 'if that's what He wants, there's none should say 'tis wrong. Now then, Merry,' Maggie said as she put a finger to her lips, 'shhhh, promise?'

'I promise.'

That night, Merry didn't sleep a wink. If anything happened to Mammy, she thought she'd die.

Please God, I'll do anything, anything, *even kill Britishers, but please let Mammy live!*

'Maggie O'Reilly is expecting again,' James sighed as he and Ambrose enjoyed a rare sunny day in the pleasant garden of his house, which overlooked the whole stretch of Court-macsherry Bay below.

Ambrose looked at him in horror.

'Surely that's a disaster! She's just written herself her own death sentence.'

'We'll all have to pray that she's stronger now than she was the last time. The doctor might be wrong.'

'James, you know what this might mean for Mary, and she's doing so well at school.'

'She is indeed, and what makes it worse is that Miss Lucey came by only the other day to talk with me about her. Merry is in desperate need of superior teaching. She's surpassed everyone in the school and Miss Lucey is in a quandary as to what to do with her next year. After that, well,' James concluded, 'if her mother is having another baby, her help may be needed at home.'

'What can I do?'

'Very little for now,' said James. 'I can at least make sure the doctor puts Maggie in a hospital to have this baby. Then, if things go wrong, she has professionals around her.'

'Mary *must* continue her education, James,' Ambrose urged him. 'She's read the entire works of Charles Dickens, and last time I saw her, I gave her a copy of *Jane Eyre*.'

'Would you not think that the . . . romance side of it was a little grown-up for her?'

'There's nothing of the physical side of love in that story, James.'

'No, and we must both remember that Mary has grown up watching bulls mount cows. The children round here are innocent in many ways, yet at the same time they have to grow up so fast.'

'Not as fast as young women are growing up in Dublin. Have you heard of this new book, *The Country Girls*, by a young writer called Edna O'Brien? It's just been banned in Ireland because it talks openly of women having sex before marriage. There's been an outcry from the church, but my English Fellow friend provided me with a copy,' Ambrose grinned.

'And?'

'It's a triumph, if one is eager to break boundaries and move Ireland – and the lives of women here – forward, although I doubt it would be your cup of tea. We also have the imminent prospect of a national television service, which will again change the country as we know it.'

'Have you seen a television?'

'Yes indeed. I have a friend who lives up close to the border with the North and is able to get a picture from the British transmitter there. It's like having a miniature cinema in your own sitting room.'

'I'm sure 'twill be years before such a thing makes its way down here to West Cork,' said James.

'Are you glad about that, or not?'

James gazed down over the fields, the town beyond them, and the bay. 'I'd certainly like my flock to live above the breadline and to have advances in medicine . . . I'm all for that.'

'Even contraception?'

James saw his friend had a mischievous glint in his eye. 'We both know the answer to that. As a priest, how can I be in favour?'

'Not even when it would have safeguarded Maggie O'Reilly's life?'

'No, Ambrose. Wilfully stopping human life arriving goes against every Christian belief. It must be God's decision to give life or to take it away. Not ours.'

'This from a man who, after a few drops of whiskey last month, agreed that more wars have been fought and more millions of lives lost in the name of religion than anything else.'

James couldn't deny he'd agreed, so drained his teacup and placed it back in its saucer.

'Anyway, dear boy, we have veered heavily off track,' said Ambrose. 'Whether we like it or not, Mrs O'Reilly is having her baby in – what? Six months' time? And Mary's fate will then be known. I suppose all we can do is wait.'

'And pray for them both,' whispered James.

As the glorious summer months descended into autumn and then into winter, Merry watched as her mother's stomach grew large and sapped her energy. Dr Townsend had been to visit only last week and had advised, to everyone's relief, that mother and baby were doing well.

'However, given the damage inflicted on Mrs O'Reilly during her last labour and the fact that she's underweight herself, I must advise complete bed rest. This will give her a chance to save the energy she needs for when her time comes.'

Merry had looked at her father aghast, but he'd hardly seemed to hear what the doctor was saying. These days she rarely saw him, nor he his family. He'd be out all day on the farm, come in for his tea, then be off to either the Henry Ford pub or the Abbey Bar in Timoleague to chat with the other farmers. Merry didn't like the sound of Pa Griffin, the owner of the bar. When he wasn't pouring the stout or whiskey, he'd be off taking in dead bodies and making the coffins to bury them in, because he was also an undertaker. Merry was long in bed when she'd hear Daddy arrive home. In the mornings, when he came in for his breakfast, his eyes would be red, like he was the devil.

'What will we do, Daddy?' she'd asked him once the doctor had left. 'While Mammy has to be in bed,' she'd added in case he didn't understand.

Daddy had shrugged. 'Well so, you, Katie and Nora are the women of the house. Sure, you can sort it out between your-selves.'

When he left the kitchen, Mammy appeared from upstairs. She looked even paler than before the doctor had arrived, and sat down heavily in the chair by the range.

Katie glanced around helplessly at them all.

'Don't look at me, Katie,' said Nora. 'I'm away up at the Big House most of the time, skivvying in the kitchen.'

'You could leave your job and help me,' put in Katie.

'What? And lose the few shillings they pay me?' Nora shook her head. 'I'll be working for free here doing the same thing.'

'Your wages don't help us, do they? They just pay for your fancy clothes and your trips up to Cork City to buy them, while I do everything here,' Katie spat back.

'Girls, please!' Mammy said as Nora and Katie eyed each other furiously. 'Sure, we can work something out.'

'At least Bill will be coming to school with me,' put in Merry. 'And I'll make the breakfast before I leave.'

'But there's minding Pat, an' all the washing and the cooking and the cleaning and the pigs! Who'll do the pigs?' Katie's eyes were full of tears.

'We won't be taking every word the doctor said seriously,' said Mammy. 'I can rest when Merry and Bill get back from school.'

'Mammy, we must do as the doctor has told us, mustn't we, Katie?' Merry implored her.

'Yes,' Katie replied reluctantly. 'But, Nora, you have to be helping when you're here.'

'Are you saying I don't help now? 'Tis a lie, Katie O'Reilly, and—'

'I—'

'Stop!' Merry butted in before another argument could start between them. ''Tis only a few weeks until the babe is born, and I've the Christmas holidays from school too. I'll help all I can, I swear.'

'I'm not having you doing housework instead of homework, Merry,' said Mammy firmly. 'I'll ask Ellen to come in every day to help us.'

'Oh Mammy, she'll be bringing her own babe up here and then 'twill be a madhouse,' Nora complained.

'Will all of you stop it!' Mammy said, and Merry saw tears in her mother's eyes. 'Now, can one of you be laying out the plates for our tea?'

Later, up in their bedroom, Merry and Katie discussed the situation.

''Tis all very well Mammy saying she'll find a way, but for a start, she can't be working on a Monday for Father O'Brien,' said Merry. ''Tis a big old house and Mrs Cavanagh gets so cross if she doesn't leave it sparkling. *And* spreads gossip around the place about how bad at cleaning Mammy is.'

'Oh, don't you be minding her; everyone knows she's an evil old witch. One day her cold heart will turn her to stone and she'll be in hell for all eternity.'

'Maybe I could do the cleaning at Father O'Brien's house,' Merry thought out loud. 'Just one day of missing school wouldn't be too much of a bother. Our John left at my age to help Daddy run the farm.'

'But farming's what he's born to do, Merry. Everyone knows you're cleverer than anyone else around these parts. And how much you love your learning. Father O'Brien wouldn't be hearing of it.'

Merry sighed, then turned out the light on the little wooden night stand that Daddy had made for them one Christmas.

'Merry?' came a voice out of the darkness.

'Yes?'

'Do you . . . do you think Daddy is a drunk?'

'Why are you asking?'

'Only 'cos I heard Seamus O'Hanlon laughing about Daddy being too fond of the bottle. You know 'tis often John that's up and into the shed to start the milking. And he's driving the cart with the churns to the creamery most mornings, because Daddy's still asleep downstairs.'

Merry lay there thinking how Katie always said out loud what she only dared to think. Of course she'd noticed, but what could she do?

Nothing, was the answer.

During the next two months, Merry and Katie did their best to help Mammy rest. They shared the early morning chores, making sure everyone was fed before Merry and Bill left for school. If Nora wasn't working up at the Big House, she would mind Pat, although, as usual with Nora, she often couldn't be found when she was needed.

'I'd reckon she's meeting a fellow on her way home,' Katie told Merry. 'That Charlie Doonan lives near to the Big House, and she's always been sweet on him.'

Mammy would sit in the leather chair next to the range and teach her younger girls how to make soups and stews from the vegetables they grew in the field. Merry decided that when she grew up, she'd never cook another turnip again as long as she lived. They'd also had to learn how to break a chicken's neck, which was awful as the girls fed them every morning and had named them all. Even though Mammy had also been teaching her how to make sweet things like brack and scones, Merry despaired as all her mixtures came out of the range wrong. So she left Katie to take over those because she was so much better at it.

Often, Mammy insisted on coming downstairs more than she should to supervise them.

'I'm your mammy, girls, and I'm not ill, just carrying a babe,' she'd say when they chastised her for being in the kitchen.

Ellen had temporarily taken on Mammy's duties at Father O'Brien's house, so Mammy could return to the job once she'd had the new baby.

'I need that job, girls,' she'd said one night as the three of them had sat in front of the fire in the New Room, knitting booties and bonnets for the babe. 'See, the wages I've saved have paid for the wool to make sure this babe never goes cold.'

Now it was the start of the Christmas holidays – the baby was due during Christmas week itself – and Merry despaired that there was no walking up the hill to the priest's house with Mammy, to sit in front of the fire with Ambrose to talk and read. All the books he'd given her were still there in Father O'Brien's study, and she'd read everything they had at school, which were mostly books for babies anyway.

Please come soon, Baby, Merry thought miserably as she dragged herself out of bed one rainy morning to go downstairs and cook the goodie. As it was thickening, she crossed the hallway and went to peep in at the New Room. Since Mammy had got pregnant, Daddy had again taken to sleeping downstairs, because now he had a long sofa to stretch out on. Sure enough, there he was, snoring away with his boots still on and the room smelling like a whiskey bottle. She'd heard John earlier, getting up to milk the cows and the clop of the donkey and cart as he took the churns to the creamery.

'Daddy?' she whispered, but got no response.

'Daddy! Will you not be getting up now?' she asked more loudly. 'John's away up with the churns already.'

He stirred, but stayed asleep. Merry sighed and rolled her eyes. At least, she thought, as she closed the latch behind her, John was steadfast and hardworking and never complained about all the extra work he had to do. The family didn't speak about Daddy's fondness for the bottle, but Merry always made sure she gave John an extra spoonful of sugar on his goodie in the morning. It was hard on him too.

Katie arrived into the kitchen yawning, with Pat and Bill in tow.

'Pat bangs that drum Ellen got him for his birthday the moment he wakes,' Katie grumbled as she looked out of the window. 'It doesn't feel like Christmas is coming, does it?'

'Everything will be better once the babe has been born, Katie.'

'Why does it have to be due at Christmas?'

'Maybe 'tis the new baby Jesus,' Merry giggled. 'This farm will become like Bethlehem, and we'll be charging thousands to pilgrims wanting to see where he was born.'

'That'll be at the Bon Secours Hospital then,' Katie replied pragmatically.

'Holy Mother, I'd not want to go and have my babe delivered by nuns!'

'There's doctors there too, Merry, and it's safer for Mammy.'

'Talking of Christmas, have you been adding the whiskey to the fruitcake every day?' Merry asked her.

'I've tried, but every time I go for the bottle, 'tis always empty. Where is Daddy now?'

'Asleep in the New Room. It might as well be called Daddy's Room these days.'

'Could you not wake him up? 'Tis past seven,' Katie suggested.

'I tried, but he wouldn't wake, so,' Merry shrugged. 'He'll be in when his tummy is growling.'

'Daddy should be out there with John. His son should be helping *him*, not the other way around. Like Nora should be up helping us.'

'I know, Katie, but 'twill all be sorted again when the babe comes, I swear.'

'As long as nothing goes wrong,' Katie said, a grim expression on her face as she doled some goodie into a bowl. 'I'm off to take this up to Mammy and fetch the washing from the boys' room. You should see the state of it – those boys live like pigs. I'll give Nora a kick too,' she called as she left the kitchen.

As Merry gave the goodie another stir, she thought that her sister had unknowingly voiced exactly why it didn't feel like Christmas: everyone in the family was holding their breath until this baby was safely born.

With only a week to go until Christmas, Merry let Dr Townsend in.

'Good afternoon,' he said as he took his hat off. 'I'm here to see your mother. How has she been?'

'I . . .' Dr Townsend frightened Merry, even though he was perfectly nice and Father O'Brien had said he was to be trusted. 'She's been all right, sir, although she did say she was suffering a bit from headaches and complaining her ankles were swollen, but that's just the weight of the babe, isn't it? Would you like a cup of tea, sir? And a mince pie, maybe? My sister made a batch this morning.'

'That would be excellent, thank you, Katie. I'll go up and see your mother first, and be down for one after.'

Merry didn't correct him on confusing her name with her sister's. The fact he'd bothered to try made him a little more human in her eyes.

Ten minutes later, just as she was taking the warmed mince pie out of the range and the tea in the pot was perfectly brewed, Dr Townsend came into the kitchen.

'There you are, Doctor,' she said, pointing at the cup and saucer (Mammy had said they must serve him tea in one of the two china cups they owned). 'Please, sit down.'

'Thank you, Katie. Is your father around?'

'I'd say he's in the milking shed,' Merry answered as she poured the tea for him.

'Good. While I drink this, would you be able to run and fetch him? I need to speak to him.'

'O'course. Is there something wrong with Mammy?'

'Nothing that we can't sort out, so please don't worry. Off you go, there's a good girl.'

A few minutes later, Merry was back with Daddy and John, and Bill and Pat in tow. Katie appeared from the scullery, and Nora arrived from work. Merry was only glad that it was early enough in the evening so that Daddy hadn't disappeared off on his nightly trip to the pub.

'What is it, Doctor?' Daddy asked, and even though the worry in his eyes frightened her, there was a part of her that was glad to see it, because it meant he wasn't drunk. She handed him a mug of tea, then poured some for the rest of the family.

'Please don't be alarmed, Mr O'Reilly. As I said to your daughter, it's nothing that we can't sort out. And by the way, Katie,' Dr Townsend said, turning to Merry, 'you were right to mention your mother's swollen ankles. It's a condition called oedema and is very common in a lot of women when they are near their time. However, given the fact Mrs O'Reilly is also suffering from headaches and has a previous history of problems, I'd like to make arrangements to take her into hospital now, so that we can monitor her closely up to the birth. If it's acceptable to you, Mr O'Reilly, I'll drive up to Father O'Brien's to use the telephone and let the hospital know Mrs O'Reilly is coming in.' He turned to Merry again. 'Perhaps you could pop upstairs and pack a bag of things your mother might need, like a nightgown, slippers and a dressing gown. And, of course, things for the baby. I'm presuming you have no transport?'

'No, sir, only a donkey and cart and a tractor,' Daddy said.

'Then I'll be back in an hour to drive your wife to Cork City. I'll see you later,' Dr Townsend said, then left.

A silence hung over the kitchen.

'I'll be running upstairs to sort out Mammy's things,' Merry said. Reaching the door, she glanced back at Daddy's face. He looked terrified, because everyone around these parts knew that you never went into the hospital unless you weren't going to come out again.

Stop it, Merry, you always knew Mammy was having the babe there. She's just going a little early, that's all.

She tapped lightly on Mammy's door before walking in. Her mother had hauled herself upright and was sitting on the side of the bed, cradling her huge tummy. She was deathly pale and her forehead was beaded with sweat.

'I've come up to help you pack your bag for hospital.'

'Thank you, Merry. My spare nightgown is in the press over there, and . . .' She directed her daughter around the room to collect all the items she needed.

'Have you ever been in a hospital before, Mammy?'

'No, but I went once to Cork City with Daddy. 'Tis very big.'

Merry thought she looked like a frightened child.

When the bag for her and the baby was ready and she'd helped Mammy into one of her smock dresses, Merry came to sit on the bed next to her and took her hand.

''Tis good you'll be looked after, Mammy.'

'What will those grand city women think of me?' Mammy swept a hand down her old maternity dress.

'It doesn't matter. All that does is that you and the babe are safe and well. Father O'Brien says 'tis a very good hospital.'

Maggie took Merry's head in her hands and kissed the top of it.

'You're a good girl, so, Merry. Whatever happens to me, you must listen to Father O'Brien and Mr Lister. They'll help you, I know they will.'

'Yes, Mammy, I will, o'course, but you'll be home soon enough.'

Maggie took her daughter in her arms and held her tight, like she couldn't bear to let her go.

'Just remember to follow your dreams, won't you? You're special, Merry, and don't you go forgetting you are. Promise?'

'I promise.'

It was the last conversation that Merry would ever have with her beloved mother.

32

It was a bitterly cold January day when Maggie O'Reilly was buried with her newborn baby in the graveyard at Timoleague church. Father O'Brien took the service, and Merry held Pat on her lap, her brothers and sisters tight around her, all numbed with grief. Pat still hadn't understood that his mammy had gone; the rest of the family had been unable to explain to the five-year-old what had happened.

Merry was relieved when Nora took him from her during the wake up at the farm, and carried him upstairs. She could still hear Pat screaming his little lungs raw, asking where his Mammy was.

'I can't bear the noise,' muttered Katie, as she put out another plate of scones for the mourners. 'What'll we do now, Merry? What'll happen to our family?'

'I don't know.' Merry scratched distractedly at the high neck of her black funeral dress, too devastated to think straight.

'Did you see all the people in the church?' said Katie. 'I've never seen some o' them before in my life. Who was that old man walking with the stick? And that fierce-looking lady on his arm? Did Mammy know them?'

'Katie O'Reilly, keep your voice down,' hissed Ellen as she came up behind them, holding her two-year-old daughter, who she'd named Maggie after their mother. 'I think that lady was Mammy's mother,' she whispered.

'Our grandmother, you mean?' Katie asked in shock.

'I remember seeing her once in the street years ago, when I was with Mammy in Timoleague,' said Ellen. 'Mammy looked at her, and just as the lady was about to walk straight past her, she called out to her and said, "Hello, Mammy." The lady didn't answer, just carried on walking.'

'She didn't say hello to her own daughter?' Merry breathed in disbelief. 'Why?'

'I'd not be knowing,' Ellen shrugged, 'but the least that woman could do is to come to her daughter's funeral,' she muttered angrily, then turned away to fill the mourners' glasses.

Merry stood where she was, too numb to summon up the energy to ask more. It felt like the house was stifling hot and full of people. While all their friends and neighbours had come, Bobby hadn't. He had caught her at Inchybridge the day before on her way back from getting some shopping in Timoleague.

'I'm sorry about your mam, Merry. I wanted to tell you that my mammy said my sister and me are to stay at home. Maybe 'tis since my daddy died that she's not been wanting to go to any funerals. 'Tis no disrespect to your mammy, Merry, or your family.'

She'd nodded, close to tears for the thousandth time since Dr Townsend had arrived with Father O'Brien to tell them all the terrible news.

'It doesn't matter, Bobby. 'Tis kind of you to explain.'

''Tis to do with our families, I think. Something that happened a long time ago, but I don't know what. I'll be seeing ye.' Then he'd given her a hug the only way he knew how, squeezing her hard round her middle.

Merry felt as though she might suffocate where she stood. She needed to get away from the crowds of people that were milling around the New Room and the kitchen. Outside, she could hear the cows lowing in the barn, continuing on as though everything was normal, when it really wasn't. And never would be again, because Mammy was never coming back.

'Good Lord, what a wretched day,' muttered Ambrose as he looked out of the window, the sky pendulous with heavy grey clouds. Like most people in northern Europe, he'd always loathed January. As a child, going back to school after the Christmas holidays had always been the most miserable journeys of his entire life. Nothing to look forward to, the weather dreadful, just as it was outside now. Up to his knees in mud as he staggered across a rugby pitch, waiting to be attacked by one of the larger boys, which, given how short he was, meant just about everyone on the pitch.

And now, all these years on, he had different reasons for feeling as miserable and helpless as he did today.

'So, where do we go from here?' Ambrose said as he sat down and stared at James, sitting opposite him in front of the fire in his study. It was a week since Maggie O'Reilly's funeral, which he'd been desperate to attend, but James had said his presence would attract too much attention in the close-knit farming community.

'Sadly, I doubt there's much we can do, Ambrose,' said James.

'The family must be heartbroken.'

'How else would they be? 'Twas Maggie who held that household together. Especially after John O'Reilly began drowning his misery in whiskey.'

'How is he now?'

'I tried to speak to him at the wake, but he wasn't saying much.'

'Does Mary know what it will mean for her?' said Ambrose.

'Ah, sure, all the girls know there'll be hard work ahead.'

'But what about her schooling, James?'

'I'm afraid that round these parts, education doesn't win over two little boys needing care, let alone feeding the chickens, doing the washing, shopping and cooking, tending the cows and helping to bring in the harvest.'

'But . . . it's mandatory for all children to go to school.'

'Only to primary school, up to the age of eleven, which Merry is now. And even then, especially down in a rural place like this, teachers would be expecting a number of absences from children of Merry's age.'

'What you're saying is that Mary's formal education could stop in six months' time, when she finishes primary school?' Ambrose shook his head in despair. 'To see that bright, enquiring mind reduced to baking cakes and washing the family's smalls is simply a travesty! And I won't have it!'

'Of course I agree, but I can't see how it can be averted,' said James.

'James, in my role as quasi-godfather, all I wish to do is to protect her and educate her. Do you understand?'

'I do, of course . . .'

'You know I have the funds to help. Can you see any way in which I could?'

'I'd say that any money you handed over to John would only be used for one thing, and that would not benefit Merry or the rest of her family.'

'Then what if I took her back to Dublin with me and put her into school there? Surely Mr O'Reilly couldn't complain?

I'd be taking one of his children off his hands, relieving him of an extra mouth to feed . . .'

James took a deep breath to calm himself and gather his thoughts before he spoke. There had been many times the two of them had disagreed over the years, but the subjects that provoked those disagreements, such as politics or religion, did not take the form of an eleven-year-old child *or* her family, who were part of his flock.

'Ambrose, would it not occur to you that John O'Reilly might actually love his daughter? That Merry's brothers and sisters love her too? And, even more importantly, that she loves *them*? She is grieving for her mother. From what I've seen, Nora, the eldest sister left at home, is a self-absorbed young lady, who finds a way out of everything that needs to be done. Which places the burden of running the house and looking after the younger brothers squarely on Katie and Merry's shoulders. Is it fair on Katie to remove Merry from her home? I too love her dearly, but I must consider all members of the family.'

'Is there not a relation who could step in at this point? Surely John O'Reilly has an extended family? Everyone in Ireland does, especially down here.'

'There is family on both sides, but they are . . . estranged. 'Tis a long story, but like most things around these parts, it goes back a long way,' sighed James. 'I've learnt in my time here that old wounds run deep. It is, after all, the area where Michael Collins lived and died.'

'I see, but what about friends and neighbours?'

'We'll not get friends and neighbours to take on another family's domestic situation, Ambrose. They've enough managing their own.'

Ambrose took a sip of his whiskey. 'It makes me wonder when Ireland will stop looking to the past, and begin to see the future.'

'I'd say it will take a good few more years than we have now. Tales are told of family heroes in the War of Independence to the young seated around the hearth, which often sows the seeds of hatred in the next generation.'

'Still, none of this solves the problem with what to do about Mary,' said Ambrose.

'I think you must accept that for now, there is nothing you can do. Merry is still grieving; she needs her family around her and they need her.'

'But if she misses out on her education now, she'll have no chance of getting the university degree I know could be within her grasp. It would change her life, James.'

James reached out a hand and placed it on Ambrose's. 'Trust me, leave it for the moment.'

There was a tap on the door as it opened, and Mrs Cavanagh appeared. James immediately pulled back his hand.

After a moment's pause, Mrs Cavanagh's beady eyes pulled themselves up from James's hand to his face. 'Excuse me if I was interrupting, but I was wondering what time you wanted your tea?'

'Mr Lister will leave to drive back to Dublin in twenty minutes or so. I can make myself a sandwich later,' James said abruptly.

'Very well,' Mrs Cavanagh nodded. 'I'll be off then, and we'll be having to find a permanent replacement for Mrs O'Reilly soon. Ellen O'Reilly isn't reliable, in my opinion, and I need my day off. Goodnight, Father,' she said, then nodded at Ambrose and added, 'Sir.' The door shut behind her with a thump.

'That woman never ceases to remind me of Mrs Danvers in Daphne du Maurier's *Rebecca*,' Ambrose sighed. 'And you're right, my friend, I must be off.' Ambrose stood up. 'Will you telephone me as soon as your thoughts on Mary have coalesced?'

'I will, and please try not to fret. I won't be letting your beloved girl's brain stultify,' he said as he followed Ambrose out of the study and to the front door. 'May God take care of you until we meet again.'

'And may you take care of Mary,' Ambrose muttered under his breath as he climbed into his Beetle, ready to drive through the West Cork rain and home to Dublin.

James left the conversation he needed to have with John O'Reilly for another two months. In that time, he consulted with Miss Lucey at Merry's school, who was also anxious to see her star pupil continue to blossom.

'She's a gifted child, so, Father,' Geraldine Lucey said, as James sat in her parents' parlour eating what he considered (and he had extensive knowledge of the subject) to be excellent brack cake made by Miss Lucey's mother. He understood now why all seasoned priests were carrying extra weight.

'She's still coming to school with her little brother Bill, but she looks like a ghost. I'd say she's taking on extra chores at home, because her homework is never done. That's all right for now, Father, she's ahead anyway, but if she stops school in June to help on the farm full-time, all her potential will be wasted.'

'Yes, it would be tragic,' James agreed.

Geraldine shook her head and exhaled in agitation. 'I understand how it is here, but . . . this is 1961, Father! The dawn of a new decade. You should see some of the pictures in magazines of what the girls are wearing in London, and even in Dublin! Trousers, and skirts above their knees! Emancipation is coming, it truly is, and I believe that Merry O'Reilly has the makings of a fine school teacher in her, and perhaps more. She has a brain that needs stimulation.'

'I agree, Miss Lucey, but emancipation has yet to reach the south-west of Ireland. Well now, perhaps I could help for the foreseeable future.'

'How? As I mentioned to you before, Merry's after reading through every book in the school library.'

'I'd be willing to lend you some from my own library. I've Lamb's *Tales From Shakespeare*, some Austen and Brontë. And what do you think of introducing her to some modern poetry? T. S. Eliot, perhaps?'

'I'd say she was ready for it, Father, and I would, of course, take great care of them, and lock them up in my office after Merry has read them.'

'I'd only be able to do this if the books were to be offered to every other child in her class.'

'They would be, Father, but there is no eleven-year-old who'd want to take them; most of them are still struggling to put their words into a sentence. Other than one boy: Bobby Noiro is as bright as a button, but what a troubled soul he is,' Miss Lucey sighed.

'He comes from a troubled family, as you know. Anyway, regarding the books, there's no harm in offering them to the other children at least.' James gave Miss Lucey a smile. 'Now, I must be off, but I'm grateful for your support and your discretion on this matter.'

Climbing onto his bicycle, James rode away from the gaily painted house that stood halfway up the hill along the winding streets of Timoleague. Looking at the steep slope and then down at his bulging stomach, he pedalled with determination up the rest of the hill to home.

Ambrose arrived for his monthly visit, bringing all kinds of books to help further Merry's education.

'She must learn of the world around her,' he said, as he stacked the last of several leather-bound volumes onto James's desk. 'This is the full set of the *Children's Britannica*, only published last year. They are for children aged seven to fourteen – an offshoot of the adult encyclopaedia – and I had them sent from Hatchards in London. They cover most subjects and will help feed Mary's enquiring mind.'

James studied the title and gave Ambrose a wry smile. 'I'm not sure the word "Britannica" will go down well around these parts.'

'Goodness, James, this is the most comprehensive compendium of collective knowledge it's possible to read in English! Surely no one need worry about its nationality? The Irish have their republic now, and they still speak the same language after all!'

'I shall leave it up to Miss Lucey's discretion. Perhaps she can keep them in her office, and the children can read them when they wish.'

'Whatever you and Miss Lucey think best. Now then, how is Mary?'

'Still devastated by her mother's death, as is all the family. Last time I saw her, she told me that school was all that was keeping her going. At least the older sister Nora is back full-time at the farm, because the shooting season is over and she's no longer needed to help in the kitchens at Argideen House. And . . . I did hear something that may be of use. Bridget O'Mahoney, who's a classmate of Merry's, is being sent to boarding school in Dublin next September. Her mother is originally from Dublin and went there herself. The family is wealthy and they want Bridget to have the best education money can buy.'

'Ah . . .' said Ambrose as he sat down in James's study and looked up at his friend expectantly.

'Now, the fees are exorbitant, but the school does offer scholarships to bright Catholic girls from poor backgrounds.' James looked at Ambrose. 'What do you think?'

'I think . . . I think that you may have just solved the problem, James. You are a genius!'

'Hardly, Ambrose. For a start, Merry has to win the scholarship. Added to that, she herself must want to go. And then there's the issue of her father agreeing to it, although the fact Bridget will be attending will help enormously. The O'Mahoneys are very well respected around these parts.'

'As I said, you're a genius, James. So, what happens next?'

A week later, James had gone for his regular visit to the school. Afterwards, he'd summoned Merry into Miss Lucey's office. The child looked exhausted and had lost weight, so her huge blue eyes stood out in her pale, gaunt face.

He explained the idea to Merry, and watched her expression go through a gamut of emotions.

'What do you think, Merry?'

'I'd say 'tis not worth thinking about it, 'cos I'm not clever enough to win anything, especially against girls from Dublin. They'd be far cleverer than me, Father.'

'Well, Miss Lucey, Ambrose and I all think you are quite clever enough to give it a try, Merry. 'Twill be just like a test that Miss Lucey gives you. And she'll make sure you have lots of practice.'

'But even if I did win a scholarship, I'd not want to be leaving everyone here, Father. I'm needed to help at the farm. And Dublin's a long way away.'

'Ambrose lives there, as you know, and I used to as well. It's a beautiful city too. And remember, Bridget O'Mahoney will be going.'

'Yes, but . . .'

'What, Merry?'

'Nothing, Father.'

James watched Merry bite her lip, and knew, of course, that the child did not want to speak ill of a classmate in front of him.

'Might I suggest that you have a try at the scholarship? After all, if you think you will fail anyway, then what do you have to lose?'

'Nothing, I s'pose,' Merry whispered. 'But if Bridget knew I hadn't passed, she'd be teasing me, because she's going anyway.'

'Well, why don't you keep this test a secret for now? Then, if you don't pass, nobody has to know.' James realised that he was stepping out of his remit as a priest to suggest this, but needs must.

'Yes, Father. That would be a better idea. Thank you.'

During the next few weeks, helped secretly by Ambrose to compile what Merry should be studying, Miss Lucey set her star student to work.

Merry had never felt so exhausted. Every day, she was taking books home to study once she'd finished all her chores.

'Why is your satchel so heavy?' Bobby asked her one rainy afternoon as he held it while she climbed over the fence. 'You got some ammo in here or what?'

'You say some really stupid things, Bobby Noiro,' she said as she snatched her satchel back from Bobby, once she'd helped little Helen and Bill over too. 'Who'd I be trying to kill?'

'The British doctorman who sent your mammy into that hospital to die?'

'He was trying to help her, not to kill her! Will you shut up with your stupid talk?'

'You can say 'tis stupid, but I've been reading my granny's diary, written during the War of Independence and—'

'I said, stop your chatter about wars! Come on, Bill,' she said, grabbing her brother's hand and pulling him off across the field.

'See you tomorrow, Merry,' Bobby called, and Helen raised her small hand in a wave.

Merry didn't bother to respond.

The day of the scholarship exam came, and Merry was put in Miss Lucey's office to take it.

'There you are, Merry,' Miss Lucey said when she arrived, 'a nice hot cup of tea with sugar, and one of my mother's homemade shortbread biscuits.'

'Thank you, Miss Lucey,' Merry said, her hand shaking so much that she had to put the cup down.

'You try and drink up now and eat that biscuit. You need the sugar for your brain.'

Merry said a quick prayer before it was time to turn the test paper over. When she did so, she was surprised to see how easy many of the questions were, and she finished with twenty minutes to spare.

Miss Lucey walked in. 'All done, Merry?'

Merry nodded, and quickly wiped her eyes with her hands.

'Ah now, was it very hard?'

'No . . . I mean, I don't think it was, because I finished ages ago and . . . I must have answered them wrong or something,' Merry sobbed.

'I doubt that, Merry,' Miss Lucey said as she collected the papers from the desk. 'Sometimes, things are easier than you'd imagine them to be. Now then, dry your eyes and eat that biscuit. You've done your best and we can only wait and see.'

'What were you doing all morning in Miss Lucey's office?' Bobby asked her that afternoon.

Merry had the answer all prepared. 'I was in trouble for stealing Bridget's rubber, so I had to do lines.'

'Don't believe you,' said Bobby, as he waited for her, Helen and Bill to catch him up.

'I don't care what you believe, Bobby Noiro,' she said, too tired to argue with him.

'Well, I know you and I know when you're lying, Merry O'Reilly. You an' me, we're the same, we are.'

'No, Bobby, we're not the same at all.'

'We are, Merry, you'll see. We'll be knowing each other for a long, long time!' he shouted at her as she took Bill's hand and, using up the last strength she had left, marched on towards home, not looking behind her.

33

On a bright March morning, James opened his front door to find Geraldine Lucey standing outside.

'Hello, Father, sorry to be bothering you, but I've news about Merry O'Reilly.'

'Right. Do come in.' James ushered her through to his study, then indicated one of the leather armchairs by the fire.

'From the look on your face, I suspect it's not good news.'

'Oh, it is, Father, I mean, Merry has won the scholarship, but . . .'

James found a lump in his throat. He swallowed hard, knowing it would be inappropriate to show such emotion over one young member of his flock.

'That is wonderful news, Geraldine! Just wonderful. So, what is the problem?' he prompted.

'The problem is, Father, that even though the scholarship covers the school fees, there's nothing there for extras. Look.' Geraldine pulled an envelope out of her satchel. 'Her uniform's included, but she'll be needing a whole long list of other things: a gym kit, all kinds of shoes, a camogie stick, nightgowns, a robe, slippers . . . never mind the train fares from here to Dublin. Oh Father, we both know John O'Reilly barely has the money to feed his family, let alone to buy Merry all this!'

'No, he doesn't, but . . . Listen, would you be so kind as to give me some time to think about it? There may be a way to find the money needed.'

'Really? From where?'

'As I said, leave it with me. Don't say anything to Merry just yet. We don't want to raise her hopes, only to have them dashed.'

'Of course, Father. Shall I leave the paperwork with you? We have to tell them whether Merry will accept within fourteen days.'

'Yes, thank you,' he said as Geraldine stood up and he walked her to the door.

'Oh Father, I so hope she can go. She deserves the best teaching there is.'

'I know, and I shall do my very best to make sure she gets it.'

'Well, of course I will pay! Good grief, James, you didn't even have to ask,' said Ambrose on the telephone later that day. 'I could not be more delighted Mary has won the scholarship. We should be celebrating her success, not worrying about details.'

'They might be "details" to you, Ambrose, but to her father and her family, Merry's possible departure most definitely isn't. I have to find a way to convince John O'Reilly this is the right thing to do.'

'I know, James. Forgive me, but I can't help but be utterly relieved and thrilled. So, how do you plan to go about it?'

'I'm not sure yet, but I shall pray for guidance as always.'

'Well, if God suggests you throw in a new tractor to help heal the pain of John losing his daughter, then please do let me know,' Ambrose chuckled.

Having prayed, but found no direct answer, James decided he must let his instincts lead the way. The following Sunday after Mass, he asked a bleary-eyed John whether he'd be able to call on him the following evening.

'Six o'clock would suit, Father. I have . . . things to do from seven. Is anything wrong?'

'Not at all. In fact, it's very good news.'

'I'll be needing some o' that just now. Goodbye, Father.'

James watched the man wander over to the long line of O'Reilly graves in the cemetery surrounding the church. The rest of his family were kneeling over the plot where their mother and her tiny newborn baby had been interred. It was still waiting for a headstone and the sight of Maggie O'Reilly's children placing posies of spring flowers picked from fields and hedgerows brought tears to his eyes. Even Bill and little Pat had laid a squashed handful of wild violets upon the mound, still yet to grow a full head of grass.

'I trust you, Lord, but sometimes, I'm not understanding the way you work,' James muttered as he walked back inside the church.

'So, that's the situation, John. The question is, what do you think? As Merry's father, it's ultimately your decision.'

James watched as various emotions passed across John O'Reilly's face. It was a long time before he spoke.

'Is it your friend Ambrose Lister who'll be paying?'

'No. Merry won the scholarship fair and square. It's a huge achievement, John, and all credit to her.'

There was another long pause.

'I – and Maggie – we love her so much. Maggie always said she was special. Merry has the brains, but a kind heart too, and some fierce strength inside her. She's the one who's comforted the small ones and slept with them in their beds when they've been crying for their mammy. Nora and Katie might be better at the washing and the cooking, but 'tis Merry who's kept this family's spirit going since . . .'

James could only watch as John put his head in his hands.

'Sorry, Father. I loved Maggie from the moment I laid eyes on her at a *ceilidh* in Timoleague. Our parents weren't for the match; her mammy and daddy refused permission, but Maggie and me, we married anyway. She gave up everything to be with me, and what did I give her? A life o' hell, that's what! Her life was no better than if I'd chained her in a cellar on rations. And then . . . Jaysus, Father, I killed her by putting that babe inside her, but me and Maggie, as well as love, that . . . side of us was one thing we always had in our marriage.'

'You also have seven beautiful children that were made out of that love,' James said quietly. 'And you must thank the Lord for that.'

John looked up at him. 'I don't want to lose Merry, but is it my decision to make?'

'You're her father, John, so yes, it is.'

'What does Mr Lister say?'

'That she should go. But then, he's all for education, teaching as he does at a famous university. He thinks it's an opportunity for Merry to better herself.'

John paused again before he spoke. 'Then better herself she should. It's what my Maggie would have wanted. Even though 'twill break my heart.'

'She'll be home for the holidays, John. And Bridget O'Mahoney is joining her there, so at least she'll be going with someone she knows. They can ride to Dublin on the train together. Do you want to tell her, or shall I?'

'You, Father. I'd not be knowing what to say.'

As James left the room, he caught a glimpse of John reaching down the side of his chair for the whiskey bottle. And felt such sorrow for a fine, good man, broken by the harsh life God had chosen for him to live.

Merry and Katie were in the kitchen setting out the table for tea when Father O'Brien came in and asked to speak to Merry outside. He beckoned her to sit down on the bench in the courtyard.

'Have I done something wrong, Father?'

'No, no, Merry, not at all. Quite the opposite in fact. You've won the scholarship.'

'I've what?' Merry stared at him as though he'd told her she was about to be shot.

'You've won the scholarship to the boarding school in Dublin.'

'I . . .'

Then she burst into tears.

'Merry, please don't cry. It's wonderful news. You beat girls across the country to win it. It means you're very clever.'

'But . . . but there must be a mistake! I know I failed. 'Tis a mistake, Father, really, it is.'

'No, Merry, it isn't. See, here's the letter.'

James watched her read it, her expression changing to astonishment, then back to misery.

'So, what do you think?' he asked.

'What I think is that 'tis nice of them to offer it to me, but I can't go.'

'Why not?'

'Because Nora and Katie and the small ones need me here. I wouldn't leave my family. What would Daddy be saying?'

'I've spoken to him and he's said yes to you going. He's as proud as punch of you, Merry.'

'He wants me to go?'

'Yes. He thinks it's a wonderful opportunity. Like I do, and Ambrose,' he added.

'But it's Dublin, and so far away.'

'I understand, but you'll be back in the holidays, and . . .' James paused, wanting to choose his words carefully. 'Merry, the world is so much bigger than down here in West Cork, and it is becoming even more so for young women. With a proper education, you could have a wonderful future ahead of you. Ambrose has always believed you do.'

'Can I . . . can I think about it?'

'Of course you can. Let me know when you have decided.'

In bed that night, Merry confessed to Katie what Father O'Brien had told her. Expecting her sister to react with rage, declaring that she wouldn't let her leave because she would have more work to do, Merry was shocked when Katie nodded calmly.

''Tis what you need, Merry,' she said.

'No! I need to stay here and help you and Nora take care of Pat and Bill and Daddy and the farm . . .'

'And you'll do that by going off to Dublin city and becoming even more clever than you already are, and making this family rich,' she said. 'Ellen showed me some of her magazines – Merry, girls in Dublin drive cars! And dance at rock concerts, not *ceilidhs* . . . Maybe I could even come and visit you sometimes and see for myself. We'll be grand here without you. We'll miss you something fierce, but we'll have you back plenty enough in the holidays.'

'Oh Katie, I'm scared. Dublin is a big city and I know I'd be getting homesick for all of you.'

'I know,' she said, taking her sister in her arms. 'But I'll be telling you something, Merry O'Reilly: when I grow up, I'm not staying in this life we have now. Mammy died 'cos of it, and look at Ellen: she's married a farmer's son, and already has one babe and a second on the way. She's swapped one hard life for another and I'll not be doing that. My way out is my looks and yours is your brain. Use what God has given you, Merry, like I will, and then neither of us will be spending the rest of our lives cleaning out pig shite. Think what Mammy would have wanted for you. I know she'd say 'tis the right thing for you to do.'

With her beloved sister's approval, and her father, Miss Lucey, Father O'Brien and Ambrose all saying she should go, Merry finally agreed.

A celebration was held at the farm and, for once, Merry didn't mind Daddy drinking whiskey, because he took out his fiddle and played as the children danced around the New Room.

Little Pat didn't really understand why everyone was happy and dancing, but it didn't matter, Merry thought, because it was the first time she'd seen her family smiling since Mammy died. All except Nora, who'd glared at her when Daddy had announced the good news. But everyone knew she was a jealous eejit, so Merry ignored her.

At the beginning of September, dressed in her new school uniform, Merry went out into the courtyard to say goodbye to all the animals. Bridget's daddy would soon be arriving in his car to drive them both to the station in Cork City so they could take the train to Dublin together. It would be Merry's first ever time on a train, and when she had confessed this to Bridget, she hadn't laughed at her as she'd expected, but had said that they would have a grand time, as her housekeeper would pack her a picnic with plenty of sandwiches to eat, and a big bar of chocolate for afterwards.

'There'll be enough for the two of us to share, promise.'

Perhaps they could be friends after all, Merry thought.

It was warm in the cow barn, and there was the familiar rustling of young calves.

'Merry!' shouted her brother, who was changing the straw. 'Don't you be getting any muck on your fine new clothes. Get on with you, out of here!' He shooed her into the courtyard, then gave her a big hug. 'You're not to be taking on any airs and graces now and coming back with a soft Dublin accent,' he said. 'You take care of yourself up in the big city.'

'I will, John, I'll see you soon.'

After she'd said goodbye to the pigs and the chickens, Merry walked across the field to say goodbye to the cows, then climbed up on a fence and looked over the valley. She tried her best not to feel frightened at the thought of her new life in Dublin, because at least she knew that Ambrose would be there. He had said she could stay at his home during what the school called 'exeats'. Ambrose had explained it meant pupils were allowed out of school for the weekend, and 'twould be too far to travel home.

'I've been waiting for you, Merry.'

She jumped as she heard a voice from behind her.

'Bobby Noiro!' She turned round to look at him. 'Why can't you be saying hello like a normal person?' Merry complained.

'You're leaving today?'

'Yes, Bridget's daddy is driving us to the train station in Cork.'

'He's a British sympathiser,' he scoffed. 'That's how he made all his money.'

'Might be, but 'tis better than dragging my case to the station on foot,' she said, by now immune to his barbed comments.

'I've got something for you,' he said and reached inside his trouser pocket to pull out a small black book. ''Tis a very special book, Merry. 'Tis my grandmother Nuala's diary. The one I told you about. You read this and you'll understand.' He put the book in her hands.

'Oh Bobby, I can't be taking this! It must be very precious to you.'

'Well, I'm giving it to you because I want you to know about her life and see what the British did to us, and how my family fought for Ireland and freedom. 'Tis my gift to you, Merry. Read it, please.'

'I . . . thank you, Bobby.'

He stared at her for a while, the irises of his dark blue eyes almost black. 'You'll come back, won't you?' he asked eventually.

'O'course I will! I'll be home for Christmas.'

'I'll be calling you the missing sister till you're back, like in the Greek story you told me once about the Seven Sisters and Iron,' he said. 'And I'll be needing you back here, Merry. You're the only one I can talk to.'

''Tis Orion, and sure, you'll be grand without me,' she replied.

'No.' Bobby shook his head fiercely. 'I need you. We're different to everyone here. Bye now, Merry. You take care of yourself up there in Dublin city. And remember, you're mine.'

With a shiver, Merry watched him run off across the field. And for the first time, felt glad she was going far away.

Hearing a car, Merry saw Bridget's daddy driving up the hill towards the farm, so she jumped off the fence and ran back across the field.

John, Katie and Nora had come out to say goodbye with Bill and Pat, the younger boys' hair brushed and their faces scrubbed so they wouldn't embarrass themselves in front of Emmet O'Mahoney. Merry felt tears prick her eyes as she saw that Daddy had come out of the house in a fresh shirt too. He walked towards her and placed a rough kiss on her cheek.

'Your mammy would be proud of you, Merry,' he whispered in her ear. 'And so am I.'

She nodded, not able to reply because she was too choked up.

'You take care of yourself in Dublin city, and make sure you do lots of learning.' She felt him slip a coin into her hand and hug her, and she suddenly wanted nothing more than to stay at home.

She got into the car, sitting on the plush leather back seat next to Bridget, and trying not to cry. As the car drew out of the courtyard and she waved goodbye to her family, she remembered her mother's last words to her:

You're special, Merry, and don't you go forgetting you are. Promise?

She had made her mother a promise. And she would do her best to keep it.

Merry
Dublin
June 2008

34

'And from then on, when I went home for the holidays, Bobby always called me the missing sister,' I sighed. I felt exhausted; I had been speaking for over two hours, with Ambrose helping by filling in the gaps about the part he and Father O'Brien had played behind the scenes.

'It must have been devastating when your mum died.' Jack shook his head sadly. 'You were so young.'

'It was. I still think about her every day, even after all this time,' I admitted. 'I adored her.'

'Maggie was a truly remarkable woman,' said Ambrose, and I saw that his face looked grey. 'Seeing your family grieve, and knowing there was so little I could do to help you all . . .'

'But you did help me, Ambrose, and I'm only starting to learn how much. So it was you that gave Miss Lucey the *Encyclopaedia Britannicas*? I always wondered.'

'Yes, and it was a pleasure, Mary. You were such a strong, cheerful little girl, and you grew by leaps and bounds once you were at boarding school in Dublin, with the right teachers and resources to help fuel the fire of your curiosity. Although I have often wondered if it would have been better for you to stay with your family, with the love of your brothers and sisters around you.'

'Ambrose, I have no regrets about going to school in Dublin,' I reassured him. 'I know I was only eleven, but I did have a choice even then and I know I made the right one. Had I stayed in West Cork, I never would have gone to university. I would most likely have married a farmer and had as many children as my mammy,' I joked weakly.

'I'd love to meet your – *my* family,' said Jack. 'It's so weird to think that a few hours from here are people who share our blood.'

Ambrose stood up and began clearing our glasses.

'Don't worry about all that, Ambrose,' I said. 'I'll wash everything up before we leave.'

'Mary, I'm not that decrepit yet,' he said, but I could see that his hand was shaking as he picked up my empty water glass. I stood and gently took it out of his grasp.

'What's the matter, Ambrose?'

He gave me a sad smile. 'You know me well, Mary. I . . . there are . . . aspects of your past that I know I should have discussed with you when I gave you that emerald ring all those years ago. Back then, there was always tomorrow, but you disappeared for thirty-seven years. And now, here we are, and I am still to explain to you all that occurred.'

'What do you mean?'

'Oh dear, as you can see, I do indeed feel very weary. Why don't you and Jack return tomorrow, when all our minds are refreshed?' he suggested. 'As long as you can promise me you'll be back?'

'Of course,' I said, and drew him into a hug, feeling the guilt of having left this man, who had been nothing less than a father to me, weighing heavily on my shoulders.

Once Jack and I had washed up the glasses and cups from the sitting room and made sure that Ambrose was settled back in his chair, we stepped out of the house and into the warm evening air. Merrion Square was quiet and the streetlights had only just come on, the long summer evening light still casting a gentle glow.

Jack and I had a quick meal of fish and chips in the hotel restaurant, my mind so full of memories of my family that I barely heard Jack speaking.

'Mum, you know what?' he said, breaking into my thoughts. 'You're right: I think Mary-Kate should be here in Dublin with us. I reckon we're going to be in Ireland for a while, and you should ask her if she wants to fly over. Whatever this puzzle of the missing sister is, I'd feel a lot better if we were all here together.'

'Yes,' I agreed, 'you're absolutely right. She should be here, just in case . . .'

'In case of what, Mum? Won't you tell me what it is that has so frightened you? You stopped your story just when you went to boarding school, so what happened after that? Was it something to do with that weird Bobby character who called you the missing sister?'

'I . . . you wanted to know about my childhood, Jack, and how Ambrose fitted into it. I've told you now. So, no, Jack, I can't tell you any more. Not until I've found out some facts for myself.'

'But if Ambrose hasn't seen or heard from you since you left, there must be a reason for it?'

'Please, Jack, that's enough questions, I'm very weary too and I just need some sleep. As my darling mammy used to say, things will be better in the morning.'

We finished dinner in silence, then walked towards the lift together. 'What floor is your room?' I asked as we stepped inside it.

'It's just down the corridor from yours, so any problem, just give me a buzz.'

'I'm sure there won't be,' I said, 'but will you give Mary-Kate a call and ask her if she'd be able to fly over as soon as she can? Here.' I dug in my bag, fished out my purse and handed Jack my credit card. 'Pay for the flight on that, and whatever you do, don't panic her.'

'As if.' Jack rolled his eyes. 'I'll just tell her that our mum's going on a journey of self-discovery and she should be here to see it. Night, Mum.' Jack kissed me on the forehead then turned along the corridor in the direction of his room.

'Sleep tight!' I called.

'And don't let the bed bugs bite,' he chanted, as he had since he was a small one.

I went into my room, undressed, did my ablutions and climbed into the marvellously comfy bed. I made a note to change the thirty-five-year-old mattress the moment I returned home to New Zealand – I still had the one Jock had bought just after we were married. I lay there and closed my eyes to try to sleep, but there was so much buzzing around my brain, it felt like a hive of bees had colonised it. I realised that there were names that had been mentioned in Nuala's diary that I was now remembering from my own childhood.

There's no point in trying to work it all out tonight, I told myself, but still, sleep did not come.

I used the relaxation techniques I'd gleaned over the years, even though they left me more tense because none of them ever worked. In the end, I got up to find my bottle of duty-free whiskey, and drugged myself into an uneasy slumber.

'Right,' said Jack as he joined me downstairs for breakfast the next morning. 'MK's flight is already in the air, and what with all the stopovers and the time difference, she should be here sometime after midnight,' he said as we sat down to eat.

'The wonders of the modern age,' I smiled. 'All that way across the world in a day. How far we've come as human beings. In my childhood, that would have been regarded as a miracle.'

'From what you told me yesterday, it sounds as though you had a very tough upbringing,' Jack said tentatively as he stood next to me at the buffet and piled bacon and eggs onto his plate.

'We certainly never had breakfasts like these, but we never went hungry either. Yes, life on the farm was hard and we all had to do our chores, but there was a lot of love and laughter too. I missed it so much when I went away to boarding school, even though there wasn't pigs' muck to be cleared out of the sty on wet winter mornings. I could never wait to get home for the holidays.'

'Did your brothers and sisters not resent you for having a better education than them?'

'No, not at all. I think they all felt sorry for me. I had to be careful not to come back from Dublin with any "airs and graces" on me, as they put it. It was Katie I missed the most,' I sighed. 'We were very close when we were young.'

'It sounded like it, from what you said. Yet you haven't kept in touch. You just dropped everyone from your past when you left. Why, Mum?'

My son looked at me, his blue eyes urging me to explain.

'As I said, I will tell you everything, just not yet. Now, let's go and hear what Ambrose has to tell me.'

'Okay. I'm quickly gonna grab my mobile from my room and call Ginette at the *cave* in Provence, to tell her I'll be away for a while.'

'Please, Jack' – I caught his arm before he left the table – 'if you're needed back there, I promise I can do this alone.'

481

'I know you can, Mum, but the harvest isn't for over a month, and this is much more important. I'll meet you in the lobby in fifteen, eh?'

As we approached Ambrose's front door, I had a premonition that he wanted to tell me something important – even life-changing. I rang the doorbell and felt a surge of trepidation run through me.

Ambrose welcomed us in, but as he led us into the sitting room, I thought he looked every one of the eighty-five years he'd spent on the earth.

Jack and I settled ourselves onto the sofa as we had yesterday.

'Are you feeling well today? You look a little pale, Ambrose,' I said.

'I admit to not sleeping as soundly as I normally do, Mary.'

'Could I make some coffee for you? Tea?' offered Jack.

'No, thank you. I have water, which, after the amount of whiskey I drank yesterday, should reinflate the vital organs that we're all so reliant on. Putting it bluntly, I have no ailment other than a mighty hangover,' he smiled.

'Would you prefer us to come back later? Give you some time to sleep it off?' I offered.

'No, no. I feel that whilst I have breath left on this earth, and you are actually here, I should tell you the truth. The alternative being a letter sent by some nameless solicitor after my death. Which is what I was planning to do until you turned up on my doorstep,' he chuckled.

I reached instinctively for Jack's hand, and he squeezed mine. 'Ambrose, whatever it is, it's best said, isn't it?'

'It is, my dear. When I heard you speak so lovingly of your

childhood and your family yesterday, I knew that what I had to tell you would be so very difficult, but—'

'Ambrose, please, we've agreed, no more secrets,' I entreated him. 'I mean, there's nothing that you could tell me or Jack that I don't already know, is there?'

'As a matter of fact, there is. When I gave you that ring on your twenty-first birthday' – he gestured to my hand – 'I'd sworn that I would tell you the truth about its provenance. But, at the last minute, I did not.'

'Why? And why is the ring so important?'

'I am about to tell you, but I rather fear that the story you told me yesterday about the people you believe are following you from hotel to hotel has something to do with it.'

'I'm sorry, Ambrose, you're not making sense.'

'Try to understand that objects can become symbols of importance to different factions. These women who arrived on your daughter's doorstep in New Zealand, talking of Mary-Kate being the missing sister of the seven, is not, I believe, directly to do with your time here in Dublin before you left.'

'Ambrose, you can't know that . . .'

'My dear Mary, it may or may not come as a surprise to you that I had an inkling of the situation you had got yourself into. Especially during that last year. You were living under my very roof, remember?'

I had the grace to blush. 'Yes. I'm sorry, Ambrose. But this ring . . .' I held up my hand for Jack to see. 'You told me that the seven points around the diamond were for each of us seven sisters and brothers, with our mother sitting in the centre.'

'I did, but sadly, Mary, and to my eternal shame, it was a lie. Or more accurately, I invented a story about its design that I knew would appeal to you, because of your fascination with the Seven Sisters myths and the fact you were one of seven siblings.'

I stared at him, shocked to the core that this man whom I had so adored and trusted above any other had lied to me.

'So' – I swallowed hard – 'where is the ring from?'

'Before I tell you both how I came by it, I should set the scene. Perhaps the first thing that you need to understand, Jack, is that even though the Irish were victorious in achieving their dream of independence, it was on the British government's terms. They partitioned the country into the British-run North and the Irish Republic in the South. Not a lot had improved for the poor on either side of the border. By the time you were born in 1949, Mary, Ireland had just become a republic, but the levels of poverty here were more or less the same as they had been in the 1920s. Many had immigrated to America, but those who stayed were suffering from the effects of another depression, which hung across Europe after the Second World War. They were dark times in Ireland; as you experienced, families like yours lived on subsistence levels only – in other words, using what they grew to feed and clothe their families. And for Irish women in particular, almost nothing had changed.'

'You're saying that Ireland was stuck in the past, even though things had changed politically,' said Jack.

'It was certainly true of rural areas such as West Cork,' Ambrose nodded. 'At the time of your birth, Mary, I'd just completed my DPhil here at Trinity and had only just been promoted to Research Fellow. As you heard yesterday, I regularly travelled down to Timoleague to see my dear friend James – Father O'Brien – who had recently taken his first position as priest of a parish that encompassed Timoleague, Clogagh and Ballinascarthy. I had few friends and even less family, and James was my closest friend and confidant.'

'It was a long drive for you, wasn't it?' I put in.

'Even longer before you were born, my dear, as I didn't have my red Beetle then. I took the train down, and I remember Mrs Cavanagh, the housekeeper at the priest's house, greeting me as if I was a stinking bundle of seaweed washed up on the shore,' he chuckled.

'Mrs Cavanagh didn't like anyone,' I said with feeling.

'Indeed not. Now, Mary, it was on one such visit to see James that my life changed. So, let me take you back to West Cork and the time that was then, to the moment of your birth in November 1949 . . .'

Ambrose and James

West Cork

November 1949

An Cros Cheilteach
The Celtic Cross

35

Father James O'Brien jumped awake and sat upright. A crying baby had filled his dreams and, as he listened, he realised he could still hear it. Pinching himself to make sure he wasn't still asleep, and realising he wasn't, he stepped out of the warmth of his bed, walked to the window which faced the front of the house, and pulled back the curtains. He could see no one on the path or in the garden – he'd been expecting a young mother with an already big brood to look after, who had come to him for comfort because she was finding it difficult to cope. Pulling up the sash, he leant out and looked down in order to make sure there was no one at the front door, and then let out a gasp of surprise. Lying in what seemed to be a wicker shopping basket was a wriggling bundle of blanket. Which was most definitely where the crying was coming from.

James crossed himself. Babies had sporadically been left on the presbytery doorstep in Dublin, but Father O'Donovan, his priest there when he'd been a deacon, had always dealt with them. When James had asked him where they were taken, he had shrugged.

'Down to the local convent orphanage. The Lord help them all once they're there,' he'd added.

With Dublin being the size it was, it was hardly uncommon for such things to happen when young ladies got themselves into trouble, but here in such a tight-knit community, where James had learnt in the six months he'd been here that everyone knew everyone's business better than they did their own, he was surprised. He dressed hurriedly, pulling on a thick Aran jumper to ward off the West Cork winter, then did a mental check of his parishioners. Yes, there were a number of young women expecting, but they were all married and resigned to the prospect of their new arrivals. As he opened his bedroom door, walked along the corridor and then downstairs, his mind ran through any teenage daughters in the parish.

'Dear Lord! Where is that squalling coming from?'

James looked behind him and saw his friend Ambrose standing at the top of the stairs, wearing a pair of checked pyjamas.

'There's a baby been left on the doorstep outside. I'm just about to bring it inside.'

'I'll collect my robe and be down in a jiffy,' Ambrose said as James unlocked the bolts and drew the front door open.

The good news was that at least he already knew from the screeching that he would not pull the blankets from a child already blue and lifeless. Shivering in the chill wind, he picked up the wicker handle and lifted the basket inside.

'My, my. Now, this package might be even more interesting than the parcels of books I'm sent from Hatchards,' Ambrose said as the two of them stood over the basket.

'Right then,' James said as he took a deep breath and prepared to uncover the baby, only hoping the poor creature was not so disfigured that the mother had abandoned it.

'There's a thing indeed,' Ambrose said as they both stared down at what looked like – even to two amateurs – a perfectly formed, if rather red in the face, newborn infant.

'Girl or boy, I wonder?' mused Ambrose, pointing to the piece of cloth covering the child's genitals.

'We shall find out, but before we do, let's take it into my study and light the fire. Its tiny fingertips look blue.'

As James laid the basket on the mat in front of the hearth and lit the fire, Ambrose continued to stare down at the baby, whose screaming had now abated to the odd yelp of displeasure.

'There seems to be something rather wrong with its belly button,' said Ambrose. 'There's a bloody grey stalk sticking out of it.'

'Don't you remember your biology classes?' James clucked. 'That is what remains of the umbilical cord which attaches the mother to the baby.' He knelt down by the basket. 'From the look of it, this little dote is no more than a few hours old. Let's see whether it's a girl or a boy.'

'I'd bet a few punts on it being a girl. Just look at those eyes.'

James did so, and even though the skin around them was blotched red from crying, the eyes were huge – of a deep blue, framed by long dark lashes.

'I'd say you were right,' James agreed as he timidly pulled away the damp, soiled cloth to reveal that yes, the infant in the basket was female.

'What a shame, now you can't name the child Moses,' Ambrose quipped. 'You think she's a newborn because of the umbilical cord, but she's really rather large. Not that I'm any expert on these kinds of things,' he added.

James looked at the plump little arms and thighs – babies' legs always reminded him of frogs' – and nodded. 'True, this child does look more well nourished than most of the scrawny mites I baptise around here. Now then, can I trust you to mind her while I find a cloth from the kitchen to replace this sticky mess of one?'

'Of course. I've always loved babies, and they like me too,' said Ambrose. 'There now, little one,' he soothed the child as James left, 'you're safe with us now.'

By the time James returned, having resorted to the hot press and tearing apart one of Mrs Cavanagh's immaculately laundered sheets, the baby was staring up at Ambrose as he muttered softly to her.

James chuckled as he listened. 'You're speaking Latin to her?'

'Of course. It's never too soon to start learning, is it?'

'As long as it keeps her quiet and calm, whilst I deal with the other end of things, you can use any language you want. We need to lift her out and put her on the towel so I can clean her.'

'Let me hold her . . .'

James watched in genuine surprise as Ambrose took hold of the baby's head with one hand and slipped another under her lower back, then placed her gently on the towel that James had laid out close to the fire.

'Seems like you do have a knack with the small ones,' James commented.

'Why on earth shouldn't I?'

'True. Now, I'll do my best to make a napkin, although it'll be my first time.'

As Ambrose continued to talk to the baby – this time in Greek – James struggled to clean and then secure the piece of torn sheet around the baby's plump little bottom.

'That will have to do,' he said as he tied a knot just below her belly button.

'Was there a note of any kind left in the basket?' Ambrose asked. 'Or some clue as to who the mother might be?'

'It's not likely there will be, but . . .' James shook out the blanket that had accompanied the baby, and a small object fell to the floor. 'Oh my,' James gasped as he bent to pick it up.

'Is that a *ring*?' said Ambrose.

Together, they went to the light on the study desk to inspect the item in the palm of James's hand. It was indeed a ring, unusually made in the shape of a star, with emerald stones set around a central diamond.

'I've never seen anything like it,' Ambrose breathed. 'It's got seven points, and the colours of the emeralds are so clear and vibrant . . . it can't be costume jewellery, James. I'd say that this is the real thing.'

'Yes.' James frowned. 'You'd think that someone who could afford this kind of ring would be able to keep their baby girl. Rather than answering questions, the ring has simply raised more.'

'Perhaps she's from a well-to-do family, the product of a forbidden love, and the mother had to dispose of her lest she face recrimination from her parents,' Ambrose suggested.

'You've obviously been reading too many romance novels,' James teased him. 'For all we know, the ring might be stolen. Whatever its provenance, I shall keep it in a safe place for now,' said James. He fetched a small key and the leather pouch in which he kept the silver cross his parents had given him on his confirmation from his desk drawer. He slipped the ring inside with the cross, and then went over to his bookcase to unlock a cupboard set under one of the shelves.

'Is that where you hide your whiskey from Mrs Cavanagh?' Ambrose chuckled.

'That, and other things I don't wish her to find,' said James, as he slipped the leather pouch into the cupboard and locked it.

'Well, one thing's for certain,' Ambrose said, gazing down at the baby, who was now lying quietly on the towel, 'it appears that our little girl is special indeed. She's very alert.'

However, even Ambrose's gentle attentions no longer held

sway as the baby realised her tummy remained empty and she started to scream again. Ambrose swept her up into his arms and rocked her gently, to no avail.

'This girl needs her mother's milk, or anyone's milk, for that matter,' said Ambrose. 'And that's not something either of us can provide. What are we to do now, James? Kidnap the nearest cow and stick an udder in her mouth?'

'I've no idea,' James sighed helplessly. 'I'll need to send word to Father Norton in Bandon and see what he would suggest.'

'I'm not meaning what will happen to her eventually, I'm talking about now!' Ambrose raised his voice. 'Ah, baby, how can a tiny mite make such a loud noise!'

Just as both men were on the verge of panic, there was a knock at the study door.

'Who on earth is that at this time of the morning?' Ambrose demanded.

'It must be Maggie, my domestic help on Mrs Cavanagh's day off. Come in!' called James.

A pair of large, emerald-coloured eyes, set in pale Irish skin dotted with freckles, appeared around the door. She had glorious red hair that tumbled across her shoulder in ringlets, held back by a headscarf.

'Hello, Father . . .'

'Come in, Maggie, come in,' said James. 'As you can see, we have a guest. She was left in a basket on the doorstep some time in the night.'

'Oh no!' Maggie's eyes opened even wider in shock and surprise.

'Did you . . . do you know any young women locally who may have, um, well . . .'

'Got themselves into trouble?' she finished his sentence.

'Yes.'

Maggie frowned as she thought about it, and for the first time, James saw the beginnings of lines etched on her young face – brought there by the sheer physical hardship of the life she lived. He knew she had four small ones at home and was pregnant again. He noted also that the skin around her eyes was reddened, as if she had been crying recently, and there were dark patches of exhaustion underneath them.

'No, Father, I can't think of anyone.'

'Are you sure?'

'I'm sure,' she said, looking him straight in the eye. 'That young 'un needs feeding,' she commented on the obvious. 'And that cord needs seeing to.'

'Do you know of anyone who is nursing presently around these parts? And would be prepared to take on another just until we find a place for her to go? That is, if we can't find her mammy.'

There was a pause as Maggie stared at James. 'I . . .'

'Yes, Maggie?'

'Oh Father . . .'

James watched as Maggie put her face in her hands. 'My babe passed into God's hands only yesterday, so . . .'

'Maggie, I'm so very sorry. I'd have come up to give last rites. Why didn't you tell me?'

When Maggie looked up again, James could see the fear in her eyes.

'Please, Father, I should ha' told you, but me and John, we couldn't afford a proper burial. She came a month early, see, and she . . . she breathed her last inside me, so . . .' She took a deep, gasping breath. 'We . . . put her in with her brother who died in the same way, under the oak tree in our field yesterday. Forgive me, Father, but—'

'Please.' James's ears were beginning to ring from the racket the baby was making, and the horror of what Maggie had just told him. 'There is no need to ask my forgiveness or God's. I will come to the farm and say a Mass for your baby's soul.'

'You would?'

'I would.'

'Oh Father, I don't know how to thank you. Father O'Malley would have said the babe's soul was damned to hell for not being buried in hallowed ground.'

'And I will tell you, as His messenger on earth, the baby's soul most assuredly is not. So now, Maggie, are you telling us that you have . . . milk?'

'Yes, Father, it comes as if she's here and waiting for it.'

'Then . . . would you be prepared to feed this child?'

'To be sure I would, but I haven't lit the rest of the fires, or the range, or—'

'Don't worry about any of that. I am sure we can manage for a while whilst you take care of the baby. Eh, Ambrose?'

'Of course. Here.' Ambrose handed Maggie the baby. He watched as Maggie looked down at the child with such devastation that it almost broke his heart in two.

'I'll take her to the kitchen to feed her, so,' she said, recovering herself.

'No, the kitchen is freezing,' said James. 'You sit there in the chair by the fire. Let us know when she's had her fill.'

'Are you sure, Father? I—'

'Completely. We'll see to everything, won't we, Ambrose?'

'Of course. Take as long as you need, my dear.'

The two men left the study.

Ambrose sat in a chair in the kitchen, a blanket wrapped round him as James re-stoked the range and waited for the kettle to boil so they could have a cup of tea.

'Are you all right, my friend?' James asked him. 'You look quite pale.'

'I confess that I'm shocked by the morning's events. Not only at the arrival of a baby on your doorstep, but young Maggie . . .' Ambrose sighed and shook his head. 'She buried her newborn only yesterday, and yet here she is at work, despite what must be considerable physical exhaustion and inexorable grief.'

'Yes.' James warmed his hands on the range as he willed the kettle to hurry up and boil. He too needed solace, and it could only come in a cup of hot, sweet tea. 'Here, human life is cheap, Ambrose – you must realise that you and I are very privileged in our different ways. At my church in Dublin, I was protected by my priest, whereas out here, I'm on the front line. And if I'm to stay and survive, I must understand the ways of the flock I serve. And that flock is mostly poor and struggles to stay alive.'

'From what I've seen this morning, surely it will test even your faith in God?'

'I will learn, and hope I can bring solace to those affected by situations that I can't even begin to imagine. It does not test my faith, Ambrose, it strengthens it, because I am God's hands here on earth. And the little I can do for them, I will do.'

The kettle finally gave a weak whistle and James poured hot water over the tea leaves.

'And what of the baby? That precious new life?'

'As I said, I must send a message to Father Norton; he will know the local orphanage, but . . .' James shook his head. 'I was once sent to administer last rites to a child dying of tuberculosis at the convent orphanage close to my old Dublin parish. 'Twas a dreadful place; I can't say it wasn't. The babies were three to a cot, filthy from their own mess, their skin alive with lice . . .'

'Maybe couples should desist from the activity that brings

them here in the first place,' said Ambrose as James put a mug of tea in front of him.

'I'd hardly say that could ever be the answer,' James cautioned. 'It's a natural human instinct, as you well know. And the only form of solace some of these poor young couples have.'

There was a timid knock on the kitchen door.

'Come in,' James called and Maggie appeared with the baby fast asleep in her arms.

'She's taken a full feed and is quiet now. I was wondering, Father, whether I may take some salt from the pantry, and some hot water to bathe the babe's cord, lest it turns septic.'

'Of course. You sit down, Maggie, and I'll find a bowl and mix some salt water in it.'

'Thank you, Father.'

'Ambrose will get you some tea, Maggie. You're very pale, and only a day after giving birth yourself, never mind the grief of losing your child. You shouldn't be here.'

'Oh no, Father, I am well and healthy and able to work today, so.'

'How are your children coping?' James asked.

'They don't know yet. When I felt the babe was coming and that something was wrong, I had my eldest, Ellen, take them to our neighbours. I . . . . I haven't fetched them back yet to tell them as I was up here working today. I'll get right back to the cleaning, Father.'

'Please, rest for now,' Ambrose said to her as he placed a mug of tea in front of her and James went to the pantry in search of the salt. 'Why don't you give me the baby, whilst you drink it?'

'I am well, sir, really,' Maggie reiterated.

'Even so, I'd like to hold her.'

Ambrose took the child from Maggie's arms, then sat down and cradled her in his arms.

'She's very beautiful,' he said as he looked down at the sleeping baby.

'That she is, sir, and big too. Fatter than any of mine, so. Must'a been a difficult birth for the mother.'

'You have no idea whose baby it could be?'

'None, sir. And I'd be knowing every pregnant mother round these parts.'

'Then the baby must have come from outside the village?' Ambrose queried.

'I'd say so, yes.'

James came back with salt and a basin and followed Maggie's instructions to take a little hot water from the kettle and mix it with cold. He was amazed as Ambrose insisted on holding the baby for Maggie while she tended to the cord.

'There, it's clean now. 'Twill dry out in a week or so, then drop off,' she said, re-covering the baby in the blanket. 'Now, if you don't mind, I must get on with my work, or Mrs Cavanagh will have words with me next time I see her.'

Maggie gave a small bob and left the kitchen.

'Surely she should be in bed resting, just a day after burying her child? She's terrified of losing her position here, isn't she? And of Mrs Cavanagh,' commented Ambrose.

'She is, yes, and we will both try to make her rest as much as possible today. Of course, those few extra shillings she gets for her one day a week could make the difference between her family being fed or going hungry.'

'I wonder who minds her children when she's here?'

'I dread to think, Ambrose,' James shuddered. 'They probably mind themselves.'

'How she could hold this perfect healthy baby in her arms and let it feed on the milk meant for her own dead child is truly beyond me. Such bravery, I . . .'

James could see tears in his friend's eyes. He'd never seen

them there before, even when he'd been badly bullied at school.

'Is an orphanage really the only route for this poor, innocent child?' Ambrose looked up at him. 'I mean, you saw that ring, perhaps we could find out who it belonged to, track down her family . . . Or if not, there are childless women, desperate to adopt – my English Fellow friend was telling me that American couples come over here to adopt from the orphanages.'

'Well, if the Irish are normally good at one thing, it seems to be giving birth to fine healthy children. Shall I take her from you? I can lay her upstairs on my bed, and I'm sure Maggie will be able to feed her again later.'

'What will you do now, James?'

'I will speak to Father Norton after Mass to find out the protocol on these things down here.' James lifted the baby out of his friend's arms. 'There now, I'm taking her away before you adopt her yourself.' With a sad smile, he left the kitchen.

36

While James went to Timoleague church to perform morning Mass, Ambrose took himself off for a walk down the hill, to Courtmacsherry Bay below it. Today it was filled with millpond-still water, and the breeze was gentle as he walked along the seafront. It was a crisp, bright November day – the kind Ambrose loved – and even though he could not imagine how faith alone in an invisible being could tempt his soulmate away to this godforsaken part of Ireland, he could occasionally appreciate its raw natural beauty.

Ambrose had known since the day he'd met James – even at eleven, tall and almost roguishly handsome – that this boy who would become the beautiful man he now was had promised his life to God. He remembered sitting on the hard, uncomfortable pew of Blackrock College chapel, always with a slim paperback to hand in order to surreptitiously read all the way through the endless dirge of Evensong. He'd sometimes glance at James sitting next to him in the pew, his head bowed in prayer, with a look on his face that he could only describe as ecstasy.

Ambrose knew that he could never talk about his lack of spiritual belief in public; after all, he was at a Catholic boys' school and taught by devout monks. The Holy Ghost Fathers, the order that ran the school, were preparing their pupils to become missionaries in West Africa. Even as a young boy, the idea of travelling far across the seas to an unknown land had terrified him. If he mislaid his glasses, he was immediately tumbled into a blurred, indecipherable world. Unlike James, whose constitution could withstand the wettest, coldest days on the rugby pitch, after a single match, Ambrose could be laid up in the sanatorium for days with a bad chest.

'Be a man,' his father was always saying, especially as Ambrose was the heir to an Anglo-Irish dynasty, or at least what was left of it. The family had once owned half of Wicklow three hundred years ago, as the masters of the Catholic poor. But through his ancestor's philanthropic work for the tenants and their farms at that time, the family had come to be loved. Lord Lister had passed the ethos on to his son, who had taken it one step further and in his will had left the land to his tenants. This act had left future generations of Listers with only a vast mansion and little means of supporting it. Yet that generosity had saved the place from being burnt to the ground like so many other grand houses had been during the War of Independence. And there, his father still lived to this day. Ambrose was technically an 'Honourable' as heir to the dynasty, with only a gold signet ring given to him on his twenty-first birthday to mark his noble ancestry. His father also rarely played on his own heritage, unless he needed to impress an Englishman, who he joked may regard him as an 'Irish navvy'. Ambrose always chuckled when his father returned from England and said this, because despite everything, he had a cut-glass English accent.

Ambrose wouldn't be at all surprised if Lister House wasn't mortgaged to the hilt. At the age of eleven, he was certain already that the Lister dynasty was doomed to end with him, because he would never marry. His mother had died young, leaving him a substantial trust fund, inherited through her own family. With his father still alive and drinking through what remained of his Lister heritage, she had sought to protect her son. Ambrose harboured dreams of selling Lister House to some *nouveau-riche* Irish family who'd made money out of the war, and buying himself a small, cosy apartment near Trinity College, where he could surround himself with his books and, most importantly, be warm . . .

Which he definitely wasn't now.

'Oh, how I hate the cold . . .' he muttered as he turned back towards the village, with its pretty pastel-coloured houses, many of whose owners earned their keep from the shops they'd established on the ground floor within them. As always, the Catholic church towered over the village – there wouldn't be a soul in Timoleague or its surrounds that would miss Mass on a Sunday. Often, James said, there'd be standing room only, even though the church could seat at least three hundred people.

Ambrose then looked down to his left at the far smaller Protestant church, built just below the enormous breadth of the Catholic church of the Nativity of the Blessed Virgin Mary. Here for certain, a very unholy war had taken place and still rumbled on. Even since Partition, when Northern Ireland had been split from the rest of the new Republic of Ireland, there was anger that the Protestant British ran part of the island. And yet, wasn't the act of Communion at the centre of both Catholic and Protestant communities?

'Dear James,' he breathed, 'I do love you so very much, but I also fear you've wedded yourself to an empty promise.'

However, Ambrose accepted that, like the Franciscan monks who'd built Timoleague Friary over seven hundred years ago, his beloved friend wished to do good while he was here on earth. As he thought about that precious newborn baby – the way he'd felt as he'd held her in his arms, knowing he would never hold one of his own – Ambrose felt a tug at his heart.

Turning back and bracing himself for the rest of the walk up the hill, he headed back towards the priest's house.

'How's the little one?' James asked Maggie as she set the table for lunch.

'Grand altogether, thank you, Father. I fed her again and she's sleeping tight on your bed.'

'And you, Maggie? You must be exhausted.'

'I am very well, Father,' Maggie replied, although her face told another story. 'Have you spoken to the father in Bandon?'

'No, I'm only in from Mass for a few minutes. Do you happen to know where the nearest orphanage is?'

'I believe 'tis in Clonakilty. There's a convent there and they take in babes like ours . . . yours,' Maggie blushed.

James could see she was close to tears as she stirred the soup on the hob. She opened the door to the range and pulled out a tin of something that smelt delicious.

'I've made you a brack, Father. I found some dried fruit in the pantry and thought you could have it with a cup of tea this afternoon.'

'Thank you, Maggie. I haven't had a brack cake since I was in Dublin. Ah,' he said as he heard the front door open and close, 'that'll be Ambrose. Please, serve up.'

Ambrose entered the kitchen, breathing heavily.

''Tis a steep climb indeed from the waterfront,' James said. 'Are you all right, my friend?'

'Yes, just unused to walking up hills, that's all,' Ambrose said, sitting down and drinking some water from the glass Maggie had set on the table. 'How was Mass?'

'Busy for a Monday morning. And there were a number for confession after.'

'I would guess that was to do with taking drink on God's Holy Day,' Ambrose smiled as Maggie placed a bowl of soup in front of him.

'There is also bread and butter for you both. I'll be getting on with my chores now, if you have everything you need.'

'Thank you, Maggie. This smells delicious.'

''Tis only turnip and potato, but I added an apple from the windfall pile you have in the pantry. Lends a touch of sweetness, I always think.'

Giving a bob, Maggie left the kitchen.

'This actually tastes as good as it looks,' said James as he blew on a spoon and took a sip, then cut himself a thick hunk of homemade bread and laced it with butter. 'Bread for you, Ambrose?'

'Indeed. And the soup *is* good. What a shame you couldn't get the girl to replace Mrs Cavanagh completely.'

'If only,' James sighed. 'But there'd be riots in the hierarchy, I can tell you. She looked after my predecessor for years.'

'Maggie is a real beauty too, if only she wasn't so thin,' Ambrose commented. 'Listen, dear chap, I've been thinking while I was out and about on my walk.'

'I know that is a dangerous thing,' James smiled.

'For some reason, I was pondering my own family genealogy, back to Lord Henry Lister, known in our family as the Great Philanthropist. He near bankrupted the Listers through his generosity. I was also thinking about that baby sleeping upstairs. And how you know better than I that the best she can hope for, *if* she survives childhood, would be a menial education, which would only fit her for a future in service or some other low-paid job.'

'And . . . ?'

'Well, getting to the point, I have money, James. And as I know, I will never have a family of my own—'

'You simply cannot know that.'

'I *can*,' Ambrose replied firmly. 'I'm fully aware I cannot change the world, let alone save it, but perhaps a small act of charity *could* change one life at least.'

'I see.' James sipped his soup thoughtfully. 'Does this mean you are intending to adopt the baby currently sleeping upstairs? You certainly seemed to bond with her this morning.'

'Lord, no! I wouldn't know where to begin,' Ambrose chuckled. 'However, it does seem to me, that with my help from the sidelines, a solution to this puzzle appears to be sitting right under our roof.'

'Which is what exactly?'

'We have a woman who has just lost a beloved baby. And a newborn orphan who needs a mother and her milk. The only thing stopping them from being joined together is money. What if I suggested to Maggie that I would cover all costs for the baby, and add a little bit extra to help her and her family too? What do you think?'

'I'm not sure what I'd be thinking, to be honest. You're saying you will pay Maggie to adopt this baby?'

'In essence, yes.'

'Ambrose, that sounds like bribery. For a start, we don't even know if she would want someone else's child.'

'The look in her eyes when she tended to her tells me she would.'

'Maybe, but Maggie also has a husband, who may well have other views.'

'You know him? What is he like?'

'From what I've seen of him at Mass, John O'Reilly is a good God-fearing man. There's certainly no gossip of trips down to the village to haunt the pubs, and trust me, I would have heard about it. All the same, bringing up an unknown man's child may not be an idea he would be willing to consider.'

'Then we must speak to him. What of the rest of her family? What are their circumstances?'

'They have their eldest, Ellen, who is ten, their son John, who is eight, then two girls of six and two. I've heard chatter that Maggie and John married for love, against both their parents' wishes, and they are devoted to each other.'

Ambrose smiled. 'Fortune and love favour the brave.'

'That's as may be, but it doesn't help put food on the table. The family has some pigs and chickens and a few cows on a couple of acres of land. They live in a dark, cramped cottage with no electricity or running water. Ambrose, I don't know if you appreciate the stark poverty that some families hereabouts have to endure.'

'James, I know that I am privileged, but I'm not blind to the deprivations of others. It seems to me that however poor, the O'Reilly family have the foundations that would enable them to give this child a stable future, with a little help from me. And we must act fast. Maggie said this morning she's told no one of the death of her baby, and has not yet collected her children from their neighbours. If we act quickly, we can make this all happen privately. As I said, I'm prepared to pay. Whatever it takes,' Ambrose added firmly.

James surveyed his friend thoughtfully. 'You'll have to forgive me, but your talk of a philanthropic ancestor is not going far enough to convince me of your sudden need to perform an act of charity.'

'Maybe the Holy Ghost Fathers never convinced me to believe in a God, Catholic or otherwise, but the simple innocence of that newborn girl sleeping upstairs has done more for my charitable sensibilities than they could have managed in a lifetime. I feel I've done nothing particularly good in my twenty-six years, unlike you, who does good every day. And I want to help, James, it's as simple as that.'

'Ah, Ambrose,' James sighed. 'You'd be asking a lot of me, in my position here as a priest. The babe should be legally registered in my church notes as being abandoned, and—'

'Would we be incurring the wrath of the Lord if we tried to find a better life for her than the one on offer through the church?'

'Who says 'twill be better? Maggie and her husband John are very poor, Ambrose. This new child will be amongst a number of siblings who may not even have enough to eat. She will be asked to work hard on the farm, and given no better an education than she would receive if she went into the orphanage.'

'But she will be *loved*! She will have a family! And let me tell you, as an only child, with a father who could barely acknowledge me, I'd take the harder life with a family around me, always. Especially as you – and I – will be here to watch over her as she grows.'

James stared at his friend and saw tears in his eyes. In all the time he'd known him, he'd never heard Ambrose talk of his father like that.

'Can I take some time to think, Ambrose? Maggie is not due to leave here until six o'clock, after she's served our supper. I must go to my church and pray on what you have suggested.'

'Of course.' Ambrose cleared his throat and took a freshly laundered handkerchief out of his trouser pocket to blow his nose. 'You must excuse me, James. The arrival of that baby has quite disconcerted me. I do understand that I'm asking a lot of you.'

'I'll be back in time for tea and a slice of Maggie's

delicious-smelling brack cake.' With that, James nodded and left the kitchen.

As always in a crisis, Ambrose went to his room and took out his volume of Homer's *Odyssey* from his old Gladstone bag. Its deep wisdom from many hundreds of years ago comforted him. Back downstairs, as Maggie tended to the baby, he told her to rest by the range in the kitchen and made her a cup of hot, sweet tea. He went into James's study, stoked the fire and sat in the leather armchair to read. But today, even Homer's words could not bring him solace. With the book open on his lap, he questioned his own motives for helping this child. When he'd fully understood the answer, he then asked himself whether, even if the motives were intrinsically selfish, the result was any the worse for it?

No, he was convinced it was not. The child needed a loving home and one was possibly available. And there was nothing morally wrong with that.

'How did your prayers go?' he asked as James appeared in the study an hour later.

'We spoke very well together, thank you.'

'Did you come to a decision?'

'I think we must first talk to Maggie. If she and her husband are against the idea, then there is no decision to make.'

'She is resting by the range with the baby – I insisted.'

'Then I shall go and get her.'

James left the study as Ambrose stared into the fire. For once in his life, Ambrose actually felt the urge to pray too.

James returned with Maggie in tow. She had used the other half of the torn sheet to make a sling around her, so the baby could lie tucked up close to her breast.

'Have I done something wrong, Father?' she asked as James offered her the armchair by the fire. 'The babe was fretful and I was after needing to cook your supper, so I took the sheet and—'

'Maggie, please don't upset yourself. Ambrose told you to rest,' James said as both men looked down at the little fists and feet that were appearing from the sling. 'Now,' James continued as the baby made small mewling noises not unlike a kitten, 'the thing is that . . . I'd better leave Ambrose to explain.'

'I know you've just lost your own baby, Maggie, and that she was a girl,' Ambrose began.

'Yes, sir, she was.'

'I'm so sorry for the pain you've been through. And here you are, nursing a newborn.'

Tears shone in Maggie's eyes. 'She's so much heavier than my poor babe was. Mary – me and John named her before she was born – was only a little wisp of a thing . . .'

Ambrose handed Maggie a handkerchief and let her collect herself before he continued.

'Now then, we all know where this poor child will end up if Father O'Brien contacts Father Norton,' continued Ambrose.

'I've heard orphanages are terrible places, so,' agreed Maggie. 'There was an outbreak of measles in the Clonakilty one not long ago, and many of the babes died.' Maggie looked down tenderly at the baby, then took a finger and stroked her cheek. 'But what's to be done?'

'You said you haven't told another soul about poor baby Mary's death?' James cut in to confirm.

'No, Father,' she gulped. 'As I told you, it all happened so suddenly, we decided 'twas best not to, given as we couldn't afford the wake. We're not heathens, I swear. We said prayers over her once we'd laid her to rest and—'

'I understand, Maggie, and I'm sure you are not the only parents to do the same around these parts.'

'The thing is,' said Ambrose, 'I was wondering whether you – and your husband, of course – would be willing to adopt this little one?'

'I . . . of course I'd take her in as mine if I could, but' – Maggie blushed to the roots of her beautiful red hair – 'we already have four hungry small ones, and 'tis difficult enough as it is . . .'

'Maggie, please, don't be upset,' James comforted her, seeing her embarrassment and distress. 'Listen to what my friend Ambrose has to say. This was his idea, not mine, but I said he should put it to you at least.'

Ambrose cleared his throat. 'I understand your financial predicament, and if you and your husband would consider taking her in as your own, I would be more than happy to cover any costs the baby incurs until she reaches twenty-one. That includes her education if she wishes to go further than secondary school. This amount would be paid in a lump sum to you every five years. I would then add on another sum, payable immediately for your trouble, and also for your discretion. Your friends and family must believe that the baby is one and the same as the child you were carrying. Otherwise it would put Father O'Brien in an intolerable position for not reporting her arrival through the correct channels. Now, this is the sum I am prepared to give you to cover the child's costs for the first five years of her life.' He handed Maggie a sheet of paper on which he'd written down a figure earlier. He waited until she'd looked at it, then handed her another sheet. 'And that is the lump sum I will pay you and your husband immediately for your trouble, and for any extras along the way.'

Both James and Ambrose studied Maggie as she deciphered the figures. It crossed James's mind that she may not be able to read, but the look of utter shock on Maggie's face as she glanced up at Ambrose was enough to tell him she could.

'Jesus, Mary and Joseph!' Maggie put her hand to her mouth as she looked at James. 'Forgive me, Father, for using such language, but I'm, well, I'm in shock. These numbers, have you perhaps added an extra nought to them by mistake?'

'No indeed, Maggie. Those are the sums I'm prepared to pay for you to take the child.'

'But, sir, the first amount is more than we could think of earning in five years or more! And the second, well, we could begin to build a new home, or buy a few more acres of land . . .'

'Of course, you must consult your husband, explain what I'm suggesting. But if he did agree, I could go to the bank in the village tomorrow and pay you the cash in full. Would he be at home now?'

'He'll be in the milking shed, but I know he'll think I've gone stone mad if he sees these numbers.'

'All right. Well, why don't you go home now, explain what Ambrose has proposed and, if you wish, bring your husband here so I can confirm everything?'

'But your supper, Father, I've not yet served it, or cooked the cabbage.'

'I'm sure we can see to ourselves,' said James. 'If this is to happen, it's vital the baby leaves with you tonight. We wouldn't want Mrs Cavanagh knowing about it, would we?'

'No, Father, we wouldn't. Well, I'll be off home to see Himself, if you're sure.'

'I'm sure,' said Ambrose. 'We'll take care of the baby until you're back.' He stood up to collect the child from the sling.

Once Maggie had left, the two of them plus baby went to the kitchen where James took what smelt like a meaty Irish stew out of the range.

'If it's all the same to you, I won't be cooking cabbage. 'Twill be good to have a night off from it,' said James. He looked at his friend, whose attention was focused on the baby as he rocked her gently in his arms. 'May I ask how much you offered her?'

'You may not.'

'The only reason I ask, is I'm thinking that there is a possibility they may take the baby simply for the grand sum.'

'It certainly is enough to encourage them to take the baby, and for Maggie to put some weight on that frame of hers, yet not deck it out in grand clothes. And yes, to help them live a slightly more tolerable life. The baby is really quite beautiful, isn't she?' he murmured.

'You're smitten, Ambrose. Perhaps she will finally change your mind about having some children of your own.'

'Impossible, but I'd certainly want to keep a fatherly eye on her as she grows. And so must you when I'm away in Dublin.'

'Of course, but first, let's see if the husband agrees. Now, come and try this stew. It tastes delicious.'

An hour later, Maggie was back with a brawny, handsome young man by her side. He'd obviously put on his best clothes for the occasion and was wearing the peaky, flat cap that most of James's male parishioners wore to Mass.

'Please come in,' James said as he ushered them inside and quickly shut the door, glad of the five windswept acres around the priest's house, which meant no nosy neighbours. He took them into his study, where Ambrose had placed the baby in the basket she'd arrived in. He knew that the husband might think it strange to see a man tending to a newborn.

'This is my husband, John,' Maggie said shyly.

'And this is my Dublin friend, Ambrose Lister, a Fellow at Trinity College.'

''Tis a pleasure to meet you, sir,' mumbled John.

James could see how uncomfortable he was – so many of the farmers around here spent much of the day outside on the land, and often only spoke to others beyond their immediate family for a few minutes after Mass on Sunday.

'Good to meet you, Mr O'Reilly,' Ambrose said, noting John's body stiffen instinctively at hearing his English accent.

'Shall we all sit down?' James suggested. 'John, you and Maggie take the chairs by the fire.'

James went to sit in the chair behind his desk, actively separating himself from Ambrose and the two prospective parents, because it was vital that this 'deal' did not include him. Ambrose sat down in the wooden chair in front of the desk. He saw husband and wife sit down tentatively beside the fire and stare down into the basket.

'Please, Maggie, take the baby out if you wish to,' said Ambrose.

'No, sir, I'll leave her there until . . . well, for now.'

'So, Mr O'Reilly, Maggie will have told you of my thoughts,' he began.

'That she has, sir, yes.'

'And what are yours?'

'I suppose I'd be asking you why you'd do such a thing for the babe?' John didn't meet his eyes.

'Well, that, Mr O'Reilly, is a very good question. And the simple answer is, I am a bachelor who lives in Dublin, and am lucky enough to receive a private income that supports my current studies at Trinity College. Before you ask, I am Catholic,' Ambrose added hastily, realising that even though John O'Reilly was a simple farming man from West Cork, he may well have heard that the famous Trinity College had been originally founded in the Protestant faith.

Ambrose braced himself to continue, knowing he must choose his words carefully: 'As such, I have disposable income. When this infant turned up on Father O'Brien's doorstep this morning, and he told me her fate would be an orphanage, I found myself wondering what I could do to help. And then, of course, your wife arrived and told us of your tragic loss . . . Put simply, I saw a way that the baby could be helped to receive a family upbringing, and at the same time, could perhaps relieve a little of the grief you both must feel over your loss.'

There was a pause as John pondered what Ambrose had said. Maggie was looking at her husband with nothing less than blatant hope in her eyes.

As the silence continued, Ambrose felt he should fill it.

'Of course, neither of you are under any kind of pressure to agree, but I thought that there was no harm in suggesting a possible way forward that might suit all parties. Both Father O'Brien and I were educated by the Holy Ghost Fathers, who taught us to be charitable. I have recently felt that I have not done enough to help others less fortunate than I, being busy with my studies in Dublin as I am.'

John looked up and met Ambrose's gaze for the first time.

''Tis an awful lot of money you'd be offering us, sir. What would you want in return?'

'Nothing at all. In fact, as Maggie has explained to you, any transaction that happens between us must never be spoken of again. For both your sakes, and the father's,' he said, indicating James. 'Father O'Brien cannot be seen to have had anything to do with this, and indeed, he does not.'

John's attention moved to James. 'You went to school with Mister . . . ?'

'Lister,' James confirmed, 'and, yes, I did. I can vouch completely for his character and tell you that this is nothing more than an act of charity towards a motherless child.'

'And towards us,' muttered John. 'We don't need to take that much for one small babe.'

The baby in question had been mewling all through their conversation and now burst into full-throttled screeching.

'May I pick her up and take her to the kitchen for a feed?' Maggie's eyes beseeched her husband.

John nodded his consent. Maggie swept up the child and almost ran from the room, as if she was unable to hear any more.

'I think that before you even begin to discuss the finances, the most important thing is to decide whether you are willing to take her,' James cut in from behind his desk.

'You can see already that Maggie has her heart set on the babe,' said John. 'It nearly broke in two when she lost our Mary only yesterday. And only a year since we lost the babe before that. O'course, we'd be hoping there'll be more babes of our own to come. Is this child healthy?'

'I'd say so, from the size of her,' James answered. 'And your wife certainly seemed to think so.'

John O'Reilly sat in silence for a while before he spoke. 'You're certain you'll be wanting nothing more from us?'

'Nothing,' confirmed Ambrose. 'I'm sure Father O'Brien will keep me updated occasionally on her progress, and that will be payment enough. I simply want to see the child brought up in a family and taken care of.'

'We'd do our best, but we can't guarantee to keep her safe if the measles or influenza are making the rounds.'

'I do understand that, Mr O'Reilly, I only meant that I would take an interest from afar. But if you prefer, no interest at all.'

'Well, as to the money . . . You told Maggie 'twould be in cash? And we'd have it tomorrow?'

'Yes.'

'Then I must tell you that we are a God-fearing family, and if my wife had come home and told me of the babe, and what with her still in milk, I might ha' been persuaded to take her in without your offer.'

Ambrose could see from the set of his shoulders that the man might be poor, but he was proud in equal measure. Ambrose liked him even more.

'I believe you would, Mr O'Reilly. I can see that you love your wife very much, so perhaps the best way to look at the amount you will receive is that it can be used to make her and your family's lives more comfortable than they have been.'

''Twould certainly do that, sir. The damp in our place is something fierce. I may be able to fix it, or even begin on a new farmhouse for us all. Not too fast, mind, or the neighbours would start to wonder where the funds had come from. I'd be wanting no gossip over this.'

'I'm sure you are both sensible enough to make sure that won't happen,' James interjected. 'We must remember that at the heart of all this is a newborn child who needs a home and a family. Everyone involved is performing an act of charity.'

'Yes, Father, thank you. And I'll be wise over how the money is spent. Slowly, over time, so.'

There was a knock at the door and Maggie appeared round it with the baby in her arms.

'She's sleeping now,' she said, then looked at her husband. 'See, John? Isn't she beautiful?'

John got to his feet to look at the baby and gave a small smile. 'That she is, love.'

'And?' It was as if Maggie couldn't bear to ask.

John turned back to Ambrose and James. 'Would we be taking her straight home with us now?'

'Good Lord,' Ambrose said as James returned to the study, having said goodbye to the young couple and their brand-new child. 'I feel quite overcome.'

James watched as Ambrose pulled out his handkerchief and mopped his eyes. 'What is it?'

'Oh, I'm sure it's a mixture of things,' said Ambrose. 'But mostly it's John O'Reilly: as poor as your poorest church mouse, and yet so proud.'

'He's a good man,' James agreed. 'And worships the ground his wife walks on. Which is good to see, given the amount of marriages I've conducted that feel more like joining acre to acre rather than man and wife. That is a love match for sure.'

'Would you mind if I helped myself to a whiskey? After all that excitement, I feel I need one to calm my nerves.'

''Tis a good thing you've done today, my friend. *Sláinte*,' James said as he accepted a glass of whiskey from Ambrose and toasted him. 'Here's to you, and the baby.'

'Who will be called Mary because that's what they want, which is rather a pity. I have a whole host of Greek names I rather like. Athena, perhaps, or Antigone . . .'

'Then I'm happy she was already named after the Holy Virgin,' smiled James.

'Mary is special, James, I feel it. She was sent for me to watch over.'

'I'd be agreeing that God does move in mysterious ways.'

'I'd call it fate, but I must admit the chances of my taking a trip down here, combined with the absence of Mrs Cavanagh, together with a mother who had recently lost a child herself, does make me feel as if it was all destined.'

'I'll make you a believer yet,' smiled James.

The next morning, Ambrose walked down to the village and stepped into the bank. He drew out the amount he'd promised Mr and Mrs O'Reilly, then walked back up the hill. Taking two envelopes from James's desk, he separated the amounts, then sealed the envelopes. The withdrawal would not even make a dent in his trust fund, yet to the O'Reillys, it represented financial security for the next five years at least. Mrs Cavanagh was bustling about the house, complaining at anything and everything she could find to suggest that 'the O'Reilly girl' had not been thorough in her duties, so he stuffed the envelopes into the desk drawer.

There was a knock on the study door. 'Come,' he said.

'Will you be staying for luncheon, Mr Lister?'

'No, Mrs Cavanagh. My train leaves at noon, so I'll be off to the station in fifteen minutes,' Ambrose said, checking his watch.

'Right so. Safe journey then,' she said and almost slammed the door behind her as she left. He could feel the animosity that emanated from her. Even though he'd accepted the woman was not a lover of the human race in general, her dislike for him – though he was, after all, a guest of the man she worked for – was palpable. It was obvious she thought it somehow inappropriate that the priest should have a male friend who visited him every month. He'd done his best to be as polite as he could, for James's sake at least, but he could smell that the woman was trouble.

James walked into the study and gave him a weak smile.

'You look weary, dear boy,' Ambrose observed.

'I admit to not sleeping well last night, after all the . . . activity yesterday.'

'Does it concern you?'

'Not the act itself, but the deception of it worries me. If anyone found out that I was associated with this, then . . .'

'No one will; the O'Reillys won't tell, I'm certain of that.'

Ambrose put a finger to his lips as they both heard footsteps along the corridor. 'I must be leaving now,' he said in a normal voice as he went to the drawer to show James where he'd put the envelopes.

James nodded. 'I'll give them to Maggie next Monday when she's in for work, as we agreed,' he whispered.

There was another knock on the study door, and Mrs Cavanagh appeared around it again.

'Don't forget, Father, you're due at choir practice in ten minutes – the organist changed it from Thursday, because it's fair day in town and he has to take two of his heifers along to it.'

'Thank you for reminding me, Mrs Cavanagh – I'd quite forgotten. Ambrose, I'll walk with you as far as the church.'

The two men left the house and walked the short distance to the front of the church. Already, the sound of the organ could be heard inside.

'Thanks a million for coming, Ambrose. I'll write to you.'

'Of course, and I'll do my best to come down at least once before Christmas. Keep a watchful eye over our Mary, won't you?' Ambrose whispered.

James touched him on the shoulder. 'Safe journey, my friend. Thank you.'

Ambrose watched as he swept into the church. Then he turned away to walk down the steps and head for the tiny railway station. He was always filled with a sense of loss when he said goodbye to James, but at least now, through a motherless newborn abandoned on a doorstep, Ambrose could comfort himself that they shared a secret that would last a lifetime.

Merry

Dublin

June 2008

37

As Ambrose finished his tale, I found I couldn't speak. I didn't
have the words to describe how, within the space of less than
an hour, everything that I thought I had known about myself
– my childhood, and journey into adulthood – wasn't real.

'So, Ambrose,' the calm voice of my son spoke for me. I
hadn't let go of his hand since I'd taken it as Ambrose had
begun to tell me who I was. Or, in fact, who I *wasn't* . . .
'What you're saying is that Mum isn't actually related by
blood to either of her parents, or her sisters and brothers.'

'That is correct, Jack.'

'I . . .' I cleared my throat, because it was dry from shock
and emotion. 'I don't know what to say.'

'I'm sure you don't,' said Ambrose. 'You must feel as
though your entire childhood was a lie. A lie, which was per-
petrated by myself for far too long. My dearest Mary, I can
only offer my abject apologies to you, because it is I who was
the coward. I should have told you the truth on your twenty-
first birthday when I gave you that ring. Please believe that,
however misguided, I continued to lie out of love for you. I
simply couldn't bear to destroy your love and belief in your
family. I never once thought that we'd all be sitting here now,
so many years on, with you in unnecessary pain because of
my continued deception.'

Jack turned to me. 'Mum, I know it must feel terrible at the moment, but you have to remember that you and Dad adopted Mary-Kate. She's not related by blood to any of us either, but do you love her any less because of it?'

'No, of course I don't. And nor did your dad. We both love her as our own.'

'And so do I. She's my sis, and always will be.'

'But the difference is,' I said, 'as soon as she could understand, we *told* her that we had adopted her. So she'd never grow up thinking we'd deceived her in some way. It was something that your dad and I felt strongly about.'

As I spoke the words, my heart clenched again. I knew *I* had kept *my* past a secret from my husband and my children. So did that make *me* a hypocrite . . . ?

'Mary, I understand that you must be so very angry with me, but I beg you to forgive me for what I failed to tell you when I gave you that ring. You were off to visit your family to celebrate your twenty-first, and receiving your first-class degree in Classics. How could I have spoilt your happiness?'

Even though my entire view of myself had just been whipped from my grasp, I could see Ambrose was close to tears. I was angry – of course I was – but remembering the way I'd walked out and left him thirty-seven years ago, I stood up and went over to him, then knelt down and took his hand in mine.

'I understand, Ambrose, really I do. Maybe we all lie to protect those we love. Or at least, don't tell them things that we feel might hurt or frighten them.'

'That is most generous of you, dear girl. I expect I would have told you eventually. But then you disappeared from my life so very suddenly. I had no idea where you were. As I said, I was planning to leave a letter explaining all this to you in the hope that a solicitor could trace your whereabouts. You are the sole beneficiary of my will to this day. I . . .' Ambrose removed his hand from mine to take the immaculate square of handkerchief from the top pocket of his jacket. He blew his nose hard.

'Well, as you just said, Jack, even if I wasn't their blood, the O'Reillys will always be my family.'

'You must know that I loved you from the first moment I set eyes on you,' said Ambrose.

'And I often wished that you *were* my father, darling Ambrose. What you've told me is a huge shock, but you weren't to know I was going to vanish for so long. I have to believe you would have told me sooner. Besides, you saved me from an orphanage.'

'Thank you, my dear, it is so very magnanimous of you to take the news as you have. But I also fear that I'm partly responsible for what made you leave Dublin. I was aware of what was going on, but felt it wasn't my place to intervene. You were all grown-up, an adult.'

'Shall I make some tea?' Jack asked, obviously keen to break the subsequent silence.

'Perhaps a little whiskey would be better?' I said, indicating the bottle.

'You'll have me turning into a lush! It's only just past noon,' said Ambrose, looking at the clock that had always stood in the centre of the mantelpiece. But he didn't refuse the glass that Jack offered him. He took a few sips and eventually, I saw some colour appear back in his cheeks. I went to sit next to Jack.

'Better?' I asked Ambrose.

'Much.'

'Of course, Mum, this means that if you *were* adopted, it could be either you or MK that Ally and her sisters are searching for,' Jack said.

I looked at him in surprise. 'My goodness, you're right. *If* these women are actually telling the truth about why they are hunting me down,' I added. But it did prompt me to ask Ambrose an important question.

'Do you . . . I mean, would you have any idea who my birth parents were, Ambrose?' I asked tentatively.

'None at all, Mary, none at all. You were what was once known as a "foundling", and because you replaced the Mary that had died, there was never any gossip about you. No one except the unknown person who brought you knew that you *had* been left on James's doorstep.'

'Do you . . . well, do you think my parents took me in because of the money you paid them?'

'Of course that was a worry to begin with, but I remember so vividly the look on your mama's face when she held you in her arms for the first time. And your dear papa was so very much in love with her that he'd do anything to make her happy. I watched as he grew to love you. You were very easy to love, Mary,' he smiled.

'Perhaps you'll never find out who your birth parents were, Mum,' said Jack. 'Does it matter if you don't?'

'Under normal circumstances, it might not,' Ambrose cut in, 'except that there seems to be a search taking place by a group of sisters who are determined to look at that ring of yours. As it is the only clue to your original heritage, it does indicate that they may well be genuine. Mary, might I suggest that you actually consider meeting with one of these women to discover what it is they want?'

'I think Ambrose is right, Mum,' said Jack. 'I could certainly contact Ally.'

'But you're not even sure whether she *is* one of the sisters, are you, Jack?' I said.

'The more I think about the conversations we had, the

more I think she sought me out on purpose. Anyway, there's only one way to find out.'

'I've just realised something,' I said with a shudder. 'That man I met in London – Orlando Somebody-or-other – I told him which *cave* you were staying at in Provence, and even gave him your mobile number, in case he wanted some further technical details about our vineyard.'

'Well then,' Jack sighed sadly, 'that settles it. That's how she found me.'

'It seems that these sisters are certainly resourceful.' Ambrose gave a weak smile. 'Despite your fear that their motivation is connected to your past here in Ireland, perhaps either yourself or your daughter *is* their missing sister.'

I could feel every nerve in my body tingling as I thought of the connotations of me being the missing sister. Even if Ambrose said he had an inkling of why I'd run away all those years ago, and he was certain that these women looking for me were not connected to it, I was still not convinced. I stood up suddenly. 'Would you mind if I took a walk? I need some fresh air.' With that, I turned, made my way to the entrance hall and left the house.

Outside, I took in some long, deep breaths of Irish air, then I walked determinedly through Merrion Square Park, past the couples and groups of students having summer picnics in the shade of the large trees, just as I'd once done. Walking past the Oscar Wilde statue, I followed the same path I'd trodden in my uni days. When I emerged onto the intersection between Merrion Square West and North, I saw that even though the streets were now packed with cars, and the odd new building had popped up along the way, it was otherwise unchanged. I'd always loved how green everything was here in the city centre, having missed the wide-open spaces of West Cork, and in a daze, I automatically walked down the road, past Lincoln's Inn, which had always been a popular student watering hole, then around College Park, where men in whites were practising cricket. I arrived at the smaller green of Fellows' Square and remembered how I used to meet Ambrose outside the School of Humanities to walk home together.

I saw tourists were lined up outside the Trinity Library building, waiting to view the famous *Book of Kells*, and continuing onwards, I arrived in Parliament Square and looked up at the central campanile tower, its white granite facade still as imposing as I remembered it. I smiled weakly at the tourists posing underneath it for photographs, thinking of the student superstition that if one were to walk through it while the bell was tolling, you would fail all your exams.

Student life had been full of superstitions, ancient traditions, balls, house parties and anxiety over exams, all accompanied by a good quantity of alcohol. Being here at the beginning of the seventies, a bright new decade when the youth were finding their voice, had been exhilarating – Parliament Square had frequently been filled with students protesting against apartheid in South Africa, or the republican student clubs rallying for support.

I went and sat on the chapel steps and I shut my eyes, overwhelmed by the memories evoked. I remembered sitting on these steps with my friends in my first ever pair of Levi's jeans. I'd started smoking, just because everyone else did then – we'd even had our own brand of Trinity cigarettes, sold by a man at the college front gate, who'd always flirted outrageously with any girl he saw. It was here that I'd celebrated the fact that I'd won the Classics scholarship at the start of my second year. It meant that I wouldn't have to worry about tuition fees, accommodation or meals, they were all provided for me by the college. It had been fiercely competitive, and after months of studying, I'd rarely felt more elation than I had then. We'd all drunk beer out of bottles, then gone to the student café in New Square for some more. The Beatles' 'Hey Jude' and 'Congratulations' by Cliff Richard had been on the jukebox, and we'd played them over and over. It had been one of the happiest days of my life. I'd felt young and free, as if anything was possible.

'If only life could have been frozen there,' I murmured as I watched the students coming and going, their exams over for the year and as carefree as I'd been back then, before everything had changed. Sitting here now all these years on, I simply didn't know where to turn for comfort. My mind – usually so clear and organised – was in turmoil.

'I'm falling apart,' I whispered, on the verge of tears. 'I should never have left New Zealand.'

'Mum?'

I saw Jack standing at the bottom of the steps looking up at me. I hadn't noticed his approach, because he'd blended in with the rest of the young faces milling about.

'Are you okay?' he asked.

'Not really. I just needed . . .'

'I know. I understand. I can leave you be if you want?'

'No, come and sit up here with me.'

He did so, and we sat side by side, our faces tipped up to the sun, which had just appeared from behind a grey and very Irish cloud.

'What a beautiful place. You must have loved being here at uni,' he said.

'I did.'

Jack knew me well enough not to push for any further information; he just sat quietly beside me.

'Is Ambrose all right?' I asked him eventually.

'He is, but obviously pretty devastated about upsetting you. I took him the sandwiches his "daily", as he calls her, left for his lunch. He's a nice man, I like him a lot. And he adores you, Mum, he really does.'

'He was like a father to me, Jack, and a mentor academically, not to mention that I now know he was my financial benefactor. He had great things planned for my future.'

'It sounds as though he and this priest – James – were very close.'

'They were. I asked him how Father O'Brien was, but he said he hadn't seen him for years.'

'That's sad. I wonder why.'

'Who knows?' I sighed. 'I just hope it was nothing to do with me. Father O'Brien was a very good man, Jack. Some priests, certainly back in the day, could be so frightening, but Father O'Brien was approachable. He had humanity.'

'Maybe we should take a walk and find a pub where we can get some lunch? I wanna try my first pint of proper Guinness,' Jack smiled as he stood up and offered me his hand. 'Any suggestions?'

'Definitely,' I said as I took his hand and let him pull me up. And I thought how I had never loved him more.

I took him to the Bailey pub in Duke Street, where we had gone as students. I was shocked to see how much it had changed: tables were set up outside, and men and women were eating fresh seafood in the sunshine. Luke, the dour doorman of my time, was of course no longer there, and the inside of the pub had been completely refurbished, the once battered tables and worn leather banquettes replaced by sleek new fittings, the only nod to its history being the pictures on the wall. The air smelt of delicious food, rather than stale beer and male sweat.

Jack pronounced his Guinness the best he'd ever tasted and I insisted he had colcannon and ham for his lunch.

'That's my kinda grub,' Jack said as he put his knife and

fork together, having finished the succulent ham and creamy mashed potatoes mixed with cabbage in record time. 'It reminds me of your cooking, Mum.'

'Well, Ireland's where I learnt to cook.'

'Yep. Er, Mum?'

'Yes?'

'I was thinking that maybe we should think about travelling down to where you were born. I mean, we're here, aren't we? In Ireland? It might be good to meet up with some of your family again.'

'Go down to West Cork?' I rolled my eyes. 'Oh Jack, after this morning's revelations, I'm not at all sure I'm up to that.'

'Apart from seeing your family after all these years – and they *are* still your family, even after what Ambrose told you – it's the only place you're going to get any answers about who your birth parents are. There must be someone who knows how you came to be left on Father O'Brien's doorstep.'

'No, Jack. I mean, even if somebody did know something back then, they'd be dead now, wouldn't they?'

'Ambrose is still alive and kicking, Mum, and there'll be plenty more like him still left.'

'Maybe, but I'm not sure I want to know. Would you?'

'It's a question I've never had to think about, but yeah, if I was in your shoes, I guess I would. Come on, Mum,' he urged, 'I'd love to see where you came from and meet your family – *my* family.'

'Okay, okay, I'll think about it,' I agreed, just to shut him up. 'Shall we go?'

Strolling back through the city, we walked into the lobby of the Merrion to pick up our keys, and the concierge turned round to take a note out of a pigeonhole.

'Message for you, Mrs McDougal.'

'Thank you.'

As we headed to the lift, I looked at Jack. 'Who would be sending me messages? Nobody knows I'm here.'

'You'll have to open it and find out, won't you?'

'Can you open it?'

'Okay,' he said as we entered my room.

I sat down in the nearest chair, my nerves yet again jangling. At this rate, I thought, I'd be dead from a heart attack soon and joining Jock. Bizarrely, I felt comforted by the image of my earthly remains spread across the vines with his, always together at the safe haven we'd created.

'Right.' Jack tore open the envelope and removed the short note inside.

> *Dear Mrs McDougal,*
>   *My name is Tiggy D'Aplièse, and as you might know, my sisters and I have been trying to track you down to talk to you. I don't wish to disturb you or, more importantly, frighten you, but I am staying in Room 107 and my mobile number is below. I can be contacted at any time.*
>   *With best wishes,*
>   *Tiggy D'Aplièse*

'Well.' Jack eyed me as he handed me the note. 'One thing I can confirm is that Ally and Tiggy *are* sisters, because Ally mentioned a sister called Tiggy. It's not a common name, is it?'

I glanced up at him and saw the look on his face. I'd been so taken up with these women pursuing me, I hadn't put two and two together.

'You really liked Ally, didn't you, Jack?'

'I did, yeah, even if she was only there because I'm your son and she had a hidden agenda,' he said ruefully. 'I did text her, but I haven't heard back. I don't seem to have much luck with women, do I? Anyway, apparently we have another of these sisters right here in the hotel with us. What do you want to do, Mum?'

'I . . . I don't know.'

'Well, I don't know what it is that made you leave Ireland, or why you've been scared ever since, but the one thing that I *do* know, having met her, is that Ally is a good person.'

'That's what James Bond thought about Vesper Lynd in *Casino Royale*,' I smiled weakly.

'For goodness' sake, Mum, we're not in a fictional thriller!'

'As a matter of fact, Ian Fleming based his spy stories on fact. Trust me, I know how these organisations work.'

'Maybe soon you'll tell me all about it, but for now, I've had enough of this subterfuge. Let's find out for sure, shall we? I'm gonna call this Tiggy's room and arrange to meet her. You can stay safely up here until I give you the all-clear, okay?'

'Look,' I sighed, torn between looking like a total fruitcake in front of my son, and protecting him. 'I know you think your old mum is losing her mind, but I swear, Jack, there's a good reason why I'm frightened.'

'Which is why *I* will meet this newest member of the family. Enough is enough, Mum; I can see you've lost a load of weight since you left home, and you're in a right state. Dad's not here to protect you anymore, so I'm going to.'

I watched my son stride over to the phone that sat by the bed and pick up the receiver.

'Hello, could you put me through to Room 107, please? Yes, my name is Jack McDougal.'

We both waited as reception transferred the call, me in an agony of tension, Jack perfectly calm.

'Hello, is that Tiggy D'Aplièse? Yes, hi there. I'm Jack McDougal, Merry McDougal's son. I was wondering if we could meet down in the lobby and have a chat whenever you're free?'

I watched Jack nod and give me a thumbs up. 'Right, I'll see you there in ten. Bye now.' He hung up the phone. 'So, I'm going downstairs to meet her – I doubt she'll be shooting me in the middle of a public lounge with people taking afternoon tea. I suggest you have a lie-down while I suss her out. I'll give you a call on the mobile to update you.'

'But—'

'No more "but"s, Mum, please. Trust me. For everyone's sake, we need to get to the bottom of this, okay?'

'Okay,' I nodded. What else could I say?

He strode out of the room, and even though part of me wanted to call him back because of the danger he could be in, I had never felt prouder of him. He had his father's clear, calm demeanour, and every day, he reminded me more of my beloved husband.

'Oh, Merry,' I said as I followed Jack's advice and lay down on the bed. 'What a mess you've made of your life . . .'

Of course, I couldn't sleep, so five minutes later, I was up and pouring myself a cup of tea, waiting tensely for Jack to call.

Fifteen very long minutes later, he did.

'Hi, Mum, it's Jack. I've just talked with Tiggy, and I promise, you're totally safe to come down.'

'Oh Jack, I don't know.'

'Well, I do, Mum, and you're to come. Are you wearing that emerald ring?'

'Yes, why?'

'Because Tiggy has a drawing she wants to show you. I swear, Mum, she's lovely. Want me to come up and get you?'

'No, no. If you're sure it's safe, I'll come down. See you in a minute.'

I tidied my hair in the mirror, applied blusher to my pale cheeks and some lipstick. Jack was right: I had to stop running away and face my fears. Taking a deep breath, I left my room and headed for the lift.

Downstairs in the lounge, I saw my son's blond head immediately, then took a few seconds to study the woman sitting with him. She was small-boned and slim, with a head of thick, wavy mahogany-coloured hair that fell prettily around her shoulders. As I approached them, they both stood up, and I felt instinctively that this young woman had a fragility to her, her expressive tawny eyes dominating the rest of her face.

'Hi, Mum, meet Tiggy D'Aplièse, who is number . . . ?' Jack looked at Tiggy for confirmation.

'Five of my six sisters,' she said in a soft French accent. 'I'm so pleased to meet you, Mrs McDougal, and I just want to say that really, we mean no harm.'

Tiggy smiled at me, and even with my paranoia, it was difficult to believe that this gentle young woman was here to harm me.

'Thank you, Tiggy. And please, call me Merry.'

'Sit down, Mum.' Jack patted the space on the sofa next to him.

As I did so, I felt Tiggy's eyes travelling from my face to the ring on the fourth finger of my left hand. I instinctively put my other hand on top of it.

'So, Tiggy has been explaining exactly what MK told us both after the visit she had from Tiggy's sister, CeCe, and her friend, Chrissie. If you wouldn't mind, Tiggy, maybe you can tell Mum yourself?'

'Of course I will, but I want to apologise on behalf of all my sisters. I totally understand why you must have been frightened by us trying to find you,' said Tiggy. 'I'm so sorry,

Merry, I really am. It's just that, well, as your daughter probably told you, our father died a year ago, and the six of us
are all going on a cruise to where my sister Ally – who Jack
has met – thinks she saw him being buried at sea. Recently,
Pa's lawyer received some information on someone who my
family nicknamed the "missing sister". Pa named us all after
the Seven Sisters of the Pleiades, you see, and of course, the
seventh would have been—'

'Merope,' I finished for her.

'Yes, and whenever any of us asked him why there wasn't
a seventh sister, Pa said that he never found her. So, when we
got this information from our lawyer, our two eldest sisters
contacted the rest of us to see if we could help find her. And,
if she was who we've been told she is, ask her to join us on
our pilgrimage to lay a wreath on the sea at the spot where
we believe he was buried.'

Of course, I knew this story already, but I felt calmer hearing it from this sweet girl, whose eyes shone with what I could
only describe as a kind of goodness.

'It wasn't well planned or anything,' she continued. 'We
just sent the sister closest to where Mary-Kate had said you
were travelling to. Electra lives in New York – that's the
woman Jack said you noticed in your hotel lobby in Toronto.
She discovered you were going to London next, so my third
sister, Star, was sent.'

'Yes. I did meet her. She called herself Sabrina. Is she
blonde, thin and tall?'

'Yes. That's Star. She was with her almost-brother-in-law,
Orlando. He's a little on the eccentric side, and came up with
a plan to entice you to meet him and Star by saying he was a
wine writer.'

'Well, he did fool me, so it was a good plan.'

'But it scared you too, didn't it, Mum?' Jack cut in.

'Yes, because even if he'd concocted a plausible story, he doesn't blend into a crowd. I saw him following me around London the next day.'

'Oh dear.' Tiggy gave an embarrassed chuckle and sighed. 'I can only apologise again for the disorganised and thoughtless way we've gone about this. You must have felt as though you were being hunted.'

'That's exactly how I felt, yes.'

'And then there was Ally,' Jack said. 'She had me completely fooled, until Mum told me about the other women who'd arrived everywhere she was going, and I put two and two together.'

'Now you are here, Tiggy,' I said. 'Does that mean that between us McDougals, we've met all of your sisters?' I briefly counted up on my fingers. 'Yes, what with the two Muslim women in Toronto, that makes six. Was the other one Maia?'

'You know her name?' Tiggy said in amazement.

'Mum did her dissertation on the myths of Orion. Part of that was to do with the Seven Sisters of the Pleiades, and Orion's obsession with Merope,' said Jack. 'Other kids got Snow White or Sleeping Beauty as their bedtime stories, while we got Greek legends. No offence meant, Mum,' he added suddenly. 'Or to you, Tiggy.'

'None taken,' she smiled, and as her eyes swept over me, I had the strangest feeling that I was being X-rayed. 'We obviously grew up with the stories too,' she continued. 'By the way, it wasn't Maia with Electra, it was Electra's PA, Mariam. Maia is holding the fort in Geneva at our family home which, by the way, is called Atlantis.'

'Wow.' Jack shook his head. 'I mean, isn't it a coincidence that both sets of us kids grew up with a parent obsessed by Greek mythology?'

'I don't think that coincidences exist,' Tiggy replied, as she looked at me steadily again.

'So you believe in destiny, do you, Tiggy?' I said.

'I do, yes, but that really *is* another story. Anyway, Mrs McDougal, the reason all of us sisters have been trying to get to see you was because of your ring. Here.' Tiggy pulled a sheet of paper off her knee, turned it over and placed it on the coffee table in front of me. 'That's the drawing our lawyer gave us. Star confirmed it was identical to the one you were wearing. Would you agree?'

I stared down at the drawing and then reluctantly unclasped my left hand from my right. I stretched it out so that Tiggy could see it. All three of us looked down at the drawing and the ring.

'They are identical, Mum.'

Jack spoke for all of us because, down to every detail, the ring and the drawing were the same.

We all sat there in silence for a few seconds, none of us knowing exactly what to say.

Then Tiggy put out her hand and took mine very gently in hers. She looked at me and I saw her eyes were full of tears.

'We've found the missing sister,' she said. 'I'm sure of it.'

The touch of her small hand, and her obvious emotion and conviction blew away the last remnants of any fear I had left.

'Tea anyone?' said Jack.

We drank the tea and, sensing the fact that I was overwhelmed, Jack took over the conversation, chatting about how this was his first visit to Dublin, and how he wanted to explore the city before he left. Both Tiggy and I replied monosyllabically; we were each lost in our own worlds, trying to make sense of it all. Or at least, I was, especially after the news I'd received from Ambrose earlier today . . .

I could hardly keep my eyes off the girl sitting opposite me. I felt connected to her somehow, and even though she was obviously very young, there was a wisdom, a depth to her that I couldn't put my finger on, as if she somehow knew all the answers but wasn't telling.

'Can I ask you where this information about the ring came from, Tiggy? I mean, your lawyer's source?' I asked.

'All I can say is that he told us that he'd followed many false leads over the years, but he'd been assured by our father that this ring was definite proof.'

'And what was your father's name?'

'He was always called Pa Salt at home. I think Maia or Ally named him, because he always smelt of the sea. And he did.' Tiggy nodded. 'It's a shame about the "P" for Pa in the name, because I've marked out the rest as an anagram of "Atlas".'

'Perhaps the "P" might be for Pleione, the mother of the Seven Sisters?' I suggested.

'Oh!' Tiggy clasped her hands together and tears welled again in her huge brown eyes. 'Of course! Of course. Now I have serious shivers.'

'So do I, and I'm not a "shivery" person these days,' I smiled at her.

'Well, I'd love to meet Mary-Kate, but I totally understand if you're not comfortable yet with this situation,' she said.

'As a matter of fact, Tiggy, she's arriving here tonight,' said Jack. 'Mum was worried about her, and didn't want her by herself in New Zealand whilst all this was going on . . .'

I sat there and gave my son a look that could kill. It was okay for *me* to trust this woman, but Mary-Kate was my daughter and this was information I hadn't yet wanted to divulge.

'Oh, how wonderful! I do hope I can meet her,' said Tiggy. 'CeCe said she was lovely. She fits the age perfectly; she'll be the youngest of us seven sisters.'

'I was one of seven children,' I said, trying to change the subject.

'Really?!' Tiggy's eyes lit up. 'What number where you?'

'Number five.'

'So am I! How marvellous,' she added. 'I've never met a fifth sister before.'

'Well, I had three brothers, so it's not quite the same as you.'

'No, but it feels nice anyway,' she smiled. 'One day, we'll have to talk about our shared mythology.'

'I already know the legend of Taygete. Zeus pursued her relentlessly,' I said.

'He did, yes, and, oh, it's a long story but . . .' Tiggy shrugged. 'I hope we can speak for longer some time.'

'Yes. I'd like that.'

Jack looked at me. 'Mum, you look exhausted. I know I am, and I've only sat on the sidelines of all of this. Go and get some rest before Mary-Kate arrives.'

'Yes, you should.'

Tiggy's tiny, calming hands were once again placed on mine, and I felt my heart rate slowing. This girl, whatever and whoever she was to me, was magical.

'Yes, I think I need to sleep,' I agreed, standing up. 'Would you excuse me?'

'Of course,' Tiggy said as she stood up too, 'and thank you for trusting me today. I know it's confusing, but my instinct tells me that everything is as it should be.' Then she enveloped me in a big hug. 'Sleep well, Merry. I'll be here when you need me.'

'Would you like me to come up with you, Mum?' Jack asked.

'No, I'm fine. Why don't you amuse yourself in the city this afternoon? I can recommend the *Book of Kells* in the Trinity College Library.'

'That's been on my list forever,' said Tiggy. 'Are you up for it, Jack?'

'I sure am, Tiggy. See you later, Mum.'

By the time I entered my room, I could hardly stand from exhaustion. Having put the *Do not disturb* sign on, I closed the curtains – I was never one for sleeping during the day – undressed and sank under the duvet.

'Who am I?' I whispered drowsily.

For the first time in my life, I realised I didn't know.

38

Tiggy
Dublin

'Maia? It's Tiggy here.'

'Hi, Tiggy! Ally's here, and CeCe and Chrissie have just arrived from London. Have you found her?'

'I have.'

'More importantly, have you managed to speak to her and explain everything?'

'Yes.'

'And?'

'I think I managed to reassure her. I showed her the drawing of the ring and she agreed it is identical.'

'Fantastic. And what would be your feeling about Mrs McDougal?' said Maia.

'Oh, she's lovely, although I don't think our rather slapdash undercover tactics helped – her son said she literally thought we were some organisation hunting her down, but I hope I convinced her that's not what we were trying to do.'

'What about her daughter, Mary-Kate? Like, how does Merry feel about her meeting us all?' CeCe butted in.

'We haven't discussed it yet. The good news is, Mary-Kate's

landing here in Dublin tonight, so hopefully I'll get to meet her.'

'How exciting!' said Maia.

'Please say hi to her from me and Chrissie,' said CeCe.

'You're the one with the instincts, Tiggy. Do you think we've found the missing sister?' came Ally's voice.

'Definitely, but . . .'

'What?' said all three sisters at the other end of the line.

'I need to think about something. I'll tell you once I have. Her son Jack is also lovely.'

'Hey, he's not adopted too, is he?' CeCe chuckled. 'Wouldn't it be weird if the missing sister was a guy?'

'Merry certainly didn't say he was. He talked a lot about you, Ally.'

'Did he?'

'Yes.'

'I bet he was cursing me, because now he knows I lied to get information out of him,' Ally sighed.

'He didn't do that at all, I promise you. When we went to see the *Book of Kells* together this afternoon, he said he wished that you could have seen it too.'

'Oh, come on, Tiggy, he must hate me,' Ally persisted.

'He may feel many things about you, Ally, but hate is definitely not one of them.'

'Anyway, well done, Tiggy. I'm so glad you've been able to reassure her,' said Maia. 'Do you think it's possible that Mary-Kate might be able to fly over from Dublin to join us on our cruise?'

'Let's wait and see, shall we? If it's meant to be, then—'

'It's meant to be,' chorused her sisters.

'Even though my instincts tell me that we're completely on the right track, do you think you could contact Georg to say

I've found Merry and the ring? I'd really like to speak to him about something.'

'I'm afraid Georg is away,' said Ally. 'I've already tried to reach him, but his secretary told me he won't be back until the boat trip.'

'Oh dear, that makes things more difficult,' said Tiggy. 'I mean, it's all very well us trusting him and his information, but others might not. All we have is the ring.'

'When I discovered my ancestors, apart from the likeness to my great-grandmother Bel in a painting, it was a piece of jewellery – my moonstone – that convinced me that I genu-inely was her great-granddaughter,' Maia interjected. 'Maybe it's the same with the ring.'

'I know, but we don't have a painting and there's no one on earth that can actually confirm that Mary-Kate is who we think she is, is there?'

'Unless she finds out who her birth parents were,' put in Ally.

'True,' Tiggy agreed, 'which is why I could do with some help from Georg to find out if he knows any other details. Please, try contacting him again for me, if you want me to convince Mary-Kate and her family to come with us on the cruise.'

'You're saying that Merry and Jack should come too?'

'I think they should all be there,' Tiggy said firmly. 'Right, I'll keep in touch if there's any news. I'll have to go with my intuition on this one.'

'Do you ever live any other way?' Ally smiled. 'It would be so amazing if we could have her with us.'

'I'll do my best, promise. Bye, everyone.'

Tiggy ended the call and then dialled Charlie on his mobile. These days, he was spending much less time at the hospital in Inverness, as the Kinnaird estate needed every hand to the pump. Even though he'd moved to a three-day week, if there was an emergency, he'd still get in his beaten-up Defender (Ulrika had the new Range Rover *and* the family house in Inverness, negotiated in a separation agreement) to drive the two hours to the hospital. His voicemail kicked in as it usually did, and Tiggy left a message.

'Hi, darling, I arrived safely in Ireland, and I've managed to meet with Merry. She's lovely, as is her son, Jack. Anyway, her daughter's arriving tonight, so I'll try and get back home at some point late tomorrow. Love you, miss you, bye.'

Tiggy laid her head back on the soft hotel pillow, sighed in pleasure and wondered if there was any money in the coffers to buy some new ones for her and Charlie. They'd rented out the luxurious lodge to wealthy families for the summer and were reduced to living in the poky gatehouse where Fraser had once lived. Not that she minded – but every penny that came in from the guests was going towards planting saplings, fencing and the re-stocking of indigenous wildlife, such as the European elk she and Charlie's daughter Zara had their hearts set on.

Her greatest triumph so far was that her Scottish wildcats had managed to produce a healthy male kitten in April. She'd been tempted to pet it, but of course, she knew she mustn't; if the cats were ever to be freed from the pen they currently lived in and released back into the wild, then any human contact was a no-no.

'Perhaps I'll ask Georg if I could have some money from Pa Salt's trust to help us,' she mused. At least it looked like Ulrika had decided against trying to snatch the Kinnaird estate, but she was still demanding a huge divorce settlement. When Charlie died, the estate would pass to Zara. Her step-daughter-to-be was so passionate about it, and Tiggy thought how terrible it would be if the estate had to be broken up to pay for her mother's taste in designer clothes.

'All things do pass,' Tiggy murmured as she closed her eyes

and breathed in deeply. Since her heart scare, and discovering the condition she would live with for the rest of her life, she'd become much more aware of her heartbeat. And it was definitely raised at the moment.

She'd felt something so strongly when she'd met Merry, she could hardly describe it. And her son Jack too . . . As for Mary-Kate, she'd meet her later tonight, but Tiggy was fairly certain she knew the answer already.

'Am I right, Pa?' she asked.

Yet again, there was no reply from him. Was it because he hadn't settled there yet, or was it her own emotions crowding the usually clear line between heaven and earth? There was always silence when she asked her father for help; like a void, as if he wasn't there . . .

'Maybe one day you'll speak to me, Pa,' she sighed, before turning to one of her other relatives who had passed on. She thought about the question she needed the answer to, then asked it.

'*Yes*,' came the reply. '*Yes*.'

Jack had spent the evening in his room at the hotel, jotting down notes on all he had learnt so far. He liked order, not chaos, and this situation with his mum and sister was unsettling him. How could it be possible that two worlds, which both included the Seven Sisters in one way or another, had collided? Or was it just coincidence . . . ?

Tiggy had said coincidence didn't exist. He wasn't so sure.

Shared interests, he'd written in his notebook.

Did Mum once know the sisters' father? he wrote *(which would explain shared interests)*.

Ambrose?

Father O'Brien?
Proof? The ring. (Is this enough?)
Ally: why do I keep thinking about her?

'Yes,' he said out loud, 'why do I? I mean, I must be . . . Damn!' Jack threw the notebook down on the bed in frustration. He was glad Mary-Kate was arriving soon, because he sure needed somebody to talk to about all this.

'Why is Mum so scared?' he asked the wide-screen television on the wall.

Surprisingly, it didn't answer.

'Time for a beer and some grub, Jack,' he said as he rolled off the bed, put on his trainers, and headed downstairs to the bar.

Just as he was ordering, a text message pinged on his phone.

On the 10 pm flight to Dublin. I'll get a taxi to the Merrion Hotel. C u soon, bro. MK xx

Sitting at the bar having a beer, he listened to the hum of Irish voices and wondered if this small island made up any part of his genes. If the DNA ran through his mother, it must run through him too. But given she'd just found out she was adopted, who was to know?

Ah, I miss you, Dad, he thought, *you were always the voice of reason, and boy, do I need that right now . . .*

Seeing it was past nine o'clock, he went to reception and asked them to call his mother's room to see if she wanted to join him for something to eat while they waited for Mary-Kate to arrive.

'I'm sorry, sir, but Mrs McDougal still has her room phone on "do not disturb",' said the receptionist.

'Right, okay, thanks.' Jack wandered away from the desk, wondering if he should go upstairs and knock on her door.

Deciding to leave her be – she'd looked so very pale earlier – he wandered into the restaurant and saw Tiggy sitting alone at a table.

'Hi,' he said.

'Hello there, Jack,' she replied, smiling her sweet smile. 'Want to join me? I was just about to order something for supper.'

'Thanks,' he said, sitting down opposite her. 'Me too.'

'Is your mum not hungry?'

'I think – or at least I hope – that she's sleeping. She's been through a lot in the past few days.'

'Because of us trying to find her?'

'Partly, yes, but also because . . .' Jack sighed and shook his head. 'Let's order, shall we?'

'I'm having the butternut squash soup.'

'I'll have the steak, with a side of fries,' he added.

The two of them ordered, Tiggy having a glass of white wine and Jack another beer.

'Cheers,' Tiggy said as they clinked glasses. 'Here's to new friends.'

'Yes. Although, it's just that, well, the whole thing's a bit weird. No offence to you and your sisters, but who was this man who adopted you all?'

'That is the burning question,' said Tiggy. 'None of us ever really knew – not where he came from or even what he did for a living. I think it's human nature to believe that the people you love will just live forever, so you never ask the questions that you should have done until it's too late. I think all of us sisters regret it now: that we didn't ask Pa more about himself, or why he adopted all of us specifically.'

'Do you mind me asking how old he was?'

'Again, we don't know, but I'd guess that he was well into his late eighties. How old is your mum?'

'Fifty-nine in November – and I know that for sure,' said Jack with a smile. 'She had to renew her passport last year, so that would put, what? Twenty-five, or even thirty years between him and my mum.'

'What are you thinking?'

'Only that, well, I was wondering if the two of them—'

'Could have got together at some point in the past? I've thought about that too. But then . . .' Tiggy eyed him.

'That would make *me* the missing brother!' Jack grinned. 'I'm joking. My mum and dad were devoted to each other, and I'm definitely my father's son.'

'Well, the one thing that my father was was specific. It was absolutely the missing *sister* he was looking to find.'

'Then it has to be Mary-Kate, doesn't it? She's the one who's adopted, but . . .'

'Yes?'

'Nothing,' said Jack.

'Does Mary-Kate know, or in fact, does your mum know who Mary-Kate's birth parents were?'

'I've no idea, but these days, it's probably easy for Mary-Kate to find out if she wants to.'

'And does she?'

'Tiggy, I honestly don't know, but as she's arriving in a couple of hours' time, I'll ask her.'

'And what about your mum? Who were her parents?'

Jack took a sip of his beer, knowing it was not his place to tell what Ambrose had said this morning. 'They were Irish, I think.'

'Jack, was your mum adopted too?'

He stared at Tiggy in disbelief as she calmly ate her soup. 'Christ! How did you know? My mum was only told that this morning! Who told *you*?'

'Oh, nobody, it was just a feeling,' she said. 'I have a lot of those, Jack, and when I met your mum earlier today, I *knew*.'

'Knew what?'

'Just that she was. Now it all makes sense.'

'Well, at least I didn't tell you. Seriously, Tiggy, this must stay a secret from everyone, including your sisters. Mum was pretty devastated, y'know? Even if she's never talked about her past to us kids, knowing where you come from and believing your family is your family . . . it identifies you, doesn't it?'

'Yes . . . but being adopted myself, I firmly believe that if you grow up in a loving environment, it doesn't matter what your genetic make-up is.'

'Yeah, but like Mary-Kate, you always knew you were adopted. And you made that a part of your identity. Mum has thought she came from her Irish family the whole of her life. And now, at not far off six decades, she's just been told it was all a lie.'

'That must be so very hard for her to come to terms with. I'm sure it will take her some time. Please don't worry, I'm especially good at keeping secrets. I won't say a word until I'm allowed to, but it does mean that we might have got it all wrong.'

'About what?'

'Oh, just assuming things. Anyway,' Tiggy shrugged. 'It doesn't matter.'

'Everything's a bit crazy just now, eh? Especially for Mum. I don't like craziness.'

'Perhaps there has to be a moment when everything is thrown up in the air before it can settle again, then maybe it can be even better than before. Tell me if I'm wrong, but I get the feeling your mum is frightened of something else, other than us sisters tracking her down. Is she?'

'Yeah, she is for sure. Wow, Tiggy, are you a mind-reader or what?'

'I just sensed it. Now then, shall we look at the dessert menu? I'm still hungry.'

After they'd eaten, Tiggy and Jack sat in the lounge having coffee and chatting about both living in far-flung, isolated locations when Jack's mobile rang.

'Excuse me,' he said as he answered it.

'Hi, Jack! I'm here!' came Mary-Kate's bright voice.

'Where is "here"?'

'I'm standing in the lobby, idiot! Where are you? You're certainly not answering the phone in your room.'

Jack looked at the time on his watch and saw it was after midnight. 'O'course! Sorry, I'd lost track of the time. I'll come and get you.'

'Mary-Kate's here,' Jack said as he stood up. 'I didn't realise it was so late,' he added as he began to walk towards reception.

'Jack!' Tiggy called. 'I'm going back to my room now. You need some time with your sister.'

'Okay, but why don't you come and say hi? After all, she might be your missing sister . . .'

'If you're sure.'

Tiggy stood up and followed Jack into the lobby. She saw a young woman dressed in black jeans and a hoody, her fair hair scraped up into a topknot. She watched as brother and sister embraced and felt the easy warmth and affection between the two of them.

'Tiggy' – Jack beckoned her over – 'this is Mary-Kate, more commonly known as MK. MK, meet Tiggy D'Aplièse, the fifth sister.'

'Pleased to meet you, Tiggy. Sorry I look such a wreck; it's a long way from NZ to Ireland, and I left in a huge rush to make the flight.'

'You must be exhausted, but it's wonderful to meet you,

Mary-Kate. My sister CeCe said you were very hospitable to her and Chrissie when they visited you.'

'Us Kiwis are just brought up that way, eh, Jack? But yeah, they were great and we had a fun night together.'

'Right, I'll leave you two to it and say goodnight.'

'Night, Tiggy, and thanks for the chat,' Jack called to her as she walked towards the lift. After Mary-Kate had checked in, he took her rucksack. 'Let's get you upstairs to your room, so you can get some shut-eye.'

'I'm not sure I can sleep, y'know?' said Mary-Kate. 'I'm wired; my body has no idea what time it is or what it's meant to do. Where's Mum?'

'Sleeping. I haven't woken her – I know she'll be mad at me tomorrow morning, but she's had a helluva day today.'

'Really? Is she all right?'

'I'm sure she will be,' Jack replied as they went up in the lift, then headed for Mary-Kate's room. 'Coming back here to Ireland has been a bit like pricking a boil: you gotta get the poison out before it starts to heal.'

'Lovely analogy, Jacko,' Mary-Kate commented as her brother opened the door to her room for her. 'What kind of "poison"?'

'It's all to do with her past. I'll let her tell you. Anyway, it's good to see you, sis. I'm glad you came.'

'I didn't think I had a choice, Jack.' Mary-Kate climbed onto the bed and leant back against the pillows. 'What's been going on?'

'I wish I could tell you, but at the moment, I can't. Basically, there's something – or someone – Mum is frightened of. And when this family of sisters kept turning up at her hotels trying to speak to her, she got really spooked.'

'They only wanted to meet her and identify that ring, Jack. Why would that scare her?'

'I haven't a clue,' Jack sighed. 'All I've managed to get from her so far is that *she* used to be called the "missing sister" when she was younger. Listen, I've had a long day too, even if I haven't travelled round the world like you, and I'm beat. I think we should both get some shut-eye; if tomorrow's anything like today, you'll need your wits about you.'

'Bad stuff?' Mary-Kate asked.

'Just . . . stuff. Put it this way, after years of never mentioning it, Mum's on an odyssey into her past, and it's complicated.'

'So it's nothing to do with me then? Or the fact I might be this missing sister? I was thinking on the plane that maybe she's scared she's going to lose me to some other family.'

'Maybe, yeah, but as all the rest of the sisters are adopted and their dad is dead, I'm not sure how you'd be related to them anyway.'

'What about the adoptive mum? Who's she?'

'I don't think there ever was one. Tiggy told me that some nanny brought them all up. It's all a bit weird, to be honest, but she and her sister Ally, who I met in Provence, are lovely and seem pretty normal.'

'CeCe and her friend Chrissie were great as well,' Mary-Kate agreed. 'Anyway, I've got something to tell you and Mum tomorrow. Right, I'm taking a shower and then I'll try to get some sleep. Night, Jacko.'

'Night, sis.'

39

Merry
Dublin

I woke up and lay there in the dark, thinking I was at home. I reached out for Jock's comforting bulk, but found emptiness next to me.

And remembered.

'I miss you, my love, every day more, and I'm so sorry if I never appreciated you properly when you were with me,' I whispered into the darkness.

I felt tears prick my eyes as the nightmare of my current existence began to flood back into my brain. I reached to turn the light on to stop the bad thoughts. And was shocked that the clock was saying it was ten to nine.

'At night?' I muttered as I staggered out of bed to open the curtains. I was amazed to find the sun shining high in the sky. Partly because it was rare to see such a clear sky in Dublin, but also because it meant it was morning, and I'd managed to sleep for almost fourteen hours straight.

'Mary-Kate!' I exclaimed out loud as I remembered. Reaching over, I dialled Jack's room.

'Hi, Mum. Sleep well?'

'I did, yes, but did Mary-Kate arrive? Is she okay?'

'Yeah, she's fine. I left her in her room at around one a.m.'

'Why didn't you wake me?'

'Because you needed to sleep. You had quite a day yesterday. Fancy some breakfast?'

'I need to come to first, Jack. I feel like I've been drugged. It's tea and a bath for me, but you go ahead if you want.'

'I can wait. Just give me a call when you're ready to come down.'

'You're sure Mary-Kate is okay?'

'Totally, Mum. See you in a bit.'

I lay in the bath, drinking tea and thanking God and the heavens for the gift of my two children. Coming from a big family myself, I'd hoped for more babies, but that wasn't to be.

'But you weren't from a big family, Merry, you just *belonged* to one,' I whispered to myself.

However, the thought of Mary-Kate, my precious daughter in all but blood, lying a few feet away from me, stopped me from self-indulgence. Jock and I could not have loved her any more than we did. We were her mum and dad and Jack her brother, no matter whose genes she did or didn't have.

Out of the bath and feeling calmer, I dried my hair and thought about the reason – the *real* reason – I'd decided to embark on my tour of the world. Now here I was in Dublin and even though it frightened me, I knew exactly where my children and I needed to go next.

'But first . . .' I said to the mirror as I applied the usual dab of pale pink lipstick, 'I must visit my godfather.'

'Mary-Kate, it's so good to see you!' I said as she reached our table in the dining room.

'And you,' my daughter said as we hugged. 'You look well, Mum. I was worried when Jacko called and told me to jump straight on a plane.'

'I'm fine, really, sweetheart. Fancy some breakfast?'

'Weirdly, I'm craving a glass of our Kiwi wine, preferably red.'

'Your body clock hasn't caught up yet,' Jack grinned. 'It's evening wine time in NZ. Some of this fantastic Clonakilty black pudding will have to do.' Jack indicated his plate.

'Ewww. It looks disgusting. What's it made of?' Mary-Kate asked.

'Mum says pig's blood mostly, but it tastes great, I promise.'

'I'll grab some toast, if they have anything like that here,' she said as she began to walk to the buffet.

'Oh, they do, try the soda bread with some jam!' I called. 'You'll love it.' Mary-Kate gave a thumbs up and I took a sip of my steaming cappuccino. 'They never had coffee like this when I was growing up. Ireland, or at least Dublin, has changed so much, I can hardly believe it.'

'In what way, Mum?' Jack asked me.

'In every way. I mean, Dublin always was ahead of the Irish curve, so it would be interesting to see what West Cork is like these days, but—'

'No wonder your fry-ups have always been good, Mum,' said Mary-Kate, returning with a fully loaded plate. 'I've got some toast, eggs and bacon and a bit of that pudding stuff. I'm actually starving.'

I watched my daughter as she ate hungrily, just enjoying the sight of her here with me.

'That bread is delicious, Mum,' said Mary-Kate in between bites. 'And the pudding thing is really good, even if it's full of stuff I don't want to think of.' She put her knife and fork together and looked at me. 'Jacko says you've been on a voyage of self-discovery since you've been here. What's the news?'

I looked at my watch. 'Actually, there's somewhere I need to be.' I stood up from the table abruptly. 'I'll only be gone an hour or so, and I'll tell you everything when I'm back. Feel free to go out and explore the city while I'm gone.'

'Okay,' said Jack, and I saw my children exchange glances.

'See you later,' I said, then I walked out of the hotel and headed back to Merrion Square.

'Mary, come in,' said Ambrose. He led me slowly through to his sitting room and eased himself into his leather chair. 'How are you, my dear? I've been so concerned for your state of mind after what I told you yesterday. Again, I beg your forgiveness.'

'Ambrose, please, you mustn't worry about me. Of course I was shocked. But firstly, I met Tiggy, the fifth of the six sisters who have been chasing me. She arrived at the hotel yesterday afternoon.' I explained the conversation we'd had and how it helped ease my mind. 'Then, after a surprisingly good night's sleep, I woke up feeling much calmer. Truly, I understand why you hadn't told me before. My daughter Mary-Kate arrived from New Zealand too, and having her here with me – especially as she's adopted herself – has really helped.'

'I'd very much like to meet her.'

'I'm sure you will. Ambrose . . .' I paused for a moment, collecting my thoughts. 'You know I've always come to you for help and advice, or at least I used to. And . . . I need some now.'

'Fire away, Mary, and let us hope my advice to you is better than the advice I gave to myself all those years ago, when I neglected to tell you about how James and I found you.'

'I . . . well, after Jock died, I decided that it was time to finally put my past to bed. So when I went to visit Bridget on Norfolk Island at the start of my Grand Tour, I wanted to know if she'd seen . . . well, *him* in Dublin after I left. I think you know who I mean.'

'I do, my dear, yes.'

'She said she hadn't, because she'd moved to London and, like me, hasn't returned to Ireland since, as her parents sold their business and moved to Florida. She told me it would be better to let sleeping dogs lie. Especially when the two girls showed up to see Mary-Kate at The Vinery and used that phrase, the "missing sister". And then said they wanted to see the ring.'

'I think I understand, Mary, but surely now, having met Tiggy, you can see that your past problems in Dublin have nothing to do with the sisters who've been trying to find you?'

'I'm starting to believe it's coincidence, but I can't tell you how terrified I've been. As far as *he's* concerned . . . I decided that I had to find out what happened to him. I've been searching for his name in public records offices in all the countries I thought he might have gone to if he was following me. So far, I've found no trace of him.'

Ambrose paused before he spoke. 'Mary, you never told me the whole story, so I cannot claim to know exactly what happened, but I will say that after you left, I had a visit from him here.'

'Did you?' My stomach turned over. 'Did you speak to him?'

'Briefly; he was thumping so violently on my front door that I rather felt I had no choice but to let him in. He obviously wanted to know if you were here. When I said I hadn't seen you for two days – which was the truth – he didn't believe me. He tore through here, looking under beds, searching in all the nooks and crannies and out in my tiny back garden, in case you were hiding under a pot of begonias! He then caught me by the lapels of my jacket, making threats of violence if I didn't tell him where you were.'

'Oh, Ambrose, I'm so, so sorry, I—'

'It was a long time ago, Mary, and I'm only telling you this to assure you that I understand why you left. Luckily, I'd already seen him lurking out on the street before I let him in, and had the foresight to call the Gardaí. A patrol car arrived in the nick of time and he made a run for it.'

'Did they catch him?'

'No, but he never came back here again.'

'You got my note saying that I had to leave for a while?'

'I did. Your Greek was almost impeccable; only a couple of small grammatical errors,' he said with a sardonic raise of an eyebrow. 'I still have it to this day.'

'I'm so sorry he came here, Ambrose. He'd made the most terrible threats against me, my friends, my family . . . everyone I loved. And he hated you most of all, and that ring you gave me. He called it "obscene", said it was like an engagement ring and that you were in love with me. In the end, I decided that all I could do was to disappear and cut off all contact with everyone. They weren't idle threats either; he'd told me he was involved with some violent men and, given his republican extremism and what was happening here in Ireland, I believed him. Oh dear,' I sighed, feeling dizzy as I said the words I'd kept to myself for so long, but I had to continue. 'The point is, Ambrose, I have to know if he's alive or dead and end this thing once and for all. Even though I've changed my name, my nationality and lived in the safest place you could possibly imagine, I still jump whenever I hear a car coming down the track towards our house. So the question is, do you . . . do you think I should go back to where it all began?'

Ambrose steepled his fingers and thought for a while. It was such a familiar gesture, it brought a lump to my throat.

'In my view, it's always beneficial to rid oneself of one's demons, if at all possible,' he said eventually.

'But what if he went back home to West Cork and is living there now? I think I'd die of fright if I actually saw him.'

'Do your children know your . . . situation?'

'No, nothing, although after the past few days, I know Jack's aware something's not right.'

'I'm sure he is. I presume they would accompany you?'

'Yes.'

'And you'd visit your own family?'

'I'd hope to. I don't even know if they're still there,' I sighed. 'One of the reasons I came to see you originally was because of your friendship with Father O'Brien. I always thought that would endure the test of time, and if anyone would know if *he* was still around down there, it would be him. He was the parish priest, after all.'

'Ah, sadly, that was not to be,' Ambrose replied quietly.

'May I ask why?'

'You may, and the answer is two words: Mrs Cavanagh.'

'How can I forget her? With that long, pointed nose of hers, she always reminded me of the Wicked Witch of the West in *The Wizard of Oz*. What did she do?'

'Well now, from the moment she set eyes on me, I felt her utter dislike. She didn't approve of me or my visits, and most of all, the friendship I had with dear James. After all, I was a single man with a British accent, and I was labelled by her the moment I opened my mouth. Ironic, really, considering she worked as a housekeeper at Argideen House, and was the most out and out snob I'd ever met. Well, there we are.'

'But what did she do to end your friendship?'

'Oh Mary, she was merely waiting for her chance to destroy it. When she was around, I took every precaution I could to make sure she had no ammunition. Then my father died a few years after you had left Dublin. Even though my father and I had a difficult relationship, it was the end of an era – I sold our family house only a few months later, after four hundred years of Lister occupation. I went down to see James after the funeral, and I admit to breaking down and crying in his study. James put his arms around my shoulders to comfort me, just as Mrs Cavanagh opened the door to tell us that lunch was served. The following morning, when James was out holding Mass, she cornered me and told me that she'd always felt our relationship was "inappropriate", especially for a priest. Either I left and never came back, or she would tell the bishop what she had seen.'

'Oh Ambrose, no,' I said, my eyes filling with tears. 'What did you do?'

'Well, both you and I know what a devoted man of God Father O'Brien was. If there had been any words whispered in the bishop's ear – words that she was sure to embellish – his priestly journey would have been halted then and there. It would have destroyed him; not just his career path, but spiritually too. So, when I arrived back in Dublin, I wrote to James telling him that, due to my new appointment as head of the Classics department, the workload would prevent me from coming down regularly to see him.'

'Surely Father O'Brien must have contacted you after you did?'

'Oh, he did, and I evaded and evaded, with excuse after excuse as to why I couldn't spare the time. He even came up to Dublin to see me, so I invented a lady friend.' Ambrose chuckled sadly. 'Eventually, he took the hint and I heard from him no more. Of course, now that I'm retired, I have far too much time to look back on things I'd rather not remember.'

I watched as Ambrose took his handkerchief from his pocket and dabbed his eyes.

'You loved him, didn't you?' I whispered.

'I did, Mary, and you're the only person in my entire life to whom I've admitted that. Of course, I was aware from the start that he could never love me, not in the way I wished at least. For me, it was the love that dare not speak its name, and for James, the true embodiment of my precious Plato's platonic love. Still, just seeing him regularly was a gift. I treasured our friendship, as you will remember.'

'Yes. He was such a very good man and even I could see how much he cared for you. If only—'

'Sadly life is filled with "if only"s, my dear, but there's never a day that goes by when I don't miss him.'

'I suppose you have no idea where Father O'Brien is? Or even if he's alive?'

'No. Rather like you, I felt that cutting off contact was the best thing for us. And if he *is* with his beloved God now, then I am happy for him. Well,' Ambrose sighed, 'there we have it.'

'I'm so sorry for asking you. The last thing I wanted to do was to upset you.'

'Goodness, no; as a matter of fact, it's rather a relief to speak it all out loud to someone who knew him. And his goodness.'

'Ambrose, I've just discovered that if it hadn't been for the kindness of you and Father O'Brien, I'd have ended up in an orphanage. And we all know now how terrible most of them were.'

'Luckily, James knew that already, having seen one for himself in Dublin.'

'At least Mrs Cavanagh must be a few feet underground by now. Frankly, I hope she rots in hell, and I don't think I've ever said that about another human being,' I added staunchly.

'Anyway, we've veered off track, Mary. Do continue with what you were telling me.'

'Well, only recently I read the diary *he* gave me as a parting gift when I left for boarding school. He wanted me to understand why I must hate the British too and continue the fight for a united Ireland. He told me it was written by his grandmother, Nuala. She'd given it to him apparently, so he'd never forget. Of course, I never read it back then, but given my current odyssey into my past, I decided I should. So I did, a few days ago.'

'And?'

'Well, it certainly didn't make easy reading, but it's obvious where *he* got his republican leanings.'

'You should hold on to that diary, Mary. There are so very few documented first-hand sources about the fight for Irish independence. Everyone was far too frightened of being caught.'

'You can read it if you'd like. There were names and places mentioned in it that make me think there was a family connection between us. For example, Nuala talks about her home being Cross Farm, and her brother being Fergus. Well, our family lived at Cross Farm and I know my Daddy inherited it from our great-uncle Fergus.'

'I see. So you're thinking that *he* may have been a relation?'

'Yes.'

'Well, that's hardly surprising – everyone was related to everyone down in West Cork.'

'I know, and I'm wondering if he knew too. He was never

allowed up to our farm and I'm thinking that maybe there had been a falling-out long ago. And that's why he behaved so oddly with me when I was a child. He seemed to love me and hate me in equal measure.'

'Maybe,' Ambrose agreed. 'There's only one way to find out and that is to go back to where it all began.'

'That's what I came to ask you: should I travel back to West Cork?'

'On balance, I think you should, yes. You have your son and daughter to protect you, plus a family there, who I'm sure will be delighted to welcome you back into the fold.'

'Oh Ambrose, I don't know. What if he *is* there? It would be a lot easier just to get on a plane to New Zealand and forget all about it.'

'You will find out very quickly if he is, Mary; we both know how everyone knows your business there before you do. And the young woman I once knew you to be was brave and strong, and would face her foes head on. Besides, surely now there is another reason to travel there?'

'What?'

'The fact that it's the only place to discover your original birth family. As I explained yesterday, you couldn't have been more than a few hours old when we found you on the doorstep, Mary, so your birth parents must hail from somewhere very close to the priest's house in Timoleague.'

'I suppose so,' I sighed, 'but I'm not sure I want to find them. My head's so full at the moment, I hardly know which way to turn.'

'I'm sure you don't, Mary, but my belief is that in the end, we must all go back to where we began in order to understand.'

'Yes, you're right as usual,' I smiled.

'One thing I must ask you is what happened to that nice

young man you were seeing before you left? Peter, wasn't it?'

'I . . .' For some reason, I blushed, simply at the sound of his name. 'I don't know.'

'Right. He also came to see me after you'd left. He seemed distraught – he said he hadn't received a reply to letters he'd written to you in London.'

'Did he?' My heart began to thump again against my chest. 'Well, I certainly didn't receive any. Actually, he . . . *that* situation is something else I wanted your advice on . . .'

I arrived back at the hotel and was handed a message at reception from Jack to say he and Mary-Kate had gone on a wander into the city and would be back in time for a late lunch.

Upstairs in my room, before I could even begin to process the conversation I'd just had, I did as Ambrose had suggested. I went to a leather folder on the desk, drew out some hotel notepaper, found my pen from my handbag and sat down to write.

'Jesus, Mary and Joseph!' I murmured. 'What on earth do I say?'

In the end, I decided that less was more, and what did it matter, as the chances of finding the other 'him' were tiny anyway?

I read it through once, then signed it and sealed it in an envelope before I lost my nerve. I quickly packed my suitcase and threw some essentials in my holdall, then stood up to leave the hotel and give the letter to Ambrose before I changed my mind.

'If you could store my suitcase for me until I'm back, that

would be wonderful,' I said to Ambrose as he met me on the doorstep. 'And here's the letter,' I added.

'Right,' he nodded. 'I will do my absolute best to locate him, and will let you know if I do.'

'Thank you, darling Ambrose. Oh, and I brought you Nuala's diary to read. I'm afraid the writing isn't very clear and the spelling is sometimes phonetic rather than accurate,' I said, handing him the small, black exercise book.

'Exactly what I need to keep my brain active,' Ambrose smiled. 'Now then, Mary, go with your children and try to relax. As Jean de la Fontaine said, a person often meets his destiny on the road he took to avoid it. Or she, in your case. Please keep—'

'. . . in touch,' I parroted as I walked down the steps. 'I promise, Ambrose, truly, I do.'

Then, seeing I had just enough time before the children were back, I headed for the Dublin records office.

'Hi, Mum, sorry we're late – we got lost in a few alleys off Grafton Street,' said Jack as he and Mary-Kate appeared in the hotel lobby a few minutes after me.

'Oh, don't worry, I had bits to do myself.'

'Well, I'm starving,' Mary-Kate announced.

'Then let's go and grab a quick sandwich in the lounge, shall we?' I suggested. 'The train leaves at four,' I added.

'The train to where?' asked Jack.

'To West Cork, of course. The county where I spent my childhood. You said I should go back, Jack, so we are.'

Jack and Mary-Kate glanced at each other as we sat down on a free sofa. 'Okay,' they chorused.

Once we'd ordered, I saw Mary-Kate give Jack a small nod.

'What?' I enquired.

'MK has something to tell you.'

'I do, but . . . well, I know you've had a tough time recently, Mum, and I don't want to upset you any further,' said my daughter, who could hardly look me in the eye.

'Whatever it is, just tell me, or I'll worry anyway,' I said.

'Well . . .' She looked at Jack and he gave a nod of encouragement. 'You remember we had that conversation after CeCe and Chrissie had been to see me?'

'We had a few, so remind me which one?'

Again, I saw her look at her brother, who offered his hand to her.

'The one when I asked if you knew who and where my birth family was.'

'Yes,' I nodded as I wondered how much more stress my soon-to-be fifty-nine-year-old heart could take. 'I said that we'd talk about it when I got home.'

'Yeah, well, the whole thing had obviously got me thinking, so I found the adoption agency you mentioned in Christchurch, and they had my details on file. I made an appointment last week to go and see the guy there who runs the records department. I explained the situation to him – that a woman saying I might be related to her family had turned up on my doorstep, and I wanted to know if she really was who she said she was.' Mary-Kate eyed me, obviously trying to gauge my reaction. 'I'm sorry I couldn't wait for you to come home, but, well, seeing as it had come up, I couldn't think about anything else, y'know? You're not angry or anything, are you?'

'Of course not; I'm just sorry I wasn't there with you.'

'Mum, I'm twenty-two – I'm a big girl now. Anyway, the guy was great. He said I'd have to fill out some consent forms if I wanted to trace my birth parents and they'd have to be asked as well, assuming they could still be found.' Mary-Kate let go of Jack's hand and put hers on mine. 'I swear, this will make no difference to the way I feel about you. Or Dad. I mean, you *are* my mum and always will be, but what with all this missing sister stuff, I just want to know who my birth family is and move on, y'know?'

'Of course,' I nodded. 'So, what happened next?'

'Well, I filled in all the forms, then I faxed them a copy of my birth certificate and passport. The guy – Chip – said it might take some time, so I wasn't expecting to hear anything back any time soon, but . . .'

'What?'

'I got an email a couple of days ago. They've found her! I mean, they've found my birth mum!'

'Right,' I nodded, instinctively wanting to cry, because those two words hurt my soul so much. 'And?' I said lamely.

'I typed out a quick email to her as Chip had asked me to do, saying I'd like to get in touch, and guess what?'

'You got a reply,' I said.

'Yeah. Last night, when I was at Heathrow airport. Obviously, it's all going through the agency at the moment, but I know her name is Michelle, and she's going to email me back. She wants contact. Mum, is that okay with you?'

'That's great, yes, great,' I replied, not having it in me to step up to the plate and look happy for my daughter. *My* daughter . . . The waitress appeared and I was relieved that the sandwiches had arrived to give me something to concentrate on. 'These look good,' I said as I picked one up and took a bite, even though I felt sick to my stomach.

'I think what Mary-Kate means is that at least, if this woman does email back, maybe we can get to the bottom of this whole missing sister thing,' Jack said gently.

'Completely. We all want to know whether I'm related to

those girls in some way. One thing I have thought about, Mum,' Mary-Kate said between munches, 'is whether there were other people trying to adopt me. Chip mentioned that there's not usually many Kiwi newborns going spare in the region. I wonder whether this dead father – Pa Salt, or whatever silly name those sisters call him – applied to get me and lost out to you and Dad. Or something,' she shrugged.

'That's certainly another theory,' I nodded, trying to look enthusiastic. It wasn't Mary-Kate's fault that I felt emotionally conflicted about this news, as well as just about every other thing in the current maelstrom of my life. 'So, have either of you seen Tiggy this morning?'

'Yeah, she came down to breakfast after you'd left, so she joined us for a tosh around the city,' explained Jack.

'Where is she now?'

'I think she went up to her room to pack. She's on the afternoon flight back to Scotland.'

'Right. You have my credit card, so would you pay the bill for all of us, Jack, and ask them to get a taxi to pick us up in twenty minutes?'

'O'course, Mum.'

'You come with me, Mary-Kate,' I said as I signed for lunch, then made for the lift as Jack headed for reception.

'Are you okay about all this, Mum?' Mary-Kate asked me tentatively.

'Of course I am,' I said as we walked out of the lift and along the corridor. 'I'd always known it was a possibility that one day you'd want to meet your birth family.'

'Hey, slow down, Mum. We're only going to email at the moment,' said Mary-Kate. 'The last thing I want to do, especially after losing Dad, is cause you any more pain.'

'Come here.'

I pulled my daughter to me and hugged her. She snuggled into me, just as she'd done when she was a tiny newborn of only a couple of days old.

'Right,' I said, knowing I was close to tears, 'pack up your stuff and I'll see you downstairs in twenty minutes, okay?'

'Okay. Love you, Mum,' she said as she wandered along the corridor to her room.

Just as I was about to go downstairs, there was a knock on my door. I opened it to find Tiggy standing there.

'Tiggy, come in!'

'Hello, Merry, I just wanted to come and say goodbye. Jack said you're leaving.'

'Yes. I mean, we're not leaving Ireland, just travelling down to West Cork where I was born.'

She stared at me. 'Are you looking for answers?'

'I suppose I am, yes, but whether I'll find them or not is another story. I have no idea what to expect.'

Tiggy walked over to me and again took my hand in hers. 'I'm sure you will, Merry. All of us sisters were sent on a journey into our past after Pa died last year. It was scary at times, but we each found what we were looking for and it made our lives much better. It will for you too.'

'I hope so.'

'I can feel you're frightened, but wouldn't it be so much better if you were finally freed from that fear?'

I stared at this young woman who looked so fragile, yet seemed so wise. Every time she held my hand, I felt a sense of calm sweep over me.

'I've written down my mobile number,' she said as she released my hand to reach into her jean pocket and give me a piece of paper. 'Any problem, call and leave a message and I promise I will get back to you as soon as I can. The signal's patchy where I live,' she explained. 'I've also written down my big sister Maia's number, and the landline at Atlantis, our house in Geneva. Any help you need, just call.'

'Thank you,' I said. 'When are you all leaving for your boat trip?'

'One week on Thursday. Some of us are flying to Geneva and others straight to Nice, where the boat is moored. We'd love for you to join us. All of you,' Tiggy added firmly.

'But . . . we don't even know for sure whether Mary-Kate is the missing sister, do we?'

Tiggy looked down at my ring and brushed a finger over it gently.

'*That* is the proof. Seven emeralds for seven sisters. The circle is complete. Goodbye, Merry, and I hope to see you all again very soon.'

On the two-and-a-half-hour train journey down to Cork City, I slept most of the way; just the touch of Tiggy's hands seemed to have that effect on me.

'Mum, we're pulling into the station.' Mary-Kate shook me gently.

I came to and looked out into Kent station, which I had come to know well between the ages of eleven and twenty-two. It had been modernised, of course, but it still had that grand old air of the past about it, with its vaulted iron ceiling and echo of voices and footsteps. In the early days, I'd been glad to arrive back here with Bridget for the holidays from boarding school. Her father had collected us in his shiny black car with the big leather seats, and driven us back to West Cork, because the old railway line that served it and had once taken Ambrose almost to the doorstep of Father O'Brien's house had been shut down in 1961. I remembered how I'd always let out a breath of relief when climbing into that car, because I was on my way home. Then, when I went to Trinity College at eighteen, everything had swapped around, and on my return to Dublin, I'd seen Kent station as a gateway to my freedom.

'So,' Jack said, looking at me as we stood on the main concourse, 'where to from here, Mum?'

'The taxi rank,' I pointed.

'Hello there,' said a cabby as we reached the front of the queue for a taxi. He opened the car doors and gave us all a smile. 'Welcome to the city of Cork, the finest in all of Ireland. My name's Niall, so,' he added as he stowed my holdall and the two rucksacks into the boot, then climbed behind the wheel and turned round to me. 'Now then, where'll I be taking you?'

The sound of his lilting West Cork accent brought a lump to my throat. I took my purse from my bag and handed him the piece of paper with the address of the hotel on it.

'Ah, the Inchydoney Island Lodge and Spa. 'Tis a grand hotel altogether,' he added. 'I don't live so far from it myself – it's near the town of Clonakilty. Will you be on your holidays here, sightseeing?'

'Sort of,' said Jack from the front seat. 'It's me and my sister's first time down here, but Mum used to live here, didn't you?'

I saw Niall glance at me in the rear-view mirror. 'Whereabouts would that have been?'

'Between Clogagh and Timoleague, but it was a long time ago now,' I added hurriedly. I knew how local gossip could begin with a whisper of someone's arrival, and be trumpeted around in the space of a few hours.

'I've cousins in Timoleague,' he said. 'What's your family name?'

'I . . . well, it was O'Reilly.'

'Sure, there are a few O'Reillys down in those parts. What was your homeplace called?'

'Cross Farm,' I said.

'Ah, I think I know of it, so, and I'd be betting we have kin in common. Everyone does down there.' Niall turned to Jack. 'So, 'tis you and your sister's first time here, to see where your mammy grew up?'

'Yes. We're looking forward to it, aren't we, Mary-Kate?'

'We are,' she agreed.

'You'll be staying in one of the grandest spots on the coast, but if you fancy a trip out, I'd recommend you see the Galley Head Lighthouse, which isn't so far from your mam's homeplace. Then there's the friary in Timoleague, o'course, and you should go to the Michael Collins Centre in Castleview.'

As Niall regaled my children with what to see and do, I gazed out of the window in amazement, not only at the number of cars, but at the roads themselves. We were on some kind of dual carriageway and the surface beneath us was completely smooth as we drove along. Journeys home from Dublin, even in Bridget's daddy's big comfortable car, had been bumpy to say the least. It was obvious that West Cork had finally joined the twenty-first century.

'There's the airport,' Niall was saying. 'The new terminal was only opened a couple of years back, and 'tis grand altogether! I often pop in on my way back from Cork City for a coffee, so.'

As we arrived at Innishannon, I was relieved to see that the main street of the village hadn't changed much.

'Oh look, Mum!' said Mary-Kate. 'The houses are all painted in different colours! It's so pretty.'

'You'll be seeing a lot of those around these parts, and

575

other villages in Ireland too,' cut in Niall. ''Tis something bright to look at when the rain's tipping it down in the winter, or on any day of the year.'

We entered Bandon, which Niall duly announced was the 'gateway to West Cork', and again I recognised some shops that still had the same family names painted above their doors. Then finally, we were off and out into the lush and unadulterated countryside I remembered so vividly. Gentle slopes on either side of us were peppered with grazing cows, and I caught sight of fuchsia bushes coming into bloom. The only change was the number of bungalows that had replaced the old stone ruins of cottages.

'Wow, it's so green here,' said Mary-Kate.

'Well, it is called the Emerald Isle,' I smiled, looking down at my ring.

'Am I ever going to get that back from you, Mum?' she teased me.

'Of course you will. I just needed it in case anyone I met from the old days didn't recognise me.'

'Mum, you look exactly the same now as you did in that black and white photo of you when you got your degree,' said Jack.

'Flatterer,' I said. 'Look! We're at Clonakilty Junction. There used to be a train line down here, which serviced West Cork. My older sisters used to get on it if they were off for a day of shopping or a dance in Cork City.'

'My daddy used to cycle up if there was a big GAA match at the Park,' said Niall.

'You cycled all the way we've just driven?' Mary-Kate asked.

'And many miles more too,' Niall confirmed.

'I rode everywhere on my bicycle when I lived here; it was just the way we got around back then,' I added.

'Sure, we all had calves the size of body-builders in those days, didn't we, Mrs O'Reilly?' Niall laughed.

'Please, call me Merry,' I said, not bothering to correct my surname.

'Now then, look to your left, at the car up on that plinth. This is the village where Henry Ford himself's parents lived, before they followed half o' Ireland across the Atlantic to America.'

I looked over at the stainless-steel replica of a Model T car, standing on a plinth just across a lane from the Henry Ford pub. It was a lane I knew well, for further on, it would eventually bring us to our own farm.

'So now, we're heading into Clonakilty,' said Niall. 'If you've not been here for a good few years, Merry, I think you'll spot some changes. We've a new industrial park with a cinema, and a sports centre with a swimming pool these days. O'course, Clonakilty is most famous for being the nearest town to Michael Collins's homeplace.'

'Michael who?' said Jack.

'Is he a film star?' Mary-Kate asked. 'I'm sure I read somewhere about him being in something.'

'Ah now, I think you mean you read of a film *about* him,' Niall corrected my daughter. 'The young ones don't know their history these days, do they, Merry?'

'To be fair, they were both brought up in New Zealand,' I interjected. 'What happened here and who Michael Collins was didn't really feature in their history lessons.'

'And you're telling me that you were born here and never told your small ones about the Big Fellow?'

'To be honest, Niall, Mum didn't tell us much about anything to do with her childhood,' said Jack.

'Well, I'll be tellin' you that Michael Collins was one of the greatest heroes Ireland has ever bred,' Niall said. 'He led us towards independence from the British and . . .'

Welcome home, Merry, I thought, as we turned off towards Inchydoney and I let Niall's history of Michael Collins wash over me.

Five minutes later, Niall pulled the car to a halt in front of the entrance to the Inchydoney Lodge.

'Now, Merry, what do you think of this?' he asked as he got out of the taxi and the three of us opened our doors too. 'I bet you're remembering that old shack that used to be here when you were a girl.'

'Yes, I am,' I agreed, as I admired the big, smart hotel, then turned to face the magnificent stretch of white sandy beach with the waves crashing onto it and felt the wind whip through my hair. I took in a lungful of fresh, pure, West Cork air, smelling its unique scent of sea and cow.

'So what will you be doing for transport whilst you're here?' Niall asked as I paid him in euros, rather than the shillings I'd so carefully counted when I was growing up.

'I'll rent a car,' I said. 'Where would be the nearest place?'

''Tis Cork airport – you should have mentioned it and we could have sorted it out on our way here. Never mind, I can help you until you get your own,' Niall said as he picked up my holdall and we all walked into the lobby.

'This is stylish,' Jack said as he looked around the spacious, modern reception area. 'I was expecting something beamed, like a farmhouse, y'know?'

We checked in, with Niall chatting away to the staff behind reception, who gave me the number of a hire car company based at the airport.

'Sure, I can be taking you back there early tomorrow morning. Just give me a call,' said Niall. 'Anything else you need, you have my number. I'll be seeing ye,' he said with a wave as he walked off.

'Everyone's so friendly here, Mum. Was it always like

this?' Mary-Kate asked me as we followed the porter to the lift.

'I suppose so, yes, but it was different for me living here. We were all more worried about what everyone was saying about *us*.'

'Well, they're certainly chatty,' said Jack as we walked along yet another hotel corridor.

'Here now,' said the porter, taking us into a room still flooded with soft, early evening light from the glass sliding doors, which led onto a small balcony. 'You've a grand view of the ocean.'

'Thank you,' I said as I tipped him. 'You can leave the rucksacks in here.'

'Anyone for a cup of tea?' I asked my children when he'd left.

'It's almost eight, so more beer time for me, thanks, Mum,' said Jack.

'I could kill for one too,' agreed Mary-Kate.

'Then let's treat ourselves to room service, shall we? We can sit out on the little balcony and enjoy a sundowner,' I suggested as I walked towards the phone.

'Why don't you sit down, Mum? I'll get the drinks in,' said Jack.

'What number hotel is this one, Mum?' Mary-Kate asked me as we slid the door open to the large balcony.

'I've lost count, to be honest, sweetheart,' I said as I pulled out a chair and sat down.

'You were meant to take months to do what you've actually done in the space of less than two weeks.'

'I wasn't counting on being followed, was I?'

'I still don't understand why you were running away, when I'd told you the sisters just wanted to see the ring and—'

'Could we leave it for tonight, Mary-Kate?' I sighed. 'I'd like a breather from the whole thing, if you wouldn't mind.'

'Of course, but wasn't Tiggy lovely? She was so sweet to me. She said that even if it turned out that I wasn't related to them, she'd love for me to stay in touch and to come and visit them at Atlantis whilst I was here in Europe.'

'She was lovely, yes,' I agreed. 'She even invited all of us to go on this boat trip down to Greece.'

'Well, hopefully Michelle will get in touch with me via the agency soon, and we'll be able to find out more about who I am. Chip also said that it's easy enough to do a DNA test.'

'I don't doubt that you're her daughter, sweetheart. Maybe it's just whose daughter *she* is. Or in fact, who your birth father is. He might be the one who's related to this mysterious Pa Salt.'

'Do you know what, Mum?' said Mary-Kate as Jack brought the tray of drinks out onto the balcony. 'You're right. I hadn't thought of that.'

'As I said, shall we leave all that for now? And just enjoy us all being here together in West Cork; a moment I never thought would happen,' I said.

'I'm really glad it has, Mum,' said Jack. 'Cheers!'

'Cheers,' I toasted, as I took a sip of the strong tea that tasted so much better than any other I'd tasted since I'd been on my travels. Sitting here with my children, it suddenly felt very good to be back home.

After supper in the relaxed Dunes pub downstairs, we all opted for an early night.

I climbed into bed and switched off the light, leaving the door to the balcony open so I could hear the waves crashing onto the shore.

It was a beautiful sound, and one that had been heard by

humankind since we'd begun to populate this earth of ours. And by other creatures for billions of years before that. No matter what happened to any of us in our small lives, that tide would come in and roll out, and continue until the moment when our planet and everything on it ceased to exist.

'So why *do* the things that happen to us in our small lives matter?' I murmured. 'Because we love,' I answered myself, 'because we love.'

40

Niall picked us all up at nine the next morning to drive us to the airport. Having collected the hire car, and put myself and Jack on the insurance, I took charge of the steering wheel.

'Where are we headed to, Mum?' asked Mary-Kate from the back seat.

'To my old family home,' I said, glad that I was driving so I had to concentrate on signposts rather than the final destination. Just after Bandon, I swung a left at the signpost for Timoleague and headed along what had once been a narrow lane and now was – at best – a wider lane.

'Did you live in the back of beyond here as well, Mum?' Jack asked.

'Not like we do in New Zealand, no, but on a bicycle, it certainly felt like that.'

I turned left at the Ballinascarthy crossroads, and then took a right in Clogagh village and wound my way through the country lanes completely by instinct. We ended up turning a corner near Inchybridge and almost driving into the Argideen River.

'Jesus, Mum!' Jack said as I slammed on the brakes to stop us going bonnet-first into the water – there was no protective barrier or warning sign, which actually made me smile.

'You might find it funny, Mum, but I really don't,' muttered

Mary-Kate as I reversed into a ditch on the side of a field filled with maize, which had obviously replaced the barley of my era.

'Sorry, but we're not far away now,' I reassured her.

About ten minutes later, I saw the high stone walls that surrounded Argideen House in front of me, and knew we were getting close.

'Who lives inside there, Mum? It looks pretty overgrown.'

'I've no idea, Jack. My sister Nora worked there for a while, but I'm sure the occupants are long dead. Now, let me concentrate; the farm is up here somewhere . . .'

A few minutes later, I turned into the track that led up to it. Even though I was glad the children were with me, I wished I could have taken a moment to stop the car and draw breath before my arrival was noticed. Taking the drive as slowly as I could, I saw very little had changed, only the odd concrete bungalow peppering the valley, where before there had merely been the uninhabitable stone ruins of cottages abandoned during the Great Famine.

Arriving at the farmhouse, where the washing still hung out like flags on the line, and cows were grazing in the valley that led down to the slim sliver of the Argideen River, it was almost exactly as I remembered. Apart from the modern car parked in front of the house.

'We're here,' I said, stating the obvious.

'Hey, Mum, I thought you said the house you grew up in had really low-beamed ceilings? This farmhouse looks quite modern,' said Jack, disappointment on his face.

'This is the new farmhouse that we moved to when I was six. You'll see the one we used to live in behind it.'

Looking at it now, I agreed with Jack that it was an unre-markable and small square house. Yet, moving from one side of the courtyard to the other, with all its space, light, and modern conveniences, had been a revelation for me back then.

'Okay, why don't you two stay in the car while I go and see who's home?' Before they could answer, I was out of the car and walking round the back towards the kitchen door, because I couldn't ever imagine walking in through the front entrance. Only the priest or a doctor or a British person had ever done that.

The kitchen door was made of PVC now, not wood, and I saw that all the windows had been replaced in a similar fashion too.

'Here goes.' I held my breath and forced my fist out to knock on it, because I had no idea who would answer.

There was no reply, so I knocked louder. Putting my ear to the door, I heard a noise coming from within. Testing the stainless-steel door handle, I found it was unlocked. Of course it was, I told myself; on a farm, there was always someone in. Pushing the door open, I stepped into the kitchen and looked around me. The only thing that was the same was its shape and the old press holding tableware that still stood against the wall. The rest of the room had been filled with modern pine kitchen units, the old stone floor now tiled in an orangey colour. The range had gone, and instead there was an oven with an induction hob over it. The long table in the centre was also made of pine.

I walked to the door that opened onto the narrow hall which led upstairs, and realised the noise was of somebody hoovering above me.

The door in front of me led to the New Room; the over-riding memory I had of it was of Daddy in his chair, with a glass in one hand and a bottle of whiskey in the other.

The open fire had gone, and a wood-burning stove stood in its place. There was still the long leather sofa and a box of children's toys was stowed in one corner.

Walking back into the corridor, I heard the hoovering noise above had stopped. 'Hello?' I called.

'Hello there, can I help you?'

An unfamiliar woman stood at the top of the stairs, as I stood at the bottom.

'Er, yes, my name's Mary, and I used to live here with my parents, Maggie and John. And my brothers and sisters, of course,' I added, trying to work out whether the woman could be one of my sisters grown older.

'Mary . . .' the woman said as she came down the stairs towards me. 'Now, who would you be?'

'I was the youngest of the sisters – Ellen, Nora and Katie. John, Bill and Pat were my brothers.'

Having reached the bottom, the woman stared at me. Eventually, realisation appeared on her face.

'Jaysus! You mean, *the* Mary, who everyone called Merry?'

'Yes.'

'The famous missing sister of the O'Reilly clan! Well now, what a gas! If I make one phone call, we'll have them that are here out within the hour. Come into the kitchen and we'll have something to drink, will we?'

'I . . . thank you,' I said as she led me back into the kitchen. 'Um, sorry to ask, but who are you?'

The woman laughed suddenly. 'Well, o'course, considering you've been missing for all these years, you wouldn't be knowing, would you? I'm Sinéad, John's – your eldest brother's – wife.'

Now she was close up, I glanced at her again. 'Did we ever meet?'

'I doubt it. I was in John's year at Clogagh School. We started courting a year or so after you disappeared. He dragged me down the aisle a few months later. Now so, what can I offer you? I'd say we should be opening a bottle of something that sparkles, but I don't have any in stock just now,' she smiled and I thought what a lovely warm woman she seemed.

'Um, tell me if it's too inconvenient and you'd rather not, but I've got my two children with me,' I said. 'They're waiting in the car outside whilst I found out whether the house was still owned by our family.'

'O'course, Mary, or are you still called Merry?'

'I am, yes.'

'Sure, I'd love to meet them!' she said, so I went outside and beckoned Jack and Mary-Kate in.

After the introductions, we all sat down with a cup of coffee.

'I'll be telling you, John'll fall to the ground in shock when he sees you, Merry. You haven't changed at all from the old photos I've seen of you, whereas I' – Sinéad indicated her curves – 'have filled out.'

'Do you have any children yourself?' I asked.

'We have three, so, two of them married already, and just the young fellow still at home with us during his hols from uni. He wants to be an accountant,' she added proudly. 'Either of you two wed yet? Givin' your mammy some grandchildren to play with?'

Both of mine shook their heads.

'We've four from our bunch now,' Sinéad continued. ''Tis good to have small ones around the place again. They'll often come and stay over too. Will you be joining us for lunch? Both you and John will have a lot to be talking about.'

'Really, Sinéad, don't go to any trouble for us.'

'As if it would be, Merry. 'Tis not every day a missing member of the family appears out o' the blue. 'Tis like the parable of the prodigal son, so you're getting fed the fatted calf. And it's beef and Guinness casserole for lunch!'

'Can I ask you how everyone is, Sinéad? All my sisters? Bill? Pat?'

'The sisters are grand, so; all of them married, and Pat too, though Nora's on her second husband and lives in Canada these days. She always was a flighty one, wasn't she? Ellen, Katie, Bill and Pat – who runs a farm of his own these days – are all still local and some have grandchildren of their own too. Bill's in Cork City, working for the council, no less. There's a rumour he'll be running for election for Fianna Fáil soon.'

I struggled to picture my little brother being all grown-up, with a responsible job.

'And Katie? Where is she?'

'Katie?' Mary-Kate queried.

'My sister closest in age – she was two years older than me,' I explained. 'And yes, I named you after her,' I smiled.

''Tis normal to name our kids after their families here, especially their parents,' Sinéad explained to my daughter. 'It gets complicated at family parties, mind, when everyone's shouting for a John and four of them appear,' she chuckled. 'Ah, here's your man coming up the drive. Himself will be knocked over by a feather when he walks in, just you wait.'

As I heard the door to a truck slam and footsteps walk towards the back door, I didn't know what to do with myself. In the end, I stood up as John opened the back door. He had filled out since the last time I'd seen him, but in a brawny way, and his curly hair was peppered with grey. I looked into his green eyes, inherited from our mother, and gave him a smile.

'Hello there, John,' I said, feeling suddenly shy.

'Guess who it is?' chirped Sinéad.

He stared at me, and I finally saw recognition dawn on his face.

John took a step forwards. 'Jesus, Mary and Joseph! Merry, is it you?'

'You know it is,' I said, my eyes filling with tears.

'You come here, girl, and take the first hug I've been able to give you in over thirty-five years.'

'Thirty-seven,' I corrected him as we walked towards each other and he took me in his big strong arms. He smelt comfortingly of cow and it made me want to cry.

The others in the kitchen remained silent until John unclasped me. 'I've missed the sight of you, Merry.'

'Me too,' I gulped.

'And are these your young ones? They're the spit of you!' he said, turning his attention to Jack and Mary-Kate. 'Where've you been all these years?'

'We've been living in New Zealand.'

'Well now, I'd say 'twas the moment to open something to welcome you back home. What'll you be drinking? Beer? Wine?'

'I'll have a beer, please, sir,' said Jack.

'And me,' volunteered Mary-Kate. I saw that both my children looked dazed at what was going on in front of them.

'White wine would be perfect,' I said.

'Right then, Merry, I'll be having one too,' said Sinéad. 'Beer, John?'

John nodded as he sat down, hardly able to take his eyes off me. Sinéad brought the beers and two glasses of wine to the table.

'To my missing sister, safely returned. *Sláinte!*' said John.

'*Sláinte!*' we toasted, as Mary-Kate frowned.

'It's the word for "cheers" here,' I told her as we all took a sip.

'Don't tell me your mammy hasn't been educating you in the Irish ways,' John said to my daughter.

'She never said much about her childhood until recently,' Jack said. 'All we knew was that she went to university in Dublin.'

John paused for a moment, then looked at me before he answered. 'Sometimes 'tis better not to dwell on the past too much, isn't it?'

'Yes,' I said gratefully.

'So now, tell me about your life in New Zealand. Plenty of sheep there, I've heard?' he said. 'Not as good for the milk as cows, mind,' he added with a wink at Jack. 'Have you a husband? Where is he?'

I hardly ate a mouthful of the delicious beef stew as John and Sinéad fired questions at all three of us. My kids did me proud, sometimes answering for me when they sensed I was overwhelmed.

After a homemade chocolate cake with cream was offered for dessert, and Sinéad was chatting to Mary-Kate and Jack, I leant over to John.

'How's Katie? Do you see much of her?'

'Ah, she's busy working up at the Clonakilty old folks' place. She cares for the old people around these parts that have dementia or can't cope in their own homes.'

'She has a husband?'

'She does, so. Connor was in construction and when the Celtic Tiger began to roar here in Ireland and the boom came, he made a good deal of money, that's for sure. He's retired now, sold up his firm. And lucky for him he did, what with the recession starting here. I'd be saying some of the lads that went on to work for the new boss will find themselves out of a job soon enough,' John sighed.

'The economy's not good here?'

'No. There's been a big downturn in building round these parts during the last few months. You know, I'd look at Connor sometimes, with the big smart house he built for himself and Katie, and the summer holidays they took to Tenerife, and I'd wonder what I was doing up at five every morning to sort the cows. The good news about my animals and their meat and milk is that the world continues to need them, whatever's happening in those stock market places.'

'Have you expanded the farm since I was last here?'

'We have indeed. Do you remember our neighbours, the O'Hanlons, who owned the few acres next door to us?'

'I do, of course.'

'Well, he was old and wanted to sell up, so I bought the land.'

'What about Daddy? Sinéad didn't say when I asked, so . . .'

'Ah now, I'm sure it won't be a surprise to you to learn that the drink got him eventually. He died in eighty-five. He's buried with Mammy and the rest of our family in Timoleague graveyard. I'm sorry to be the one to have to tell you.'

'Don't be, John. It was me who left, and it was you that had to pick up the pieces here. You were virtually running the farm by the time you were sixteen.'

'I can't lie and tell you it wasn't hard, but it hasn't been a bad life, Merry. Me and Sinéad are happy, so. We've all we want and need, and have our family around us.'

'I'm desperate to see Katie, and, of course, the rest of the family. Could you give me Katie's number so I can call her?'

'I can, and once she's over the shock, sure, she'll be delighted to see you. How long are you thinking of staying?' he asked.

'A few days, or maybe longer . . . I haven't got any definite plans.'

'I'll get Katie's number for you.' John stood up and went to the telephone that sat on a chest of drawers. He pulled out a black leather-bound book from one of the drawers, which I recognised immediately.

'You still have the same address book that Mammy and Daddy used?!'

'We do, so, yes. We hardly needed it in those days; we knew where everyone lived, but now 'tis useful for the mobile phone numbers. There's Katie's.'

'Thank you.'

'I'll be putting your number in the book now, just in case you're thinking of disappearing for another thirty-seven years.' He winked at me.

I recited my number and he wrote it down. Then he gave me the landline here so I could do the same.

'I can't be doing with mobiles even though I have one,' said John. 'It means that if I'm out in the meadow on a sunny day having a snooze, Herself can call me,' he sighed. 'Now then' – John raised his voice so everyone could hear – 'I've got to be off back to my tractor, though I'll be seeing you again soon, I hope.'

'I was just saying to the kids that we should have a family get-together, so they can meet all their aunties, uncles and cousins,' said Sinéad.

'Apparently we have about twenty in all, Mum! But some of them are in Canada,' said Mary-Kate.

'Don't you worry, there's enough of them to be getting on with right here,' Sinéad smiled. 'How about this Sunday coming?'

'Can we, Mum?' asked Mary-Kate.

'I'm sure we can, and it's very kind of you to offer, Sinéad. Right, kids, let's be off,' I said. 'Thank you for lunch and being so hospitable.'

'Ah, 'twas nothing. I just can't wait to tell all my sisters-in-law that I met you first!' she giggled.

All three of us had a big hug from her, then climbed into the car and followed John's tractor down to the lane. I felt so proud of my children, especially Mary-Kate, who ironically, although she didn't know it yet, shared the same circumstances as me: we both knew that those we'd just visited were not our blood family. Yet her obvious excitement at having 'cousins' meant she hadn't even thought about it.

Maybe it was simply because she'd spent twenty-two years being loved by her parents, as I had been loved by mine.

Would I tell John and the rest of my siblings that I had been 'dropped in' as a replacement for a dead baby?

No, I thought, that didn't matter. Love *did*.

'Where to now, Mum?' asked Mary-Kate.

'Back to the hotel, I think.'

'Well, as it's such great weather, I wouldn't mind seeing whether that surf school we spotted on the beach hires out their equipment,' said Jack. 'It's ages since I last surfed. Join me?' he asked Mary-Kate.

'If Mum doesn't need us, then yeah, I'd love to.'

'I'll be fine, you two go and enjoy yourselves. The sea's always freezing, mind you,' I warned them with a smile.

Back at the hotel, the kids walked off to enquire about hiring surfboards, and I went back to my room and immediately dialled Katie's number. There was a voicemail telling me to leave a message, but I had absolutely no idea what to say. I dialled the number for Cross Farm and Sinéad answered.

'Hi there, it's Merry here. Katie's not answering her mobile, so maybe I'll just turn up at her door. Where exactly does she live?'

'In Timoleague. Do you remember where the GAA pitch is?'

'I do.'

'Well, 'tis a grand big house on the other side of the lane, just beyond the pitch. You'll see it because it's painted bright orange. Wouldn't be the colour I'd choose, mind, but at least you can't miss it,' chuckled Sinéad.

Leaving a message at reception for Jack and Mary-Kate, I got back into my car and headed for Timoleague. Like Clonakilty, the village had expanded upwards and sideways, but the main street remained more or less as I remembered it. As I drove, I looked across the magnificent Courtmacsherry Bay. Passing the GAA pitch, where I could see boys practising Gaelic football, bringing back vivid memories of watching my brothers playing in the field with Daddy, I saw the big house standing up on a slope just beyond it and agreed with Sinéad that the bright tangerine colour was not one I would have picked either. 'Look at me,' the house was saying. It was obvious Katie had done very well for herself.

I headed up the drive, admiring the pristine gardens and the carefully tended flower beds. There was a Range Rover parked outside which was so shiny, the sun glinted off it and half blinded me. Bringing the car to a halt, I turned off the engine and gathered my nerve to get out and knock on the front door.

It was opened by a slim, greying but still handsome man dressed in a pink shirt and chinos.

'Hello there, can I help you?' he asked.

'I'm looking for Katie.'

'Aren't we all,' the man shrugged with a grim smile. 'She's at work as usual. And who might you be?'

'My name is Mary McDougal, and I'm Katie's sister.'

He looked at me for a while, then nodded. 'You'll be the one that disappeared then?'

'I would, yes.'

'Well, she's due back around four, in about twenty minutes. I'm Connor, by the way, Katie's husband. Do you want to come in and have a cuppa? I was just making one for myself.'

'Thank you,' I said as he ushered me inside and into the kitchen. 'Sit down, take the weight off your feet.'

I did so, looking round at what was obviously a state-of-the-art kitchen, with no expense spared.

'I can't be saying she'll be home on time,' he said as he put a cup of tea in front of me and sat down. 'As you can see, she doesn't need to work, but no matter what I tell her, her old people up at the home come first. Dedicated, she is. So, can I be asking you where you disappeared to for all these years?'

'I moved to New Zealand.'

'Now that's a place I'd love to visit, if I could ever get my wife to take a holiday. Whereabouts are you? The North or South Island?'

I told him and we chatted pleasantly about the country and the vineyard, until I heard the sound of a car coming up the drive.

'Must be your lucky day. My wife is home on time for once.' Connor stood up. 'Why don't you go and sit in the lounge across, and I'll tell her you're here, prepare her, so. 'Twill be a shock for her; I wasn't around when you left, but I know how close the two of you were.'

'Of course.' I went into the room he'd indicated, which looked more like a showpiece in an advertisement than a home. Everything, from the cream leather sofas to the faux mahogany side tables and grand marble fireplace, was immaculate. I heard low voices beyond the door, and finally my sister came into the sitting room. She looked exactly the same as I remembered her: slim, elegant and the spit of our mother. Her red hair was piled up on her head and as she came towards me, I saw her lovely pale skin was clear of wrinkles, as if she had been held in aspic since I last saw her.

'Merry.' She studied my face carefully as I stood up. 'It really *is* you, isn't it?'

'It is, Katie, yes.'

'Jaysus, I don't know what to say.' Her voice trembled. 'I feel like I'm in one of those reality TV shows where two long-lost sisters meet again.' She started to cry. 'Merry, come here and give me a hug.'

We hugged for a long time, until she finally pulled away and indicated the nearest sofa.

'My legs are shaking. Let's sit down,' she said.

We did so, and she reached towards the glass coffee table to pull a wad of tissues out of a box.

'I'd always wondered what I'd say if you ever turned up; I hated you for going and not even leaving me a note to say why or where. I thought I was your best friend? We *were* best friends, weren't we?'

Katie wiped away her tears harshly.

'I'm so sorry, Katie,' I said, gulping back my own. 'I'd have told you if I could have, but . . . I just couldn't tell anyone.'

'Not true,' she said, her voice rising. 'You left a note for that Ambrose of yours, didn't you? I know because I got hold of his telephone number and called him. The note said you had to go away, but he wasn't to worry about you. And then you disappeared for thirty-seven years. Why, Merry? Please tell me why.'

'I had no choice, Katie, believe me. I never meant to hurt you or the rest of our family. I was trying to protect you.'

'I knew you were keeping secrets from me, Merry, but I'd have never told. Ah, Jaysus, I can't stop crying.'

'I'm so, so sorry, Katie.' I put my arms around her and hugged her again as she wept.

'I'd have done anything to help you, you know I would. Come with you if that was what you needed. We shared everything, didn't we?'

'We did, yes.'

'I hate that Ambrose; 'twas him that stole you away from us all in the first place. Getting Father O'Brien and Daddy to agree to send you to that fancy boarding school in Dublin, then you staying with Ambrose all the time when you were up there. It was like *he* was wanting to be your daddy, even though he wasn't. He wasn't, Merry.'

'No, he wasn't, but the reason I left has nothing to do with him, I swear.'

'Have you seen him since you came back?' she eyed me.

'I have, yes.'

'He must be very old these days.'

'He is, but he still has his wits about him.'

'And what did *he* say when you turned up out of the blue with no warning?'

'He was shocked, but happy to see me. Katie, please don't cry anymore. I'm here and I promise, I'll tell you why I had to leave, and I just hope you'll understand.'

'I've had so long to think about it, and I'd reckon I have an idea. I think—'

'Would it be all right if we talked about it another time, Katie? I've my children here with me and I haven't told them anything about it either.'

'What about your husband, assuming you have one? Does he know?'

'My husband died a few months ago, he didn't know. Nobody did. When I left, I forgot the past. I made a whole new life and got myself a new identity.'

'Then I'm sorry for your loss, Merry. But . . . well, I've some things to tell you about *our* family, some things we didn't know as children, but that make sense now, looking back. Especially for you.'

'Then you must tell me, Katie.'

''Tis not a pretty story, Merry, but it explains a lot.'

I was just about to mention I'd read Nuala's diary, when there was a brief knock on the door and Connor appeared.

'Sorry to interrupt, but will we be having something for our tea tonight or not, Katie? There's nothing in the fridge that I can see.'

'No, Connor, I need to go shopping. I just came back here

to take a shower and change out of my uniform.' Katie stood up. 'What about I come to see you tomorrow?' she said to me. ''Tis my day off. Where are you staying?'

'The Inchydoney Lodge Hotel.'

'Oh, 'tis a lovely place that, with a beautiful view.'

'It is,' I said, sensing the tension that had appeared in the room with the arrival of Connor. 'Well, I must be off anyway.'

'Would eleven o'clock suit?' she said.

'It would. I'll be down in the lobby to meet you. Bye, Katie. Bye, Connor.'

As I drove back to the hotel, I decided that, despite the car, the perfect home and the handsome, rich husband, my sister was not a happy woman.

That evening, Jack, Mary-Kate and I enjoyed a relaxed supper at a pub in Clonakilty. Afterwards, we went to listen to some Irish music at An Teach Beag, once a tiny cottage that had now been turned into a pub. The traditional band played the old ballads, bringing back memories of my father playing his fiddle. Then we headed back to the hotel.

'Looks like the weather is set fair for some good surfing tomorrow, Mum,' said Jack, 'so if it's okay with you, MK and I will get our togs on after brekkie.'

'I'm seeing one of my sisters anyway, so that's perfect.'

'I really love it here, Mum,' Mary-Kate said as we kissed goodnight. 'Everyone is so friendly. It's like NZ, with a different accent!'

I was happy that my children liked it here, I thought the next morning, as I donned a pair of jeans and a blouse for Katie's imminent arrival.

At eleven o'clock prompt, she arrived in the lobby. Yesterday she'd been in her navy-blue nurse's uniform, but today she was immaculately dressed in tailored trousers and a silk blouse.

'Katie,' I said, standing up to hug her, 'thank you so much for coming.'

'As if I wouldn't! I might have been shocked and upset yesterday – who wouldn't be? But I know you must have had your reasons, Merry, and 'tis so grand to see you! Where are your kids?' she asked.

'Out there, braving the waves. They're both mad for surfing, so.'

I listened to what I'd just said and had to smile because, with the West Cork accent all around me, I was slipping back into it myself.

'Is there somewhere we can talk? I mean, privately?' Katie asked me.

'Is here not private enough?'

'You need to remember that walls have ears here, and my husband, well, he's well known round these parts.'

'Are you saying you're ashamed to be seen with me?' I giggled.

'Of course I'm not, but what I want to tell you . . . well, we might not be comfortable being interrupted.'

'Okay, let's go up to my room.'

We ordered cappuccinos from room service and chatted away about how modern this part of the world had become.

'Don't I know it – until recently my husband had one of the biggest construction companies here, so he's been kept very busy in the last few years,' said Katie. 'Now there's a downturn, but he saw it coming and managed to sell the business last year. He's sitting on a fortune, whilst the new owner and all those fellows who worked for him will probably watch the whole thing go down the drain. He's always been lucky that way.'

'Or a clever businessman?'

'I suppose, yes,' she agreed with a weary smile.

'Can I ask you something, Katie?'

'Of course you can, Merry. I'd never be keeping any secrets from you, anyway.'

'Touché,' I said with a slight grimace. 'Are you happy with Connor?'

'Do you want the long or the short answer to that?' she replied with a shrug. 'I mean, there was me pulling pints at the Henry Ford pub and he waltzed in one evening and swept me off my feet. Even then his company was starting to do well, so he'd all the luxuries. He showed me plans to build a grand house on land he'd bought in Timoleague, took me driving in his flash sports car and then presented me with a big rock of an engagement ring when he asked me to marry him.' Katie shook her head. 'You'll be remembering what our childhood was like and how I'd sworn I'd not repeat it, so to have a rich man offering to marry me felt like a miracle. Of course I said yes, and we had a big wedding up at the Dunmore House Hotel, and a honeymoon in Spain. He spoilt me rotten with clothes and jewellery, said he wanted me to look the part on his arm.'

'Were you happy?'

'Back then, yes. We were trying to grow a family. It took a long time, but I managed to produce a boy and a girl – Connor Junior and Tara. It wasn't long after Tara was born that I got wind of my husband's first affair. He denied it, o'course, and I forgave him – and then it happened again and again, until I couldn't any longer,' she shrugged.

'Why haven't you divorced him?'

'Knowing Connor, he'd have found a way to wriggle out of me getting much in any settlement, so once the kids had left home, I decided to go to college and take my nursing exams. It took me three years of driving back and forth to Cork City, but I got my qualifications, Merry,' she smiled proudly. 'So, for the past fifteen years, I've been working up at the old people's place in Clonakilty, and I love it there. I'm happy enough, Merry; I've learnt we all need to make compromises in life. What about your hubby? Was he a good one?'

'He was, yes,' I smiled. 'Very good. I mean, we had our ups and downs as any marriage does, and went through some very hard times financially when we were building up our vineyard—'

'Vineyard, is it? Remember how we used to steal Daddy's homemade porter? A couple of sips of that could pull the skin off a cat!'

'I do! It tasted disgusting.'

'But we still drank it,' Katie giggled. 'Sounds like we've both come a long way since our childhoods.'

'We have. Looking back, we lived close to the breadline, didn't we? I remember walking to school with big holes in my boots because we couldn't afford new ones.'

'We'd definitely be described as deprived kids these days, but then, 'twas half of Ireland at the time,' said Katie.

'Yes, and after all that suffering our ancestors went through to fight for their freedom, nothing much had moved on in reality, had it?'

'As a matter of fact, that's what I wanted to talk to you about.'

'Our past?'

'Yes. You'll be remembering that we never had our grandparents round to visit us, or any cousins either?' said Katie.

'I do, and I could never understand it.'

'No, but when I started working at the old people's home in the early nineties . . . let me tell you, you learn a lot about the old stories there. Maybe their folks have stopped listening, or maybe they tell you things because you're a stranger. Anyway, I'd one old lady who was in our special care unit, as we called it, which meant those who didn't have long left on this earth. I was on a night shift and went in to check on her. Even though she was in her nineties, she'd all her faculties on her. She stared at me and said I was the spit of her daughter, then asked my name. I told her I was Katie Scanlon, but then she asked what my maiden name had been. I told her it was O'Reilly and tears appeared in her eyes. She grasped my hand and said she was my grandmother, Nuala Murphy, and her daughter had been named Maggie. She told me she'd a story she needed to get off her chest before she met her maker. It took her three nights to tell it, because she was so weak, but she was determined to do so.'

I stared at Katie in disbelief. 'Nuala was *our* grandmother?'

'Yes, the one we never saw, apart from that once at Mammy's funeral. After what she told me, I understand better why we didn't see her. Merry, what's wrong? You're a strange colour.'

'I . . . Katie, I was given her diary a very long time ago, by someone we . . . both knew.'

'Who?'

'I'd prefer not to say just now, or we'll be off down another track and—'

'Well now, I can guess who gave you that diary. Why did you never tell me?'

'Firstly, because I only read it myself a few days ago – I know that might sound odd, Katie, but I was only eleven when it was given to me and I wasn't interested in learning about the past. Then when I got older, because of who gave it to me, I never wanted to set eyes on it again.'

'But you still kept it?'

'Yes, I did. Please don't ask me why, because I honestly couldn't tell you,' I sighed.

'Sure, I won't, but since you've read it, I'm guessing you've made the family connection?'

'No, because the diary stopped in 1920. Something happened to Nuala and she said she couldn't write anymore.'

'Maybe you could show it to me sometime. I heard the whole sorry story from beginning to end. Where did you get up to in the diary, so I won't be repeating myself?'

'I . . .' I cleared my throat. 'It was just after Philip – the British soldier – had shot himself.'

'Right. Nuala was still upset by that, along with a whole lot more that came after, including the reason why she never came to visit when our mammy married our daddy.'

'Katie, just tell me,' I said in a burst of impatience.

Katie drew a folder out of her smart Louis Vuitton shopper and flicked through a large sheaf of pages. 'I wrote it all down after she told me, so I wouldn't forget it. So, you already know the part up to when Philip killed himself.'

'I do.'

'Well, the War of Independence went on for a good deal longer after that. Finn, Nuala's husband, was a volunteer, as you know, and they were dark times as both sides stepped up the violence. Now then, let's start when Hannah, Nuala's sister, married her fiancé, Ryan, soon after Philip met his end . . .'

Nuala
Clogagh, West Cork
December 1920

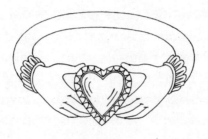

Irish Claddagh Ring

41

The wedding of Hannah Murphy and Ryan O'Reilly took place in Clogagh church, in a very different atmosphere than that of Nuala and Finn's. They had wanted something small that befitted the sombre mood that hung in the air.

Decked with holly and a candle set in each window, the church looked festive, but Nuala walked through the wedding in a fog of grief she couldn't seek comfort for. No one could know how devastated she was at Philip's death.

At the party afterwards, held in the church hall, Sian, one of Hannah's dressmaker friends, leant over to Nuala.

'Is Herself not interested in helping the cause now she's a married woman?'

'What do you mean?'

'Well, she used to be the first we'd all go to if a message needed sending somewhere. Now she says she hasn't the time.'

'I'd say her mind was on her wedding, Sian,' Nuala replied. 'Sure, she'll settle down once it's all over.'

'Maybe, but . . .' Sian had to put her mouth to Nuala's ear to whisper over the sound of the little *ceilidh* band. 'I'd reckon her man doesn't want her to be involved in our activities.'

Sian was pulled up to dance a few seconds later, but as Nuala sat and watched the bride and groom take their places in the centre of the group, she wondered whether love really was blind after all. As hard as she tried, she could not see what her strong-minded, passionate sister saw in the quiet, self-proclaimed pacifist she had just wed.

The year 1921 dawned, and over the following few months the brave volunteers did all they could to thwart the British. There were whispered reports of IRA victories, that the boys were slowly winning with their clever use of guerrilla tactics and knowledge of their own land, but the reprisals for British casualties were harsh. Nuala found relief in keeping busy running messages and helping those whose homes had been turned upside down and often set alight by the British in retaliation. There was many an elderly couple who had been forced to live in their chicken coops, too frightened to come out. Nuala rounded up as many Cumann na mBan members as she could and they met one night at a safehouse in Ballinascarthy to draw up a list of temporary accommodation for the poor souls to be billeted at. There was an air of positivity and hope that the conflict would soon draw to a close, but Niamh, their brigade captain, urged caution.

''Tis not over yet, girls, and we mustn't let our guard slip too soon. We've all lost people dear to us in this battle and 'twould be good not to lose more.'

'What about those in jail?' asked Nuala. 'I hear the conditions there are terrible, and they say they're worse up in Mountjoy Prison in Dublin. Is there a plan to get our fellows out?'

'They're under lock and key day and night,' said Niamh. 'They're the Britishers' prized possessions; they know our volunteers will think twice before launching an ambush, for fear of one of their comrades being shot in reprisal.'

She was almost numb these days to hearing terrible things, but the death of Charlie Hurley, Finn's closest friend, hit her hard. He had been shot at point-blank range at Humphrey Forde's farmhouse in Ballymurphy. Finn was devastated but could spare little time for grief. A few days later he went deep undercover with the Flying Column and Nuala didn't know when she would see her husband again. She knew that Charlie's body had been carried out of the workhouse morgue in Bandon by the women of Cumann na mBan. He'd been buried in the graveyard in Clogagh in secret at night, so that all the volunteers who had loved and respected him as commandant of the Third West Cork Brigade could be present.

The thought of all those she and Finn had lost in the fight to secure Ireland's freedom fuelled her determination to help as much as she could, which was more than she could say for Hannah. Even though she did her best to accept that Hannah had no choice but to follow her husband's lead, her sister's now open refusal to have anything to do with the cause she'd once been so passionate about cut her soul in two. The fact Hannah had told her Ryan condemned the volunteers' bravery, in the name of pacifism, had caused a deep rift between them. Often, when she was in Timoleague and saw her sister emerging from the dressmaker's shop, Nuala quickly turned and walked the other way.

The farming seasons carried on despite the war, and still no sight of Finn, apart from the odd message passed by Christy to say he was alive and sending her his love. Nuala spent time up at Cross Farm, and threw herself into any job she was given. As spring progressed, golden gorse filled the valley, the barn was full of newborn calves, and the days lengthened. At least, in the fear and grief that cast a shadow over everything, Nuala had a special secret that lit a spark of joy within her.

'Soon enough, you'll be showing yourself and there'll be

nothing can hide it,' she said as she looked down at her tummy. By her estimation, she was about two months gone, and due sometime in late December. Now over the worst of any sickness, she felt renewed vigour to win the war for her and Finn's child. She told nobody, wanting her husband to be the first to know, but was sure her mammy had guessed her secret.

As spring turned to summer and with fewer British troops visible on the roads – wary of ambushes from the volunteers – Nuala also did the rounds of those wounded in action or injured during a raid on their homeplace.

All of the fellows and their families poured gratitude on her head, offering her whatever they had to eat as a thank you. Most of her patients were barely more than boys, who'd had their bodies and their lives blown apart by the cause. They and their families humbled and moved her.

I've learnt more about nursing in the past year than I could ever have learnt from books, she thought as she cycled home one evening.

What with all she was doing, she fell asleep easily at night as the summer wore on. The talk was that the British had retired to their barracks, if they'd not already been burnt down by the volunteers. She'd heard from Christy that Michael Collins himself had sent a personal message of congratulations to the West Cork Flying Column. Next time she saw Hannah in town, Nuala invited her to sit and eat lunch with her. She wanted to tell her sister about the message to the lads, and have Ryan know too.

'Imagine that!' Hannah said to her dreamily as they sat on their favourite bench overlooking Courtmacsherry Bay. 'A message from the Big Fellow himself!'

'He's behind the boys and all they're doing, Hannah,' she said pointedly. 'I hope you'll tell Ryan that.'

Hannah had ignored her sister's comment, instead going on to confide that she was expecting. Nuala had shared her news too, but sworn her to secrecy until she was able to tell Finn. The exchange had engendered a few moments of their old closeness, as the sisters had imagined their babies playing together in the future.

Then Nuala had asked whether she and Ryan were coming up to Cross Farm for lunch on Sunday.

'We've not seen the sight of the two of you for weeks,' she'd added.

'Sorry, we can't. Ryan's taking me on a vigil over by his homeplace near Kilbrittain. We're praying for peace.'

'And your prayers will be needed, if this war is ever to end,' Nuala had muttered.

She'd just made a brack for poor Mrs Grady next door, who was now confined to bed as her arthritis was so bad. It was an unusually sweltering June day, and she stared at the dry, unkempt patch of earth at the back of the cottage, which she'd had no time to do anything with since she'd moved in. She was just wondering if she could tidy it up and plant some pretty flowers when there was a sudden tap on her shoulder.

'Jaysus, Christy! You made me jump,' she gasped as she turned round.

'Sorry, but I thought you might like to hear the news: last night the volunteers burnt down Castle Bernard up in Bandon and took Lord Bandon hostage.'

'Holy Mother of God! They did *what*?! Were any of them hurt?'

'Not that I've heard, no. Are you feeling all right, Nuala? You're swaying where you stand.'

'Let's go inside, where you can tell me more,' she whispered nervously.

Once Christy had furnished her with a glass of water, Nuala looked at her cousin, her expression a mixture of horror and amazement.

'I can't believe they did that!' she said. 'Castle Bernard is centuries old, and Lord Bandon is surely the most powerful man around these parts. The volunteers have him as a hostage, you said?'

'Yes. And I've been sent here because he's being kept not far from where we sit, and you're trusted by the volunteers. Let's just say that currently he's a neighbour of poor Charlie Hurley, lying in Clogagh graveyard.'

Nuala opened her mouth to speak, but Christy hushed her.

'Lord Bandon needs feeding; we'll not have him reporting back that we treated him badly, like so many of ours have been when they've been "guests" of the enemy. Can you be making some food for him?'

'Me? Make food for Lord Bandon? The man is used to the finest salmon, fresh from the Innishannon River, and freshly slaughtered meat from his herd of prize cattle. I can hardly make him turnip soup now, can I?'

'I'd say that some well-cooked Irish food is exactly what the man needs. Just be remembering that he's human and shits and pisses like the rest of us, despite his grand life. I'll be taking that brack cake away up, if that's all right with you.'

Christy scooped it off the cooling tray.

'Get your filthy hands off that!' Nuala grabbed it from him, then found a square of muslin to wrap it in. 'Will I be adding a pat of butter to go with it?'

'Whatever you think is right. 'Twill do for his tea at least. I'll be back tomorrow for his lunch. Bye now.'

Christy left and Nuala watched him walk towards the schoolhouse, then turn right by the church.

Nuala reckoned she knew exactly where they were hiding Lord Bandon. The question was, was her husband with him?

That afternoon, using her precious supply of flour, Nuala made a potato and ham pie. She was nervous about the result because she was unaccustomed to making pastry, but the top came out as golden as you'd like. She'd just set the pie down on the kitchen table to cool when there was a knock on the door.

'I'm here, Christy. Just let yourself in, will you?' she shouted as she concentrated on trimming the extra crust off the pie.

'Hello, Nuala.'

She turned round, the knife still in her hand.

'Nuala, please, I come here in peace, I promise. And in secret.'

The woman removed the hood of her long black cape from her head. 'Lady Fitzgerald?' Nuala whispered in utter shock.

'Please, don't be frightened, I'm not here on business of my own, I'm here to pass on a plea for mercy from a very good friend of mine.'

Lady Fitzgerald set a wicker basket down on the table as Nuala, still holding the knife, went to the front window to check there were no military using Lady Fitzgerald as a decoy, waiting to break down the front door and arrest and torture her until she told them what she knew about Lord Bandon.

'I have come alone, Nuala, I swear. I even walked here all the way from Argideen House, so that none of my family or servants would know of my movements. May I sit down?'

Nuala gave a slight nod and indicated the one comfortable chair they owned.

'I know you have me down as the enemy, and have learnt to trust no one, but please, I beg you, you are the one person who understands what I've been through.' Lady Fitzgerald's eyes filled with tears, and Nuala knew she was thinking of Philip. 'And I'm here to talk to you today because of the bond that we forged, woman to woman. We are both risking a lot by my being here, I know, but in my cape, with my hair unpinned' – Lady Fitzgerald gave a sad smile – 'I'd doubt even my husband would recognise me.'

Nuala thought Lady Fitzgerald looked so very pretty, with her long blonde hair falling in waves on either side of her face. Her lack of make-up or jewellery showed off her natural beauty, making her look younger and more vulnerable.

'I am begging you to trust me,' Lady Fitzgerald continued. 'And you should know that I have tried to protect you and your family. Even though you and your husband are suspected, your cottage has never been raided, has it?'

'No. Well, if that's to do with you, then thank you.'

Nuala stopped short of saying 'your ladyship', and showing the appropriate courtesy to an English gentlewoman. Even if Lady Fitzgerald had been kind to her, the atrocities committed in her and her husband's and every other British person's name made the words stick in her throat.

'What can I be doing for you?' she asked.

Lady Fitzgerald eyed the pie. Then her eyes moved back to Nuala.

'A very good friend of mine came to visit me this morning. She told me that her husband had been taken hostage by the Irish, and was being kept by them in retaliation for the executions of IRA prisoners in both Cork and Dublin jails. She said that an ultimatum has been issued by the IRA, saying that if there are any further shootings of their volunteers, they will kill her husband.' There was a slight pause before Lady Fitzgerald said, 'I think we both know who I'm talking about.'

Nuala sat in silence, her lips pinned together.

'That's a very fine pie, Nuala. Are you expecting company, or is it for . . . another?'

''Tis for my neighbour, who is bedridden next door.'

'Well, she is a very lucky woman, and I'm sure she will enjoy the pie. Nuala, I come to you on behalf of a wife who is sickly and, like yourself, desperate for her husband's safe return. If there is anyone you know who might be holding Lord Bandon, could you please send her plea for clemency?'

Again, Nuala sat poker-faced, saying nothing.

Lady Fitzgerald indicated the basket. 'Inside are foodstuffs from my own pantry, which will feed the hostage in the manner to which he is accustomed. There is also a note from his wife.'

Lady Fitzgerald searched her face for a reaction. Nuala was now struggling to keep her expression plain.

'Perhaps there is someone you know who could get the basket to him. There is nothing within it that could be seen as incendiary; it merely contains love, support and comfort from his wife. May I leave it with you?'

This time, Nuala gave a slight nod.

'Thank you. I must also tell you that my husband and I are leaving Argideen House. We are packing our trunks and closing the house as we speak, then returning to England. After what happened to my friend's husband two nights ago, and the burning of the Travers' house in Timoleague, it is clearly unsafe for us to stay any longer.'

Lady Fitzgerald stood up and began to walk towards the front door. Then she turned back.

'Goodbye, Nuala. May your side prevail and your husband be safely returned to you. This is your land after all.'

With a sad smile, Lady Fitzgerald left the cottage.

After her departure, Nuala finally found the strength to move from where she sat and turned to the basket. Her fingers inched so tentatively towards the cloth that covered it, it could have contained a Mills bomb.

'And it might still, so,' she muttered.

Inside were tins of things from a shop called Fortnum and Mason's. Biscuits, Earl Grey tea leaves and a tin of salmon. There were also chocolates and a box of tiny speckled eggs that the writing on top said were apparently laid by a quail. Right at the bottom of the basket was an envelope addressed to *James Francis*. Nuala turned it over and was just about to open it when she saw Christy coming across from the pub towards her cottage. Putting everything back, she covered the basket with the linen cloth, then ran to dump it in the out-house.

'That pie is looking fit for a king, Nuala,' Christy said as she stepped back into the kitchen. ''Twill keep his lordship going for a couple of days, so.'

'I'm sure he's used to better than spuds and ham, but 'tis all I have.'

'Right then, I'll be off.' Christy picked up the pie.

'Is he a still a neighbour of Charlie Hurley?'

'The fellows are moving him around.'

'Have you seen him?' she pressed.

'No.'

'Do you know who's guarding him?'

'The lads are taking it in turns.'

'Is Finn one of them?' she asked.

Christy stared at her, and even though he didn't answer yes or no, she knew her husband was involved.

'If you see him, say his wife loves him and is waiting for him at home.'

'I will so, Nuala. Now you take care, and if any British patrols come a-calling, act innocent.'

'Would I be doing anything else? I know nothing,' she shrugged.

'I'll be back at the pub in half an hour, so you know where I am if you've any trouble. Bye now.'

'Bye, Christy.'

He gave her a wink and she watched him limp back across to the pub, thinking how glad she felt that he was only a stone's throw away. She didn't know what she would have done without him.

She poured herself a glass of water and went to sit in a shady patch in the back garden. It was plain that, despite Lady Fitzgerald's plea to deliver the basket, she could not risk passing it on.

'Forgive me, Philip, but I can't be seen to have anything to do with your mammy,' she whispered, raising her eyes to the sky.

Making a decision, she stood up and went to the outhouse to collect the basket.

An hour later, she had decanted the contents of all the tins and boxes into either bowls or brown-paper packages. Collecting the discarded wrappers, she knelt by the fireplace and burnt each one of them. Lastly, she put the letter on the flames and watched it burn. Even though she could have opened it, she hadn't. What was in there was for 'James Francis's' eyes only, and she respected that.

When she had burnt all the evidence, Nuala stood up and cut herself two healthy slices of bread, and had a delicious salmon sandwich for her tea.

The following day, she gave the same to Christy for Lord Bandon's lunch.

A week had gone past and Christy was still coming to collect food, and every day, Nuala would use a little of the foodstuffs Lady Fitzgerald had sent to salve her conscience.

'How long will they be holding him?' she asked as she and Christy drank a mug of tea together.

'As long as is needed. Sean Hales, who was in charge of the burning of Castle Bernard, has made sure that General Strickland up in Cork knows we have him. He was told that unless he stopped the executions of our fellows in prison, Lord Bandon would be shot. Not a single execution has taken place in Dublin or Cork since,' Christy grinned. 'We finally have the British by their balls.'

'So you won't be killing him anytime soon?'

'Not unless the British execute any more of our own, but I'm guessing they won't. Sean says Lord Bandon has friends and relations in the British government. They'll not see one of their own murdered by the Irish. All of us are praying they'll offer a truce.'

'As long as they don't find him first, Christy.'

'Ah now, they'll not be doing that, however hard they look,' he chuckled. 'He's never in the same billet twice, and we've scouts and guards on him night and day. So now,' Christy said, standing up, 'I'll be seeing ye, Nuala.'

Christy left with the basket Lady Fitzgerald had brought, the linen cloth covering the food. She was glad to have it out of the house.

'Can you imagine?' she said to her unborn baby in wonder. 'Peace might be coming.'

It was ten more days before Christy burst into the cottage and enveloped her in an embrace.

'It's happened, Nuala!' he said as he finally let her go. 'We've a truce agreed with the British! It's over, 'tis really over. Now what do you think of that?'

'But . . . just like that? What will happen to Lord Bandon?'

'It's been agreed by our side that he'll be returned safely to his home tomorrow.'

'He has no home now.'

'No, the castle is burnt to the ground, so maybe he'll feel the pain thousands of us Irish have felt as they burnt our homeplaces and left them in ruins.' Christy looked at her. 'You're not feeling sorry for the man, are you?'

'Of course I'm not . . . I just can't believe it, so.'

'Come outside and see what's happening.' Christy offered her his hand, and the two of them walked out of the front door. Nuala saw the residents of the village opening their front doors timidly and standing in the street, dazed from the news that had obviously spread like wildfire.

There was a lot of hugging and kissing, and nervous glances to either side in case the whole thing was another British joke on them, and they were going to be shot by the Black and Tans or the Essex Regiment, rumbling into the village on their death trucks.

'Is it true, Nuala?' asked one of her neighbours.

''Tis true enough, Mrs McKintall. It's all over.'

John Walsh at the pub came out to announce free beer for all and the little village gathered together outside and in, toasting the victory with glasses of porter.

''Tis a victory, isn't it?' she asked a filthy, pale Fergus, who had appeared out of nowhere to join in the celebrations.

'It is indeed. Sean Hales said the truce will hold for six months, and in that time men like Michael Collins and Éamon de Valera up in Dublin will be negotiating with the British on how things will work.'

'I just can't take it in! Will we have a republic? I mean, are they really giving us our own country back?'

'They are, Nuala. Ireland is free! It's free.'

Later that day, Fergus drove her and Christy on the pony and cart into Timoleague to collect Hannah, so that the whole family could be reunited at Cross Farm to celebrate the victory together. Even Ryan had agreed to come, and there was much whiskey drunk and laughter and tears and toasts for all those who had contributed so much to the fight, but were no longer here to celebrate with them.

Even though Nuala had joined in with the celebrations, she felt distracted.

'Do you mind if I drive the pony and cart back home now, Christy?' she asked her cousin, who'd had a good few too many whiskeys.

'O'course. I'm in no fit state to drive the cattle into the barn, let alone a pony and cart,' he chuckled. 'But I'll come back down to Clogagh with you. Sure, John will need some help clearing up in the pub tomorrow morning.'

Nuala left the rest of her family to their joy, and was glad to see Ryan chatting away happily to her father about how Mick Collins would sort everything out for Ireland peacefully.

On their journey down to Clogagh, there was a strange hush on the roads, and they did not meet a single car or truck.

Nuala released the horse from the cart and took the animal into the field next to the pub. Christy was still punching the air, and swaying as he sang an old Irish ballad.

'Time for your bed, Christy, but I'll be seeing you tomorrow,' she smiled.

'Goodnight, Nuala, and I'm sure your man will be back with you soon,' he said, as he leant heavily on his stick, then staggered through the pub door, the place still full with customers.

'I can only pray he will be,' she murmured as she let herself into the cottage.

For the next twenty-four hours, while it seemed like the whole of Ireland was letting out its breath, Nuala was still holding hers. She'd hardly slept a wink, listening for the sound of the back door opening. But it hadn't come.

By the evening, she was beside herself with worry as she watched thin, dishevelled volunteers appearing back in the village and embracing their loved ones.

'Where are you, Finn?' she whispered. 'Please come home to me soon, or I'll be losing my mind.'

By bedtime, Nuala was too exhausted to change, and fell asleep in her clothes on the bed. She didn't hear the back door open, or the footsteps up the stairs.

Only when his voice whispered in her ear, then took her into his arms and held her close, did she know her prayers had been answered.

'You're home, Finn. God love you, you're home.'

'I am that, darlin', and I swear I'll never leave your side again.'

42

Over the following few months, the atmosphere in Ireland was jubilant. The British troops moved out, and life resumed a semblance of normality. As Nuala's pregnancy progressed, Finn went back to teaching his children at Clogagh School. Summer turned into a wet and windy autumn, which couldn't dampen Nuala's spirits.

In November, during Sunday lunch at Cross Farm, all talk was of the truce negotiations currently happening in London between Michael Collins and the British Prime Minister David Lloyd George, supported by his team of seasoned politicians. Collins had been sent as Ireland's advocate and had promised to bring back a treaty that would give Ireland their republic.

'I'm surprised Éamon de Valera didn't go himself to negotiate with the British,' said Finn as he tucked into the beef and stout stew Eileen had made. 'After all, he's our president, and more experienced at all that than Mick.'

'Mick Collins will bring us the peace we've been yearning for,' said Ryan tersely, and Nuala could still feel the underlying tension between the soldier and the pacifist.

'I'd reckon that de Valera is after using Mick Collins as a scapegoat. He's always been good at making sure he's out of the way of things when they go wrong, then taking the credit if they go right,' said Daniel. 'Look at how he left Mick to fight the British while he sailed off to America to raise funds. I'd not be trusting that man an inch. I'm glad 'tis Mick who's there for Ireland.'

Nuala saw Finn about to speak and put a hand on his leg under the table to stop him. The war was over, and Nuala wanted peace at the family lunch table as much as she wanted it for Ireland.

By the beginning of December, Nuala was heavy with child, and eager for the babe to arrive. She was glad that her sister was only a month behind her, and the two commiserated over their aches and pains.

''Tis only a few more weeks.' Nuala gritted her teeth as she lowered herself into a chair. She was up in the kitchen of Cross Farm with Hannah and her mother, knitting hats and booties for the two babes. A gust of cold wind blew in as Daniel swept through the kitchen door, waving a newspaper over his head, with Fergus behind him.

'We've got a peace treaty!' he cried. 'Mick's done it for Ireland!'

As the family hugged each other and cheered at the news, Daniel opened the *Cork Examiner* and began to read out the terms of the Treaty. As he read, the excitement in his voice turned slowly to anger. When he'd finished, he sat down heavily at the table, the family crowding round him to read the details for themselves.

'This can't be true,' Daniel murmured.

'It is, Daddy. It says here that Ireland is to be a "self-governing dominion" of the British Empire,' said Hannah.

'But we wanted a republic,' said Nuala. 'Does this mean

we'll still be swearing allegiance to the feckin' King of England?'

'Nuala!' her mother reprimanded her. 'Well, Daniel, does
it?'

'Yes,' said Daniel, his excitement completely vanquished.
'And that part of the North of Ireland is being kept under
British control.'

'Jaysus Christ!' murmured Fergus. 'How can Mick Collins
have agreed to this?'

'I don't know, but surely they can't carve up our country?!'
cried Nuala.

''Tis a travesty,' said Daniel, slamming his fist on the newspaper. 'Mick Collins has had the wool pulled over his eyes by
the British negotiators.'

'He calls it "a stepping stone to Irish peace",' said Hannah.
'Maybe he always knew he couldn't get a republic out of the
British immediately. At least this is a start, and we'll have our
own legal government here in the South.'

'Yes, and the British will govern part of the North! 'Tis a
stepping stone to hell more like, Hannah,' raged Daniel.
'Seven hundred years of British dominance, and it seems we're
no further on.'

'De Valera should have gone to London,' said Nuala. 'Mick
Collins wasn't the right man for it.'

'You say that now, but you were cheering him on during
the summer when we got our truce!' said Hannah, still loyal
to her hero. 'He's done his best to protect us, bring us peace
and an end to the killing!'

'And at what price?!' Nuala retorted furiously. 'Having
part of *our* island chopped away, and the South still a dominion of the United Kingdom?!'

'Girls!' said Eileen. 'Calm yourselves. The Treaty hasn't
been approved by the Dáil government. The newspaper says

de Valera is against it and will put up a fight. Just be glad the war is over.'

But what was the point of it all if we don't have our republic? Nuala thought as she watched her red-faced Daddy reach for the whiskey bottle.

The plans that had been made to celebrate not only peace but the first Christmas free from British occupation were put on hold, as Ireland became a divided nation once more. The chatter in the villages and pubs was all of who was for Mick Collins and his pro-Treaty followers, and who stood firm with Éamon de Valera and his anti-Treaty faction of the Sinn Féin party.

'Hannah just told me she and Ryan are staying home for Christmas lunch,' Eileen said to Nuala as she dropped in to see her at her cottage for a cup of tea.

'What was her excuse?' asked Nuala numbly.

'Well, she's close to her time and—'

'Mammy, so am I! Closer, in fact, and I'm still riding up with Finn to Cross Farm to spend the Holy Day with my family! 'Tis that Ryan; he's knowing we're all anti-Treaty and for de Valera, while he's for his precious Mick.'

'They are for peace, Nuala, as are many others. You can't be blaming them for that,' said Eileen.

Finn and Nuala welcomed their daughter Maggie safely into the world just after Christmas. Hannah and Ryan's son John was born at the beginning of January, amid Irish politicians shouting furiously as they debated the Treaty in the Dáil.

Despite her new babe, and the happiness she felt at being a mother, Nuala feverishly followed the news, praying that de Valera's anti-Treaty faction would triumph. When Mick Collins and the pro-Treaty lot won the vote in the Dáil, Éamon de Valera stepped down as president, in protest at parliament approving it, and was now putting his full energy into physically fighting it. An election was looming, the first of this strange new 'Irish Free State' that the South had become. Political turmoil continued in Dublin throughout the spring, and the IRA, which had ballooned with new recruits during the months of the truce, was now turning against itself, as weary soldiers declared which side they were on. Led by de Valera, anti-Treaty soldiers began to take matters into their own hands and seized state buildings, including the central Four Courts in Dublin, where the Easter Rising had begun in 1916.

'How dare they act against the law like this?' Hannah fumed, as she and Nuala sat on their bench overlooking Courtmacsherry Bay, John and Maggie on their laps. 'Can't they see that this Treaty is giving us the freedom to achieve freedom?' Hannah parroted the slogan that Mick Collins had been spreading to garner support.

'He's in the pockets of the British now,' Nuala scoffed. 'Finn told me he heard what Collins said after he'd signed the Treaty – that he'd just signed his own death warrant. He knew true Irish republicans would denounce it, so.'

'Are you saying I'm not a true Irish republican?' Hannah bristled. ''Twas me who brought you into Cumann na mBan if you remember, sister.'

'And 'twas me and Finn who fought to the very end of the war,' retorted Nuala. 'I can't be talking to you any longer if you insist on swallowing Mick Collins's propaganda.' With that, she stood up, put Maggie in her sling and walked home, fuming all the way.

It was in June, when little Maggie had just started on solid food, that Nuala read the newspaper with a sinking heart.

'De Valera and the anti-Treaty representatives have lost. The pro-Treaty Collins lot have won the election!' she cried out to her husband, who was coming down the stairs, doing up his tie in readiness for his day at Clogagh School. 'The Irish people voted for his despicable Treaty, Finn! How could they, after all they've – *we've* – done to fight for a republic?!'

Nuala laid her head on the table and sobbed.

'Ah, Nuala, darlin', I know 'tis a disaster. But if politics fail—'

'War begins again, and this time 'twill be brother against brother. Jesus, Finn, I can't even think of what that'll mean. Families around these parts are already divided over the Treaty. Look at our own,' she added as she stared up at him, tears still streaming down her face. 'Hannah told me proudly she and Ryan had voted for Michael Collins! She'd better not be showing her face round here after this! I'll drag her up to Cross Farm and get her to curtsey to the King of England in front of her Fenian father! And her brother Fergus, and you and our friends and neighbours who risked their lives for a republic!'

'I know, Nuala, I know . . .'

''Tis even worse than fighting the British! Now we're a land divided against ourselves.'

'Well, at least *we're* not divided. Now then, try and keep calm and see to that babe of ours over there. She's wanting her breakfast.'

As Finn doled out some porridge from the pot sitting warm on the hearth, Nuala swept up six-month-old Maggie and placed her in the wooden feeding chair Finn had made during the Easter holidays.

Maggie smiled at her, which melted her heart. She was a beautiful babe – the irony being that she'd inherited her Auntie Hannah's red hair, and was the spit of her.

'Pass me her porridge, Finn.'

Finn did so, hoping that their daughter would act as a calming influence on his distraught wife.

'So now, I'll be seeing you both later,' he said and, placing a kiss on the top of the dark head of his wife and the red-gold of his daughter's, he left the cottage.

'I'll tell you, Maggie,' said Nuala, 'if that sister of mine comes round here crowing about the pro-Treaty lot winning the election, I'll be having to slap her hard.'

Maggie gurgled and opened her tiny mouth for more porridge.

'Maybe later we'll walk across to see your Uncle Christy, will we? He'll be feeling it like I am.'

Just as she'd laid Maggie down for a sleep, Christy arrived on her doorstep. 'Have you heard the news?' he asked as he walked in.

'I have indeed. Maggie's asleep with a tummy full of porridge, so shall we take a glass outside?'

'Of what?'

'Whatever you want.' Nuala lifted up a bottle of whiskey, as Christy took his arm from behind his back to raise a bottle of porter.

'I brought my own,' he said and followed her outside into the garden. 'Thought we might be needing it after what's happened.'

'Remember walls have ears,' Nuala whispered nervously.

'Unless poor Mrs Grady next door will rise from the grave we both saw her buried in three days ago, I'd be thinking we're all right.' Christy gave her a weak smile. 'If we're worrying about that, then we really are back to the old days.'

'I'd say with the pro-Treaty lot winning the election, we are.'

'Yes,' Christy agreed. 'There's fellows in the pub already this morning, so I'll not be here long, but they are singing the same song as us, and it isn't in support of Mick Collins. There's a lot around here who'd fight on for the republic we dreamt of. I've been hearing tales that Protestants round these parts are already packing and heading up to the North. There's talk of closing the border.'

'We won't be allowed into part of our own country?' Nuala gasped as she took a sip of whiskey.

'Ah now, I don't know how 'twill work, but many will go, just in case.'

'But what about the Catholics living across the border in the North?'

'They'll be trying to come south if they can, but like our own family, many will have land they farm to survive. What a bloody mess it all is.' Christy shook his head and knocked back a great gulp of porter straight from the bottle.

'How will we ever start a war against ourselves? Would you be willing to fight your friends? Your kin? I . . . don't know.' Nuala put her head in her hands. 'With Daddy being a Fenian, he'd continue the fight for a republic to the death, and Mammy would support him as she always has. Fergus would too, but Hannah . . .'

'Don't be too hard on her, Nuala. She has to stand by her husband, and there's many around here that were voting for peace, not war, whatever the consequences.'

'We had peace before with the British ruling us, and where did that get us? We were so close to being free and we lost so many doing it. Surely we owe it to those who died to continue the fight?'

'Even though 'tis an unbearable thought, I'd agree, and 'tis one we volunteers will all be debating the next time the Third West Cork Brigade meet. Sean Hales won't be present – he's already made it obvious he's pro-Treaty, the traitor! He's even in Dublin working with Mick Collins to recruit a national army. Tom Hales will stand with us and support fighting on.'

'How can Sean Hales support the Treaty, when his own brother Tom was beaten and tortured by the British?!' Nuala raged.

'Look now, we're not there yet. Try not to worry, Nuala. Mick Collins doesn't want war against his own just as much as we don't. Let's see if he can work his magic politically, and we'll take it from there.'

It was only ten days later that newspapers reported that the Dublin anti-Treaty headquarters, set up in the Four Courts with Éamon de Valera at its head, had been attacked by Michael Collins's new National Army.

> After requests for the anti-Treaty men to surrender their position at the Four Courts, the order was given to attack. Pro-Treaty forces bombarded the building with heavy artillery.

Rather than slamming her fists on the newspaper, Nuala took it in her hands and began to rip it to shreds. Finn walked in from his day in the schoolroom to his wife tearing paper and a screaming child.

'Have you heard? Collins has attacked the Four Courts! The fighting's still going on, but the paper says Collins has got help from the British, with them supplying cannons and artillery and . . . Oh Finn, please tell me I'm dreaming,' she said as she walked into the comfort of his arms.

'Nuala, we triumphed before and we can do it again. Christy just told me there's a meeting for our brigade tonight. Now's the time to show whether a man is with us, or with the pro-Treaty government. Darlin', we'd not be wanting Maggie upset, would we?'

Nuala shook her head and went to calm her crying babe.

'You're to concentrate on being a mammy, Nuala, and leave the rest to your husband, all right?'

'But if things get difficult, sure I'll have to work with Cumann na mBan again, and—'

'No, Nuala. 'Tis one thing risking your life when you've no one depending on you, another when you've a family. This time, you're to leave this to the men. I'll not have us leaving Maggie an orphan. D'you hear me?'

'Please don't say that! I'd rather me die than you.'

'And leave me to change Maggie's napkins?' Finn chuckled. 'Now, is there a bite to eat in this house of ours before I go out?'

Finn came in late that evening, but Nuala was still awake. 'What happened at the meeting?'

''Tis looking good, Nuala,' Finn said as he undressed and climbed into bed next to her. 'We've almost everyone with us, so it's the pro-Treaty lot who should be watching their backs in these parts. I've heard that Rory O'Connor himself is coming down from Dublin to Cork to take control of our anti-Treaty forces. We have to defend ourselves against this new Irish National Army that Mick Collins has recruited. I hear him and his government are calling *us* the republicans these days!' Finn shook his head and grimaced. 'It has to be faced, and we will face it; we've experience on our side, and men like Tom Hales with us.'

'With Sean Hales in charge of this new army?'

'Yes. Ah, Nuala, it looks like we're headed for more difficult times. Let's get some sleep while we can.'

As Finn disappeared off again to volunteers' meetings and drills, Nuala read that the Irish National Army, headed by Sean Hales – who'd fought side by side with Finn and been responsible for burning down Castle Bernard, which had brought about the truce – was travelling by boats supplied by the British to make landings on the southern coast. Aware of the way that the volunteers had blown up bridges and railways when Sean was fighting with them in the last war, landing the National Army by sea was a clever ploy.

She was only thankful for Maggie, who kept her busy. She was on tenterhooks every moment Finn was away. It felt like the nightmare was happening all over again. With Maggie strapped to her chest, she drove the pony and cart into Timoleague. In the shops, there was nothing but talk of what was happening, most of the residents horrified by the new turn of events. There was a palpable air of uncertainty and fear.

''Tis civil war now and there's no denying it,' said Mrs McFarlane in the butcher's. 'I've heard that Sean Hales landed the army in Bantry yesterday and they're marching towards Skibbereen. What will it all come to?' she said as she handed over the stewing steak and some bacon to Nuala.

Walking down the high street, Nuala saw that the pubs, which had been full since the truce had been agreed and the

British had withdrawn from the area, were now empty, apart from old men drowning their sorrows. On the way to collect her pony and cart, Nuala saw Hannah come out of a shop right in front of her.

'Hello there, Nuala, how are you? And the little one?' her sister asked.

'We're grand altogether. How's your small one?' Nuala replied, as if she was addressing a stranger.

'Sure, John's coming on well, thank you.'

'Well, 'tis a while since we've seen you up at the farm for Sunday lunch. Will you and Ryan be joining us?' Nuala asked.

'Ah now, with feelings running so high, Ryan says 'tis best if we stay back till the whole thing's sorted. He knows too well how my family feels about the Treaty.'

'And how do you feel, Hannah?'

'I just want peace, like Ryan. Now, I need to get back home to my babe. Goodbye, Nuala.'

Nuala watched her sister turn away from her and walk down the street towards the little house she and Ryan had moved into just after John had been born. There was no more watching their babes grow up together; all that had stopped since the fighting had begun.

'All because of Uncle Ryan,' Nuala said to the sleeping Maggie, cradled peacefully against her chest. As hard as she tried, she could not forgive her sister for what she saw as nothing less than treachery.

Luckily, the school holidays had just begun and Finn was free to join the other anti-Treaty volunteers in the fight. He had said the National Army were now heading towards Clonakilty.

'The home of Michael Collins himself,' Nuala said to Christy when he popped over for a chat.

'Is Finn going there? I'd be worried if he was, for even if they're anti-Treaty, there's many in Clonakilty that'll come out in support of the Big Fellow. He's one of their own.'

'No, Finn's on his way up to Bandon with the rest of the brigade. They think that's where the army will head next.'

'Well, the lads know what they're doing, and they're on their own territory,' said Christy. 'Try to remember, the National Army are just ordinary Irish folk like us, in need of a wage to feed their families. Besides, whatever we may feel about Sean Hales being pro-Treaty, he's a man of peace. He doesn't want to kill his fellow men in the same way as the British did. He'll show mercy, Nuala, especially in West Cork where he and his brother Tom were born.'

'I can only hope you're right,' Nuala sighed. 'Are you joining us for lunch at the farm after Mass on Sunday?' she asked him.

'Sure, and we'll listen to a few Fenian songs of your daddy's on the fiddle, to remind us what we're fighting for, eh?' Christy smiled. 'I need to be getting back. I'll be seeing ye, Nuala.'

As Christy left, Nuala pondered why a man who – apart from his bad leg – was such a fine figure of a fellow, and so kind and clever, had never found himself a wife.

The following Sunday, with Finn away fighting to hold Bandon, Christy drove Nuala and baby Maggie in the pony and cart up to Cross Farm after Mass. It was a beautiful July day, and Nuala looked up at the blue, blue sky above her.

Wherever you are, Finn Casey, I'm sending my love and all my blessings to you.

Talk at Cross Farm was all of the battle in Bandon. News had filtered through to her father that despite the anti-Treaty volunteers defending it bravely, the National Army would take the town.

'At least the loss of life was far less than it would have been if we'd been fighting the British, and we must thank God for that,' her mother commented as she and Nuala served lunch.

'Ah, but there were still some casualties, and what's your man Sean doing using British warships and artillery to fire on his own?' Daniel roared from the end of the table. 'And Mick Collins sanctioning it?!'

''Tis a tragedy and that's all I can say,' sighed Eileen.

'The enemy know our tactics, because they once used them themselves not so long ago. They're taking West Cork easily, and we're sitting around and watching it happen!' Daniel continued in his rant.

'Finn isn't sitting around, Daddy,' said Nuala defensively. 'He's out there fighting for our republic.'

'That he is, Nuala, along with our Fergus,' said Eileen. 'And may God bless both of them.'

After lunch, Daniel took out his fiddle and played some rousing ballads from the old times, then newer ones he'd learnt, like 'The Ballad of Charlie Hurley', Finn's closest friend, who had died so tragically during the last war. As his rich voice soared through the moving words, Nuala felt calmer. They weren't just fighting for their republic, but for all those who had lost their lives to the cause.

Finn came back from Bandon a day later, exhausted but unharmed.

'Towns across West Cork are falling to the National Army

– towns where we won against the British to get the truce for Ireland. But are we now to go in and blow up a garrison full of our Irish brothers?' he sighed. 'Word is, the National Army are off to take Kinsale, and unless we start putting up more of a fight, they'll have that town and the rest of Ireland surrendering before the month is out.'

'Will you continue, Finn?'

'To the end, Nuala, you know that.'

'Did you . . . did you kill anyone during the Bandon battle?'

''Twas dark, and I couldn't be seeing, but yes, there were some men lying injured in the street, but I've no idea whose they were, or which gun fired the shot. Jaysus, I'm tired and for my bed. Are you coming?'

'Of course, darlin'. I'll take all the chances I can to hold you safe in my arms,' Nuala whispered as she snuffed out the oil lamp and followed Finn miserably upstairs.

43

By the middle of August, the National Army had Cork City and all the major towns in the county under their control. Michael Collins and his pro-Treaty government were triumphing.

'If they've taken Cork, what's the point of continuing?' she said to Finn, who had arrived home, filthy and dejected from another fruitless fight. 'We've lost, and that's all there is to it. And if there's no hope, I'd be preferring to live with this travesty of a Treaty than without my husband.'

'Nuala,' Finn said as he knocked back a drop of whiskey, 'we all agreed we'd fight for a republic, didn't we?'

'Yes, but—'

'There *is* no "but". If you asked all the people around here to put their hands on the Bible and say what's in their hearts, they'd all be for saying no to the Treaty. And we're all Ireland has left to make that happen. I couldn't live with myself if I didn't give my last breath to the cause.'

'So you're saying you'd prefer to die, Finn? That the cause is more important than me or your daughter?' she demanded.

'Now then, where is this talk coming from? There was none of it last time. You stood with me, and 'twas your love and belief that got me through.'

'Yes, 'tis true, but our lives have changed. Look at you,

telling me I wasn't to be involved with Cumann na mBan because of our Maggie. We're a family now, Finn, as you said yourself. That's what matters most, isn't it?'

Finn looked at her and sighed. 'I'm too tired for this, Nuala. I'm off to clean myself up.'

Nuala took the sleeping Maggie from her cradle and hugged her to her breast, looking down at her young daughter's face.

'What's to become of us, little one?' she whispered. Maggie continued to sleep peacefully in her arms.

It was decided that all members of Finn's brigade should once more take to the hills and become the shadows they had been last time around.

'Are you saying the pro-Treaty lot will come and arrest you on your doorstep like the British did last time?' Nuala asked Finn when he came home.

'Some of ours have been arrested and thrown into the jails by the National Army during the skirmishes, but if they want to push further to clear out the troublemakers, well, they'll be knowing where we all live, won't they?' he pointed out. 'And where our safehouses were, because they used them themselves in the old days.'

'How many of you are left, would you say?'

'Enough,' said Finn. 'But there's news come down from one of our spies in Dublin that the Big Fellow might be planning to pay a visit to West Cork.'

'Mick Collins would come here?!'

''Tis where he was born, Nuala. 'Tis his place, and there's many around these parts that might be anti-Treaty, but still see Mick as a god, the hero that saved Ireland. 'Tis ironic, isn't it?'

'What?'

'West Cork and Kerry probably contributed more to the winning of a truce with the British than any other part of Ireland. We all fought for Mick, believed in him because he was one of our own, but that passion makes us the most anti-Treaty area in Ireland. 'Tis madness, it really is. Anyway . . .' Finn tied the belt of his trench coat and heaved his haversack onto his shoulder. 'I'll be off.' He took her face in his hands and kissed her gently on the lips. 'Remember how much I love you, my Nuala. And how I'm doing this for you, our small ones and their babes to come.'

'I love you too, and I always will,' she whispered as she watched the door close and her husband leave her again.

Two days later, Nuala saw a number of villagers walking down the street or on their ponies and traps.

'Where are they going?' she asked Christy, who had popped over for his now habitual cup of tea before the pub opened its doors.

'The talk is that Michael Collins will be in Clonakilty this afternoon. I heard some chat last night in the pub that he'd passed through Béal na Bláth. His convoy had to stop and ask directions outside Long's pub from Denny, who works there.'

'What!' Nuala put her hand to her mouth. 'Did Denny tell them the way?'

'Sure he did,' nodded Christy. 'There were a few of our boys in the pub, as there's a brigade meeting later at Murray's farmhouse nearby. Tom Hales was up there, and I also heard that de Valera himself was travelling down from Dublin for the meeting. 'Tis said they're deciding whether to continue with the war or not. And there, bold as you like, our sworn enemy, Mick Collins, passing by just a few miles from where they all were, not suspecting a thing.' Christy shook his head and chuckled.

'Are you sure Denny saw Mick Collins in the car?'

'Yes, Denny would swear on the Bible 'twas him. He was sitting in an open-topped car, and now half of West Cork has got wind that he's down here. Word has it he'll be visiting all the towns that the National Army has taken, and everyone has taken a bet he'll stop at Clonakilty near his homeplace.'

Nuala watched the flurry of activity in the street gaining momentum.

'You'll be giving it a miss, will you, Nuala?' asked Christy with an ironic smile.

'I will indeed.' There was a pause as Nuala took in the ramifications of what she'd just been told. 'If our lot know he's here and will most likely return the way he came, will they be planning anything?'

Christy turned his head away from Nuala. 'I'd not be knowing. Seems to me that today, all the chickens have come home to roost.'

It was late evening by the time Nuala saw the villagers and those who lived beyond Clogagh returning. They obviously had drink in them and wanted more, as many of them parked their carts, bicycles and themselves outside the pub. Unable to resist, she opened her front door and listened as the crowd milled about outside with pints of porter or drops of whiskey.

''Twas at O'Donovan's Mick bought me a drink . . .'

'Ah now, it was drinks on the house at Denny Kingston's place. He waved at me!'

'Mick asked after my small ones, he did!'

Nuala recognised men and women who'd been passionate IRA volunteers during the revolution. With a sad shake of her head, she closed the door. Then she poured herself her own whiskey.

At just past midnight, Nuala was roused out of a whiskey-induced slumber by the creaking of the back door opening. She heard footsteps coming upstairs and sat up, holding her breath until she saw Finn enter the room.

'Nuala, oh Nuala . . .'

She watched as Finn staggered towards the bed, then almost fell forward onto her and began to sob.

'What is it? What's happened?'

'I . . . what a mess, Nuala, what a mess.'

Nuala could do no more than wait for her husband to stop crying. Then she handed him some whiskey from the bottle and he drank it straight down.

'Can you tell me what's happened?'

'I . . . can't speak the words, and I've run many miles through the night to get back to you. Let me sleep in your arms, Nuala, and I'll tell you in the . . .' Finn fell asleep mid-sentence, his head on her chest.

Whatever it was he had to tell her, she didn't care, for her husband was safe home.

The following morning, Nuala left Finn in bed and went downstairs to feed Maggie. Finn joined her an hour later, looking gaunt and haggard, as if he'd aged ten years since she'd last seen him.

'Porridge?' Nuala asked.

Finn could only nod as he slumped at the table.

'Get that down you,' she said quietly.

He finished the bowl in a few gulps and Nuala, who'd been too exhausted herself this morning to bake bread, used the rest of yesterday's loaf and lathered it with jam.

'Ah Nuala.' Finn finished the bread and jam, then wiped his hand across his lips. 'My head is spinning this morning, I . . .'

'Tell me, Finn, you know 'twill go with me to the grave if that's what you ask. I heard chat from Christy that Mick Collins was expected in Clonakilty yesterday. Was an ambush planned on his convoy?'

'It was. Me, Tom Hales and the boys were up at the Murray farmhouse for a meeting with the Cork brigades. When we heard from Denny Long that Collins was likely to come back along the same route he'd arrived by, Tom directed that we should plan an ambush. We laid in wait for hours around the crossroads at Béal na Bláth, but the convoy didn't appear. Tom decided we should call it off because of the weather – we were soaked to the skin from the rain. So me and some of the other men left, but there were a few who stayed just in case, including Tom. I was coming home across country when I saw the convoy beneath me. I crouched down in case they saw me, and then, about ten minutes later . . .'

He stopped and took a shuddering breath before he was able to continue.

'I heard shots ring out from where I knew some of the men were still waiting. I began to run back to find out what had happened, and met a couple of volunteers sprinting towards me. They told me that the weather was too bad to see who they were firing at when the convoy passed, but that Collins had gone down. The rest of the convoy had fired back, but had soon stopped when they'd seen Mick lying there.'

Finn looked up at her, his blue eyes filled with tears. 'He was dead, Nuala. The only one in the convoy that was.'

'Mick Collins?! Dead?! I . . .' Nuala stared at her husband in shock and disbelief. 'Do you know who shot him?'

'The man I was talking to – and I'm giving no names now – was hardly making sense, other than to keep repeating that "Mick's dead, Mick's dead!" Jesus, Mary and Joseph, shot by his own down here in West Cork.'

Finn began weeping again, and all Nuala could do was to stand up and put her arms round him.

''Tis one thing to fight for a proper republic, but another to be part of an attack that killed the man that originally led us to victory and a truce. God only knows what will become of Ireland now, without the Big Fellow.'

'Where was de Valera? Did he know about the ambush?'

'I'd say he did, yes, but he left West Cork early yesterday to get back to Dublin for a meeting.'

'Did he order the attack on Mick?'

'Word is 'twas Tom Hales, who cried like a baby when he found out Mick was dead. You know what good friends they once were before the Civil War.'

'I . . . just don't know what to say.' Nuala shook her head, unable to stop her own tears from falling. 'Where will we go from here?'

'I don't know, but there's not many around these parts, whatever side they were on, who won't be shedding a tear today. I tell you something, Nuala, 'tis over for me. I've not the stomach for any more now that Mick's gone.'

'I understand, Finn,' she replied eventually. 'I wonder how many others will feel the same, so.'

'Most of us. I'm frightened, Nuala, for the first time; I'm frightened that people will find out that I was part of the ambush that killed Michael Collins, and that they'll come after me.'

'But you weren't part of it, Finn; you told me just now that you'd already left and were coming home to me. There were so many out on the streets last night, who'd travelled back from Clonakilty with a bellyful of porter, so drunk they could hardly stand up. They'll not be knowing where you were. If anyone asks, you were here with your wife and child last night. I'll swear to it on the Bible if I have to. Sure, there'll be Masses said for Mick all over Ireland and we should go.'

'We should, yes, and I'll say a prayer for a man that I didn't kill with my own hands, but will forever feel as if I did.'

'Well, you didn't, Finn, and you must try to remember that you were just following orders, like any soldier in battle.'

'You're right, of course.' Finn wiped his hands harshly across his streaming eyes. 'I'd doubt Tom Hales or a single one of us thought for a moment 'twould be Mick that would get it. We just wanted to have a go at the Dublin lot, remind them that there were many of us still out here, fighting for the republic we'd dreamt of. Jesus, Nuala, Mick was the head of our new government! Why was the man riding around in an open-topped car? And where were the soldiers who were meant to protect him when they were needed?'

'I'd say that Mick didn't think anyone down here in West Cork would want him dead. He was amongst his own, wasn't he?'

'Yes, or so he thought.'

'And from the state of those back from their drink with him last night, he and the soldiers must have downed a few with them. They weren't on the lookout, were they?'

'You're right, Nuala. Mick was always one for the party and a drink. Whatever their politics, people loved him down here. *We* once loved him; he was one of us . . .' Finn began to cry again.

'Now then, how about I fill the tub with some nice warm

water and you go clean yourself up? Then I'll lay out a shirt and some trousers and you, me and Maggie will take a walk outside, so our neighbours can see that you're here and mourning for Mick with them. You're respected, Finn, you teach the children at the village school. Sure, no one's going to want to see you harmed.'

Nuala spoke with a confidence she didn't feel, but whatever it took to console her devastated, frightened husband, she'd do and say.

As she made to move, Finn caught her, drew her roughly into his arms and kissed her hard on the lips. When he eventually pulled away, his eyes were wet again. 'God help me, Nuala Casey, I'm spending the rest of my life being grateful for the woman I have for my wife.'

The mood in the week after the ambush that killed Mick Collins was sombre. Everywhere she went, Nuala saw windows hung with the black of mourning, and grown men weeping in the streets. The newspapers were full of tributes to the man who'd been born on West Cork soil. There was a great deal of local upset when Michael Collins's body was buried in Dublin, rather than locally where he'd been birthed.

Nuala, Finn and Maggie joined a Mass held in Timoleague church on the day of his burial. She had never seen the church so full, and recognised many of the men who had been fighting against him. Her whole family was present, joined together in grief for a man who'd given them the belief, strength and courage to begin the revolution. And had now made the ultimate sacrifice himself, aged only thirty-two, and already Chairman of the Provisional Government of Ireland.

Outside the church, both Hannah and Ryan were inconsolable. As Nuala passed her sister, Hannah reached out and grabbed her to whisper in her ear.

'I hope you and that husband of yours are happy. You've both got what you wanted, haven't you? Don't be telling me Finn wasn't involved in the ambush – I know very well he was and so do many others around these parts. *He's* the one who deserves to be lying in a grave, not the saviour of Ireland,' she hissed through her tears.

Nuala didn't tell Finn what her sister had said, as there was no point worrying him any more than he was already.

Two nights later, he told her he was going out to a brigade meeting.

'You're not to be fretting, Nuala, I'm telling them the fight is over for me. I'll not put you and Maggie at risk any longer for a cause that's already lost.'

As it was a warm August evening, Nuala sat outside in the garden. Maggie – who was just sitting up – sat on a blanket, playing with the toy dog that Finn had carved from a piece of wood.

'Perhaps that'll become Daddy's new hobby now he's retiring from war,' she said to her daughter. Despite the tragic events that had occurred, and the fact they'd lost the dream of their beloved republic, part of Nuala felt relieved. Ireland's path was still unclear, but she could now imagine a more peaceful future, without the terrible lump of fear that had sat in her stomach for so long. At last, the three of them could concentrate on being a family, and with the prospect of Principal O'Driscoll at Clogagh School soon retiring, Finn would take over and they'd have more money to spare.

'Maybe your mammy could think about getting a part-time job in the local pharmacy, what with her nursing training,' she cooed to Maggie, as she picked her up to get her ready for bed.

Finn had not arrived back by eleven, but Nuala did her best not to panic.

He's probably got caught up chatting, she told herself, as yet again she mounted the stairs alone to bed.

Exhausted from the past few days, Nuala fell asleep easily. It was only when she heard a loud banging on the front door that she woke with a start.

Looking out of the bedroom window, she saw Christy with Sonny, another man from the village, standing below.

Running down the stairs, she opened the door.

With one glance at the expression on their faces, she knew.

'Finn's been shot, Nuala, up near the Dineen Farm,' said Christy.

'I found him in my field as I was walking home from the meeting. He'd been thrown into a ditch,' said Sonny.

'I . . . is he alive?'

The men bowed their heads. 'Nuala, I'm so sorry,' said Christy.

Christy caught her before she fell. She could hear someone screaming from far away. Then the world went black.

Finn's funeral took place at the little church in Clogagh, the day after he had been waked. If she could have done, Nuala would have only allowed her family to be there to support her, as they prayed for his immortal soul. No one had come forward to confess to shooting her husband, and even though there'd been plenty of rumours as to who it might have been, Nuala had ignored them. Her husband's murderer was probably sitting right here in the church, pretending to be sorry for not only ending Finn's life, but her own and her daughter's too.

On the journey up to Clogagh graveyard, which sat in an idyllic spot at the top of the Argideen valley a good half-mile away from the village, the coffin was borne by the volunteers Finn had stood side by side with. Nuala walked in front of the coffin, supported by Christy. With his volunteer's cap on the top of it, Finn had been interred into the ground next to Charlie Hurley, his closest friend. Then the Clogagh company had fired off a seven-gun salute to their fallen comrade.

At the gathering afterwards, held up at Cross Farm, Nuala had smiled and nodded at the condolences from friends and neighbours.

Realising who was missing, she excused herself and went to find her mother. 'I didn't see Hannah and Ryan at the church. And they're not here either.'

'No, they didn't come.' Eileen did her best to control her anger. 'Don't blame your sister, Nuala, 'tis that husband of hers who's the problem.'

'Well, she married him, didn't she?'

In that moment, in a heart already scarred with loss, Nuala felt a part of it turn to stone.

That night, staying in her childhood bedroom, with Maggie lying next to her in the bed she used to share with Hannah, she came to a decision.

'God save me, but I can never forgive Hannah for this. And I never want to see her again for the rest of my life.'

Merry
West Cork, Ireland
June 2008

An Crann Bethadh
Celtic Tree of Life

44

'There now, that's the story that Nuala told me only hours before she left this earth,' said Katie. "Twas emotional for both of us when she told me the family connection.'

I did my best to come back to the present, still enveloped in the utter tragedy of Finn's death, and all that Nuala had suffered.

'So Nuala was our mother Maggie's mum . . . our grandmother? The one we never saw when we were growing up, apart from at Mammy's funeral? And what about our grandfather? Finn died. So who was that man with her, who walked with a stick?'

"Twas Christy, her cousin who worked at the pub across the road. She married him a few years after Finn died. You can see why she did: Christy was always there for her. They had shared experiences,' Katie replied, then paused as she stared at me. 'Christy's surname was "Noiro".'

I stared at her in utter shock. 'Noiro?'

'Yes. As well as her daughter, Maggie, Christy and Nuala went on to have a son, Cathal, who married a woman called Grace. And, well, they had Bobby and his little sister, Helen.'

'I . . .' My head was swimming. 'So we shared a grandmother with Bobby Noiro?'

'We did, yes.'

'But why didn't Bobby ever say?'

'I don't think he knew, to be fair.'

'Why didn't Nuala and Christy ever visit us?'

''Tis complicated,' Katie sighed. 'Our great-uncle Fergus was running Cross Farm before our daddy; he inherited it when Fergus died.'

'Fergus was mentioned in the diary I read. He was Nuala's brother. Did he ever marry?'

'No, so the farm went to our daddy as the eldest boy of the clan. We never met his parents – our other grandparents – because they both died before we were born. Our grandmother was named Hannah, and our grandfather was called Ryan.'

Katie gave me a meaningful stare as I tried to compute what she was saying. 'So now, Nuala was Mammy's mother and Hannah was Daddy's! Our grandmothers were sisters! Which means . . .' Katie produced a sheet of paper. On it was a family tree. 'See?'

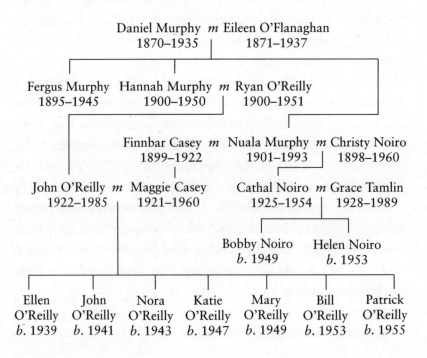

I took it from my sister to study it, but a raft of names and dates danced in front of my eyes and I looked up at Katie for guidance.

She pointed at two names. 'John and Maggie – our mammy and daddy – were first cousins. It isn't illegal here in Ireland, even these days – don't worry, I checked. With such big families often living in isolated communities, 'twas common, and still is, for cousins to mix socially and fall in love. And after Hannah didn't turn up for Finn's wake or funeral, Nuala never spoke to her sister again. You know 'tis an awful thing not to pay your respects to the dead, especially here in Ireland, and 'twas the icing on the cake, after her sister had said such terrible things to her.'

She raised her eyebrows at me and I nodded in agreement. It was one thing that had struck me when I had moved to New Zealand – that there didn't seem to be any long-running family feuds that had been passed down through the generations, just because a great-grandfather had once insulted his cousin's fiddle-playing.

'Old wounds run deep here,' I murmured.

'They do,' Katie agreed. 'Now, when our parents – Maggie and John – met and fell in love, Nuala and Hannah must have been horrified. 'Twas like *Romeo and Juliet*. Nuala said she'd told her daughter that she'd disown her if she married John, but Mammy loved Daddy so much, she went ahead. Ah, Merry, Nuala couldn't stop weeping as she told me how she had cut our mammy out of her life. And how much she regretted it looking back, especially when Mammy died so young. She said she just couldn't bear to set eyes on Daddy – Hannah and Ryan's son. She asked my forgiveness for not being there for all of us kids after Mammy died.'

'Oh my God . . .' I muttered, tears springing to my eyes as I thought about the diary I hadn't read for all those years. The story of a brave young woman who had been my grandmother, who through the pain of war had lost her husband, but who had also been prepared to cut not only her sister but her beloved daughter out of her life.

'So now, I went to Timoleague church to look through the records and put the tree together.' Katie pointed to it.

'There's Bobby,' I whispered. 'All those stories he used to tell of his grandparents fighting the British in the War of Independence . . .'

'Yes. I remember, Merry,' Katie nodded grimly, 'and I think it explains why Bobby was the way he was. With Nuala and Christy as his grandparents, Bobby would have been brought up as pro-republican as you can be. Nuala's hatred for the British, for Michael Collins and "his gang", as she called them, passed down through the generations. After all, the Treaty that Mick Collins signed with the British government in London sparked the Civil War, which killed her husband, Finn. He was the love of her life.'

'Yes.' I spoke quietly, as my chest felt so tight I could hardly breathe. 'Which must also mean that I – *we* – are closely related to Bobby and Helen Noiro.'

'We are, yes. He's our first cousin. And o'course, his daddy, Cathal, was half-brother to Mammy.'

'We knew that Bobby's daddy, Cathal, died in a barn fire, didn't he? So Nuala lost her son as well,' I sighed. 'What a sad life she led.'

'I know so, 'tis tragic, but it's interesting working with the old folks. They took death to be part of life back then, because they were used to it. These days, with all the newfangled medicine, 'tis a shock when anyone dies, even if they're very old. What I've learnt is that life was cheap back then, Merry. I went to Nuala's funeral at Timoleague church. There weren't many there, just a couple of old friends and Helen, Bobby's little sister.'

'Bobby wasn't there?' I held my breath for an answer.

'No, he wasn't.' Katie eyed me. 'What happened in Dublin, Merry? I know 'twas something to do with Bobby. He was obsessed with you from the first moment he set eyes on you.'

'Please, Katie, I can't talk about it now, I just can't.'

'But he was why you ran away, wasn't he?'

'Yes.' Tears jumped into my eyes as I spoke the words.

'Ah, Merry.' Katie took my hands in hers. 'I'm here now, and whatever happened then is long in the past. You're safe back home with me.'

I put my head against my sister's chest, gulping back the tears because I knew that once they began, they'd never stop. I needed to hold it together for my children. There was one last question I needed to ask.

'Has he . . . have you seen him around here since I left? I was wondering whether he comes back to visit his mum. She was called Grace, wasn't she?'

'Helen Noiro told me at the funeral that her mammy was long dead, and as for Bobby, I've only seen him once, and that was soon after you'd vanished from the face of the earth. He came tearing up to the farm, wanting to know if we'd seen you. When we said no, he didn't believe us, and went raging through the house, opening all the presses, looking under beds until Daddy came along – he had to threaten him with his rifle . . . Bobby was frightening, Merry. The rage on him . . . 'twas like he'd been possessed.'

'I'm so sorry, Katie. He did the same at Ambrose's flat too.'

'But you weren't there?'

'No, I'd already gone. I had no choice, Katie.'

'Well, part of me is glad you disappeared, Merry, because

I thought to myself then that if he found you, he'd kill you. Though I'd have liked to have known whether *you* were dead or alive sooner, so.'

'It wasn't just me he was threatening to kill, Katie, but . . .' I shook my head. 'I promise I will tell you everything, just not now, okay?'

'O'course, and I hope what I've told you today has helped in some way. Old scars never seem to heal here, do they? And 'tis so unfair when they're inflicted on the next generation. Ireland's been too good at looking back at its past, but now I'd say we're getting better at looking to the future. Things have finally moved on.'

'Yes,' I agreed as I dug in a pocket to find a tissue. 'I really feel that. Even though part of me still wants to see the ponies and carts on the roads and the old cottages rather than all the modern bungalows, progress is a good thing.'

'So you don't know where he is, Merry?'

'No. I've checked the records in Dublin and London to see if I could find out whether he was still alive, but there wasn't a single Robert or Bobby Noiro registered as dying since 1971. So, unless he moved somewhere else abroad and died, he's still alive, out there somewhere.'

'And that frightens you?'

'I can't tell you how much, Katie. He was partly the reason I decided to come on my Grand Tour after my husband died. I thought it was time to put the past to rest.'

'Did your husband know about it?'

'No. I agonised about telling him, but knowing Jock, he'd have gone to hunt him down and the whole nightmare would have begun again. I just wanted a completely fresh start. I haven't told my children either, but I'm going to have to tell them now, Katie. They both think I've lost it, which I have a bit recently. The strange thing is, as I set out to find Bobby, some other people were trying to find me too,' I confessed. 'And I thought . . .'

'That Bobby was after you again. Jaysus' – Katie raised her eyebrows – 'you've certainly led a more interesting life than I have. So, who are these people trying to find you?'

'That really *is* a story for another day.' I checked my watch. 'My kids will be back at any moment. Please don't tell them what we were discussing this morning. When I find out what's happened to him, I will.'

'I'll just say we were talking of the old times, which is true. Take that with you, Merry,' she said, pointing to the family tree. 'Have a look at it in more detail another time . . .'

There was a knock on the door. 'Come in!' I called.

'Hi, Mum, the surf was fantastic out there!' said Jack, walking into the room with Mary-Kate. His eyes fell on Katie, who smiled and stood up.

'Hello there, you two. I'm your long-lost Auntie Katie, and you are?'

'I'm Jack.'

'And I'm Mary-Kate. So you're the sister I'm named after?'

'She is,' I smiled as Katie embraced Jack and then Mary-Kate.

'What a legacy you've been given: named after the both of us. Sure, you've the best qualities of your auntie, and the bad ones of your mammy.' Katie winked at my daughter.

'I don't have any bad qualities, do I, kids?'

'Of course not, Mum,' said Jack as he and Mary-Kate rolled their eyes.

'Maybe you two can tell me more about what my naughty little sister's been up to in the past few years,' Katie chuckled.

'We'd be up for that, wouldn't we, Jacko? I love the colour of your hair,' Mary-Kate added.

'Ah, thanks. I'd be having to get the red roots from a bottle these days, mind. I always wanted the blonde curls of your mammy when I was younger. Now so, I'm starving. Shall we treat ourselves to some freshly caught fish at An Súgán in town?' she suggested.

Over lunch, at a lovely pub-restaurant in Clonakilty, Katie regaled them with stories of our childhood, some of which Jack had heard already.

'She was always the clever one, see, and she won a scholarship to go and be educated properly at boarding school in Dublin.'

'When she got older, did she have many boyfriends?' Mary-Kate asked.

'I'd say your mammy was more for her books than she was boys.'

'But your auntie always was a one for the lads, weren't you? There was always some fellow hanging around,' I teased her, relishing the relaxed atmosphere after the tension of our earlier conversation.

By the time Katie had dropped us back at the hotel, I felt utterly exhausted.

'So, your Uncle John's already been in touch – all of us who are here around these parts are invited up to the farm on Sunday night, including grandchildren. No sign of kiddies for you yet, Jack?' Katie asked.

'I just haven't found the right woman to be their mother yet,' Jack shrugged. 'Bye, Katie. It was a pleasure meeting you.'

'And you. Never thought I'd see the day.' Turning to me, she said, 'Call me, Merry, and we'll talk some more, okay?'

'I will, thanks, Katie.'

Inside the lobby, I told the kids I was going for a rest, and handed Jack the car keys.

'Go and explore, but stick to the main roads for now. They're not big on signposts around here.'

'Okay. Are you all right, Mum?' asked Jack.

'Yes, I'm fine, sweetheart. See you later.'

Up in my room, I took the family tree out of the file Katie had left for me. Taking it over to the bed, I studied the names on it. Even now, knowing that I wasn't blood-related to any of them, I realised that the dreadful legacy of war and loss that Nuala had passed down had radically altered the course of my life.

Then I thought of Tiggy; how she had said that even though it had been hard sometimes to come to terms with the journeys she and her sisters had taken into the past, it had changed their lives for the better. I only prayed it would be the same for me, because every instinct in my body told me the answers to the questions I had lay down here in West Cork.

If only I knew where *he* was, then . . .

The hotel phone rang by my bed and I picked it up.

'Hello?' I said tentatively, doing a mental tally of the people who knew I was here.

'Mary, my dear girl,' came Ambrose's clipped tones. 'How are you finding being back in your homeplace, as they say down there?'

'Grand altogether,' I said, smiling into the receiver. 'I've just been with Katie . . . oh Ambrose, it's been so wonderful to see her.'

'I'm happy for you, Mary. This call is simply to tell you I located the address you were after. And it was quite a surprise, let me tell you,' Ambrose chuckled. 'I posted your letter to him immediately. Let's see if he replies.'

'I . . . oh my goodness! Thank you, Ambrose, I can't believe you found him!'

'It's the least I can do for you, Mary. Do let me know when you are returning to Dublin.'

'Of course I will, Ambrose, and thank you. Bye.'

Putting the receiver down, my heart racing, I once again longed for Jock to be here beside me. But . . .

Why did you never tell him, Merry?

You saw him as second best, a safe haven . . .

In retrospect, I could see that I'd been too preoccupied hankering after a love I'd lost, a love that had been so passionate and exciting and forbidden that I truly believed there was nothing that could ever match up to it. And because it *had* been lost, I'd built it up into some grand *coup de foudre* . . .

I'd counselled and consoled both my children through their own various break-ups with people they'd believed were the love of their lives, but eventually they'd recovered and moved on.

When I'd been their age, no one had been there to counsel me – Ambrose had not been a person I could turn to on affairs of the heart. And as for Katie . . . I knew she and my family would never approve because of who he was. And because of what had subsequently happened, I'd had no 'closure', as the kids would say.

And all along there'd been Jock, who had loved me deeply and always protected me.

Now here I was, missing him so desperately that it physically hurt.

Well, I thought, the closure I'd always wanted might possibly be within my grasp . . .

Yet the truth was, it wasn't true love for *him* I'd discovered since I'd left New Zealand; it was for my husband.

45

Atlantis

'Any news from Ireland?' CeCe asked as Ally walked into the kitchen.

'No, nothing. Merry, Mary-Kate and Jack all have the Atlantis number and our various mobile numbers, so the ball is in their court.'

'But, Ally, you said we had to leave next Thursday morning at the latest to have any chance of getting down to Greece to lay Pa's wreath next Saturday. Which means they all need to be in Nice by the middle of next week to join us on the *Titan*. Can't we contact them?' CeCe urged.

'No,' Ally replied firmly. 'Tiggy said that there's things both Merry and Mary-Kate need to find out, and we shouldn't interfere.'

'To be honest, I think we probably have to accept that we're not going to have Mary-Kate with us,' Maia sighed.

'Besides, there's only one person who can confirm it's her and that's Pa. And he's dead.' CeCe looked up at her older sisters' faces and saw them cringe. 'Sorry, but he is, and this cruise is all about us saying goodbye to him properly. I mean, Chrissie and I really liked Mary-Kate; she was lovely and the right age to be the missing sister. But she – and her family –

never even knew him and . . . Hi, Ma,' CeCe said as she walked in.

'Hello, girls. I . . . oh dear, Claudia's been called away to visit a sick relative. Christian's taken her to Geneva on the speedboat. Which means we'll have to cope here domestically without her.'

'That shouldn't be a problem, Ma,' said Ally. 'We're all completely capable of cooking for ourselves these days.'

'I know, but with the others arriving, well, I don't know how I'll manage without her,' Ma admitted. 'It could not be worse timing. If all your partners come, there will be at least eleven of you, plus Bear, Valentina and Star's little Rory . . .'

'Really, Ma, we'll be fine.' Maia offered a chair to her. 'Sit down, please, you look very pale.'

'I feel it. I don't think any of you realise how much I – and this household – depend on Claudia.'

'Remember, most of the others will be joining us directly in Nice,' said Ally. 'I'm sure Claudia will be back by the time we're home at Atlantis after the cruise.'

'It'll be fun, Ma,' CeCe put in. 'We can have a rota on the fridge, like we had for the washing-up when we were kids.'

'Which you always managed to get out of, CeCe,' Maia teased her.

'She still does, don't worry,' remarked Chrissie.

'I think we should each take a night and make a dish from where we all live now,' suggested Maia.

'Which means we'll get a hot dog from Electra,' giggled Ally. 'See, Ma? It'll be fun. Anything you need us to do?'

'No, thank you, Ally. All the rooms have been prepared and are ready for the guests and Claudia said she'd left a salmon out for tonight.' Ma looked round at the four women. 'Does anyone know how to cook it?'

'I think that's my night on the rota,' Ally smiled. 'Fish is what you might call a Norwegian staple.'

'I just wanted you all to have a rest from your busy lives, be looked after here at home,' Ma sighed.

'Maybe it's you who should be taking a rest,' Maia replied, putting a hand on Ma's shoulder.

'Chrissie and I are going for a swim in the lake. Anyone want to come?' CeCe asked. 'Chrissie used to be a state champion!'

'I might take the Laser out and race you,' challenged Ally. 'But first, let me help you with the dishes, Maia.'

Alone in the kitchen, the two sisters fell naturally into the rhythm of washing and drying up.

'When does Floriano leave Rio with Valentina?' Ally asked.

'The day after tomorrow. It's ridiculous, I know, Ally, but I'm nervous about seeing him.'

'Why?'

'Because we discussed getting married and starting a family, but not, well, immediately. I'm not sure what he'll say. And then there's Valentina. She's been so used to having us to herself that she might not like the idea of a younger sibling.'

'Maia, I understand why you're nervous about telling Floriano, but I can't believe there are many seven-year-old girls who wouldn't love having a real-life baby to play with. I'm sure she'll love it.'

'You're right, Ally, and forgive me for worrying about this, when you couldn't share your pregnancy with Theo.'

'Don't apologise, I understand. Although as I admitted to you before, now all the partners are about to arrive, I wish I had one of my own . . . Someone in my corner, you know? I called Thom today to check on Felix – who is fine – but Thom definitely can't make the cruise. Anyway,' Ally said, changing the subject, 'isn't Chrissie great? And she puts CeCe in her place when she needs to.'

'She does, and CeCe seems far more relaxed than she's ever been.'

'It's going to be quite a gathering, isn't it?' Ally smiled. 'Let's hope everyone gets on okay.'

'We've all got to accept that we won't get on with some of them as well as others, but that happens in all families. Pa would have loved to have seen us all here together. It's just so sad he won't be there.'

'Yes, but not wanting to go all Tiggy on you, he'll be there in spirit, I'm sure,' Ally comforted her.

46

Merry
West Cork

I had just started to stir awake when my room phone rang.
'Hello?'

'Merry, it's Katie. I haven't woken you, have I?'

'Yes, but that's all right. What is it?'

'I'm just about to go in to work for my shift, but I had a
couple of thoughts last night after we'd spoken. About Bobby,
and you wanting to find out what's happened to him. I still think
it's worth contacting his younger sister, Helen. When I saw her
at Nuala's funeral, she told me she'd moved to Cork. Noiro isn't
a common name, so you might find her in the telephone directory. Sure, you could ask reception – they're bound to have one.'

'Thanks, Katie.' I could hear my voice already wavering
with nerves at even the thought of it.

'Strikes me that you need to put this to bed now, Merry.
Let me know how you get on. Bye now.'

'Bye.'

Just after I'd finished dressing, there was a knock on my door.

'Who is it?' I barked.

'It's me, Jack.'

I opened the door and he came in, shaking his head.

'Honestly, Mum, who were you expecting, other than me, MK or housekeeping?'

'I'm sorry, I'm just a little paranoid at the moment.'

'You're telling me. Now listen, the sooner you explain what is spooking you, the better.'

'I will, Jack, I will. Are we going down for breakfast?'

'We are, but I just wanted to tell you something first. Last night, MK checked her emails and . . . well, she found one from her mum. I mean, this woman that—'

'I know what you mean, Jack, it's all right. I suppose you're here because she's worried about upsetting me?'

'Yes.'

'Right, I'll go and speak to her.'

I brushed past Jack and walked down the corridor to Mary-Kate's room.

'Hi, Mum,' she said, lowering her eyes as she opened the door to me.

'Jack's just told me your news. Come here,' I said as I stepped inside, then opened my arms to wrap them around her. When I finally pulled away from her, I could see her eyes were wet with tears.

'I just don't want to upset you, Mum. I mean, the only reason I decided to find out in the first place was because of the whole missing sister thing.'

'I know, sweetheart, and you absolutely do not need to feel guilty about it.'

'You mean, you don't mind?'

'I'd be lying if I said I wasn't apprehensive, but our relationship has always been special, and I have to trust that. Hearts are big spaces if you let them be. If your birth mum wants to be part of your life in the future, then I'm sure yours can make room for her in there too.'

My daughter's gaze finally met my eyes. 'Wow, Mum, you're amazing. Thank you.'

'Please don't thank me, Mary-Kate, you don't need to. Now then, what did this email say?'

'Do you want me to read it to you?'

'Why don't you just give me the general details?' I said as I walked over to a chair and sat down in it. Despite what my mouth was saying, I only hoped that my heart really could be as generous as I was telling my daughter it was. Jack stepped into the room, obviously having waited outside in the corridor until he could hear that our emotions had settled down. He sat down on the bed beside his sister, who had opened up her laptop to find the email.

'Well, her full name is Michelle MacNeish, and she's of Scottish heritage originally, like Dad. She lives in Christchurch and was seventeen when she got pregnant with me. The long and short of it is, she ignored it for the first few months and was too scared to tell her parents. At the time, she was about to go to uni because she wanted to train to be a doctor . . .' Mary-Kate consulted the email. 'She says, "I did tell my parents eventually, but because they are quite religious we had a massive showdown. In the end, they agreed to support me through university as long as I had the baby, then gave it up for adoption."

'She goes on to say that she didn't feel that she was equipped to have a child so young, especially as the dad – her boyfriend at the time – wasn't interested in having a family with her. They split up soon after and apparently my biological dad is married and works as the manager of a hardware store in Christchurch. Michelle's a fully fledged surgeon these days, Mum. She's also married with a couple of young kids.'

'So . . . how do you feel?'

'About the fact she gave me up? I'm not sure yet, but to be honest, if that had happened to me at seventeen, just when I was on the verge of leaving home and going off to uni, I don't think I would have been too chuffed to find myself pregnant either. I guess I understand why she did it. At least she *had* me,' Mary-Kate shrugged, 'she could have got rid of me.'

'Yes, she could have, sweetheart, and thank God she didn't. Does she want to meet you?'

'She hasn't said. She just asked me if I'd like to email her back and tell her a little about myself. But she says there's no pressure or anything. I mean, if I don't want to.'

'Do you think you will write back?'

'Maybe, yeah. It might be interesting to meet up with her eventually, though I'm not, like, desperate or anything. But what that email also means is that I'm probably not the missing sister that CeCe and the other sisters were looking for. Michelle is definitely my biological mother and my biological father is local too. She says there are hospital records of my birth and everything. It makes me a bit sad, actually; I'd got into the idea of being part of that big family of adopted girls.'

'So, you're not blood-related to the sisters' adoptive father, even if they thought you might be. Of course, as you said before, it's possible this Pa Salt guy wanted to adopt you too, but Mum and Dad got there first,' Jack shrugged.

'You mean, perhaps Jock and I were approved by the agency and he wasn't?' I asked.

'Something like that, yeah,' said Jack, 'but who knows? And I'm getting to the point where I want to say, who cares? It's only relevant if this Pa Salt is a proper relative, isn't it?'

'True,' said Mary-Kate, biting her lip. 'And I suppose I do have new siblings now through Michelle . . . How weird.'

'It's okay to take all this slowly,' I said to her, 'and as a matter of fact,' I added, making a decision, 'I have something I need to tell you. About me, I mean. It's nothing to worry about, but after what you've just said, it's relevant. So why

don't we go and have some breakfast and I'll tell you while we eat?'

'Hold on a minute' – Mary-Kate's forkful of bacon and egg hung suspended between her plate and her mouth – 'you're telling me that you were dumped on a priest's doorstep as a newborn? And then this priest and a man called Ambrose gave you to their cleaner, whose baby had just died, to save you from life in an orphanage?'

'That's about the size of it, yes. I was only called Mary because the poor baby I'd replaced was too.'

'And they pretended that you were her,' Jack added.

'Which was a good thing actually, or Ambrose would have chosen some outrageous Greek name for me,' I chuckled.

'So, Mum, how are you coping with the fact that your family isn't your family, after all these years of thinking they were?' Mary-Kate asked.

I smiled inwardly, because it was the one area in which my daughter had far more experience than I did. And I'd taken a chance that sharing the fact I was also adopted might help her too.

'It was a shock at first,' I said. 'But a bit like you, when I met my brother and sister again after all these years, the blood bit didn't matter.'

'See, Mum?' said Mary-Kate. 'It doesn't, does it?'

'No, and especially because I have no idea – and nor does Ambrose or anyone else – who my biological family are.'

Mary-Kate gave a small chuckle, then wiped her mouth with her napkin. 'Sorry, Mum, I know it's not funny but, like, how the tables have suddenly turned. I now know where I came from, but can we help you find out who you really are?'

'At nearly fifty-nine, sweetheart, I think I know who I am. Genetics aren't important to me. Although looking back now, I knew that I was different. When I went away to boarding school and then university, everyone back in West Cork used to tease me about being the missing sister, not because of the Greek myth like Bobby, but because I wasn't at home anymore. And then I really was missing for thirty-seven years.'

'It's all a bit of a coincidence, isn't it?' countered Mary-Kate. 'I mean, this whole family that thinks I'm related to them in some way, but it's actually you who really *has* been the missing sister.'

'Yes,' I sighed, 'but for now, I suggest we forget all about them. Let's try and actually enjoy the three of us being down here in this lovely part of the world and getting to know my family again.'

'Will you tell your brothers and sisters, Mum?' asked Jack. 'About you being parachuted into their family?'

'No,' I said, with surprising certainty. 'I don't believe I will.'

The three of us spent the rest of the day driving along the coast, then enjoying a relaxed late lunch at Hayes Bar overlooking the almost Mediterranean-looking Glandore Bay. We returned through Castlefreke village, where the ruined castle stood in its dense forest, and I recounted the ghost stories my parents had told me about it. Taking the byroads along the coast, we found a tiny deserted cove near a village called Ardfield, and both my kids immediately put on their swimming gear and ran into the freezing cold sea.

'Come in, Mum! The water's fantastic!'

I shook my head lazily and lay on the pebbles looking up at the sun, which was so graciously making a rare appearance.

I'd never told my kids I couldn't swim and was hideously afraid of the ocean, like many Irish of my generation. But so much of what was then wasn't now, and after hundreds of years of stagnation, it seemed that Ireland was reinventing itself in every way. The mass poverty and deprivation I'd known when I was younger seemed to have lessened considerably. The Catholic Church – such a huge part of my upbringing – had lost its claw-like grip, and the hard border between the North and South had come down after the Good Friday Agreement was signed in 1998. The Agreement had even been voted for in a referendum across Ireland. And – mostly – it had held for ten years.

I picked up a pebble from beside me and, sitting up, clenched it in both hands. Whoever I really was, there was little doubt I'd been born here on this land. For better or worse, there was a big part of me that would always belong right here, on this beautiful but troubled island.

'I have to know what happened to him before I leave,' I muttered. Then I saw my children running towards me, so I collected their towels and walked to meet them.

Back at the Inchydoney Lodge, as the kids went off to find hot chocolates in the pub, I asked the receptionist if I could borrow a telephone directory. I took it over to one of the comfortable sofas and, with trembling hands, found the 'N's.

N-o . . . N-o-f . . . N-o-g . . . N-o-i . . .

My finger landed on the one and only 'Noiro' listed. And the initial was 'H'.

My heart beating fast now, I scribbled down the number and the address. 'Ballinhassig,' I said to myself, the name sounding familiar. Handing the telephone directory back to the receptionist, I asked her if she knew where Ballinhassig was.

'Sure, 'tis a small village – well, not even a village really – this side of Cork airport. Here now.' The woman, whose name badge said she was called Jane, took a map of West Cork and pointed it out.

'Thanks so much.'

Then I went into the pub to join my children and have a cup of tea.

'MK and I were thinking we might go up to Cork City and look around tomorrow morning if that's okay with you, Mum,' said Jack. 'Fancy coming along?'

'Maybe. There's actually a friend I want to visit who lives near there. I'll give her a call, then I can drop you two in the city and go and see her. Okay?'

They both nodded and then we all went upstairs to our rooms to freshen up before dinner. Taking the piece of paper out of my handbag, I sat on my bed and laid it nervously by the phone. As I picked up the receiver to dial Helen Noiro's number, I could see my hands were shaking.

She probably won't even answer, I told myself. But a female voice did, after only two rings.

'Hello?'

'Oh, er, hello,' I replied, wishing I'd rehearsed what I was going to say. 'Is that Helen?'

'It is indeed. Who's speaking?'

'My name's Mary McDougal, but you might remember me as Merry O'Reilly. We used to live quite close to each other when we were younger.' There was a pause on the line before Helen answered.

'I do remember you, o'course. What can I be doing for you?'

'Well, I've been abroad for a long time and I'm looking

up . . . old friends. I'm coming up to the city tomorrow morning and I wondered if I could drop in?'

'Tomorrow morning . . . Hold on whilst I check something . . . Okay, I have to be out of the house by noon. How about eleven?'

'That sounds perfect.'

'Grand. If you're driving, it's easy to find; as you're coming down from Cork past the airport and into the village, look for the garage on the left-hand side. I'm the white bungalow next to it.'

'Okay, Helen, I will. Thanks for that, and see you tomorrow. Bye.'

I put down the receiver and scribbled the directions underneath the address. I didn't know what I'd been expecting, but it wasn't the casual reaction Helen had just given me.

Maybe she didn't even know what had gone on between me and her brother. Or maybe she did and thought I was just a girl from the past that Bobby had long since forgotten.

'Maybe he settled down and is married with a few kids,' I muttered to myself as I stood up, applied a little lipstick and left the room to go and have supper.

Having dropped the kids off in the centre of Cork the following morning, I headed back towards the airport. As we'd gone through the village of Ballinhassig on the way there, I'd glanced around and noticed the garage Helen had mentioned. It took no longer than twenty minutes before it came back into view.

There was a small, white-painted bungalow next door, and I pulled into the drive that had an attempt at a patch of garden to one side of it.

Switching off the engine, I suddenly wished someone was

with me. What if Bobby actually *lived* with his sister? What if he was inside this nondescript bungalow and would come for me, then hold a gun to my throat . . .

I sent up a quick prayer begging for protection, then opened the car door and walked to the front entrance. I tried the bell, but it didn't work, so I knocked instead. A few seconds later, a woman dressed in a smart navy-blue suit, her shiny dark hair cut into a bob and her make-up perfect, answered the door.

'Hi there, Merry . . . Everybody called you that in the old days, didn't they?' she said as she ushered me through the door.

'They did, yes, and still do.'

'Come through to the kitchen. Is it coffee or tea you'd be wanting?'

'A glass of water will do me fine,' I said as I sat down at a small table. The kitchen was as nondescript as the bungalow and not nearly as smart as its resident.

'So, what brings you to these parts after all this time?' Helen asked as she poured some coffee from a machine into a mug and came to sit down next to me, handing me a glass of tap water.

'I thought it was time I visited some friends and family. And, well . . .' I brought out the family tree that Katie had given me. I'd decided that the familial connection between us should be the initial pretext for my visit.

'Ah, don't tell me you've been living in America and wanted to come back to explore your roots? A good few tourists that pass through the duty-free shop are after that *craic*.'

'That's where you work?'

'It is indeed. I do all the promotions for them, like hand out tasters of whiskey or portions of a new local cheese we're selling,' she shrugged. 'I enjoy it and I'm after meeting some interesting people there too. So now, what have you to show me?'

'Maybe you already know this, but it looks like we shared the same grandparents.'

'Yes, my mammy told me before she died. She said that your mam and my dad were half-siblings.'

'They were.' I turned the tree around and pointed to Nuala and Christy's names. 'If you follow the tree, there's your daddy's parents and there's you. And Bobby.'

Helen's glossy nails traced a path down the tree.

'It means we're cousins. Mind you, 'tis hardly surprising, is it? Everyone in that area is a cousin of someone.'

'I only ever saw a glimpse of Nuala, my – *our* – grandmother, once. And that was on the day of my mother's funeral when I was eleven. Nuala and Hannah were estranged.'

'Oh, I know all about that. We saw a lot o' Granny Nuala when we were younger,' said Helen. 'She and Granddad Christy were always up at our cottage, singing the old Fenian songs. When he died, and then my daddy, Granny came to live with us. What a load o' chat she filled Bobby's head with,' she sighed. 'You remember those walks home from school.'

'I do,' I said, hardly believing we'd moved on to this topic so quickly.

'Would I be remembering right if I said that you were at Trinity College, while Bobby was at University College, in Dublin?'

'You would be,' I nodded.

'And wasn't he always sweet on you?'

'Yes,' I said, feeling like the mistress of understatement. 'Um, how is he?'

'Well, 'tis a bit of a story, but sure, you'd already be knowing that he got mixed up with the republican crowd at university?'

'I would, yes.'

'Jesus, the venom inside him and the stuff he used to come out with . . .' Helen gave me a direct gaze. 'Do you remember how angry he got? He was so passionate about "the cause", as he called it.'

'Is he dead, Helen?' I asked, not able to bear the suspense any longer. 'You talk about him as though he's in the past.'

'No, he's not dead, or at least he hasn't left this earth. But to be honest, he might as well have done. I thought you were up in Dublin in the early seventies? Surely you'd have heard?'

'I left Ireland and went abroad in 1971. Bobby told me he was going on protests in Belfast with the northern Catholics. I even heard a story that he was shielding a Provisional IRA man on the run down in Dublin.'

Helen looked at me uncertainly, then sighed. 'Listen now, it isn't a subject I'd be wanting to talk about to just anyone, but seeing as you're family . . . Wait there.'

I did, because even if she told me to leave, I wouldn't have been able to. I felt weak all over, and though my body was still, I could feel the blood rushing through my veins.

'There now, read that,' she said as she returned and handed me a sheet of paper.

I saw it was a page photocopied from an old newspaper, dated March 1972.

UCD STUDENT JAILED FOR ARSON ON PROTESTANT HOUSE

Bobby Noiro, a twenty-two-year-old student of Irish Politics at UCD, has been sentenced to three years in jail for attempting to burn down a house in Drumcondra. Telling the court he was a member of the Provisional IRA, Mr Noiro pleaded guilty to arson. The house was unoccupied at the time.

During sentencing, Mr Noiro had to be restrained as he attempted to break free of the guards. During the struggle, he shouted IRA slogans and made threats against leading members of the Democratic Unionist Party, the DUP.

On sentencing him, Mr Justice Finton McNalley said that he was taking into account Noiro's youth and the fact that he may have been influenced by his peer group.

Judge McNalley also cited the fact that nobody was injured in the fire. The Provisional IRA has denied any part in the attack.

'Helen . . .' I looked up at her. 'I don't know what to say.'

'Does it surprise you?'

'If I'm honest, no. Was he released after his three years?'

'Well, when Mammy first went to visit him in prison, she came back in bits, crying buckets. Said Bobby had been ranting and raving, and the guards had had to take him away. "He's not well in the head, like your daddy," I remember her saying. And sure,' Helen sighed, 'he caused so much strife in the jail that they moved him to a high-security prison where he could be better controlled. When he was released, they tried to re-introduce him to society, but he accused one of the men at the halfway house of being a "bastard Proddy" and tried to strangle him. After that, he was assessed and diagnosed with paranoid schizophrenia. He was moved to the psychiatric hospital in Portlaoise in 1978. He's never come out,' she said grimly, 'and nor will he. After Mammy died, I went up to see him. I'm not sure he recognised me, Merry. He sat there and cried like a baby.'

'I . . . I'm so sorry, Helen.'

'Turns out the madness runs in the family. You won't be knowing this, but Cathal, our daddy, committed suicide; he set fire to our barn, then hung himself inside it. Mammy also told me that our Great-Uncle Colin – Christy's brother – was stone mad too, and ended up in an asylum. That's why Christy came to live on the farm after his mammy died of influenza and grew up with Nuala and her brothers and sisters.'

'Bobby told me your daddy had died in a barn fire, an

accident,' I breathed. 'Maybe that's what he was told by your mammy.'

'Yes, we both were, Merry, though I was just a babe when it happened. Did Bobby ever . . . how can I put this? Hurt or threaten you?'

'He did, yes,' I said, and the words came out of me like a boulder that had held back a river of emotion. 'He'd found out about . . . something I'd done that he didn't approve of. He had a gun, Helen, which he said had been given to him by the Provisional IRA. He put it to my throat . . . and . . . and said that if I carried on seeing this boy he didn't like, h-he'd have him and all my family sh-shot by the people he knew in his terrorist organisation.'

'And you believed him?'

'Of course I did, Helen! Back then, the Troubles were just beginning. Tension was running high in Dublin, and I knew how passionate Bobby was about the North being returned to the Republic of Ireland, and his anger at the way the Catholics were treated across the border. He'd joined one of the more radical student groups at UCD and was always asking me to go with him on his protests.'

'Merry, I think he must have used the old pistol that had belonged to Finn, our grandmother Nuala's first husband. She kept it and passed it on to our father, Cathal. When he committed suicide, it passed into Bobby's hands. So now, I suppose he wasn't lying to you if he said that it had been given to him by the IRA, but it certainly wasn't during the recent Troubles. 'Twas ninety years old, Merry, and I doubt Bobby knew how to load it, let alone fire it.'

'Are you sure, Helen? I swear he was involved with what was going on at that time.'

'As a student rebel, maybe, but no more. If he had been, the Provisional IRA would have taken great pride in announcing they were responsible for the burning of that Protestant house in Dublin. When I came up to support Mammy during the trial, I met one of his friends from UCD. We went for a chat and Con told me that everyone who knew him had been worried about his mental state. He'd lost his girl; I'm realising now he might have meant you . . . ?'

'I . . . I think he probably did but, Helen, I was never "his girl". I mean, Bobby was a childhood friend,' I sighed, 'but everywhere I went, he seemed to be there. My friend Bridget used to call him my stalker.'

'That would be Bobby, all right,' said Helen. 'He'd have fixations and would have believed that you *were* his girl, and that he was part of the Provisional IRA. But it was all in his mind, Merry, and as the psychiatrists I've talked to since have told me, it was part of the delusions.'

'I never, ever gave him any kind of sign that I wanted to be with him in a romantic way, Helen, I swear,' I said, gulping back tears. 'But he wouldn't take no for an answer. And then when he found out about me and my boyfriend, *and* that he was a Protestant, he said he'd kill us and our families. So I left Ireland and went abroad. Ever since then, I've lived in fear, because he told me he and his friends would hunt me down wherever I tried to hide.'

'Leaving was probably the sensible thing to do,' Helen nodded. 'There was no doubt Bobby was a violent man when he was in the grip of one of his episodes. But as for his IRA terrorist friends hunting you down – 'twas all nonsense. His friend Con confirmed that. When the police interviewed one of the real Provisional IRA mob after the fire, he swore blind he'd never even heard of Bobby Noiro.' She took a sip of coffee, sympathy in her eyes. 'So you left, but what about your boyfriend? Him being Protestant and all – now that was like a red rag to a bull for Bobby.'

The boulder had settled back in my stomach again, and I could barely speak. 'We lost touch,' I managed, because that was a different story. 'I married someone else and was happy in New Zealand.'

'Ah, 'tis good you found a home and a husband, so,' said Helen. 'There now, Merry, you have every right to be upset,' she said, reaching out to put her hand over mine. ''Twas terrible what Bobby put you through,' she continued, 'but the signs were always there, weren't they? Like on all those walks home, he'd be racing like a mad thing across the field ahead of us, hide in the ditch, then as we passed by, spring out and shout, "Bang! You're dead!" 'Twas a childhood game that became a lifelong obsession, fuelled by our grandmother and all her talk of war. I don't often go to see him, but now Mammy's dead, 'tis me who gets the reports from the hospital. He still talks about the revolution, as if he's part of it . . .' She shut her eyes for a moment and I took a deep breath, simply glad to be with some-one who understood exactly who the person that had haunted me for so long actually was.

'Did he harm you, Helen?'

'No, thanks be to God, he didn't, but I'd learnt from the cradle to be invisible. If he was in one of his tempers, I'd take myself off and hide. Mammy protected me too; what a terrible life she had, what with Daddy not right in the head, then her son. I do remember her saying . . .'

'What?'

'Well, how upset she'd been that your mam, Maggie, hadn't come to Daddy's funeral. He was her half-brother after all – Nuala's son with Christy. I'd reckon that was the reason we were never allowed to come near Cross Farm.'

'Family members not turning up for funerals has caused a lot of grief in our family,' I sighed.

'Listen now, Merry,' Helen said, 'I have to be off soon – my shift at the airport starts at one – but would you be able to come back and see me? I'm happy to answer any more questions you might be thinking of, so.'

'That's very kind of you, Helen, and I can't thank you enough for being so open and honest with me.'

'What's there to lie about? All these years you've been living in fear, thinking that real terrorists were after you, and yes, Bobby *was* a threat to you then, but if only you'd known that a year later he got locked up and will stay that way for the rest of his life . . .'

'It would have made a huge difference.' I gave Helen a glimmer of a smile.

'I'd no idea he'd been after you, but I moved away up to Cork City after Mam died,' she said. 'I wanted to make a fresh start. You know how it is,' she added as we walked to the door.

'I do. So, you live here alone?' I asked.

'I do, so, and 'tis just fine by me. I've a way of picking the wrong fellow, but now I've my work, my girlfriends and my independence. You take care now, Merry, and give me a bell if you need anything.' She gave me a brief but firm hug.

'I will, and thanks a million, Helen.'

I walked to my car on wobbly legs and sat down heavily behind the steering wheel.

Bobby's securely behind bars, Merry. He can never hurt you again, I told myself. *He never* was *able to hurt you for all these years, and everything he told you was a product of his imagination . . .*

I steered the car out of the drive, then took the first lane I saw. Parking my car between two large fields, I climbed over the fence and walked fast and hard between grazing cows. Rain was threatening, and grey clouds were hanging low overhead, but I sat down on the rough grass and began to sob.

It's over, Merry, it's really over . . . He can't ever hurt you again. You're safe, you're safe . . .

It took me a long time to cry out all the tension, after holding it in for thirty-seven long years. I thought of all that had been lost because of it . . .

'And found,' I whispered, thinking of my beloved children and dear, dear Jock, who'd swept me up in his capable arms and put a blanket of security and love around me.

Looking at my watch, I saw it was almost one o'clock and I was late to meet the children for lunch. 'Children!' I muttered to myself as I brushed myself down and headed for the car. 'Jack's thirty-two, for goodness' sake!'

Deciding that he really was a big boy now and perfectly capable of getting them both back to the hotel in a taxi, I called him and said I had a migraine – which wasn't a lie as my head was thumping – and drove slowly back to Clonakilty. As I passed Bandon, I saw the turning to Timoleague, and on instinct I took it. There was somewhere I wanted to go.

I wended my way through the familiar streets and parked the car next to the church. It was a huge building for such a small village and there was something moving about the tiny stone-built Protestant church just below it and then the ruins of the Franciscan friary standing right out into the water.

'What suffering has come from the differences in how we worshipped our God,' I said out loud. Then I walked into the church where I had prayed and taken Mass every Sunday, and seen my mother lying in her coffin.

Walking down the aisle, I genuflected and curtseyed automatically at the altar, then turned to my right where a frame full of votive candles stood, their flames flickering in the draught creeping through the old windows. Whenever I'd come back from boarding school, I'd always been comforted by lighting one for my mother. Today I did the same, then dropped some more cents into the box as I lit another one for Bobby.

I forgive you, Bobby Noiro, for all you put me through. I'm sorry for your continual suffering.

Then I lit one for Jock. He'd been a Protestant by birth, coming from a Scots Presbyterian background. We'd married at the Church of the Good Shepherd by Lake Tekapo, under the magnificent Mount Cook. It had been interdenominational, welcoming people of all faiths through its door. At the time, I could hardly believe such a thing existed, but the fact that it *did* had made the day even more wonderful. We'd invited a small group of friends and Jock's sweet and welcoming family, and the ceremony had been simple but beautiful. Afterwards, there'd been a drinks party on the Hermitage Hotel terrace, where we had first met and worked together.

I went to sit down on one of the pews, and bent my head in prayer.

'Dear God, give me the strength to no longer live in fear, and to be honest with my children . . .'

Eventually, I stepped out into the church graveyard, where generations of the family I'd believed was mine by birth had been buried. I went to my mother's grave and knelt down on the grass. I saw that a spray of wild flowers was arranged in a vase and presumed it was one of my sisters or brothers. Beside her was my father's grave, the stone less weathered.

'Mammy,' I whispered, 'I know everything you did for me, and how much you loved me, even though I wasn't your blood. I miss you.'

Wandering along the lines, I saw Hannah's and her husband Ryan's graves, then Nuala's. My grandmother had been interred alongside Christy and the rest of our clan, not with her beloved Finn up in Clogagh. I sent up a prayer, hoping that all of them rested in peace.

After meandering through the family graves, I looked for Father O'Brien's headstone, but couldn't find it. Eventually, I drove home, my mind feeling curiously empty. Maybe by allowing myself to acknowledge the trauma I had been through and its physical and mental effects on me over the decades, now I could finally begin to heal.

'No more secrets, Merry . . .' I said to myself as I arrived at the hotel, parked the car and walked inside. A note in my pigeonhole told me the children were already back from Cork. I went up to my room and downed a finger of whiskey. It was time. Summoning Mary-Kate and Jack to my room, I closed the door behind the three of us.

'What's up, Mum? You look very serious,' Jack queried as I indicated they should both sit down.

'I feel it. This morning I went to see somebody, and after I talked to her, I decided that, well, I needed to tell you a bit more about my past.'

'Whatever it is, Mum, don't worry, we'll understand. Won't we, Jacko?' said Mary-Kate.

'Course we will,' Jack smiled at me encouragingly. 'Come on then, Mum, get on with it.'

So I told them the story of Bobby Noiro, and about how he'd come up to uni in Dublin while I'd been at Trinity.

'Trinity was, and still is, a Protestant university, and University College was Catholic,' I explained. 'These days, of course, it hardly matters, but back then, when what the Irish have always called "the Troubles" were beginning, it mattered a lot. Especially to somebody like Bobby Noiro, who had grown up in a household with an intrinsic hatred for the British, and what he and many Irish republicans saw as the theft of Northern Ireland for their Protestant citizens. Catholics who ended up stuck across the border in the North often weren't well treated and were always last in line for new housing and any jobs on offer.' I paused, struggling to simplify what was such a very big story. 'Anyway, I settled into university very well, and absolutely loved it – what with Ambrose teaching Classics there, and me studying the same subject, it was what you two would call a no-brainer for me to follow in his footsteps. However, Bobby didn't approve – I think I mentioned him to you when I was telling the story of my childhood in West Cork, Jack.'

'You did. He sounded like a really weird kid.'

I then told them what had happened in Dublin.

'All these years, I've lived in fear that he'd find me, or send his friends in the IRA to hunt me down. I know it sounds ridiculous, but he was terrifying,' I gulped. 'And as I told you, he was imprisoned for burning down a Protestant family's house. Well, that's why I left Ireland and ended up in New Zealand.'

Mary-Kate came and sat down next to me on the edge of the bed where I'd been perching and put her arm around me.

'It must have been terrible for you, thinking that he was after you for all these years, but it's all over now, Mum. He can never harm you again, can he?'

'No, he can't. Today is the first time I actually know that.'

'Why didn't you tell us any of this before?' asked Jack.

'Let's be honest, even if I had, would you have been interested in listening? Is any child ever really interested in hearing stories of their parents' past? I used to hate it when Bobby went on about the Irish revolution, singing those Fenian songs. My mum and dad never said anything about their past, because of the family rift.'

'What family rift?' asked Jack.

I was very tired now. 'It's a long story, which if you *are* interested, I'm happy to tell you one day. However, tomorrow morning, I'm packing both of you off to the Michael Collins Centre up at Castleview. At the very least, you can learn about the local hero who originally released Ireland from the grip of the British.'

Mary-Kate rolled her eyes, which made me smile.

'See?' I said. 'You're not interested. But as he did have a big impact on my own upbringing and subsequent life, you'll just have to put up with it for a couple of hours.'

'Was this Michael Collins Bobby Noiro's hero?'

'As a matter of fact, Jack, quite the opposite. Anyway, let's get something to eat, shall we? I'm starving.'

When I returned to the room, I saw the message light was flashing on my phone. It was from Katie, just asking me how I'd got on, trying to track down 'your friend', as she put it.

I dialled her mobile number and she answered on the second ring. 'Well?' she said.

'I'll tell you when I see you, but the good news is, that even though Bobby isn't dead, he's certainly never going to come after me again.'

'Then I'm so happy for you, Merry. You must feel quite a weight off your shoulders now.'

'Oh, I do, Katie, yes. Also, while you're on, I popped down to the church in Timoleague this afternoon and I was wandering round the family graves. Then I looked for Father O'Brien's, but I couldn't find him. Do you know what happened to him?'

'I do indeed, Merry. As a matter of fact, I saw him myself only this afternoon.'

'What?! How?'

'He lives at the old people's home in Clonakilty where I work. He never budged from his Timoleague parish, even though I know he was given offers of promotion. Anyway, he finally decided that he was getting too long in the tooth to carry on, and he retired five years ago when he turned eighty. You'll be remembering that draughty old presbytery he lived in, so a year ago, despite protesting he could take care of himself and he wanted to die in his own bed, he was brought to us. Would you like to see him?'

'Oh, Katie, I'd love to see him! Is he . . . all there?'

'You mean, does he have all his marbles? He does, 'tis only his body that's after letting him down. Riddled with arthritis, he is, God bless him, from all those years o' living in that house, I shouldn't wonder. They've built a new one for the next priest, which is sheltered from that evil wind which rattled through the panes.'

'I'll come to visit him tomorrow morning then.'

'Grand job. I'm up at John and Sinéad's, baking for the family hooley on Sunday.'

'Katie, please, there's no need for everyone to go to a lot of trouble.'

''Tis no trouble. A family get-together is long overdue anyway, and there'll be plenty of room for all the kids to run around outside.'

'The forecast is for rain tomorrow.'

'Ah, sure it is, but 'twill be warm rain at least.'

'Oh, just before you go, I was wondering if I could invite Helen Noiro to the party. I mean, she is related to us and—'

''Tis a grand idea, Merry. Bye now. I need to go check on my pie.'

Going over to draw my curtains and seeing there was a puddle of water on the floor from the rain blown inside by the wind, I shut out the roar of the waves. In bed, I tried to file away everything that I'd learnt today, but I was so exhausted, I fell asleep immediately.

47

The old people's home was light and airy, even though that particular hospital smell of disinfectant lingered strongly in the air. I asked for Katie at reception and she bustled through, giving me a big smile and a hug.

'He's in the day room, and look now, I haven't said who his visitor is. I'd say he's in for a grand surprise. Ready?' she asked me as we stood outside the door.

'Ready.'

We threaded through the chairs occupied by elderly men and women who were chatting or playing board games with their visitors. Katie pointed to a man looking out of the window.

'See him there in the wheelchair? I've put him in the corner, so you two can have a little privacy.'

I studied Father O'Brien as I approached. He'd always been a handsome man, as my mammy and the rest of the young women used to whisper to each other. His thick head of dark hair had turned white and had receded somewhat, but he still had a good amount of it. The lines etched onto his face gave him an added air of gravitas.

'Father, here's your visitor,' Katie said, ushering me forward. 'You might remember her.'

Father O'Brien's still brilliant blue eyes gazed up at me and slowly, the look in them altered from disinterest, to puzzlement, and then eventually to amazement.

'Merry O'Reilly? Is that you?' Then he shook his head as though he was dreaming. 'Sure, it can't be,' he muttered to himself, turning away from me.

'It *is* me, Father. I was Merry O'Reilly, but I'm now Mrs Merry McDougal.'

I squatted down so I could look up at him, just like I'd done when I was a little girl on the visits to his house that had meant so much to me. 'It really is me,' I smiled, taking his hands.

'Merry . . . Merry O'Reilly,' he whispered, and I felt his warm hands tighten on mine.

'I'll be leaving you now to chat,' said Katie.

Still clasping his hands, I stood up. 'I'm sorry if I've given you a start.'

'You've certainly got my heart beating faster than it has done for a while.' He smiled at me, dropped my hands and pointed to one of the plastic-covered easy chairs. 'Please, pull that chair closer to me and sit down.'

I did so, gulping back the tears as I felt his wonderful calm and secure essence wash over me. I realised it reminded me of the way Jock had made me feel: that I was totally safe in his presence.

'So, what brings you back to these parts after so long, Merry?'

'It was time to come home, Father.'

'Yes.'

He gazed at me, and in one glance, I felt as if he knew everything he needed to know about me. I supposed that he'd spent so long both contemplating and dealing with the human soul and its complex emotions that he could probably see into my mind.

'Unfinished business?' he said, confirming my theory.

'Yes. I'm so very happy to see you, Father. You look well.'

'I am very well, thank you.' He cast an arm around the room. 'Sadly, many of these dear people have no idea whether it's 1948 or 2008, so it doesn't always make for good conversation, but all my needs are taken care of,' he added quickly. 'And the staff here are wonderful.'

There was a long silence as both of us struggled to know what to say. I'd no idea whether I'd meant as much to him as he had always meant to me.

'Why didn't you ever come back, Merry? I know you were in Dublin, but often visited your family here. And then suddenly, you didn't.'

'No, I moved away, Father.'

'Where to?'

'New Zealand.'

'That *is* a long way away,' he nodded. 'Was it because you were in love?'

'Sort of, but it's a very long story.'

'The best ones usually are, and I've heard many of them in my confessional, I can tell you. But of course, I never would,' he said with a wink.

'From what Katie said, it's obvious you're very well loved around here, Father.'

'Thank you for saying that, and sure, I have plenty of company still coming to visit me here, but it's not my home. Ah well, I mustn't complain.'

'You're not, Father. I understand.'

'I've nowhere to put my books, you see, and I miss them. They were a love that both myself and my friend Ambrose shared. You remember him?'

He looked at me and my whole heart almost broke in two at the yearning in his eyes.

'I do, Father, yes. Where are your books?'

'In a storage facility in Cork. Never mind, I always have the good book at the ready if I need it.' He pointed to the low table between us and I recognised the small leather-bound copy of the Bible that he'd never been without. 'So, tell me, did you ever marry? Have children of your own?'

'I did, and they're both here with me. I've sent them off to visit the Michael Collins Centre. It's about time they learnt of their mother's history.'

'That man and what he did for Ireland were certainly part of yours, Merry. I was saddened to bury your grandmothers Nuala and Hannah. They both pleaded for God's forgiveness over their feud at the end. 'Tis a sad story.'

'It is. I only know of the rift between them since my sister Katie told me about it yesterday. I finally understand a lot of things,' I added, 'and I'm so glad I came back.' A tea trolley was being brought round and the echo in the room seemed to grow louder. I wanted to tell him I knew what he'd done for me all those years ago when I was a tiny baby left on his doorstep. But this was not the place or the time to bring up such a subject.

'How are you both doing?' The tea lady, with her jolly smile, had reached us. 'Tea or coffee for either of you?'

'Nothing for me, thank you. Father O'Brien?'

'Nothing, thank you.'

There was a pause as she wheeled the trolley away and we collected our thoughts.

'I'd love to meet your children,' he said.

'I'm sure that can be arranged, Father. I'd love you to meet them too. I—'

It was Katie's turn to bustle over. 'All good here?'

'Yes,' I said, wishing she would go away and give us some peace to continue the conversation I felt we both wanted to have.

'I'm sorry to interrupt but 'tis time for your physio session, Father,' she continued.

Father O'Brien's eyes filled with resignation. 'Of course,' he said. 'Can you come back another time, Merry? Bring your children?'

'Definitely.' I stood up and kissed him gently on the cheek. 'I'll be back, I promise.'

I collected the children outside the Michael Collins Centre.

'Wow, Mum,' Jack said as he buckled his seat belt and we drove off, 'I've learnt so much. I had no idea about the Easter Rising of 1916 that sparked the Irish revolution against the British. Ireland finally became a republic in 1949 – the year you were born! Did you know that?'

'I did, yes, but I wasn't old enough to take in its significance at the time.'

'I understand now why so many Irish people were angry back then,' Mary-Kate put in from the back. 'Jacko and I went halves on a book and we're both going to read it, aren't we?'

'We are. I didn't realise how much religion played a part in it all. We never even think about whether we're Protestant or Catholic, do we, MK?' said Jack. 'It doesn't matter in New Zealand.'

'Well, here there's still die-hard Catholics and Protestants on both sides,' I said.

'What's amazing is that everyone here seems so happy and friendly. You'd never know what the country's been through from the people you meet,' commented Mary-Kate. 'The suffering was so terrible – I saw the stuff about the potato famine and . . .'

I listened to my children chatting about my homeland and

the turmoil it had been through in the past. And suddenly felt an enormous pride in just how far it had come since I was born.

Back in my room at the hotel, I sat out on the balcony, having a cup of tea. A thought had come to me since my meeting with Father O'Brien.

The question is, is it really my place to interfere?

Then again, Merry, you've spent your life hiding behind your husband and your children, never making decisions for yourself . . .

'Come on, Merry,' I told myself out loud, '*do* something for a change.'

I walked inside, telling myself the worst that could happen was that he would say no. Picking up my mobile, I dialled the number.

The phone rang three or four times before it was answered. 'Ambrose Lister here. Who's speaking, please?'

'Ambrose, it's Merry. How are you?'

'Very well indeed, thank you. And you?'

'I'm fine, thanks. Ambrose. Actually, I was just wondering if you were busy in the next couple of days?'

'Mary, I'd be lying if I said my calendar was full, but Plato awaits, as he always does.'

'I was wondering if you would consider coming down to West Cork. I . . . well, I need your help.'

'West Cork? I don't think so, Mary, it's a long journey for these old bones.'

'I promise you, Ambrose, things have improved since the last time you drove down here in your bright red Beetle,' I smiled. 'It's motorway or dual carriage and certainly tarmac all the way. How about I book you a taxi? I have a man here who I'm sure would be delighted to come and get you.'

'Mary, I would rather not, I—'

'Ambrose, I *need* you. And we're staying at the most wonderful hotel overlooking Inchydoney Beach. You remember, the huge one near Clonakilty?'

'I do remember it, yes. And the shack that stood above it. I wouldn't say it looked terribly inviting.'

'Well, this hotel is modern, with every facility you could imagine. It would also give you a chance to meet my daughter before we go back to New Zealand. Please, Ambrose, there's a mystery I need solving and only you could possibly know the answer.'

I'd now run out of ammunition to persuade him. There was a pause on the line. 'Well, if you really need me to come all that way, I have to believe that it's for good reason. What time would this taxi collect me?'

'I still need to confirm it, but how about we say eleven o'clock tomorrow morning?'

'And I shall no doubt arrive in time for a cup of bedtime cocoa.'

'Nonsense, Ambrose. It'll take you three hours at the most, so I'd hope you'd be in time for afternoon tea, taken with a gorgeous view of the Atlantic. I shall book you a lovely room and look forward to seeing you tomorrow.'

'Very well, Mary. I will see you then. I have something to give you that arrived here only this morning. For now, I will say goodbye.'

Switching off my mobile, I threw it down on the bed and then gave a little whoop of triumph. There was a knock on my door and I went to open it.

'Hi, Mum, you look happy,' Mary-Kate said as she wandered inside.

'I feel it, actually. Or at least, I think I do,' I shrugged. 'I've just done something that I hope will make the lives of two people I love very much better. Anyway, are you okay?'

'Yeah, I'm good. Listen, Mum, I was just having a chat with Jack and . . .'

'What is it?'

'Well, we both feel we should let Tiggy and her sisters know that I've found my birth family. And it's unlikely that I'm the missing sister they're looking for.'

'You don't know that for sure, Mary-Kate. Your birth parents could have some connection to this dead father of theirs.'

'Maybe, but the point is, I feel I should at least give them the name of my birth mum. Then they can investigate themselves whether there's a connection. It's obvious they're desperate to find the missing sister so she can join them on their cruise. Would you mind if I gave them a call?'

'Of course not, sweetheart. It's your decision to make, not mine.'

'Okay, thanks. And . . .'

'What is it?' I asked. I could see she was about to broach a sensitive subject by the look in her eyes.

'Would you mind if I also told them that you were adopted too? I mean, Jack and I were saying that the emerald ring was yours originally and . . . Mum, the missing sister could be you.'

'I doubt it – those adopted girls are all a similar age to you and Jack. No.' I shook my head. 'I realise you'd like to have a connection to them, but unfortunately for you, I'm not it.'

'So you don't mind if I tell them you were adopted then?'

'Go ahead,' I sighed. 'It doesn't matter to me one way or the other. I'm sorry, sweetheart, but seeing they've managed to ruin my Grand Tour, in truth, I just want to forget all about them.'

'I understand, Mum, but thanks anyway. See you at dinner.'

Giving me an apologetic smile, Mary-Kate left my room.

48

Atlantis

'I have news,' said Ally, arriving on the terrace where Maia was serving up a Brazilian stew.

'What?' CeCe asked.

'That was Mary-Kate. She called to tell us that she's found her birth parents.'

'Wow, that *is* news,' whistled Chrissie.

'It is and it isn't, because obviously, until Mary-Kate has established proper contact with her mum, I don't think it's our place to start investigating her parents, and she won't do that until she's back home in New Zealand.'

'Which will be way after the cruise,' said Maia. 'Sit down, Ally, before the food gets cold. Maybe if we could get in contact with Georg, he'd at least be able to make some discreet enquiries.'

'I tried his mobile earlier and he's not picking up,' CeCe shrugged. 'Maia, this is delicious. Thanks, Ma,' she added as Ma poured wine into the women's glasses and then sat down herself.

'It is,' said Ally. 'There's also something else Mary-Kate told me.'

'What?' Maia asked.

'She told me that her mum, Merry, has just found out that she was adopted too.'

The entire table looked at her in total silence.

'How come?' said Maia. 'Tiggy said they were off to visit her long-lost family in the south-west of Ireland.'

'Mary-Kate didn't go into detail, but Merry was apparently found on a priest's doorstep and replaced a baby that had just died.'

'Right. Well, does that mean it could be her that's the missing sister?' CeCe asked.

'But she's old, isn't she? Far older than you guys anyway,' Chrissie pointed out.

'Be careful, Chrissie, Merry and I are only middle-aged these days,' Ma smiled.

'Sorry, but you know what I mean,' Chrissie blushed.

'Of course. But we must remember the ring was Merry's originally,' Ma added.

'You're right, Ma,' Ally breathed. 'So, do we have two possibilities for the missing sister now?'

'Maybe, but with two Marys, who have both owned the ring, we need to speak to Georg.' Maia took a sip of her water.

'So, do we hold to our invitation and have Merry and her two children on the cruise anyway?' Ally asked the table. 'I mean, if the ring is the proof – and Georg was adamant it *was* – one of them has got to be the missing sister.'

'I don't know,' Ma said softly. 'This is a very big occasion for all of you. And these women—'

'And Jack, Mary-Kate's brother,' put in Ally.

'Well, the three of them are strangers.'

There was silence around the table as the girls ate and thought.

'Ma's right,' said Maia eventually. 'We knew and loved Pa

so very much, and they didn't know him. It will be an emotional time for everyone.'

'Does that mean Chrissie and the other partners who didn't know him aren't welcome, then?' CeCe fired back.

'Don't be silly, CeCe, of course Chrissie is welcome, as are all the partners of you girls, and the children,' said Ma. 'There will be quite a crowd on board.'

'There's plenty of room at least,' said Ally. 'It's what the boat was made for, and the McDougals are only a short flight away. Personally, I'd like them to come.'

Maia studied Ally. 'Why don't we all think about it? Maybe call the other sisters tomorrow and see what they say?'

'Tiggy invited them all in Dublin and Star was definitely up for it when I last spoke to her,' said CeCe.

'So that only leaves Electra,' said Ally.

'Let's sleep on it, shall we?' suggested Maia.

CeCe and Chrissie followed Ma upstairs after supper, while Maia and Ally tackled the washing-up.

'What time does Floriano land tomorrow?' Ally asked her sister.

'He and Valentina will land in Lisbon tomorrow morning. As long as they make the connection to Geneva, which they should, Christian and I will pick them up from the airport after lunch.'

'Fancy a nightcap on the terrace?' Ally asked as Maia turned on the dishwasher. 'I think I'll have a small Armagnac – I have a taste for it since I came back from France. You?'

'Just water will be fine. I love it here in the evening,' Maia said as they sat down. 'It's always so calm and quiet and safe.'

'It was only a year ago that you were living here full-time. Look at you now.'

'I know. Ally, can I ask you something?'

'Of course you can.'

'This Jack . . . You got on well with him, didn't you?'

'I did. He was a genuinely nice guy. I mean, he's still single and in his thirties, so maybe there is something wrong with him.'

'Excuse me,' Maia reproached her. 'I am also approaching my mid-thirties and have only just found the one.'

'And I found mine and lost him.'

'I know . . . but at least you have Bear.'

'I do, and you know what's odd? I feel ashamed to tell you this, but . . . for some reason, even though I told Jack about losing Theo, I didn't say that I'd had his baby.'

'Right. Do you think maybe that's because – subconsciously, of course – you were worried that he might be put off by it?'

'Yup, and how awful is that?' Ally sighed.

'Not awful at all. It just meant that you *did* like him, that there was a connection.'

'Maybe there was. I've definitely thought about him a lot since, which makes me feel even more guilty, like I'm betraying Theo as well.'

'From everything you've said about him, Ally, I'm sure that Theo would want you to be happy. What happened was so terrible, but for both you and Bear, at some point you must take the decision to live again. Please, don't do what I did and make the mistake of shutting yourself and your heart off from love. I wasted years because of Zed, although I'm glad that I was here for Pa, at least.'

'Yes. It meant we could all go off and live our lives, knowing you were at Atlantis with him.'

'Ally?'

'Yes?'

'You would like it if the McDougals came on the cruise, wouldn't you?'

'Yes, though Jack will probably never speak to me again after he's found out I didn't come clean about who I was.'

'He's probably guessed already, after speaking to Tiggy,' Maia pointed out.

'Maybe,' Ally sighed. 'Anyway, I don't want to talk about it, to be honest.'

'Okay, I understand. I just wish that Georg were here to tell us which of the two Marys she is. It's just bad luck he isn't available to ask.'

'Well, he isn't, and you also have to remember that we're not in control of this situation – Mary-Kate and her mum are. Now, I'm going upstairs to try to get some sleep before my usual early morning call,' said Ally. 'Coming?'

'I'll be up in a minute.'

'Okay, night, Maia.'

Maia sat there a little longer, thinking of Floriano arriving tomorrow and how exactly she would tell him he was going to be a father again.

And where . . .

The thought carried her along the softly lit path to Pa's garden. She went and sat on the bench in front of the armillary sphere, and took a deep breath of the still warm summer air, scented with the roses that grew on the arbour all around her.

'Maybe here,' she whispered to herself. Standing up, she walked towards the sphere. Uplighters had been placed around its edges since she'd last been here, which meant it glowed against the darkness of the garden. She ran her fingers over the bands, then she stopped and leant down to see her own inscription.

'*Never let fear decide your destiny* . . . Oh Pa, you were so right,' she whispered. She was just about to walk away when something odd caught her eye. Leaning down again, she checked the name on the band and what was below it and gasped.

'*Mon Dieu!*'

Without pausing, Maia turned tail, ran as fast as she could into the house, then raced up the stairs to the attic floor.

'Ally! Are you asleep?' she panted as she knocked on her sister's bedroom door, then opened it.

'Nearly . . .'

'Sorry, Ally, but this is important.'

'Shhh . . . don't wake Bear. Let's go outside,' Ally whispered, collecting her hoody from the back of the door. 'What is it?'

'Ally, you've been here quite often in the past year. When did you last look at the armillary sphere?'

'Um . . . I don't know. I do sometimes take Bear to sit in Pa's garden, so maybe a couple of days ago?'

'I mean, looked at it really closely?'

'I don't understand what you're saying. Of course I've looked at it, but—'

'You have to come with me. Now.'

'Why?' asked Ally.

'Just come!'

Back downstairs, Maia collected a notepad and pen from beside the phone in the kitchen and the two of them ran towards Pa's garden.

'I hope this is worth only having two or three hours' sleep for,' Ally complained as Maia led her towards the armillary sphere.

'Look, Ally, look at Merope's band.'

Ally bent down to see what Maia was pointing at.

'Oh my God!' she said as she stood upright and gazed at her sister in shock. 'Someone's added a set of coordinates to it. But when?'

'I don't know, but more importantly, Ally, where in the world do they point to?'

'Pass me that pad and I'll write them down. My laptop's on the kitchen table. Let's go and see where they lead, shall we?'

Back in the kitchen, while Ally fired up the laptop, Maia paced up and down. 'Ma must know when that inscription was put there, Ally.'

'Surely if she did, she would have told us.'

'She must know far more than she's telling.'

'If she does, she's a very good actress. Ma's the most honest and straightforward person I know, so I'd be surprised if she is keeping anything back from us girls. She'd want to help us in any way she could. Okay, so . . . here we go.'

Maia stood behind her sister and watched as Google Earth did its miraculous thing.

'Oh, wow, how interesting, it's not gone to New Zealand, it's closing in on Europe, on the UK and . . . Ireland!' Maia gasped.

'And down in the south-west too, where the McDougals are now. It's closing in on what looks like a lot of farmland – oh! There we go. There's the house.' Ally picked up her pen. 'Argideen House, Inchybridge, West Cork,' she read. 'So.' Ally looked up at Maia. 'It looks like our missing sister is Irish and not a Kiwi, which means . . .'

'It's Merry. It's Mary-Kate's mother! She's our missing sister.'

49

Merry
West Cork

That evening, Niall drove us up to Cross Farm in his taxi so we could all have a drink. As the taxi turned up the lane towards the farmhouse, I could see that the drive was already full of cars and a hubbub of laughter and conversation rang out through the valley from the open windows. As Jack, Mary-Kate and I stepped out of the car, John and Sinéad came out to greet us.

'So now, I'll be back to pick you up later,' Niall said to us with a wink before driving off. As we entered the kitchen, the crowd in the room turned to look at us.

'Merry!' came a voice, and a plump woman with steel-grey hair emerged from the crowd. 'Oh Merry, 'tis me, Ellen!'

'Hello,' I gulped as she engulfed me in her arms and hugged me tightly.

She pulled back to look at me. 'You haven't changed a bit and I've missed the sight of you,' she said with tears in her eyes. 'Do you still giggle like a mad thing?'

'Yeah, she does,' Jack put in, and so followed a chaotic round of introductions as Ellen and John guided us round the party. I was speechless to see my baby brothers Bill and Patrick grown into tall, burly men, like my father had once been, their dark hair now greying. Katie waved at me from where she was putting the finishing touches to a table groaning with food; the sights and smells of home-cooked cakes and bottles of stout, sparkling wine and whiskey laid out in a corner of the kitchen sent me falling back in time to my sixth birthday party.

'. . . And this is little Maeve, my first granddaughter,' said a red-headed woman called Maggie, holding a toddler in her arms. 'I'm Ellen's eldest daughter.'

Maeve reached out to grab a strand of my hair, and I giggled at the sweet child with green eyes so like my mother's.

'I remember when you were little, Maggie,' I said to my niece. 'And here you are, a grandmother!'

'I remember you too, Auntie Merry,' she smiled at me. 'I can't tell you how delighted Mam was when Uncle John rang to tell her you were back.'

A glass of whiskey was pressed into my hand, and I was introduced to so many children and grandchildren of my brothers and sisters that I gave up trying to work out who was whose.

I found my own children in the New Room, where Jack was chatting to a crowd about rugby, while Mary-Kate was talking to a handsome young man.

'Mum,' she called to me, 'this is Eoin, who's your brother Pat's son.'

'Will you be joining us in a song, Mrs McDougal?' he smiled at me, taking his fiddle out of its case.

'Please, call me Merry. It's been a long time since I've sung the old songs, but perhaps after a few drops of whiskey,' I said.

Bill came up to me, his face already flushed pink from the drink, and flourished his mobile phone at me.

'Merry, 'tis Nora! She's on the phone from Canada!'

I pressed the phone to my ear and immediately removed it when I heard a familiar high-pitched shriek of excitement, as if Nora was trying to shout across the Atlantic Ocean.

'Hello there, you eejit! Where have you been all these years?' she cried.

'Ah Nora, it's a long story. How are you?'

I let her chatter wash over me, as Eoin struck up a tune on his fiddle. More people gathered in the room, their feet stamping and hands clapping along. My little brother Pat pushed his two young granddaughters into the centre of the circle, and they began to dance, their identical curls bouncing as their legs performed intricate steps and hops.

'Oh my God, Mum, that's just like *Riverdance*!' Mary-Kate smiled. 'Aren't they sweet?'

'We never had the money to go and learn properly, but be glad I never sent you to Irish dancing lessons, it's brutal,' I giggled.

John offered me his hand and led me into a dance, and I was surprised as muscle memory took over and I remembered all the steps. Ellen and her husband were dancing beside us, and with a hop, we switched partners.

'Ah, 'tis the song they played at our wedding,' said Ellen's husband Emmet. 'You were only a slip of a thing back then.'

As invisible hands poured drops of whiskey into my glass, the dancing, singing and laughter went on, and my heart felt fit to burst with happiness, surrounded by my family and my own children in the house that I had grown up in, the music of my homeland thumping in my veins. And knowing at last that I was free from the man who had haunted me for thirty-seven years . . .

Later, needing some air, I pushed through the crowded rooms and made my way out of the kitchen door. Facing me across the courtyard was the old farmhouse where I'd lived up until the age of five, and where I now knew Nuala and her family had lived before us. The barn next door to it had obviously been recently rebuilt, but the sound of young calves still emanated from within it.

'What troubles this place has seen,' I whispered to myself as I wandered across to the side of the courtyard, beyond which we used to hang the washing every day. Now the area had been lawned and turned into a garden, with flower beds and a thick fuchsia hedge growing along one side to give shelter from the winds that swept along the valley. There were some children playing on the swings and slide in one corner, and I sat down in one of the ageing wooden chairs placed around a table. The view down the valley towards the river was quite beautiful, not that I'd ever fully appreciated it as a child.

'Hello there, Merry. Mind if I join you?'

I turned around to see Helen, looking as immaculate as the last time I'd seen her.

'Of course not, Helen. Sit down.'

'Thank you so much for inviting me tonight. Everyone's been so welcoming, treating me like a long-lost relative.'

'You *are* a long-lost relative,' I chuckled.

'I know, but 'tis still strange that we lived not far away from you, went to school together, and yet I've never set foot in this house before tonight. Mammy would have strung me up if I had.'

'I don't think it's possible for us to begin to know what our ancestors went through,' I sighed.

''Tis only sad that no one talked of it much outside their own families, because they were too frightened. Some of them wrote about it when they were older, or made deathbed confessions, but 'tis important for the young to know what their forefathers *and* mothers did for them and understand how long-held family grudges began.'

'I agree. I wonder what Hannah and Nuala would think if they could see us sitting here right now?' I said. 'In an Ireland that feels to me as if it's being modernised by the day. I was only reading this morning that there's been a move to legalise gay marriage.'

'I know! Jesus, who'd have thought it? I'm hoping Hannah and Nuala are sitting up there together and feeling proud of what they began. 'Twas the start of a revolution in all sorts of ways.'

'Helen? Can I ask you a question?'

'O'course, Merry. Ask away.'

'I was wondering why you've never had children.'

'Apart from never finding the right fellow, you mean?' she chuckled. 'I'll let you in on a little secret: after I researched the mental illness that ran through my family, I've discovered there's a genetic component that mostly affects the male line. So I'm glad I never did have children. The Noiro line will die out with me, and I'd have no regrets about that. Sure, 'twasn't Bobby or my Daddy or our Great-Uncle Colin's fault, but 'tis better to let the genes die with them.' Helen gave a sad sigh. 'Anyway, I'd better be off now, so. I've an early shift at the airport tomorrow morning. Nothing like the smell of whiskey at seven a.m. to turn your stomach.' She raised an eyebrow. 'But 'tis amazing the amount of people who'll take a free sample. Can we keep in touch, Merry?'

'I'd love to,' I said, as she put her arms around me. 'If you ever fancy a trip to New Zealand, I'd be so happy to have you visit.'

'Well now, being young, free and single and all, I might take you up on that. Bye, Merry.'

'Bye, Helen.'

I watched her wander off towards her car and thought how I'd never have believed before a couple of days ago that communication, let alone a warmth and potential future friendship, could be established with Bobby Noiro's younger sister. She'd said little about what she'd suffered because of him, and that made me warm to her even more. She was made of strong stuff – and I needed to take a leaf out of her book.

I heard a rousing round of applause as everyone cheered and stamped for my brother John to play his fiddle – the one that had once belonged to Daniel, the proud Fenian and the great-grandfather Helen and I shared – and I went inside to join the party.

I woke up the following morning with a thick head, which was all of my own making. I only hoped Niall had made it up in time to go and collect Ambrose from Dublin, because it had been past two in the morning when he'd picked us up from Cross Farm.

After a cup of tea and a hot shower, plus a couple of para-cetamol, I called Katie on her mobile, wondering how on earth she was at work this morning. She answered after a few rings.

'Hi there, Merry, 'tis all organised this end. I'll be bringing him over to the hotel at two p.m. He's very excited about meeting your kids.'

'Perfect, I'll speak to you later.'

As I ended the call, I saw I had a missed one, as well as a voicemail. Pressing the right buttons to retrieve it, I sat down on the bed to listen.

'Hi, Merry, it's Ally D'Aplièse here. You met my sister Tiggy in Dublin, and she gave us your number. Could you possibly call us on the home number at Atlantis? You've probably got it already, but if you haven't . . .'

I did have it already, so I didn't worry about writing it down.

'There's some new information that's just come to light, so

call us as soon as you can. Thanks, Merry, and I hope you're okay. Bye.'

My mobile then rang again. I saw it was Niall the taxi driver, and answered it immediately.

'Hello?'

'The cargo's on board and ETA is around two fifteen.'

'Thanks, Niall. See you then.'

I sat there, debating whether to phone the Atlantis number back before deciding not to. Just now, I had more important things to think about than any tenuous connection to some strange dead man and his adopted daughters.

There was a knock on the door.

'Hello, Jack, how are you feeling?' I smiled as my son came into the room.

'I'm upright, so that's something,' he said. 'That was quite a piss-up last night. The Irish sure know how to enjoy themselves. Maybe a fry-up would help.'

My own stomach turned at the thought. 'Maybe. Have you heard from Mary-Kate?'

'Not yet. She was in a worse state than I was. Even you were a bit tipsy, Mum,' he grinned.

'I admit that I did knock it back a bit.'

'Well, it was great to see you relax and laugh like you used to when Dad was alive. Besides, it's known across the world that the Irish can drink, so we couldn't really leave without participating, could we? Right, I'm off down to brekkie. You coming?'

I nodded and Jack led the way.

After some coffee, toast and jam, I felt better. It was a sunny day again and Jack decided that an hour on the waves would clear out any cobwebs.

Back upstairs and seeing the time, I called Mary-Kate's room.

''Lo?' said a muffled voice.

'It's Mum, and it's almost noon, sweetheart. Time to get up.'

'Mmph . . . Not feeling well.'

'Okay, well, sleep a bit longer and I'll give you a call in an hour. Remember, my friend Ambrose is arriving this afternoon, and I don't want him to meet my daughter for the first time with a hangover.'

''Kay, Mum. Bye.'

'I only hope I've done the right thing,' I muttered as I took myself off for a walk across the dunes.

At two on the dot, Katie's car drew up in front of the hotel.

'Right, Father O'Brien is here,' I said to my children as we stood up from the sofas in the reception.

'I thought it was Ambrose we were meeting?' Mary-Kate queried.

'It is, but Father O'Brien was a big part of my childhood too. I'll go and help him inside.'

I hurried outside and saw Katie unfolding the wheelchair from the boot.

'Hello there, Father, isn't it a beautiful day?' I said as I opened the front passenger door.

'It is indeed,' he answered.

I watched Katie expertly manoeuvre him out of the car and into the chair. She wheeled him into the hotel as I walked alongside him.

'Remind me of the names of your children?' he said.

'Jack and Mary-Kate. I'm afraid they're not feeling too well this morning. My brother John and his wife threw a party up at Cross Farm, so we could meet up with everyone again.'

'And sure, a good time was had by all?' Father O'Brien chuckled.

'Exactly. They're over there,' I pointed as we wheeled him over.

'Hello there, I hear you've been given a baptism in how to enjoy yourself the Irish way. I'm Father O'Brien and 'tis a pleasure to meet you. You're the image of your mother,' he added to Mary-Kate.

'Thank you.' My daughter threw me a look and I gave her a slight shake of my head. There was no reason for him to know just now.

'Why don't we go up to my room and I can order some tea up there?' I said. 'It's a bit more private, isn't it, Father?'

'Ah, I'm just as happy down here, Merry. Please don't go to any bother.'

'It's no bother. You go with Katie and we'll follow.'

I handed Katie my key card, then she pushed Father O'Brien into the lift. As the doors shut behind them, my mobile rang.

'Hello there, it's Niall. We're just approaching the hotel. Will I bring your man into the lobby?'

'Yes, perfect timing. I'll meet you there. Kids, go up and chat to Father O'Brien and order some tea. Don't say a word about Ambrose arriving, okay?'

'Okay, Mum,' Jack shrugged as the two of them took the stairs.

Hurrying towards the lobby, I saw Ambrose being escorted through the entrance by Niall. He looked his usual dapper self in a checked jacket, pressed twill trousers and shiny black brogues.

'Here he is, Merry, safely transported from Dublin. There now, it wasn't as bad after all, was it, Mr Lister?'

'No, although it's still an awfully long way,' said Ambrose. 'How much do I owe you for the ride?'

'It's all taken care of,' I said as I slipped Niall a wad of euros. 'I'll let you know when he's returning.'

'Grand job. We'd a good chat on the way, didn't we?' Niall smiled as he headed off. 'I'll be seeing ye.'

'I'd query the fact we had a good chat. That would take two of us, after all, and I hardly got a word in edgeways,' muttered Ambrose.

'You must be exhausted,' I said as I linked my arm through his.

'What I could do with more than anything else is a nice cup of tea. It is that time of day, after all.'

'That's perfect then,' I said as we stepped into the lift and I pressed the button to take us upwards. 'I've just ordered some to my room. Jack and Mary-Kate are up there too.'

'Well, even if you have dragged me halfway across Ireland, it will be a pleasure to see Jack again and to meet Mary-Kate.'

'What do you think of this hotel?' I asked him as we emerged onto the second floor and walked slowly along the corridor towards my room.

'It's certainly a step up from the shack that used to be here,' he agreed as we came to a halt in front of my door.

Feeling breathless with nerves, I knocked and waited for Jack to open it.

'Hi, Mum. Hi, Ambrose. It's good to see you again. We're just pouring the tea to take out onto the balcony.'

'Perfect,' I nodded at him.

Katie gave me a nod and I saw that Father O'Brien's wheel-chair was on the balcony, partly concealed behind the curtain at the window.

'This is my sister Katie, and my daughter, Mary-Kate,' I said to Ambrose. They all said hello, and then Katie looked at me for instructions.

'Now, Ambrose, why don't you come and sit outside? We'll bring your tea out to you.'

'I might as well make the most of the sea air before it starts bucketing down with rain, which is what it usually does here,' he commented as he refused my arm and walked with his stick towards the open glass door. I followed him, not wanting him to trip on the ridge between the room and the balcony, and held my breath as he stepped across it. I watched as he turned towards the man sitting in the wheelchair.

Both men stared at each other for some time, and from my vantage point hidden behind the curtain, I could see Father O'Brien's eyes filling with tears. Ambrose took a step closer, as if his already compromised sight was playing tricks on him.

'Ambrose? Is that really you? I . . .'

Ambrose staggered a little and caught hold of the back of the chair in front of him.

'It is, indeed. Dear James . . . I can hardly believe it! My friend, my dear, dear friend . . .'

Ambrose held out his hand across the little table. Father O'Brien raised his to meet it.

'What's going on, Mum?' Mary-Kate whispered. 'Do they want some tea?'

'I'll take it out to them, and then I think we should leave them alone. They have a lot to catch up on.'

Armed with two teacups, I stepped out onto the balcony and placed one in front of each man. They were still grasping each other's hands, so lost in a lifetime of memories that they didn't even notice me.

I stepped quietly back inside and ushered my children and Katie out of the room.

'Are they okay?' Katie asked an hour later as I joined her back in the lounge downstairs, having discreetly checked on the two men.

'They seem fine. I asked them if they wanted anything and they said no. Where are the kids?'

'In their rooms. I think they're still getting over the hooley last night,' she smiled. 'So, why did Ambrose and the father's friendship end all those years ago?'

'Do you remember that old battleaxe of a housekeeper called Mrs Cavanagh, who used to work for Father O'Brien?'

'How could I forget her?' Katie rolled her eyes. 'A fierce old witch she was, for sure.'

'She threatened Ambrose with the fact that she'd seen them hugging just after Ambrose's father died. Father O'Brien was simply consoling his beloved friend after his loss, but she said she was going to tell Father O'Brien's bishop of their "inappropriate behaviour".'

'So the old bat was twisting it into something more than it was?'

'Exactly,' I sighed. 'Ambrose had no choice but to walk away. He knew any sniff of scandal like that would end Father O'Brien's career. I believe it broke Ambrose's heart, Katie; every time he was there at the presbytery, the two of them would talk for hours, mostly arguing about the existence of God. Ambrose is an atheist, you see.'

'Do you think that, well, there *was* anything inappropriate going on?'

'No, I don't. Absolutely, categorically not. I know that you've never liked him, but Ambrose always knew and respected that the love of Father O'Brien's life was God. And he could never compete. Who could?' I shrugged.

'Well, whatever I feel about Ambrose, 'tis a beautiful thing you've done, Merry, bringing the two of them back together.

'Tis hardly much of a life for the father up at the old people's home, that's for sure. Now then, I'll be having to take our fellow back before they call the guards out for him. I hate to break them up, but . . .'

'Of course,' I agreed. 'I'm sure that Ambrose will stay on down here longer now he knows why I asked him to come in the first place.'

Upstairs, we both crept into the room, feeling almost as if we were voyeurs. I was only relieved to hear laughter coming from the balcony.

I stepped out onto it and looked down at both at them.

'Have you had a good catch-up?' I asked.

'We have indeed, Merry,' said Ambrose, 'and may I say that you're a very naughty girl, bringing me here under false pretences. My poor old heart almost stopped when I saw James here.'

'Well, you'll just have to forgive me, won't you? Now, Father, I hate to break up the party, but it's time for Katie to take you back home.'

'I'd hardly be calling it home,' Father O'Brien shrugged sadly.

'You'll be here tomorrow, won't you, Ambrose?' I asked him. 'He wasn't sure whether he actually wanted to stay down here overnight,' I said as an aside to Father O'Brien.

'As we've only reached 1985 so far, I rather feel I must,' said Ambrose. 'What time are visiting hours?' he asked as he stood up and stepped back to make room for Katie to wheel Father O'Brien inside.

'For the father, any time you please,' said Katie with a smile.

'Until tomorrow then, dear James,' said Ambrose, stepping into the room. 'Until tomorrow.'

The look in Ambrose's eyes as Katie wheeled Father O'Brien out of the door brought a lump to my throat.

'Good grief! Well, that certainly got the blood racing around my old veins,' he murmured. 'I feel quite wrung out.'

'You must be hungry, Ambrose. Shall I order you something?'

'First of all, Mary dear, please escort me to the nearest facility. I haven't used the bathroom since we stopped off in Cork three hours ago!'

Having taken Ambrose to his room, he opened his Gladstone bag – a relic I remembered from his days with Father O'Brien – and pulled out a letter.

'This is yours, I believe,' he smiled, as he handed it to me.

I looked down at the writing, feeling I should recognise it, but I didn't. Why should I? There had been no need for correspondence between us all those years ago.

'Thank you. Why don't you have a lie-down and call me on my room phone when you want to have supper?'

'I will. Thank you, my dear, for what you did today.'

'Ambrose, it was a pleasure.'

Back in my own room, I put the letter to one side and sat on the balcony to check my mobile. Three voicemails had been left for me.

I listened to them, finding they were all from Ally D'Aplièse, and urging me to call her back. With a sigh, I found the Atlantis number and did so; after all the anticipation and emotion of the afternoon, I really wasn't in the mood for any further drama.

'*Allô? C'est Atlantis.*'

The unfamiliar voice speaking French threw me for a second and I hunted around my brain for the words I needed to reply, as I hadn't used French for so very long. In the end I gave up.

'Hello, this is Mrs Merry McDougal here. I've had a message from Ally D'Aplièse to call this number.'

'Ah! Of course!' the woman replied immediately in English. 'It is a pleasure to speak to you, Mrs McDougal. My name is Marina and I have looked after all the girls since they were small. I shall just go and find Ally for you.'

As I waited, I could hear the sound of a baby crying in the background, and wondered whose it was. At the same time, there was a knock on my door. I ran to open it and saw Jack standing there with his mobile phone in his hand.

'Mum, I've just had a text from Ally. She's desperate to get in touch with you,' he said as I sped back to pick up the receiver.

'Hello?' said a voice at the other end. 'Is anyone there?'

'Yes, sorry about that, Ally. It's Merry here. I got your messages and Jack's just come in to tell me you sent him a text too.'

'Yes, I did. I'm so sorry if you feel hounded, but we didn't want you to leave West Cork before we'd spoken to you.'

'Oh, why would that be?'

'Because, to cut a long story short, some information has just turned up that we wanted you to know about.'

'What is it?'

'Well, it sounds a little strange, but each of us were given a set of coordinates telling us where we'd originally come from, so we could go back and trace our biological roots if we wanted to. All ours have been accurate so far. Last night, we found the missing sister's coordinates, and they pinpoint a place in Ireland. So, we believe it must be you rather than Mary-Kate who they refer to. Shall I confirm with you where they lead to?'

'Go on then,' I sighed, 'surprise me.'

'Mum!' Jack frowned at the cynicism in my voice.

'Well, it's in an area called West Cork. I'm not sure where exactly you are at the moment, because I know the region covers a large area, but the address the coordinates lead to is called Argideen House, near the village of Timoleague. Does that mean anything to you?'

I gulped in astonishment and sat down abruptly on the bed. How *could* she know?

Eventually, I found my voice. 'I . . . yes it does. My family home here was originally part of the Argideen estate, so maybe that's what the coordinates point to.'

'We can see on Google Maps that the Argideen estate still covers a few hundred acres, but the coordinates we have point specifically to Argideen House,' Ally replied.

'Right. Okay.' For some ridiculous reason, I wrote 'Argideen House' down on the pad next to the phone, as if I might forget it. 'Well, thank you for telling me. I'm sorry I haven't got back to you sooner, but it's been a very busy day. Goodbye.'

I shuddered suddenly, hating the thought of this unknown, dead man telling his adopted daughters the whereabouts of *my* birthplace.

'Mum, what is it?' Jack stared at me.

'They've had some new information and apparently they know where I was born. How do they know? How *can* they know, when even I don't?'

'I dunno, but where is it then?'

'It's very near here actually, only a couple of miles from where we were last night – the farm where I was brought up. Which means they could have made a mistake with the coordinates, as I told her.'

'What's the name of the place?'

'It's called Argideen House, but in my day it was always known as the "Big House". My grandmother Nuala worked there for the rich Protestant family who owned it during the revolution. And actually' – I frowned and cast my mind back – 'so did Nora, my older sister, for a while when I was young.'

'I suppose it makes sense that it's local, doesn't it? I mean, is this house close to Father O'Brien's house in Tim . . .' Jack looked to me for help.

'Timoleague. Yes, it is. Very.'

'Who lives at Argideen House now?'

'I've absolutely no idea. And do you know what, Jack? After this afternoon and last night, I feel too exhausted to even think about it.'

'Of course, Mum.' Jack came to sit on the bed next to me and put his arm around me. 'All this has been really hard on you. We can talk about it tomorrow maybe. But whether or not you decide you want to have anything to do with Ally and her gang in the future, surely for your own benefit, while you're here, it might be interesting to find out a bit more about this Argideen House?'

'Maybe,' I sighed. 'I feel awful now for being rude to Ally. Could you speak to her and apologise, say I've had a long day, or something?'

'O'course, Mum. And you've had a helluva time in the past few weeks. I'll explain that to her, don't worry. I guess you're not up to eating downstairs tonight?'

'No, and the good news is that this is one of the only hotels I've stayed at where the room service menu has sensible things on it, like toast and homemade jam. I'll give Ambrose a call and see if he wants any company tonight, but I somehow doubt it. It's been a very big day for him.'

'Yeah, and you made it all possible.' Jack hugged me. 'You just take it easy, okay? Give me a call if you need anything, but otherwise, I'll see you in the morning. Love you, Mum.'

'Thanks, Jack, love you too.'

As the door closed behind him, I found myself on the verge of tears again.

Simply because I felt so lucky to have given birth to such a wonderful human being. 'Now all he needs is the love of a good woman,' I muttered as I went to start the bath running. But for now at least, I was glad to have him by my side.

Having taken a bath, I called Ambrose, who said that he felt too exhausted to do anything more than have some sandwiches in his room, so I ordered a platter for him, and toast and jam for me. Then I switched the television on and watched a bad Irish soap in an attempt to turn off my brain.

However, it didn't work, and as I slid under the duvet, I couldn't shake off what Ally had told me:

Argideen House . . .

Countless times on my cycle rides to Timoleague and walking home from school, we'd gone past the never-ending stone wall that cut the Big House and its residents off from the rest of us. I'd never seen the house myself; the chimneys were only visible in winter when the trees that shrouded its perimeter had shed their leaves. I knew my brothers had often climbed over the wall, looking for the apples and figs that grew there plentifully in the autumn.

Then I suddenly remembered the letter Ambrose had handed me was still sitting in my bedside drawer, as yet unopened.

Why are you so frightened? He loved you . . .

Yet, the whole point was that maybe he hadn't, and I'd spent thirty-seven years picturing a thousand versions of a tragic love story that never was . . .

'Just open it, you silly woman!' I told myself, as I sat up and opened the drawer next to me. Tearing the envelope open, I took a deep breath and read the letter inside.

He had responded in the same guarded way I had written to *him*. Except he had included a telephone number.

Please do call me with a suitable date and time for us to meet up.

I stuffed the letter back inside the drawer, lay down and switched off the light.

But sleep wouldn't come, and why should it? I'd just had contact with the man who had haunted both my dreams and my nightmares for so long.

Then a thought made me giggle out loud. Wouldn't it be the most ironic thing if I, brought up in a staunch Catholic family, whose life had been under threat because I'd fallen in love with a Protestant boy, had been born into a Protestant house myself?

With that thought, I finally fell asleep.

'Would you kindly give me a lift up to this old people's home where James lives?' Ambrose asked us over breakfast the next morning.

'Of course we will,' I said.

'I must admit, I've rather a phobia of such places,' he said with a shudder. 'Dear James did say – in confidence, of course – that half the residents are often chatting away to him as if they are still living in the 1950s. At the very least, both of us have our little grey cells still intact, even though our bodies are failing us by the day.'

Jack agreed to run him in to the home, saying he had a couple of errands to do in Clonakilty. So Mary-Kate and I sat finishing our coffee together.

'Feeling better today?' I asked her.

'Yeah. You know I don't drink much usually, and certainly not whiskey. Oh, by the way, Eoin, one of the cousins I met at the party who played the fiddle the other night, is a musician and songwriter, and gigs around the local pubs. He says I should come down and join him one night at the open mic session they have at a pub called De Barras. He's just lost his female singer apparently, because she went off travelling.'

'That's wonderful, Mary-Kate. It's traditional Irish music, is it?'

'God no, Mum,' she giggled. 'It's modern stuff. Eoin says that there's a huge live music culture down here and across Ireland. I suppose it helps that there are so many pubs. We have nothing like this in NZ.'

'Certainly not in the Gibbston Valley, no. Will you take him up on it?'

'I can't, can I? I'm presuming we'll all be heading back to Dublin soon. Have you thought about when?'

'To be honest, I'm just living from day to day at the moment, but there's no reason why you couldn't stay on here for a bit, Mary-Kate, even if Jack and I leave.'

'Maybe,' she shrugged. 'Who knows? If someone will give me a lift at some point today, I might go to his studio and listen to the type of stuff he writes. Oh, and changing the subject, Mum, I had another email from Michelle yesterday. She's sent a photo that was taken of the two of us just after I was born. I . . . well, if it wouldn't hurt too much, would you mind taking a look at it for me? I just want to make sure that the baby in the picture looks the same as the ones you have of me at that age. So there's no doubt or anything. I mean, I know all babies look the same but—'

'Don't worry, darling, I'll know immediately if it's you or not,' I confirmed. 'Whilst we're waiting for Jack to come back, why don't we go up to your room and you can show it to me?'

Upstairs, it took me one glance to know that the newborn child lying in her mother's arms in the photograph was now my daughter.

'You were even wrapped in the same pink blanket when you were given to me and your father.'

'How old was I?'

'No more than a few hours, sweetheart. That photograph was probably taken just before she had to say goodbye to you. It must have been very hard for her.'

'She said in the email that the weeks afterwards were terrible – that she coped by thinking I would be given a better life than she could have given me at the time. I think she feels really guilty, Mum.'

'Do you resent her for making the decision she did?'

'I don't think so, but that's partly because I was lucky enough to come to you and Dad and have such a great upbringing. She wants to . . . well, meet up whenever I feel ready to.'

'Do you think you will?'

'Maybe, yes, but I don't want to become part of her family or anything; I have my own. I know it sounds weird, but she was so young when she had me – if I do end up having any kind of relationship with her, I'd see her more as an older sister. I mean, Jack's only a few years younger than she is. Sooo . . .' Mary-Kate looked at me with a glint in her eye. 'Seems like I'm out of the running for being the missing sister, Mum. Jack told me last night about the coordinates that had appeared on Merope's band of the armillary sphere at Atlantis. They're close to where you were brought up as a child, apparently.'

I stared at Mary-Kate in confusion.

'Sorry, I've no idea what you're talking about.'

'Surely Ally told you about the armillary sphere that appeared at the sisters' home just after their father had died?'

'I vaguely remember her mentioning it, but can you explain again, please?'

'Well, CeCe told me that their father had a special garden at their house in Geneva, and this armillary sphere appeared in it overnight, just after he died. There were bands on it for each of the sisters, and each of the bands had a quotation engraved on it and a set of coordinates to where they were found by their father.'

'And . . . ?'

'Ally told Jack that Maia – the eldest, and the sister who none of us have met so far – was wandering about in the garden a couple of days ago, and saw that a set of coordinates had been engraved on Merope's empty band.'

'What?! This whole thing gets more far-fetched by the second.' I rolled my eyes.

'Oh, come on, Mum! Stop being such a cynic. You're the one who's been a self-professed addict of Greek mythology the whole of her life. Obviously their dad was too, and the armillary sphere was his way of passing on information. As Ally said to Jack last night, it was what they all needed if they wanted to find out where he'd found them. Maia was adamant that unless this information was completely accurate, it wouldn't have been engraved on the armillary sphere.'

'So when did this information appear?'

'Jack said Ally wasn't sure. I mean, she said that both she and Maia and the other sisters had gone to sit in the garden where the armillary sphere is, but none of them had studied it closely for a while, so it could have been months, or just a few days ago. I'm not sure that's the point, though, Mum. The more important thing is that it can't be complete co-incidence you were put in a basket on a priest's doorstep, which is only a mile or so from where the coordinates said you were born.'

I felt my daughter studying me, waiting for a reaction.

'So this father – with no name other than a nickname – apparently found me there? If he did, why on earth did he then put me on a priest's doorstep?'

'I don't know, Mum, and nor does Ally or anyone else. But taking Pa Salt and the sisters aside, wouldn't it be interesting to find out who you really are? Who your birth parents were?'

'This from the child who told me only a few minutes ago that she wasn't bothered about meeting her own birth family?' I smiled.

'Yeah, but the difference is, I can if I want to,' Mary-Kate countered. 'You're frightened, aren't you, Mum? Of knowing the truth?'

'You're probably right, Mary-Kate, but the past few weeks since I left home have been rather a roller-coaster. Perhaps one day I'll want to know, but like you, it's only those that I love and that love me – my family – that really matter, and I'm quite happy with the one I've got, especially after just meeting them all again.'

'Yeah, I understand completely, Mum.'

'I'm sorry if that sounded like I was commenting on any feelings I have about you and your adoption,' I added quickly. 'I swear that these are completely my *own* feelings. Even if this bunch of sisters has a missing one, which they now think might be me, I can't cope with another family just now.'

'I get that, Mum, and please don't apologise. It's actually Jacko that seems keen to find out stuff. Remember, if you *are* related – or your story is anyway – to this other family, then he might be too, because he's your and Dad's biological son.'

'Actually, you're right,' I said, suddenly feeling terribly selfish. 'Just because I'm not interested in knowing, doesn't mean he isn't. Thank you, sweetheart, for pointing out that this is Jack's history too. And yours.'

'No problem, Mum. Well, I'm with him – I'd like to get to the bottom of all this. It's like the best mystery ever! I know exactly where Jack is at the moment, and it's totally up to you if you want to come along and see this house. We're gonna go take a look – whoops! That must be Jack, checking in from Clonakilty.' Mary-Kate swooped to answer her mobile. 'Hi,

Jacko, yup. Okay, I'll ask her. I'll be in the lobby in half an hour.' She put the phone down.

'So, we're off to see Argideen House. Wanna come along?'

'Why not?' I answered with a grim smile.

'I know exactly where it is,' I said to Jack as we set off. 'We don't need the satnav.'

'Okay, I just got the feeling that maybe you weren't up for it. Sorry, Mum,' he added, turning the satnav off.

'No need to apologise. How was Ambrose?'

'Much more jolly than he was when I first met him in Dublin. You did a good thing there, Mum. I saw our Aunt Katie when I arrived at the home and she said she'd call when Ambrose wanted to be collected.'

'Okay. Turn right here, Jack,' I directed. 'Where were you this morning?'

'Oh, just around Clonakilty.'

'How is Ally? Mary-Kate said you spoke to her last night.'

'She's good. All the rest of the sisters are arriving for the cruise in the next few days. Their boat is sailing down from Nice to Greece on Thursday morning.'

'That's nice,' I said. 'Okay, right round the roundabout and then follow the road until I tell you different.'

We sat in silence for a while, so I looked at the countryside speeding by. I felt numb, as though my brain had switched off, because it simply did not want to know or be involved with the place where I was being taken. As if somehow, seeing it and knowing that I was connected to it would change my life forever. That it mattered.

And I so didn't want it to.

'Turn right here,' I almost barked at Jack.

Stop it, Merry! Remember, you're here for Jack, for your son. It's his story too . . .

The lane twisted, turned, then became narrower as we drove towards Clogagh.

At this moment, I felt it was a metaphor for my life:

What if I was to turn left instead of right in my own life at this moment? Is all life simply a series of twisting and turning paths, with a crossroads every so often when fate allows humanity to decide their own destiny . . . ?

'Mum, where to now?'

The road had narrowed even more as we arrived at Inchybridge and I told Jack to keep going a little further, then turn right.

'That's the stone wall which is the boundary to Argideen House,' I announced.

'It goes on for miles, Mum,' said Mary-Kate from the back.

'They wanted to make sure they kept us peasants out,' I smiled. 'The main entrance is just up here on the left.'

Jack slowed down as he approached. Opposite, a field of maize was growing high in the fertile soil that took nourishment from the Argideen River below it.

'That's the entrance,' I said.

Jack slowed down and then parked in front of it. The majestic old iron gates were open and the driveway beyond was covered in weeds. The trees surrounding the border of the property inside the stone wall had turned into a forest. It reminded me of the enormous thorn bushes that had grown up around Sleeping Beauty's castle.

'Shall we get out and take a look?' asked Jack.

'We can't! We might be trespassing,' I replied.

'I spoke to a local this morning and they said no one's been living here for years. It's empty, Mum. Promise.'

'Well, it's still owned by someone, Jack.'

'Fine, you stay here then.'

I watched Jack climb out of the car.

'I'm coming too,' said Mary-Kate as she opened the back door.

'Oh, for goodness' sake,' I muttered as I got out too. We all circumnavigated the huge nettles that had sprung up along the drive. Ironically, I found it comforting how, without human interference, nature would so quickly start taking back its own.

'Ouch!' Mary-Kate winced and hopped as a nettle found its mark between her trainer and jeans.

'The house should come into view at any minute,' I said from behind them. And a few minutes later, it did. Like all Protestant houses around here, it was a squarely built, elegant Georgian building. Its frontage was vast – eight windows wide on both the ground and the upper levels and surrounded by what would once have been beautifully manicured parkland. As it was, even if the facade was still standing, I could see the rotting wood around the windowpanes, and the ivy on its constant crawl upwards from the base of the house. The feeling of neglect was palpable.

'Wow!' said Mary-Kate as she looked up at the front of it. 'This must have been amazing in its day. Do you know who lived here, Mum?'

'I can tell you who it was one hundred years ago, but I know the Fitzgeralds returned to England during the revolution. They were English, you see. And Protestant,' I added. 'I'm sure someone else bought it just after the war. The Second World War, that is. One of my sisters, Nora, worked here in the kitchens during the shooting season, but I don't know what the family was called.'

'You're right, Mum, the Fitzgeralds went back to England in 1921, and the house was empty for a while.'

'How on earth do *you* know that, Jack?'

'Because Ally, who's a bit of an expert in researching family histories, suggested I looked up solicitors' practices locally, as they would probably have handled any sale of the property. The solicitor I found in Timoleague told me it wasn't him who had dealt with the sale of Argideen House, but he gave me the name of who had. So I visited them in Clonakilty earlier.' Jack shook his head. 'This area is amazing, Mum; everyone knows everyone else, or knows someone who does.'

'And?'

'The guy I spoke to made a call to his dad, who made a call to *his* dad, and apparently the house was sold by the Fitzgerald family in 1948 to a new buyer.'

'Who was that buyer?' Mary-Kate butted in.

'He doesn't know. Or at least, his grandfather doesn't. He was asked to send all the title deeds and related documents to London.'

'Do you have an address for wherever they were sent?' I asked.

'Apparently it was a post office box address, and I've no idea what that actually is.'

'We'd have called it a PO box,' I explained. 'It basically means envelopes or parcels go to the post office to a locker with a specific number attached to it, and the recipient collects them from there.'

'So it means that the person wants to remain anonymous?' said Mary-Kate.

'Yes, in essence, it does.'

'Do you have the PO box address?' I asked Jack.

'I do, and it's a place in somewhere called Marylebone. I checked out the post offices there online and called around them all. Basically, the number doesn't exist anymore.'

'Surely they had the name of whoever had opened that PO box account?' Mary-Kate asked.

'They did, but as Mum just explained, the whole point of having a post office box is to remain anonymous. They weren't going to give the owner's name out to a stranger over the telephone, that's for sure,' said Jack.

'This is such a beautiful house,' Mary-Kate said dreamily.

'My grandmother Nuala looked after a young British officer who lived here and who'd been injured in the First World War. She talked in her diary about how wonderful the gardens used to be. Sadly, he committed suicide soon after Nuala left.' I shuddered then and turned away from the house. 'I'm going back to the car. I'll see you there.'

As I trekked through the undergrowth, I could hardly believe that the story which had moved me so much and had taken place here had possibly been part of *my* history too. Yet, there was just something about the house, an atmosphere – an energy – that was unsettling me.

Not prone to anything spiritual, even I felt as if a darkness hung about Argideen House; although there was no doubting it was – or had once been – beautiful, I knew that tragedy had taken place within its walls and still left its mark until this day.

I began to run, tripping over the weeds and the roots that had pushed up along the drive, until I passed through the gates panting, and taking gulps of fresh air.

Whatever my connection was with Argideen House, I knew I never wanted to pass through those gates again.

50

Having dropped Mary-Kate off in Clonakilty, where she'd arranged to meet her new friend Eoin at his studio, Jack and I went to collect Ambrose.

'You're upset, aren't you, Mum?'

'A bit,' I admitted. 'I can't really say why. But seriously, Jack, it's nothing you've done. I just don't like Argideen House, that's all.'

'But you've never been inside the walls before today?'

'No, never.'

'By the way, when are you thinking of leaving?' he asked me.

'I haven't thought about it, to be honest. I think it depends on Ambrose. We can take him back to Dublin with us.'

'Okay. Well, if it's all right with you, MK and I are thinking of going to Dublin tomorrow, then flying on to Nice via London. You know that all of us have been invited on the cruise down to Greece. I get that you don't want to go, but . . .' – Jack shrugged – 'I'd like to. Maybe I could investigate for you, Mum, find out what all this missing sister stuff is about, if that's all right with you?'

'Of course it's all right, Jack. You're a grown man and you can do what you want. As Mary-Kate pointed out to me, if I'm related to them in some way, then so are you.'

729

'Yeah, I would be.'

'So, be honest, Jack, how much of your eagerness to go is to do with Ally?'

There was a pause as he thought about it. Or at least, thought about what to say to *me*.

'Quite a lot, actually. I mean, I'm obviously interested in finding out more about the whole situation, but yeah, it's been a long time since I met a woman who I just felt . . . well, an immediate bond with.'

'Do you think she feels the same way about you?'

'I don't know; she might just be texting me because of the whole missing sister thing, but when we spoke last night, we laughed, y'know? I get her and she gets me and that's all there is to it.'

'Then you absolutely must go, Jack. Right,' I said as we pulled up in front of the old people's home. 'I'll go in and get Ambrose.'

Katie came out to reception to meet me. 'How have they been?' I asked her.

'Ah now, I'd say they haven't stopped chatting since Mr Lister sat down.'

'They've had a lot to catch up on.'

'They have, so. I'll go fetch him now.'

'Oh, by the way, Nora worked at Argideen House when we were younger, didn't she?'

'She did, yes.'

'Do you think you could ask her if she remembers the name of the family she worked for?'

'I will. If I remember rightly, 'twas some foreign couple,' said Katie. 'I'll give her a bell when I'm home tonight.'

'Thanks,' I said, as she gave me a smile and walked off. As I stood in reception waiting for Ambrose, I thought about the six sisters' strange surname, which I'd already worked out was an anagram of 'Pleiades'.

D'Aplièse . . . I pulled a pen out of my handbag, asked the receptionist for a piece of paper and wrote the word down.

As Ambrose appeared with Katie, there was a definite spring in his step that hadn't been there in Dublin.

'Good day?' I asked him.

'Apart from the less than private surroundings, it's been most pleasant. Thank you, Katie, it's been a delight to make your acquaintance again, and rest assured, I'll be back soon,' he said to her.

'Can you check with Nora that this wasn't the name of the family up at Argideen House?' I said to her, handing her the slip of paper.

'Of course,' she said as she tucked it into her uniform pocket. 'Bye now.' She gave me a smile and walked off.

'I don't know how James copes with living there,' said Ambrose as I helped him into the car and we drove off. 'And yet somehow he bears it. I'd rather be with my maker.'

'I didn't think you believed in God?'

'I said "my maker", dear girl, which could technically be my parents, and therefore, at the very least, my earthly remains will lie with theirs.'

'You're splitting hairs, Ambrose.'

'Maybe so, but . . . Merry dear, would you be available for a chat once we get back to the hotel? I've drunk more tea today than I think I've drunk in a week, and I may treat myself to a glass of whiskey.'

'I'll go and collect Mary-Kate when she calls,' said Jack as we parked in front of the hotel. 'See you later at dinner.'

'Your children are utterly delightful, by the way. Now then,' he said, as Jack moved off to find a parking space, 'how about we sit outside on the café terrace, whilst the sun is gracing us with an appearance?'

Over a pot of tea for me and a whiskey for Ambrose, we

sat enjoying the sound of the huge waves breaking on the shore below us.

'What is it you wanted to talk to me about?' I asked him.

'It's about James, of course. I mean, I know he is in a wheelchair and needs help with his daily ablutions, but I don't feel he should see his golden years out in that home. So I was thinking . . .'

'Yes?'

'Well, I'm hardly getting any younger, am I? And even though I hate to admit it, I'm beginning to struggle with the stairs down to my bedroom and bathroom. I've been thinking for a while that I should sell the flat and move to a modern apartment block with a lift, and everything I need – including a walk-in shower – all on one floor. Let me tell you, there are plenty of those types of places available in Dublin these days.'

'I see. And?'

'You can imagine that selling the home I've lived in for so very long will be something of a trauma. But seeing James's current situation has given me the spur I needed. So when I get back to Dublin, I intend to put my little half of a house on the market and buy something more sensible with three bedrooms. One for myself, one for a live-in carer and, well, one for James.'

'Goodness!'

'What do you think, Mary dear?'

'I think it's a wonderful idea in theory, Ambrose. However, it would be a huge wrench for Father O'Brien. He's lived down here for most of his adult life, and even if his living circumstances are not quite what they should be, he has many of his old parishioners popping in to see him.'

'Parishioners who he's seen every day for the past sixty odd years. He might be glad of a change.'

'Have you actually asked him?'

'I have, yes, as a matter of fact. Or, putting it another way,

I've hinted at the idea to him. My plan is that I make the move, and then have James up to visit me when I have found a carer who can live in with us. And perhaps—'

'He will never want to return to West Cork,' I finished for him.

'Exactly. And there's no reason why we couldn't take somewhere down here every summer, if he felt the need of some fresh sea breezes.' Ambrose pointed to a separate building adjacent to the hotel. 'I've enquired and discovered the apartments are let out to families needing a self-catering space.'

'Goodness, Ambrose, you've certainly got it all worked out,' I smiled. 'I do know that he misses his privacy and his books around him.'

'I shall, of course, have shelves made especially for those. Truth to tell, I'd move down here if that is what he wished, but no doubt tongues would wag. Whereas in Dublin – the big city – no one would notice or even care about two old friends seeing out their twilight years together. Would they?'

Ambrose looked at me for reassurance.

'I'm sure they wouldn't, although you'd better make sure the apartment's near a church. I'm sure that James will wish to keep in touch, so to speak, when he's in Dublin.'

'Well, the moment I get back, I shall begin to put my plans into action.' He smiled, then turned to me. 'Thank you, dearest girl, for what you have done. I will remain eternally grateful,' he added, his eyes full of tears. 'You've given me a reason to live again.'

'Oh Ambrose, don't thank me, please. After all you've done for me, there's no need to say anything.'

'I wanted to say it anyway. Also, Mary dear, have you read your letter yet?'

'Yes.'

'And?'

'And . . . I don't know. I mean, it was quite formal, like mine to him. He left me a telephone number that I could contact him on, but—'

'Mary, for goodness' sake, go and see him! He – and the other one – have haunted you for all these years! If there's one thing life has taught me, it's that it's too damned short!'

'Yes. You're right, of course. Okay, I will. And while we're here, I should tell you all about "the other one", as you've just called him . . .'

Forty minutes later, Ambrose had gone for a nap and I was back in my room. He'd listened intently as I'd told him what had happened to Bobby, then placed a hand on my arm.

'So, finally the past has been put to bed and you can start to breathe again,' he said.

'I can, yes.'

'Dear Mary, if only you'd have told me at the time, I might have been able to help.'

'No, Ambrose. Nobody could,' I'd sighed. 'But at least it's over now.'

'And just this to go,' I murmured as I took out his letter and dialled what I knew was a British code. He answered after a few rings and the two of us made an arrangement. Very formally, like we were having a business meeting. Putting the receiver down, I folded the piece of paper on which I'd written down what time and where, and put it in my purse.

'Why didn't he sound guilty?' I asked myself. The answer was, I didn't know.

'So, Mum, how long are you going to stay in Ireland?' Jack asked me that evening as we all ate in the smart restaurant upstairs, which had a panoramic view of the sea.

'I'm coming back to Dublin with Ambrose and you two tomorrow, then after that, I want to spend some time with my family down here.'

'Are you sure you won't come on the cruise, Mum?' asked Mary-Kate. 'You've always wanted to see the Greek islands – the birthplace of all your beloved mythology. Ally sent Jack a picture of the boat – it looks amazing!'

'You should think about it, Mary dear,' Ambrose piped up. 'Your daughter is absolutely right. I haven't been back to Greece since my last trip to Sparta, over twenty years ago now. The theatre is something to behold at sunset, with Mount Taygetus forming the backdrop.'

Ambrose gave me one of those looks I remembered so vividly from my student days.

'Named after Taygete, the fifth of the Seven Sisters of the Pleiades, and mother of Lacedemon, sired by Zeus,' I parroted, just to assure him I hadn't forgotten. He gave me a slight nod of approval. 'Tiggy's name is short for Taygete – she's the fifth sister in her family,' I continued, 'and ironically, I'm the fifth child in my adoptive family.'

'Or maybe the missing sister in Ally's family,' said Mary-Kate. 'Oh Mum, please come,' she urged me again.

'No, not now, but maybe I'll add Greece to my list of places to see on my Grand Tour. So, anyone for dessert?'

When I arrived back in my room, I saw the red message light was flashing on my hotel telephone, and that there was a voicemail on my mobile. Picking up my landline message first, it was Katie asking me to call her back.

Turning to my mobile phone, I listened to my voicemail messages. The first was – coincidentally, after our dinner conversation – from Tiggy, asking how I was and saying that she was hoping to see me on the cruise with Jack and Mary-Kate.

I then called Katie.

'Hi, it's Merry. Is everything all right?'

'Yes, grand altogether, thank you. I just wanted to let you know that I spoke to Nora, and she said she couldn't remember the name of the family that she worked for up at the Big House, but she'd have a think. Then she called me back to say she'd remembered it. I was right, 'tis a foreign sounding name, but not the one you gave me. I'd better spell it out for you. Got a pen and a pad?'

'Yup. Fire away,' I said, pencil at the ready.

'Right, she thinks she's got the correct spelling, so it's E. S. Z. U.'

I read the letters back to myself.

'Eszu,' I said. 'Thanks a million, Katie, and we'll speak tomorrow.'

51

Atlantis

'Have you heard anything back from Jack about who owned Argideen House, Ally?' asked CeCe, walking into the kitchen, where Chrissie was preparing a supper of steak, with all the Aussie-style trimmings.

'No. I asked him to let me know if Merry's sister remembered what it was. Obviously she hasn't,' Ally sighed.

'Did he say if his mum's still refusing to come on the cruise?' said Maia, who was sitting in front of a laptop, checking her emails.

'She wants to stay longer in Ireland, apparently. Well, I think we all have to accept we've done our best to find the missing sister. If the ring's the proof, plus the fact Merry was adopted, along with the address of where she was found being so close to the priest's house, we've found her. But if she won't come on the cruise, we can't make her.'

'No, but it's such a shame, because everything fits,' Maia said.

'Apart from her age,' Ally countered. 'We all presumed we were looking for a much younger woman. At least we'll have her children with us, which will just have to be good enough.'

'Right,' Maia said, jotting down some notes on a pad

beside the laptop. 'Tiggy and Charlie's flight lands in Geneva at eleven thirty on Wednesday, Electra's confirmed that she's going to fly straight to Nice, and so will Star, Mouse and Rory. Then there's Jack and Mary-Kate, who are yet to confirm when they'll arrive.'

'So how many bedrooms do we need for tomorrow?' said Ma, who was ferrying glasses and cutlery out onto the terrace.

'Just one for Tiggy and Charlie,' Maia said, standing up. 'Please relax, Ma. You have to remember we're all here to help you.'

'We sure are,' Chrissie said as she turned round from her station at the range and smiled at Ma. 'Although how anyone can cook anything on this ancient gadget, I have no idea. Good job we decided to have a barbie and cook the steaks on that, isn't it, Cee?'

'Ma, why don't you sit down and we'll get you a glass of wine?' Ally steered her towards the table and pushed her gently into a chair. 'Let us look after you for a change.'

'No, Ally, that is not what I am paid to do, and I cannot bear it,' Ma protested.

'You were never paid to love us, but you did for free, and now we're loving you back,' CeCe said as she plonked a glass of wine in front of Ma. 'Now drink it,' she ordered, 'and stop flapping, okay?'

'As I said to Star when I visited her in London last year, without Claudia by my side, I fall apart; she is truly the engine of Atlantis.'

'Well, maybe we never appreciated her enough,' Maia said, then smiled as she saw Floriano and Valentina walk in through the doors from the terrace. They had both been taking a short nap in the Pavilion, having only arrived from Rio de Janeiro via Lisbon that afternoon.

Ally studied Floriano as he held tight to his daughter's

hand. He had tanned skin, dark hair and expressive brown eyes, his teeth flashing a smile on his handsome face. Valentina looked up at all the adults, her huge brown eyes wide, shyly twisting a strand of her shiny long hair around a dainty finger.

Ma stood up immediately. 'Hello, Valentina,' she said, walking over to the little girl. 'Are you feeling better after your sleep?'

'Yes, thank you,' the little girl answered in thickly accented English. Maia had said that, being bilingual himself, Floriano had taught her English from the cradle.

'Would you like a drink? Coke, maybe?' Ma continued, looking up at Floriano for guidance.

'Of course she may have a Coke,' agreed Floriano.

'I am *verrry* hungry, Papai,' she said, looking up at her father.

'Supper won't be ready for perhaps thirty minutes, so why don't you come with me and we'll see if we can find a snack for you, to keep you going until then?' Ma offered her hand to Valentina, who took it willingly. The two of them walked in the direction of the pantry.

'Straight back into mummy mode,' Ally smiled as she rolled her eyes.

'Where she is happiest,' said Maia as she went to Floriano and gave him a kiss on the cheek. 'Would you like a beer?'

'I could kill for one,' he said as he put his arm around her shoulder.

'One for the chef too, if there's any going, please,' called Chrissie.

'I'll get them,' said CeCe, heading for the fridge.

Ally poured a glass of wine for herself, and when everyone was furnished with a drink, raised it. 'To Floriano and Valentina, for making it all the way here from Rio to join us on this very special occasion.'

Everyone toasted, and Ally thought how wonderful it was to see the Atlantis kitchen not only full of her sisters, but also their new partners and family.

She watched Valentina spot Bear, who was lying on his playmat in a corner of the kitchen.

'*Aí que neném bonito!* May I play with him, Maia?'

'Of course you may,' Maia said, looking at Ally as Valentina put down her Coke and made her way over to Bear. She knelt down next to him, then gathered him up in her small arms. The two sisters shared a smile.

'Would it be okay if I took Floriano to see Pa's private garden?' Maia asked the kitchen in general.

'Of course,' said Ma, moving towards Valentina and Bear. 'I will watch over the children, don't worry.'

'Thank you.' Maia took Floriano's hand and led him out of the kitchen.

'We'll whistle when it's ready, Maia,' CeCe shouted after them. 'I should think the barbie's nearly hot enough to go now, Chrissie.'

'Well, I'll come with you, otherwise you'll burn the steaks to a crisp as usual,' Chrissie quipped as the two women walked outside.

'Isn't it wonderful to see CeCe so happy?' Ma said as she sat down in the easy chair, next to where Valentina was playing with Bear.

'Absolutely, and just look how maternal Valentina is.'

At the mention of her name, Valentina looked up at Ally questioningly.

'You like babies?' Ally asked her.

'I like babies *verrry* much,' she agreed as she gently put a wriggling Bear back onto his mat.

Fifteen minutes later, CeCe gave a shrill whistle to let Maia and Floriano know that supper was ready, as the rest of the girls took the bowls of salad and a large tureen of French fries onto the terrace table. Ally sat down, watching for any signs of Maia returning. She knew why her sister had wanted to catch Floriano alone as soon as she could. Eventually, she saw them walking hand in hand towards the terrace. Maia's head was resting on Floriano's shoulder and just before they reached the table, he stopped, turned towards her and put his arms around her so tightly that he lifted her off the ground. He kissed her on the lips, and the beam that spread across his face meant that Maia's news had been received more than positively.

As everyone sat down and Chrissie began to serve the steaks, Ally heard her mobile ringing in the kitchen. Dashing back inside, she saw it was Jack.

'Hi there.'

'Hi, Ally,' he replied as a burst of laughter came from the table outside. 'I'm not catching you at a bad moment, am I?'

'Actually, we're just sitting down for supper.'

'Okay, well, very quickly, I just called to say that Mum's sister, Nora – the one that worked at Argideen House – has remembered the name of the family that owned it. It's a weird one, I can tell you, something foreign. I'm not even sure how to pronounce it properly.'

'It isn't D'Aplièse, is it?'

'No, no, it's . . . well, I think I'll spell it, rather than say it. Have you got a pen?'

'Yup,' said Ally, reaching for one. 'Fire away.'

'Okay. It's E-S-Z-U.'

Ally wrote the letters down, and it was only when she looked at the word on paper that she struggled to gulp in air. Jack was saying something, but she wasn't listening as she mouthed the surname to herself.

'Ally? Did you get that? Did you want me to repeat it?'

'No, I got it. E-S-Z-U.'

'Yup. Told you it was a weird one.'

'It is . . .' Ally sat down heavily in a chair.

'Hey, Ally, you okay?'

'I'm fine.'

There was a pause on the line before Jack spoke. 'That name means something to you, doesn't it?'

'I . . . yes, it does, but how it fits into everything, I really don't know. Listen, I've got to go and have supper now, but I'll speak to you later.'

'Okay. Speak later.'

Ally stood up and realised she was sweating with . . . what? Surprise, or fear . . . ? Deciding she wouldn't share the news with anyone just yet, she went to the sink and splashed her face with water, then stepped outside to join the diners.

After supper, everyone except Ma, who was upstairs putting Bear to bed, joined in with the clearing up.

'I guess it went well, then,' Ally whispered to Maia as they stood side by side, drying the saucepans as CeCe and Chrissie stacked the dishwasher.

'It did,' Maia whispered back. 'He was thrilled, Ally, and I'm just so relieved!'

'I certainly don't think you need to worry about Valentina's reaction either, given the way she already adores Bear. I'm so happy for you, Maia, I really am. I just hope you can be happy for yourself.'

'Now I've told Floriano, maybe I can be. I'm not going to say anything to anybody until we're all gathered together on the boat, although I think that—'

'Ma already knows,' they both whispered together, then smiled.

'Was that phone call earlier from Jack, by the way?' Maia asked.

'Yes, it was.'

'Any news?'

'Yes, but it wasn't important,' Ally lied. 'You go off with Floriano and Valentina and enjoy your special evening, okay?'

'Okay. I'll see you tomorrow.'

'Sleep well, Maia.'

'I think that finally I will. Goodnight.'

Taking Valentina by the hand, Maia and Floriano left the house to head for the Pavilion.

'I think we'll have an early one too,' said CeCe. 'It's gonna be a busy day tomorrow. Night, Ally.'

Chrissie and CeCe left the kitchen and Ally watched as Ma entered it and began preparing Bear's bottle for the night-time feed.

'Honestly, Ma, I'll do tonight. I think you need a full night's sleep before tomorrow. I'm feeling so much better since I came back from France. Seriously.' Ally almost grabbed the bottle from her and put it on the table. 'I'll do it,' she repeated.

'Perhaps a night's sleep will do me good. These last few weeks have made me realise I'm getting old, Ally. When you were younger, I could exist on almost no sleep and did for years. But now . . . well, it seems I can't.'

'Ma, you've been absolutely wonderful and I don't know what I would have done without your help with Bear. Now, go to bed and enjoy the peace while you can.'

'All right. Will you come up with me?'

'I . . .' Ally was desperate to confide in someone. 'Ma?'

'Yes?'

'I need to get hold of Georg, but he's just not answering his mobile. Do you know for sure when he'll be back?'

'As he is coming on the cruise with us, it must be tomorrow. May I ask why?'

'I . . . oh Ma, Jack told me something earlier and it's really shaken me. Normally I'd tell Maia and we'd work out what to do. But under the circumstances, I just couldn't tell her. Especially not tonight.'

'Tell me, *chérie*. You know it will go no further. What did Jack say?'

'That Argideen House, which is the place the coordinates for Merope point to, was once owned by a family called Eszu.'

Ally registered the shock on Ma's face. 'Eszu?'

'Yes. Jack spelt the name out for me. It's identical, Ma. I mean, over dinner I was thinking that maybe it could just be a coincidence, but it's such an unusual name, isn't it? Especially in Ireland. Do you know if there was any connection between Pa and the Eszu family in the past?'

'Truly, Ally, I have no idea. However, I do know that you believe you saw Kreeg Eszu's boat close to where you think your father was buried. And then, of course, his son, Zed . . .'

'The father of Maia's child,' Ally spoke in a whisper, just in case CeCe or Chrissie came down for a mug of something to take up to bed. 'I hope you understand why I didn't want to say anything about it tonight.'

'Of course I do. She told Floriano she's pregnant, didn't she?' said Ma.

'She did. But you mustn't tell anyone, Ma.'

'Of course I won't. I'm so very happy for her.'

'Do you think that Georg might know anything about the Eszu connection?'

'Ally, please believe me, I know no more than you, but he worked so closely with your father, so he might well, yes.'

'You really don't know where he's gone?'

'I swear, I have no idea. I am sorry I cannot help you further – I would if I could. I'm going up to bed. Goodnight, Ally.'

'Goodnight, sleep well.'

Ma left the kitchen just as Ally's mobile rang. 'Hello?'

'Hi there, Jack here again. You're not in bed or anything, are you?'

'No, not yet. How's things in Ireland?'

'They're well, thanks. The taxi's booked to take me, Mary-Kate and Ambrose – my mum's quasi-godfather – and Mum, of course, back to Dublin.'

'Are you sure you can't persuade your mum to join us? I'm hoping that our lawyer, Georg, will be back tomorrow and then hopefully he can confirm for certain it is your mum who is the missing sister.'

'No can do, I'm afraid, Ally. She's adamant that she wants to spend more time here in Ireland. Mary-Kate and I will fly from Dublin to London tomorrow afternoon, then our plane for Nice leaves early the next morning. We'll meet you on the boat, is that right?'

'Yes, I'll send a car to pick you up from the airport, then I'll see you aboard the *Titan* with . . .'

Ally stopped herself, realising she hadn't yet told Jack she had a baby son. 'With the rest of the sisters,' she added quickly.

'Okay. Well, sounds as if it's sure gonna to be an adventure. Mary-Kate's excited to meet the rest of you girls.'

'And I'm excited to meet her. Okay, let me know if there's any delays, and if not, I'll see you in Nice.'

'Yeah, and I'm really looking forward to seeing you again, Ally. Night.'

'Goodnight, Jack.'

Grabbing the milk bottle from the table to take upstairs in case she needed to supplement for Bear, and switching off the kitchen lights, Ally headed for bed. As she lay down, ready to sleep, she thought about her conversation with Jack.

I'm really looking forward to seeing you . . .

Ally felt a little bump of excitement at the fact Jack had said that, but then squashed it immediately when she heard Bear give a tiny snore from his cot.

'Even if he does seem to have forgiven me for not coming clean on who I was, he's hardly going to be interested in a single mother, is he?'

Doing her best to push down any silly flutters in her stomach, Ally fell asleep.

52

Merry
Dublin

I sat in the back of the taxi next to Mary-Kate, with Ambrose on the other side of me. We'd offered him the front seat, but he'd declined, saying that Niall might talk him into an early grave, so that honour had gone to Jack. Yet again, my children had tried to persuade me to come on the cruise, but given that the meeting I had waited thirty-seven years for was only hours away from happening, I had yet again declined.

'Another time,' I'd said, 'but you both go and have a wonderful holiday. It all sounds very glamorous.'

Reaching Merrion Square, Jack helped Ambrose out of the back of the taxi, as Niall collected my own and Ambrose's luggage from the boot.

''Tis a pleasure to have met both of you,' Niall said. 'You have my card now, Ambrose, so any time you're wanting to come down to West Cork again, you be giving me a ring, so.'

'I will, and thank you again,' Ambrose said as he turned and, using his walking stick, manoeuvred his way up the steps to the front door.

'Bye, Mum.' Both Jack and Mary-Kate hugged me – they

were going straight off with Niall to Dublin airport – and I felt tears prick the back of my eyes.

'You two keep in touch, won't you?'

'We will,' said Mary-Kate. 'And if you're down in West Cork when the cruise is over, I might come back and join you.'

I saw the faintest hint of a blush appear in my daughter's cheeks and knew immediately the meeting with her new musician friend, Eoin, had obviously gone well.

'If you change your mind, Ally says there's plenty of room on the boat,' Jack urged for the last time.

'No, Jack. Now, you'd better get back in that taxi or you'll miss your flight.'

I said goodbye to Niall and stood on the pavement waving them off, then followed Ambrose inside.

'Cup of tea?' I asked him.

'My goodness, I could murder one,' he said.

Fifteen minutes later, we were in his sitting room drinking tea and eating a slice of a very good fruitcake his daily had left for him.

'So, are you still set on selling this, Ambrose?'

'Absolutely. Even though I love the dear old place, and whether or not James will join me somewhere new, it's time.'

'I'm sure he won't take that much persuading, Ambrose. It was wonderful to see the two of you reunited after all this time.'

'It felt wonderful, too, Mary. I'd forgotten what it was like to laugh. We did an awful lot of that. So, I shall invite some auctioneers to come and value this and up for sale it shall go. Now then, and far more pressingly, are you sure you want to go tonight? You're most welcome to stay here, Merry.'

'I know I am, but I've never been to Northern Ireland before and I feel I'd like to see it.'

'As you are aware, the last time you were in Ireland, Belfast wasn't a safe place to visit, but recently, I hear there's been major regeneration in and around the city.'

'You know,' I said quietly, 'if any Provisional IRA bombings were reported on television or in our New Zealand newspapers – which, as you know so well, happened a lot in the seventies and eighties – I wouldn't look. Or read. I just . . . couldn't. But then in 1998, I actually sat in front of my television in Otago and cried my eyes out when I saw the *Taoiseach* sign the Good Friday Agreement. I couldn't believe it had finally happened.'

'It did indeed, but of course, it will never be enough for some republicans, who won't stop until Northern Ireland is reunited with the South and back under our Irish governance, but I *do* believe the next generation have been brought up to define themselves as human beings first, rather than Catholics or Protestants. That certainly helps, and a broader education too, of course,' he added. 'I find it quite amusing that I'm one of those rare old people who doesn't look back to the past and think how perfect it was, and despair of the world we live in now. In fact, quite the opposite. The human race has taken quite remarkable strides in the past thirty years, and I rather envy the young, who live in such an open society.'

'Both of our lives would have been very different if we were young in this generation,' I agreed, 'but, well . . . I'd better be thinking about leaving soon. I'll pop downstairs and get changed.'

In the basement, I opened the door to the bedroom that had once been mine. And felt choked when I saw that Ambrose had not removed my books or the bits and pieces I'd collected as a teenager. The wallpaper – which he had had sent over from England for when I began to stay with him – was of the flowery pink variety, and the same lace counterpane lay neatly across the bottom of the wrought-iron single bed. I remembered that when I'd first seen the bedroom, I'd almost cried in pleasure, not only because it was so very pretty and feminine, but because it was all mine. Certainly through all those years of boarding school when I had a short weekend exeat and it was too far to travel home to West Cork, this bedroom had provided a refuge. Then I'd moved in fully when I'd started my Masters, which I'd never completed . . .

I opened the wardrobe, wondering if all my clothes from the early seventies – mini-skirts, bell-bottomed trousers and tight, ribbed polo necks – would still be hanging there, but they weren't. Of course they weren't. I'd left decades ago, so why should Ambrose keep them?

Shivering suddenly, I sat down on the bed and my mind immediately sped back across the years to the last time I'd been in here and Bobby had arrived on the doorstep. He'd banged so hard and was shouting so loudly that I'd had no choice but to let him in.

With his long jet-black hair and intense blue eyes, along with his height and muscled torso, he'd been a handsome man. Some of my friends who'd met him when he'd gate-crashed our group having drinks in a pub had found him attractive. But to me, he was just Bobby: the angry, mixed-up but highly intelligent little boy I'd known since childhood.

As he'd pinned me against the wall, I'd felt the chill of steel pressing into my neck.

'You'll stop seeing him, or I swear I'll kill you, Merry O'Reilly. And then I'll go after him and his family, as well as yours. You're mine, do you understand? You always have been. You know that.'

The look in his eyes and the sour smell of stale beer on his breath as he'd pressed his lips to mine would never leave me.

With my life under threat, of course I'd promised him that I'd stop seeing Peter, that I'd join him in his terrorist crusade against the British.

I'd been terrified out of my wits, but at least I knew how to calm him down – I'd had years of practice after all. Finally, he'd removed the gun from my neck and let me go. We'd agreed to meet the following night and I'd just about managed to stop myself from vomiting when he'd kissed me again. When he eventually walked towards the door, just as he was about to open it, he turned round and stared at me.

'Just remember, I will hunt you down, wherever you try to hide . . .'

It was after he'd left that I'd decided I had no choice but to leave. And I'd come down here to my bedroom and begun to pack . . .

'It's all over, Merry, Bobby can never hurt you again,' I told myself as I tried to quell the familiar panic attack symptoms that had begun automatically for thirty-seven years every time I'd thought of him. I was sure, given the hundreds of times I'd relived that moment, that a psychiatrist would tell me that I was suffering from post-traumatic stress. I had no idea whether coming back to where it had happened would actually help, but I had to believe that one day, I'd manage to convince my brain that it was all over and I was finally safe.

I heaved the large suitcase I'd brought with me on the Grand Tour onto the bed, opened it and tried to concentrate on what to wear to my 'meeting' tomorrow.

Not that it matters, Merry . . .

I pulled out some clothes. Should I look sophisticated? Casual? I just didn't know.

In the end, I plumped – as I usually did when I wasn't sure – for my favourite green dress, folding it carefully into my holdall, alongside my black court shoes. After changing into my usual travelling attire of jeans, a shirt and a Chanel-style bouclé jacket that added a touch of class and just seemed to go with everything, I packed my washbag, some clean underwear and a book for the train, then zipped up the holdall.

Back upstairs, I left it in the corridor and went into the sitting room to say goodbye to Ambrose.

'I've left my big suitcase downstairs, along with a pile of laundry which I'll sort out when I'm back tomorrow. I hope that's okay?'

'Of course it is, dear girl. It means that you must return to collect it, though given you left a wardrobe full of clothes last time, I suppose that's no guarantee. They're all here, by the way.'

'What are?'

'The clothes you left behind. I packed them into a suitcase and put it in the bottom of one of my wardrobes, just in case you might be passing one day.'

'Oh Ambrose, I'm so, so sorry.'

'Don't be. *Je ne regrette rien*, as the French say so succinctly. You are back now and that is all that matters. Oh, and with everything that has happened recently, there's something I keep forgetting to tell you. I've read Nuala's diary. Your grandmother was a very brave young lady.'

'Yes,' I said as I watched him tap it gently on the round table next to his leather chair. 'She was.'

'It was a struggle to make out some of the misspelt words, but goodness, what a story. It moved me to tears at certain points,' Ambrose sighed. 'One thing I must tell you is that Nuala writes about the parlour maid, Maureen.'

'The one who betrayed her?'

'Yes. Now then, you remember Mrs Cavanagh, James's famous housekeeper? He told me she worked at Argideen House before she kept house for James. Guess what her first name was?'

'No, Ambrose . . .'

'Maureen. Maureen Cavanagh. One and the same woman who betrayed young Nuala, and who also betrayed myself and James years later.'

'Oh my God,' I breathed.

'What a sad, bitter woman she was. Poor James told me he had the job of presiding over her funeral. He said that only three people attended, and you know how many people usually turn up for such events here in Ireland. She lived alone and died alone. And perhaps that was her punishment.'

'Perhaps, but if I had ever met her, then I couldn't be held responsible for my actions,' I replied fiercely.

'Dear Mary, you could never hurt a fly, but I appreciate the sentiment,' Ambrose chuckled. 'Although perhaps one day you might think of publishing Nuala's diary, especially as you now know the end of her story. There aren't enough factual accounts of that moment in time, and the anguish it caused so many families afterwards, and certainly very few written from a female perspective. The role Cumann na mBan played in freeing Ireland from the British barely gets a footnote in history.'

'I agree, and maybe I will. In fact, confronting my past has also made me remember my love for academia. I was thinking downstairs that I never finished that Masters I started, because I had to leave . . .'

'I still have your half-finished dissertation in there.' Ambrose indicated his desk. 'It – and you – were becoming something quite brilliant. Now then, shall I call you a taxi to take you to the station?'

'I'll walk down to Grafton Street and find one. I shall be back tomorrow, Ambrose darling. Wish me luck, won't you?'

'Of course. I can only pray that you will finally be able to put the past to rest.'

'I hope so too. Bye, Ambrose,' I said, then picked up my overnight bag and left the house.

The train to Belfast – which was rather aptly named the Enterprise – caught me by surprise, as it was so modern and comfortable. I watched as countryside flew by, wondering if I'd see a sign when we crossed the border into Northern Ireland. In the old days, there'd been border controls on all forms of transport. Yet today there was nothing, and just over an hour into the two-hour journey, we were stopping across the border at Newry, a place I knew had seen such violence during the Troubles. In August 1971, six civilians, including a Catholic priest, had been shot dead by the British army in Ballymurphy. News of the massacre had only added another spark to light Bobby's already flammable touchpaper. I had realised that that incident, plus the fact he'd seen me in a bar with Peter, had almost certainly been what had sent him over the edge, and it had happened very close to here.

Today, it looked like any other station that serviced a small town, but back then, it had been the scene of an old conflict brought back to life by extremists like Bobby. So many times he'd set off at me in the pub, raging about the plight of the Northern Irish Catholics and how the IRA would bomb 'the bastard Proddies' into extinction. I'd said to him over and over that the way forward was negotiation, not war, that surely a way could be found to make the situation better through diplomacy.

He'd accused me of sounding like Michael Collins himself.

'That traitor spun us all a tale, told us that signing the truce would be a stepping stone to an Irish republic. But the North is still in British hands, Merry!' he'd railed at me. 'You watch and see how we'll fight fire with fire.'

I had watched, as the Provisional IRA had done as Bobby

promised they would, bombing targets in the North and then heading to the British mainland. 'The Troubles' had lasted for almost thirty years, and all through them, I had imagined Bobby being part of the death and destruction that the new war had wrought.

No wonder I couldn't watch the news bulletins on television . . . they had fuelled my own fire of fear. Yet all those years, Bobby had been sitting in an institution, believing he was back in 1920 . . .

Well, here we were in 2008, and yes, Northern Ireland was still part of the United Kingdom, but the fact that I had just sailed at high speed across the border had to be a sign of progress, surely.

It felt ridiculous even to myself when I looked out of the window and was surprised to see that the surrounding landscape looked very similar to that south of the border – *As if a manmade line could change anything*, I thought – but coming here to the area that had seen so much bitter conflict was yet another demon in my head that I was trying to tame by facing it.

The train arrived exactly on time at Lanyon Place station in Belfast. Walking through to the exit to look for the taxi rank, I heard the lilt of an accent that was familiar, yet unique to this Northern Irish part of the United Kingdom. Climbing into a taxi, I directed the driver to the Merchant Hotel which, so my guidebook told me, had once been the headquarters of the Ulster Bank.

I looked out of the window fascinated, as we drove into the city that no longer showed any signs of its terrible wounds, on the outside at least.

'Here you are, madam,' the driver said, pulling up in front of the Merchant Hotel. 'It's a fine wee establishment.'

'How much do I owe you?'

'That'd be ten pounds, please.'

Pounds . . .

I hunted through my purse for what was left over of my British money from my London stay.

'There you go, thank you.'

I walked up the steps and into a very modern lobby. I checked in and the porter took me and my holdall up to my room, which was beautifully decorated in a cosy, rather chintzy way.

'I'll certainly have had my fill of hotels by the time I get home,' I sighed as I lay down on the bed.

I checked the time and saw it was past seven o'clock. Calling down for room service, I ordered the soup of the day and a bread roll. I then had my usual moment of feeling bad for spending so much money on smart hotels, but then, what were savings for? Jock and I had put a bit aside every month for the past thirty years and, given we had never taken a holiday outside New Zealand, I didn't think he'd mind.

'But he might mind about tomorrow,' I muttered.

I hung up my dress to take out any creases, then I switched on the television as I ate my soup. BBC One was showing *EastEnders*, a British soap that Mary-Kate had found on a channel of our satellite package back home.

It all felt very strange here, to still be on the island of Ireland, and yet so definitely in a tiny parcel of land that was distinctly British.

I took a long, leisurely bath in the free-standing tub and wondered how I'd feel when I was back in my farmhouse in the Gibbston Valley, which was certainly homely, but had none of the fine furnishings or modern appliances I'd become used to.

After my bath, I watched a terrible romcom about a bridesmaid, trying to do anything to distract myself from thinking about tomorrow. I took out my bottle of Jameson's, which was now three-quarters empty due to me plundering it each time there had been a new revelation to deal with. Just maybe, after tomorrow, I could get back on that train to Dublin, knowing that I'd finally put my past to rest. Slipping under the crisp white sheets, I set my alarm for nine o'clock, just in case, and lay back on the soft pillows. Lying there in the dark, my arm instinctively reached out towards Jock.

'Please, darling, forgive me for never telling you about any of this, and for meeting him tomorrow . . .'

I woke with a start to the sound of the alarm clock. I had tossed and turned into the small hours, wondering how I'd feel when I saw him, and thinking about all the things that I wanted to ask him, but equally knowing there was only one question I needed answering.

'In under an hour's time, you'll be finding out,' I said as I reached for the bedside telephone to dial room service for a cup of tea and some toast.

While I waited, I dressed and gave myself a quick wash and brush-up, then put on some mascara, adding a little blusher to my cheeks. My hair was doing what it always had done, waving in places it shouldn't wave – oh, how I had always longed for straight, easy to manage locks – but having tried it in an elegant bun and then some combs, I gave up and let it hang naturally in a wavy bob around my face. Last time I had seen him, my hair had been long – almost reaching to the bottom of my back. My 'mane', he used to call it. I drank the tea, but I was so nervous that I almost choked on the toast and gave up on the third bite. I checked my watch. A quarter to ten. In less than ten minutes, I needed to walk downstairs.

'Calm down, Merry, for goodness' sake,' I told myself as I applied my usual pink lipstick and gave my hair a last quick brush. 'The onus is on him, not you, remember?' I said to my reflection.

I walked to the door, opened it and headed for the lift that would take me downstairs to meet him for the first time in thirty-seven years . . .

The receptionist pointed me in the direction of the Great Room and I walked towards it, my legs like jelly beneath me. As I entered, I saw the most enormous chandelier hanging down from a high atrium in the centre of an incredible room. Pillars bedecked with cherubs and golden cornicing held up the intricately decorated ceiling. I was still gaping up at it when I heard a voice from behind me.

'Hello, Merry. Amazing, isn't it?'

'I . . . yes.' I dragged my eyes away from the chandelier and turned to look at him.

And . . . he looked exactly the same: tall and slim, albeit with grey peppering his sandy hair and a number of thin lines etched across his face. His brown eyes were just as mesmerising as I remembered and . . . here he was, standing next to me after all these years. The world spun as a wave of dizziness engulfed me. I had no choice but to reach out a hand to his forearm to steady myself.

'Are you all right?'

'Sorry, I'm feeling a little dizzy.'

'It's probably standing there, craning your neck back to look at that chandelier. Come on, let's get you sat down.'

I half closed my eyes as further waves engulfed me. I clung on to him as I felt his arm go round my waist to support me as we walked.

'Can you bring some water over?' I heard him ask, as I felt him sit me down.

I'd broken out in a sweat and I sucked in some air to try and steady my breathing. 'Sorry, sorry . . .' I muttered, hardly believing that, after all this time, my plans to be cool, calm and in control had gone out of the window before I'd even begun.

'Here, drink some of this,' he said and I felt a glass being thrust between my lips. My hands were too shaky to hold it myself, and he emptied so much water into my mouth that I choked and began coughing and spluttering.

'Sorry,' he said, as I felt a piece of cloth being dabbed round my mouth and then patted down my neck. At least the water on my skin cooled me down, even if I wanted to die of embarrassment.

'Can you bring us some hot tea?' I heard him say. 'Or maybe a whiskey might help more? Tell you what, bring both.'

I laid my head back against the soft covering of the banquette that I'd been placed on and took some long, deep breaths in and out. Finally, my body stopped doing the strange tingly thing and the black spots in front of my eyes began to recede.

'Sorry,' I said again, pointlessly.

'Tea with plenty of sugar, or whiskey?'

I heard that familiar ironic smile in his voice. I shrugged.

'Right, whiskey it is. Can you hold the glass?'

'Maybe.'

He placed it into one of my hands and then steered it towards my mouth. I took a small sip, and then a larger one.

'Honestly, Merry, any excuse for an alcoholic drink at breakfast.'

'That's me,' I agreed. 'I'm a lost cause, but at least I'm feeling better.' I opened my eyes fully and the world finally stood still. I placed the whiskey glass on the table in front of me, then looked down at my front, which was spattered with water.

'I'll pour you some tea too, in case you want that.'

'Thank you. I apologise again.'

'Seriously, there's no need. It's actually very muggy in here as well, not a feeling we tend to be used to in Ireland, is it?'

'No.'

'Global warming and all that . . . A few offices I know are beginning to put in air conditioning. Can you believe it?'

'No, considering I spent most of my childhood not being able to feel my toes. Anyway,' I said as I turned to him, unable to keep my own eyes away from his, yet terrified that if I looked into them again, I'd be as lost as I had been the first time I'd met him.

'Anyway,' he smiled. 'It's very good to see you after all these years.'

'And you.'

'You haven't changed a bit, you know,' he said.

'Thank you, but I doubt you'd be saying, "Jaysus, Merry, you've turned into an old bat!" now, would you?'

'I suppose I wouldn't, no,' Peter chuckled.

'Just for the record, you haven't changed either.'

'That's an out and out lie. My hair is almost entirely grey—'

'At least you have some, which is more than can be said for a lot of men your age.'

'My age, is it, Merry?'

'You are two years older than me, remember? In your sixties . . .'

'Yes, I am, and feeling every bit of it too. I may look all right on the outside, but I certainly can't run around a pitch kicking a ball like I used to do. Now I have to hit it against a wall in a squash court – the game of city-dwelling old men,' Peter added as a waiter approached our table.

'Can I offer you any breakfast?' he asked us. 'It's last orders, I'm afraid.'

Peter looked at me and I shook my head.

'No, thanks.'

'Are you sure?'

'Positive. I'll nibble on the biscuits they brought with the tea.'

'I'll have a croissant and a double espresso, to soak up the whiskey,' he said with a raise of his eyebrow as he reached for his glass. '*Sláinte!*'

'*Sláinte*,' I parroted without picking mine up. My head had spun once this morning and I certainly didn't want it to happen again.

'So, how have you been?' he asked me.

'I . . .' We caught each other's glance and, given the situation, we both began to chuckle at the ridiculous inanity of the remark.

'I've been . . . well, I've been fine, really,' I said, and then we chuckled some more, which turned into a good few minutes of uncontrollable laughter.

We both ended up wiping our eyes on our napkins, which meant I had probably smudged my mascara all over my face, but I was past caring. One of the reasons Peter had so attracted me in the first place was his sense of humour, which, levelled against the intensity and seriousness of Bobby, had been a relief. Peter had worn life lightly back then.

When the waiter returned with the coffee and croissant, we both tried to get ourselves under control.

'Do you think he's going to chuck us out for bad behaviour?' I whispered.

'Possibly. My reputation here will probably be destroyed – it's close to my office, so I use the hotel for the occasional meeting – but who cares?'

'What do you do?'

'Why don't you guess, Merry?' he challenged me.

'Well, you're wearing a suit and tie, which wouldn't mark you out as a circus performer, so we'll cross that one off the list.'

'Correct.'

'You have a leather document holder with you, that's useful for putting papers in when you have meetings.'

'Correct again.'

'And the third and most important clue is that you were studying law at Trinity, then doing your articles when I last saw you. You're a lawyer.'

'Correct. You could always read me well, couldn't you?' he said as he picked up his espresso and eyed me with amusement over the top of the cup.

'Perhaps, but why don't you try to do the same with me?'

'Ah, now that's far harder. So . . . let me see.'

I felt his eyes scan over my face and my body, and for my sins, I blushed. 'Clue number one: even though women tend to age far better and are able to keep themselves much fitter than they could in the old days, it would not strike me that you followed your own mother down the path of having nineteen children, or however many it was.'

'Seven, actually. Correct. Continue.'

'Given the fact that you are wearing a wedding ring, I assume you're married.'

'*Was* married. My husband died some months ago, but I'll give you that.'

'I am sorry, Merry. I had a similar tragedy when the woman I'd lived with for ten years died. Anyway, given I already know you haven't been resident here on the island of Ireland for many years, or London in fact, or ended up in Canada as we'd planned – I've checked the register – I'd reckon, taking all the circumstances of thirty-seven years ago into account, that you went elsewhere. Somewhere far flung, like Australia, maybe.'

'Ooh, you're hot,' I replied, then felt a further blush rise to my cheeks, as it wasn't appropriate to call someone 'hot' these days.

'New Zealand then.'

'Correct. Very good.'

'Perhaps you pursued an academic career at one of the universities over there?' he said. 'It was certainly where you were heading in those days.'

'Wrong, completely wrong. You've failed, Mr Lawyer,' I smiled. 'I actually built and then ran a vineyard with my husband down in the back of beyond on the South Island.'

'Okay, even if I couldn't have ever guessed that, I suppose it does sort of fit,' he said. 'I mean, you were brought up on a farm in West Cork. That was the back of beyond too, and you're certainly used to working on the land, although it's a shame that you didn't pursue your academic career, Merry. You were destined for great things.'

'Thank you for that. Life had other plans, but yes, I'd be lying if I said I don't sometimes regret not following my dream.'

'If it makes you feel any better, I *did* follow mine and – especially recently – I've begun to regret it. Don't get me wrong, it's provided me with a very good income and quality of life.'

'But?'

'When I qualified, I chose to go into corporate law, which was the golden nugget financially. I moved to London and worked my way up to being an in-house adviser at a large oil and gas company. Spending my days telling them how they could achieve X-million pounds in tax breaks every day for twenty-five years was probably not the right career choice for a self-proclaimed aesthete, but hey, it bought me a nice suit, didn't it?' Peter gave a 'grin-mace', as we'd always called his ironic smile.

'I thought you were all set on becoming a barrister?'

'I was, but my father talked me out of it. Said it wasn't secure in comparison to taking articles and becoming a solicitor in a nice steady job, not just being as good as your last case in court. Everybody has regrets, I fear, by the time they get to our age. I was pensioned off at fifty-five, so I decided that I'd finally do my bit for my fellow man and ended up here in Belfast.'

'Really? And what do you do here?'

'I've actually been working in an advisory capacity for what's now known as the Titanic Quarter of Belfast. There's a massive regeneration project in progress on Queen's Island, and in fact, not that you'd probably know about it, as you haven't been around in Ireland recently, the tourism minister, Arlene Foster, has just announced that the Northern Ireland Executive is going to provide fifty per cent of the finances for the Titanic Signature Project, with the other fifty per cent coming from the private sector. We've got an incredible American architect who will come on board and hopefully create something to reflect the great shipbuilding history of the city. You know, of course, that the *Titanic* was built here,' he added.

'Somewhere in the back of my mind I did, yes. Wow, Peter, that all sounds fascinating.'

'And a bit weird?'

'No, not at all,' I said.

'Well, you might remember I've always been a hybrid – English Protestant mum and Irish Catholic dad – born in Dublin, following my mother's line and being baptised as a Protestant. Not that either of them were interested in their religion, just their love for each other,' he shrugged. 'The good news is, I've now lived and worked in England and in the North and South of Ireland, and after years of struggling with my identity, especially during the Troubles, I've arrived at my own personal – and very simple – conclusion: that who you are has everything to do with whether you're a decent human being or not.'

'I totally agree, of course, but extremist indoctrination from the cradle can definitely hamper one's personal development, can't it?' I said.

'It certainly can, and let's face it, there aren't many of us who can live without a cause of some kind, be it work or family. I made work my cause for far too long. At least now I feel I'm using my experience to make a difference to a city that was in such desperate need of regeneration. If in some small way I can provide – through my knowledge and skill set – help to make that happen, it'll make all the years of grind worthwhile.'

'I'm sorry you weren't happy, Peter, I really am.'

'Oh, I was fine, Merry, just playing it safe, which was my *own* family form of indoctrination. Everyone from my lower-middle-class background was told by their parents to go into a profession that would see them safe and secure financially. Doctors and lawyers were where it was at, unless you were aristocratic, of course, and there were certainly a few of those at Trinity, weren't there?'

'There were, yes,' I chuckled. 'Do you remember that guy who drove around Dublin in his open-topped Rolls-Royce? Lord Sebastian Something-or-other. It was awfully smart at Trinity in those days, wasn't it? All those wealthy, bright young things who were there for the social scene rather than the degree.'

'Well, I'm pretty sure my mum always thought that I'd

meet some Anglo-Irish heiress and end up living in a draughty mansion, surrounded by dogs and horses, but—'

'I've always hated horses,' we both said at the same time and laughed.

'Where did we both go wrong, Merry?' He shook his head in mock-sorrow. 'I mean, the British and Irish are obsessed with the nags.'

'Only if they're groomed to a shine by a minion, who will also muck out the dirty hay when the wealthy behind has had its ride and leads it back into the stables.'

'Or when the owners are holding the Winner's Cup on Derby Day, when it's the trainer and jockey who have done all the hard work.' Peter rolled his eyes. 'Or maybe that's just jealousy, Merry. Both of us were bright, of course, but from poor backgrounds and had to work. So, how is your family?'

'They're mostly well, but I hadn't seen them since the last time I saw you, up until a few days ago. My daddy died over twenty years ago of the drink, which was sad. He was a good man, destroyed by a hard life. Though actually, I found out recently that they weren't my blood family. I was simply dropped into their midst as a newborn, but that really is another story.'

Peter looked at me in shock. 'You mean, you were a foundling?'

'Apparently I was. It was Ambrose who told me – remember him?'

'Of course I do, Merry, how could I forget him?'

'Well, he and his friend Father O'Brien persuaded the O'Reilly family to adopt me. Or in fact, take the place of a dead baby they'd lost. Called Mary,' I added.

'Goodness, I don't know what to say.'

'At this moment, Peter, nor do I, so let's not talk about it, shall we? What about your family?'

'My mother's still alive, but my father died a few years ago of old age. I think he lost the will to live when he retired from the railways. He loved that job so much. Apart from my old mum, that's it. I have no family.'

'You never had children of your own?'

'No, and that's another regret I have. But for some of us, it just isn't to be. After my girlfriend died, I took a company transfer over to Norway to make a fresh start and I was briefly married to a Norwegian girl there. It didn't last long – in fact, I think the divorce process lasted longer than the actual marriage, but hey, that's life, isn't it? We all make mistakes. Do you have kids?'

'I do, two of them. One boy and one girl.'

'Then I'm envious. We always wanted kids, didn't we?'

He looked at me and I knew that the game of pussyfooting around was now at an end. However much we'd both enjoyed it.

'We did. I think we named them something ridiculous,' I responded.

'You mean, *you* named them something ridiculous. What was it now? Persephone and Perseus, or some such. I was quite happy with Robert and Laura. Ah,' he said as he picked up his whiskey glass and drank the remains of it, 'those were the days, eh?'

I couldn't answer then, because yes, they had been 'the days', but I needed to ask the question.

'Why didn't you come and meet me in London as you'd promised to, Peter?'

'So . . .' He eyed me. 'Here we are, finally on to the meat of the matter.' I watched as he signalled for the waiter and ordered two more whiskeys.

'Will I need another?'

'I don't know, Merry, but I certainly do.'

'Please, Peter, just tell me what happened. It's a long time ago and whatever the reason, I promise I'll understand.'

767

'I think you're clever enough to know what happened, Merry.'

'Was it him?' I forced the name onto my tongue. 'Bobby Noiro?'

'Yes. After you left for England, I'd done as we agreed that night and made a point of being seen in that bar where he'd first spotted us together, to make sure he didn't think I had anything to do with your disappearance. I don't know whether he saw me, but then, just the day before I was about to get on the boat to England, he turned up at my parents' front door – he must have followed me home from the bar – pinned me against the wall with a gun to my throat and told me that if I disappeared too, he'd make sure Mum and Dad wouldn't live to find out where I'd gone. That he and his "friends" would make sure of it by burning down the house. He said he'd be keeping a watch on it to make sure I was there at home every day, going out in the morning and coming home at night. And he did, Merry, for months.' He took a sip of his whiskey and gave a deep sigh. 'He made sure I saw him too. What could I do? Tell my parents they'd been targeted by the Provos? A terrorist gang that, as we both know and history can attest to, would stop at nothing to get what they wanted.'

'I waited for three weeks in London at Bridget's place. And heard nothing from you. Why didn't you *write* to me, Peter? Let me know what had happened?'

'But I *did*, Merry, and I even have the proof. Let me show you.' Peter reached for his leather case, unzipped it and pulled out a bunch of old airmail envelopes. He handed them to me and I stared down at the top one.

My name and the address in London were crossed out, and in big letters was written *Return to Sender*.

Then I looked at the address he had sent it to.

'See? Look at the stamp at the top,' he pointed. 'It's dated August the fifteenth, 1971. Turn it over, Mary.'

I did so. It had Peter's Dublin address, in his neat handwriting, and a note beneath it: *Person not known at this address.*

'That isn't Bridget's writing,' I said. I frowned and, turning it over to the front, I reread the address.

'Oh no!' I gulped in horror and looked up at him. 'You got the address wrong! Bridget didn't live in Cromwell Gardens. She lived on Cromwell Crescent! I told you that!'

'What?! No!' Peter shook his head. 'I swear, Merry, as you were packing to leave, you told me it was Cromwell Gardens. It was indelibly inked on my heart – why would I ever forget? When we decided we needed to go, that address was the only means of communication we had. I swear you told me it was Cromwell Gardens . . .'

'And I swear I said Cromwell Crescent.'

I forced my mind back to that night, when Bobby had paid me a visit and threatened me and mine. Peter had arrived an hour later and I'd taken him down to my bedroom to tell him we'd been seen by Bobby in a pub the night before. I'd been hysterical, as I'd sobbed in terror and thrown God knows what into a suitcase.

'Did I not write it down for you? I'm sure I wrote it down,' I said, desperately trying to recall the details of telling Peter I was going to Bridget's flat in London on the morning ferry, and parroting the address she'd given to me when I'd called her earlier.

'Merry, you know very well you didn't. You were in a terrible state, and to be fair, so was I.' Peter gave a heavy sigh. 'Well, one of us made a mistake that night,' he shrugged. 'And ever since, I've never known whether that maniac had caught you, murdered you and thrown you into the Liffey, or whether you had just decided it was best if we ended it.'

'You know I'd never have ended it, Peter! We were secretly engaged, had all our plans set out for a new life in Canada . . . It was a decision that was only pre-empted by Bobby and his threats. I thought *you'd* changed your mind, and as I knew I could never come back to Ireland because of Bobby, I had to go on. Alone,' I added.

'So you went to Toronto as we'd arranged?'

'Yes. After delaying my passage three times to see if you'd come. The fourth time, well, I got on board.'

'And how was it? Canada, I mean.'

'Terrible,' I admitted. 'I headed for the Irish Quarter in Toronto as we'd agreed – Cabbagetown, it was called. It was little better than a slum and there was simply no work available other than literally selling my body. A girl I met there told me she'd heard that they were desperate for young workers in New Zealand and there were plenty of jobs, so I used the last of my savings and went with her.' I looked down at the letter that I was still holding in my hands.

'Can I open it?' I asked.

'Of course you can. It was written to you, after all.'

I looked at it again and then at him. 'Maybe I'll save it for later. What does it say?'

'It says what I just told you – that your Bobby had paid me a visit at home and threatened to burn down my parents' house. That I had gone to the police to tell them about him and his threats, and that they said that they'd look into it. I was hoping that they'd take him in for questioning and charge him with threatening behaviour, but I didn't even know where he lived.'

'If I remember rightly, he was squatting at the time, with his fellow "comrades".'

'Exactly. So I wrote that I'd have to wait before I came to London, but that I'd write as often as I could.' Peter shook his head sadly. 'It seems ridiculous, doesn't it, in the age that we live in now, that my parents didn't even have a landline installed in their house, because they simply couldn't afford it? In all the panic, I hadn't given you my address either. I said I'd write to you with it, and I did.' He indicated the pile of letters.

'The schemes of mice and men . . .' I said quietly.

'I did all I could to find you, Merry. I went to visit Ambrose and he said he'd had a note written in Greek telling him you were going away. He knew no more than I did.'

'Oh God, Peter,' I said. 'I . . . don't know what to say. But even if you knew where I was, what could we have done? You couldn't have left and put your parents at risk. That was the point – Bobby had threatened to kill everyone I loved. And I believed him.'

'No, but at least when the situation here really started to heat up, Mam wasn't comfortable with staying in Ireland any longer – there were bombs going off in Belfast constantly and even Dublin was under threat. They were vulnerable anyway, what with their "mixed" marriage, so she persuaded my dad to move to England. I moved with them to Maidenhead, where Mum had relatives, and managed to find a job at a solicitors' practice there, where I could continue my articles. Of course, I went to up to London and to Cromwell Gardens, but they'd never heard of either you, or Bridget. I swear, I was half out of my mind with worry.' Peter gave me another 'grin-mace'. 'I then heard a few weeks later that some madman called Bobby Noiro had burnt down my parents' old rented house, and that they'd locked him up for it.'

'When Bobby's sister Helen told me only a few days ago about Bobby being imprisoned for burning down a Protestant house, it did cross my mind it could have been your parents'.'

'At least no one was hurt,' Peter sighed. 'He really was a

total headache, wasn't he? Him and his friends in the Provisional IRA.'

'He was a headcase, yes, but he didn't have friends in the Provisional IRA,' I sighed, suddenly feeling completely exhausted. 'What a mess it all was. One stupid, misheard word, and here we are thirty-seven years later, thinking the other had . . . well, I imagined just about everything, that's for sure.'

'So did I. But at least I knew my family was safe when Bobby Noiro was put behind bars, but not you. I never forgot you, Merry . . . A year on from the burning, someone at my law firm recommended I find a private detective. I saved up to pay for a company to look for you in London and Canada. To be honest, I assumed the worst. Merry, there *was* no trace of you.'

'Forgive me, Peter, that's how I needed it to be. For the safety of everyone I loved. I didn't even know that Bobby had been locked up until a few days ago, when his sister told me. Maybe if I had, I'd have come back. But who knows?'

There was a pause as both of us sat, lost in thoughts of the past and what might have been.

'At least it sounds as though you've been happy, Merry. Have you been happy?'

'Yes, I think I have. I married a lovely man called Jock. He was a good few years older than me and, if I'm honest, I do think part of the initial attraction was the fact that I felt protected by him. But as the years passed, I honestly grew to love him, and when he died a few months back, I was completely devastated. We were together over thirty-five years.'

'Far longer than I ever managed.' Peter offered me a wry smile. 'But I'm glad you found someone to care for you, I really am.'

'And I cared for him. With the kids coming along too, I was

contented. Yes, I was,' I said out loud, mainly to myself. 'But I also realise now I was always holding something back from him emotionally, and that was because of you. I learnt from my kids that first love can be overwhelming – a grand passion, if you like – but often that love comes to its natural conclusion. Ours never did; in fact, quite the opposite. There was always the "what if" scenario. And because it was forbidden, what with you being Protestant and me a Catholic at that moment in Ireland, not to mention Bobby . . . Well, it gave the whole thing the feeling of an epic romance, didn't it?'

'You're right, it did, and it has continued to do so for the whole of my adult life,' he agreed. 'I admit to not sleeping properly since I received your letter, or being able to concentrate on anything much. I could barely speak when you called me and I heard the sound of your voice, so forgive me if I sounded formal. When I saw you here earlier, actually in the flesh, looking up at the chandelier, I seriously wondered if I was dreaming.'

'Oh, I know, I was completely terrified! Yet, when you think about it, we were only actually together for six months and never out in the open. You never met my family and I never met yours.'

'Well, if you remember, I was planning to introduce you to my parents, who wouldn't have minded in the slightest about our different religions, as they'd intermarried themselves. I've spent the last thirty-seven years kicking myself for not being more together that night. I should have given you the telephone number at my lawyers' practice, but we didn't think about all that, did we?'

'No,' I sighed. 'I was in complete shock, so it was probably me who gave you the wrong address. I did pick up the receiver in a call box in London a couple of times to dial Ambrose and see if he'd heard from you, but then I remembered how Bobby had threatened to hurt him too and I felt I just couldn't put him at risk. If he'd have known where I was, I'm sure Bobby would have beaten it out of him, so I thought it was safest not to contact him at all, then he'd have nothing to tell. The bottom line was that I just never thought you wouldn't come,' I shrugged. 'It was as simple as that.'

Peter took a sip of his whiskey and looked at me. 'I've sometimes wondered if it would have lasted . . . you and me.'

'That's something neither of us will ever know the answer to, isn't it, Peter?'

'Sadly, yes. So, wanting to meet up with me today, is this all about what they call "closure" these days?'

'Yes; I left New Zealand on a mission to try and track down both you and Bobby. It was time, if you know what I mean.'

'I understand. You really did lose everyone you loved when you left, didn't you?'

'I did, but remember, I'd known Bobby since I was a little girl, and he and his obsession with the Irish Revolution – and *me* – had always frightened me. It actually turns out that we shared the same grandparents – we were cousins through our grandmothers, who had been sisters. But they were estranged – as many families were – during the Civil War of 1922. It turns out mental illness ran in the family. I'd always been told about Bobby's crazy dad, then I met up with his younger sister Helen, as I said, who told me their great-uncle, Colin, ended up in an asylum. She decided she didn't want any children, so that she couldn't pass whatever gene Bobby and his forefathers shared on to the next generation. All that talk about him being in the Provisional IRA was rubbish. It all came out of his psychosis. The whole thing's so, so sad.'

'Psychosis or not, it didn't make him less dangerous. He was an extremely violent man. As a matter of fact, I went to visit him at St Fintan's some years back.'

'Did you? Oh my God, Peter. That was brave of you.'

'Well, he was handcuffed to an iron bar on the table and I had two burly guards in there with me. I suppose I too wanted to put the past to rest, after he'd terrified the life out of me and then tried to murder my family. I actually walked out of there feeling sorry for him. I remember thinking he'd probably be better off dead than in that living hell. He was so drugged up, he hardly knew his own name. Anyway, what's done is done. Life's about the future, not the past, isn't it? Now, how long are you staying in Belfast?'

'As long as I'm here with you. Then I'm on the train back to Dublin to spend a little time with Ambrose. After that, I'm going to go back down to West Cork to get to know my family again.'

'That'll be nice, and so long overdue.'

'Well, there was a lot of us to begin with, but now they've all had families of their own, it'll take me a good couple of weeks to get round to see all of them,' I smiled.

'And then?' he asked.

'I don't know, Peter. I've only thought as far as meeting you today, to be honest. I'll go back to New Zealand eventually, I suppose.'

'If that's the case' – Peter looked down at his watch, then back up at me – 'could I take you to lunch? I'd love to hear more about your life and this journey you've been on in the last few weeks.'

'Okay,' I smiled at him. 'Why not?'

53

In transit: Geneva to Nice

The private jet touched down smoothly at Nice airport, as its occupants looked out of the windows in either anticipation or trepidation.

'We've landed,' Maia said to Valentina, who was strapped into the seat opposite her, her eyes wide as she continued to grip the armrests. 'What did you think?' she asked in Portuguese.

'I preferred the bigger plane, but this is nice too,' she said politely.

Ally was sitting opposite Floriano, with Bear strapped into his child safety harness on her knee. She was very proud of him, as he hadn't cried once.

'The key is to feed him a bottle as we ascend and descend, because the sucking stops the air pressure hurting his little ears,' Ma had advised her before they'd boarded, and sure enough, it had worked. As the plane taxied to a halt, Ally's nerve endings jangled. Only a short ride away sat the majestic *Titan*, anchored just outside the port and ready for its last guests to be ferried out on the gig to join it.

Waiting on board would be Star, Mouse and his son Rory, Mary-Kate *and* Jack.

Ally's stomach turned over and she grimaced at the mere thought of the look in his eyes when he saw her. *Yet another lie . . .*

'Anyway, why should it matter what *he* thinks,' she whispered to Bear as she unstrapped his harness and lifted him into the papoose.

The doors opened and the friendly ground-staff officials welcomed them all to Nice. Ma walked towards the front of the cabin and greeted them both as Floriano and Charlie – who had arrived with Tiggy at Atlantis last night – helped everyone reach for their bags.

Ma was led down the steps by the ground staff, followed by CeCe and Chrissie.

'Can I help you with anything, Ally?' Charlie asked her.

'Could you take that nappy bag?'

'Of course,' he nodded as he picked it up.

The fact that this man had delivered Bear into the world a few months ago made Ally feel comforted by his presence.

'Ally, are you okay?' Tiggy asked as Charlie descended and they were left alone in the cabin.

'Yes, why?'

'Please don't worry,' she smiled at her as she indicated Bear. 'I promise Jack won't mind at all. Now, you two first.'

Ally descended into the gorgeous light, warmth and smell that was so intrinsic to the Côte d'Azur, with Tiggy bringing up the rear. After a short walk through passport control, their bags were loaded into two limos and they were whisked out of the private terminal and into the Nice traffic.

'Where's Electra?' Ally turned to Maia. 'I'm sure she said she was meeting us here, not at the boat.'

'I just got a text to say her plane landed early so she's – or should I say *they*, as Miles is with her – have headed straight for the port.'

'So she's brought her man with her – isn't it wonderful?' said Ma.

'It is,' Maia agreed, as she put a protective arm around Valentina and smiled at Floriano, sitting opposite them.

Forty minutes and a serious amount of traffic congestion later, they arrived at the Port de Nice. Ally felt her blood pound in her veins, awash with conflicting emotions. As a child and then a young woman, the annual summer voyage on the *Titan* with her sisters and her father had been the moment she'd looked forward to more than any other. Now, the person that she'd loved most in the world was gone, as was Theo, who hadn't lived to see this day. Yet now, someone who seemed to matter to her far more than he should was waiting for her to arrive.

Shaking herself, she turned to Ma. 'Will Georg be there?'

'I hope so,' Ma said. 'His secretary said he would meet us on board.'

'Please, Ally, don't stress.' Maia put a hand out to her sister, sensing her obvious tension. 'Everyone who needs to be there will be there.'

'I'm sure you're right, Maia. It just all feels a bit odd, doesn't it?' she sighed.

'It feels different, yes, and sad too, because this was always the moment when we were reunited with Pa from wherever we were. But we must try to celebrate his life, and also the many positive things that have happened to all of us in the past year.'

'I know,' Ally replied, experiencing just the slightest sense of irritation as she felt her older sister was patronising her. Which was completely unfair, as Maia could not have been sweeter in the past few weeks. 'Where are we meeting everyone?'

'On board,' said Maia. 'It's all organised, as it always is.'

Their limo, and the one behind them carrying the other sisters, drove through the harbour to a pier, at the bottom of which floated two gigs that would take them out to the *Titan*. Given the time of year, the port was packed with boats bobbing on the water, and many larger craft were sitting out in the bay.

Stepping out of the limo, the heat of the day hit Ally and she pulled Bear's tiny sun hat down over his eyes.

'*Bienvenue à bord du* Titan.' Hans, the captain who had skippered the boat for as long as Ally could remember, greeted them as their bags were unloaded by two deckhands, smartly dressed in white. Everyone was offered a cooling towel and led along the pier towards the gigs.

'Can I take your arm, Ma?' said Charlie, sweeping in from behind, as she attempted to descend the steps.

'Thank you. I should have remembered to leave my court shoes at home and put on a pair of deck shoes, shouldn't I?' she said, as she did every year.

Once everyone was on board the gigs, the engines were started and the short trip out towards the *Titan* began.

'Wow,' said Chrissie, as the gigs navigated out of the harbour then picked up speed on the blue of the Mediterranean Sea. 'This is the way to travel!'

'Pass me those binos, Ally,' CeCe called to the front of the gig.

'The *Titan* is just over there,' said Ally as she did so.

CeCe fixed the setting on the binoculars and then passed them to Chrissie, who looked through them.

'Oh my God! You're actually joking, aren't ya? That's not a boat, it's a cruise liner!'

'Yeah, it's pretty big,' CeCe agreed as they drew closer towards it.

'Now that,' said Charlie, indicating the *Titan* to Tiggy, 'is what my father would have called a floating gin palace.'

'I'm not sure if that's a compliment or an insult, but yes, we do have an occasional gin and tonic on board,' Tiggy grinned.

'I don't ever think I've properly realised until coming to

Atlantis last night and now seeing this today just how rich your father was.'

'Yes, he was,' Tiggy agreed.

'Do you know what makes me really happy?'

'What?'

'That my dear ex-wife would have probably given up anything to be invited on one of these for a summer cruise on the Med. And as it turns out, it was the "hired help" – as she always calls you – whose father actually owns one.' Charlie gave a chuckle. 'We'll have to take lots of photos and leave them lying around the next time Ulrika arrives to collect Zara, just to annoy her.'

Tiggy looked up at the *Titan* as they drew alongside it, and realised that yes, it did indeed look majestic. At over seventy metres long, the Benetti superyacht rose four levels out of the water, the radio tower reaching into the cloudless azure sky.

A deckhand helped Ma on board first, followed by the rest of the passengers. Two very excited faces stood on the aft deck to receive them.

'Hi, guys! Star and I were thinking about not waiting for you all and just sailing off, but hey, here you are!'

And there was Electra, looking as insouciantly beautiful as she always did, in a pair of denim shorts and a T-shirt.

'I love your short hair,' said Maia as she took her turn to hug Electra.

'Yeah, well, it's a new me in all sorts of ways. Now, come and meet Miles.'

'You're here!' Star said from behind her, as CeCe and Chrissie stepped onto the deck. Star put her arms around both of them. 'It's so good to see you both. Hi, Tiggy, and this is?'

'I'm Charlie, pleased to meet you, Star.' He shook her hand.

'And you, Charlie,' Star smiled. 'This is Mouse, my other half. Now, have a glass of champagne and make yourselves comfortable,' Star continued. 'Rory, Mouse's son, has been taken off by our first mate to see the bridge about twenty minutes ago, and we haven't seen him since.'

The sun deck, with its comfortable canvas-covered soft furnishings, was suddenly full of milling people. Out of the corner of her eye, Ally spotted Jack and a young blonde woman standing slightly apart from the rest of the sisters and their other halves.

'Okay, Bear,' she whispered to the baby fidgeting in his papoose. 'Here goes.'

'Hi, Jack, how are you?' she said as she walked towards them.

'I'm good. This is Mary-Kate, my sister, and . . . ?' He looked down at Bear, surprise in his eyes. 'Who is this little guy?'

'My son, Bear. He's just about four months old.'

'Hi, Ally,' said Mary-Kate, 'nice to meet you. Jacko's told me a lot about you. And oh,' she said as Bear continued to wriggle, 'he's sooo cute! Isn't he, Jacko?'

'He is, yeah. Very.'

'He's getting hot and bothered in his papoose,' she said. 'Could you lift him out for me, Mary-Kate?'

'I'll do it.' Jack reached his big hands into the papoose and pulled Bear out of it. 'There you go, little one. That's better, isn't it?' he said as he gave Ally a quizzical look over the top of Bear's head.

'Jacko's very good with babies, aren't you, Jack?' said Mary-Kate. 'He had a summer job as a manny to one of our neighbours when he was eighteen.'

'Yeah, I did, for my sins,' he said, 'and I detect a familiar pong from this little guy. Which, from my expertise, I deduce belongs to a full nappy,' he chuckled. 'Here you go, Mum,' he added, handing him back to Ally.

'Thanks. I'll take him downstairs and change him. Maia?'

Ally called across the deck. 'Come and meet Jack and Mary-Kate.'

With her sister taking over the helm, Ally walked into the main salon, where the bedroom plan was always pinned to a cork board inside a metal case.

Deck Three, Suite Four, she read and went down a flight of stairs to find it. Having changed Bear and given him a quick feed, they were just leaving her cabin when she saw Georg walking along the narrow corridor towards her, still dressed in a suit and tie. He was on his mobile and looked agitated. Spotting her in front of him, he said something in German, then ended the call.

'Ally! How are you?'

'I'm well, thank you, Georg. How are you?'

'I'm . . . well. Many apologies for having been absent in the past weeks. I had matters to . . . attend to.'

Ally studied him, thinking he looked suddenly older. His skin was grey and there was a gauntness to his face that suggested he'd lost weight since she'd last seen him.

'I'm glad you're here, Georg. You look exhausted, if you don't mind me saying. Hopefully you can take off your suit and tie and start to relax.'

Just as she and Bear were about to ascend and join the others, Georg put a hand gently on her shoulder to stop her.

'Ally, may I have a word? In private?' Georg indicated the door that led into what they called the Winter Salon, which was a cosy lounge used when the weather was bad.

'Of course.'

Georg opened the door into the salon, and both of them moved to sit on a couple of sofas placed on either side of a low drinks table, with lovely views through the portholes onto the sparkling Mediterranean Sea.

'What is it, Georg?'

'Well, I have met both Jack and Mary-Kate upstairs on deck, but I hear that Mary-Kate is not the "Mary McDougal" you originally thought she was?'

'No, she's the adopted daughter of her mother, who is also Mary McDougal, or Merry, as she's more commonly known.'

'Atch!' Georg said in frustration. 'We – I – did not foresee such a thing. All I'd heard was that Mary had been located and had agreed to join us on our cruise.'

'Yes, but in the past few days, Mary-Kate has made contact with her birth mother, and it turns out that her mother Merry was actually adopted too. Well, she was a foundling, anyway.'

'So, let me get this straight.' Georg pulled out a miniature leather-bound notepad and a fountain pen from the inside pocket of his jacket. 'The daughter, Mary-Kate, is how old?'

'Twenty-two.'

'And born where?'

'In New Zealand.'

'And she has recently identified her birth mother and father? Who are also from New Zealand?' he asked.

'I believe so, yes.'

'And Merry, the mother, how old is she?'

'Fifty-nine this year.'

'And she has just discovered that she was adopted?'

'Yes. Merry just found out that she was put in the place of a dead baby, and brought up as part of that family. But that originally, she'd been a foundling.'

'From the south-west of Ireland?'

'Yes. We did try and contact you, Georg, because we needed more information about Mary McDougal and which one of them it might be, but we didn't hear anything back from you. Then, just by coincidence, Maia happened to be in Pa's garden and saw a set of coordinates had been added to Merope's band on the armillary sphere. I looked them up on

Google Earth, and it turns out that they pointed to a big old house, very close to where Merry was put on the doorstep of a local priest down in West Cork.'

'I . . .' Georg looked up at Ally in horror. 'You mean, you had only just seen that set of coordinates?'

'Yes. I'd been in the garden sometimes when I was home, sitting on the bench under the rose arbour, and looked at the armillary sphere, but never that closely.'

'*Mein Gott!*' Georg thumped the table. 'Ally, those coordinates have been on the armillary sphere for months. I myself gave orders to have them engraved only a few weeks after we all saw the armillary sphere for the first time. I'm amazed that none of you girls had noticed them. And when I came to see you . . . I took a call, if you remember, and had to leave immediately.'

'But why would we have seen it, Georg? Maia had left for Brazil and the rest of us were only going home sporadically. If we did look, it was only at our own band.'

'Then this is all my fault,' he said. 'I assumed that you *had* noticed it, and to be perfectly honest, my mind was on other things. So why is this Merry not here with her son and her daughter?'

'Jack told me she didn't want to come,' Ally shrugged. 'I'm not sure of the reasons why. Georg?'

'Yes, Ally.' Georg had stood up and was pacing around the salon.

'So, the mother of Mary-Kate – Merry – is definitely the missing sister?'

'As far as I am aware, she is, but after all this, she is not here! And neither is the ring. This is all my fault, Ally,' he said again. 'In recent weeks, I have been . . . distracted, but still, I should have told you how old she was, checked if you had seen her coordinates on the armillary sphere. But I wasn't expecting that there would be *two* Mary McDougals. I . . . aatch!'

Ally watched him, this man who had always seemed so cool and calm, never showing any emotion. Yet now, she saw that he was utterly beside himself.

'Do you know who used to own that old house in West Cork?' she probed. Georg turned round, stared at her and nodded.

'Yes, I do.'

'Then why didn't you tell us?'

'Because, because . . . Ally, as always, I was only following orders . . .' Georg sat down opposite her and wiped his sweating brow with his white handkerchief. 'Giving you that information from the start might have upset certain . . . members of the family. It was thought best for you, or in fact, Mary McDougal, to discover it for yourselves.'

'You mean, because Maia's son is Zed Eszu's child? And because he pursued Tiggy and Electra?'

'Exactly, but still, this is all my mistake, Ally, and I must rectify the situation immediately.'

'Why? I mean . . .' Ally's head was spinning. 'How?'

'Where is Merry now?'

'Jack said she was staying in Ireland to spend some time with her family.'

'So she is still down in West Cork?'

'No, I'm pretty sure she travelled back to Dublin with Jack and Mary-Kate, but we can ask them. She has a godfather there apparently, called Ambrose.'

'Right, then I must sort this out before it's too late. Excuse me, Ally.' Ally watched as Georg marched out of the salon.

54

Merry
Belfast, Northern Ireland

'More wine? Or maybe an Irish coffee to finish? I bet it's a long time since you had one of those,' Peter said to me across the table.

'It was, at least up until a few days ago when I treated myself and the kids to one down in West Cork. Anyway, the answer is sadly no; I've drunk far more than is good for me, especially at lunchtime. I'll end up sleeping the afternoon away.'

'Well, it's not every day you meet a long-lost love again after thirty-seven years, is it?'

'No,' I smiled.

'It's been so wonderful to see you again, Merry, even though I was dreading it.'

'That makes two of us, but yes, it's been wonderful. Now I really must go, Peter. It's half past three already and I have to get myself back to Dublin.'

'You can't stay on another night?'

'No, I promised Ambrose I'd be back, and given that he's paranoid I may suddenly disappear again, I must. I wasn't even intending on staying this long.'

'He knows where you've been?'

'Of course. It was him I asked to try and help trace you after I could find no records of you in Ireland, England or Canada. He suggested he contact an old student of his who works in the records office at Trinity, to see if you still had a subscription for *Trinity Today*, the university alumni magazine. He took a look at the records of subscribers and there you were, with an address in Belfast!'

'Full marks to Ambrose for excellent sleuthing,' said Peter as he signalled for the bill. 'It's a real shame you can't stay longer, as I'd love to have shown you around more of the city. Everything you remember from your TV screen in the seventies and eighties is not how it is now. It's beginning to thrive, and once the Titanic Quarter is completed, Belfast really will be a destination city.'

'I'm so happy it will be, and that old wounds are beginning to be mended,' I replied, as I took out my wallet and offered Peter a credit card. 'Let's go dutch?'

'Don't be silly, Merry. I've waited a very, very long time to take you out for lunch – besides, you put the whiskeys and my coffee and croissant on your hotel bill this morning.'

I agreed, and ten minutes later, we left the restaurant and wandered past the great mass of St Anne's Cathedral.

'It's very impressive,' I commented. 'What is that long steel pipe coming out of the top?'

'That was installed only last year, and it's called the Spire of Hope. It's illuminated at night, and actually, I love it, and what it stands for. Merry?'

'Yes?'

'I . . . I mean, obviously it's up to you, but I'd love to see you again before you go back to New Zealand. Today has just been, well, fantastic. It was so good to laugh like we used to.'

'It was, yes. As I said, I have no real fixed plans yet and I'm still getting over the loss of Jock, so . . .'

'I understand,' he said as we entered the hotel. 'But this time, we'll take out our mobiles, swap numbers and emails and addresses, then double-check we both have them written in correctly, deal?'

'Deal,' I smiled as I walked over to the porter's desk and handed in my left luggage tag.

While we waited for them to retrieve my holdall, we did exactly as he'd suggested.

'Do you need a taxi, madam?' asked the porter.

'I do, yes please.'

Peter and I followed the porter back down the steps outside, and watched as he whistled to attract a cab's attention.

'I hate saying goodbye when we've only just said hello. Please think about coming back here, Merry, or I can come to you in Dublin. In fact, anytime, anywhere.'

'I will, I promise.'

He took my hand and kissed it, then enveloped me in a hug. 'Please, take care of yourself, won't you?' he whispered gently. 'And don't you dare lose touch!'

'I won't. Bye, Peter, and thank you for lunch.'

I climbed into the cab and waved at him as we set off into the traffic.

Due to the build-up of tension, the emotion of actually seeing Peter again after all these years, plus the amount of wine I'd downed over lunch, I slept for most of the journey back to Dublin, only waking up when the man next to me nudged me to let him out.

In the taxi to Merrion Square, I felt half drugged, and

could hardly believe that I'd actually just been with Peter after all these years.

Letting myself into Ambrose's flat, I put down my holdall and walked into the sitting room, where he was in his usual chair.

'Hello, Ambrose, I made it back safely,' I smiled at him.

'All went well then?'

'Oh, it did! I was so unbelievably nervous, I literally fainted into his arms and . . .'

I suddenly became aware of the fact that we weren't the only two people in the room. I turned to look behind me and there, sitting in the corner of the sofa, was a man I'd never seen before. As my gaze fell on him, he stood up. I saw that he was very tall, immaculately dressed in a suit and tie, and probably in his early sixties.

'Do excuse me, sir, I didn't notice you were there. I'm Merry McDougal, and you are?' I asked him as I held out my hand.

For what seemed a very long time, the man didn't answer, just stared at me as if he was mesmerised. His grey eyes looked a little wet, as if they had tears in them. My hand still reached towards him, but as he didn't seem inclined to take it, I let it fall. Eventually, he seemed to shake himself out of his hypnotic state.

'Do forgive me, Mrs McDougal. You bear a striking resemblance to . . . someone. I'm Georg Hoffman, and I am so very pleased to meet you.'

The man spoke perfect English, but with a pronounced accent I placed as German.

'And . . . who are you?'

'Please, won't you sit down?' Georg indicated the sofa. I looked over at Ambrose for reassurance.

'Do sit down, Mary. Can I offer you a whiskey?' he asked me.

'Goodness, no, I've had far more than my fair share of alcohol today.'

I sat down tentatively, as did Georg Hoffman. I saw that he had a slim leather case very similar to the one Peter had brought with him this morning. He pulled a plastic file out of the case and laid it on his knee. I sighed, because after the day I'd had, I simply wanted to have a quiet cup of tea and a sandwich with Ambrose, tell him of my meeting with Peter and then slip down the stairs to bed.

'Are you here to see me, or do you and Ambrose know each other?' I asked.

'Mary, Mr Hoffman is the lawyer of the dead father of all the sisters that have been trying to trace you recently,' said Ambrose.

'Please, call me Georg. I believe it was Tiggy you met here in Dublin.'

'Yes, it was. But I've also met other sisters and their . . . partners around the world. That is, they've been trying to track me down.'

'Yes, they have. And I'm here tonight because I now realise it should have been me who came to you in the first place, because I had more . . . details of your origins than my client's daughters. But when the girls – as I call the sisters collectively – came up with a plan to track their missing sister down, I took the decision to let them find you. They had been very successful in finding their own birth families, you see, and I had other matters to attend to. Let me now apologise for any inconvenience or worry I – and they – have caused you in the process.'

'Thank you. The situation has caused me some distress, especially as I booked a Grand Tour to try to get over the loss of my husband.'

'Mary, my dear, do forgive me, but that isn't quite true, is it?'

I looked at Ambrose, wondering why on earth he was defending the behaviour of a set of sisters whom he knew had completely terrified me.

'What I mean, Mr Hoffman, is that at the same time, Mary – and I do hope you don't mind me speaking for you,' Ambrose continued, 'was also on a search for her *own* past. Ironically, as the sisters were trying to find her, she was searching for someone too. Someone that frightened and terrorised her as a young woman. Unfortunately, the two lines of enquiry became confused. Do you understand?'

'Not completely, but enough to know that you, Mrs McDougal, did not welcome the sisters' pursuit of you.'

'Please, call me Merry, and no I did not, but you still haven't answered the question: why are you here tonight?'

'Because . . . forgive me, Merry, if I sound as though I'm talking in riddles. To be honest with you, I never expected this moment to arrive. I have worked for the girls' father—'

'Whom they call Pa Salt,' I butted in.

'Yes. He's been like a father to me ever since I have known him. I have worked for him for the whole of my career as a lawyer, and he has always talked of the fact that there was a missing sister, one he could never find, however hard he searched. I joined him in that search when I was old enough to do so. Occasionally, he would call me with a promising lead as to her whereabouts and I would employ a trusted team of private investigators to follow that lead up. Every time, they led to nothing. And then, this time last year, finally, my employer discovered new information, which he assured me was almost certainly accurate. I had very little to work on, but work on it I did.'

I watched the man pause for a moment, then lean forward to pick up the glass of whiskey on the table in front of him. He drained the glass, put it down and looked at me.

'Merry, I could sit here and tell you the pains that I and the private investigators went to in order to discover who you had become, but . . .'

I watched him as he shook his head and put his hand to his brow, obviously embarrassed to be showing deep emotion.

'Excuse me one moment . . .'

He fumbled in the file on his knee. Accepting and rejecting various pages, he finally drew one out and turned it round to face me.

'If only I had known how simple the puzzle of identifying you would eventually be, then I could have spared you all you've suffered during these past weeks. After all this, we didn't even need that emerald ring.' Mr Hoffman pointed to it sitting on my finger, then handed me the sheet of paper. 'Look,' he said.

I did look, and once my brain had made sense of the image, I performed the cliché known as a double-take, because I looked again in disbelief.

On the page in front of me was a charcoal portrait of *me*.

I looked closer, and discovered that yes, maybe the shape of my jaw was heavier and my eyebrows were a little lighter than the drawing in front of me, but there was no doubt.

'It's me, isn't it?'

'No,' Mr Hoffman whispered, 'it isn't you, Merry. It is your mother.'

In the following twenty minutes, I couldn't remember much about what I'd said or what I'd done. That face, which was mine yet wasn't, stirred in me some primeval reaction I'd been unprepared for. I wanted to stroke the drawing, then I wanted to tear it into shreds. I accepted a whiskey that I didn't want but drained the glass, and then I cried. Torrents of tears for the mess my life seemed to have become. Whatever I thought I had solved, each time a new puzzle had appeared in its place, along with a gamut of emotions that ended with me in Ambrose's arms on the sofa, and the lawyer watching from the leather chair.

'Sorry, sorry,' I kept saying as I dripped tears all over the charcoal drawing of the me that was my mother.

Eventually, I stopped crying and with Ambrose's handkerchief, dried my eyes, my cheeks and then patted the photocopy of the face that had apparently borne me into the world. Which was now smudged and ugly.

'Please, do not worry about that. It is a facsimile of the original,' said Georg.

As my senses began to return to normal, I moved out of Ambrose's embrace and sat upright.

'Merry, if you please, could you give me a little tug upwards?' Ambrose asked. 'I think some tea is in order for all. I shall go and make some.'

'Ambrose, really—'

'My dear, I'm perfectly capable of making a pot of tea.'

Georg and I sat together in silence. There were so many questions I wanted answers to, but I struggled to know where to start.

'Georg,' I managed as I blew my nose for the umpteenth time on Ambrose's sodden handkerchief. 'Could you please explain why, if you knew which year I was born, you pursued – or the sisters pursued – my daughter, who is only twenty-two?'

'Because I had no clue that your daughter would be called Mary too. And that you would have passed the ring on to her on her twenty-first. During the past two weeks when the search for you was continuing, having established that they

793

had found Mary McDougal, I was then . . . unavoidably detained elsewhere. Out of contact with them.'

'I'm very sorry, Georg, but there are so many things I don't understand. You say that this charcoal drawing is of my mother?'

'Yes.'

'How do you know this?'

'Because of the drawing that has hung on the wall at Atlantis, my employer's house in Geneva, for many years. He had told me who it was.'

'Did she die? Giving birth to me, I mean?'

Yet again, I could see the man's indecision at revealing what he knew and didn't know.

Just as Ambrose brought the tea in, Georg stood up and went to retrieve his leather case. I watched as he removed a padded brown envelope from inside it. He sat down in Ambrose's chair and laid the package on his knee.

'Do you take sugar, Georg?' Ambrose asked.

'I do not drink tea, thank you. Merry, this package is for you. I believe it will answer all the questions that I cannot. But before I give it to you, I entreat you now to come with me and join your children and the sisters on the *Titan*. You will be fulfilling their father's long-held dream, and I cannot leave here without begging you to come. A private jet sits on the runway at Dublin airport, waiting for us to board and fly to meet the boat.'

'I'm so tired,' I sighed. 'I just want to go to bed.'

I turned to Ambrose as I sipped my tea, at nearly fifty-nine years of age, still looking to him for guidance.

'I know, my dear, I know,' Ambrose replied, 'but what is the price of a night's sleep, as opposed to discovering your true heritage?'

'But it's all so surreal, Ambrose.'

'That is simply because so far, your experience of the sisters has been so fractured. Plus the fact that you have had so much to contend with recently, but even your own children are on the boat. They are sailing towards Greece, the land that you never visited, but always wished to, and from what Georg has said, where you may find the answers that you seek. I too, as the man who first laid eyes on you at only a few hours old, then watched you grow into a remarkable young woman with a passion for philosophy and mythology, beg you to go and discover your *own* legend. What do you have to lose, Mary?'

I stared at him, wondering how much had been discussed between him and Georg before I'd arrived. Then I thought of my children, already ensconced in this strange, disparate family, somewhere on the sea sailing towards Greece, the land that had always held such a special, magical place in my mind . . .

I reached for Ambrose's hand. And took a deep breath. 'All right,' I said, 'I'll go.'

An hour and a half later, I was on the kind of private jet I'd only ever seen in movies or magazines, sitting in a leather-covered seat, with Georg opposite me on the other side of the slim aisle. At the front of the plane, I could see the two pilots getting ready for take-off. Georg was on his mobile, speaking to someone in German. I only wished I could understand what he was saying, because it sounded urgent.

A male steward appeared and asked us both to fasten our seat belts and turn off our mobiles. The plane began to taxi, and then within the space of perhaps only a few seconds, the jet picked up speed and we were suddenly airborne. I gazed out of the window, wondering what madness it was that yet again, I was abruptly leaving the land where I had been born and raised. The lights of Dublin twinkled below me, and then almost immediately there was darkness as we began to cross the Irish Sea. I closed my eyes and tried to focus on the fact I was flying *to* my family – Jack and Mary-Kate – and not away from it, like the last time I had left Ireland.

There was a ding from above me, then the steward arrived and told us we were free to take off our seat belts.

I watched Georg as he reached for his leather case. He pulled out the brown padded envelope.

'This is yours, Merry. Inside, I hope you will find the answers to the questions you have asked me. For now, I will leave you to take some rest.'

As he handed it to me, I saw the glimmer of tears once again in his eyes. He then summoned the steward. 'Mrs McDougal wishes to have some privacy and sleep. I will move forward.'

'Of course, sir.'

'Goodnight, Mary. I will see you when we land,' Georg nodded.

The steward duly pulled out two panels from either side of the cabin, which formed a partition between the back and front of it. He then handed me a blanket and a pillow and showed me how to form the seat into a bed.

'How long is the flight?' I asked him as he placed a glass of water in the holder beside me.

'Just over three hours, madam. Would you like anything else at all?'

'I'm fine, thank you.'

'Please press the bell beside your seat if you need anything. Goodnight, madam.'

The panel doors slid closed behind him and I found myself in total privacy. I experienced a moment of sheer panic, because I was flying to God knows where and had a brown package on my knee that apparently contained the secret of my true heritage.

'Ambrose trusted Georg, and so must you, Merry,' I murmured to myself.

So here I was, suspended somewhere between heaven and earth. The Greek gods had chosen Mount Olympus, the highest mountain in Greece, as their home, perhaps wishing for the same feeling. I looked out of the window at the stars, which seemed so much brighter up here, shining down like astral torches.

I turned my attention to the parcel on my lap and stuck a finger under the seal to pull the large envelope open. I reached inside and took out a thick and somewhat battered brown leather book, and an accompanying cream vellum envelope. Placing the book on the little table in front of me, I looked down at the envelope and read the three beautifully scripted words on the front of it:

For my Daughter.

I opened it.

> *Atlantis*
> *Lake Geneva*
> *Switzerland*

My darling daughter,

I only wish I could address you by your given name, but sadly I do not know what it is. Just as I have no idea where in the world you might live. Or if you still live. Nor do I know whether you will ever be found, which is an odd thought for both of us if you are reading this, because it means you have been, yet I am gone from this world. And the two of us will never meet on earth, but in the next life, which I believe in with all my heart and soul.

I cannot voice or begin to explain the love I have felt for you since I knew of your imminent arrival. Nor can I tell you in this letter the lengths I took to find you and your mother, who were both lost to me so cruelly before you were born. You may well believe that you were abandoned by your father, but that is far from the truth. To this day – and I write to you as I have written to my six other daughters, because I am close to death – I do not know where your mother went, or whether she lived or died after you were born.

How I know you were born is also a story that can only be explained in more pages than I have the energy to write here.

However, write it I did, many years ago, in the journal that I have instructed my lawyer, Georg Hoffman, to give to you. It's the story of my life, which, if nothing else, has been eventful. You may well have had contact with my adopted daughters and I would ask that, once you have read it, you share my story with them, because it is their story too.

Read it, my darling girl, and know that there hasn't been a day that has gone by without me thinking and praying for both you and your mother. She was the love of my life . . . everything to me. And if she has passed on to the next life, which some deep instinct tells me she has, know that we are reunited and looking down on you with love.

Your father,
Atlas x

To be continued in

Atlas: The Story of Pa Salt

To be published Autumn 2022

Author's Note

I'd always known that I would set *The Missing Sister* predominantly in my home territory of West Cork, Ireland. Given the coronavirus pandemic, it was as if it was meant to be: I'd already secretly visited Central Otago in New Zealand and Norfolk Island before Christmas 2019. Then, only a few weeks later, I was locked down in West Cork with the research I needed for once at my fingertips. I'd believed I knew quite a lot about the past turbulent one hundred years of Irish history, but as I began to do my usual in-depth research, I realised that I'd only scratched the surface. I also noticed that the scarce personal accounts of those who were directly involved in the Irish War of Independence were written by men, and mostly penned many years after the fact. I decided that, to get as true a picture as possible, I'd need to turn to my family, friends and neighbours, whose ancestors had fought for freedom at the time. Out of this, a picture of wartime West Cork and the huge contribution its brave volunteers – nearly all rural farming people, mostly aged between sixteen and twenty-five, with no fighting experience and outnumbered in their thousands by trained British soldiers and police officers – made to winning what, on paper, was an impossible fight.

It is only due to all the locals prepared to give up their time to help me that I was able to write what I hope is a relatively accurate portrayal of what happened in West Cork back then and throughout the rest of the twentieth century. My biggest thanks must go to Cathal Dineen, who (when we were 'unlocked') drove me all over, into the *back* of the back of beyond to meet men like Joe Long, who Cathal had heard still had Charlie Hurley's original rifle, which he did! Then up to the remote Clogagh graveyard, to show me the vault beneath an enormous Celtic cross sitting on a gravetop, where Lord Bandon had reportedly been placed when he was held hostage for two weeks. My spine tingled when I looked around and saw bones visible in the eroded coffins still lying on the shelves around me. Nothing was too much trouble for him or anyone he contacted, and if they didn't know, normally there was a grandparent or older relative available to ask who'd had parents alive at the time or had kept newspaper cuttings. Tim Crowley, who runs the Michael Collins Centre at Castle-view, is a relative of the Big Fellow himself. He and his wife Dolores were not only able to help factually, but actually let me hold the very briefcase that Michael Collins had used for his papers when he journeyed to London to negotiate the long and rocky road to eventual Irish independence with the British.

I'd read of Cumann na mBan, but again, there were and still are few books/papers published on the organisation, and they didn't relate specifically to West Cork. Through my friend and owner of my local bookshop in Clonakilty, Trish Kerr, I contacted Dr Hélène O'Keefe, an historian and lecturer at University College Cork, who put me in touch with Niall Murray, a long-time journalist with the *Irish Examiner*, his-torian and current PhD candidate at the university, researching the Irish Revolution in urban and rural districts of County Cork. He suggested visiting the Irish Government's War Pen-sion Files website to discover who from Cumann na mBan in my local area had applied. This opened the door not only to how many local women were involved in providing invaluable support to their men, but also to the real and present danger they were prepared to encounter, while still working on their farms and in the local post office or dressmaker's. I can only pay tribute to each and every one of these unsung heroines.

My wonderful friend Kathleen Owens also went in dogged pursuit of the smallest details, aided by her Mammy, Mary Lynch, her husband Fergal, and her son, Ryan Doonan. Mary Dineen, Dennis O'Mahoney, Finbarr O'Mahony and Maureen Murphy, who wrote to me from New York where her family had emigrated after the Civil War, are just some of those in my kind local community who contributed so much colour to this book. However, this book is categorised as a work of fiction – but peppered with real historical figures and set against an all-too-real fight to the death to achieve freedom from the British. As always, history is subjective, being reliant on human interpretation and, in many cases throughout this book, memory. Any 'mistakes' are mine and mine alone.

Also, in New Zealand, heartfelt thanks go out to Annie and Bruce Walker for their tour around beautiful Norfolk Island and their stories of NZ and island life, plus, of course, a taste of true Kiwi hospitality.

Huge thanks must go to my 'home' team, who have given me amazing support in their different ways. Ella Micheler, Jacquelyn Heslop, Olivia Riley, Susan Boyd, Jessica Kearton, Leanne Godsall and of course my husband Stephen – agent, rock and best friend – have all been there when I've needed them. Tribute must also go to all my many publishers around the world, who have walked the extra mile to get the books out to their readers, especially in these unprecedented times.

My tight cluster of close friends, who all know who they are and never fail to spur me on with honesty and love. And of course my children – Harry, Isabella, Leonora and Kit – who will always remain my greatest strength and inspiration.

On another point, I imagine that some of you might be sitting reading this letter in shock and perhaps disappointment that so many of the underlying mysteries throughout the series remain unsolved. This is simply because, as I started to write *The Missing Sister* and her own story grew, I realised that there just wasn't the space to tell the 'secret story' properly. So yes, the eighth and truly final instalment of *The Seven Sisters* series is yet to come . . .

Thank you for bearing with me, and I promise to begin writing book eight as soon as I've put *The Missing Sister* 'to bed', as they say. It's been in my head for eight years, and I can't wait to finally get it down on paper.

Lucinda Riley
March 2021

To discover the inspiration behind the series and to read about the real stories, places and people in this book, please visit www.lucindariley.com.

Bibliography

Munya Andrews, *The Seven Sisters of the Pleiades* (Spinifex Press, 2014)

Sebastian Balfour ed., *Trinity Tales: Trinity College Dublin in the Sixties* (Lilliput Press, 2011)

Tom Barry, *Guerilla Days in Ireland* (Mercier Press, 2013)

Alan Brady, *Pinot Central: A Winemaker's Story* (Penguin, 2010)

Tim Pat Coogan, *Michael Collins: A Biography* (Head of Zeus, 2015)

Dan Crowley, *My Time in My Place* (Michael Collins Centre, Castleview, 2013)

John Crowley, Donal Ó Drisceoil and Mike Murphy, *Atlas of the Irish Revolution* (Cork University Press, 2017)

Tim Crowley, *In Search of Michael Collins* (Michael Collins Centre, Castleview, 2015)

Liz Gillis, *The Hales Brothers and the Irish Revolution* (Mercier Press, 2016)

Da'Vella Gore, *This Blessed Journey* (Da'Vella J. Gore, 2009)

Patrick Radden Keefe, *Say Nothing: A True Story of Murder and Memory in Northern Ireland* (William Collins, 2018)

Anne Leonard ed., *Portrait of an Era: Trinity College Dublin in the 1960s* (John Calder Publishing, 2014)

Ken Loach et al., *The Wind that Shakes the Barley* (London: Sixteen Films, 2007)

J. V. Luce, *Trinity College Dublin: The First 400 Years* (TCD Press, 1992)

Ann Matthews, *Renegades: Irish Republican Women 1900–1922* (Mercier Press, 2010)

Charles River ed., *New Zealand and the British Empire: The History of New Zealand Under British Sovereignty* (Charles River Editors, 2018)

Charles River ed., *The Maori: The History and Legacy of New Zealand's Indigenous People* (Charles River Editors, 2018)

Marianne Slyne, *Marianne's Journal* (Michael Collins Centre, Castleview, 2015)